Also by Bruce Wagner

Force Majeure

I'm Losing You

I'll Let You Go

I'll Let You Go

A Novel

Bruce Wagner

Villard / New York

I'll Let You Go is a work of fiction, and all of the events, situations, incidents, and dialogues contained in it are products of the author's imagination. Other than those well-known persons whose inclusion is incidental to the plot, the characters in the work are inventions of the author, and any resemblance to actual persons, living or dead, is entirely coincidental. Where the names of actual persons are used, or symbols or names of actual entities are referred to, the situations, occurrences, and descriptions relating to them, and the statements and dialogues attributed to them, are completely fictional and are not to be construed as real.

Copyright © 2001 by Bruce Wagner

All rights reserved under International and Pan-American Copyright Conventions. Published in the United States by Villard Books, a division of Random House, Inc., New York, and simultaneously in Canada by Random House of Canada Limited, Toronto.

VILLARD BOOKS is a registered trademark of Random House, Inc. Colophon is a trademark of Random House, Inc.

Library of Congress Cataloging-in-Publication Data
Wagner, Bruce.
  I'll let you go : a novel / Bruce Wagner.—1st ed.
    p. cm.
  ISBN 0-375-50002-2 (alk. paper)
  1. Beverly Hills (Calif.)—Fiction. 2. Los Angeles (Calif.)—Fiction. 3. Homeless persons—Fiction. 4. Social classes—Fiction. 5. Rich people—Fiction. I. Title.
PS3573.A369 I45 2001
813'.54—dc21   2001026729

Frontispiece Illustration: Sandow Birk c/o Koplin Gallery

Grateful acknowledgment is made to the following for permission to reprint previously published material:

Carcanet Press Limited: "Warning to Children," from *Complete Poems*, by Robert Graves. Reprinted by permission of Carcanet Press Limited.

Chronicle Books, San Francisco: Four lines from "The House that Crack Built," from *The House That Crack Built* by Clark Taylor. Copyright © 1992 by Clark Taylor. Reprinted by permission of Chronicle Books, San Francisco.

Scribner, a division of Simon & Schuster, Inc. and A. P. Watt Ltd.: Five lines from "The Song of the Happy Shepherd," from *The Collected Works of W. B. Yeats,* Volume 1: *The Poems, Revised,* by Richard J. Finneran. Rights outside of the United States are controlled by A. P. Watt Ltd. Reprinted by permission of Scribner, a division of Simon & Schuster, Inc., and A. P. Watt Ltd.

Villard Books website address: www.villard.com

Printed in the United States of America on acid-free paper

9 8 7 6 5 4 3 2

First Edition

to my mother

Warning to Children

Children, if you dare to think
Of the greatness, rareness, muchness,
Fewness of this precious only
Endless world in which you say
You live, you think of things like this:
Blocks of slate enclosing dappled
Red and green, enclosing tawny
Yellow nets, enclosing white
And black acres of dominoes,
Where a neat brown paper parcel
Tempts you to untie the string.
In the parcel a small island,
On the island a large tree,
On the tree a husky fruit.
Strip the husk and pare the rind off:
In the kernel you will see
Blocks of slate enclosed by dappled
Red and green, enclosed by tawny
Yellow nets, enclosed by white
And black acres of dominoes,
Where the same brown paper parcel—
Children, leave the string alone!
For who dares undo the parcel
Finds himself at once inside it,
On the island, in the fruit,
Blocks of slate about his head,
Finds himself enclosed by dappled
Green and red, enclosed by yellow
Tawny nets, enclosed by black
And white acres of dominoes,
With the same brown paper parcel
Still unopened on his knee.
And, if he then should dare to think
Of the fewness, muchness, rareness,
Greatness of this endless only
Precious world in which he says
He lives—he then unties the string.

—*Robert Graves*

So let me sing of names remembered,
Because they, living not, can ne'er be dead,
Or long time take their memory quite away
From us poor singers of an empty day.

—*William Morris ("The Earthly Paradise")*

CONTENTS

PRINCIPAL CHARACTERS

The Trotter Family

LOUIS AHERNE TROTTER (*"the digger"*), *patriarch and benefactor.*
BLUEY TWISSELMANN TROTTER, *his wife. A socialite.*
KATRINA BERENICE TROTTER, *their daughter, a designer of gardens.*
MARCUS WEINER, *her husband.*
TOULOUSE ("TULL") TROTTER, *the offspring of Katrina and Marcus.*
DODD TROTTER, *son of Louis and Bluey; brother of Katrina.*
A billionaire like his father.
JOYCE TROTTER, *his wife. A philanthropist.*
EDWARD AURELIUS TROTTER, *their son, a brilliant invalid.*
LUCILLE ROSE TROTTER, *their daughter. A budding author.*
PULLMAN, *a Great Dane.*

Servants

WINTER, *the Trotter's longtime nanny and helpmeet.*
THE MONASTERIOS:
EPITACIO, EULOGIO, CANDELARIA *housemen and housekeeper. They are siblings.*
"SLING BLADE," *a cemetery worker and part-time Trotter family employee.*

Other Noteworthy Characters

AMARYLLIS KORNFELD, *a homeless orphan.*
WILL'M AKA "TOPSY," *an English eccentric. The orphan's protector.*
SAMSON DOWLING, *a detective and Trotter family friend.*
JANE SCULL, *a deaf and dumb girl.*
GEO. FITZSIMMONS, *a former caseworker.*

I'll Let You Go

CHAPTER 1

Born Toulouse

The boy took long walks in the countryfied Bel-Air hills with Pullman, the stately Dane—ears like membranous tepees, one eye blue, the other a forlorn and bottomless brown, jowls pinkening toward nose, arctic-white coat mottled by "torn" patches characteristic of the harlequin breed, the whole length of him an inkspot archipelago— even though the animal didn't seem particularly fond of such locomotion. Great Danes were majestic that way. They could take their jaunt or leave it.

When people learned what each was named, they usually said the two had it wrong—better the noble, gigantine champion to bear the burden of whimsy (Best of Breed to *Trotter's T. Lautrec*) while his master coupled to Pullman, steady, scholar'd, sleeping car Pullman, nostalgically trestle-trundling under bald hills and starstruck sky, velour shadow of midnight passengers murmuring within. Not that "Pullman" fit so well for the boy, though it might: twelve-year-old Toulouse was thin and dreamy, with the requisite bedroom eyes. His tousled red hair verged on blood-black, and his skin was so clear that the freckles seemed suddenly evicted, their remains the faintest of blurred constellations.

So: Toulouse—etymology unknown. He suspected it had something to do with his dad, as most things cryptic or unspoken usually did. They had christened him Louis, after Grandpa Lou (Mr. Trotter, to the world), and his grandfather was the only one ever to call him that. For all the rest he was Tull. His mother had started it. An abbreviation in his own life, she was a connoisseur of abridgments. *Toulouse:* the boy always used *that* name in his head, the way one thinks in a different language. A father tongue.

There are no sidewalks in Bel-Air to speak of, and though his mother, Trinnie, forbade it, the boy and his dog regularly ventured from Grandpa's estate on Saint-Cloud Road to walk the musky, sinuous asphalt lanes—baked warm as loaves—against traffic, so as not to be run down by neighborhood denizens in careering, souped-up Bentleys and polished, high-end SUVs or by celebrity-hunting tourists, who traveled at less speed but were likelier to remain at the scene of an accident. If Pullman was struck, Tull suavely imagined, there'd be victims galore. Like plowing into a mule deer.

They always found themselves at the strange house down the hill, on Carcassone Way. Well, from the road there was no house at all, no sign of the living, not even a graveled drive; merely a filigreed gate with the obscure and rusted barely discernible motto LA COLONNE DÉTRUITE. The entry's metal wings, fastened with a cartoonishly oversize padlock, were under siege by a dusty, haughtily promiscuous creeper, evoking melancholy in the boy—the crass finality of a dream foreclosed. They discovered another way in. He rode the dog's back through a desiccated hedge, the scratchy privet andromeda of a once finely pruned wall, until Pullman reached a clearing—quiddity of lawn smooth as the brim of some kind of wonderland bowler hat.

Inside, the sudden magical oddness of a centuries-old park. The empty, vaulted space, so queerly "public"-feeling, was serenely at odds with the neighborhood's proprietary nature. Intersecting rings of a sundial armillary sphere sat atop a pedestal of English portland stone, and though Pullman drew near, it was not to relieve himself. Rather, he became instantly mindful and mannered; each time they broke in, the animal invariably yawned, downplaying his bold, jungly efforts. Tull Trotter's heart sped, as it did with any adventure to this meadowy place, dipped as it were in trespasser's spice. Mother being a landscape architect of world renown, his catchall mind knew its flora—there, in the green all-aloneness, he communed again with the elegantly attenuated pyramid of the Cryptomerias and pines; the billiardist whimsy of great clipped myrtle balls so carefully, carelessly scattered; a cutting shed made of morning glory; the junipers and wisteria that flanked the still, square ponds; then began his saunter toward the ominous allée of flat-topped Irish yews.

He knew where those ancient columned soldiers led.

As he entered, the air chilled and darkened. Pullman had vanished as surely as a magician's offering. Tull walked through a phalanx of sentries until far enough in to see the wild, weird thing, two hundred yards off, set apart on a hillock . . . a stout, ruined column, fluted as Doric columns should be, rent with fissures, at least fifty feet in diameter, proportions suggesting it was all that remained of a temple forty stories tall. Whatever peculiar god had made this base had provided it with crazily bejeweled windows too, oval, square and pentagonal, then snapped the tower off five floors up, where tufted weeds sprang from its serrations like hair from an old man's ear. What could he make of it? The boy had never even gotten close enough to peer in. Now he moved inexorably nearer, at once cool and febrile, the capricious breath of open fields rushing at him like a breezy compress on the forehead during a sickbed hallucination.

Now he could see white, tented forms—furniture?—in the rooms within, but was interrupted when a daymare shape came from nowhere shouting, "Little fucker!" Tull was startled enough that he couldn't read any features, though it *was* wearing bib overalls, the perfect parody of a ghoulish Mr. Greenjeans. In a blink, the figure rudely tumbled, care of a certain Dane; the terrified man, having met a fair match for the Olympian pedestal's remains, retreated to the severed column while Tull made a sprinting Hardy Boy getaway. Regal and unruffled, Pullman strutted a beat in his master's direction, then paused, slyly turning with calm eye and tarry muzzle to fire a last warning shot toward the groundskeeper—the astonished head of whom already appeared in an upper portal of the cylindrical mirage. Then, like a Saturday-morning-television creation, the aristocratic beast leapt toward his charge, through the chilly gantlet of yews, past the huge myrtle balls leading to the brambled entry that would carry them back to Carcassone Way and the homely, reassuring traffic of the world.

CHAPTER 2

The Digger's Tomb

Since this is a book of houses—shelters for the living and the dead—it should not be unusual that our narrative approach the boulevards of Westwood and Wilshire, epicenter of what is still nostalgically called the Village; an unlikely place for a cemetery. Yet there it exists, sewn behind the back alley of Avco's smoky glass façade like a spare black button beneath a lapel, a stone's throw from Qwikcopiers and cineplexes, barbers and Borders, middling lunch crowd sushi bars, oversize pet boutiques and the smug bone-white ridges of formidable crosswalks linking high-tower marble REIT palaces. Strolling the memorial's smallish grounds, one notes a rustic, dignified intimacy, unexpected considering the outlandishness of its bright, blandly civic context. Though the parkland's beginnings are for some other history, we will soon become familiar with its laconic caretaker—the one with the JESUS IS COMING! LOOK BUSY bumper sticker on his sun-warped maroon Marquis; the one unmaliciously called Sling Blade, because of a casual resemblance to the sentimental creation of a well-known Hollywood hyphenate. We will learn to embrace him, as he does so honorably his extended family of dead.

At dusk, at least three times a week, he watches the arrival of an impeccably dressed old man. The car rolls to its same position and a chauffeur midwifes its passenger's entry to the world, albeit a sunny netherworld; Mr. Louis Trotter then stands before a pricey five-hundred-square-foot patch, the largest family plot in the yard, spotted hands clasped at small of back, pensive captain on a ghost ship prow, well-oiled skin the color of ivory, visionary orbs the singular, crustacean blue of the epic self-made. Hairless, save for bushy tangle of eyebrow, charcoal thicket of inner ear and friar's whitish fringe peeking from collar like a threadbare angora wrap. The enormous gnomish space between nose and upper lip has the piquantly poignant effect of making him soft and beasty, fragile yet full of hope, imperious and obeisant. Like Monet's haystacks (one of which hangs on the wall at Saint-Cloud), his cunning face, open to the endless translations of moving sunlight upon still life, invites scrutiny; one could make a vocation of its study, as of a rock or an illuminated text. Perhaps the answer to the riddle of its magnetism is that it provokes something exquisitely, abominably parental—you focus on its moods, growths and grandeur as a precocious child madly, futilely attempting to learn the catechism of his father.

Mr. Trotter is an animal who speaks—no, *chuffs*, literally, the way a dog does—Tull sometimes observed him and Pullman greet each other that way, muzzle to muzzle, a fraternal clearing of throats by the amicably encaged. But the old man holds dominion and, like the wild place of his sovereignty, is primordial as well. Nothing governs him: he chuffs when and where he pleases. The despotism of such a quality is, for most of his subjects, irresistibly charismatic. In his presence one feels like a strop, a worn leathery thing waiting to be rubbed against, the more for Mr. Trotter to hone or drop his quills. His ability to enlist fascination continually surprises—he mesmerizes, for while changing constantly, he remains unchanged. Paid underlings and blood relatives alike journey roughly through the seasons, hanging on for their lives, for *his* life, renewing themselves each day so that *he* might be renewed, willing the old man to be cozily predictable, as one wills the same of all one's fellow men. (He nearly gives them what they want, and in so doing binds and grafts those close, addicts them, even minor players—and sometimes, too, by another eccentricity: he is a perversely lavish tipper.) The minions swig morning lattes, already beginning their time-clock day by dreamily nudging him toward Good Boss and Benefactor, Good Father and Mentor, but it is *their* dream and theirs alone, dreamers trying to undream something that they, with inferior twitching animal noses—why, they can't even properly chuff!—sense is not quite right. All efforts come to naught and the strop gets its workaday workout; he will not be tamed. To make things worse, he's something of a dandy. His bald-faced buck-toothed mien, hovering above faintly absurd ascots and greatcoats, could not be more touching and inscrutable.

Mr. Trotter likes it here. Nothing showy: no Gardens of Ascension or Harmony Hills, Whispering Glades or Resurrection Slopes, no Babylands or Vales of Memory. He sees someone looking but takes no mind. Sling Blade and Dot, the park's chatty, efficient manager, have watched him pace his plot for almost two years, himself a movable monument, pharaonically obsessed by a single thought: who would build his tomb?

The old man has spent a decade quietly researching locus and method. He considered cremation but felt it too forced, too sudden; as big a fan of fire as he was, he wished a slower, less radical denouement. He consulted with Buddhists, who could arrange to dice him up, mixing crushed bones with barley flour and the milk of the dri, the more easily to be digested by vultures on Tibet's rock-strewn plateau—the idea being that buzzards, those infernal landlords, would expediently ransack the house, tossing soul-tenant out onto street, "perforce accelerating reincarnation." The Parsis did the same in India, *sans* plateau; the dead played hide-and-seek within round stone dokhmas called towers of silence.

It had all been great fun, hell of an education for an unschooled man, but in the end Louis Trotter decided to go the way of the Jews (he'd always admired the Jews) and be laid out in a plain pine box. But where? For the first time in his life, he was daunted. The irony was that his fortune came from waste management—quarries and fills were his métier. In the trade they called him a geomancer, legendary for his sixth sense of the land. He chuffed aloud and mordantly sniggered: *having a bit of trouble with the eighteenth hole.*

He found an architectural book on Tallum, a cemetery in a forest south of Stockholm, and impulsively flew there on his son's BBJ. The memento mori above chapel portico was worth the trip: a Brothers Grimm oak zealously overtook the plinth of a columned temple, and between its pillars was carved HODIE MIHI CRAS TIBI (*Today Me, Tomorrow You*) . . . yet so far away, in the cold Swedish ground! What could he have been thinking? Besides, all those ramrod trees and open spaces reminded him of the freakish cloister he had made for Katrina as a gift on her wedding day. Fifteen years had passed since he'd created the storybook meadow, with its perfect replica of the famed folly of Désert de Retz—La Colonne Détruite. He sometimes wandered there, but made certain she never knew.

A gypsy, a nomad, a vagabond of death, Mr. Trotter had loitered the twenty-six cemeteries of greater Paris (for a seven-figure fee, a dubious realtor promised a shadier berth at Père-Lachaise near one of two pairs: Abélard and Héloïse or Gertrude and Alice B.)—on to Venice, then Campo Verano in Rome—Malta and Milan, Staglieno in Genoa and Almudena in Madrid—St. Petersburg, Cambria, Prague, Turkey, Cairo, Scotland . . . Brompton, Kensal Green and Highgate (they'd plant him, said yet another Underworld broker, "not sixteen meters from George Eliot") with jaunts to the thirty-one necropoli of New Orleans—Metairie, Lafayette and Odd Fellow's Rest—then on to the song-line haunts of the Outback—squatter-infested mausoleums of Manila, Ecuador, Brazil and beyond the infinite. Yet all roads led to Westwood, and he had to laugh. Wasn't it always like that? If his soul was in Bel-Air, then its gloved hand could the more easily reach over to that humble little place in the Village; you-can't-go-home-again be damned. Here would lie Louis Trotter, in a mildly meditative, sedately urban place, proximal to the variegated myths of his life. Yet who would build his tomb?

As usual, the quandary made him chuff; Dot's chafing panty hose, sounding not unlike sandpaper, made him turn.

"We haven't seen *you* in a while!"

She was a plain, doughty nurse and he tolerated her well enough—no sense alienating the afterlife custodians. (Once, he'd almost done just that by proffering her a hundred-dollar bill to leave him in peace.) She wore a heinous frock, one in a series which he detested and thought almost an incentive to be elsewhere interred.

"I've been traveling," he said, with a wince.

"*I* used to have the travel bug. But it's important to be safe, don't you think? World's become such a dangerous place. I'd like to go to New York, where my sister Ethel lives; they've done a marvelous job getting the murders down. Nothing could be as terrible as *this* town—my Lord, you're as likely to be killed by the *police* as you are by a rapster. The police used to be *helpful,* but now, well they gun you down for jaywalking. Plant dope on you without batting an eye. But the terrorists! I think the McVeighs, the *homegrowns,* are worse than the Jackal types any day— that's what Ethel says and I agree. There was a man on the morning show, his entire job is smuggling guns through airport metal detectors, looking for weak spots. Works for the government. Even *he* said there's nothing you can do. Did you read in the *Times* about the man who impersonated a pilot? *Everyone* knew him at LAX—well, he stole baggage and came and went just as he pleased for five years! Lived in Venice. Police found a whole room full of Tumi luggage; he took them right off the conveyor! They said once he even got in the cockpit. Now, what in the world would he be doing in a cockpit? Just chatting away! The man on the morning show was saying that kind of thing wasn't even the problem. It's the *viruses*—and I'm not talking computer. Oh, I am sick to death of the viruses! Did you know that if someone blew a cloud of anthrax in over Manhattan—and believe me, they're out there figuring out how to do it—it would be three days before anyone even got symptoms?"

The old man smiled and floated backward like a jack-o'-lantern putting out to sea; she went after him with a long pole.

"This was on the morning show, can you imagine? I'm not sure I want to start my day hearing it. Anyway, he said that by then—by the time they even found out about it—a lot of folks who were exposed would've already disappeared and gone back home: you know, tourists flying all around, some of 'em right back to Westwood for all we know. And the way the planes recirculate the air—well if someone in the last row of coach so much as clears his throat, first class gets it right in the lungs at the speed of sound. You're minding your own business watching one of those dreadful movies or munching on honey-coated peanuts—I love those things!—and well now evidently with anthrax— and this is what the morning-show man said—with anthrax the infection starts with a little cold, but then you get all better. There's even a medical term he used for that . . . what was it? The 'eclipse' or something. Yes! The anthrax eclipse. Well it goes away, then before you know it you're sick again, but this time instead of a cold, it's a terrible hemorrhaging pneumonia. I think syphilis is like that too—I mean, with an eclipse. The man on the morning show said people clutch their throats and die right in the middle of a sentence, like bad actors in a play. And the *doctors*—well your doctor won't have a *clue*. Did you know that when Ethel had shingles, it took him a full week to diagnose? Mind you, he's a cardiologist, so that's partially explainable. But when it came time to prescribe, she said he had to peek inside a book—the older ones don't even know how to use the Internet. Now, this is a top doctor, a Park Avenue man. And we're not talking anthrax, we're talking *shingles*. And Ethel said that whatever he gave her made it worse!"

"Yes! Well!" he said, backing off as if she had the pox herself. "It's a difficult time! The world can be very unpleasant! And *you*, Dot, you have a good afternoon!"

He bared a bucktooth, winced, chuffed and slunk off.

"Mr. Trotter," she called out. "What a marvelous coat! Never *saw* such a fabric."

"Thank you," he said vainly, pleased at being out of her clutches; he had almost reached the car. "A tailor found it, in London. Bespoke, of course." He instantly regretted the use of the word.

"What?"

"The ensemble—it was custom-made. *Custom-made!*"

"I'm reserving a place for you in Dot Campbell's Best-Dressed Hall of Fame—and that's a hard thing to achieve!"

"Thank you!" he said, shivering at the rebarbative honor, doffing and chuffing and shambling toward the black-sapphire Silver Seraph, where Epitacio waited dutifully by open door. The eavesdropping Sling Blade still raked at the lawn; Mr. Trotter caught his eye, nodding as he climbed in.

The tinted window came down and the old man made sure to see Dot's back before gesturing him over. Sling Blade approached and looked in, where the visitor sat as if floating upon the French navy–piped Cotswold hides; perched on a shiny ascot, the elfin face twisted up and fairly twinkled, an odd vintage brooch in a velvety box. He pressed a business card and some green to Sling Blade's hand and smiled perspicaciously. A secret covenant had been made—the car sped away.

It was almost time to lock the gate. The caretaker strolled to his benefactor's plot. A shallow wind cinematically stirred the leaves while he stared at the grass, wondering what stony monument would there be born.

CHAPTER 3

Saint-Cloud Road

By the time they reached home, Pullman had long overtaken him; the boy ran till he feared his heart would burst, never looking back. The gates of his grandfather's house, electronically controlled and far more massive than the corroded ones of Carcassone, were, thankfully, open. A dirty vintage BMW meant his mother's "friend" was there.

Pullman lingered, then peeled off, disappearing past a fountain, while Tull opened the front door, heavy enough that Grandpa Lou had installed sensors and tiny motors to help it along. The interior of the Wallace Neff–designed estate, built for a silent-film director in the twenties, and the design of its sixteen hilltop acres will later be revealed; they held no interest for the hungry boy scudding over terrazzo floors, headlong toward the kitchen.

Ralph sat on a stool, across from a Sub-Zero the size of a giant's armoire. The handsome, mordantly stubbled face with dimpled chin, hollowed cheeks and tormented eyes reminded Tull of a monk in flight from a monastery—never mind that Trinnie had decked him out in Dries and motocross Menichetti and in six scant weeks addicted him to Keratase emulsions, Hortus Mirabilis elixirs, Lorenzo Villoresi aftershaves and the arcane almond pastes of Santa Maria Novella. Today he wore an absurd Edwardian tux that made Louis Trotter look positively staid. The popinjay's head hung heavily, mocked by the pots and pans that dangled around him in cheerful, coppery profusion.

"Hey, Ralph."

He looked up, annoyed. "*Why* do you call me that?"

"Sorry. I forget."

With a grunt, Tull broke the vacuum'd death grip of the Sub-Zero and began to forage.

"Do I fuck with *your* name? Do I call you 'Teal'?"

Tull phonily mused. "You can call me that." That was bogus; it would have irritated him no end. Lugging Tupperware filled with Southern-fried leftovers from the shelves, he changed tack. "Did you hear about the tapir? It pulled off a zookeeper's arm. It was on the news."

"There's a rocky island near San Francisco," said Ralph smugly, "where some naturalists live. They saw a sea lion wash ashore, its ass bit off by a shark, clean. It lived for days, shimmying along on the front fins—whenever the thing tried to rest, a gull would come give it a little peck and it'd move on. This went on for *days.*"

"That's rad."

"A perfect marriage of Beckett and Bosch." He simpered, then dementedly shrieked, "Teal!" like a sadistic gull himself. The boy recoiled, glowering.

"Oh! Then there's the *whale* that got trapped too far inland when the water started icing up—Alaska or something. The polar bears just sat in a ring around the hole swiping at it while a shark had his way from underneath. Oh, the natural world! How pristine and unforgiving! Like Hollywood, no?" He wriggled and sneered and cockadoodled: "Teal! Teal!"

Tull lost his cool. "If you want your name pronounced *Rafe*, then why don't you just spell it that way? With an *f* instead of an *l*?"

While it wouldn't be fair to say that Tull baited his mother's "friend"—the latest, most tolerable of a line of friends stretching as far back as he could remember—he wasn't exactly indifferent.

"How would *you* know how I spell it?" asked the poseur.

"Mom said."

"Oh. In your many discussions. Of me."

"We were talking about Ralph Fiennes, the actor"— Tull used the *l* again, as in *Ralph's Foodmarket*, and egregiously rhymed Fiennes with *Viennas* —"and she said you pronounced yours the same way."

"It's *Rafe!*" he furied, nostrils flaring. *"Rafe Fines!"* The thirtysomething self-anointed screenwriter from Colorado drew a hand through long, gel'd hair. "In this town, unless you're very lucky, unless you're *Ron*

Bass"—he spat the name out like pus—"you need something else, some-thing small and subliminal. What the Jews call minor shtick." Tull greedily set upon half a cold chicken, green peas and whipped potatoes. "Take 'Rafe Fines.' *You* brought him up. *'Rafe Fines'* "—he called out the name as if he were announcing the nominees for the Golden Globes—"is a 'double hit.' You *read* 'Ralph,' but you *hear* 'Rafe.' You *read* 'Fee-ehn-nez' but *hear* 'Fines.' The *juxtaposition* makes it memorable. It oscillates. And that's especially true of a 'double hit.' "

"Where's Candelaria?" asked the boy offhandedly.

"I sent the servants home," answered Ralph, deliberately camp. "Mirdling's Name Theorem: the small, strange thing that perceptually sets you apart. There's something so *rune-like* about Rafe, so *rarefied*. When you take that rune-like, rarefied thing and make silk from the sow's ear, 'Ralph'—"

"You know what? You're getting to be like the nutty professor. And who's 'Mirdling'?"

"My last name."

"You should change it. Where's Mom?"

"Getting ready. Your cousins are here, you know."

"What's with the tux?"

"Black-tie gala for ten thousand, to honor . . . *Ron Bass*."

"What is your problem with Ron Bass?"

"I don't have a problem."

"You're always going off—"

"Going off?"

"He doesn't even fit your theorem."

"Oh yes he does. There's 'Bass'—you read it much more than you hear it. An inner voice forever asks: fish or tone? Add the confounding banality of *Ron* to the oscillating fish-music of *Bass* and you've got a cognitive dissonance—"

"I still don't know why you're so freaked."

The Beau Brummell squealed, kicking up his python boots in a re-tarded jig. "Did you know Ron Bass's first nine films took in a billion dollars worldwide? Or that he gets up at three forty-five in the morn-ing to write, seven days a week? That's why his company is called Predawn Productions. And I'll tell you something else: Ron Bass skips breakfast because digesting food makes him *logy*. Ron Bass doesn't use a computer—huh-uh. He writes on yellow loose-leaf with number-two

Sundance pencils made by Blackfeet Indians. Ron Bass, as you probably know, is a legendary mentor, with an inner circle of story-structuring Pradacunts who paste and fax and generally *work* those three acts like crack whores on a cock. 'I'm not comparing myself to Mozart,' said Ron Bass in a recent interview with the *L.A. Times,* 'but is the Jupiter Symphony any less magnificent because he worked so much and so fast?' Do you want to know what Ron Bass does on weekends? I'll *tell* you what he does on weekends: he writes! And then he takes his German shepherd to the farmers' market in Santa Monica on Pico and buys hummus. (Gerry the German shepherd—could have used some help writing *that* name!) Ron Bass likes to go to movies on the weekend; he'll see three in a day. He likes to see movies with the *public.* 'You really know how good it is,' sayeth Ron Bass, 'when you're in the dark surrounded by strangers.' On Friday or Saturday nights, Ron Bass likes to have French-onion soup at 5 Dudley or branzino and green lasagna at Vicenti. Ron Bass likes to drive down to Orange County to see opera for a Sunday matinée—"

"Jesus, you're obsessed! It's just Ron Bass! He's not even Robert Towne."

"Did you say . . . Robert *China*towne?" He spun around impishly, in fresh rodomontade. "Did you *hear* Chinatowne on KCRW, discussing 'the sound of the shammy'? Polanski understood the importance of 'the sound of the shammy,' he said. Oh, how lucky for us all! Oh, 1974, if we could just go back! Do you know—are you *aware*—of what the Council of Elders—*the professors of screenwriting*—call that script? 'The grail.' Literally. They're just like Trekkies—with their Grand Wailea Maui Waui seminars and Callie Khouri–Nora Ephron champagne brunches, laughing and clinking glasses while hooking you for thousands. And don't think Mr. *China*towne isn't rewarded *monetarily* each time some weekend warrior writes a check—oh, the Council makes sure they all get their fat number-two Sundance-pencil'd checks!—don't think he isn't cut in by the *pantheon*—the story-structure gurus—*groupies* still coming in their pants over *Sleepless in Seattle*—"

"You're getting crazy."

The soberest of smiles quickly normalized him. "Tull, you can't think I'm serious."

"Well, you seem awfully serious."

A thoughtful intake of air, reminiscent of a politician reflecting on a benign opposing view. Then: "Tull, when can we meet—to discuss?

There's trouble around page 50—no, 63, 64—that I can't put my finger on. Maybe up through 80 or 81—at least toward the end of the second act. You know: the limo driver's 'false crisis.' It's affecting the whole *tone*—"

"Maybe Saturday."

He had surreptitiously skimmed Ralph's latest draft of *How to Marry a Billionaire,* the po-mo screwball *Notting Hill* clone, and erred by making a few casual, goading observations—concise and lucid enough to convince the absurd, desperate writer that the boy was a savant.

When Ralph further pressed, Tull took the stairs, shouting, "On the weekend!"

*T*he hallway was dark; the cracks around her bedroom door blazed. It was actually a child's room of epic proportions—she'd grown up there—the only place his mother ever stayed while alighting from the colorful, ragtag rest-stops she sardonically called the Fourth World. Her son knew by name the drabber exotica of those faraway countries—Connecticut and Minnesota included—a landscape of famous rehabs and less famous halfway houses.

"Mother?"

Tull knew she couldn't hear; he edged the door open and crept into a shambles of incense, perfume, cigarette smoke and discarded clothes. He made a beeline to her blasting Bose, still in its stylishly beat-up gray-cloth portable battery pack, and lowered the volume.

"Baby?" she called from the toilet.

"It's me."

Tull scrunched his face, ticcing it this way and that with the excitement and distress of being near her.

"Oh, *baby.* Would you turn the music back up?" He didn't budge, struck dumb by the sheer smell of her. "Did you know you're going to see Grandma after dinner? At Cedars."

Trinnie swept into the room in trademark strands of Tahitian black pearls—otherwise nude as a peach—and gave a goony flasher's grin. He looked away, frowning with the effort not to ogle. From the corner of his eye, he watched this creamy, high-voltage half-moon as it fished through mounds of couture—hand-painted satin-lined toile, copper-wire camisoles and furry capes, beaks of Blahniks peeking out from under like a dominatrix's smothered chicks.

"What's she in the hospital for?"

"Angioplasty. Catheter in the heart. Used to be a big deal, now it's outpatient. But Bluey—*dear* Grandma Bluey has to have the celebrity suite at Cedars. She is obsessed."

Usually she wore vintage suits, dark flues that ended in a glorious ignition of orange hair, even while working on her knees in clients' gardens—but tonight she would sport a pale gray silk-faille jacket, Galliano for Dior, topped with a Steven Jones feathered hat that might have been the fanciful lid of a great and cordial eagle's teapot. She was nearly forty, with her son's cool Celtic skin and emerald-green eyes, the see-through lids subtly dilating just before she laughed, which was often. Trinnie tantalized. She was a stormy, beautiful, damaged thing and she was irresistibly his mother. Details of the ancient hurt—the death of his father—went assiduously unspoken, for all practicality expunged from the Histories. Tull was certain Grandpa Lou was part of the puzzle—he could tell by the way the old man watched her, the keen vigilance of his face reflecting back his daughter's emotions. There was something inextricable about them. It was clear she was the only human being his grandfather had ever loved; nothing incesty about it, Tull knew that in his bones—only that rarest of rare things, an unconditional affection for her mind, her body, her blithe broken spirit.

"Lucy and Edward are here," she said, while excavating a stiletto.

"Where are you going with Ralph?"

He acidly mispronounced the name, but she couldn't have cared less. He loved her a little more for it.

"They're raising money for CAT scans—for *animals*, can you believe? You know: when Kitty gets that titty lump or Fido has lymphoma. They care more about fucking animals than they do about people. I'll give them animal," she said, twirling around. "How's *this*?"

He finally turned—there the hell-raiser stood, tall and fabulous, arms righteously crossed beneath princessy sneer—Russian sable open just enough for a redundant, fiery wink of bush.

As he ran to his cousins, the child (for he was still a child) was ecstatically certain he could devise a way to keep her home forever. Yet each time he warmed himself to the thought, like a moth drawn to spectral mother's flame, he was singed awake by the knowledge that there were no strategies to deploy—all was doomed. Like his grandfather, he was helpless and unmoored before her.

Lucy called out as she leapt from the shadowy pergola and dashed to the maze, Pullman barking furiously from within. Tull strode to the topiary sundial, where, on a granite bench at ten o'clock, sitting Buddhalike in his titanium body brace, was the most mysterious, most admirable, bravest, brilliantest creature he knew he would ever meet: his ten-year-old cousin Edward.

CHAPTER 4

The Labyrinth

*H*e wore a sort of embroidered pillowcase on his head, as if hiding a cockeyed bolster, its open edge ending beneath the nose so that only his lips, with their funky mob of yellowish teeth, were revealed. The jaw jutted like a thirties movie tough's—too much bone. A slick bar of light metal rose from his collar, and the chin, with a scintilla of scar where a nurse had once dropped him, sat stalwart in its rubber rest (the neck alone would not have supported the outsize skull). Cutout holes for the eyes, lined in silk or leather, varied in shape and size. Edward designed each hood himself and was much praised for his efforts.

It excited Tull to see him. As usual, he was eager to gauge his cousin's mood.

"What's happening?"

Edward shrugged, pursing his mouth à la Early Cher.

"He's upset with Trinnie," said Lucy with the smugness of an off-duty medium.

The self-described bespectacled "girl detective" had the lambent cheeks of Aunt Trinnie, who, incidentally, had long ago taught her how to weave her hair into mandala-like plaits. Almost thirteen now, she had never trimmed a lock; today, braids dangled down to non-hips.

"I'm upset with your mother," Edward said.

"You are? I mean, really?"

The gangster-cousin mouth roiled and twisted.

"She didn't do it for spite, Edward," said his sister. "Anyhow, the world doesn't revolve around *you*—it revolves around me! Didn't you get the memo?" Lucy tittered as her brother coughed up a snigger. Tull smiled; if Edward was sniggering, things couldn't be so bad.

"Well, what did she do?" asked Tull.

"It's the *maze*," said Lucy.

"What about it?"

"He's just amazed with it!"

Edward folded his arms outside the thin bar of the brace and glared. "It isn't a maze, it's a labyrinth. There's a difference."

"Ah! So solly."

"A maze has tricks and dead ends. A true labyrinth's only dead end is the center."

Pullman shot from the hedge and lay down at the sundial, where he stretched and shivered. Lucy took a seat in Edward's custom golf cart; with fringed canopy and fat white tires, it looked a little like a time machine—half-buggy, half-lunar mod. She put her hands on the wheel.

"You're mad at my mom for designing it?" offered Tull, by way of opening a dialogue.

"That's right."

"But it was Grandpa's idea."

Lucy drove the quiet car in an arc around the earthen clock's edge, the dial itself being a tall bush sculpted in the form of an enormous harp.

"Come on, Tull, don't be naïve. She knows how much time I spend at Saint-Cloud. And *we* know what the labyrinth held, don't we?"

"The minotaur," said Lucy, cool as a cucumber.

Tull let this sink in. "I don't see the connection."

"Then let me clarify: I *am* the minotaur. The *monster*, OK?"

Lucy flinched. "Oh, Edward, give it up!"

"You *know* what they call me at school. Dilbert—and Cat-in-the-Hat. And don't forget their favorite: Headward the First. Which at least has wit."

"My mother would never make fun of you, and you know it."

"I even played the minotaur at school, remember? Trinnie even filmed it."

"You *wanted* to play it," said Tull.

"I didn't do it for *them*. They're retarded. Afterward, they came up—the worst Headward offenders—and said, 'That was so cool!' All of them talk like kids in bad teen movies. But why begrudge them their little heartfelt charitable moment?"

Lucy laughed, loving his rancor; his impersonations were always dead-on toxic.

"Anyhow, your *mother*—her little verdant puzzle has me feeling . . . sorely mocked." He set his arms in a favorite Jack Benny pose, and at last, Tull knew he was being had.

Without fanfare then, let it be said: it was the presumption of medical experts that Edward Aurelius Trotter would not exceed the age of five (he and Pullman bore that in common, Danes being notorious for their short life-span)—and that the boy had already lived twice that long had dumbfounded the very same, who had expected him to at least have the courtesy and forbearance to remain under house or hospital arrest. But the victim of Apert Syndrome refused to play the invalid game.

It is not for us to present a study of what M. Apert in 1906 identified as acrocephalosyndactyly here; neither shall we delve into the flattened occiput, bregmatic bump, mandibular prognathism, high arched palate or anti-Mongoloid palpebral fissures incurred by those unfortunate genetic heirs. Suffice that Edward's feet and gloved hands, though eminently usable, were webbed, and his skull had what the technical books called a turret or tower-shaped effect, cracked as surely as Carcassone's La Colonne. To add—or detract—from his misfortunes, he handily shared an artistic streak with Aunt Trinnie that showed itself in the swankly poetic hand-sewn hoods (naturally, she had tutored him in the art) that on occasion sported papier-mâché prosthetics: a beak, an ear or some such excrescence. To his credit, Tull reveled in his mother's attentions toward his cousin, for he knew Edward took her absences nearly as hard as he.

And how *was* the precocious cousin treated at school? As noted, he was first tormented by "Gimme head, Headward!" and its varied variations—then Special Ed, Dilbert, Cat-in-the-Hat and, finally, Casper (the boy, when stung, could be less than friendly and more than trenchant). Only once, around a month or so after he'd begun to wear the self-stitched hoods, had a bored and motley crew unveiled him; ever stalwart, Edward replaced the hood and claimed not to be bothered. His stoicism, and the fact that he never reported the crime, duly impressed—from then on he was watched over and given tender respects and, because of his vast intellect and sagacity, consulted and revered.

"Edward," said Tull with a frisson of relief. "There's something I don't get. If a labyrinth doesn't have dead ends, how can someone get lost?"

"You can't. It's impossible. The myth's a metaphor—we don't *want* to get out. We're hardwired for failure. It's in our genes. Even flies want to fail."

"What do you mean?"

"Put a hundred flies in a jar and leave the lid on awhile. Take it off and only a few escape."

"What does that prove?"

"Psychologists say the flies suffer from 'premature cognitive commitment': meaning, the commitment that they're still trapped."

"That is *so brilliant*," said Lucy as she maneuvered the buggy into a harbor of manicured bush. "See? Fits perfect. Though I'm not sure it'll turn."

"Back up, Lucy!" said Tull with proprietary zeal. "You'll ruin the hedge."

Like the Tin Man, Edward swiveled on the bench to watch while she threw the buggy in reverse. "What's a $400,000 hedge?" He shrugged, nonchalant.

She cleared it, then turned back to her brother. "Tell him about Joyce." Then to Tull: "Our mother has a pet project."

"Animal CAT scans?" asked Tull, pleased to elicit a smile from the invalid.

"Mother Joyce has been searching for a calling," said Edward. "The middle-aged need their passions, you know."

"We were *hoping*," said Lucy, eyes atwinkle, "that it would be in the form of a personal trainer."

"Or pool man."

"That would have been the *best*."

"At first, we thought she'd adopt a disease, but that's tricky. *My* particular anomaly's too shamelessly grotesque to build a telethon around. Too obscure. *Unphotogenic*." Lucy chortled, then nudged a tire against Pullman's back; he twitched an ear. "Then Mother read an item in the *Times* about a baby in a dumpster. A drive-by: someone tossed it in and the thing died. People don't leave kids on doorsteps anymore—they'd have to park the car, God forbid. Park and toss and you're ahead of the game. And what does Mother do when she reads about said odious crime? Remember, this is no ordinary woman! This is a filthy rich woman with too much time on her hands! She goes to the morgue to claim it, that's what. But they won't just *give* it to her, they make her *wait* thirty days. I, for one, find it comforting to know the finders-keepers rule has such broad and universal application. Voilà! a month later, there she sits, morgue-ready, far away from the Hills of Holmby. Comes the Man— from her emotionally charged description, we read between the lines and deduce the deputy to be a burly cretin with, no offense to you, Tull, sweaty, orangish body hair. From the distant end of the hall, Franken-sheriff walks toward her. *Clump clump clump.* And what does Franken-sheriff do? Hands Joyce a Hefty bag dripping with the baby's remains!"

"Edward, that is *gross.*"

"You're serious," said Tull, happily playing straight man.

"And Mother vows—this being the first in a series—Mother vows the next time she comes, she'll do things a little differently. Two weeks later, she makes good. Hands the sheriff one of those humongous Hermès scarves from a few seasons back with an African theme, because the next little dead baby's *black.* Oh, Mother Joyce thinks of every-thing! Frankensheriff appears in said distant hall—*clump clump clump*—*weeping* as he approaches, *sobbing* as he hands it off! He's caught the spirit! Touched by an angel! Frankensheriff stands converted!"

"But what does she *want?*" asked the incredulous Tull. "What's she going to *do* with them?"

"She wants," chimed Lucy, "to bury them."

Pullman rose indifferently, and in doing so, violently jostled the buggy, whose tire had been resting on his flank.

"Weird," said Tull.

"And the perfect thing is that it's not even an original thought! There's a woman who's been burying throwaways for years—that's where Mother got the idea. From *People* magazine. You see, her tragedy— and ours—is that Mother Joyce cannot even be original in her Buddha Compassion phase." Edward yawned with boredom, circling back to his aunt. "You know, there were *so* many things Trinnie might have done besides build a fucking maze. I mean, she could have gone Versailles: some conical hedges, a *hegemony* of hedges—big drippy grotto with water-works automata—no Hefty bags here! Maybe *un grand escalier* . . . I *did* see them haul in a Rodin, but your mom assured it wasn't the centerpiece; that'd have been *such* a cliché. She's too clever by half." He clutched his hands theatrically to his bosom. " 'Aunt Trinnie, this is too cruel!' I said. 'A *labyrinth*—and here *me*, with my deformity—Mini-Me the Mini-Minotaur!' "

"And how did she respond?" asked Tull, playing along.

"With something very . . . Trinnie-like," answered the cousin.

"I believe," said Lucy, "it was: 'Edward, shut the fuck up.' " Her brother rasped and hooted, then Lucy got a grand idea. "You know what we should do? We should just drive in! Come on, Edward! Journey to the center of the labyrinth—I dare you!"

"We'll tie some yarn to the cart," said Tull. "In case we get lost."

"I'll pass."

"He's afraid," shouted Lucy gleefully. "Edward's afraid!"

"That would be you," said the cousin. "I've seen how far *you've* gotten. You won't even go in with Pullie."

"That isn't true," she said defensively. As impossible as it may seem, the Trotter children were, in regard to the maze, wary of exploration.

"Then *no* one's been to the center," said Tull.

"What? Not even you?" asked Edward, a bit stunned.

"Well, when would I? They only just finished it."

"Nearly two weeks ago, they did," said Edward, thoroughly pleased. "Well, well, we *are* a timid group!"

"Then let's do it," said Tull. "What's the big deal?"

"The big *deal* is what your mother put in the middle of the damn thing."

"The Rodin?"

"Guess again." He paused, striking his Benny pose. "A dumpster fetus—what else?"

While Tull and Lucy laughed, exhaustion darkened Edward's face like a cloud, and his sister sprang to help. They walked from bench to buggy, supporting him on each side. Lucy got in to drive and smiled at Tull, pained and poignant; Edward would need to skip a few days of school to get his strength back, and she hoped he wouldn't have to go to the hospital. Pullman cantered about the carriage, then licked Edward's hand, but the cousin twitched it away. As Lucy drove the serpentine path to the house, the Dane galloped toward a rakish figure on the hill: Grandpa Lou.

Trinnie shouted at the children that it was time to see Bluey, then

Ralph shouted to *her* that they would be late and she hurried off. As they entered the living room, Tull called out hello, but the old man didn't hear.

He was already down on all fours, chuffing with Pullman at the door of the Palladian doghouse.

CHAPTER 5

A Lucy Trotter Mystery

*A child should always say what's true
And speak when he is spoken to,
And behave mannerly at table:
At least as far as he is able.*

—*Robert Louis Stevenson*

*A*fter they dropped Edward at the cousins' home on Stradella Road, they descended Saint-Cloud in the four-wheel Cadillac truck that took them to and from school. The gentle driver, Epitacio, was aptly named; he rarely spoke, and when he did, one could imagine the words being his last. The children were enormously fond of him.

"Epi, can we stop at Rexall for nonpareils?" The chauffeur shrugged as if to disappoint, then toothily grinned. Tull turned his attentions to Lucy. "So what's going on with Edward? Seemed like he had a fever or something."

"He's OK." She tapped her fingers and stared out the window. "He might have another surgery. No biggie."

They sat quietly while Epitacio guided the SUV toward Cedars, down, down, down through the stone West Gate.

"That *is* weird about your mother and those babies."

"My parents are kind of insane, if you haven't noticed. The whole Trotter *dynasty*—and that means you, too. And ever since this *Forbes* thing—"

"How high was your dad on the list?"

"Like, the eighteenth-richest person."

"How much?"

"Nine-point-four."

"Billion?"

"Duh."

"Whoa."

"He's been on this giant binge."

"What do you mean?"

"He got totally freaked when someone told him Ted Turner was the biggest private landowner in the country."

"Like how much?"

"Turner? Like a million and a half acres."

"In the U.S.?"

"And the world. Argentina, I think."

"Whoa."

"Dad doesn't really *want* that. I think he visited a few ranches for sale in Wyoming, but—can you imagine my father on a ranch? So he started buying . . . really *strange* things instead."

"Like?"

"Buildings. Big, empty buildings. Foreclosure stuff. You have no *idea* how many empty buildings there are."

"For investing?"

"He doesn't *do* anything with them—they just sit there with *home-less* people inside."

"Squatters."

"Whatever."

"He probably has a master plan." Tull fiddled with a mahogany air vent. "Lucy . . . do you think Edward's serious about all that maze stuff? You don't think he actually thinks my mother would—"

"Oh, don't be so paranoid. We *have* to take him into the maze, we *all* have to go, right into the middle—just to get it over with. Put him in a wheelbarrow! I'm writing a mystery about it, you know."

"About what?"

"*The Mystery of the Blue Maze*—Mr. Hookstratten said the school would publish five hundred copies to sell at the fund-raiser. And the lady said I could sell them out of Every Picture Tells a Story."

"What's that?"

"A store for kids' books. Mr. Hookstratten says it's a natural. He said publishers love it when a real kid writes a book, it could be a fran-chise. He said I should make it a little hard-edged, like maybe the girl's grandma is dying."

"That's depressing."

"It's *real*. He said that's the trend."

Lucy glanced out the tinted window at the Beverly Center as they swooped toward the drugstore. She surveyed it with abstracted hauteur—

as if she owned the dun-colored retail fastness and all the serfs who desperately congregated within. A man with an aluminum crutch stood outside the Hard Rock with a sign: SOMEONE HELP ME.

"That's sort of why I wanted to come tonight. For research."

"But Bluey isn't dying."

"I *know* that," she said disdainfully. "It's still good for research. Mr. Hookstratten says the *When a Grandparent Dies* books do really well in the marketplace." Tull frowned at his cousin's mercenary ways. "*The Mystery of the Blue Maze.* Isn't that cool? Mr. Hookstratten said it's better when you put a color in the title."

"Shouldn't it be green? A green maze?"

"That's the *cliché*," she said, sounding much like her brother. "Anyhow, green looks blue in the dark. I already have the cover—I get all my ideas that way. I always start with a cover. Want me to describe it?" Without waiting for an answer, she hunched like a witch ready to conjure. "It's midnight, and a girl—I *may* name her Lucy—creeps toward the dark mouth of the maze. I'm calling it a maze, not a labyrinth, because Mr. Hookstratten said maze is less complicated. That with children's books you could be *ironic* but not *complicated.* Anyway, Lucy—if that's what I decide to name her—is in a long, flowing robe. She glides across the lawn, carrying a brass taper in her hand. The flame flickers across her thin, anxious, pretty face—"

"Did you hear about the tapir at the zoo?" he asked impetuously.

"I mean *taper,* as in *candle . . .*"

"It tore off the keeper's arm."

"I really don't care."

The spell was broken; her expression curdled as Tull gave rein to a diabolically mischievous impulse. Impious and inspired, he leaned across the front seat and reached upward. "Let's talk to the *man!*" Epitacio smiled as the boy pressed a button on the roof console; a little arpeggio played, like the one that languorously strummed when he turned on his ThinkPad. Then came a Voice from the mystical GPS ether.

"Good evening, Mr. Trotter!" the Voice greeted, setting Tull to giggle. "How may I be of assistance?"

Lucy crossed her hairy arms and fumed.

"Trotter Junior here. Can you tell us our location?"

"Right now we have you on San Vicente and La Cienega," said the Voice, absurdly mispronouncing the latter boulevard.

"And where are *you?*"

"Detroit, Michigan, sir!"

They pulled into the Rexall; Tull could barely contain himself. "We're, uh, looking for someplace to eat."

"All right, Mr. Trotter . . . let me just check my guide. . . . I have a Locanda Veneta, on Third? Let's see—just bear with me, Mr. Trotter, while I pull this up—if you're in the mood for meat, there's Arnie Morton's, on La Cienega . . ."

Tull, in the firm grip of a virulent strain of silliness, merely gaped at his cousin. Lucy violently froze him out.

"We're actually in the mood"—now Tull looked at Epitacio as he said it—"for a *Cedars* salad. Where do you think we could get a nice *Cedars* salad?"

After a few moments' interchange, he jumped out.

When Tull returned with his bag of Sno-Caps, the voice from the satellite had apparently long since departed. They doubled back to the hospital. Lucy waited until they were upstairs in the enclosed pedestrian bridge before speaking.

"Tull," she said in low tones. "There's something I wanted to talk to you about—about your father."

"What about him?" he asked hesitantly.

"I'm thinking of using it for my story."

"What story?"

"The Mystery of the Blue Maze."

"Using what?"

"Do you mind if I ask you about him? For research."

"Go ahead."

They entered a kind of hushed sitting area, bordered by a wall of lithographs. He felt suddenly uneasy, and it wasn't solely from the subtle shift in the balance of power.

"Well, would you mind—and you don't have to answer—would you mind if I asked how he died?"

"You know how he died."

"I have to ask—for journalistic reasons."

"But you're writing fiction."

"It's just the way you have to ask when you're researching. So, do you want to talk about it or not?"

"In a snowmobile accident."

"Where?"

"Where what?"

"Where did he pass away?"

"You *know* where he passed away. In New Mexico."

"When?" She paused, then said, "You don't have to answer if you don't want to."

"Why wouldn't I want to, Lucy?"

"I don't know. I just don't want you to be uncomfortable. I'm not that kind of writer—I don't believe in *forcibly* interrogating a subject. You never get the truth that way."

"This is bullshit."

"Fine. You don't have to answer."

"March, the year I was born. 'Eighty-eight."

"Then he passed away right after you were conceived."

"That's obvious, isn't it?"

"Mr. Hookstratten said *nothing* is obvious. And what did your father do? I mean, for a living? You don't have to answer."

He wondered what she was up to. If it was payback for his earlier high jinks, she'd gone overboard.

"He studied the classics. He went to the Sorbonne in Paris."

"A scholar. *Really* . . ."

"Why do you want to know?"

"My parents were having an argument. They were talking about Aunt Trinnie—you know, Mom's always been jealous, she always thought Dad paid her too much attention or something. Anyway, Mom and Dad were having this fight. I think what happened was, Mom called to ask Trinnie if she wanted to name one of the dead babies—they give them names before burying them—and you can imagine what Trinnie said. Probably something really mean and funny. So Mom ran back to Dad and said she was trying to be friends with Trinnie but Trinnie was being a major bitch and that Trinnie should just get *over* it and get a life. Mom said Trinnie was putting on a big act and all that Dad and Grandpa Lou ever did was indulge her and she'd never get off drugs that way. Then Mom started talking about the tragedy of Edward and how much courage it took for them to raise him and how Trinnie could never face anything like that herself and was always running away—that it *was* sad what happened with Marcus—your dad—but that she had to take some responsibility, because *she* picked him in the first place and people don't wind up together for no reason and Trinnie was probably better off it happened right away instead of later."

"That *what* happened?"

"That he left the way he did."

"By dying—"

"But he *didn't* die. He *never* died. That's what I'm saying. That's the whole point of the story."

CHAPTER 6

The Great Race

The two cousins visited Bluey awhile, ensconced in her twenty-five-hundred-dollar-a-day high-roller suite—twenty-five hundred above Blue Cross, that is—with the concealed cardiac monitor wiring, silent infrared call system, marble bath and sitting room with parquet floor, Scalamandré brocaded sofa under Jasper Johns collage, orchids—*Rhyncostylis gigantea*, smelling of cinnamon and nutmeg—and faux Chippendale desk and chairs. It was even nicer than Mount Sinai's 11 West, where Mr. Trotter once stayed with his pneumonia. She was attended by Winter, Trinnie and Dodd's erstwhile nanny, but occasionally a "floor concierge" (trained, courtesy of the Laguna Ritz-Carlton) poked his head in, bearing fresh linens and imported magazines, anime for the kids and doctor-approved treats Bluey had bused in from Frenchie's, her favorite downtown bakery. The hospital bed, its quilt and duvet brought from home, was covered with obituaries from the *Times*, both coasts'. Winter busied herself by placing the ones not under current scrutiny in a suede photo album, its cover bearing the Trotter family arms within an embossed cartouche.

In fact for most of the children's visit Bluey was on the phone with her son, the aforementioned eighteenth-richest person in the United States, reading death notices aloud like they were funny pages. Bluey was strong as an ox; the memorials were a tonic. She'd been an aficionado for years and now included Dodd in her enthusiasms, tracking him down to announce a public figure's controversial or banal demise (actually, the figure needn't be all that public to qualify). If he'd already heard it on the news, Dodd liked to feign surprise. At first, he thought it macabre, but since he'd never had easy ingress to Bluey's heart, he let her build this supernal bridge of bones; before long, mother and son stood on the great span and warmly communed, watching a back-page parade of departed souls.

Tull supposed that his cousin got enough "research" watching Bluey—what with her preternaturally keen eyes darting like Pixar bug antennae as she jotted things down in the green leather Smythson of Bond Street ms. notebook with the whimsical gilt heading: BIRD NOTES. He listlessly pushed tarragon around on the rack of lamb (Lucy had kimchi) delivered from the hospital's gourmet kitchen by a bow-tied black-jacketed server, and was glad Grandma was preoccupied with her call, because his braided friend had delivered a blow from which he had not, nor ever would, recover.

He went to bed early, like an invalid. The sudden notion of his father being alive had conferred a strange new sickness, and his head grew as heavy as Edward's. Swathed in six-hundred-count Pratesi sheets, a goose-down pillow over his face, Tull sweatily descended—first imagining himself in the labyrinth, shuffling through narcotic mist to mysterious middle, then on to more prosaic fields—a dark school playground, where cottony smoke also swirled. His dreams were unsettling that night. He had shed his innocence; Lucy had fired the pistol and the perverse, arduous race of life had officially begun. Twitching in troubled sleep, Pullman's was the only familiar face, but even the Dane was creepily confabulated, a dog patch of ill-fitting body parts amid Tull's tule fog REM. The rest of the supernatural school yard's denizens were strangers, more phantom than corporeal, and filled him with anguish and apprehension. It seemed as if they were beings of pure emotion, pure feeling, but the emotions and feelings of luminous deep-sea creatures whom he could never know.

～

Grandpa Lou chuffed awhile with "my Danish friend" before retiring to the library to look over the maquettes of his future grave.

The walls of the vast "Withdrawing Room," three thousand square feet in area and two stories tall, were fronted by an ornately paneled restoration of fifteenth-century Italian wood intarsia. Trompe l'oeil murals of Piranesi's *Imaginary Prisons* hung in other spaces: mossy, forbidding underground expanses. Amid thousands of vellum volumes were priceless gouaches and oils—smallish Bonnards, Twomblys and Klimts—old spheres and compasses, a letter and poem written in French in van Gogh's hand—

> Tell me the story simply, as to a little child.
> For I am weak and weary, and helpless and defiled. . . .
> Tell me the story always, when you have cause to fear,
> That this world's empty glory, is costing me too dear

—a scale model of Vanbrugh's Temple of the Four Winds (appropriated for the cover of his grandchildren's private school's literary magazine), a similarly scaled version of Le Corbusier's chapel at Notre-Dame-du-Haut that he'd picked up while in Paris with Trinnie and her fiancé, a shrunken eighteenth-century Louis XVI mahogany armchair, a sixty-year-old potted two-foot-high grove of bonsai juniper trees ($23,000, from Dimson Homma in Manhattan), an original pilaster from the Pantheon and a minuscule copy of the Bacchus Room at Villa Barbaro. Among gaudy torchères were a clutter of miniature "stairways to heaven," their atheistic steps ending as abruptly as a hangman's scaffolding. Mr. Trotter commissioned such a spiral for his grave; the cabinetmaker David Linley did a mock-up, delivering it with a Carlton House–style writing desk, gratis. Knowing his client's taste for follies, he painstakingly built a detailed replica of the famed Russian grotto at Kuskovo to span the tabletop's length.

Which brings us to the finely detailed tomb fantasias—twenty-five to date, on pedestals—and he walked among them, chuffing and musing. The idea came to him after visiting the Hollywood Forever Cemetery near Gower. The handsome young midwesterner who owned the place told Trotter that a family mausoleum could be had for around two hundred thousand "off the shelf," though available models were rather wretched. It was then that the old man recalled a contest in Copenhagen, a kind of peacock affair, in which architects submitted plans for a series of shed-size garden pavilions, and luminaries such as Graves, Botto and Isozaki had applied. The concept was a bit precious (like those books that feature celebrity doodles), but when he saw photographs of the eclectic, somber, spirited results, he heard his calling and came closer to solving an endgame puzzle too; he would make a contest to design his grave.

In short order, the "Trotter Funerary" became one of architecture's hot cynosures—handling the big themes on a small, elegiac scale was a natural for the vanity portfolio, even if the designs remained unbuilt. Mr. Trotter personally contacted the world-class talents whose aesthetic captured his fancy. He would have them create miniatures of projected works—temple, sculpture, earthwork—the only requisite being that each was no larger than 300 square feet. Anything could be submitted: a pile of "sacred" rocks would do. He remembered the megalithic slabs of Avebury, in the bare, chalky downs of southern England's Wiltshire . . . let the tourists troop down *Westwood*'s Wilshire to see the Trotter Stones, a ring of nineteen just like those at Penzance, waist-high in broom sedge and gorse, hard by the graves of Marilyn and Burt, Dean and Natalie and John (Cassavetes). Oh, he *liked* it. Let there be tors and barrows, hollows and cairns! It had all gone swimmingly, even though he couldn't for the death of him make up his mind: so far, the only entry taken out of the running was Richard Meier's; Trinnie gibed that selected future wags would call his crypt "a Getty gift shop adjunct." There it sat, withdrawn in the Withdrawing, a small, slick white-tiled elephant.

Here they were, then: Gehry's neoclassical bowl-shaped marble carp, an homage to Louis XIV's obsession as much to the gefilte fish of his youth; George Hargreaves's loamy waves of rattlesnake- and blue-grass; a tiny replica of the incestuous tomb of Halicarnassus (built for Mausolus and Artemisia, a married brother and sister); a pistachio-colored room built by Renzo Piano, its floating roof's aluminum petals powdered and powered by the sun; a Frank Stella "Dresden" folly with entrance through a berm; a copper barrel-vaulted "dwelling" by Bartholomew Voorsanger from a drawing by Mies, with climate control, olive wood interiors and walls of gneiss hewn from one of Mr. Trotter's own quarries; Charles Jencks's *Alice in Wonderland* miniature golf course plot of sliced ponds, carved crescent tumuli and grassy ziggurats; a "mouth of Hell" martyrium; Len Brackett's mortise-and-tenon tea-house, inspired by the Pine-Lute Pavilion (wood planed so smoothly it required no sealant); a cunning replica of the James Smith–designed mausoleum at Greyfriars churchyard in Edinburgh; Rafael Moneo's stone ruin of a seventeenth century–style cloister, with echoes of his own Our Lady of the Angels still taking shape in downtown L.A.; Rem Koolhaas's stainless-steel cage and huge rusty oculi with ghostly elevator that silently motored to the roof; another stairway to nowhere from

Predock, made of water and riverstone; Herzog and de Meuron's nod to their famed Yountville winery, with more gneiss, ground up and held together by signature mesh—the old man loved the way the light filtered through the arrowhead shards into the sanctum; two curved walls that formed parentheses, after a children's area conceived by Noguchi for a park on the island of Hokkaido; Robert A. M. Stern's playful Palladian villa (the only one Trotter had had built to scale, for chez Pullman); a Hellenistic pyramid, typical of those found in Constantine and Tripolitania, stretching skyward into obelisk sleekness; a sixth-century Palmyrene tower-tomb, four stories tall, with burial compartments on each level; various bronze maidens weeping over TROTTER-emblazoned sarcophagi; an angel leading a downcast naked man of formidable physique into a stained-glass tomb; Tadao Ando's Gordian sluice of bamboo-shaped aqueducts; Lauretta Vinciarelli's classic enfilade of slick aluminum sheds; Zaha Hadid's symbolic, mournful tekton bridge; Daniel Libeskind's zinc-clad bunker, stabbed eerily by unframed window openings (you peered in and saw empty vitrines, as if in an abandoned museum. Dodd liked this one best); Shodo Suzuki's Zen garden of pine, bamboo, irises and azaleas; and Trinnie's favorite, after a tomb at cobblestoned Lachaise—a painted couple staring out from the crypt's window frame with a kind of haunted, remonstrating indifference.

That was the image he turned over while drifting to sleep in the master bedroom of the main house. The California king felt good; he hadn't slept on it in years. What brought him back there tonight? His wife would be home from Cedars tomorrow. Tomorrow, like a mad scientist, he would return to the "bespoke" Murphy bed that sprang from the vast study's muraled wall.

We have described how Louis Trotter and the boy closed the night. But what of Trinnie?

Ron Bass had, in fact, been at the gala. Inadvertently introduced to Ralph Mirdling, he was most gracious and kind, even correctly pronouncing his name. Thus charmed, the fledgling screenwriter unraveled.

Home from the Animal CAT-scan Ball, she sent the boyfriend back to his Koreatown single and promptly went to bed. Couldn't sleep. Threw on clothes and raced down the hill, tucking the old chocolate-brown

Cabriolet beneath a suppurating magnolia. Through a bosk of cotton-woods was a hillock with a culvert, but the drain wasn't real. There was a wad of chain link deep inside the baffle, and a lock for which only she had the key.

Under mysterious moonlight (much like Lucy's taper girl, but wearing a Y's bis LIMI box-coat) she made her way to the broken tower. The wind blew wild and the yews' brushy applause made her hair stand on end, a commotion that covered the startled exhalation of a man in pressed bib overalls; he saw she wasn't a trespasser and hung back, charting her progress from the blind of a myrtle ball. She entered the column, snubbed by the lonely groups of dusty white tents within, then clambered up a corkscrew stairwell to the fourth-floor bed. Everywhere was mildew, and bad smells; weeks ago, a possum died up there, seeping fluids into the faded, hand-printed Indian-patterned toile de Jouy.

She got into bed, drew the cold cover to her collarbone and fell quickly to sleep.

CHAPTER 7

Song of the Orphan Girl

*W*e should leave the Trotters awhile; they'll do well enough alone. An essential part of our story takes place downtown—the jump from riches to rags, admittedly shopworn, cannot be helped.

The buttery treats Bluey favored herself at hospital could only be found at Frenchie's, a homely shop on Temple Street. They were something relatively new, made from pomegranate grains dressed with almonds by the affable, rail-thin Gilles Mott, Mrs. Trotter's longtime confectionary confidant. She'd met him years ago, detouring from a museum walkabout; a sugary courtship had begun.

But this isn't the moment to speak of the exuberance with which the baker donated fresh pastries to local missions and shelters (his favorite being St. Vincent's, called Misery House by habitués) or of the 255-pound homeless schizophrenic named Will'm, who asserted a steady appreciation for those donated goods, not to mention a profoundly nuanced affinity for baking them too—who lived beneath an overpass in a customized dwelling made from wedded squads of GE refrigerator boxes etched and blotted with finely wrought ink-and-Crayola murals—Will'm (for that is how he pronounced it, and those around him followed suit), who spoke fluently of a Victorian circle of friends and lovers in a voice that could boom, if he chose, which rarely he did, like a god's or beast's among men. It *is* time to speak of Amaryllis, age eleven, toffee-colored, ravenous, rapturous nail-biter, leonine head of hair, self-taught and more than capable of reading the entire *Los Angeles Times* in a two-and-a-half-hour go; who keeps a cigar box, its thin trapdoor-mouth shut by straight pins, filled with favorite clippings; whose tiny breasts, beneath vintage tatterdemalion Natalie Imbruglia sweatshirt, are discolored by burns and scarified by cutting—one ruined nipple chronically leaking clear fluid—whose thighs and buttocks are blistered by a shiny field of keloids: all this, one way or another, courtesy of her mother, Geri, who not so long ago stopped being thirty-three. Dark-skinned, ash-blond and ashen, she lies with broken larynx on the mattress, having hemorrhaged into the strap muscles of her neck, with attendant fracture of the greater cornu of the left hyoid bone. So the coroner's report later said.

Amaryllis sits at Geri's bedside (not too close) four or five times a day. She peers at the body, looks away, then back; away—listening to the Muzak of everyday life, the shouts, coughs, thumps, canned TV laughs—then back, watching a whirligig of light and shadow on her mother's sparkless face, torso propped awkwardly in death almost a week now. A knotted sheet loops under chin and the corpse endures the prop with dignity, like a vaudevillian undergoing a zany toothache cure. Staring thus, Amaryllis is sometimes unsure of what she sees, as when finding a word in the paper she cannot decipher, though it be goadingly familiar. Young siblings sleep in kitchen on flattened cardboard while she sprays 409 around the body, already draped in extra sheets and anchored by pillows to stanch the smell.

Friday, when Amaryllis first discovered her, she knew something irrevocable had happened. Yet if she called 911 or brought someone to look and it turned out Geri was only sleeping, she would dearly pay. So the girl sat and stared instead, thinking: *If she doesn't wake up for my birthday, she's really dead.* The time for commemoration came and went.

The sheet snakes over headboard and catches the neck before returning whence it came. During her vigil, kneeling like a supplicant before the bed, Amaryllis contemplates the creamy cable of linen whose underbed origins are too spooky to imagine, let alone investigate. What, exactly, did this sheet want with her mom? It was like something out of that movie she saw on TV—alarm clocks, blankets and dustpans flying around behind bedroom doors as if they had minds of their own (that little midget woman came to save the day). But Amaryllis is busy enough hushing and feeding and changing the babies to dwell: been busy like that for years. The babies are good and beautiful and she loves them with all her heart. She sings made-up lullabies, and, when they finally sleep, goes out to forage.

The giant gave her food and pastries. At first, she thought he wanted to touch her, but he never did. Topsy—that's what Will'm wished her to call him—was a scavenger himself and provided the girl with cooked meals in hard plastic containers covered with aluminum foil, courtesy, he said, of chefs at the Biltmore. Sometimes the unlikely couple ate high-end spoils under the 4th Street Bridge, where he lived; he threw scraps to a confederate's dog, a mangled pit bull called Half Dead. He spoke British and the sound of the words was rich and full and coarse and it seemed to her he'd shatter the air itself if ever he gave full voice.

Topsy hailed from a village called Essex, a place "now terribly Cock-nified and choked up by the jerry-builder." The house he was evicted from had been (might still be) called Woodford Hall, and he said he longed to go back—though he sometimes referred to the childhood seat as Elm House or Red House, Kelmscott Manor or Horrington; Bexley-heath in Kent, the Retreat at Hammersmith, Queen's Square or Merton Abbey on the River Wandle near Wimbledon. Among many peculiar things he spoke of were his "beastly, wondrous" adventures in Iceland, his beloved wife, Jane, and Jenny, their epileptic daughter; and a current labor of love, the Society for the Preservation of Ancient Buildings. Topsy loathed anything modern, and it seemed to Amaryllis he had the impression the year—*this* year of Our Lord—was 1840 or '60 or '80 or sometime "bigly twixt." He used words she read in the newspaper but had never understood, and took the time to tell her what they meant (she thought that explaining the English language was all part of being an Englishman).

He lived in a box on which he'd painstakingly drawn a colorful woodsy scene. Underbridge denizens had dubbed this nomadic place the Cadillac because of its capacious dimensions and luxury; Topsy called it the Manor. She had never seen such a lovely thing—graced by a mural filled with bounteous trees and birds and fruits, leaves and blossoms, fly-ing insects and little branches. On sallow windblown trompe l'oeil ban-ners, Topsy had inscribed

> i once a king and chief
> now am the tree bark's thief
> ever twixt trunk and leaf
> chasing the prey.

He never asked her inside, and of that she was *almost* glad, but Amaryllis heard its sturdy corrugated cardboard furnishings had been fashioned by his able craftsman's hands. When visiting, Topsy made sure they sat out of sight of the street; the police, he said, mostly left the encampment unbothered, but the presence of a young girl was something they'd be forced to look into. The underbridge wasn't gloomy— airy as Union Station, its hilly carpet of dirt was packed clean and firm. On sunny days, a breeze like the sigh of a secret garden blew through. There were sleepy dogs (other than Half Dead, who never seemed to sleep at all), well-behaved "town-birds"—that's what Topsy called them—and bleached white dishrags that on closer inspection showed themselves to be large rats the English colossus had poisoned and deposited by the gray concrete stanchions like so many houseplants. Most of the time, the two didn't take a formal meal; he gave her the boxes to bring home, offering samples from each, along with simple, civilized lectures about their individual ingredients as she tasted. He knew something about her, because she'd told him things over the months. He knew about her brother and sister and gave food for them that was easy to chew: butter-squash soups, marmalade and mashed potatoes. (She always made certain to bring the containers back, neatly scrubbed.) Lately, when he asked after her mother, Amaryllis lied.

When she tired of Geri's bedside and the babies were napping or settled and there was no more gathering to be done, Amaryllis sorted through her treasured "classifieds"—the cigar box of pages torn from yellowing newsprint and magazines. There was a sheaf about the child-goddesses of Nepal that told of a Special Council of Selectors, who went from village to village looking for little girls. If the parents agreed, the child was plucked from the family house and put in a palace. Her face was painted and her body adorned with golden robes and she was then called the Royal Kumari. The Royal Kumari was allowed out only during holy festivals. The Royal Kumari couldn't play with other children, because if she cut herself, her godly powers seeped away with the blood. Amaryllis thought she would like to be chosen, but when she read that the Special Selectors wanted a child with unblemished skin, she cried. They would probably want the girl to be virginal, too.

She reread another brittle bundle—this one about Audrey, the Massachusetts girl who'd been asleep with open eyes for the past eleven years. She had fallen into a backyard swimming pool when she was three and had been in a magical coma ever since. Audrey never spoke, but seemed aware of her surroundings; when the family said mass in the house, they noticed that blood sometimes appeared on communion wafers and light-colored oil dripped down statuary. Soon, people made pilgrimages to gaze at her through a big window. Audrey had become a "victim soul," who took on the suffering of those who came to ask for intercession with God to hear their pleas. Though she would be performing a valuable service without having to do much—without having to do anything, really—Amaryllis didn't relish the idea of being half asleep, stared at by strangers all day. She looked up at her mother, imagining for a moment that Geri was Audrey and they were separated by candles and a pane of glass.

She kept her very favorite at the bottom of the pile: the dossier on Sister Benedicta, formerly known as Edith Stein, a "Jewish" who converted to Catholicism and was killed at a place called Auschwitz. The article said that Edith Stein was on a "fast track" to sainthood. When she first read about her, Amaryllis didn't understand. For one thing, she didn't even know saints came from people; she thought they came from angels or myths. When she read about this mere girl, this Jewish who the pope wanted to canonize—which, to Amaryllis, meant shot into sainthood—whole worlds opened up. The orphan was smart enough to know there wasn't such a thing as a Jew saint (her mom had told her), so when she learned Edith was "eligible," it was confusing. But then she grew hopeful; she wanted in. If a Jewish who died not so long ago—a *girl*—could officially become a saint, why not Amaryllis Kornfeld, a half-Jewish herself? Was not the name of their very motel—corner of 4th and Los Angeles—the St. George? Was this not a sign and a wonder? (St. Amaryllis Motel would have been more of a sign, but it was still something.) A quotation read in a *Reader's Digest* left in the lobby clinched it: *If they, why not I? If these men and women could become saints, why cannot I with the help of him who is all-powerful?* A man named Saint Augustine had said it, obviously before he'd been shot through the canon. Amaryllis's father was a Jewish and her mother, part African, but maybe none of it even mattered.

One of the *Times* religion articles was long and detailed, and she set about learning the rules and regulations by heart. Inside the Vatican lived a Congregation for the Causes of Saints, somewhat like the Special

Selectors for the Royal Kumari. In the Congregation for the Causes of
Saints there was a "postulator," who did the nominating. The postulator
was the one who needed to come up with evidence of the holiness of
whoever was elected. He needed to find examples of what they called
heroic virtue and did that by interviewing people who knew the nominee. Once the person was found to have heroic virtue, they received a
declaration from the pope allowing them to be called Venerable. They
could then be venerated in their local community. Amaryllis thought
the Congregation could interview Topsy, who would attest to her overall
humility and general hardships, and made a mental note that if she received a declaration, she would be in a stronger position to nominate the
charitable Englishman himself. But first things first: if all went well, she
might eventually be allowed to carry the title of Venerable Amaryllis
Kornfeld of Los Angeles. The Congregation usually waited until the person to be sainted actually died, but *this* pope had waived all that and
in the case of Mother Teresa already had an archbishop working on
beatification—*this* pope seemed to be in such a hurry that the rules were
constantly changing or being broken. Anyhow, Amaryllis didn't think it
was important if, when crowned, she was dead or alive, but thought it
would probably be more fun to be alive, at least for a little while.

Some people said Pope John Paul II was hurrying to make new
saints because he didn't think he had long to live and wanted to spread
the Gospel of Christ far and wide. Because he moved with such dispatch,
the clippings spoke of his sacred mandate as if it were an evangelical car
race—the process had been "streamlined" and "overhauled," becoming
altogether "speedy." Things certainly were moving along at a fast clip.
For example, in olden days there used to be a Promoter of the Faith,
whose entire job was to argue against new nominees to ensure that no
one unworthy became a saint. The Promoters were called Devil's Advocates, but John Paul, in all his streamlining, had sent them packing. Another example of speediness was the beatification. After a person was
declared Venerable, the next step to being crowned was beatification,
which *used* to require two miracles, but now you only needed one unless
you were a martyr, in which case you didn't need a miracle at all (they
never explained what a martyr was, but Amaryllis reasoned it must be
something good). It had to be what they called a "healing" miracle,
something science couldn't explain.

After beatification, all that was left was to be canonized, which also used to require two miracles, but because of John Paul, the Congregation for the Causes said they'd be happy with just one: now it was *one* miracle for each step, plus *no* Devil's Advocate! Amaryllis hadn't yet come across any child saints, but this pope was a maverick and anything seemed possible. He had already beatified something like a thousand people, "eclipsing the 20th-century record of Pius XII, who only beatified twenty-three." Nominees were pouring in every day. One of the articles even said the next pope might be from Mexico or Vietnam.

She stared at the picture of the Blessed Edith Stein, dark and sad, her long handsome face framed by a halftone wimple. She'd been beatified a few years before Amaryllis was born, on the basis of the 1987 case of the daughter of a pastor, who overdosed on Tylenol samples she'd thought were candy. When the girl fell into *her* magical coma, the family prayed for Blessed Edith to intercede with God on their behalf; when she awakened, her Jew doctor was surprised. He was summoned to the Vatican to be interrogated by the Congregation for the Causes. The doctor said he didn't believe in miracles per se—reading aloud, Amaryllis pronounced it "percy"—and that in his heart he had never expected her to recover. (Amaryllis thought that wishing patients the worst was maybe the way of Jew doctors.) There was a photo of the saved girl, with big features like Amaryllis's but lily-white.

Before going out, the novitiate knelt by her mother, a demon who had sold her for drugs and held her down to be raped and burned by a tubercular woman. Amaryllis shut her nose to the putrescence and closed her eyes, willing Geri to come alive; she would perform a healing miracle that the Congregation would need acknowledge "percy." She would make her mother live. And if she *didn't* rise, there were other "proofs" science could not explain—wasn't Amaryllis's survival a miracle in itself? The Congregation for the Causes of Saints would come and see that the babies were well cared for; under her hand they had bloomed, with defiant unruly innocence, like succulents in hell. There were manifest miracles from which the Congregation could choose.

She closed the door behind her and made sure the Korean busybody manager wasn't in the hall. She stooped to stuff paper under the door, damming the fumes. Her heart swelled as she left the St. George, soaking in the light. She clung to the rosary of words *People* magazine said had been so dear to the Blessed Edith Stein: *Secretum meum mihi.*

This is my secret . . .

CHAPTER 8

Concentric Circles

*A*maryllis set out for the bridge. She'd been thinking that if she told Topsy about her mother, he might have an idea what to do. She passed a mission, then cut down Winston Street—sometimes he loitered on the sidewalk outside Misery House and made cardboard begging signs for the men in his distinctive calligraphic hand. He wasn't there. The orphan kept a darting, furtive lookout as she moved; she didn't want to be picked up for truancy.

On Grand Avenue, trucks and trailers lined the curb. Pedestrians gathered in curious clumps to watch, but there was nothing to see, at least so it seemed. Amaryllis slowed, wending her way toward the blaze of lights that came from the desiccated lobby of the Coronation, one of the bigger SROs. A distant shout of "Quiet!" and a baffled roundelay followed, each voice handing off to the next, all coming closer, some electronically enhanced—"Quiet!" Then another cavalcade. But instead of "Quiet!" this time they yelled, "Speed!" A girl with purple hair and a ring through her nose like a bull glared fiercely at Amaryllis, gesturing her to be silent. She froze. A voice crackled over a radio: "We! Are! Rolling!" Then, the final chorus: Rolling!—Rolling!—Rolling! The little girl quaked, waiting for a bomb to go off, certain that's what was happening. Under her breath, she beseeched: *Benedicta Benedicta Benedicta . . .* and the world stood still. She prayed that if she died then and there, an angel's emissary would get to the babies and keep them from harm. She even wondered what a person who'd been blown to bits looked like in heaven. Then, the crackling voice tore into her reverie: "And . . . cut!"

The woman with the bull ring echoed, with great purpose but to no one in particular, "Cut!"—then turned on her heel, leaving Amaryllis to fend for herself.

There was much coming and going and people laughing, and she was certain the bomb had been defused. The blinding lights still shone in the window and she made her way toward them. As she threaded the crowd, it was as if she were invisible. She passed a bum, who smoked and wore sunglasses. He rested a hand on his leg in regal fashion and guffawed, phlegmy and herniated, while a smiling, serious boy with headphones handed him a Styrofoam cup of coffee.

"All right!" someone yelled. "Here we go! Last looks!"

When Amaryllis got *very* close to the Coronation lobby lights, she hid behind a truck and watched a strange scene: a beautiful girl of about thirteen sat on an upturned wooden crate, hair brushed and combed by two bizarre-looking women with beehives and tattoos. The beautiful girl chattered with someone the orphan couldn't readily see. Then a man came along to powder her face while another smoothed the pleats of her dress and primped a collar. It seemed to Amaryllis everyone around the beautiful girl was polite and reserved and happy and the beautiful girl had made them so—just as she imagined life among the entourage of the Royal Kumari. Then she saw with whom the girl was gossiping: two friends sitting opposite on a shared milk crate, only theirs was horizontal to make them closer to the ground than she who was illuminated. Her companions were a boy and girl, both fair, red and pretty, and the girl's braids dangled so they nearly touched the grotty, gum-flattened sidewalk.

"Is that part of the movie?" asked the boy of the beautiful girl.

"Is what?" she said.

"The snot." He pointed to her nose. "Are you supposed to have snot?"

The beautiful girl grew serious as finger flew to nostril; then she looked at the boy with narrowed, beady eyes and he laughed. "I *hate* you, Tull! I hate you!" she said, but she wasn't really mad and the man powdering her backed off to fetch a Kleenex, which he then applied to the beautiful girl's upper lip until she seized it, completing the job herself. The other adults continued to brush and fluff and straighten and comb—the finishing touches of merry, manic elves.

"*Qui—et!*" came an anonymous voice.

And another: "Quiet, everyone!"

"First team!"

More scurrying. More commands, and the adjusting of machines.

"And . . . roll sound!"

"We—are—speeding!"

"Roll camera!"

"Rolling."

"*And* . . . We! Are! Rolling!"

The voices made their way to the outer reaches, where Amaryllis had stood in frozen repose only minutes before. Within an instant, the beautiful girl had stopped laughing and risen from the crate, which was neatly whisked away; her helpers lingered like bees reluctant to leave a flower. A gangly man stood by, listening to someone through headphones while holding a long pole, the end of which wobbled over the beautiful girl as she smoothed her own skirt. Then, a sudden, perfect silence. A man with long, stringy hair said: "Action, Boulder!"

At which the beautiful girl took a deep breath before walking determinedly toward the lobby door. A short muscleman type followed her with a camera strapped to a thick belt on some sort of hinged pivot; trailed by the man with stringy hair and then by the *other* man, gangly and serious-looking, the long pole held high over his head, along with assiduous minions who crouched and slinked noiselessly beside the beefy one with the pivoting camera, some holding aloft cables in his wake as if attending a rubbery bridal train—but the actress's entrance to the hotel was blocked by the bum Amaryllis had seen earlier. This time his dark glasses were gone. He carried a bottle of brown-bagged wine instead of a Styrofoam cup.

"Out of my way!" she shouted.

"*Your* way!" said the bum, hissing. "You've always had it *your* way, haven't you, Missy?"

"I'm looking for my mother!"

More stumblebums appeared.

"Hear her, boys? She's looking for Mother!"

They cackled and howled, rolling over the word in their mouths like pirates molesting a treasure chest.

In the midst of all this, the redheaded boy on the crate caught Amaryllis's eye. She grimaced and later regretted not softening her features when he smiled. As if aware of her discomfort, he turned back to the scene at hand. The beautiful girl vigorously pushed aside the lead bum, then stormed into the SRO. Apparently, this was the funniest thing in the world, because the bums let loose with an explosion of rollicking huzzahs; the man with the stringy hair watched like a giddy child at a puppet show, then yelled, "And . . . *cut* it!" They repeated the exact same sequence at least five times, the spaces between "Cut!" and "Action!" filled with a kind of wild yet militarily controlled commotion.

Finally, the stringy-haired one spoke animatedly to the sweat-soaked muscleman, who tried to listen but was mostly interested in the progress of those unburdening him of the camera, which they finally did, lifting it off like the saddle of a tired and finicky mule. A voice called out, "Checking the gate!" while the gangly man peered into the lens. Then someone said, "Gate is clear!" and there were bursts of laughter all around. A familiar chorus of voices called "Lunch!" in the same staticky, concentric, fading circles. The girl with the long braids leapt up to join her beautiful friend, already set upon by the bees or elves or what have you, each of whom seemed to have bottomless pockets filled with small, significant items for every possible need. The redheaded boy—more orange-headed, really—turned again to catch Amaryllis's eye before she walked slowly backward, fading into the general disorder.

⌒⌒

Tull, Lucy and Boulder were escorted to Edward's MSV by the second assistant director.

The Mauck Special Vehicle was built in Ohio with the cousin's needs in mind, at a cost of $275,000. Its gull-wing front doors rose up with frank, freakish efficiency. Within, calfskin recliners sat upon a walnut Hokanson carpet, telephones graced Corian countertops and a huge flat-screen panel downloaded DirecTV from a rooftop dish. Concealed abaft was a state-of-the-art hydraulic docking berth for Edward's golf cart—he could drive right in.

Lunch awaited the guests as they clambered aboard the orchid-filled cabin. Edward was already enthroned in his custom Donghia captain's chair watching soundless CNN, a vast linen nappie tucked between chin and brace. He wore his gloves and "Mauck mask," a lounge-around hood made of festive yellow silk lightly embroidered by his own hand. The cousin sipped leek-and-potato soup with sautéed langoustines and black truffles, FedExed frozen from Lespinasse's 55th Street kitchen, while trays brought by craft-services sprites stood on individual teak stands in readiness; under straining cellophane, industrial-strength

paper plates were heaped with standard Friday film-set fare—barbecued
chicken, biscuits and beans, blackened swordfish and black-eyed peas,
yams and limp salads smeared with yogurty dressing, happy fruit and
less happy cottage cheese. Still another tray was filled solely with desserts: Joyce's precious lemon tarts from Ladurée (Edward had swiped
them from the Stradella freezer), Häagen-Dazs'd brownies, American
apple pie and Everyman's peach cobbler. All in all, not too bad a spread.
In his wisdom, the ever cordial host had adorned placemats with tiny
brown La Maison du Chocolat hatboxes from Neiman's, each one tied
with their distinctive satiny, dark-brown ribbons.

"Oh my God!" said Boulder as she bounded in, wide-eyed at the cor-
nucopia. "Edward, you are amazing!"

"I was going to bring food from home but for some reason it didn't
happen."

"It happened for *you*," said Tull, raising a gentle eyebrow at the
cousin's non-communal meal—minimalist though it was.

"It's just soup." He brought a spoonful to his tiny mouth then wiped
a trickle from the titanium, patting down the protuberant chin with the
bib. Tull thought the veil made him look like a deranged harem girl.

"And who's *that* for?" asked Lucy. She referred to a tray that sat by itself, with food maturely arranged.

"Mr. Hookstratten."

"*He's* coming?" called Boulder with a full mouth, cross-legged on the
Hokanson. "Doesn't he teach today?"

"He's tutoring Dad," said Edward.

At the mention of Uncle Dodd, Tull's heart fluttered—this was the
Forbes coverboy who not only knew unthinkable secrets about his father
but had dared blurt them out to his gossipy girl-child. Of all the people he
could have told! If *Lucy* knew, it was likely *everyone* did. The thought
jolted him. She smugly watched him squirm; he could tell their tacit
agreement not to discuss the recent revelation was near unraveling and
that gave him another hideous frisson. Tull switched to conversational
autopilot.

"What do you mean, tutoring?" he said blandly.

"The fact is," said Lucy (and it seemed to Tull she was at this
moment savoring life to the fullest), "that Father maintains a bit of an
inferiority complex about his abysmal high school GPA. So Mr. Hookstratten comes over and they read the classics. I think it's sweet."

Boulder dabbed at some barbecue sauce that had found its way to the woolen weave.

"Like which classics?" offered Tull. The tension surrounding Lucy and the potential public airing of his uncle's disclosure had the effect of both zombifying and nauseating him, at once.

"I'm sure they'll be taking a look at one of Lucy's faves," laughed Edward. "*When a Grandparent Dies!*"

"Very funny," she said.

Tull winced, remembering how he had upbraided Lucy for her journalistic methods. It was now his prime objective to keep her displeasure at a minimum; he didn't want her provoked by *anyone,* and present company was a volatile mix—Boulder liked to jump on Lucy with as much relish as did Edward. Tull's morbid fear was that if the redhead was teased too much, she might suddenly spill the beans about his father, merely to deflect negative attention—not that Tull could be sure it still *was* a secret. Lucy had always had a crush on him, and that was the only bit of leverage he had in terms of her doing the right and decent thing: keeping her trap shut.

"Seriously, Edward," said Tull, rushing to Lucy's aid with delusional chivalry. "Who are they studying?"

"Oh, you know—Tolstoy, Chaucer . . . Steve Martin's *Shopgirl* . . . all the heavy texts. Daddy pores over it, then Professor Hookstratten deconstructs. Hookstratten *gets busy!*"

Boulder asked if the teacher was going to Europe.

"Europe? For what?" wondered Tull, overeager.

Edward squinted at his friend, annoyed. "You're awfully inquisitive today."

He would have to watch himself; the cousin was onto him. He could smell Tull's fear. "Dad's taking Third-Tier Honors on holiday," sneered Lucy. "Well his plane is, anyway—the Boeing." She gave Tull a contemptuous once-over. "Don't you know *anything?*"

Boulder flipped through a teen girl's fanzine called *All About You!*—ironically, she was on the cover. "I really want to go to that beach in Belgium," she said, bored with the "Star Poll Picks." Boulder said there was a beach in Belgium where if a person wanted to face the sun, they had to turn their back to the ocean; apparently, it was the only beach like that in the world. Lucy said that was weird and Pullman farted. Everyone burst out laughing. At the end of the jag, something caught Tull's eye through the Mauck window.

"Hey," he said. "It's the girl."

"What girl?"

"From the set."

Lucy joined to watch. At odds with herself, the urchin moved inexorably toward the specialty vehicle as if pulled by a great magnet. The reflective glass made it impossible to see her audience.

"Look! She can't help herself," said Lucy. "We're the monolith from *2001*."

"You're about as flat," said Edward.

"What's a monolith?" asked Boulder, blasé.

"She's *sweet*," said Lucy, earnest and patronizing.

Boulder glanced through the window, then flopped onto a $10,000 Costa del Sol Alcazar nightspread. "I hate it when crew bring their fucking kids to the set."

"I don't think she—she looks kind of homeless."

"Maybe she has AIDS."

"Boulder," said Lucy. "That is so mean!" She tended to be exclamatory around her famous friend.

"Or hep C—*everyone's* got hep C. Or scabies! Oh God, do you *remember*, Lucy?"

"I so hated having scabies."

"Well," said Tull, "I'm going to ask her in for lunch."

"*Please* don't!"

"Boulder, we *have* to. I'll use it for my essay."

"What essay?"

Lucy put on her girl-detective/bestselling-author face. "It's research. I'm getting credit for writing about visiting you."

Boulder sighed. "I so hate the homeless."

"Oh my God, Boulder, that is so vile!"

The movie star laughed devilishly and tickled Lucy until she begged for mercy.

"Edward," said Tull. "*You* decide. It's your Mauck."

"*It's my Mauck*," sang Boulder, "*and I'll cry if I want to!*" She did a spastic dance and laughed another starry, bigger-than-life laugh.

"You're *stoned*," said Lucy.

"Well what say, Eddikins?" ventured Tull, in a terrible rendition of some upper-crust character. "Shall we ask her in? Are you a man or are you a Mauck?"

"I say," said the cousin, hand poised thoughtfully to chin brace, "that we haul her unwashed homeless butt aboard."

Boulder beseeched the unsavory visitor be kept at the door with her back to them, like at the Belgian beach.

The sight of her crushed him. Why had he set all this in motion? Tull felt like one of those World War II GIs on the History Channel giving candy to children amid the rubble of cities—only he was about to lure the little one to a death by embarrassment at the hands of his rarefied friends. He hung back in the passenger seat, afraid she'd run.

"Hi," he said. "I'm Toulouse."

He *never* called himself that.

"Tull," he corrected. "Tull Trotter." He felt ridiculous. "What's your name?"

The girl said nothing.

"Do you want—would you like some lunch?"

He hated himself. She just kept staring. Then:

"Amaryllis."

"What?"

An eternal pause, in which he thought she'd bolt.

"My name is Amaryllis."

"Like the place in Texas?" Another massively dumb thing. Again her ancient stare, like the bas-relief of a child's tomb. "My friends—my friends want to meet you." Epic dumbness. Silence. She twitched. He'd blown it. "We have tons of food. If—if you're hungry."

Nothing to do now but retreat. She came closer, like Edith Stein to concentration camp gas. Lucy effusively threw an absurd, corn-fed "Howdy!" at the girl. Tull gave her a look and his cousin demurred. Then he went inside and strode to Mr. Hookstratten's pleated seat, tearing the cellophane off the absentee tutor's tray, wanting to feed her right away. After a minute or so, Amaryllis poked her head under the gull wing, trembling. Tull beckoned and she clambered in. She stood before them, a muted cable news anchor laughing beside her head.

"You must be *so hungry*," said Lucy, coaxing. "What's your name?"

"It's Amaryllis," said Tull.

"Can't she talk?" said Lucy.

Boulder rolled her eyes, shook her head and picked up *Teen People*.

"Your name is Amaryllis? That is *so* pretty!"

"Would you like some chocolates before lunch?"

The orphan turned to see where the voice had emanated from, then focused on the seated apparition ladling soup into its mouth behind a gossamer yellow hood. Astonished, she moved backward, falling. Tull rushed to her aid while the others tittered like munchkins.

"Don't mind Edward. He's, uh, disabled."

The beautiful girl who had played for the camera had spoken. She was lying on a quilted bed, languidly flitting through an old *Weekly Variety*. Her beauty—her luminescence—had a strangely comforting, nearly soporific effect upon the visitor.

"Disabled but still able to *dis*," said Edward.

"Oh, just come and sit," said Boulder to the girl imperiously. "Don't make us beg. It's not attractive."

Amaryllis obeyed. She moved toward her seat and promptly stepped on the dozing Pullman. She shrieked. Barely stirring, the animal broke wind. Amaryllis smiled as everyone laughed, then grew self-conscious and sat grimly, as if reprimanded. Tull was amazed by what that smile did to him.

He took her greasy backpack and hung it from a peg. With his artful encouragements, she began to eat while Lucy and Edward peppered her with questions. Where did she live? (Nearby.) Where did she go to school? (Not far.) Why wasn't she in school? (Getting medicine for her mother.) And what did her mother do? (Worked. Sick today.)

Amaryllis had hardly taken her eyes off Boulder; finally, the stare became fixed.

"Are you an actress?"

"Sometimes."

"She doesn't know who you are!" said Lucy, delighted. Perversely, Boulder made as if she liked that. Lucy turned back to their guest. "She's a very *famous* actress."

Edward watched Tull hover. "God, Tull, cut her food, why don't you."

"When you work for Disney, you don't *act*—I mean, not really. You're sort of . . . animated. You need to look *cute*."

"Which you always do," said Lucy.

"When oh when, *please* can someone let me do an indie?"

"Do you go to school?" asked Amaryllis.

"Oh my God, I'm being interviewed! Mostly on the set. I have a teacher."

"But when she doesn't," said Lucy, "she deigns to attend Four Winds with the pleh-*bee*-enz."

"Four Winds?"

"It's a school," said Tull. "In Santa Monica."

"We all go there."

Amaryllis turned to Edward and asked, "What happened to you?"

The cousin chortled. "Oh, I *like* that! Let's put that on a T-shirt! *What happened to you?* We'd sell millions! I love it!"

"He's got Apert's," said Lucy.

"Big Head Disease," said Boulder. "That's all you need to know."

"He's the smartest boy on earth," said Tull.

"He's a saint," said Lucy.

"They streamlined the process," blurted Amaryllis with enthusiasm, immediately wishing she hadn't. She was rusty. She hadn't spoken with other children for so long—with anyone really, except for Topsy and the babies—and these were like no children she'd ever met . . . but now, she had better go on or they'd think her crazy. "They streamlined the process for becoming a saint. John Paul made it easier. Everyone's on a fast track."

Lucy and Boulder exchanged secret looks and Tull winced, wishing to protect the girl from the half-assed cruelties of the world. He was having major feelings, all of which his braided tormentor noticed with customary alacrity.

"Amaryllis is such a *pretty* name," offered Lucy again, somewhat poisonously.

Tull detected the hint of an English accent and hoped nothing lurid was coming.

"I hate it when you start doing Anna Paquin," said Boulder.

"Does it mean anything?" posed the unflappable inquisitrix. "I mean, the name?"

"It's a flower," said Amaryllis. "From South Africa."

"Is that where you're from?" asked Lucy, brightening. "I mean— Africa?"

Tull bridled and Amaryllis meekly shook her head.

Edward stood from his chair. "Amaryllis, do you like orchids?"

"What are they?" she asked. Boulder rolled her eyes at Lucy again.

"This," said Tull, plucking a flower from a slim celadon vase, "is an orchid." She held the stem in her hand and stared.

"A *hybrid*," said the cousin.

A large white petal stood up like a bishop's miter; beneath it, a pouch in the shape of the chin of a cartoon Mountie—or the chin of the boy called Edward.

Bisecting both was a leafy mustache, speckled with polka dots.

The invalid proffered a discrete flower, with movie-star-red lips. "This one *is* from South Africa—like your name," he said. "It grows on waterfalls."

"You know," said Lucy, "you should really come to Four Winds and visit." She turned to the others. "Don't you think?"

"It'd be great!" said Boulder, rather affectlessly.

"We're doing a homeless project," she continued while Tull glared. "We're building sidewalk shelters—I mean, that's not *why* you should visit. It's just that if you've ever had that *experience* or know someone who *has* . . . We're using really strong, light materials—space-age. And laptops to design them."

"*We* were homeless once," said Boulder.

"The earthquake doesn't count."

"It killed our beach house."

"You had *two* beach houses."

"It killed them *both*."

"She stayed in a hotel for three months."

"A hotel is not a home."

"You stayed at Shutters."

"That's a beach hotel," said Tull for Amaryllis's edification—then hated himself some more.

"That's where I live," chimed the orphan, then frowned. Again, she wished she hadn't spoken. "A motel. The St. George—with my mother and brother and sister."

"A motel! The St. George?" queried Lucy. "I haven't heard of it. Now, is that near the Bonaventure or the Biltmore? Is it four- or five-star?"

Before the torture could continue, there was a sharp rap at the door and Amaryllis nearly jumped from her skin. The arrival of Mr. Hookstratten—Four Winds teacher of the year, private tutor to moguls and occasional on-set educator—was not unexpected, but the children (all but Edward, of course) scurried about as if they'd been up to great mischief. The balding scholar beamed from the driver's side, hand of a raised arm gripping the Mauck wing, blinking in through bulgy, light-sensitive eyes. Boulder and Lucy rushed forward, trying to distract from the sight of Tull, who shadowed the orphan girl as best he could while she seized her backpack and made her way to the passenger-side portal whence she had come—clinging all along to the walls like a tiny cat burglar.

"And who's this?" Mr. Hookstratten cheerily inquired. Boulder said she was the daughter of a grip; Lucy said she was part of "the research project"; Tull said she had helped bring the food trays—all in unison, while Amaryllis quit the luxuriant specialty vehicle, vanishing into the brightness of day.

*W*hen she got to the St. George, there were patrol cars and sedans with revolving red lights stuck on khaki-colored roofs. The babies were already in one of the backseats, with a policewoman fussing over them; the froggy front-office Korean pointed at Amaryllis and the men set after her. She had never run like that before, and prayed to Edith Stein no one would catch her.

She would *have* to find Topsy now. He'd give her shelter, and she would finally tell him everything.

CHAPTER 9

Squatters

*F*ive in the morning. Will'm stood among ovens and large iron machines, unfurling canvas stored in a hard long tube. The hawk-nosed baker, Gilles Mott, held the bird-and-berry scene (the very same depicted in the "Cadillac" 's mural) carefully in flour-dusted hands, an auctioneer apprizing maps of a medieval world.

"It's *very* detailed," he remarked. "Is it a painting?"

"*Fabric*, man—one of our more popular patterns. We call it the Strawberry Thief. Indigo-discharge on block-printed cotton. That's what stained me blue!"

He waved his arms, which, at shoulder joint, were thick as cadets' thighs, but Gilles saw no dye. The baker *did* think it an amazing business, though: this colored parchment with inked green foliage shot through by cocky thrushes, their beaks cadging strawberries hung from tendrils like swollen lanterns.

"Will'm . . . you've been to France, no?"

"I'm not fond of the Frankish tongue nor Frankish things."

He rolled up the "Thief" and replaced it in the scabbard. For a moment, the baker worried his segue had offended, but an old memory stubbornly asserted itself.

Will'm unceremoniously began mopping the concrete. For this and other chores, Gilles paid him minimum wage plus bread, scones and other delectables. Once in a while, the mystery man announced the urge to bake; on such days, his startled benefactor wisely sat back to watch artistry unfold. Tossing off scintillating ciabatta and pane pugliese as if it were child's play, his skill with sweet things was elysian—it was during one of those rare incursions that Bluey's recent favorite, the mille-feuille of almonds and pomegranates, was born, and christened The Perse-phone. (*If only the old woman knew,* thought the baker, *the circumstances of its preparation.*) Yet whenever Gilles offered steady work, the prodigy angrily balked. He soon gave up his entreaties, fearing the man would never come around again.

"You'd look amazing there," said Gilles. "I mean, in France. The French would love you. They wouldn't know what to *make* of you, but they'd love you. That pattern made me think of something. My fiancée and I were having a look around Paris. An arrondissement near the Père-Lachaise—the famous cemetery. *Every* cemetery in France is fa-mous. We thought we could run into Marlene Dietrich, who supposedly lived in an apartment house nearby; we were a little drunk. We finally found the place and stood knocking for fifteen minutes." A polite lis-tener, the transient leaned on the mop to hear him out. "We were just about to leave when a middle-aged woman came to the door. *Not* Mar-lene. What I remember were her eyes: dilated. One of those opium eaters. She looked like a fish coming at you from twenty thousand leagues. We followed her down—she *floated* down—to a six-hundred-year-old wine cellar. Well, we turned the corner and eighteen people looked up and stared. An amazing *shock.* Their eyes peeked over napkins; they were covering their faces like dignitaries caught in a raid. And for-mally dressed! Very *Discreet Charm,* do you know Buñuel? He was a Spaniard—an Andalusian, actually. Well, can I tell you what the occa-sion was? We later found out. It was a bunch of rich gourmands, and they had paid a *huge* amount of money to eat these songbirds. Little songbirds! *Completely* illegal—the birds were on the endangered species list. Very Kosinski, do you know him? Killed himself in the bath. Never had a tastier treat in my life: sweet, crunchy . . . bitter, too. My fiancée said they kept them in dark cages for months—"

"The dinner guests?"

"The birds! Gorged them on millet, then drowned them in snifters of Armagnac. And the reason they held up their napkins, so they said, was because you were supposed to eat the birds *hot.* You just popped them in and chewed with your mouth open or else you got burned."

"That *is* the Frankish way, isn't it? Murder a thrush behind veils of civility! Truth be told, the French *are* a dishonorable and troublously shoddy race."

Gilles Mott had known the hulking homeless man for six months. He found him to be thoughtful, gentle and diligent at menial tasks, of which he neatly did a baker's dozen. Gilles was something of a scholar of the fractured souls who wandered from dark and dirty wings onto his stage; of all the players he'd known, the one called Will'm was the most "accomplished." He *looked* magnificent—his face had the ruddy plein air nobility of a streetwise sage, without the astringent lunacy in the eye. He was truculent but never uncivil. The hair swept back like a Big Sur poet's (he said he was nicknamed for his locks; friends got Topsy from the slave girl in *Uncle Tom's Cabin*), and his beard grew like cliff bush over tweedy layers of dress, its wiry, earthen, sun-bleached colors blending with sport coat, vest and wan-pink debuttoned Brooks Brothers blouse fastened at collar with twine. How clothes were found to fit the dimensions of this man remained, for the baker, a puzzle. His voice too was distinctive, a contained whisper emanating from the citizens of a thousand nodal villages sitting upon cords buried deep as transatlantic cable within a meaty, blushing throat. Gilles thought of the self-averred Oxford-educated wanderer as a ghost who walked the urban heath, otherwise imagining him a character from H. G. Wells dislocated in Time. He worried about this tender mountain and keenly wondered about the origins of his elaborate personal myth. Like the student he was, Gilles nudged and probed, but not too hard—the baker's wife, a volunteer caseworker herself, had cautioned him against it.

"Will'm," he said, cutting dough for croissants. "Where exactly were you born? I mean, if you don't mind."

"All that's public knowledge!" he snapped, mopping with new resolve. "If it must be said again, I came into this world in Elm House, Walthamstow—dead on Clay Street."

"But when?"

"That, man, is also for the record: March of 'thirty-four."

"*Nineteen* thirty-four . . ." said the baker, the slight emphasis giving him away.

Will'm stopped his chores and horse-laughed. Gilles was actually relieved—mindful of his wife's admonition, for a split second he'd seen himself tossed to the floor and gutted.

"If that *is* the case, then something's *very* wrong indeed!"

"So it's eighteen thirty-four then—"

"Man, are you daft? Of course eighteen. We're not in Utopia yet, are we?"

"Most certainly not! But well—could you—can you *tell* me about it? *Some*thing—say, about where you were raised?"

"Epping Forest, man! That's where we moved, when I was six. That's what's most vivid. A mystical place: boon and balm to a child. Lived at Woodford Hall. Now, *that* was fifty acres and six hundred pounds to let, six hundred the year. For the rest of my *life* I never paid more, not even at Kelmscott. So you can see how lavish it was. Father'd made his fortune in copper, so we were set." His eyes crinkled and gleamed. "Had my own coat of armor as a boy. A smithy did it up, all to my design—well, perhaps I 'borrowed' one or two touches from a Negrolian 'bat-wing' burgonet—quite the swashbuckler I was! We (all the garrulous *Waverly* boys) lived and breathed Walter Scott. Rode ponies past blue plums and pollarded hornbeams to watch low-slung craft loiter on the glassy river: then on to Shooter's Hill and the wide green sea of marshland at Essex."

Maybe, thought Gilles, *Will'm had been a professor, a professor at Oxford who was visiting the States (one somewhat eccentric to begin with), whose mad cow virus kicked in halfway through term at Claremont or USC, the insidious Bovine Spongiform Encephalopathy herding him to skid row and such.* Maybe if he got to the bottom of it, Gilles could help.

"But *how,* Will'm—how did you get *here?*"

"Do you mean the Abbey?"

"Well . . . yes! If that's where we are now."

"Then if *you* don't know—!" He began to laugh.

The baker, yet again mindful of his wife and seeing himself pummeled and bleeding as the morning's first cheerful customers arrived, thought well enough of today's session being done. So they worked in relative silence, with Topsy back to his mopping, on occasion muttering epithets toward "those bilious Frankish people," until the store opened and the lapsed don discharged.

Watching him leave, Gilles Mott ruminated awhile on Paris and that long-lost fiancée; someday if possible he would make amends. Until then, he felt like one of those characters he read about in the paper, who, ensconced in happy second lives, await authorities to enter the workplace and handcuff them so they may at long last answer charges from another time.

* * *

*T*here was too much to do. There were designs for textiles that crowded his head like vernal snowflakes; the medieval cathedrals—and St. Mark's, in Venice—that needed to be cataloged by his Society for the Preservation of Ancient Buildings; a mental inventory of stained glass and tile, wood furnishings and tableware; correspondence to be kept up, with Ruskin and Rossetti and Georgiana Burne-Jones; fresh lectures on socialism and the decorative arts; and the charting of his daughter's seizures and wife Jane's infidelities. Most important, he must continue his life's work, a book written in his own fine hand, a book called *News from Nowhere.* He kept it in a downtown locker and went there to work on it three times a week. And so it began

This is the picture of the old house by the Thames to which the people of this story went. Hereafter follows the book itself which is called News from Nowhere or An Epoch of Rest & is written by William Morris.

For that is who he thought he was: William Morris, robust, protean, Promethean William Morris, the Victorian genius of design.

While it has become simple for laymen to know a ruined mind when they see one—any worthwhile psychotic hears voices through teeth or television—the gods of madness are surely in the far-fetched details that often astonish with the fabulous, unexpected poignancy of cracked new worlds revealed. Those unhinged men and women, having left the ocean of our experience, now reside in stagnant pools and brackish backwaters, encamped by polluted river or stream from which there is no return. Before his descent (until we know his Christian name, we will oscillate between Topsy and Will'm), a friend at his workplace found him acting strange. When told as much, Will'm recounted a dream he'd had that affected him in a most peculiar way. A group of ghouls, he said, asked if he would please to consider the newly formed position of Chairman of the Disembodied. The co-worker laughed uncomfortably, before asking how he replied. "I told them yes," said Will'm. But his addendum is what set the listener's teeth on edge: "Because I knew I would soon have time on my hands."

Now he *did* have time—Time, like a blue-indigo stain on arms and hands, on beard and triple-E feet: time to rove and decorate cardboard Manor, time to send dispatches of news from nowhere on the onionskin paper of a hand-stitched cloth-bound book, time to dream (as William Morris had a greater century ago) of Iceland and its heroic sagas, time to worry over daughter and wife—time to appropriate a "troublous" life of startling historical richness.

When Topsy got to the 7th Street Viaduct, there was nothing left— the Cadillac had been razed—and Half Dead and Fitz, his one-legged keeper, whose very skin matched his faded seersucker suit and who wore the aspect of an accountant-turned-assassin, stood skittish sentinel. If street rumor had it that George Fitzsimmons was a legendary Department of Children and Family Services caseworker turned out by crack cocaine (rendering him a rather too baroque cautionary tale)—if such talk remained unsubstantiated, then scabby sores from relentless scratchings and general dermatological reconnaissance *could* be confirmed as easily as the absence of his left limb. The owner of Half Dead, though not quite half, was definitively not quite whole, thanks to diabetes and the great white hacks of County General. One of the mission wags had bestowed on the man and his dog a sobriquet: Half 'n' Half.

"I'm telling you, Will'm, the Department had one very large, ugly hard-on for your personal effects! I told 'em: *Hey! Fold the man's Cadillac down and he'll be by to pick it up.* This is the man's *home. Would* not do it. Proud little shits took *every*thing away. 'Most killed Half Dead while they were at it."

The deformed pit bull chased a rat. He limped from broken bones never properly healed and his coat oozed, in spite of Fitz's unfailing application of vitamin E and antibiotic creams that an outreach worker had wheedled from a sympathetic veterinarian. In glory days, the hapless animal was the warm-up act in South Central dogfights—featured warriors chewed on him in prelims to get their blood up. Fitz had liberated the beast from the pound; the neighborhood handle, with variations, stuck.

"C'mawn, Baby Half," he chastised. "Don't you play with them dirty old things."

He loped over while Topsy stood on the patch of earth where his house had been. He closed his eyes and imagined the crosshatched honeycomb on the boxes—bugs and marigolds, hawthorn and snakes-head, hummingbirds, cabbage and eglantine that took weeks to evoke. He sighed; his enormous chest heaved skyward. He would not go to Misery House tonight. There was another place he knew, with rooms towering high above the city. As he set out, Half Dead barked halfheartedly while his master ranted against Sanitation and all Departments thereof.

Dusk: a zealous menagerie of untouchables traversed the bridge in a parody of corporate commuting. Where were they bound? Some gesticulated, some nearly loitered, most just rushed along. At least they might take the same direction—but this was a dystopian crusade, all fervor and no cause. At night they built fires at the curbs; by day, they were ticketed for jaywalking by latex-gloved police.

It was close to suppertime and he waded past Misery House and the Midnight Mission with their long lines of the wretched of the earth. A daffy civic-center sign—TOY DISTRICT—loomed on a sidewalk pole, the city's lame, futile proclamation of a "famous" area. A few of the disenfranchised called hello from their boxes, for the man in tweed was well regarded on the street, and respected for his prodigious physical strength.

Someone-Help-Me gave a shout. Hassled by cops, he had abandoned his stint at the Hard Rock Cafe. He needed a new sign; Will'm made the last, a real crowd pleaser. The vagrant wanted it spruced and was not pleased his greeting went unreturned.

The hulking figure rounded the corner of St. Vibiana without glancing at the notice on the wall: CATHEDRAL CLOSED.

Darkness fell as he reached his destination, a beleaguered ten-story sandstone-finished façade, vacant for decades—brass knobs and piping long since purloined, with shardy windowpanes whose twisted blinds looked as if they'd gone mad before dying; a smell that knocked at the solar plexus, then gusted low over a hellish carpet of syringes, diapers and tampons, soiled to a man, gracing the once illustrious entrance of the Higgins Building, put up in 1910 by the eponymous Thomas H.—who'd made his fortune in copper, as, we may remind, had the father of the original William Morris. *Our* Will'm arched his neck to read the spray-painted legend

Isa 23—Howl, ye ships of Tarshish; for it is laid waste, so that there is no house, no entering in then closed his eyes and imagined: *saw* women in high collars pass to and fro and bowler'd men from trolleys they called Red Cars: then buggies, bustle and Arrows (Arrows he had gathered from library visits). The main entry, reluctant to admit squatters who blackened marble and checkerboard mosaics with casual fires and human waste, had been welded shut, but Will'm knew another way—the alley.

Only a cat could slip through the twisted iron; so he twisted it more with brute hands, and took a minute to shimmy his large body through. Like a circus strongman, he closed the metal back behind him and went in, letting eyes adjust to the dark.

He made his way to the lobby, where the remnants of an announcement from a previous incarnation was glued to a long faux-wood slat:

COU TY OF LOS ANGEL S DEPART ENT   F PUBLIC SOCI L SE VICES

PLEASE DO NOT
GET IN LINE
UNTIL YOUR
REPORT TIME
WATCH THE CLOCK

Debris, shit and more shards. Tumbleweeds of newspaper flecked with concrete dust amid tangle of fluorescent tubes in cool dead brittle bunches. A gang of sullen, sleepy pigeons as he took the stairs, their panicked population increasing on the upper floors, where he headed. Perhaps *they* were the ones he'd find strutting on lintels in bowlers and high collars—then he'd know once and for all he was truly mad.

What did this place remind him of? Rather, to what place did he let himself drift back? The ruins of the gabled "old stone Elizabethan house" he called Kelmscott Manor . . . that place was near a bridge, too—Radcot Bridge, on the baby Thames. He thought of the estate as he climbed the littered steps, conjuring drawing room and attic, with rugs and upholstered furniture of his design: motifs of rose and thistle, corncockle and windrush, lily and pomegranate. His blood boiled recalling his dear friend Rossetti's carryings-on with Janey . . . dear friend! Beautiful wife! That rankled him and, losing his footing on a droppings-slick landing, he stepped into a crowd of hot, feathered bodies and roared, sloppily killing two with a swat as they rose to escape.

He found a room on the ninth floor he had once used when the night was inclement. Will'm stood by the window a moment, peering at St. Vibiana's battered cupola; wearily, he lowered himself onto scarred tiles. He heard voices of faceless old cohorts on the telephones and for a moment was not himself. *I might yet work myself back,* he thought—but what did "back" mean? From what? His duties as Chairman of the Disembodied? And *to* what? He puzzled, then something stirred behind a closet of besmirched and frosted glass—he would have to rout the animal out before sleep. He stood, opening the warped door to let it scamper: there crouched a wild-eyed girl. She saw his face and dissolved.

"Topsy!" She smiled, then began to laugh. "I was so *scared*—"

He reached out, and she tumbled to his arms. Her laughter turned to sobs. He held the orphan to his tweedy breast as she cried and cried, and (to his surprise) he along with her.

CHAPTER 10

Shelter

After a storm of tears, they laughed and wept until laughter won out, and were forever bound.

Amaryllis told him how her mother had been a dead person all this time and how she had been afraid to tell anyone, even Topsy himself, who had been so kind and with whose food she had nourished the babies. How she was *going* to tell him but was sidelined by a strange troupe of children who were making a movie—a know-it-all girl, a crippled tall-headed boy with mask and gloves, and a wisecracking flaxen-haired star—the orphan waved *All About You!* before him to prove the celebrity's pampered, extolled existence. (Amaryllis wasn't sure why, but she withheld mentioning the boy who on first introduction called himself Toulouse, and Tull ever after.) Then she told him how the police took the precious ones and the Korean gave her away and she'd only managed to escape by dint of what she now felt to be a miracle—or hoped would eventually be recognized as such. And how, because St. Vibiana's was impregnable, she had come to this place for sanctuary instead . . .

Topsy listened, moved to sweet astonishment, running oversize fingers through friendly tangle of beard. He had in his vest pocket, visible through a foggy Ziploc'd window, some crushed notes of almond and pomegranate seed, residue of croissant plucked from a dessert song. He spread the sack open and the starved thing dipped in two nail-bitten fingers.

Suddenly, her voice broke. Where did they take the babies? she asked plaintively. They'd be so frightened without her! She sobbed again and couldn't catch her breath.

"There, there," said Topsy, patting her shoulder. "They'll be fine—just fine. And right along, and right along."

He made her tug from a tap-water canteen, then watched as she cried herself to sleep.

*H*ours later, Topsy started to a ruckus: someone coughed, stumbled and cursed in the adjacent hall. A shout and filthy flurry of sleep-drunk birds roused the girl, who shrieked as he stood like a colossus to repel the invader. Whoever it was had candlepower, and that meant official trouble. As the beam pierced their room, Topsy snatched the flashlight, punched the interloper's stomach (which gave the giant no pleasure), hoisted Amaryllis up and fled. The night was moonless; once recovered, the guard would be slow to leave.

She felt secure holding on and was unaware that he held her, too, arm bent behind him in support like a pale, muttony wing. He took the stairs in gulps; he was magnificent. She sweated, and his coat scratched her face as she clung. More than once the orphan girl thought she'd be pitched into blackness of space and die if she didn't hold tight.

The lobby was vaguely lit by street lamps. Outside, he set her down by the bent iron, then pulled her to shadow as two squad cars wailed and bleated by; they were meant for some other poor souls. Amaryllis climbed through and stepped to the sidewalk as delicately as a girl at cotillion, while Topsy took longer, doing some damage to the gate. He shouted at her to come back toward him, out of the light. Free of the Higgins now, he took things in full-scope. Where would he go? at four in the morning, with a child on the street? Then it came to him: but if he wasn't careful, the little sweetheart would land in gaol and they'd throw him in stocks or worse. Kidnapper! Deviant! *Monster . . .*

He lifted the girl to his back again then cloaked himself so that his jacket fell over her like a tarp—under cover of night, to an idle observer, she might be a mindless backpack of belongings, queerly squirreled away.

Topsy left the alley in unbreakable stride. For a while it seemed there was someone behind them, but whatever it was soon fell away, swallowed up in his powerful wake. Amaryllis imagined herself the Royal Kumari, freshly absconded, scooped from village seat by a Special Selector—what adventure! She thought of the Congregation for the Causes of Saints

and how in fact Topsy *was* a worthy nominee: he was humble and had
endured great hardship; he was full of heroic virtue and venerated by
the homeless community; and he had now performed the miracle of
spiriting her away. From 2nd to Broadway he marched, over streets
dream-like and bereft. In the duo's presence, the Hall of Records remained unfazed. The steam-engorged Central Heating and Refrigeration
Plant appeared ignorant of their passing, as did the democratic wooden
fence that fronted the burgeoning Cathedral of Our Lady of the Angels,
postered over with an orderly procession of schoolchildren's acrylic
saints (Edith Stein not among them). The sepulchral Hall of Administra-
tion slept; the Board of Supervisors and Health Department Administra-
tion buildings yawned, then shut their granite eyes.

As the leviathan and his charge ducked beneath the 110, Topsy felt
the whole of downtown rise off him like a corroded weight—but they
were in danger, because there were no more buildings to hide in and the
infamous Rampart station was yet to come.

He slowed so as not to seem in flight past lumpy fields and grassy
hillocks on both sides of the wide macadamized road. He could hear the
furtive, alien rustle of encampments as they rushed by (Fitz and Half
Dead in there somewhere, for all anyone knew). "It's fine, child, it'll be
right fine," he said, like a lullaby, turning his whiskery head so she'd
hear. "There, there." When taxis or trucks passed and they were alone
again, he let slip the coat from his shoulders so her head struck fresh air.
A naked man crouched in the middle of the street defecating, like a figure in an outlandish prehistoric diorama; Topsy thought it a neat diversion for his and the girl's potential pursuants.

Now, who else roamed this strange place? It *was* not Epping Forest!
How must the entirety of it have looked to a man like William Morris?
Tonight, the Victorian age was but a vapor between him and the vast
metropolis. The girl had seen to that—the sweet turtleshell stuck on
his back had crimped his delusions, the pure unselfishness of his concern for her leeching air from the bubble within which he normally
moved. He nearly heard the hiss. He accelerated past the blurred, sleepy
storefronts—Salon del Reino de Los Testigos de Jehova—SIGNS-BANNERS—
Botanica—Psíquica—Carniceria—Panadería—to a street called, most
curiously, East Edgeware. Topsy broke a cool sweat as they swept past the
abandoned hotel with the faded advertisement painted on its side—ALL
ROOMS WITH BATH & SHOWER $2.50 UP. FIREPROOF—around the stucco face, its

crumbly chicken wire disabused by a hundred careless fenders. Another alley: and then he let Amaryllis down behind the shop. They walked a few paces and huddled in the shadow of a dumpster.

Dawn came with usual rosy-fingered treachery. A white Volvo station wagon turned, nosing into its space behind the bakery. With a smile Topsy noticed that his sometime employer, may he be blessed, wore a white mushroomed chef's hat even as he drove.

"All right, listen," he whispered urgently. "That man there will help. He's an ample soul, and his wife is a worker for the public good."

"But you won't come?"

A heartbreaking puff of cold came from her tiny mouth.

"It's no *good* with me there. He'll take *care* of you, girl—him and his wife—but you mustn't say I brought you here, understand? I *know* 'im, understand? He's good and he'll get me word of what's happened to you and I'll come." Tears again between them, and he dried her eyes with his sleeve. "Go ahead now, there! I'm watching you, child! You'll do right well with 'im. This man's my *friend.* Understand? But you mustn't tell him it was me. Now, right along, right along!"

She nodded and stared at the ground, her lower lip jerking about. He kissed her cheek, turned her around and sent her off like a toy soldier. She took a few steps, then gazed at him in a way that broke his heart again; but *he* did not break, and urged her on.

The car's engine shut off, and Gilles walked to the trunk and rooted around inside. She was fifteen feet from the Volvo, and again turned back—again, he urged her on.

The baker saw her.

"Hullo?"

He stood up straight in his loose bleached clothes and came near. "Hel-lo . . . here now, what's wrong? What are we doing all alone?" He looked around but saw no one. "Do you live around here? Where's Mommy and Daddy? Do you know where Mommy and Daddy are?"

She shook her head, fighting the urge to run to her friend.

"Are you hungry? Do you like cake and pastry? Would you like to come inside, where it's warm, and have some pastry? Sure you would! Come. Come inside."

She looked back one last time—the shadow of Topsy was gone.

Amaryllis went to the baker, head bowed like a votary. He knelt and spoke to her with great kindness. The vagrant tucked thoroughly away, strained to hear, but the voice was low and indecipherable. Gilles led her inside.

The morning lifted like a curtain as he retraced his path. The cityscape stirred, stretching itself under a still-cool sun; his step quickened as he entered the tunnel. There would be coffee waiting at Misery House.

CHAPTER 11

Last Looks

*K*atrina sat on a bench in the middle of the maze in a purple Viktor & Rolf midi, a $27,000 brain coral–clasped torsade wrapped about an ankle. Her foot, shod in Jimmy Choo, tapped nervously—wearily—on the stone base.

Her father proudly called her a landscape architect, but Trinnie always told people she was "just a gardener." He thought that well enough true—his daughter had made topiary designs of startling scientific whimsy for the duke of Roxburghe and the marquess of Bath, and been engaged by whole cities to memorialize spirit of place in elegant, leafy riddle. She grew puzzles of verdure beside abbeys and ancient almshouses; one of her labyrinths for a private Swedish estate consumed twelve thousand emerald boxwoods and 150 tons of peach-colored Raisby gravel alone (Mr. Trotter pretended to be piqued that she hadn't used a family quarry). As signature, Trinnie always hid sacred spaces in the branchy creatures of myth sculpted within—her "secret meditation zones."

But not here: not at Saint-Cloud. *This* one, shaped like a Fabergé egg, was without artifice, a final, transcendent maze for the ages (you'll excuse the author when he says it didn't hedge). Mr. Trotter had been after her to grow one forever, but understood his daughter's reticence—it was too close to home or, rather, too close to where home might have been: the virid mother of all maze and meadow, La Colonne Détruite. How could she ever top what had pulled the world from under her?

At the unveiling of the Saint-Cloud labyrinth (for the forty-odd months it took to sufficiently mature, Trinnie kept the magical grid sequestered by a Christo-like muslin curtain), the old man couldn't help but think the end was near—that father and daughter had completed their tomb—and began to regret the commission.

For years, she had barely managed to stay on deck; her body clock stormily ticked maritime. She knew the marriage to drugs and hospitals (she cheated on one with the other) was bottom-line tawdry: just another circle-of-hell party girl. What was she *really* in the grip of? a man? a phantom? a middle-class fantasia?—was *that* what murdered her? But how? Yes, she adored her husband. She was certain—convinced—that her love—*their* love—matched, gale force, the greatest loves in the history of the love-long world. Then came that silly, horrifying, Dickensian *thing*—that deformed moment—absurd old literary saw come to life replete with falling-down Havishamian villa—except in Trinnie's case, there *was* a marriage . . . so which was worse? Perhaps all of it, all the heartbreak and weirdness, was merely her excuse for a fabulous thirteen-year debauch. Before him—even before Marcus—hadn't her body longed to be fucked and held, honey'd, moneyed and opiated? Wasn't she always this way? From nowhere came this dream of domestic life—such as it was—the old Carcassone dream . . . a cockeyed, hillside family life. He was crazier than her, and smarter too, and that was new and it calmed her. Trinnie could *see* herself settling down—and then, when he vanished . . . —yet how could she have done that to her precious son? She with her Year of the Pig heart, vast as the sea? It was one thing to torment her dad; Louis was a digger, a scarab, a burrower who could book his own passage. And Bluey—well, Bluey never suffered, at least not conventionally. Trinnie envied her for that. But Tull!— small, living thing, with scrunchy bones and soft smelly feet, who loved her, a wizardly child she made, then abandoned. That kind of cruelty was a dissolution sidebar; she felt like a pervert. When he needed her, when he cried and hated and wet his bed for her, she lay in the arms of jackals with pleasure palaces, jet-flown to inconceivable houses in every place on earth—Moroccan hunting lodges and Vietnamese retreats, lava-island belvederes and ranches in Tulum, festive cottages in Mustique, Compass Point flats and Christchurch aeries, sprawling pavilions in Biarritz and Jaipur, Chamonix and Amazonia, Negril, Margaret River, Lake Como, Faux-Cap, Madagascar—until, stoned and panicky, she moved on—to spa and hotel, monasteries and rainy sacred ground—and on—posh sanatoria (at one three-week stint, she found herself at

the castellated Priory arranging flowers beside General Pinochet)—
and when her son was dying for her, or when he was laughing with
friends and not even thinking of her, she sat in the wide dayrooms of
Hazelden or The Meadows listening to tales of woe from athletes and
drunks, cabbageheads and kings. And for what? A sailor now fallen from
grace, she walked slowly to dock and stood over, looking down on gelatinous waters. The perorations of those rooms would soon be—must be—
drowned by the waiting sea.

She heard heavy breathing and the staccato crush of pebble under
paw and looked up. Pullman charged, then, as if bowing for a minuet,
adroitly backed off. He licked her hand and lay down like a griffin. Now,
more crush of stone, with approach of a slower gait. Her son appeared,
face flushed, a ragamuffin who looked like his ears had been boxed by
the yew.

"Tull?" She stood. "What is it, darling?"

He inhaled, gathering ragged lungfuls, then stormed her, clutching and kneading her fashionable waist. That tiny, desperate, expensive
waist . . . his small-mouthed frame shook, keened and bellowed, and for
a moment she was afraid—for both of them—and even Pullman was
roused, coming over to sniff the boy.

Abashed, she stroked her son's head while he wept; the dog looked
Trinnie square in the eye as if to shame her.

*T*hat night, in the exotic fortress of the Withdrawing Room, she
told him everything.

Tull refused to sit. He stood throughout, as if enduring a reprimand
in the study of the Four Winds headmaster. He didn't feel at all well. Only
hours ago, he had been at the school library searching on-line for the
St. George Motel in blissful denial, mooning over Amaryllis; he fantasized trolling downtown streets in Mauck or Escalade until the girl was
found. Yet his daydream had been overtaken by a combustible sense of
urgency, and at the final bell, he fled campus, feeling Lucy's ambivalent
eyes on his back. He walked to the beach, then took a cab home from
Shutters before finding his mother in the maze.

He stood before them—Trinnie and Grandpa Lou—chin quivering,
jutting ticcishly forward so that it looked like Edward's. (The imperson-
ation comforted him.) He was oddly remorseful for having pursued any

of this now—as if caught in one of those dreams where one feels like a patient trapped in some sort of nefarious clinic.

His grandfather paced languorously before the Piranesi backdrop, hands clasped behind him, suppressing a chuff, pretending to study the detail of his maquettes (he paused an inordinately long time before the Sir Norman Foster) while actually listening with great intensity to his beloved Katrina. Earlier in the afternoon, he'd been at the cemetery when Epitacio walked over to hand him the phone; an opportune time, to be sure, for at that very moment Dot was upon him, eager to impart a bit of recently gleaned pop paranoia. He waved her off with a cadaverous smile, which Sling Blade, raking leaves behind them, thought amusing. Without ceremony, Mr. Trotter climbed into the car and sped off.

As they made their way to Bel-Air, he listened to his daughter's voice through the receiver, a voice he hardly recognized—deliberate and sorrowful, a slow elegy for brass. He had always known one day that his grandson Toulouse would come into "a piece of intelligence" and that it would be Trinnie's duty to make full disclosure, the one responsibility from which he would not abide her run. Trinnie knew as much and long dreaded it. She would do what she had to, and if accounts were not settled, then at least the books would be opened—here, now.

Her mother, tipped off by Mr. Trotter, was initially averse to such overheated summitry—then indifferent. She elected to sit in bed with Winter, organizing the album of obits.

Trinnie looked dazed but sat erect. Her gown was abraded and still bore dust from when she chased her son as he fled the maze. Her long, pale arms were scratched; even her face had been smacked by tough little leaves. At first, still worrying her waist with small, slender hands, Tull stopped crying long enough to ask if his father was alive. When Trinnie said no, he pushed her over and sprinted. Pullman ran interference as she chased after—well, this was too much! She took off her shoes and swatted the Dane, shoving the animal aside with an oath more than once. Ralph loomed from the terrace in a rage over actors-turned-directors, and it wasn't long before he saw something was amiss. Trinnie pushed him away, too, and he stood to one side with the chastened Pullman, partnered. She pinned her son to the ground, shouting at him to be still. By now, the entire staff—a disapproving Winter included—gathered to watch from afar. The boy wriggled but was quiet enough to hear her say that she would tell him what he wanted to know after supper. First they must eat, she said. And Grandpa would have to be there; she would need to call him. She took Tull to the house and gave him water. She felt ruffled and terrified and strangely empty, because she was about to be unburdened. (She did not feel like swallowing a drink or a pill.) She told him to take a warm bath. She would see him again in Grandpa's study, she said, at eight o'clock. It was now a quarter past that hour.

"Your father didn't die in a snowmobile accident."

"Then why did you say it?"

"Your father was . . . the most amazing man I ever met."

"Then why did you say he was dead?"

"Because—I was so hurt. And I'm sorry. I should have told you the truth."

"But why? Why were you so hurt?"

"He was . . . older." The declaration was meaningless, but Trinnie knew not where to begin. "I thought I'd found—I *had* found the person I wanted to be with. To spend my life with. And after a little while—a week or two—I moved in. He had a place in West Hollywood, on Alfred. We were so *happy*. Papa met him—Bluey too . . . I never introduced my boyfriends to them."

He turned to his grandfather. "Did you like him?"

"Marcus was a good man," he said without taking his eyes from Mr. Gehry's metal gefilte fish. "But I wasn't glad about what he did to your mother."

"What *did* he do?"

The more conversational things became, the more Tull's anxiety mounted.

"He asked me to marry him. I thought it was a mistake—we'd been having such a good time! See, I wasn't the marrying kind. I was already twenty-eight and had plenty of offers. I guess I was . . . superstitious. He wanted to elope, but I said, No, if we're going to get married, we're going to get *married*. Let's have a big wedding, I said—like a fool. We did. It took ten months to plan. Papa built us a house." She looked wistfully at her father. "A beautiful house. A strange and beautiful house."

"The boy should see it."

"It was a copy of a real place—an eighteenth-century garden outside Paris, where your father and I had once been. Though 'copy' doesn't sound quite right, does it, Papa?" The old man smiled humbly. "Your dad and I came upon it during our meanderings and fell absolutely in love with the place—and Grandpa built a . . . *re-creation,* right in the middle of Bel-Air. The most beautiful wedding present anyone could ever—" Again, she looked toward her father, eyes swollen with tears. Her pain was lancing, and the old man steadied himself against the vitrine that held a knockoff of Le Corbusier's chapel at Notre-Dame-du-Haut. "But Grandpa kept it a secret. He had artisans from all over the world working around the clock. I used to complain, didn't I, Papa? 'What is going *on* down there on Carcassone?' That's what I used to say. The whole *neighborhood* was in an uproar, but Grandpa kept smoothing things over. God knows who and how much he had to pay to keep everyone happy!"

"I never spent a dime on that sort of thing," he said, letting loose a gentle chuff or two.

"I'll bet you didn't," said Trinnie sardonically, the smile returning to her face, along with some color. "Six hundred people came to the wedding . . . I bought my wedding gown last minute, do you remember, Papa? At Christie's—"

"Oh yes."

"—Cristóbal Balenciaga himself had cut the material. Everyone arrived in horse-drawn landaus. *La Colonne Détruite*—that's 'the broken column'—it was so beautiful, there was no reason to leave for a honeymoon."

"They threw rice," said the old man, prompting.

"We stood on the steps and threw rice on the guests as they left." She gathered herself, nervously smoothing the lap of her gown. "That night, you were conceived. I fell asleep in your father's arms." Now her face darkened as the life went out of it. "When I woke up, he was gone."

"Where—where was he?" asked Tull, trembling.

"It was so quiet! I'll never forget that. It was the first time—the only time!—we slept there overnight. So you have that funny sleepover feeling—vulnerable. You don't really . . . you know that disoriented feeling where your body—where you don't really know where you are? And nothing's familiar? The grounds were so huge, so you really *did* feel like a trespasser in a park . . . We didn't have staff, because no one had even been hired. I listened for sounds of him—nothing. I don't know *what* I thought at first. I was still floating from the night before! I thought he was in the bathroom or the kitchen. I waited awhile, then went out to find him. I was certain he'd be walking around, but he wasn't . . . maybe he'd gone to Nate 'n' Al's for deli, to surprise us—breakfast in bed—he used to love that—but the cars were all there. I went back to our room to wait. His wallet and pants were in the upstairs bath, and a book too, thrown facedown on the floor like he'd been snatched off the toilet! I laughed—oh, I thought he was just being evil, evil. Hours and hours and hours went by. I started to feel trapped, like I was losing my mind . . . I was afraid to call anyone. Then I got angry and then I got scared and then I got *mad*—at *myself*—for *being* mad—and then I got angry and scared all over again and finally called your grandfather."

The old man wandered closer now. "I had a feeling."

"You loved him!"

"Yes, Katrina, I loved him. But I had a feeling when you called."

"What kind of feeling?" asked the boy.

His grandfather's chest expanded as he took in a long breath. "I knew we would never see this man again."

Tull nearly swooned with the drama of it.

"Grandpa called an old friend of the family, a detective. I was—I was *worried,* of *course* I was worried, that something terrible had happened to him—but in the back of my head—this *thing,* this *jilting* thing—I was ashamed to even think it possible this man who I *loved* and just *married* had actually *disappeared*—"

"What did the detective do?"

"Looked for your father," she said.

Before Tull could ask, his grandfather said: "The gentleman was unable to find him."

The old man sighed, settling into the Louis XVI.

"But where did he go?" Tull could do nothing about the pleading whine in his voice; he was at their mercy.

"That, my dear grandson, we were not able to ascertain."

He turned to his mother. "Did—did my father give me my name?"

She smiled. "When we came back from France, he began calling himself Toulouse—demanded everyone at work do the same. He was quite serious about it. Said he was going to get a tattoo: NÉ TOULOUSE. Do you know what *né* means? 'Born.' That was your father's little joke: *Born Toulouse.* But you were named after Grandpa too—'Louis' is in 'Toulouse'—"

He wished he were someplace else; remembering his ghostly peregrinations on Carcassone Way, he felt the chill of the profane; he wished

Cousin Lucy dead. Yet he no longer felt a fist in his chest, though the weight of the world seemed upon him. His jaw ached from being stuck cut, and he dug his fingers into the points beneath each ear for relief.

"Do you know why we were in France?" his mother asked rhetorically. "We were there to visit a film set. One of your father's clients was a famous actor. We were in a beautiful train station there."

"The Gare de Lyon," offered the old man.

"They were shooting a scene where two people say good-bye. We hid behind the camera, watching. It was drizzling—*très Parisienne.* The actress stood on the platform while her 'boyfriend' boarded the train. The cars were already moving. You know: a real movie good-bye. She put her hand on her heart and ran along the track as he waved. He was standing in the door, on a step. No one smiled—the director didn't want them to. She stopped running and the train kept going. They held the shot until the car was out of sight. The director called, 'Cut!' and everyone waited until the train came back to the station to its original mark. After a while, someone yelled, 'Last looks'—that's what they say when they're about to shoot again. 'Last looks! Final touches!' The last chance for wardrobe and hair and makeup. Then the scene began again and the actress ran after the train and he waved and no one smiled and then she stopped just where she did before, and put her hand over her heart. Again, the train came back to its original position. 'Last looks!' More waving and chasing and chasing and waving, again and again and again. Finally, it was over and your father looked at me and smiled and squeezed my hand. I didn't remember that until years later."

CHAPTER 12

The Well

*I*n the days following the meeting in the Withdrawing Room, Tull went to school like a somnambulist—scattered, so to speak, to the Four Winds. He finally understood what Edward meant when summoning the word *postictal* (pronounced post-*ik*-tal, always with great flourish) to refer to the emptied, euphoric state that came over him in the wake of an Apert seizure. That is to say, Tull walked about in a kind of gauze; he felt an overall generic thankfulness; colors and scents seemed more vivid. As he floated indolently from class to class, building to building, ethereally benevolent toward his fellow students, the once cynically regarded campus revealed itself as a quaint and inconsequential place, a warm and fuzzy manufacturer of future nostalgia.

Lucy and Edward were the only ones aware of the facts behind Tull's "seizure." Though Edward was perversely thrilled by the development, his poor sister grew morbidly beside herself. Deeply ashamed to be the snitching source of Tull's pain and fearful to approach him, the redhead kept her distance. Unable to concentrate on the detective-book project, she sat at desk torturing herself for having delivered the coup de grâce—it was only a matter of time before a distant chorus of screams would announce that Tull had gunned down a dozen students or been found hanging from the top metal slat of the folding bleachers of the multimillion-dollar DODD AND JOYCE TROTTER GYMNASIUM. The truth would out and she'd soon be (nationally) marked: Lucille Rose, spoiled scion, had destroyed her adored first cousin because while on the way to visit their hospitalized grandmother (whom she was exploiting in the name of "research") he had not paid enough attention to the prattling précis of her pathetically still unwritten *Mystery of the Blue Maze*. The horror of such ruminations came to a head when she startled herself awake with a reflexive gasp in the middle of European History. Boulder turned to scowl at the creepy little outburst—the outburst of a loser.

Tull still thought of the homeless girl, and fantasized that the reassuring voice of the GPS would direct them to her. He would invite Amaryllis and her mom to Saint-Cloud for dinner and make Grandpa Lou give them money so they could move from their motel—to Malibu or the Marina. After his grandson's recent trauma, how could the old man refuse?

By dreamy smile and odd disaffection, Tull not so subtly advertised the intimate, intensely private revelation that had knighted him with its from-left-field melodrama. At such a tender age we're as innocent as we are vain, and while it's true Tull had his share of weepily beleaguered moments, he was not above considering himself the irresistibly charismatic star of a new school play called, say, *The Wounded Boy.*

Having thus left the door open, it was inevitable that his nastier contemporaries would gather, as Grandpa Lou would say, a piece of intelligence, on their own; predictably, *l'affaire Colonne* still lived on in the memory of those peers of Trinnie's who had begotten children way back when—such were the vagaries of coming of age in the town one was born. Hence, like an ungainly, standoffish bodyguard, Lucy found herself shadowing the boy she loved and had so casually betrayed. "Stop it!" she shouted when tormentors made their retarded Bride of Frankenstein/Invisible Man jokes about his father that cut Tull like daggers—"You better shut up!" They laughed until she cuffed the biggest one, hard. The bully almost struck back, but her coldly measured comment—"*Touch me and my father will fuck your family*"—dissuaded him. (The aggressor, like most of the student body, had laid curious eyes on Dodd Trotter, the bullet-headed billionaire, at the formal dedication of the gymnasium; and though his *own* father was a cruel Century City litigator, instincts told him not to call her bluff.) Reveling in the martyrdom of his "second act," the Wounded Boy allowed Lucy to vent. If not exactly righting a wrong, she could at least salve her guilt.

Things changed at home, too. Ralph stopped pestering him for comments about his script, and that was definitely a plus.

As for his mother, Trinnie seemed at once lighter and heavier, like a ballasted ghost. She dressed elegantly, as always, but without the usual frivolity. She joked less, more droll than outrageous. Though she spent most of her time in the gardens, she had a warm, missionary smile for anyone who came along—she was effortlessly, agonizingly present. Even Bluey was surprised when her daughter moved from the bedroom that had been hers as a child into a guest cottage, which she kept uncharacteristically clutter free. Trinnie no longer had wine with dinner, and when speaking to Tull made sure to lightly touch his arm or hand, shoulder or cheek, like an otherworldly healer infusing with balm. She looked into his eyes when he answered; her own were clear as bells.

And each day, Tull thought: *my father* must *be dead.* They'd hired a detective . . . yet how was it a body was never found? Didn't they say a body always had to be found? Grandpa Lou would have scoured the ends of the earth, dug the deepest hole with spindly, spotted hands until he broke to the other side—he would have done that for Katrina, Tull knew. No: he *must* be dead, or good as. What a mediocre denouement for the drama of a gifted child! He raged at the walls while headphones blared Slim Shady, feebly rapping to slang he didn't fully understand, a psycho Gilbert-and-Sullivan blizzard of miniature passion plays about duct-taped women thrashing in car trunks.

"*T*here's someone here to see you," said Winter. He stood bathed in the light of the Sub-Zero picking at cold Cuban chicken. Lucy appeared in the kitchen door, frail and diffident. The old nurse ducked out.

"Tull . . ." she stammered. "I'm—I'm so sorry! You have to forgive me! I didn't mean to—"

She cried, and his heart opened up. The smell of her perspiration was animal, as if she'd been chased to Saint-Cloud by predators.

"It's all right, Lucy, really—"

"No, no, it isn't! It isn't, it isn't, it isn't! It was so *sadistic*—all because you wouldn't listen to my stupid book cover!"

"It *isn't* stupid. I *like* your book cover."

"You are *so sweet!*" Deliriously, she kissed him, and he blushed. "Why do I *do* things like that? Edward says I have a mean streak, like Mom." She dried an eye with the butt of her palm. "Then you'll forgive me?"

He nodded, then sat forlornly on the stool Ralph favored during culinary rants and raids.

"So: what are you gonna do?"

"About what?"

"You want to *find* him, don't you?"

"There *is* no finding him."

"That is bullshit, Tull." He narrowed his eyes menacingly.

Lucy quickly apologized, fearing she'd lost all the ground she had gained. "But you *could* find him, if you—"

"He's dead."

"No one knows that for sure."

"I said he's dead!"

She let him breathe for a minute—well, maybe five seconds. He'd been through so much. "But did you talk to Grandpa?"

"He said he hired a detective but they couldn't find him."

"What did your father even *do?* I mean, for a living."

"I don't know."

"Did you ask?"

"No." Tull wondered what else she knew, and was withholding for the sake of rapprochement. "If my father were alive, Grandpa would have found him."

"I don't think that's necessarily true."

"What do you mean?"

"Grandpa Lou would *not* be terribly anxious to find someone who hurt your mother the way that man did." He admitted she had a point. "But *you* should find him, for your own peace of mind."

"I don't care," he said, unconvincingly.

"You don't *have* to—but you should probably still make the effort. You need closure."

"Closure?" he said, with suspicion. "Maybe *you're* the one who needs closure—for your *book*. You know—for *research*. I know how *thorough* you like to be. Because you're such a *great writer*. Maybe *you're* the one who needs closure so you can figure out how to end your book!"

She listened to the tirade, eyes glued to the ground. "I guess I deserved that."

Tull thought that maybe he'd been a bit rough. He poked at the soggy plantains. "Besides," he said, "I wouldn't know where to start. I'm no good at 'Missing Persons.' "

Lucy tap-tapped psychedelic decal'd nails on the marble cutting board, squinting her eyes—the girl detective again. "The trail is cold, but the Internet, you know, is . . . *hot.*"

*N*ot far away, in a modernist villa on Stradella Road, cousin Edward lay in bed attended by his mother. A Gucci scarf pinned to a goose-down pillow shaded his head, its hem stopping short at the brow. Liquid brown eyes watched her sponge his small frame; today he was too tired for the tub.

Joyce Trotter was older than her husband by nearly fifteen years. Approaching sixty (having had Lucy at forty-five and Edward at forty-seven), she carried herself with the presumption of an actress who had retired in her prime and was now only rarely glimpsed, someone of whom the world might say: *Still so gorgeous!* She had mitigated the tragedy of her son's unhappy lot with the compulsive maintenance of her own body. Though she desired to prolong and enhance her femininity, Botox and herbal wraps hadn't really softened her—Ashtanga and kickboxing instead bestowed a Brentwood warrior's mannish, sinewy glow. Sclerotherapy erased spider veins and Autologen was injected into nasolabial folds (a lab in New Jersey was busy farming collagen from three millimeters of skin taken from behind her ears); the men on Roxbury Drive had rolled up AlloDerm, an implant made from the dermis of human cadavers, surgically inserting it in her lip, and applied erbium laser to forehead. Mistakenly diagnosed with Lyme disease, Joyce flew to New York on the BBJ to have her blood pumped with a synthetic amino acid. Horrified that she leaked urine during a particularly torturous Pilates session, she immediately had a "designer" vaginoplasty and anterior colporrhaphy to restore the dropped bladder to normal position.

But dark clouds hung overhead that would not disperse. They had tried so long and so nobly to have children. Joyce saw a hundred specialists, but nothing worked; she combed Russia and China for little ones, but could never commit. Then came the magician of Santa Monica. He was going to use her womb as an incubator for another woman's eggs— Joyce was giving herself preparatory injections when by mistake Lucy happened. Well, why not? She knew plenty of fortysomethings who were knocked up. What was modern technology for? Then she wanted another, and the magician made it happen. Presto: eyebrows were raised—there were always the doomsayers, including her mother-in-law, who wasn't thrilled from the beginning that her son had chosen *une femme ancienne*. Is it safe? they would ask. Are you sure that you *want* to? You were so lucky with Lucy . . . so *blessed*. What if the child—and she knew he was damaged, of *course* she knew, because the magician had told her so, but then she met with Father de Kooning and was certain she would have it. *She would have it.* And people were not happy! Years later, the Four Winds Mommies, scourges of the silent auction/Pediatric AIDS/carnival-booth charity circuit, tacitly indicted her for Edward's plastic fantastic skeletophantasmagoric woes . . . she could *feel* it. She smelled it in their eyes, their hair, their smiles, their very teeth as they pushed thousand-dollar prams stuffed with bawling bundles of gorgeous DNA. (Since Apert's wasn't a "recessive," the odds of Lucy having a child so afflicted were astronomical . . . as were those of Joyce and Dodd if it were possible for them to have another, which of course it wasn't. Wasn't that a consolation?)

"Think he'll snap?"

"Who?"

"Tull."

"Edward, don't be silly."

She used a little bit of alcohol to swab beneath the brace, then rubbed his pale skin with Camelia Iris from E. Coudray, his favorite. Say what he would to Lucy and Tull, he secretly adored her. These were the only times—her touching him—that Edward felt alive.

"He's been acting pretty weird since he found out."

"I think that's normal—an attention-getter. The whole thing has been quite a shock, I'm sure."

"Have you talked to Trinnie?"

"Yesterday."

"And Grandpa Lou?"

"Today." She smiled. "What are all these questions?"

"Is Grandpa Lou angry that Tull found out?"

"I think he's relieved."

"What about Trinnie?"

"Seems better than ever."

"She isn't mad?"

"Why *would* she be?"

"At you and Dad. For snitching."

"No one *snitched*, Edward."

"*Lucy* did."

"It's better that Tull know. He's of age—he would have found out. He *should* have been told. How can you keep a thing like that quiet?"

"*You* couldn't."

"Very funny," she said, smirking. "I always thought it was handled poorly."

"Mommy"—that's what he called her when they were alone— "what would make someone leave like that?"

"I don't know. Marcus was always kind of a nutjob."

"He didn't love her? He didn't love Aunt Trinnie?"

"I'm sure that he did."

"Did you know him?"

"Not very well."

"What was he like?"

"Edward, I'm late."

She screwed the lid on the iridescent green lotion, then drew the thin down quilt over his whiteness, gently kissing his cheek.

"Are you going to another funeral?"

"Yes."

"I never told you this before," he said, clearing his throat. "But I—I really respect the work you do."

"Thank you, Edward."

She kissed his bare cheek again, just under the hem of the scarf.

"I guess," he said, "you can't explain certain things—what makes someone leave. Tull's dad . . . or what makes someone throw a baby into a dumpster."

"No—you can't explain."

"Guess that's just the world, huh?"

"*Part* of the world. An ugly part, but just a part."

*J*oyce Trotter stood at the Castaic grave near Grasshopper Canyon. The breast of her son still flitted before her like a haunted, broken bird's.

"Can you hear the freeway?" asked Father de Kooning. "It sounds like a fountain. Jesus was tired, and stopped at a well—Jacob's well. He asked a woman for water, and she said, 'You are a Jew and I am a woman. How can you ask me for water?' Jesus said, 'If you knew who I am, you would ask *me* for water. With the water in this well, you will still have thirst. With the water I give you, you would never know thirst again because it would be like a fountain inside you.' "

There were about forty gathered there. She had dressed down for the burial, in simple earrings and black Donna Karan sheath; the sun high-lighted the chalky outline of water stains from the sponge bath. The small box about to be lowered into the earth held a two-year-old, found in the trash. Joyce had been informed that as in some infernal *Rugrats* episode, the diapered boy had scaled the garbage and draped himself over the metal side of the bin before dying in balanced repose, like a tiny-tot prisoner shot in mid-escape.

"Thomas Aquinas wrote," said the pastor, " 'It is *me* who Jesus was looking for—not water. It is *me.' "* He crossed his hands over his chest. "It is *you*"—he nodded to the mourners. "It is the seven buried children Jesus was looking for when he sat at the well."

There *were* seven now—seven anonymous babes she had helped bury in as many months. Today's child, Joyce had named Jakob. It still tore at her to know that in the eyes of the law, the new christenings were only symbolic; the interred must remain Jane and John Does, forever.

They stood listening to the indifferent fountain of the freeway while a young girl walked forward with a basket and released a dove, for Jakob. It hovered there, taking Joyce's breath away. Another basket released six more that soared above as the mourners arched their necks. The lone dove rocketed to the others—as if choreographed by a maudlin god, they moved this way and that in unison, a school of wondrous flying fishes in a topsy-turvy sea before erasing themselves in the smog of infinity.

As Joyce drove back to Bel-Air, it occurred to her with a shudder: she had never named him. Fourteen weeks in the ICU and her son had had no name. Then one day, her husband suggested Edward. Depressed and spent, she acquiesced.

CHAPTER 13

Imaginary Prisons

*D*odd Trotter was, as his precocious daughter averred, the eighteenth-richest person in the world—or thereabouts, given market fluctuations.[†] If his total worth, as construed by available SEC filings, were divided by America's GNP (a financial monthly had merrily done the math), his estimated personal wealth would equal a rough 0.19 percent of the U.S. economy. That is how this sort of money multiplies: it rises and converges, thunders, pelts and showers, then, like a perfect storm, leaves rainbows all around.

He became another poorly groomed, badly dressed coverboy of the money rags—*Fortune, Portfolio, Tycoon*—though one especially beloved, for it was Dodd's spectacular feat to have made the greatest amount of dollars in the shortest amount of time in the pecuniary history of man. This centerfold anomaly, comely string of ciphers beneath silky spread-sheets, was responsible for the birth of *Forbes*'s infamous MPH graph, where IPO booty is half-whimsically measured in "millions per hour." Like geeky campfire tales, bizarre analogies and goosebumpy stats abounded: such as how the man's annual take matched the incomes of a hundred thousand blue-collar workers combined—or how it wasn't even worth his time to stoop to pick up a $20,000 bill, if there were such a thing, because he'd make more than that in the seconds wasted by the effort.

[†]For the careful—or skittish—reader, we can assure that a fortune of Dodd Trotter's magnitude, shepherded by a man of his skill and temperament, was destined to remain one of the great fortunes of our time. If that same reader needs more assurance, suffice it to say, the prescient CEO had invested heavily not only in real estate but in energy, the "go-go" field of the new millennium.

When Dodd met his wife (Joyce Gilligan was his father's "second" secretary, a sad sack resigned to spinsterhood) he was still working for Trotter Waste Systems. To get out from under, he invested $13 million in the fledgling start-up of a once high-flying industry, which the reader has by now surely inferred. He renamed the company Quincunx, at the suggestion of his sister—the golden calf could have been called ePiss or iShit for all anyone cared—and within three years he was Dodd Trotter the Eighteenth and we'll leave it at that. Once, details of the acquisition of vast personal fortune were revelatory, offering insight and inspiration; those times are no more.

Now he walks through a building, earbud wire slacking to a phone hidden in his pocket. He does not have the fashion sense of his dad; balding since he was thirty, he shaves his own head, usually missing meadowy patches of hair at the base of the skull. He is in the mood to buy an empty shell of a structure, another in the strange series his daughter Lucy already avouched. Today, his real estate consultant has steered him to a Beaux Arts husk: the Higgins Building at 2nd and Main.

What was it about vacant buildings that captivated him? He shared the idiosyncrasy with his father—both engaged in epic searches, one seeking new edifices for the dead, the other dead edifices once for the living. For Dodd, it had begun with a magazine article about an abandoned nineteenth-century asylum in Connecticut. He'd bought it sight unseen, then moved on to rusted refineries, desecrated churches, ghostly downtown movie palaces—all of which he determinedly refused to develop. Consortiums built private prisons in hopes of landing government contracts; when that didn't happen, the bankrupted jails still stood. Dodd had already snapped up three such institutions and had no other plans but to let them sit.

He obeyed Joyce's command to see a specialist, who immediately prescribed Prozac for Obsessive Compulsive Disorder, 100 mg, once a day; BuSpar, also for OCD, 15 mg, twice a day; Seroquel (an antipsychotic he took for sleep), 100 mg, once at night; Tegretol (mania), 200 mg, three times a day; Neurontin (mania), 300 mg, twice in the morning, once at noon, twice at night; and Lamictal, for "rapid cycling" between poles of mania and depression, one tablet, twice a day. He cheated with Prozac, adding 100 mg in the afternoons. The specialist said Prozac tended to "elate" a manic.

"I'll get you archive photos," said the consultant, shuffling through lobby debris. "Everything's from the thirties," he said. "It was all marble— before the scavengers got to it . . . make a great loft building." He pointed to the ceiling. "All this was copper conduit. Brass doorknobs everywhere, engraved with HB. Clarence Darrow used to rent a whole floor."

"Hello?"

"Clarence Darrow used to have offices—"

"Hi, Mom."

"I'm not disturbing you, Doddy?"

"Not at all," he said, continuing his walkabout. Realizing that Mr. Trotter was taking a call, the consultant moved away to give him privacy. Dodd pushed the earbud further in as he spoke into thin air. "Just looking at property."

"What else is new?" said Bluey, sardonically.

"How are you feeling?"

He knew she was calling to discuss the day's obits.

"Well, Winter told me a marvelous joke."

"Is Winter doing stand-up now?"

"Don't you be silly," she laughed. "Would you like to hear, Doddy?"

"I would. Yes, I would, Mother, very much."

The consultant cautioned him to take care as Dodd poked around at the base of the stairs. A solitary pigeon watched their lazy progress.

"We were going over my album and Winter suddenly says, 'God was sobbing on a cloud.' Well, her delivery was so natural, Doddy, that I had *no* idea what she was saying. I said, 'Winter, what on *earth* are you talking about?' 'God was sobbing on a cloud,' she said, cool as can be, 'when an angel floated up and said, "What's the matter? Why are you crying?" And God says, "I'm in love with an atheist—but she doesn't even know I exist!" ' Isn't that marvelous, Doddy?"

"Wonderful."

"I thought it a delightful thing. And Winter—well, I never *knew* her to tell a joke. And she doesn't know where she heard it, but it *must* be Thurber or Wilde. It does *sound* like Wilde, doesn't it, Doddy?"

"It's very witty."

"Oh, Doddy, did you read about the poor little girl killed in Brentwood?"

A fifteen-year-old who went to school in the Palisades had been struck by a car in a Montana Avenue crosswalk; Lucy had already told him, but he didn't let on.

"Tell me what happened."

"The father saw her get hit—how awful! How could you ever get over seeing something like that? An old man, who shouldn't have been driving. Ninety-four years old! They showed the shrine on the news. That's what they do now, the friends and neighbors tape letters and flowers to telephone poles until they rot away. Do you remember the Deutschmans?"

"Howard and Lillian."

"Well, Howard just dropped dead—at a hundred and three! At St. John's. Born in St. Petersburg. Did you know he played bridge? The article says he was an expert, even wrote a couple books. Now that, to me, is marvelous . . . the things you find out, Doddy, *after* they're gone! Howard was a great friend of Sybil Brand—*there's* a jail you could probably have for a song! It's closed now, did you know? Where do they put all the prisoners, that's what *I* wonder about. What do they *do* with them? You know, your father and I used to see the Deutschmans all the time at the Hilton, for the benefits. In the grand ballroom—oh, that was long before Merv moved in. *Long* before. Howard had a degenerative hip. And you'd better believe Lillian's still cutting a rug, at ninety-one! Who did the Deutschmans know? The Bloomingdales, the Darts, the Jorgensens— now, there's another one! Earle *just* died, at a hundred and one. Didn't I read you that? Do you know what the paper said, Doddy? That he was working out with a personal trainer three times a week and playing tennis before he died. At a hundred and one! It said that Earle Jorgensen spent three days on a schooner watching San Francisco burn after the earthquake—in 1906! Now, *that's* old. Did you know Marion—Earle's wife—did you know that Marion's son is Donald Bren? He's got almost as much money as *you* do, Doddy. Land in Orange County: the Irvine Ranch. And of course Howard and Lillian knew the Annenbergs—*everyone* knew the Annenbergs. The Deutschmans were *very* much a part of the Sunnylands Christmas crowd. Walter always called Sunny 'Mother'— ugh! Don't you ever call Joyce that, Doddy, don't you ever!"

She went on like that while he made his way to the sidewalk. The consultant followed and they climbed into the Arnage.

His mother was on to another obituary, and he let her talk all the way to Beverly Hills. It was comforting to hear her chattily cogent, because of late there had been some reason to worry. A few days after the release from Cedars, Winter had found her standing in the hall in frozen repose. Startled, Bluey pretended she was trying to recall where she misplaced a book, but it was clear to Winter that the old woman was literally lost. Dodd phoned their dear friend Dr. Kindman, who suggested she be evaluated for Aricept; the billionaire had seen the Alzheimer's drug promoted in *National Geographic,* next to an ad for a pill that was supposed to help your dog remember better when he began having trouble responding to his name. He thought that odd.

He eased his mother off the phone as they neared Beverly Vista, the grade school he had attended as a boy.

Back in the sixties, the Trotters lived on Bellagio Road (they always seemed to live on a road), just outside the eligibility zone of the Beverly Hills school system. Louis could have sent his kids to Buckley or Oakwood or Westlake—could have sent them anywhere—but wanted them in public school instead. So he bought a house on Roxbury, south of Wilshire, and Winter stayed there with the children during the week. Dodd and Trinnie could walk to grade school; that way, when they graduated, they could walk to high school too, even closer but in the other direction. His father liked the unpretentious small-town feel of that. Hadn't Beverly High's "trapdoor" swimming pool been famously filmed in *It's a Wonderful Life?*

His alma mater had turned to him for help. BV had been badly damaged in the Northridge quake; since then, the lovely orange-brick California Romanesque revivalist-style buildings were entirely fenced-in, with students housed in "temporary" school-yard bungalows. The district wanted to demolish the school and build state-of-the-art facilities, but there was opposition, both nostalgic and fiscal.

The Board of Education came up with an Environmental Impact Report that provided four suggestions. The first was to do nothing—they called it the No Project Alternative, meaning the bungalows would remain. The second was the Auditorium Rehabilitation with New Construction Alternative; the third, a Partial Historic Rehabilitation with New Construction Alternative; and last, a Historic Rehabilitation Alternative—restoration of the school as in its heyday. The fight was between the PTA, who wanted to tear the thing down, and the preservationists, who reminded that all schools in the precious Beverly Hills system were official historic landmarks. The feud had lasted years.

Marcie Millard, former treasurer of their eighth-grade class and now honorary president of the PTA, had charmingly approached Dodd at a scleroderma fund-raiser. She looked the same as he had always pictured her, hair upswept and old-fashioned, as it had been in the school production of *The Music Man*. She made sure to refer to such shared touchstones—long-ago plays, outings, cultural ephemera—when they spoke, yet Dodd had the perverse sense she didn't really remember him, and had found out by chance (or the Internet) that he was an alumnus. Sometimes her words and manner seemed too scripted and eager, but maybe that was just her way. Marcie's kids were now at BV and she expressed her disgust and contempt for "the scandal of district politics" that had caused the near seven-year delay in renovations. The children, she said, were the ones who suffered. She wanted to know if Dodd would be interested in funding a new campus, ballsily suggesting the school might even bear his name as a result of his largesse.

So there he was again, walking through another shell, this time retracing smaller steps taken more than thirty years before. The group—Marcie and her carefully selected PTA brethren: architect, dentist, restaurateur—wore hardhats and missionary smiles, as if the mere presence of Dodd Trotter, *their* Dodd Trotter, class of '71, completed—*sanctified*—the dream team. Their billion-dollar angel.

Passing through the condemned halls spooked him. He went to the rest room, and Marcie called after, "Not sure the equipment's working too well in there!" He stood on the spidery-fissured diamond-patterned tiles and peered through the wire-cage windows. The architect came in, trying a faucet, which erupted in a rusty geyser. When the water cleared, he washed his hands and reminisced about a field trip they'd taken to Paradise Cove. Dodd said he'd never been to Paradise Cove and the architect had to admit he'd confused him with Tim Gaspard, a brainy boy who played the harp.

Before he left, Marcie made a final plea. She hoped, she said, they could create an environment as creative and technologically sophisticated as the campus at Four Winds, where Dodd's children were enrolled. *Oh, she's good,* he thought.

The consultant waited in the car while Dodd took a slow walk around the school's circumference, ringed by stucco'd condominiums and duplexes in the French Normandy or Spanish Colonial style, their attractive leaded-glass bay windows presiding over tiny lawns like great dark open mouths. His attention turned to the playground. The prefab bungalows were hideous; how bizarre that parents had tolerated them all these years. A bell rang and children poured out. He was startled how a generation had changed the complexion of the student body from garden-variety Jew to Benetton: Korean, Latino and Persian.

They all looked happy enough.

*E*arlier, had Mr. Trotter looked back through the Bentley's smoky rear window as it pulled away from the historic Higgins Building— had he had *cause* to look back—he might have seen a fiftyish detective in a serge suit rounding the corner. The gentleman had a homeless man in tow, or rather was towed by the homeless man; they'd just come from the St. George, where only yesterday the badly decomposed body of a woman had been found in bed, strangled by her own sheets.

The wily Sherpa was none other than Someone-Help-Me, who, rebuffed the night before, had discarded the spoiled custom-made sign that had provided his name. It was Will'm's misfortune the beggar had chosen that very night to camp in an alcove across from the venerably decrepit Higgins "plant." Awakened by a caroming warble of sirens from black-and-whites, he had poked his head from the cardboard; it was then that he saw an alley child in the light of the street lamp, and heard an unmistakable shout calling her back to darkness. A large, charcoaly figure appeared and lifted the girl to his back, covering her with a greatcoat before galloping off.

The vagrant and the detective walked from alley to sidewalk, scrutinizing the crime scene.

"Did the girl seem to be in any distress?"

"That time of night . . . little girl that age. *I'd* be distressed. Not in bed with her toys all safe. *I* would be—"

He rasped his words, interposing repulsively guttural clicks, grunts and snickers.

"Was she fighting? Did he *force* her—"

"—wouldn't be playing no kinda game *that* time of night."

"But he *shouted* at her," said the detective, mildly exasperated.

"A *command*—and you better listen. 'Come 'ere, girlie!' All 'Engli-fied,' too, like he Michael Caine! Shit, that one's a *bear.*"

"You saw her face."

"Not too well. But I'd know her. Yep, I'd know her!"

"And the man?"

"I didn't so much *seen* him but *heard* him."

"Then how could you identify?"

"That one hard to miss! Big as a house—I *know* that one. Chased after him awhile, too. Couldn't keep up, me with my leg . . . Never thought he go *that* way, not with *kids.* Them who fuck kids is pure shit."

"Which way did he run?"

"Down Broadway. *I* didn't go no further. He was *movin'* and *groovin'*—the girl on 'im like a papoose!"

"Now, you know this man?"

"Name Will'm but some call 'im Topsy."

"And you know where to find him?"

"Give me *heehaw* and I'll know, know what ahm sayin'?"

One-legged Fitz passed by and Half Dead nipped the informer's ankle, drawing blood.

"Mother *fuck* you, spunion! Old crackhead *bitch!*" He lowered a fist down on the dog's spine and the thing trundled off. "I'll *kill* that mutated peesuhshit!" He pounded the air with a gnarly fist. "Kill *you too,* Half Man!"

Fitz skedaddled as the dog dodged a bike messenger, who threw them an oath.

Someone-Help-Me rubbed his bitten ankle as he cane-lurched after the laughing detective on the short walk back to the St. George.

CHAPTER 14

Little Search Engines That Could

*L*ucy Trotter had a mission.

She would help her cousin, the boy who was first—next to Edward, of course—in heart and in blood. She would do this large and amazing thing for him *and* be Author in the process. She had finally solved the Mystery of the Blue Maze—or was at least well on her way, for the riddle now had a designation: Marcus Weiner, long-lost father extra-ordinaire. She had pried the surname off a reluctant Winter, then backed away from further interrogations. Vanity would not let her take the easy route.

So, she Yahoo!'d and Google'd, fidgeted and stressed; there were a million pages to sift through on the Web. She back-slashed, skidded and WWW'd her way from Net Detective 2000 to The Skip Tracing and Locating Missing Persons Resource Center, The Hollywood Network's Missing Persons CyberCenter, How to Find Anyone Anywhere, Tracing Missing Heirs, Missing Persons Throughout the World, and TrackStar Inc.—America's Missing Person Locator (an Infotel Company). Each site offered Certified Missing Persons Investigator courses and on-/off-line seminars in locating specialized detectives (the latter would have been a cheat). Lucy staved off tears of anxiety, frustration and boredom—YOU ARE VISITOR 193,784—mailing in subscriptions to *PI* and *Pursuit* magazines and *Professional Repossessor* once she got her seventh wind.

The free sites were filled with suggestions on how to track down the vanished through genealogy, local 411, voter registration, birth and civil records, criminal and military, real estate and alumni, news archives, former husbands, former wives, licensing bureaus, hospitals, et alia.

There were Netherlands databases and comprehensive national White Pages and what seemed to be an infinity of pathetic, once-poignant notices from those looking for loved ones stretching all the way back to the birth of the Net—how could she possibly sort through it? She enlisted her phlegmatic brother to root out Social Security numbers on Lexis-Nexis while she, with halfhearted incompetence, tackled property deeds. It felt hopeless.

There *were* certain obvious details that would have made things easier. For example: what, at the time of his leave-taking, did Marcus Weiner actually do for a living? Until she hit the PowerBook wall, Lucy made a pact with herself not to approach her parents—a true girl detective would never need to resort to such tactics. After conferring with AltaVista (there were 608,540 pages found pertaining to "Marcus Weiner," many of which were translated from other languages), she decided to do a little flat-footing at the Beverly Hills Library to check local newspapers; one of them *must* have reported the Weiner-Trotter nuptials. But it was rainy that week, so Lucy found herself glued to the enormous screen of Joyce's unused G-4 instead. Truth be told, there *were* some Webby diversions from her main cause—per usual, the pigtailed researcher was IM'd so many times that she couldn't make much headway; a veritable fusillade of "creaking doors" and harmonic tantaras announced that endless Buddies were on-line. Along the way, she surprised herself by becoming seriously obsessed with the Boulder Langon homepage, a development the actress herself found hysterical.

Whenever the thought of approaching her mother with a few queries reared its torpid head, she stubbornly ruled it out. Anyway, that wouldn't have been easy: an unnerving secrecy had dropped like a veil after Aunt Trinnie sat her son down and told all—as if there were nothing more to reveal! The party-line spin on "closure" was sorely artificial. Mysteries abounded, and the body of Marcus Weiner floated, pickled and unquiet—like the story she had read during an epic Internet tangent of a teenager who slipped and fell into a river in Georgia. Lucy and her Buds were riveted: trapped beneath the surface, wedged vertically between rocks for months, the teen's body was impossible to retrieve save for damming the waters. Locals said leave the river alone, it would "give the girl up" in its own time; but that wasn't good enough for the girl's father—and *not* good enough for Lucille Rose, who loved Cousin

Tull more than she could ever admit, even to herself. She would not wait for time or the river *or* Bel-Air to give Marcus Weiner up. She could see the crown of his head just below the surface and would do anything in her power to pull him ashore, and to rest. She was convinced Tull would one day thank her for kayaking him through such a watershed; it might even make him drop a knee and propose.

Meanwhile, the boy around whom these rapids swirled couldn't be bothered. He became irascible, and refused to pay homage to Lucy's night-surfing or the double-clicks of her anxious heart. Whenever she made the mistake of alluding to her ongoing detective work, he lashed out, leaving a jellyfish sting of hurt. She forgave him everything.

He raged. He plastered bumper stickers—MY KID SHOT YOUR HONOR STUDENT—on faculty cars. He stole hard-boiled eggs and batteries from 7-Eleven and a Schwinn from outside Borders on the Promenade. He provoked fights with stronger, wilier boys and for the first time felt the exhilarating, nauseous pain of hard knuckles against cheekbone, sinus, gut. He was winded and bruised, snide and weepy. He was all over the place. When Mr. Hookstratten beckoned him into his office, Tull said go to hell. At home, on the labyrinth's cold stone benches or in the narcotized darkness of the cavernous living room, enfolded by walls with shutters of macassar ebony, sprawled on the Jean Royère sofa between Ming-style cabinets of gold-leafed *wenge* wood, under the Chardin or black-gold Rembrandt, he let his mother stroke his tousled hair, smelling her skin and clothes while he cried all over the fine bushy hairs of her arm.

But no one took him seriously, not even himself—his anger being merely a plot development of *The Wounded Boy*, Act Two. When a Four Winds Care Team suggested the boy be medicated (they'd carefully interviewed him after a rumor spread that he had a "hit list"), his mother went ballistic. Half the school was on Zoloft, Effexor or Serzone; Tull knew a twelve-year-old who'd been on Prozac since age five. Trinnie was of a mind to pull him out of there. Lackadaisical assholes! With their much-hyped zero-tolerance policy for drugs (whenever a child was caught using, power parents brought in attorneys and the school caved)—Hypocrites! Pushers! Sleazy *fucks*—she knew all about their fund-raising tactics too: a mom whose kid had been rejected told her how she and her husband were taken out to lunch as part of the "en-

rollment process" and hit up for half a million because a TRW on an estranged relative had shown income in the high nines. *That's* how much
the Care Team cared!

With what then besides a fresh delinquency was he left? The idea of
a newly minted father, at first intriguing, now disgusted. King of dead-
beat dads, a man who'd botched visitation on a heroic scale . . . Tull conjured a face floating in the air like a newsprint terrorist's: Marcus the
Jackal. He watched the sadistic groom flee in white tux and tails from
that strange cracked column while his martyred mother slept. The
jackal had ruined her, and Tull would make him pay. As he gamboled
with Pullman through the sculpted grounds of Saint-Cloud, he imagined his father blowing up Buddhas with the Taliban—then, in a weaker
moment, as the subject of an A&E hagiography—speedily supplanted by
a careering, poorly lit chase and capture on *America's Wildest Police
Videos.* Authorities would usher the boy like a dignitary to his father's
cell. There, shackled, Marcus X (Lucy had not yet vouchsafed the last
name) stood cowering in his dirty formal wear and sleepless coward's
eyes as the boy sent a gob of spit his way. The guards laughed approvingly and steered him out by his small shoulders while dearest Dad sank
in supplication, old cold hands on cold steel bars.

"*A*n amazing feat," crowed Edward from the quaint, cozy middle of
the Black Lantern Book Shoppe. "Replicating a folly as complex
as that—and all in a year's time! Look! Look here—"

He motored excitedly toward the reticent Tull, a pristine volume
of the Amazon FedExed history of Le Désert de Retz in his gloved hand.
La Colonne itself graced the cover, while the tower of Edward's *own*
head wore a blousy façade of red silk; his face the delicate half-mask of a
raccoon-like beast he'd fashioned out of feathers and bamboo.

"But what I find *so* truly weird is how you found your way there! I
mean, before *knowing* any of this."

"And why you didn't ever *tell* us," whined Lucy.

"Pullman took me," said Tull, his casualness a bit contrived.

The magnificent animal could be heard cavorting on the streets
of the small European-style village where Edward lived. His father had
built the fantasia for his son's convenience and amusement—Edward
called it Olde CityWalk—on an acre or so tucked behind the property on

Stradella Road. The mobile invalid thought the corny "village" conceit trying, yet its ramps and customized dimensions *did* make it extraordinarliy livable. A full-time nursing staff was housed in a cobbler's storefront; the workshop where Edward designed vizards and prosthetics from clay, wood and papier-mâché occupied the Boar's Head Inn, with his private apartments above. Black Lantern was the perfect model of an English den of antiquities, its shelves stocked with both contemporary fare and volumes two centuries old.

"I mean, Pullman found it."

"And *you* kept it all to yourself. Rather elitist, no?"

"How *could* you, Tull? I *hate* you!" said Lucy, unconvincingly.

"Still," said Edward, "it *is* an astonishing coincidence."

"There are no accidents," said Lucy, sagely peering over from her celery-green Smythson steno pad. One thing was certain: she was thrilled to see her brother excited again, about *anything*—until the discovery of the broken Bel-Air column and its French counterpart, he'd been inscrutable and queerly unenthusiastic about the business of hunting for Mr. Marcus Weiner. "All is predetermined."

"Then it's settled," Edward said, snatching the book from Tull's hands. "You *have* to take us."

"*Vive La Colonne!*" shouted Lucy.

"A major field trip is in order."

"Fine," said Tull, his languidness sounding more staged than he would have liked. If it weren't his cousin who was asking, he'd have flat-out refused.

"You don't really have a choice—this whole *father* thing has you backed into a square corner. That's a phrase pilots use: it's when you run out of ideas at the same time you run out of experience. *No bueno!*"

"I'm not afraid to go," Tull said, "but it won't be easy for *you*. It's not exactly wheelchair-friendly."

Edward stared at the picture book a moment, like a preacher absorbed in a favorite verse before looking up at the flock. "La Colonne Détruite . . ." he mused, practically licking his chops. "Created on the eve of the Revolution by François Nicolas Henri Racine de Monville, gentleman of fashion. The most extraordinary folly in Europe, visited by everyone from Marie-Antoinette to Thomas Jefferson to famed Surrealist André Breton. *Vive l'ancien régime!* Nestled within a vast park of sycamores and chestnuts, lindens and blue cedars—oh! and let us not forget the imported Virginia tulips! The 'shattered column': an image common to the iconography of late-eighteenth-century Freemasonry. And who do we have to thank for this relocated heaven on earth? Why, none other than Grandpa Lou! Our very own Grandpa Lou! How crazy is that! Oh! How absurd! I knew Grandpa was a genius, but this! And kept *secret* all these years! Hidden! From even the architectural cognoscenti! How, how, how? I tell you, nothing short of astonishing!"

*W*hile the children made their plans, Bluey's birthday was celebrated in the main house. The honoree, in her beloved Oscar de la Renta sequined jacket, sported a vintage Frances Whitney millinery *mobile* spiraling neatly off her head like a junior Guggenheim, from which it was inspired.

"But wouldn't it be fun," said Joyce, "having your old grade school named after you? I think it'd be a hoot."

Hoot was a word Trinnie loathed. Though she *did* think her sister-in-law looked particularly becoming, sort of the way she remembered Claire Bloom—sexy in that rock-hard cold-mountain-stream sort of way. All the primping and preening had paid off; tonight, the skin and hair stars were definitely in alignment.

"Oh," said Dodd. "I think that was bogus—you know, something that popped into Marcie's head. She doesn't have any say about that. The district would never consent."

Trinnie fidgeted with her South Sea pearls. She wore a marabou-trimmed cardigan and a crocheted halter dress as green as her eyes; piercing her brother with the latter, she said, "You *hated* that school."

"But why *would* he?" interjected Bluey. "It was *wonderful.* And that wonderful Dr. Janklow!"

"Yes," chuffed Louis. "Extraordinary. Wonderful educator. Sensitive man. We had him to the house for dinner."

"He came to dinner because he was a *fag.*"

"Oh come on, Trinnie."

"Dr. Janklow," said his sister witchily, "was interested in Dodd because Dr. Janklow was a *fag.*"

Her brother smiled, amused.

"And *who* was Dr. Janklow?" asked Ralph.

"The school psychologist," replied Trinnie. "My brother spent *lots* of time with the school psychologist." She turned on him again and sneered. "*Dodd Trotter Elementary*—why would you even *dream* it?"

"It was just a funny concept. I mean, come on, Trinnie, don't you think it's funny? Isn't that your style of black comedy? Having the school you attended as a child named after you? Marcie said—" He swiveled to include Bluey. "Mother, do you remember Marcie Millard?"

"A little red thing? Like our Lucille? Oh yes. A go-getter! Father an *ophthalmologist*, no?"

"Mother! I'm shocked you remember," said Trinnie.

Louis nodded enthusiastically while chewing the veal. Such demonstrations of his wife's mental alacrity comforted—he hoarded them as evidence to present at some future sanity trial.

"Wasn't he a councilman?" asked Dodd.

"The *mayor*," said Trinnie. Then, in an aside to Ralph: "Beverly Hills used to be very Andy of Mayberry. The family eye doctor was actually the mayor."

"He died," said Bluey, her brow crinkling in concern. "Didn't he? Didn't the Millard man pass away?"

Louis chuffed, thinking it a tad early in the evening for obits.

"Yes," said Dodd. "While jogging. One of the very first to be claimed by the craze."

Ralph spoke up. "Aren't the Beverly Hills schools completely Iranian now?"

"Well," said Dodd, "Marcie showed me a PTA flyer that was printed in Farsi, Korean, Russian, Hebrew and Spanish. She said the children of the district came from fifty-seven countries and speak forty-six languages."

"You don't see that on *Dawson's Creek*, do you?" said Ralph. "Or is that show not even on anymore?" The flâneur was emboldened by his first dinner *en famille*—and loaded for bearish faux pas. "You don't see it in the teen masturbation flicks: no Muslims or Bahai's shagging apple pie, no *sir*. They're all rich and they're all white!"

"Perhaps it's not in their interest," chuffed the patriarch, cryptically.

"When Dodd and I went to BV—*and* Beverly—there were pretty much only Jews," Trinnie said.

"There was one black," her brother solemnly corrected. "His name was Elijah—do you remember Elijah, Mother?"

"*I* do," Trinnie exclaimed, her memory jogged. "Ralph, it was *so weird.* He was this skinny little kid, like, made-to-order: sweet and small and talented . . . *completely* inoffensive—I know this sounds *terrible,* but he was very . . . *minstrel show*—like a little Sammy Davis."

"That's horrible!"

"I am *not* being racist. It was the high school that was racist. It was like they—like the District literally cast a part."

"I would have thought you'd have gone to private school," said Ralph.

"Papa thought public schools were good enough."

"Indeed they were!" piped Lou.

"Papa bought us a house in the flats."

"I've always thought it amazing Mr. Trotter did that," said Joyce. She had called him Mister ever since the halcyon days at Trotter Waste.

"Well, the kids at school didn't think so," said Trinnie.

"No, they didn't! Oh God, Doddy! Mercy," said Bluey.

"Everyone thought it was freaky. Like: why would someone with so much money not send their kids to school in Switzerland? Or wherever. And at the same time, they were—I don't know, jealous."

For a moment, the group ate in silence.

"Did you know," said Dodd, again turning to Ralph, "that the Velvet Underground played at lunch, for a special assembly? The principal pulled the plug when Lou Reed sang 'Heroin.'"

"Incredible," said Ralph. "And now they get *Curtis Hanson* or *Michael Bay* to drop in—Tull told me Four Winds even had Robert Towne giving a lecture! What do kids want to be hearing from Mr. Chinatowne for? What are they going to learn from that *high-brow Ron Shelton?* At least Ron Shelton isn't *pretentious*—well, not as pretentious as *Chinatowne,* anyway . . . and let's not forget Callie Khouri!—oh, all you aspiring riot-grrrl-screenwriters have *so* much to learn from Callie Khouri!" Trinnie smiled at this arcana; the rest of the Trotters remained impassive. "By the way, what exactly does Callie Khouri *do*—aside from having her picture taken every month for the WGA Newsletter, and jacking off with her Oscar? I'll *tell* you what Callie Khouri does! She's on the *guru* circuit with *Thelma and Louise!* Asshole-buddies with the Council of Elders! Callie Khouri—Bride of Chinatowne!"

"You're gonna hate this," said Trinnie, eyes twinkling. "But next week they're having Ron Bass."

"Who is?"

"Four Winds."

"No!"

"Because he's an attorney. He can talk about writing *and* entertainment law."

"Well . . . Ron's OK. At least the man knows what he is."

"You mean he's OK now that the two of you are having cozy little Buffalo Club lunches." She put the needle in a little further. "Hey, Ralph, did you know that Four Winds also has a mentor program going? Something called Young Storytellers—"

"Oh God, that makes me ill," he said, ashening.

Having achieved the desired effect, she turned to her brother. "That school's getting *so* crazy. And don't you *dare* put those kids up at the Hassler—he's flying Tull's *entire class* to Rome," she explained to those not in the know, "to which I am *highly* opposed."

"It's not the whole class," said Dodd impishly. "It's Third-Tier Honors. And it isn't Rome anymore. It's . . . the *world.* All the places with roads that *lead* to Rome."

"Whatever it is, it's much too much."

"I think it's wonderful," offered Joyce.

"It's *bullshit* already. Those kids are *so* twisted—there's no sense of reality *whatsoever.* Last week, I was waiting at the curb to pick up my son."

"You picked up Tull?" said Dodd incorrigibly. "Epitacio must have been on his deathbed!"

"I sat there, forced to endure listening to *Boulder Langon* and her fucked-up friends—"

"What do they give her per movie now?" Dodd asked earnestly.

"Two, maybe three," said Trinnie.

"She's *very* talented," said Joyce. "Did you see that fabulous film she did with Susan Sarandon?"

"It was *shite,*" said Trinnie.

Dodd laughed, and Joyce wasn't pleased. The old man inclined his head, cuing his daughter to enlighten him. "Boulder Langon is Lucy's best friend. She's twelve years old, and they give her three million a movie." His eyebrows knit dramatically as he chuffed at the figure. "So I'm parked at the curb listening to this *horrible* little girl and her clique from hell dish some punk actor. They want to know who he's dating, and Boulder says, 'A nobody.' They keep pressing for the girl's name until

Boulder—this *twelve*-year-old—says, 'A nobody! She's a pedestrian!' A 'pedestrian,' can you *believe*? And the *sex*. My God, the sex! You know what they say? They say, 'Did you run barefoot?' That's what they ask each other. *Did you run barefoot?* Know what that means? Did you sleep together without protection—*that's* what it means. And these aren't even teenagers! So what kind of message are we sending when you load them up on the BBJ and—"

"Joyce," interrupted Bluey. "How are your dead children?"

The room fell silent. Pullman barked at something from far away as a servant entered to clear.

"You mean . . . the babies?" Joyce cleared her throat, taken aback. "Things are going very . . . *well.*"

"How great," said Trinnie mindlessly, trying to smooth the moment.

"Yes! People seem to be quite moved. I mean, by the program."

Mr. Trotter gesticulated to the servant, who leaned over while the old man spoke briefly in his ear.

"We've talked about this, Bluey," Joyce said gently. She looked to her father-in-law for help, but he simply smiled and stared benevolently at his plate, as if to wait things out. "We're looking for a larger cemetery," she continued, feeling that at this point the broader strokes would be welcome. "I'd like to set aside a bigger space, that's not so remote—that's the goal, anyway. We'd like to do it in every state. And have them change the law so the names we give the children are permanent and legally binding." She'd given the speech many times before, and tonight it came in handy.

"Well," said Louis, "just don't put them in the Westwood!"

The others laughed. They hoped Bluey was through; she wasn't just yet.

"Joyce—were there obituaries for any of the children?"

"We always put a notice in the paper."

"I haven't seen any. Are any of them well known?"

"Mother," said Trinnie, exasperated in spite of knowing better. "These are infants!"

"Mother means famous, case by case," said Louis, stroking his wife's arm. "Don't you, darling?"

"Yes," she affirmed.

Louis smiled at the others, as if to say, See? Perfectly compos mentis!

Another servant brought the cake. A ragged if uneventful blowing out of candles ensued. Dodd encouraged his guests to adjourn to the terrace for coffee and plates of mousse au caramel et aux poires.

⌒⌣

After a brief and cordial discussion of the pronunciatory variants of *Ralph*, and after complimenting the latter on his "wild suit" (a quilted Issey Miyake), Dodd Trotter affably quizzed the fop on his latest screenwriting gig. Ralph was shy around the billionaire, whom he in fact viewed as a potential source of capital for various projects as yet unrealized. Wishing to please his sister, who actually couldn't have cared less, Dodd tried to make conversational inroads by mentioning how, with Mr. Hookstratten's help, he had been delving the poetic and practical depths of *The Art of War*—which, he said, he'd gathered had become a kind of how-to manual for Hollywood theatrical agents and such. Ralph informed him that the military classic was actually passé, the hot new book being Aristotle's *Poetics:* Richard LaGravenese, Steve Zaillian, Callie Khouri and Gary Ross all swore by it, he said—as did the whole fucking WGA. Dodd didn't quite know what to make of that except to say *The Art of War* had proved insightful to him as a businessman.

Ralph said he was now more interested in directing than writing for film. The latter, he said, was a loser's game. Digital technology made it feasible for anyone to realize his vision; desire and a middling electrocardiogram were all a director required. The seriously stroked out Michelangelo Antonioni and Christopher Reeve, valiant quad though he was, both had films in the can, not to mention everyone from third-string DPs to casting directors to special-effects wizards to earnest morons like Kathy Bates, Kiefer Sutherland and Diane Ladd. Nepotism was rampant. Ralph Fiennes had a sister, Martha, who'd turned proud "helmer"; Ridley Scott's, Larry Kasdan's and Walter Matthau's sons all directed. Ralph had read in the trades how Charlie Matthau bought the rights to a thirty-year-old screenplay by one of the late *Vertigo* scribes—*that's* what Hollywood wanted: scripts by dead persons "helmed" by the weak-minded and well-born. A brief conversation ensued regarding some of Dodd's newly acquired properties, with Ralph paying special attention to the empty prison in the Mojave. The budding auteur had the idea to shoot a DV ensemble piece à la Dogme 95.

With distracted eyes on the distant lights of Olde CityWalk, Trinnie and her father strategized about Bluey. Louis in particular had become worried she might hurt herself during a nocturnal meandering. The two of them sighed; the evening had drawn to a close.

"Well, *here's* the man you ought to talk to," said Bluey as husband and daughter approached. The old man's face lit up supportively while Joyce's shrank to a pale rictus.

"Talk to, Mother?" he chuffed inquisitively, patiently putting an arm on her elbow. "Yes, of course! But what about?"

"*You're* the one with the quarry, Louis . . . my God, Joyce, your father-in-law has a twenty-two-acre open pit, 641 feet deep. It's in Atlanta, but hell—that represents I don't know *how* many millions of cubic yards of waste."

"What does it mean, darling?" he asked tenderly, the soul of kindness itself.

"The *babies*, Louis! We're talking about the babies! Joyce is looking for space to bury the babies and you've got space to burn."

A servant was duly dispatched to gather up Tull and his harlequin friend.

*H*ome at last, he tumbled to bed.

The envelope his cousin had slipped him as they left the Black Lantern for Edward's apartments was tucked deep inside his overcoat.

Tull flicked on a nightstand lamp. Slung over a chair like a phantom, the cashmere garment suddenly gave him the creeps; he plucked the letter from its pocket, and ran back under the covers.

He pulled out a page dated June 30, 1988. Sentences had been whited out and he wondered if his cousin was to blame. The document attested to progress made in "the case," difficulties encountered, et cetera.

He moistened his fingers to free the page stuck behind—a Xerox'd note written in cursive. On the letterhead was a personal monogram, M and W intertwined.

Mr. Tabori,

If I was shocked at the reckless insinuation of your employee, I was absolutely dumbfounded by the letter from your attorney which my office received today.

I have referred the matter to my own counsel, who would probably object to my sending this note. I suggest that you retract your
slanderous allegations, or you will find this former customer to be a
litigious one.

Sincerely,
Marcus Weiner

He read it aloud a half-dozen times, then put it beneath his pillow.
Sincerely, Marcus Weiner . . .
Just how much did Cousin Edward know?
Something in him was afraid to ask.

CHAPTER 15

Revolution's Eve

*T*hat week, Trinnie invited him to go along on a job. She had never done that before; the gesture was a coming-of-age for both of them.

Mother and son were met in the lobby of the Motion Picture and Television Hospital by Tim de Kooning, the pastor there. The Trotters were well known, and Father de Kooning said it was a happy coincidence to have recently met Trinnie's sister-in-law in connection with a "quite amazing program for orphaned children which Joyce—I'm sure you know!—has spearheaded."

Upon entering the grounds, Trinnie felt as if in a geriatric Shangri-la. Like most Angelenos, she had only a dim awareness of this place, and (until now) thought of it as "the old actors' home" rather than a modern medical facility. Her parents, along with their friends the Wassermans and the Douglases, had been generous to the institution throughout the years. Trinnie could remember being at a benefit listening to her mother and Debbie Reynolds chat about the Woodland Hills sanctuary, saying it was where both wanted to be when it was time to "wrap things up." (Bluey had always loved show people.) Strolling through the cafeteria with its waiters and white linen, the pastor pointed out wizened cowboys and ex-vamps in dainty gloves carving up racks of lamb—here, a renowned cinematographer seated beside an early effects wizard; there, a mistress of Howard Hughes, now a hundred years old. The place had a hazy, anomalous Garden of Allah vibe that instantly drew her in. The Rockwellian town square, with its architectural nod to gazebos, bandstands and calliopes, finished off the effect.

They were on their way to Harry's Haven, the unit for those suffer-ing from the disease of forgetting. Father de Kooning liked going over to speak after Sunday chapel services. A gift from Kirk and Anne Douglas, the "Alzheimer's cottage" had been built in memory of the actor's father.

They followed him in to a large room off the main corridor, where nurses had assembled about a dozen residents. Trinnie and Tull sat near the back while the pastor spoke. The boy watched the goings-on, wide-eyed. A hawk-like man with crossed, hairy arms corrosively decon-structed Father de Kooning's monologue, then abruptly fell silent, like an actor on a stool upon a stage. In the back row, a painted woman kissed the hand of a fey, embarrassed galfriend. "You're marvelous!" she hissed with maudlin zealotry. "You're just sensational, and you know it!" A Babe Paley type, displeased by the outburst, turned to stare the painted woman down—the former resembling a socialite who'd been forced to endure Bedlam itself as some kind of charity stunt.

Undaunted, the pastor homilized. "It was a dark and stormy night," he said, putting on a bit of the evangelizing dog for Trinnie, "and a father and son headed home. They came to a bridge, but the bridge was washed out. As the wind howled and rain poured down, the man lifted his son and walked across a log that straddled the raging river." He paused, for effect. "The boy awoke in his warm bed the next morning. He told his fa-ther that, back at the river, when he lifted him up he had fainted dead away, afraid they both would die."

"And I was afraid you *wouldn't!*" interjected the hawkish scold, who then turned instantly to stone.

The pastor was undeterred. "'Why be afraid?' asked the the boy's fa-ther. 'That's what death is: you fall asleep in a storm—then suddenly, you're home.'"

Given the milieu, Tull thought the story inappropriate—not that anyone in the room had anything to say about it. Anyhow, who gave a shit? It wasn't exactly the Crystal Cathedral. He looked at Trinnie, amazed to see tears in her eyes. Maybe her mind was on something else entirely. *Maybe she's just missing heroin,* he thought maliciously.

The pastor walked them to the garden and bid his adieu.

⌒

Trinnie took a draft of air as she scanned the site.

"They call this a wandering garden," she said, in teaching mode, "because people with Alzheimer's like to *wander.* Have you ever seen a walking labyrinth? They go way back to medieval Christian churches. That was my original thought for Saint-Cloud . . . there's one in San Francisco—Grace. It's based on the labyrinth at Chartres, thirteenth-century. Haven't we been there, Tull?" He wouldn't dignify it with an answer. "I can't believe I never took you to Grace!"

"I can," he said, unable to resist.

"Of course, there isn't room for something like that *here;* the idea is to create the *feeling* of flow, without the formalism of concentric rings." She stopped to touch the leaf of an overhanging tree. "The fun part is, all flowers must be edible. I am told that people with Alzheimer's like to forage."

An old crone gained on them, her purplish-spotted arm extended as if to hail a cab. "Hey! Hey!" she shouted at Trinnie. "You're sensational! You're just sensational and you *know* it! You *know* it!" She picked up speed and overtook them, a contender in a crazed derby.

"Maybe I should build a little grotto—and dovecotes. I need to find out if the sound of pigeons or water is a no-no for Alzheimoids. The birds'll probably shit everywhere, and that's no good . . . this really *does* remind me of the park Proust's uncle made—the Pré Catelan—at Illiers-Combray. You know: 'lost time' and all. Kind of thematically perfect, huh. But is it pretentious?" Listening to his mother prattle sickened him. "Did I ever tell you," she said conspiratorially, "that I *stole* something from the Proust Museum? Oh my God! A butter dish. I've never told *anyone* that; I wasn't 'well' at the time—I think I was AWOL from somewhere. I need to send it back, *anonymously,* but I've never been able to *find* the damn thing. I only hope to God they had the sense not to leave the *real* dish out for John Q. Public . . . or should I say *Jean Q. Publique*—"

"Is Grandma going to live here?"

"No," she said smugly, as if such a thing were out of the question.

Tull nodded at the squawking crone as she came around on another lap. "Is that what's happening to Grandma?"

"We don't know what's happening to Grandma."

"Then why are we here?"

"Because I'm redoing the garden. Grandpa's paying for it."

"Why?"

"Because the Douglases asked him to."

"If Grandma's going to live here, you should just tell me."

"She's not—OK?"

Trinnie shot him a look that said, I've already told you my secrets—get *over* it.

They kept walking.

"It'd be interesting to plant a little *Cosmos atrosanguineus*—that's Latin for 'black blood.' They're from Mexico and they smell like hot chocolate. Though I'm not so sure they can be *eaten*," she said, besotted with herself.

Tull's finger felt the soft outline of the folded cryptogram he'd committed to memory and carried in his pocket all week long. *If I was shocked at the reckless insinuation of your employee, I was absolutely dumbfounded—*

"Why were you crying?" he asked.

"Crying?"

"Inside—when he told the story."

"It made me sad."

"A retarded Sunday School story made you sad," he said acidly. "Are you born-again now, on top of being AA?"

"Look," she said, stopping in her tracks. "I brought you here because I thought you might be curious about what I *do*—and have compassion for what's happened to these people. But all you're doing is giving me shit."

"Fuck you!" he shouted. "You're not even *here*! You think that because you told me about Marcus—*your version*—you couldn't even do it *yourself*, you needed Grandpa there!—you think that because you tell me some *bullshit*, suddenly you're the *great mother*? You're just a drug addict!"

"No one's 'just a drug addict,' Tull," she said wearily.

"You think because you get chauffeured to AA meetings, that makes you a *great mother*? That because you pay someone to come to the house and show you how to *meditate* that makes you a *great mother*?"

"I wish you'd stop saying that."

"That you've been *sober* six weeks? Who cares! At least he *left*. I never had to even *meet* him—but *you*—you keep—coming—back! Keep coming back! Keep coming back!" He shrieked, flapping his arms in furious mockery of the famous slogan. "You don't even *care* what it's like to—for me to try to *find* you and you're just *gone*! You don't give a *shit* about me! When were we supposed to have gone to San Francisco to see some cathedral? *When*, Trinnie? That is *such a joke!* You don't even know who I *am*—all you care about are your clothes and your drugs—"

"I'm not taking drugs."

"But you *will!* You *will!*"

"Thank you, Tull. Thanks for the vote of confidence."

"And Grandpa gives you *money*, like, *every day.* And you *hate* him! You *hate* your father—"

"Don't project on me, Tull."

"You hate everyone but *yourself.* Don't tell me about *compassion* when you don't even care about your own *parents.* You've done nothing but practically *kill* them! All they do is *worry* about you, you think Bluey doesn't have any feelings, but Bluey just doesn't *show* it like Grandpa does. If it wasn't for them, I'd be dead! You don't care about anyone! Not *me* or stupid *Rafe* or *Grandma* or *Grandpa* or *Pullman*—Pullman cares more about me than you *ever* did! You fucking make me *sick!*—"

She slapped him, and he stared at her in shock.

Sobbing with anger, he tried to leave the garden, but the gate, like all doors, locked from inside to corral the guests. He put his foot on a tree and boosted himself to scale the fence, dropping down on the other side.

Trinnie watched, heart in throat, as he ran up the hill of the former onion field. She couldn't help but notice the valley oak at its crest, fairly rare for Southern California.

Trinnie thought: *Everything he said is true.* And if then and there the gods had transmuted the very dirt to morphine, she'd have sunk to her knees and choked on the earth.

*W*hile the drama played out in Woodland Hills (ending with the winded Tull's safe on-ramp apprehension), another scene unspooled at a Westwood cemetery with which the reader is already familiar.

The old man stood on his parcel. Instead of the Silver Seraph, the plush Mauck had been maneuvered past the gate; it did not present a serious encumbrance, for today park tourists were scant. Edward sat in his buggy a few paces away, ramrod straight thanks to the trusty titanium brace, which Lucy had adorned with decals of wasps and figs. Sling Blade, leaning on a rake to watch the summit from afar, completed the tableau.

The cousin smiled as beatifically as possible, while a fawning Dot discoursed. His grandfather tolerated the woman with a customary wince. Her flannel dress, to the old man's offended eye, looked like a stained tent cinched at the waist by a thrift-store belt and pinned by a fun-house brooch—a medal given to the sartorially challenged.

"What an honor it is to meet you!" she said, pumping his webbed little hand. Edward's mood was markedly Zen. "Those gloves! That marvelous veil! Are they—what was the word Mr. Trotter used?—'bespoke'? You're *just* like your grandpa—so *stylish.* You are *definitely* going to be added to Dot Campbell's Best-Dressed Hall of Fame, and *that's* a hard thing to achieve!"

"Mrs. Campbell, *please*—"

"It's all right, Grandpa! She's a wonder!"

"Don't mind me—it's just that you're so *personable.* May I ask what exactly is wrong with you? Physically, of course."

"Oh God!" eructed the old man.

"Not at all, you may ask and ask away! They call it Apert Syndrome."

Dot looked deep within herself. "Never heard of that one. My sister Ethel—who'd *adore* you—sent me an article about a special school in Long Island for children with deformities. 'Inner Faces,' they call it. They put on theater pieces—*extremely* talented. There's a few with cleft palates; you don't see those much anymore. You don't see cleft palates or clubfeet. One of the kids had—what did they call it? Möbius Syndrome! The muscles in her face *completely* paralyzed—"

"Good Lord, Mrs. Campbell," cried Mr. Trotter, who had by now reached the end of a long, low string of chuffs—so low, only Pullman might have registered the last. "That's quite enough!"

"Grandpa, it's fine. Seriously."

"Then tell me," said Dot, eyeing him intently. "Why do you cover up your face?"

"Personal choice. I suppose I'm vain. The eyes *are* a bit far apart. Dentition is . . . *eruptive.* Forehead veiny and elongated, with a 'bregmatic bump.' "

"Apert, did you say?—"

"Yes. Like Herb Alpert, without the 'Herb' or the 'l.' "

"Now, Edward, is that—is Apert's by any chance an 'orphan' disease? The ones not enough people actually have for them to go and commit research funding? They make television movies about them, it's *terribly* unfair. Oprah even did a show on 'orphans'—they do amazing things with prosthetics now. I read in *People* about a girl with a hole in her face—"

"Oh God!" muttered Mr. Trotter as he strode off.

"Are you sure you don't mind us talking like this?" whispered Dot to her new friend.

"Not at all."

"I feel so *comfortable* with you, you have that *gift*. Besides, it's much better to be frank—that's the way we learn." She spoke softly now, taking him into her confidence. "I *do* worry about your grandfather sometimes. He's here so much—even at night. I don't think it's healthy. To provide for oneself, yes, but well . . . you know, Edward, my sister Ethel would *love* to meet you, you're so *poised*. There was that girl in *People* with a cancer. They took her nose, poor thing—and her left eye, part of the forehead, part of the cheek and part of the sinus. Left a hole the size of a papaya. Now, evidently, there's a Romanian doctor who specializes in *maxillofacial* surgery. Makes 'clip-on' prosthetics—they drill screws right into the skull and the thing just *snaps on*. Though for the life of me I don't know how they get the screws to *stay*. Ethel says—"

"They're titanium. Titanium bonds with bone."

"Yes! That's what they said on *20/20*, the faces clip on like sunglasses—*so* beautifully done. The quality of a Tussaud's!"

The old man took Sling Blade aside while Dot and his grandson continued their colloquy. As he imparted whatever it was that he imparted, he held the caretaker's elbow and pressed money into his hand, a lavish, almost involuntary gesture repeated that very week with a Supercuts barber, a Montana Avenue haberdasher, even the humble, sweetly flummoxed receptionist for Dr. Bloore, his Bedford Drive dentist.

Early after the purchase of his plot, the digger had had a dream about Sling Blade, and some small omens since had shown promise for his eventual entwinement with the Trotter *familia*. For example, Mr. Trotter recently noticed an abrasion on Sling Blade's forehead. When questioned, he explained that it was an injury incurred while moonlighting as a guard at a building downtown—the Higgins, to be precise—the very landmark Dodd told his father he had in escrow.

The main detail of the story, that during rounds he'd been assaulted by a burly trespasser, held no interest for the old man.

*   *   *

*W*hen the Mauck reached La Colonne, the gates were already open. The vulgar Mr. Greenjeans stood waiting, mustered and tamed. He'd added a nitwitty canvas pith helmet to his regalia, and if Tull hadn't been so agitated, he might have been sarcastic about it. After all, this was the man who once chased him down.

Lucy was so excited she forgot to bring her Smythson. The young detective sat beside her brother in the locked-down buggy ready to be launched once the MSV reached the tip of the driveway, a small bulb intruding on the vast parkland space. Edward was dressed, well, Edwardian for the event—a three-piece "reworked" pin-striped suit by Matsushima, a retro Etro paisley vest, studded gloves and a translucent Trinnie-donated tattooed Kobayashi blouse, which he wore as a veil. Pullman, noble, copacetic specimen that he was, placidly drooled on the carpet, where lay his handsome, ham-size head.

A gentleman of protruding jaw sat comfortably in one of the calfskin swivel chairs near the front of the Mauck, his back to Epitacio, who drove. Edward introduced him as Sling Blade, and the latter showed no signs of feeling teased by the appellation. Tull felt as if he were in a dream, a feeling certainly not foreign during the last few months. He didn't think to ask about the stranger, or even who exactly had given them official ingress to the rarefied site. (Nor had he inquired of his cousin the provenance of the monogrammed letter let alone any details of the presumed cache from which it been extracted.) Initially, Lucy wasn't thrilled with Sling Blade's presence, but she grew tolerant, then positively ebullient, on realizing he would make a perfectly colorful cameo in *The Mystery of the Blue Maze.*

They entered the meadow and drove slowly through, Mr. Greenjeans trotting along beside.

The party of five—six, really, including Pullman—disembarked and Tull oriented himself. It was a different vista than that afforded from his usual illicit entry; it seemed impossible he and Pullman had never explored this side—the perspective his parents would have had when shown the place for the first time. The view of the wedding guests.

Someone had taken great pains to lay floorboard over the grass (the same had been done on location during Boulder's film, so the camera could wheel over uneven ground). The buggy lowered pneumatically;

Epitacio and Sling Blade guided it to the first plank of Yellow Brick Road. Mr. Greenjeans caught up, grabbed hold and helped them jump the curb. The two caretakers then eyeballed each other, neither coming up to measure. The gardener was not at all happy to see Pullman, and paled when the Great deigned sniff his leg.

Edward nodded for Tull to come, but the boy shook his head and hung back. Sling Blade got in and the buggy ascended the low hill. Epitacio leaned under the shade of a gull wing and smoked a cigarette; it was obvious to Tull that for him La Colonne was old hat. Mr. Greenjeans shadowed the buggy as it passed through the first set of myrtle balls, and kept apace from twenty yards.

The air chilled, covering him with goose bumps. What were they doing here? Tull watched the surrey climb at the creepy pace of a roller-coaster car once the safety bar dropped over passengers' laps; then set off to join them.

The formal entry, as the cousin had already described from the Le Désert de Retz book, was a faithfully replicated grove of sycamores, chestnuts, lindens, blue cedars, maples and ash. Beneath the chirping of birds and rustle of leaves was a dead quiet. Pullman remained loyally at Tull's side even when a large, still pond hove into view; then, oddly, the familiar allée of yews appeared, and the two were somehow back to their usual approach to the tower. They passed through—it was darker and colder than Tull remembered. He had a fleeting, terrible thought: one didn't have to be in a maze to be swallowed up by darkness, never to escape.

Seeing the buggy stop ahead, he sped up.

Edward stood beneath the canopy staring at the prospect that for all its brooding melodrama might well have been a painting of nearly fetishistic romanticism. The sky blackened and trees shook nude limbs like upended broomsticks tickling the clouds, egging them on, daring them to rain down for the sheer joy and mischief of it—and there, squatting at the end of the field like a ravaged rotunda, was the still-distant, broken Babel.

The cousin took it in with flooded concentration. For Lucy and Tull, the spectacle was not so much the Castle of Sleeping Beauty, as Edward told them a writer named Colette had called it, but the sight of the cousin himself transfixed, briefly lifting his veil to see what he could see. The ground was level now and the buggy zoomed toward Oz.

Slouching ahead, Tull nervously populated the grounds with wedding-day people: lanterns appeared, strung in the dusk, landaus with glass-encased torches burning, high-booted footmen amid pastoral gaiety, grass-stained children with flowers and bugs in their silken hair. The wind sizzled a friction of branches, and he heard the wedding music of an absurdly imagined clavichord. Edward had loaned Tull enough sci fi for him to be able to readily muse on the transitoriness of Time, the wormhole nature of it all—the smallness of himself in the scheme of things. So, the scene became more real: he saw his mother there, younger, handmaids and tailors tweaking her Balenciaga, and his father, lanky and rakish, tender and kind, drinking with male friends, who laughed in gutsy, premarital chorus. In his mind, Marcus looked like a Jewish man with tousled hair, a cross between Steven Spielberg and Ralph Mirdling, wild-eyed and gaunt. He shook off his reverie, close to the castle now. The buggy was at the front door. Sling Blade carried Edward in like a bride.

The light inside was the same as in the Poussin of Grandpa's Withdrawing Room. They allowed fairy-dust motes stirred by their arrival to settle before awakening any spirits. The white tents Tull spied before were now up close—a bedouin camp of covered furniture and figurines. Mr. Greenjeans said "the lady" had wished nothing moved. (Mr. Greenjeans being suddenly loquacious.)

"'An armed prowler would not dare stay here at night,'" said Edward out loud, again quoting this person Colette. "'How to convince yourself that in this dungeon-like darkness, a rosewood headrest and the remains of a commode are not positively evil?'"

"I don't think it's evil at all," offered Lucy, shakily.

As in the original Colonne, there were four aboveground levels, including the lobby—in the basement, which no one was in a hurry to explore, Edward said that the castle's onetime Freemason residents were intent upon alchemizing the bones of Pascal into gold (both Lucy and Tull assumed Pascal to be a dear, lamented friend of Colette's). The braided authoress pushed aside her fears and began to warm to the place; she flitted like a moth, powdering the edges of the protective drapes.

"Careful!" hissed Mr. Greenjeans. "Nothing must be moved or broken!"

Lucy started a moment, then laughed, gleeful. What fun it was being a writer! And what a wonderful character would this mad gardener make!

Edward told Sling Blade he wished to go up—the column was bifurcated by a spiral staircase—and the strong-armed cemetery worker obeyed. His sister followed.

Pullman lay at the foot of the stairwell. While the others went exploring, his master stepped over him, craning his neck. A skylight nestled high above in the jagged edges of the snapped-off "pillar," plant life sprouting from the latter like a weedy tiara. Tull took the stairs, numb. He wondered if his parents had roped off the bedroom that wedding-day night, barring access to revelers.

So these were the stairs his parents had climbed—the same his father had crept down that morning without her. She would have come later, barefoot, lover's face lit by a puzzled smile as she stared out at the rolling hills. Katrina Berenice Trotter Weiner thought for certain she would see her husband there, playfully naked, turning to make a rutting run at his brand-new bride in this blue-green heaven, outraged at their love and good fortune. The smile, Tull thought, would have stuck to her face as she wandered, searching, calling his name . . . tiring, she may have said aloud: It's a game! He's been watching me, and now's gone back in . . .

He heard Lucy's and Edward's treasure-hunt voices some floors above—and shot past, for Edward's progress was slow, and, besides, the cousins were distracted by the eerie stillness of each new floor. The structure was vast, even larger, if that were possible, than it seemed from outside. With unexpected verve, Tull bolted to the remaining level.

Ralph once told him about fire beetles—insects drawn to forest fires that flew through flames to lay eggs in charred tree bark—and though its door was shut and told nothing of what it hid, that is how Tull flew to the boudoir. He could smell his mother there, her shock and her sorrow, addictions and adorations. When he entered, he saw them for a moment entwined—then all he could see was her alone, blissful, awakening, yawning her newlywed breath, stretching, womb-starred, squatting on the toilet, then standing on tiptoes to spy from one of the mosaic porticoes, scanning for her beloved somewhere in the landscape below. He saw her put on slippers and say his father's name . . . then descend, calling out at each floor, mixing in lyrics of a sweetly improvised song as she floated down corkscrew stairs until finding herself at the front door, already flung open, *he* had flung it open, staring out at the rolling hills, smile stuck to radiantly doomed face—when Lucy suddenly appeared, exalted and fairly wheezing, already sucking the thin air of bestseller-dom. Tull blocked her way as she tried to come in.

"No!" he said. "You can't! *No* one can!"

She thought at first it was a joke, but Tull was shaking and crying and she backed off.

"It's *not* for your stupid book, so get out! *Get out*—"

She put her hands up to calm him. At that moment Edward arrived, with entourage.

"What's happening?" he asked from Sling Blade's arms. The care-taker looked like a ventriloquist. He set the boy down.

"I said no one goes in there!" Tull slammed the door in their faces. Pullman barked from below.

"We won't," called Edward respectfully. "Don't worry . . ."

"This was a *mistake*," shouted Tull. "We shouldn't have come here!"

"Then," said Edward, "we'll just turn around and go."

Lucy had never seen her brother so calm and collected, so gracious. Like one of those crisis negotiators.

"If anyone comes in here," said Tull dramatically, "I'll kill them!"

Sling Blade swept the boy up and the party retreated.

Tull of course stayed behind, heart pounding madly. It was only when their steps left the echoing cylinder at ground level and he heard circumspect voices outside La Colonne that he allowed himself to breathe again. His body, rigid since spitting its words, relaxed and his mouth began to jigger uncontrollably, tears scalding as he emerged from the wedding suite and walked down.

He thought of leaving by the old, secret way—through hedge of privet andromeda—but then thought better, to make certain the others had gone. So he raced ahead with Pullman and stood across the road until the Mauck edged from the drive.

Lucy stared at him through the window of the MSV as it swept past, her face riven by pain. Tull was ashamed and confused. He didn't want his cousins—especially Edward, who'd been so excited about the castle—to be traumatized on his account. Lucy had been trying so hard to help . . . and Edward—he would not want to injure his fragile, mystic friend. He'd call them later to make things right. For now, all he wanted was the gate of La Colonne Détruite to clang shut, its padlock restored.

The Mauck turned the corner and vanished. Mr. Greenjeans unraveled the chain and sealed everything up, then he too receded. All that was left was a nip of wind to sting Tull's eyes.

A station wagon of tourists cruised slowly down and stopped.

"Excuse me, but do you know where Nic Cage lives?" asked the driver, a sunny man in short sleeves.

"He moved," said Tull.

The man turned to his wife and said, "Apparently, he moved." The wife turned to the kids and said, "He moved." "Where?" asked an older boy. "Yeah, where!" said the girl. "I don't know," said the mother, glancing down at her *Maps to Stars Homes.* She turned back to her husband. He was about to ask again, but the boy and his steadfast friend had already begun the lonesome trudge to Saint-Cloud.

CHAPTER 16

Advocates

An Amaryllis is one of the easiest
plants to grow as well as to save
from year to year. Only a few
simple procedures are needed.

—*www.plantconnection.com*

When we left Amaryllis last, it was dawn. Gilles Mott had invited her into his East Edgeware bakery, which she entered like a prisoner led to gallows.

Instead of wooden steps and rope, she was greeted by metal trays heaped with tarts, even day-olds she recognized as items Topsy had shared during underbridge idylls. She pecked at the almond-and-pomegranate treats and remembered bringing them home to the babies—thinking of them suddenly, alone in the void, pierced her heart so that she swooned; Gilles, already on the phone to his wife, said a few words, then hung up, coming to comfort as best he could.

Lani Mott, being a trained, sworn-in volunteer advocate, was required by law to call the child-abuse hotline, and thus set in motion a series of events we will roughly sketch. On this day, the dependency system worked with unusual efficiency. The police arrived at Frenchie's within the hour (Mrs. Mott had preceded them) and Amaryllis was taken to Rampart Detectives—the very precinct she and Topsy circumvented an eternity ago. Lani followed in her Saab.

In transit, the crying girl huddled against the shoulder of the policewoman in back of the squad car. The officer tried to engage her—she had a daughter of her own—to no avail. At the station, Lani and little Jane Doe were taken to a snug room next to the homicide suites. There, a utility table sported neatly arranged rows of stuffed animals, books and crayons, and a near–life size plastic gorilla. An aged TV was fixed high on the wall. The policewoman turned on cartoons before making a last, futile effort to learn her name, where she lived and how her parents might be reached. When the lady left, Amaryllis sheepishly asked if this was the place where her babies had been brought. She clammed up when Lani dug deeper.

In time, the presence of a county social worker was announced; a pale, bespectacled child-woman appeared not twenty minutes later. She seemed to Lani more a rookie kindergarten teacher than a person who potentially held the life of a child in her hands. Lani explained about her husband finding the girl and how fortuitous it was that she, Lani Mott, "just happened to be a court-appointed special advocate for children." At first, the clueless social worker assumed Lani had somehow—in whatever capacity—already been assigned the case. It was obvious she was just another overworked CSW who had never even *heard* of the illustrious advocacy program to which the baker's wife belonged; most social workers hadn't, even though volunteers like Lani made their lives so much easier. Who could blame them? County caseloads were so heavy that they barely remembered their own names.

When the paperwork was done, the CSW and her ward—who had by now officially declared herself Edith Stein—traveled to a DCFS building on 6th Street. Lani and Amaryllis found themselves in yet another room with utility tables and disorderly rows of stuffed animals. This one had peppy sky-blue walls, beanbag chairs and a real live boy, who had the slack, glazed look of an airport toddler studying strangers while they alit. During a lunch of take-out McDonald's, Amaryllis made further inquiries about her brother and sister, but the CSW, who for some reason now referred to herself as a "clients'-rights manager," could find no record of the "Stein" siblings in the computer. ("It's really unusual to find Jews in the system," she said offhandedly, and Lani thought that inappropriate.) The orphan, in a great war with herself, nearly exposed the babies as Kornfelds to expedite their discovery; but in the end, reasoned that might put them in danger.

At the end of the afternoon, having advocated and managed all manner of prickly clients' rights, the CSW announced that a "suitable placement" had been found. Mrs. Mott gave aka Edith a hug and the girl followed her to the hall like a stray when she left. For Lani, that was the worst part.

They crawled through downtown traffic, onto the Harbor Freeway. Amaryllis wondered what was meant by "placement"—and a suitable one at that—but was afraid to ask. A placement was not quite a *place;*

that meant she was going to a not-quite someplace. Or maybe it was even *more* than a place . . . She angrily gritted her teeth at the thought of Topsy dropping her off like a package, shooing her toward the stranger in the silly cook's hat, cruelly sealing her fate. Then, seeing his hairy face and kind, cookie-size eyes float before her like a genie's, remembering how all those weeks he had fed her and soothed her then run with her in the night; watching herself turn traitorously on her only friend in the world, she wept with shame. Seeing her tears, the woman reached for a teddy—the backseat was chock-full of the furry placebos, shoveled in by the truckload.

If the Department of Children and Family Services could be counted on for anything, it was stuffed animals. A child might collect dozens even as his soul was being killed; suchwise, the Department would not fail. It was a child's inviolable right to bear arms and bear legs and bear tummies, to have and to hold and to clutch and to sob against a sad, soft donated thing staring back with synthetic, understanding eyes that could do no harm. (In protecting the rights of bears and child-bearing, the Department inarguably stood in the vanguard.) She handed a cub to Amaryllis, who instantly drew it to aching, purulent breast. Caressing the bereft girl's head, the CSW hassled her with kindness, tongue clicks and gentle shooshing *I know*s (as if she really did), coos and moans and *It'll be all right*s (as if it really would).

Wide-open spaces now. She asked where they were going and the woman said Tunga Canyon. A canyon!—another place to get lost in . . . another place not to find her precious babies. She may as well have said Alaska.

They arrived in darkness at the house on Chimney Smoke Road, greeted porch-side by the folksily winning Mrs. Woolery, sixtyish and straight out of a Knott's Berry Farm parade. "It's *Earlymae*—none uh Mrs. Woolery for *my* kids. Call me Earlymae!" she said, squatting eye to eye with Amaryllis. "*Grown-ups* the ones call me Mrs. *Woolery.*" Crystel Hallohan, a brunette the same size and age as the newcomer, attached herself to Amaryllis like a barnacle. An anarchic, gleeful boy in decal'd bike helmet and flannel PJs ran from the house jubilantly screaming. As Mrs. Woolery led them to the front door—drying Amaryllis's tears with a sleeve as they went—a bruised green-brown Wagoneer pulled up, disgorging a smiling Latino in ill-fitting sport coat, tie and teeth. He carried a mess of grocery bags, paper-in-plastic. Mrs. Woolery introduced him as Jilbo, then laughingly told him to "hup to." Grinning, he made a mock dash to the front door while the helmeted boy dervished after, spinning and shrieking and scrimmaging.

It was close and cluttered inside. There were so many nooks, knick-knacks and promise of rooms that Amaryllis felt she'd entered a honey-comb hive. Mrs. Woolery entreated Crystel to please finish cleaning for their guest—she said the place was in a bit of a shambles, which it wasn't—but first the girl walked Amaryllis over to the flowery couch and set her down like a fragile, favorite doll.

The professionals immediately set about finalizing documents. The boy whirled about in his test-pilot helmet, taking all the dips, turns and tangents of a rubber band wind-up plane; Mrs. Woolery told him for heaven's sake to come in for a landing, while occasionally calling to the kitchen to goad Jilbo into "hupping it with dinner" unless he wanted them all to starve. After one such encouragement, she winked at the CSW, remarking how Jilbo was "short for Gilberto. I give *everyone* a name. Now our Jilbo is what they call a slow mover—not like our *friend*," she said, indicating the fly-boy with a hitchhiker's jab of her painted thumb. She had a smoker's pulmonary laugh, even though she'd quit years back. "That's *Dennis*—I call him Dennis the Phantom Menace!" Laughing again, one heard the gritty gear-teeth of bronchi engage, her thick white Maidenform corseting a bosomy round-the-clock excavation of wheezing water, quartz and steam.

The benumbed Amaryllis watched MUTE flash on the big-screen tele-vision over QVC faces. After a brief absence, Crystel reappeared and du-tifully presented her with a bouquet of Barbies. Mrs. Woolery peered benevolently from half-glasses and told Crissie Fits—"We call her *Crissie Fits* 'cause she always *fittin'*. But she's a good ol' girl"—not to bother the "newbie," but the CSW said it was sweet and encouraged Edith to say thank you. ("We *think* that's her name," said the social worker.)

Amaryllis demurred, limply taking a doll by its thin, hard, dirty nude leg. Dennis flew to the rear of the house and screamed so shrilly that dogs outside began to bark. Mrs. Woolery rolled her eyes and shouted for Jilbo to "Hup the food now, 'fore Dennis the Menace blows a gasket! *Vamanos caballero!*"

When they finished signing the aforesaid papers, the CSW knelt and told Amaryllis she probably wouldn't be seeing her again very soon.Which meant never. Her job was to help children find nice homes during times of emergency and now, she said, another person would be coming "for follow-up." Amaryllis almost asked right then about the babies, but didn't have it in her. Mrs. Woolery palmed the orphan's forehead and said with some concern, "You're warm as a toaster." She told Crystel to get some Bayer's and start a cool tub. Jilbo came from the kitchen grinning like a square dancer to see the social worker off.

She didn't feel like taking a bath and was glad Mrs. Woolery led her straight to bed without a fuss, tucking her in with tender words. It'd been weeks since she slept on a mattress. The lights went off; suddenly Amaryllis was alone and afraid. She shut her eyes and felt heavier than a stone. After falling like that awhile—it was not unpleasant—she suddenly felt the presence of another. A small hot hand touched her wrist, but her eyes wouldn't open. A voice told her not to worry . . . Crystel's voice. She would stay by her side, she said, until sleep came. The girl didn't have long to wait.

The orphan dreamed of the St. George. Her mother smelled so bad it was time to move, but when she went to the kitchen to collect the babies, they were gone. Then she was running through the dark, with Topsy and the froggy Korean chasing her sister and brother up ahead; Amaryllis lagged behind. "Courage!" he shouted, his big tousled head turning back. "Courage, or you'll never see them again!" As she ran, her chest ached from its wounds and she'd had enough. When she gave up pursuit, the policewoman escorted her to a movie set and the boy who first called himself Toulouse took her hand. They raced through a crowd of adoring faces; she felt warm and giddy as he pulled her along. "You're late!" he said, sternly.

Amaryllis was starring in a movie and she was late.

*P*itch-dark night. A night and a place that did not belong to her. Mrs. Woolery's night . . .

Breathing sounds. She blinks, accustoming her eyes. Low ceiling above. No: another bed—she's on a bottom bunk. Breathing's louder now, warren-like, communal. Rasp, cough, suspiration. Germy close-quarters smell. Bright mote of moonlight reflected on helmet of sleeping boy. Her chest throbbing, infected nipple. Stomach spasms and at first she does not know why; roiling onslaught of tears, which she stanches. She cannot afford that. *Where is my mother?* she wonders, drawing air through mouth so as not to make a sound. *What happened to my—* someone stands in door now, *not* Mrs. Woolery, staring. Floats closer. Amaryllis trembles, gathering courage to bolt, shrinks back instead, spine to wall, pillow to chest. A pretty, reed-thin black girl engulfed in a XXXL jersey stands at the bunk and ducks down for a better look with hollow eyes.

"What do you want!" Amaryllis exclaims.

The wraith smiles, then retreats. As she exits, the boy with the helmet shifts and snorts from his futon. A jack-in-the-box head hangs before her upside down, causing Amaryllis to gasp—Crystel, from the upper bunk.

"That's Shanggerla. She always walks around at night. Sometimes she sleeps in the kitchen."

Amaryllis coughs. Crystel hops off the bed and brings her a Big Gulp. Amaryllis sucks the tepid soda from a fat straw.

"You don't *look* like an Edith."

"How long have you been here?"

"Ten months."

"Do you have a social worker?"

"A man, but you won't get him. He never comes. Everyone gets different ones. Do you have meds?"

Amaryllis didn't know what she meant.

"Where were you before?"

"With my mom."

She pulls Amaryllis from the bed by the wrist. "Come on!"

"Where are we going?"

"You're hungry, aren't you?"

"What if they wake up?"

"Earlymae don't *stay* here—and Jilbo comes in the morning. At night, we *party!*"

⌒‿‿⌒

The fluorescent kitchen shocks her eyes. An unplugged refrigerator, girdled by thick chain, is studded with Polaroids pinned by animal magnets—feisty former residents. Stucco walls wear a caved-in band just below eye level, courtesy, says Crystel, of the prolific, helmeted skull of Dennis the Phantom Menace; some parts colored by spongy swatches of dried blood. All the cutlery drawers are missing and the cabinets have no doors, excepting one made of metal bolted to the top of the padlocked fridge.

The girl in the XXXL lists into shiny, stale air, her long, smooth olive arm hovering over the hairline-fractured counter like a dowser. Esurient eyes, emeralds veiled in mucus, periodically widen, twitched by electrical current; when they close, she smiles as if listening to voices. Crystel moistens Shanggerla's lips with a paper towel.

"She's on so many meds! Aren't you, Shangg?"

The eyes widen, twitch, vanish. She smiles inwardly. The spidery arm dowses.

"Shanggerla means paradise—that's what Earlymae says. Shangg's a sniffer. Tell her what gang you're from."

She bends at the waist so that she's nearly parallel to the ground. "The Rollin' Tens!"

"And what is 'Ten' short for?"

"It mean ten thousand."

"Ten thousand *blocks*," said Crystel, translating for Amaryllis. She turns back to Shanggerla. "Tell Edith where the Rollin' Tens are from."

"Rollin' Tens from Venus. They Crips."

"Venice isn't big enough for ten thousand blocks, nigger!"

"Venus! They taggers from *Venus.*"

"The planet," adds Crystel, winking at Amaryllis.

"Venus spin backward," she giggles. "The Rollin' Tens is from Mar Vista!"

"You mean *Mars* Vista!"

"Vista del Mars!"

"And who are the Tens at war with, Shangg?"

"Crystel, it so *sad,*" says Shanggerla, face unexpectedly contorting in tears.

"Shangg loves Venus Williams."

"Yes I do. And her sister too."

"She likes *anything* called Venus. Tell Edith your placements, Shangg."

That word again . . .

Her long body hovers as she prepares to respond.

"Well, uh, Vista del Mar . . . and Mac. And Penny Lane. Pride House and Passageways. CLI—and Sanctuary. Orangewood. Irvine! An' Hudson-Lyndsey!"

"Family Solution?"

"Family Solution!"

"Were you at VisionQuest?"

"*Summit* Quest."

"Olive View?"

"I was, you know, Olive *Crest.*"

"They should have put you in Venus View and Venus Crest!"

"Penis View." She laughs out loud.

"*Dennis* was Olive Crest—I think."

"Dennie was at Family *Solutions* and COPES. And New Alternatives. Dennie the Mennie was maybe at Five Acres—that's where he start bangin' his haid."

"He almost burned that place down. Now they bring him to Charters whenever he cracks his skull. Dennis calls hospitals 'vacation.' You gonna get him into the Tens, Shangg?"

"Dennis can't be in the Tens!"

"Why not."

"His penis too white." She covers her mouth in silent hilarity.

"He likes Charters," says Crystel, " 'cause they give him candy and the nurses give him *hugs.* Isn't that sick?"

"He suck their titties."

"What's wrong with him?" asks Amaryllis.

" 'Tension deficit. Obsess compulse. I was at COPES," she muses. "I think when I was, *two.* I *think* I was at Mac. You couldn't wear your own clothes—the girls wore shirts with little bear stamps. I was at an Olive . . . I don't know if it was Crest or View. Were you with a family, Shangg?"

"They did try that."

"Where were *you?*" Crystel asks, turning to Amaryllis.

"Just with my mom."

"What happened to her?"

"She died."

"Did he kill her?"

"Who?"

"Your dad."

Amaryllis shakes her head. "She was lying in the bed."

"Well, who *did* kill her?"

"I don't know."

"Do you *have* a dad?"

"I don't know."

AKA Crissie Fits fishes small, blondish arm into hole in the wall, past meteorites of stucco dangling in chicken wire. Like a Martha Stewart of the damned, arranges Circle K booty on paper plates with garnishings of leaves and petals: Funyun rings, Fritos Racerz, Lunchables, Li'l Angels, POWERade, Skittles, kosher dill spears, Clamato, Twizzlers, Peppermint Patties, and *two* Ben & Jerry's—warm, sopping Chubby Hubby and Chunky Monkey. Among the few nonedibles are a Cherie makeup set and an "instant" geranium windowsill basket. Crystel lays out a green terry-cloth towel and they picnic right there on the floor.

For the first time, Amaryllis focuses on the curious little girl. She is four and a half feet tall, and wears lemon-colored shadow, smudged so opposing question marks curve from eyelid to cheek, each point ending at the downturned corners of a precocious mouth. Black-brown hair bunched into berserk braids tied together with wire hanger and red twine. She is stylish, zany and spirited, and, like Amaryllis, bites her nails to the quick. The latter's eyes flit to the metal cabinet above the fridge.

"Meds," enlightens Crystel.

"What are they?"

"Dennie pee hisself from the Juice Bar," laughs Shanggerla from behind closed eyes.

Reanimated, Crystel shouts that they have to go see if Dennis peed the bed or Earlymae will kick their ass. Shanggerla stays cross-legged on the floor, meditations—and medications—unknown. Crystel grabs Amaryllis's wrist again and races down the hall.

"Look, look!" she squeals, flipping on a light. "He shit, he shit, he shit!"

The boy lies in the position last seen. A hastily fastened diaper could not absorb the coiled, watery discharge; it has spilled onto the futon, which was, fortunately, wrapped in lawn and leaf–size Glad bags. She asks if Amaryllis wants to see his head, ignoring the orphan's pleas not to remove the helmet.

"Thorazine makes him shit," says Crystel, setting upon the strap and delicately lifting off the hard shell. Though bristled hair has spottily grown, the crown resembles a moon pelted through millennia by all manner of celestial debris.

Amaryllis backs into the bunk—aftertaste of beggar's banquet, nauseating closeness of room, stench of unconscious boy and sight of perky wolfish girl looming over has done her no real good. Crystel, ever attuned, iterates that Dennis is sleeping and no harm has been done.

Then, as if to make amends—to the boy and to her new friend, whom Crystel already loves and is determined to advise and protect— she sets to cleaning up the mess.

CHAPTER 17

When a Child Dies
in the Home

*W*hich is more onerous, politics or sentimentality? It is difficult to choose. To suggest that the perils of Amaryllis Kornfeld might have been relieved by courageous legislation is naïve; likewise, the easy fetish of emotion makes for cheap martyrdom. Let neither road be taken—pray that makes all the difference.

On Friday, they went to court, as required by law; the details of their visit will later be aired. For now, we are ready to tour the communal home of Earlymae Woolery. Dawn light is conducive to exploration, and the children are asleep. The white Sedan DeVille of the matron of the house won't pull into the driveway until ten (and then, only because of the new immigrant). Usually, each morning from seven till noon, Jilbo alone is entrusted with the brood.

Mrs. Woolery lives with her spouse under a different roof on a cul-de-sac of ranch houses in La Cañada Flintridge. Her neighborhood is lush and quiet, fluffed and fine-tuned by a discreet cadre of private gardeners and city workers. Her own children are grown; her affable hobbyist husband is nearly deaf; that is probably enough personal history, for this woman will not stay long in our lives. A realtor and professional foster parent, she has over the years acquired four other homes, including the one on Chimney Smoke Road, each with six beds. The government pays a monthly stipend per child, in Mrs. Woolery's case higher than the norm because of her willingness to process children in extremis, at all hours. She feeds, clothes and enrolls her charges in school, and if needed (it is always needed) arranges for a Special Education Plan, the child's right by law. Sometimes, if necessary (it is always necessary), Mrs. Woolery has psychotropics prescribed by phone; she has a warm and lucrative relationship with a retired psychiatrist, who will even make a house call for a personal interview with the newcomer if indicated (it is never indicated). If, in short order, it is determined that the child is too disruptive for the public school environment (it is always determined), Mrs. Woolery is thereby so ordered to tutor the ward at home, a task for which she is, conveniently, licensed. When such is the case (such is always the case for the wards of Mrs. Woolery), the government grudgingly pays a multiple of its original fee; for Mrs. Woolery, this translates to around $30K per residence. It is harder than it might seem to maintain four foster homes on $120,000 a month, but it's doable.

The house on Chimney Smoke Road wears a sweeping, pleasant façade upon a smile of manicured grass. The living room is furnished by the stodgily inviting Ethan Allen; many a social worker—many a clients'-rights manager—has been plied with cookies and coffee on its deep-dish couches and frill-fringed chairs. There is even a small magazine rack such as found in Christian Science Reading Rooms, stocked with parenting magazines and carefully folded schedules from a two-year-old Doubletree Hotel (formerly Red Lion Inn) WE ARE LIFE CHANGERS training conference featuring such topical seminars as *Microwave Cooking—Quick and Easy Meals Kids Like, Hair and Skin Care for Multi-Ethnic Children,* and the modern classic *When a Child Dies in the Home* ("A panel of three persons who have each experienced the death of a child in their home will talk about the worst of this situation. They will discuss what to expect from the bureaucracy, coroner, licensing and investigation, and of course answer any questions.")[†]

Gone are the days when officious CSWs diligently took stock of fridge and pantry or ventured into children's rooms to note the presence of stuffed animals and other surefire indicators of loving care. To the DCFS, Mrs. Woolery is a veteran, well known to have a child's welfare at heart. Still, when last glanced, even *she* felt the kitchen's dishevelment had gone too far; if the plastering could wait, the drawers should at least be retrieved from the trailer and shoved into their sockets—

[†]In this regard, Mrs. Woolery's expertise was such that she had no use for that of others. It's a fair certainty her present boarders began their extirpation long ago; and can even be said without overdramatizing that the boy Dennis, sometimes disparagingly called "D-Rate" by Mrs. Woolery, after the code for special-needs children—and who would live ten years beyond this writing—was already dead.

she'd get Jilbo to "hup" it. Only baking soda and mold graced the inside of that ungodly, humming icebox; per Mrs. Woolery's orders, Jilbo hijacked the groceries so showily brought in last night, rerouting them to another house. Though, to be fair, he *did* leave relish, frankfurter buns and a jumbo bag of M&M's blues.

But we are running out of time: let us take the meds from the locker that sits above the Kenmore and line them up.

In a half-dozen shoe boxes sprawls a town of tubular buildings with dates long expired, some missing their roofs, vacant interiors powdered from a crowd of old tenants now dispossessed—and newer ones too: refills with hard white childproof porkpie hats. What makes up this sad orange forest frontier? Meds: for depression and anxiety, OCD and ADD/ADHD, seizure and mania, insomnia, psychosis . . . a child's secret garden and cabinet of wonders. Mint-flavored, liquid, Caplet and mist: wishing-Wellbutrin, whole lotta Luvox (FDA-approved for the under-twelve set), peek-a-BuSpar (Shanggerla called it Juice Bar), tireless old standby midnight-rider Dexedrine, one-eyed hypervigilant Cylert (for bed-wetting; though children's-court judges don't like it prescribed anymore because of deleterious side effects), poison puff Adderall, hallucination-buster Haldol, whispering Risperdol, outmoded mellow-yellow Mellaril—and of course the anomalous Thorazine, great god Thor, inveterate vanquishing Viking of yesteryear. Kid, interrupted.

More dusty tenements in crypts that once held Roots clogs: squat round play-organ pipes with faded labels of forgotten names of all the thrashed little girls and boys—fruitless Day-Glo warning stickers and yellow CAUTIONS on the fresh-painted promise of Depakote; on man on the flying Trazodone and saber-toothed Tegretol; on tell-me-a-Ritalin; on bleachy Clonidine (to counter insomnia caused by the former); on catacomby Catapres; on a toy streetcar named Desyrel. It should be added that child-strength Motrin, Dimetapp (great for *calming*), Sav-On antihistamines and a hundred antibiotics (everyone is at all times on low levels to manage group head colds) are scattered in the boxes, like sleeping vagrants; over- and under-the-counter syrups and spent FloVent inhalers also trespass within, but, unlike the others, possess no gravitas and are accorded no real status.

Last but not least a sturdy Kenneth Cole contained this multiethnic low-rise ghetto drugscape: Cogentin, Ambien, Tofranil, Elavil, Pamelor, Asendin, Lidiomil, Anafranil, Nardil, Parnate, Tenex, Tractan, Remeron,

Serentil, Loxitane, Moban, Trilafon, Navane, Stelazine, Prolixin, Norpramin, Orap, Dalmane, Symmetrel, Akineton, Effexor, Neurontin, Ativan, Doxepin, Prilosec, Librium, Zoloft (been good to know you), Clozaril, Vistaril, chloral hydrate and phenobarb—the rainbow of a decade of storms, prescribed by a certain eighty-three-year-old medic, a Gahan Wilson vampire as real as anything, who fancies Mrs. Woolery and whom she deftly, flirtily avoids.

The rest of the house never saw visitors and would not know how to greet them. Cold and barren, by now it loves only the children it harbors and the memory of those formerly berthed—loves them more than it could Mrs. Woolery or Jilbo or even the kindly, deaf Jane Scull, who comes weekdays to baby-sit and clean. Two of its bathrooms are used for storage, tubs filled with soiled clothes and broken toys. Jilbo thoughtfully removed the toilet seats; there is no water in the lurid, scummy bowls. A third (master) bath has a laminated précis hammered to its door.

Attention Deficit Hyperactive Disorder

1) Frequently fidgets or squirms in seat
2) Has difficulty remaining seated when required
3) Is easily distracted
4) Has trouble waiting to take his or her turn
5) Shouts out answers to incomplete questions
6) Has problems following instructions
7) Has difficulty staying "focused"
8) Frequently fails to complete tasks
9) Talks excessively, often interrupts others
10) Doesn't seem to listen carefully
11) Engages in physically dangerous activities without considering the consequences
12) Often loses or misplaces things

A mobile home sits in the backyard, jacked-up on boards and stripped of accoutrements—it is the children's domain. The gouged-out Airstream's origin and reasons for abandonment are murky; perhaps Mr. Woolery once soldered slot-car chassis there.

Saturday morning and the pearl-white DeVille now comes. There she is, stepping out. The children (except for Dennis) are stirring. The fuzzy old charcoal Chanel suit pinned with a too-big tree-shaped brooch enters in a cloud of Bvlgari. She carries pills in her purse; she won't need to visit the ancient locker.

Amaryllis wakes up disoriented. Crystel snores beside her—sometime in the night, she dropped down to the lower bunk. Dennis wheezes in his helmet. Hearing Mrs. Woolery's footsteps in the living room, the foundling is seized by dread. Moments later, Shanggerla appears at the door, fresh-faced and juvenile. "Miz Woolery here!"

With that, Crystel Hallohan opens an eye, then another, and catapults from the bed, nearly stepping on Dennis's small arm. Jarred, he opens his eyes for a moment, then shuts them again to dream.

Crystel and Shanggerla greet their benefactress.

"Well, look what the cat drug in," she says—the sort of scary genial hillbilly thing that is her trademark. Mrs. Woolery is alive with the atoms of the outside world, and the girls are excited at the airy, wicked *newness* she brings to a room. Amaryllis, frightened and hungover from yesterday's epic pilgrimage, creeps to the hall and listens. "How's Newbie?"

"Good," says Crystel.

"Y'all have breakfast yet?" Crystel shakes her head. "Well that's good, 'cause Jane Scull's bringin' Mickey D." She screws her nose at Shanggerla and sniffs. "You on your period, Paradise?" The gangly girl nods. "You stink. I would like to see you bathe today."

Shanggerla casts sleep-encrusted eyes to carpet.

"Yes, ma'm," she says.

"You bloody too?" asks Mrs. Woolery of Crystel, who solemnly nods. "All you people do here is bleed." She shouts to the newbie: "Hey! You a bleeder?" Amaryllis doesn't answer. Then, more to herself: "She will be soon."

"Her tits hurt," says Crystel.

Mrs. Woolery tightly sets her jaw and grits it around. "You can phrase that another way."

"In her shirt—she was crying."

"Well, we'll see." Mrs. Woolery turns to Shanggerla. "Get the first-aid kit. In the master bath."

"Come on out now," calls Mrs. Woolery to the still-unseen newbie. "I ain't gonna bite." Crystel makes a mini-move toward the hall, but Mrs.

Woolery stops her. "Let her come herself. Won't go nowhere with you clucking over her like a hen."

Amaryllis slowly emerges, barefoot.

"There she is! C'mere, sweetheart—it's all right." Amaryllis stands trembling in the doorway. "Suit yourself."

Mrs. Woolery sits in the fringy chair and sighs. Amaryllis fixates on her hair, frozen on the head like silvery meringue. There's something about her face that is unassimilable—the features are large and over-painted, and though she isn't a tall woman, she strikes Amaryllis as giant, big as Topsy. Voice deep, clacking nails fire-engine-red, eyes ice-floe blue, teeth bright rows of graves.

"What's your *real* name, Newbie? Sure as hell ain't Edith. Might as well say it—they *will* find out."

"Amaryllis."

After all her vows, it comes out: just like that. What is the power of this woman?

"*That's* a mouthful. We'll call you Armadillo! Know what an armadillo is, Crissie Fits? Funny-lookin' little armored creatures—usually get runn'd over. Are you roadkill, Dillo?" Amaryllis shakes her head. "Well you surely are not. But you could be, couldn't you, if you don't mind. But you will—*mind*, I mean. You're a minder. She's a minder, isn't she, Shangg?" Shanggerla smiles at the ground while Mrs. Woolery fishes in her purse. "A mind is a terrible thing to waste, ain't it, Shangg?"

"Yes, ma'am."

"Mind over matter, mind over matter," she mutters, to no one in particular. "I don't mind; you don't matter. Crissie, git some water." She obeys, shouting, "Crystal Geyser! Crystal Geyser!" which elicits a small laugh from Mrs. Woolery, who then turns to Amaryllis. "Dillo-girl, I want you to take these." She holds three pills in her hand—a yellow Caplet, a pentagon flecked with baby blue and a tiny pink sphere that slides down the lotioned crease of her proffering palm.

"What are they?"

"Them's *good* things. Doctor things—don't you worry too much about it. Curiosity killed the 'dillo."

Crystel hands the glass of tap water to her friend. "Why did you say you were Edith?" she asks.

"*Uh*-oh—good Lord!" laughs Mrs. Woolery. "Betrayed! Look out!

You watch her live up to her name, Dillo! Lookit! She gonna have a Crissie fit!"

Crystel darkens as Dillo the Newbie works up the courage to take her pills. "Are you Earlymae because you were born in May?" she asks ingratiatingly.

"No, *December*," says Mrs. Woolery, mouth buckling in disgust. "Well *uh course* I was born in May! What do you think, stupid?" She laughs and so does Crystel; Amaryllis tries to smile. "May *third* to be exact. I'm a Taurus and that ain't no bull. Now swallow 'em, Dillo—swallow 'em up. *Hup* it!"

Jane Scull appears at the screen door with bags of McDonald's, and Crystel eagerly lets her in. (Shanggerla makes her own entrance, carrying a tackle box filled with bandages, disinfectant and bug spray.) A sweet, heavy girl with wet, whitish acne and double hearing aids. "You smell worse than Shangg," says Mrs. Woolery while Crystel greedily takes the bags and Shanggerla sets the table with Golden Arches paper and plastic.

Mrs. Woolery tells Amaryllis to come over. She says it again and the girl obeys. "What's this about your upper part?"

She shyly retreats, but Mrs. Woolery insists. Lifts her blouse.

"Lord, what happened *here?*" The others stand around goggling, and each time Amaryllis tries to lower her shirt, Mrs. Woolery stops her. "Better call someone about that 'fore they say *I* did it. Good Lord, that is ugly." Shoos the girls back to the table, insisting Amaryllis eat because she's going to give her a Percocet for pain. "I'm gonna have to put something *on* that mess and don't want you cryin'."

A living room feast: Mrs. Woolery allows them to have their repast on the Lemon Pledge–polished Ethan Allen table. What a pretty picture for clients'-rights managers the nation over! Sweet-faced sucklings tucking into Egg McMuffins on a sleepy Saturday morn . . . but soon Amaryllis was feeling odd. Tongue dried up and heart began to race. Stopped eating—just plumb stopped in her tracks—and was dimly aware of others commenting on that, laughing about it too. Then she was on the couch, woozy, heavy-lidded, cotton-mouthed, Mrs. Woolery daubing her chest with alcohol-soaked tissues while Jane, Crystel and Shanggerla looked on. Pain stabbed at her as the nipple was roughly disinfected, but foremost there was nausea; as the poor soul ran to throw up, Shanggerla comically chased after, holding slender caramel catch-basin hands under Amaryllis's chin—the newbie chose not a sink but one of the dead toilet bowls (which infuriated Mrs. Woolery). The salty innkeeper trudged in not long after, reaching behind the porcelain tank to turn the water on so the McBarf could be flushed. Assuming the lion's share of meds came up with the food, she decided to give the girl another round. By this time, Dennis the Phantom Menace was lurking, on best behavior. Then he whined and cried because the food was gone and Jane Scull gave him fries and the rest of her McMuffin.

Amaryllis was lifted to bed. She panicked because with the second wave, she didn't know what to do with her arms; it was as if they belonged to someone else. She thought of Edith Stein and other Blesseds throughout the ages—Hildegard and Theresa, and the virgin martyr Cecilia and the hardships *they* endured, and of course thought of her babies too. Unexpectedly, Boulder Langon popped into her head in time to say some harsh, untranslatable thing before Amaryllis fell asleep to the giddy horseplay screams of roommates beyond.

Snapshots: darkness at noon. Stranger in a strange land—Mrs. Woolery's land. To the bathroom again, but this time Shanggerla leads the way. Amaryllis on the bowl, making a torrent. The pee smells funny. Shangg brings her back to bunk. An interlude—duration unknown—then bathroom again. This time she's left there sitting long after her business is done. Now led to living room, where Dennis and Crystel play raucous games with Jane Scull. Mrs. Woolery gone. Jilbo opens screen door, sullen in a bad C&R suit. Jane, stricken to see him. He goes to kitchen locker and gets Shangg and the boy pills. Jilbo gives some to Crystel, who hands them to Amaryllis. Dillo swallows. Jilbo storms down hall and shouts. Shangg hurries to rip befouled Glad bags off futon while the helmeted boy wheels and whirls his way to the Airstream.

Amaryllis sleepy on kitchen floor. Crystel reaches into wall—party plates with M&M's, Fritos and Dimetapp. Her mom's in jail for cooking speed. She says the bushes and dirt around the house used to catch fire. Stands up to chase the shrieking Dennis. Jilbo gone. More games with Shangg and Jane Scull. They prop Amaryllis on the couch.

Bunk and bathroom with Shanggerla again. Dennis sticks a hand under while she pees. Puts tip of finger inside her hole, then runs out laughing. Shangg laughs too.

On living room couch, shirt bunched under chin. Bandage off, nipple lactating pus. Jilbo stares, rubbing his crotch. Jane red-faced, squirmy, dumb-sobbing. Crystel watching from hall blank-faced as Jilbo suckles bacterium. Porky Jane thrashes and mutely wails, a widow in a silent film.

Darkness—real darkness, outside too. Pills worn off enough to wander. No one on the futon . . . freshly "made" with new lawn-and-leafers. Creeps into living room, where E. Allen props adorn the deserted stage. A thought occurs: *Leave! Now! Hurry! Through the front door . . .* —but she cannot. To the back of the house she goes, and into the night. Dim lights burning in shell. She *has* to find Crystel . . . but why? To tell her—maybe she'll come with. She is the only familiar thing. Walks toward trailer . . . what if it's Jilbo inside? Hears Airstream laughter of a child. Britney on radio. Walks up steps and goes in. Trailer musty, close, incense-filled. Dennis on his back, helmet intact and Crystel astride, stuffing in the soft little dick. Sings and laughs along to the Britney—and Shanggerla with something inside her. She takes it out and nudges it to his butt-hole, then puts it back in her mouth, then buzzes back to his butt-hole then back inside her. *Penis Rollin' Tens . . .*

Crystel sees Amaryllis.

"He *likes* it," she says, heading off judgment. Amaryllis comes closer, mesmerized. Dennis the Phantom Menace looks at her and laughs. Fuck me! he says. Crystel laughs. Fuck me! says Crystel, laughing and grinding anew. Shangg is laughing too. They all watched Jilbo's porn tapes. Fuck me! Fuck me! say Crystel and Dennis. Fuck my juicy pussy with that fat white cock! My pussy is so wet! Make me come! Can you make it come? Make my pussy come! As Amaryllis backs out, Crystel grabs the dildo from Shanggerla, rusty with blood, and shoves it in herself. Like a tagged wrestler she scampers to the boy, pinning and laughing and sucking—

Out!—through the driveway, under cover of shivering trees, hugging the shore of lawns and bushes as she goes, choking and crying. The main road looms. Winds up beside the trash bin of Kanyon Korner Mart. She thinks of Topsy standing beside her that morning at the bakery— Topsy! The very name makes her yelp in the chill air. A car parks and a teenager gets out.

Amaryllis hears her own voice: "Excuse me, miss, but do you know the time?" The girl looks at her as if she's mad. "Nine-thirty." Amaryllis thanks her. Chest is burning and she has to pee; a low wave of pharmacological inertia washes over . . . She thinks of asking the girl for money when she comes out; maybe she'll go in after her. Jolts awake: what if Jilbo's shopping inside? Or Mrs. Woolery! She begins to run—yelping and crying, toxins excreting through hot tears, straight down the middle of the brightly lit boulevard. *Anyone* could see her: any cop or concerned citizen . . . even Earlymae. She was convinced that woman didn't sleep and spent the night trolling the streets for children, ricocheting between residential homes.

Amaryllis felt superhuman as she ran, like the day she fled the St. George; maybe the earth would give way and she'd fly off into space. Her shadow overtook her body, and she wished she were back with her mother, who after all this would now surely mend her ways! Topsy would take them to the special part of the rescue mission reserved for single women with children, and they'd have turkey and gravy and pomegranate pastries. She was sure that if the postulator of the Congregation for the Causes of Saints could see her run, he would favorably assess her worthiness; she would slowly ascend, walking on starry black air just as Jesus walked on water—*that* would be the miracle to beatify her. *Secretum meum mihi . . .*

Then a shape bulleted toward her from across the street, grunting freakishly. Its trajectory was certain, but the thing itself uncoordinated, like a sack filled with tomcats falling from a bridge. Numb with terror, Amaryllis ran off the highway and up a hill, but the thing pursued and she was no match. It tackled her, and she screamed as it gurgled, lurched and spat into the air, holding her to its big, dirty bosom so she couldn't breathe.

It was Jane Scull who held her down.

CHAPTER 18

Little Girl Lost

The orphan stopped struggling.

After a few smelly, apocalyptic moments, Jane Scull gripped Amaryllis's shoulders and held her away, the better to scrutinize; having discerned no damage done, she kissed the girl's crown and fussed over her, snowcapped whiteheads glistening with tears and perspiration.

But Amaryllis did not find her rank—no: Jane Scull was merely one of the tribe, the underground railway of lumbering misfits to whom the girl felt entrusted. She was certain the saints had similar helpmates, making sure this was noted with proper humility so as not to get puffed-up. Topsy and Jane were her *people*, rough and elemental as the earth itself, with hearts the size of moons: circus types, raucous, itinerant acrobats of superabundant poise and poignance and avoirdupois, grand grotesques shot through with cathedral light—thrones and seraphim, eccentric angels of virtue, stamina and spirit.

Jane Scull took the girl's hand and power-walked into the night, singing an indecipherable song. They arrived at a bus shelter and she dispatched Amaryllis to its recesses. Then Jane stood alone, waiting. Whenever a car would pass, her protectress deftly pivoted, blocking the child from view. Amaryllis shivered and stared at the movie ad encased in the shelter's foggy frame: scratched by graffiti, the pigtailed girl wore a mustache, and swastikas were carved onto her sheepdog companion's coat. It made her think of Boulder Langon—in fact, it *was* Boulder Langon. But Amaryllis didn't have the energy to fully conjure those faces, or that famous afternoon.

The bus was empty when it arrived. Jane Scull led them to the middle. She ticked off significant streets as they drove, guttural and slurred, enraptured: Pennsylvania became *Ensilanee!* Montrose *On Nose!* Verdugo *Errugo!* La Cañada *Ahkahnahduh!* San Fernando *Anurnanoh!*—then Avenue 26 and Figueroa and suddenly WHOOSH on the archaic Pasadena and Amaryllis too knew the exhilaration of her own magical mystery tour. It was even a revelation that buses traveled on freeways.

Close to midnight, they alit on Chinatown. Jane Scull moved quickly now and without regard to the girl she had rescued. Her gait was fluid and her strides so huge Amaryllis imagined her on Rollerblades; before long, as in her dream of Topsy, she ran after but failed to catch up. The quiet drizzle became a downpour and the child involuntarily squealed with the sensation she was again going to be left behind (but this time, no baker). Like a movie rewound, they strode—or rather Jane Scull strode while Amaryllis scrambled and faltered—past the very landmarks by which Topsy had carried her scant days ago, though by now time was a jumble. Her chest heaved like a failing engine as they passed the Central Heating and Refrigeration Plant, but this time the Cathedral of Our Lady of the Angels brought no saints to bear.

In the middle of Temple Street, Jane Scull turned and waited for the girl. Then she clasped her once more. *"Anku!"* she cried, heaving with sobs. *"Anku Amuhwiss!"*

She kissed Amaryllis's cheek, then ran off.

The orphan watched this uncaged creature berserk with freedom, head bent to sky, gummy sea lion maw wide open, pelted by the filthy, exorbitant rain, dizzy, gamy and exalted. *There are other circuses,* she thought, whispering good-bye—for that is where she imagined her friend to be headed. Circuses and caravans, with elephants marching tail-to-trunk . . . Jane Scull was rapidly receding so the girl raised her voice: Good-bye! Good-bye! *Good-bye good-bye good-bye*—whole body trembling with emotion. Her organs felt sludgy and her mouth tasted like blood and metal, liverish from Mrs. Woolery's Rx.

The fleeting thought of that horrible woman was enough to send her running back to the shadows. "I'm watching you, child!" she heard Topsy bellow. "Courage! Courage, or you'll never see the babies again!"

Sheets of water—like in a movie—as she neared the St. George, a weak wet bird flitting past stands of boxes shrouded in plastic tarp, end-of-the-road tenants sleeping within. A hand reached out and encircled her ankle: she clawed it and ran—toward the place where she'd find the

Korean—but why? What was she doing back there? . . . wild with grief, revisiting the raided nest to smell her vanished babies! The St. George was dark and locked for the night; rain had washed the infants' scent away. She stole toward the cupola of St. Vibiana's deserted diocese, soon to be demolished. Still no entry, else she would have liked to have stayed. She drifted across the street instead, again to that fated place.

The alley entrance used for their escape was glued shut. Fresh plywood had been nailed over chinks in the Higgins armor, but the girl was small enough to slip through an already damaged plank. She made her way to the lobby and stood dead still—no sound of pigeons or trespassers. In the half-light of a pleuritic moon, it looked like someone had made nominal efforts at clearing out debris. As the exhausted child climbed the stairs of the cold copper tower, her heart sank; she knew Topsy would not be in residence.

When she reached the place of their reunion, Amaryllis was not wrong. It was dank and freezing; *she* was dank and freezing, and determined never again to move or stir. She slumped against the wall, uncaring of her fate or anyone else's.

As fatigue and Mrs. Woolery's soldier-stragglers drew her to dreamless fields—to Minotaur's maze—Jane Scull danced across the screen of her eyes and Jane Scull only: dear Jane with her big white hearing aids, spinning into Forever like an ensorcelled top.

*M*orning—noon. The world outside shiny and new, hung to dry in the sun. She stirs, then sleeps two more effortless hours. Awakens, feverish. Chest aches. Thirsts and shivers, clothing damp. Slowly, she walks downstairs. There are pigeons and they gladden her.

"There, look!"

She seizes, choking.

Someone-Help-Me points with a cane.

"She the one there!" he shouts, advancing. "Come here last night— try to grab her foot but she too fast! Scratch me up good!"

Peering at the child from his side of the broken slat is a handsome, world-weary man in white shirt and tie, stylish sport jacket slung over his arm. In comic contrast to his guide's histrionics, Samson Dowling squints like a bird-watcher at some point above Amaryllis's head, which must have seemed a goad to the vagrant, who wished the little fugitive's apprehension to be handled in a more Most Wanted fashion.

"Wull," he says, turning to the detective. "*Get* her!"

Amaryllis sprints on cue, and Someone-Help-Me pimpily gives chase. The investigator, shod in tasseled Church's English, takes casual, graceful flight. "You! Idiot! Stop!"

He commands the bum, but the little girl, arrested by the powerful voice, can run no longer—and collapses.

Someone-Help-Me does a victory jig and the detective tells him to disappear, his tone menacing enough so the snitch is gone in the briefest time imaginable.

Detective Dowling kneels, bunching his expensive coat under the girl's fainted head.

～

When they got on the freeway, she became agitated—certain he was taking her back to Mrs. Woolery's.

"Were you staying at the motel, Amaryllis?" A nauseating lump grew in her throat—for she hadn't yet told him her name. "Were you staying at the St. George?"

"The babies!" she cried, broken. "Where are the babies?"

He reached out to pat her head; he was awkward with kids. "The boy and girl? They're fine, fine. Don't cry, now."

"How do you *know*?" she snarled. A ray of hope pierced through: "Have you seen them?"

"Not personally."

"Then how do you *know*?" She hated him again. He had hairy, muscular arms and reeked of cologne and she held him in the utmost contempt. "How do you know anything *about* them—"

He laughed, not unkindly. "Because I know the detective who made sure they were safe. A female officer," he said, then corrected himself. "A woman. She really took to those kids. They're your brother and sister, aren't they?"

Now she was possessed of a new torment: the babies were bonding with one of their captors! They would love the policewoman and not even recognize her when she came to their rescue. "When can I see them?"

"Soon, I'd imagine. First we need to get you well and on your feet. You've had a rough go of it, haven't you? It couldn't have been wonderful sitting with Mom all that time the way you did. You're a brave little gal."

They rode awhile in silence. He cracked a window, because the smell of her was overwhelming—like the worst, infected whores he'd found in crackhouses, or half dead in littered fields. He asked about the man—"a big, tall fellow" whom a "witness" saw carry her off into the night. Went by the name of William, he said, or Topsy . . . He wanted to know where the man had taken her, and if he was a friend of her mother's.

There *is* no man, she said. And where are we going?

"A place called MacLaren."

"Is it in the Canyon?"

"It's in El Monte. What canyon?"

"Is it a house?"

"MacLaren? In a way, though it's a lot bigger. There's a school and a gymnasium—even a swimming pool. Lotsa kids your age."

Amaryllis scanned the interior: the dash-mounted beacon on a curved, creepy metal neck . . . battered computer wedged between them . . . shotgun rack—prison! He was was taking her to prison!

The detective's insistence this MacLaren place wasn't a jail did little to ameliorate her terror. The children who lived there, he explained offhandedly, were *not prisoners*—why, there weren't even locks on the doors! He went on to say that in point of fact at MacLaren locks on doors were "against the law"—of course there were *some* locks, he clumsily amended, to prevent strangers from coming *in,* not to stop kids from going *out,* a system so designed to protect the "pop" ("short for 'population'") from unhappy parents, who in very *rare* cases may wish to do their children harm—

With each botched blandishment the detective dug a deeper hole for himself and his detainee, multiplying her paranoia tenfold until the looming sight of Mac's outer wall—the highest, thickest wall Amaryllis had ever seen—delivered the final blow. The only thing stopping a leap from the moving car were the babies. They were there, at the place called MacLaren, like prisoners in a deathstar. She *knew* it. They had to be.

Then it all blurred. She was taken to the infirmary, where an RN peeled off layers of clothing and gasped, hand to startled mouth. Other nurses and staffworkers gathered to gawk. Doctors were called; wounds were cleansed. She was examined for pelvic inflammatory disease and tested for TB, strep, syphilis, HIV, chlamydia, clap. They poured penicillin in her veins, and Demerol for pain.

Amaryllis slept for three days. In a languid flirtation with consciousness, she heard the stealthy footfalls of children arriving for daily meds. They poked their heads around the curtain to look before being chased away.

When some of her strength returned, a woman from "intake" came bedside to announce she could make two phone calls, adding that both would be "monitored."

"Who would you like to talk to?" she asked cheerfully.

*A*ll this time, Will'm lay low in Angelino Heights, the grateful guest of Fitz and his maimed pet. The peculiar trio put up in the garage of a Queen Anne Victorian on Carroll Avenue. The owner (one of Fitz's former supervisors at the DCFS) had hit a financial bump in mid-restoration; chain link surrounded the property. Fitz was on-site to ward off vandals.

The architecture was to Will'm's liking. It reminded him of Red House at Bexleyheath in Kent, the dwelling built for Janey on occasion of their marriage—with its humble demi-courtyard garden, rose-entwined wattle and decorative well house with conical roof, he felt he was truly home again. There were two stories, plain and spacious, and polished, set-back porches. By light of day, he explored the Gothic-arched drawing room of this earthly paradise and made secret plans to paint a mural on a hall cupboard, the one he had begun so long ago but never finished: *Morte d'Arthur.* This time he would include Fitz and Amaryllis among the likenesses of Lancelot and Tristram, and even work in Half Dead.

At night, while Fitz smoked his chemical pipe in the garage and ranted about the Department of Children and Family Services, Will'm paced the *hortus conclusus,* square plots of lilies and macerated, streetwise sunflowers, reciting verse from *News from Nowhere* (which he need soon retrieve from its Olympic Boulevard storage bin)—

I know a little garden-close
Set thick with lily and red rose,

Where I would wander if I might
From dewy morn to dewy night,
And have one with me wandering.

To be frank, he hadn't slept well since giving up the girl. The small face, with its rough cherub's mop, tugged, calling him to seek her out; he made resolution to reconnoiter the bakery and look in on her progress. But skid row tom-toms soon brought news of her capture by police—and Someone-Help-Me's perfidious involvement in the dragnet. Will'm was undone. Discreet by nature, he decided to gather Fitz into his confidence, bringing him up to speed on all that had transpired between him and Amaryllis, culminating with the freedom flight from Higgins to East Edgeware alley.

Fitz focused his rage upon the malignant beggar, for whom no love had been lost. "Why, that cocksucker snitch; he ought to be murdered!" At this moment, the once honorable George Fitzsimmons looked more than ever like one of those sociopathic eggheads from thirties heist films who plan bank jobs but don't dirty their hands. "He brought that cop to the *Higgins,* Will'm, don't you see?"—Fitz had heard it all from Misery House cronies—"so the weasel could've seen you that very first night you were with the girl. Now, *I* know you didn't do anything with her; nothing but love and protect her. But *they'll* accuse you of *molestation,* and God knows what else. That's their game!"

Will'm was in a daze. "But how did she leave Frenchie's? How would they let her wander away?"

"Never mind *that*—there was a *murder,* Will'm, a murder in the *motel.* The St. George! The girl's *mother* they think was killed—that's what the boys on the street tell me. And they've *got* her now, they've got the *girl.* They don't like unsolved murders on the books, Will'm. If they can jail us for walking outside a crosswalk, then they'll jail you for this, believe me! By the time they finish, she'll turn on you herself!"

Will'm grabbed him by the shirt while Half Dead lamely launched himself at the aggressor's calf. "Don't you say it, Mr. Fitz! Don't you say it, ever!"

"Oh, I don't *mean* anything, Will'm"—he reached for the giant's implacable wrists to loosen the grip—"Hell, she's a *kid*—I *know* what happens to frightened kids when the goons get hold of 'em. Before you know it, it's the mob after Frankenstein. You'd never be able to defend yourself."

"I need to speak with Mr. Mott," said Will'm, entering a trance again. "To find out what happened . . . how could it have come to this? What was she doing back at Higgins, in the dead of night?" He began to pace and sweat, kneading his hands like a heart-shaped motor. "And that mangy bum! That child-stealer! I'll tear his head off!"

"Don't go out there half-cocked! They'll be *gunning* for you, can't you see? You'll walk right into their web! Lay low and let me make a few calls—I'll find out where they stashed her."

But alas he found out not a thing, due to more pressing concerns with the pipe. And what if he had? What good would it have been? If Will'm stormed the palisades and spirited her out, what would he *do* with her? He'd played hero before and look what happened.

After almost a week of pondering, he could take no more. Early one morning, when Fitz had already quit the Queen Anne for coffee at Misery House, he lit out to Frenchie's. As he walked, the air was cold— having been sequestered for his own good (still hearing Fitz's admonitions), he felt like some exposed and hunted thing. He would at least find out what had happened. Could Mr. Mott have argued with the girl? And might she have been so headstrong to escape, on rebellious, childish impulse? She *was* a headstrong child . . . or could it be that Mr. Mott didn't love her, that he never took to her? No! *I'm a better judge of character than that,* he thought. Then perhaps something had happened to the bakery itself, catastrophic; perhaps Will'm would discover a charred, smoky lot with only cast-iron ovens remaining.

He looked left and right like a paranoiac and, jamming fists into pockets, tucked into the wind. Never had he bowed his head before, but now the old soul was injured or at least made vulnerable by his love for the girl. He had become the Chairman of the Disembodied.

Gray day with gray sun—looking over his shoulder for black-and-whites that might haul him to gaol. Their uniformed thugs and siren-shrieks were "abominations that oe'r the Rampart cared not twopence for hill or valley, poplar or lime, thistle or vetch, convolvulus or clematis— not twopence either for tower, spire, apse or dome."

> Forget six counties overhung with smoke,
> Forget the snorting steam and piston stroke,

Forget the spreading of the hideous town;
Think rather of the pack-horse on the down,
And dream of London, small, and white, and clean,
The clear Thames bordered by its gardens green.

When he was close to Frenchie's, his pace slowed and memories colluded. He saw himself fencing with Edward Burne-Jones at Oxford off Hell Quad, on Broad Street—arm in arm they strolled, in purple trousers, chanting Gregorians outside St. Thomas's church. (Such was his love for Arthurian legend that as a student, he had literally worn chain mail.) He was a sight then in leggings and metal, with starfish spray of hair, charging along with Rossetti and Ruskin; then one day he met her and his life was changed forever. Jane Burden was his obsession, an adulterous woman who could never have had more apt a name . . .

"Will'm!" cried Gilles, standing in dusty apron at the bakery's street-side door. In his reverie he'd walked straight past his destination. The wanderer turned with a baffled look. "I was beginning to worry!"

"Whatever for, man?"

"Well," he said, "you haven't been by."

The big man had better bide his time; it wouldn't do to just blurt things out.

"Oh, been languishing—miserable. This town is so sordid! Had to move: to Red House, near Hog's Hole and hard by the route taken by Chaucer's Canterbury pilgrims. *Extremely* medieval. Ruins of an Augustinian priory just down the road. But the *work* involved in fitting it up, Gilles, the work . . ."—he had never called the baker by first name before—" 'twas *exhausting*. I've been but a dead man knocking at a gate."

"Then come make yourself useful!"

Will'm followed him in.

Was it a dream—was it just a dream that he had dropped her there in the first place? Then he had a joyful thought: what if the skid-row grapevine had been wrong? Or, better yet, that George Fitzsimmons's gathering of intelligence had originated in the smoke of his devil-pipe! His mood lightened considerably, and while he wouldn't dare say it, his heart overflowed in anticipation of espying her there in the back room— of a sudden, he could *see* the flour-powdered shock of curls and himself kissing her chewed-up nails. He smiled, allowing the luxury (for it had been a terrible week) of conjuring her in a little apron, vaulting into his arms. He thought he'd been very clever to have steered her there for shelter from the elements, knowing she would find comfort at the source of her favorite confectionary treats; partaking of them would make her think of him and have faith that all would turn out well.

These ruminations happened in the wink of an eye, and though in a greater context a relatively short amount of time had passed since he'd dropped off his ward, it was a continual wonder how elastic that dimension could be. Yes, he had heard of her capture and lived with those squalid images for some days now; yet another part of him imagined the orphan already sprung full-blown into rosy-cheeked maiden and baker's apprentice, a busy schoolgirl with eager contingent of boyish suitors—a vital and beloved member of the community, indispensable to her proud, adopted family: Frenchie's Bakery and Fine Pastries.

As they entered the rear, his heart sank. Instead of the girl there was a woman, whom Gilles effusively introduced as his wife. Toweling one hand with the other in preparation to greet him, Lani's eyes grew large. She shook his hand, happy to finally meet one of her husband's stories—his best and biggest one—made flesh. By hirsute, tweedy bulk and sheer stylish *volume*, Will'm could not disappoint; for those of any sensitivities, he downright astonished. She cleared her throat and nervously smoothed her clothes, as if a celebrity had just stepped in. The baker positively cooed, knowing Will'm to exceed any and all expectations.

"So *this* is the secret weapon!" she said. "I'll have to admit my husband used me as a guinea pig for some of your early creations." She was referring to the pomegranate-and-almond mille-feuilles. "He wouldn't tell me they had been baked by someone else—not at first. And he's been trying to duplicate them ever since! But I'll have you know he's been an abject failure."

"Oh, I doubt that," said Will'm graciously, and Gilles was gladdened he'd rallied to his defense.

"My husband tells me you also design fabric."

"Suchwise I have been known to indulge." The words came forth, but he felt emptied out and wickedly desolate.

"Quite the Renaissance man! I'd love to see one of your patterns," she said diffidently. "When you have the time."

Gilles offered coffee and sweets—a few customers came and went—

Will'm mopped and moped—all the while pondering how to wangle things around to the girl.

"Tell me, Gilles, do you and the wife have children?"

"No."

"Well then, niece or nephew?"

"We have two nieces," offered Mrs. Mott.

"One this high?" he asked, holding an enormous hand around the height of Amaryllis's crown.

"No—why do you ask?"

"It's just that I was passing by some days ago and about to come in. And I thought I saw a child—I was afraid I'd give her a fright, so I stayed away. I *am* loud and unkempt, you know. So I kept a distance. And I was just wondering . . . well if she belonged to *you.*"

"Oh no! Heavens!" he said, looking at his wife with the realization.

"Gilles, he's talking about the *girl.*"

"The girl! *Yes.* She appeared out of *nowhere.*"

"Then there *was* a girl," said Will'm anxiously.

At ease now and happy to have a story of her own, Lani recapped their experience—how she had received a call from her husband alerting her to the emergency; how, in her duty as a trained court-appointed special advocate and occasional volunteer at children's court, she had phoned the child-abuse hotline (legally required, she added); how the police had come to the bakery, then taken the girl to the precinct; how Lani held her ground so that she was allowed to stay while the child was interviewed by the social worker, who was "rather green" (just then Gilles reached over and proudly patted her hand); how Lani then accompanied both girl and CSW to yet *another* building until "suitable placement" was procured—

"But," stammered Will'm, "but where is she *now?*"

"Now? Well . . . we—we don't know," said the baker, turning toward his wife. After all, she was the professional.

"With a family, I suppose," said Lani. "Hopefully, a *nice* one." This last, she smugly directed to Gilles.

"But—but why did you call the *police?*"

"She already said. She had to."

"I am required—by law," answered Lani defensively. "As a court-appointed special advo—"

"—but why didn't you take her in *yourself*—"

"You can't just 'take in' a child, Will'm," said Gilles, shoring up Lani with a cocked eye. "They put you in jail for that sort of thing."

"That's a *very* long process. And besides, Gilles and I—we're not set up for that." Meaning (not that it was anyone's business) that adopting a child wasn't an option. Lani set about her chores again in contrived fashion, wishing she were someplace else.

"The girl will be all right," said Gilles, vacantly. He ascribed their visitor's overweening interest in the castaway's cause to sheer eccentricity; all the man needed was to be reassured. "She'll be *fine*. We did the right thing, Will'm—by the book!"

"She will *not*—she will *not* be all right. And by *whose* book, sir!"

Lani stopped and beheld him. She was quaking.

"You say they'd put *you* in gaol—when it's *her* they put in there! They chased her down and shackled her up like an animal! The girl was meant to be *here*, that's what I *told* her—that you were my *friends* and would let no harm befall her! Now I see I've done the *worst* thing—sold my girl to the murderous police! The police, who give twopence for hill or valley or heart or soul! 'You'll do right well with him'—*him* meaning *you*—I told her. I *swore* to her as the poor thing looked straight in my eye. She'd have jumped through a hoop from a *building* if I'd told her—and now it looks as if she has, into deep space! See what's done? My girl's *alone* out there! And me a dead man, knocking at a gate!"

He stomped and snorted, and with that he was gone.

"Well, how do you like that?" said Gilles, setting down his mug. "So *he's* the one who dropped her off! Now, how would he even know a child like that? Standing around with us playing dumb . . . and what did he mean 'she's in jail.' We should probably call the police, Lani, no? Don't you think? Maybe he knows her folks. Maybe he—" A lurid brainstorm darkened his face, cheapening its features. "Lani . . . do you think there was something *funny* there? 'My girl,' he called her. Something 'Fritz Lang'—you know the Peter Lorre film—I mean, going *on*—between him and—?"

"No," said his wife, still trembling. "No, Gilles, I do *not*."

Shaken by the homeless gentleman's tirade, she steadied herself against one of the steel mixing machines and was overcome by shame, the shame of what she already knew: that her entire life she'd taken pride in doing the right thing—"by the book." The useless right thing.

*   *   *

Carroll Avenue was cushy, but the once right and honorable George Fitzsimmons knew it would not last forever; he was under the 4th Street Bridge sussing old digs when an unmarked car pulled over.

"Hi there—can we talk a moment?"

Seated beside the detective was Someone-Help-Me, who, having successfully brought hunter to quarry (he knew Fitz and Will'm were "tight"), busied himself with a grotesque celebratory lap dance *solitaire*, a seizure of freakish, self-satisfied gesticulations.

Samson Dowling stepped from the car and approached. Fitz put both hands on his crutch, cockily casual. The dirty dynamo got out too, sneering and twitching and muttering, and Fitz was not unhappy when Half Dead, gray rag of rat in his jaw, flew from the concrete stanchioned underslope and leapt at the traitorous fucker, knocking him backward.

"Mutant peesuh*shit!*" He frothed and feinted as the mongrel went for a mouthful. "*Kill* 'im, I will, crackhead Half Man!"

"I'll suck your dick first."

"You!" barked the detective at his scurvy partner. "*Outta* here—*now. Now!*"

Someone-Help-Me lurched toward the L.A. River, peppily escorted by man's best and mangled friend; the duration of Doppler'd vocalization made it apparent the dog's enthusiasms took more than a moment to diminish. That the detective cared not a whit about the attack (really only bluster) and seemed near the end of his tether with this varminty vermin, viz. the cocksucking snitch, endeared him to Fitz just a little. For Fitz had no great love of the Man.

Dowling cordially introduced himself, adding that he'd seen Fitz on the streets the last year or so. Something about his interrogator put him at ease, which of course made him more defensive than ever.

"It's my understanding you know a man who goes by the name of William."

"I do not."

"He has a nickname—Topsy."

"I don't know a William and I don't know a Topsy."

"Are you sure? Tall fellow, British. Bearded. Seems he'd be hard to miss! Not sure how *I* have. Used to go to St. Vincent's now and then, but they haven't seen him there lately. I heard *you* have. Heard he was your running partner."

" 'Running partner'!" he spat contemptuously, withdrawing a civility already overextended. "May I go about my business, *Detective?*"

"Wears strange . . . suits. Are you sure, Mr. Fitzsimmons?" The one-legged transient, mildly startled to be addressed in such a way, let it ride. "Are you sure you haven't seen him?"

"I don't run with nobody."

"You *have* been seen in the past with someone of that description."

"Seen? By who?" He nodded toward the river. "The scumbag snitch?"

The detective laughed. "*And* others. I heard the two of you shared an encampment—"

"I ain't asshole buddies with *no* one."

"—right around here, no? Look, I understand you wanting to protect your friend, but there's been a murder. A little girl is involved."

"Got nothin' to tell you."

The detective changed tack.

"You used to be a caseworker, didn't you?"

"Who told you that?"

"You know, Mr. Fitzsimmons, you're something of a legend over at the DCFS. They said you were one of the finest to ever pass through, and I believe it! One of the good guys—someone who cared. Life doesn't have to be this way, George. If you want help getting off that pipe, I can take you someplace right now. Just hop in and I'll personally see you've got a bed in a detox so you can kick this thing. That's no bullshit. In six months you can be back doing your thing. Helping kids. Making a difference."

"TPR, my friend."

"What's that?"

"Termination of Parental Rights. I'm *done* with mom and dad—some of us *are*, you know: Welfare and Institutions Code, Section 366.26, Senate Bill 243, confer January first, 1989. Baby, I was *fully* successful in all hearings, petitions and permanency plans. Who did they think they were playing with? The Department willfully demonstrated neglect, cruelty, abandonment and moral depravity—and let me tell you something else, *Officer:* it was demonstrated by my attorneys as such."

"I'm going to give you my card," said Dowling, reaching into his wallet. "If you see our friend, tell him I'd like to talk to him. It's for his own good. Maybe he can help us clear some things up. And my offer to you still stands."

"Look to the parent, Detective, always look to the parent," Fitz said, shuffling after him. "If the minor has been sexually abused or there is substantial risk the minor will be sexually abused, as defined in Section 11165.1 of the Penal Code, by his or her parent or guardian or a member of his or her household or the parent or guardian has failed to adequately protect the minor from sexual abuse when the parent or guardian knew or reasonably should have known that the minor was in danger of sexual abuse"—the detective got into his car and started the engine—"and for the purposes of this subdivision 'severe physical abuse' means any of the following: any single act of abuse which causes physical trauma of sufficient severity that if left untreated would cause permanent physical disfigurement"—Fitz lit out after the Taurus as it pulled away, pulling on the crutch with all his strength—"permanent physical disability or death! any single act of sexual abuse which causes significant bleeding, deep bruising or significant external or internal swelling or more than one act of physical abuse, each of which causes bleeding, deep bruising, significant external or internal swelling, bone fracture or unconsciousness; or the willful, prolonged failure to provide—"

The car was out of sight. Fitz leaned on the crutch, panting. A broad smile came to his face and he laughed out loud. Then his brow furrowed; he would have to make sure his friend Will'm relocated—fast.

He called out: "Half? Half, baby? Darling, come . . ."

And limped toward the river.

CHAPTER 19

Gatherings

ull and the Dane still went for walks in the sheltered park of La
Colonne, yet without the innocence of earlier explorations.
They came and went as they pleased, traipsing through wild savanna
and fields of lawn sedge studded by fifty-foot purple beeches—and
tramped amid the whimsical all-in-black Mourning Garden, designed by
Trinnie between halfway-house stints. It was filled with bat-like devil
flowers, dark-blood Queen of Night tulips and bamboo "Noir" that shot
up like bayonets. Mr. Greenjeans, who seemed born to the place and
surely would die there, waved jovial greetings from afar; it was from him
Tull learned that his mother had recently passed nights in the tower's
bridal suite.

While Pullman grazed and loped and stretched, the master averted
his eyes from the cracked pillar, unable to shake the feeling that his star-
crossed parents were ensconced—she, in the kitchen preparing lunch
(though all his life the boy never knew her to be in *any* kitchen); he, Marcus Weiner, in the library napping, the biography of a poet open on his
tangle-down chest.

The sun was low and the sky bloodied. Pullman turned five today,
and a small celebration awaited on Saint-Cloud, courtesy of Grandpa
Lou. A melancholy Santa Ana hurried them out the open gate and up
the hill toward home.

As much as he wished to attend the Dane's tribute, Tull couldn't
stay.

Epitacio drove the distrait young Trotter to cousin Edward's, who wasn't well enough to make the trip to Saint-Cloud.

Among the children only Lucy paid homage, lending her writer's ear (augmented by Cartier pen and blue-paged BIRD NOTES for a *Blue Maze Mystery*); certain that a canine birthday gala would make its way into her book, she joined her grandparents and the others at a mossy set of nineteenth-century faux-bois tables and benches just outside the maze. Servants bustled about, pouring Armagnac, spooning into faience pots of silken goose liver—from Toulouse, of all places—garnishing extracts with a gelée of black cherries and leaves of chervil. (Ralph had already gotten into the star-anise-and-honey ice cream.) Soon, modest fireworks would grace Bel-Air skies for the dedication of the "Danish friend's" latest architecturally correct (the latter phrase, courtesy of Trinnie) doghouse: none other than the Pine-Lute tea pavilion, the second, after the Meier, of Trotter funerary models to be brought to full-scale life. Working-class Winter stood behind Bluey, tetchy in her tailored RN whites—uncomfortable the elaborate to-do was for a dog; a large, sweet one, but a dog nonetheless. Trinnie told her to "get over it." She thought the extravaganza "brilliant" and took special care to observe her father delightedly mooning over the drowsy Dane, who lay upon a Moroccan ottoman incognizant of his good fortune, sated like a pasha.

On the way to Stradella, Tull compulsively felt his pocket as he had ever since the document was given him, to make certain it was still there.

*H*e found his cousin relaxed and in good spirits, stitching taffeta in the workshop of the Boar's Head Inn. He wore nothing but a saffron sari and velvet Philippe Model hat, courtesy of his doting aunt; though his chin rested on the crook of the brace, he eschewed mask and gloves, so that for the first time Tull saw how the middle and ring fingers of each hand were fused. When he'd had his fill, he discreetly drew his eyes to Edward's tall, broken face.

"You know, I'm supposed to have surgery soon."

"Really? What kind?"

" 'LeFort III'—that's the procedure. *LeFort III.* What a weird thing! With Apert's, *as you've probably noticed,* the middle face grows slower than the rest. They call it retrusion. LeFort is when they go in and do grafting and bone-spacing." He shook his head resolutely. "There is just no way. There's no payoff."

"What do your parents think?"

"Same as they do about everything—Dad's laissez-faire and Mother's indifferent. You know: they want what I want. If I'm up for the surgery—fine. If I'm not—well that's fine too. But why would I put myself *through* that, Tull? It's just so fucked. And all from *one* little change in the FGFR2—that's fibroblast growth factor receptor 2, in case you were wondering. Something's wrong with the gene on chromosome 10, or some such bullshit. Well, *fuck* FGFR2 and the stem cell it rode in on. Do you know how many pages there are on the Internet about this crap? I mean, I could get *very* intimate with some punk in Denmark who shares my tragic deformity. Get jiggy with the whole codependent World Wide Webbed-finger family." The buggy sat on the carpet beside the metal roll-up; Edward stepped in. "I am telling you, there are links up the yin-yang, every fucking orphan disease on the planet. Antley-Bixler! Langer-Geidon! Pfeiffer! Saethre-Chotzen! Arhinia! Baller-Gerold! Stickler! Carpenter! Parry-Rombergs! Craniosynostosis! Goodman! Jackson-Weiss! Sagittal synostosis! Treacher-Collins! And there's an *amazingly* pathetic homepage with a gallery of kids' fucked-up faces—a permanent, floating pediatric wax museum horror-show—with 'virtual' candles burning. Whenever one of the deformed little guys croaks, his flame gets snuffed."

"Edward, I think you should chill. You're gonna stroke out."

"Yeah well, if I ever *do*, you better put a pillow over my head, cuz. Promise?"

"Promise."

"Exceptional!" he said, giving Tull his best scary Tom Cruise smile. "Now, get in." Edward pushed a button on the console and the door of the workshop zipped into a galvanized drum. They pulled out. "Sorry you're missing the birthday."

"It's OK. I did kind of want to see the fireworks, though."

"Long in the tooth, that Pullie, isn't he?"

"He's only five."

"Gettin' up there for a Dane."

"Can we please just leave him out of it?"

"For Danes, anything past birthday number six is gravy—as any true aficionado knows."

They drove along the winding path that surrounded the vast, fragrant property. There were stretches of woodsy darkness; against resistance from his wife, Dodd gave one of the farther fields over to Trinnie, who had planted tall plumed pampas grass, which shivered as they motored past, trying to tell them secrets. Tull felt his cousin's aloneness and guiltily saw himself hovering over the comatose boy with a Pratesi pillowslip. Again, he felt for the letter in his pocket.

The buggy rolled by the guest-house pool before Edward pointed it back to Olde CityWalk. He began a tired rant about his mother's "Dead Baby Society" that segued neatly into Dodd's recent mania-fueled purchase of an empty prison in Palm Desert.

All the while, in anticipation of introducing his topic, Tull's heart beat faster than he would have liked. Finally, he said: "Edward . . . the letter you gave me—"

"I was wondering when you'd bring that up."

"Where—did you get it?"

"I—well, *Lucy* and I—I have to give her credit—we made a rather *thorough* inventory of our parents' effects. Father tends to keep certain items—including eighteenth-century pornographic etchings—in a *special* drawer in his walk-in closet. I'm telling you, cousin, my parents are not well!"

"Just tell me about the letter."

"Sadly, it was the only thing we were able to come up with—you know, I'm a little surprised you haven't done any footwork of your own. I mean, *shit*, Tull, the Withdrawing Room's most probably a Tut's tomb of nostalgic puzzle-pieces! You never know *what* you'd find: stuffed in one of the maquettes, say—or the mattress of Grandpa's Murphy bed. Or hidden behind a panel of the Piranesi . . ."

"Edward—do you think . . . do you think they actually found him?"

"All I could pry from Joyce was that they hired a man—or, should I say, *Grandpa* hired a man to look for Marcus Weiner."

"I already knew that," said Tull, thrilled to know something about anything.

"But did you know it was a guy Dad went to school with?"

"What school—"

"BV—Beverly Vista. I heard him talking—Mom and him—at midnight, in the kitchen. I've got the place *wired*. There's still a few bugs, but . . ."

"What did they *say?*"

"He was telling Joyce about Marcie Millard."

"Marcie Millard?"

"The lady hammering Dad for money to rebuild their alma mater."

In the weeks after the initial revelation of his father's undeceased state—that terrible hour with Trinnie and Grandpa Lou in the Withdrawing Room—he had been loath to think of Marcus Weiner at all, let alone make inquiries of anyone who might possess the facts. A firewall had descended; even kids at school whose parents had been privy to the resurrected scandal seemed to have lost interest in provoking him. Now, something had shifted and Tull was beginning to wake up.

"But do you think they *found* him?"

The cousin grew pensive, letting the question take air. "Do I think they found your father? Is that what you're asking?"

"That's what I'm asking."

"To that, I would have to answer . . . no. No, Tull, I do not think they found your father, I am sorry or not sorry to say."

A long, sad silence ensued as they navigated the stony streets of Olde CityWalk on the approach to the Majestyk, an authentic movie house that seated seventy-five. Like all structures in Edward's world, it was built to accommodate his motorized magic carpet; the boys got popcorn and soda without having to disembark.

The cousin grew serious while steering down the wide aisle of the plush auditorium. "You know, I think Lucy's theory is sound. Why *would* Grandpa Lou want to find such a man? He wouldn't want Trinnie to be tortured again."

"But he *hired* someone," said Tull, fairly pleading.

"Unless," said the cousin, with a mildly crazed look in his eye, "unless he wanted to find him so he could *kill* him for what he did to her." Tull saw that he wasn't joking. "It *is* a possibility. I've given it some thought."

"Shit, Edward! Are you saying Grandpa wanted to murder my father? Jesus!"

"Maybe Grandpa *did* kill him—maybe he found him and killed him and now maybe he wants to be caught—maybe he wants us to catch him. *Expose* him, so he can repent. Let's say for argument's sake that it's true—that he did 'the job'—"

"Jesus, Edward!"

"It would *have* to have haunted the guy through the years, especially since it seems your mom's forgiven him—forgiven Marcus Weiner, I mean. Or at least would like to have had the chance. She's still in love with him. I mean, you *know* she goes and stays in the tower sometimes . . ." He thwacked Tull's arm in excitement. "Beginning to sound like a real Lucy Trotter Mystery, ain't it?"

They left the buggy and sank into the Majestyk's ergonomic row of Herman Millers.

"Did you bring the letter?" asked the cousin.

Tull nodded.

"Then read it."

"I already have. About a thousand times."

"Then read it *again*—out loud."

"What's the point?"

Edward glared. Tull took the document from his pocket, unfolding it like a cynical tourist would a useless map.

" 'If I was shocked at the reckless insinuation—' "

"From the beginning, Tull."

" '*Mr. Tabori,*' " he began, annoyed. " 'If I was *shocked* . . . at the *reckless insinuation* of your employee . . . I was absolutely *dumbfounded* by the letter from your attorney which my office received today.' *New paragraph.* 'I have referred the matter to my own counsel, who would probably object to my sending this note. I suggest that you retract your slanderous allegations or you will find this former customer to be a litigious one. Sincerely, Marcus Weiner.' "

Tull paused; his cousin sighed deeply.

"A bit stilted, no? His guilt is apparent."

"What difference does it make?"

"What difference? I'll *tell* you: we found him. Lucy did, anyway."

The air left Tull's lungs. "You *found* him?"

"It seems so."

"What are you *saying*? You found him *where*? How—"

"Good old gumshoe work. And the Internet, I am pleased to say, had nothing to do with it. Lucy spoke with him on the phone, plain as day—not a single e-mail exchanged! Hard man to reach, as you may well imagine."

Tull broke into a sweat and was unable to swallow. "Where is he?"

"Los Angeles area," said the cousin, coolly. "We made an appointment to see him. Tomorrow, after school."

Edward pressed a touch-panel and the lights dimmed. The heavy curtains lifted, layer by crushed gold layer.

"But, does anyone—does anyone *know?* Did you tell your—"

"God, no! And no one's *going* to. Everyone's going to keep their mouths shut. This is strictly between *us.*"

The projector was dropping from its hidden perch all along and within moments the MGM lion roared. From the blackness came a noisy choir of ticking clocks. A sundial appeared from stage left, cross-fading with an hourglass from stage right (just like in the old *Twilight Zones* Tull watched on Thanksgiving Day marathons), followed by myriad antiquey minute-repeater mechanisms, which culminated in a floating Big Ben, its watchtower face erupting in a thunderclap of light. A title bubbled up:

H. G. Wells's

The Time Machine

"I thought it apropos," said the cousin. "Except Rod Taylor's going forward—*we* need to go *backward.*"

"This isn't funny," said Tull, reaching over to lower the sound. "And I'm not sure I want anyone to be there."

"You mean, you want to go alone?"

"That's right."

"But why?" asked Edward.

Tull began to tremble. "He's my—*father,* Edward . . . and I—well, I just think it would be better if—"

"Your *father?* Oh no, Tull, no! But we'll find *him,* too—of that I am convinced. This is merely the first step."

"But you said we had an appointment—"

"We *do*—with Mr. Tabori! Tomorrow at four. Now, can we please watch the movie?"

*   *   *

*C*abori & Company, purveyor of antiquarian books, was housed in a former mortuary built in the late twenties, now sitting on the high-end stretch of Melrose Avenue. The anachronistic open-vaulted Gothic-style edifice was a jewel box of vellum and leather, its fine stained-glass panels wittily incorporating caricatures of Tabori *père et fils*, gentle brotherhood of bibliophiles.

When Emerson Tabori received a call from a girl identifying herself as Lucy Trotter, he immediately confirmed the familial connection—a call from any member of that illustrious clan, no matter how youthful, need be taken with utmost seriousness. To be safe, Lucy said she wished to procure a gift for her grandfather, cannily begging Mr. Tabori's discretion if he by chance spoke to Mr. Trotter in the interim. (The redhead knew he was a longtime customer.) She was in full detective mode.

Bearded Emerson, youngest of the brethren, stood no taller than Tull; though his satyric countenance put one in mind of that *other* Toulouse—he of Montmartre cabarets—it was impossible to think of him in the diminutive. His unflagging energy, passionate apprehension and sheer-rock-face intellect (he was a well-known monographist and prolific contributor to *The Dickens Newsletter, The Dickens Project, The Doughty Street Dickens* and *The Dickens Universe*) made him appear like a great turbine from the dawn of the industrial age, a turbine overseen, if you will, by a pair of cool blue-gray eyes from which no textual footnote might escape. His memory was prodigious and phantasmagoric: he could still quote by heart the little van Gogh–penned poem he'd sold Louis Trotter (for $700,000) along with a letter to Theo wherein the hapless artist bitched about having no money to purchase oils.

The bell at the side door rang and there was a stir among employees, as the musketeers standing at the entrance—four, including Pullman—were fairly unforgettable. Edward, outfitted in a rather demure di-aphanous Gigli cape, embroidered linen hood and the sort of delicate white cotton gloves with which one handles rare photographs, leaned like a holy invalid on both Lucy and his cousin. (Sling Blade, who had no interest at all in entering the sanctum sanctorum, stood under the gull wing of the Mauck and smoked, while Epitacio remained at Saint-Cloud, otherwise engaged.) The Great Dane made the usual unheralded, regal entrance and lay down, stretching his muscular spotted self on the ter-razzo floor at the foot of a suite of chairs renowned for having once been featured in *Gone with the Wind*. A nervous employee sashayed over to suggest the dog remain outside; before she had the chance, Mr. Tabori brought her up short with an acrid little smile. She backed off.

"How marvelous to meet you all!" he exclaimed, with retailer's out-stretched arms. But that is unfair, for he cared nothing of money.

Introductions were made and genealogy silently noted: *These two belong to Dodd, son of Louis—this one to Katrina, beloved, famously jilted, drug-addicted daughter of same.*

He took them on tour and showed them folios and autographs, and rows of buttery bindings decorated in gilt, with watered-silk endleaves. He had no idea what they had in mind, yet planted seeds in the several-thousand-dollar range according to his sense of what the old man might enjoy, such as a 1900 edition of *Days of the Dandies*, an anthology of British court life.

The curious titanium-braced fashionista pointed to this and that while his braided sister explored the shop as if it were a fabulous tree house. The one called Tull seemed saturnine, and looked as if about to flee.

They passed a vitrine of handwritten folios.

"Bret Harte," said Mr. Tabori, gnomishly enthused. "Tiny handwriting, no? That's just a fragment; what's actually called a blad—short for 'blotting pad.' You should see Poe's! He had *two* styles of handwriting, one for manuscripts, the other for correspondence. When he wrote his stories, he usually tried to approximate the typeface of a book. And Brontë! Charlotte Brontë is *worse*—almost pathological. You need a magnifying glass!"

"Mr. Tabori," began Lucy, circling back. The boys turned in anticipation. "Do you—do you have any Nancy Drew?"

All faces registered disappointment.

"I'm afraid not! Though we *do* have Edgar Rice Burroughs—in fact, we have the entire work. May I ask what you have in mind, if you *do* have anything in mind, for your grandfather?"

She smiled devilishly at her compadres; it was the moment of truth. They would now take up the challenge like men—or forever keep their mousy peace.

"Well," said Edward, uncharacteristically tongue-tied. He theatrically cleared his throat while swiveling toward his cousin. "Do you have . . . the *list*?" He meant the *letter*, which Tull simply wasn't ready to extend. Seeing he'd get nowhere with the flummoxed boy, Edward stalled for time, and turned back to Mr. Tabori. "How about Dickens?"

The girl detective frowned at their timidity.

"For me, Dickens is the most marvelous—and one of the easiest to collect." He walked them to a section of which Lucy had thought, before setting off again on her investigations, contained the most beautiful volumes imaginable. "The interesting thing about *Dickens* is, printers had certain *requirements*. You see, most of his books were 624 pages long for a reason—they came in sixteen-page gatherings, or 'quires.' Look: this one's an 'octavo,' that's eight leaves to a quire—a total of sixteen pages with inner and outer forms. When people read Dickens and say this or that passage is hurried or belabored, it's because, you see, he was *customizing*. It's the same for certain Mozart pieces, no? Were you interested in Dickens? I mean, for your grandfather? Because if I'm not mistaken, he already has the Nonesuch—"

"We're interested in everything!" shouted Lucy from the long hall, where autographs of historical figures were hung. With that, she threw the boys the evil eye, to egg them on.

"Well!" said Mr. Tabori, figuratively licking his chops. "I strongly suggest *A Christmas Carol*." He plucked it from the shelf and turned it over with caressing hands. "Chapman and Hall, first edition, first issue: i.e., 'Stave I'—foolscap octavo, green-coated endpapers, blue *half*-title, red and blue *title*. Four inserted hand-colored steel-engraved plates *by* and *after* Leech and four black-and-white text wood-engravings *by* W. J. Linton *after* Leech. Original cinnamon vertically ribbed cloth, all edges gilt, with the *tiniest* interval between blind-stamped border and gilt wreath equal to fourteen millimeters—with a perfect *D* in 'Dickens.' The slightest perceptible fading to the spine, with an early provincial bookseller's label on the front pasted down. Spectacular! At fifty thousand dollars, it's quite simply the best and brightest we've seen." He cleared his throat, realizing he'd gone too far; these were children after all. "But I'm sure that's in excess of your budget."

Lucy returned, emboldened. The toddlers clearly needed her help—if she was going to stick this episode somewhere in *Blue Maze*, a dallying narrative would never do.

"Mr. Tabori," she said forthrightly. "Have you ever had anything *stolen*? From the shop?"

Tull and Edward refused to look at her, sharpening their attention on the host, who was amiably taken aback.

"Oh, once or twice. An autograph from the wall . . . George Bernard Shaw. A Kerouac. Some American 'firsts' were stolen—Hammett and Chandler. But we got them back."

"This," said Edward, following her lead, "would have been about thirteen years ago."

" 'This'?" said Mr. Tabori, cocking his head.

Tull reached in his pocket for the letter, which he handed to Mr. Tabori.

"Yes," said the bookseller, nodding his head as he examined. "I remember."

"Was it by any chance written to *you?*" asked Tull.

"No—that would have had to have been my brother Henry-David. He died two years ago. Colorectal cancer."

"We're so sorry," said Lucy, and she really was.

"But I *do* remember—it was the sort of thing—one of those situations where—well, you see, he was a customer and we *did* know him rather well—we preferred not to call the police. We called the gentleman's *office*—by then of course we were quite *certain*—there could have been no *question*—that he 'took' the item. The gentleman didn't respond; Henry-David might have sent a follow-up note. That would have been H.D.'s way. My brother was the *least* threatening of men, so the . . . *communiqué* referred to here couldn't have been too—but the gentleman was outraged! We were doing him a *favor*, not calling the police. Finally, we had no recourse. And then—" A light shone in his eye; he cocked his head again. "The gentleman who wrote this letter. He was connected to . . . your *grandfather*, no?"

"That's right," said the cousin.

Mr. Tabori nodded and stared into space, his gaze falling somewhere over Samuel Johnson's *Lives of the Most Eminent English Poets*. "There was a scandal, no? A marriage—he was . . . a *flimflam*."

Tull spoke up. "Was it a book that was taken?"

"Yes. Nothing of excessive value."

"Did you recover it?"

"I'm afraid that one got away."

"A purloined antiquity!" huffed Lucy, authorial glands fairly salivating. "And you called the police?"

"We were about to . . . when a private investigator came out—who was it? Had a funny name. Employed by Louis Trotter. He asked a few questions, then made good on the amount that was in dispute."

"If you could just tell us more about—"

Of a sudden, Emerson Tabori gave a great sigh, as if having reached a regretful conclusion. He sat down upon one of Tara's chairs and bid the children do the same. Edward looked amazing against the high-backed red velvet throne; Pullman clambered from camp and resettled, a spotty bedouin dead to the world.

The dealer's tone became intimate, avuncular, almost morose. "I see that perhaps you came for more than just the selection of a gift. I'm not a gossip and am afraid I've spoken too much. Your grandfather is a valued client and, I like to think, a friend. Whatever happened those many years ago was a private affair. I *wish* I could help, but simply don't have the information—nor would I feel comfortable imparting it if I had."

With that he stood, a kindly smile radiating from his face. The children, who looked more like children now than when they'd come in, were downcast. Tull and Lucy helped Edward stand; and were soon joined by Mr. Tabori and staff as in the raising of the Iwo Jima flag. The crestfallen trio began trudging to the door when Tull turned back to face their admonisher.

"Mr. Tabori . . . that 'flimflam'—he was my father." The boy stood tall, and his lip quaked with passion. "For all my life I thought he was dead, but it wasn't true. Trinnie—that's my mother—Katrina Berenice Trotter Weiner—both she *and* my grandfather told me this, that he was alive, at least to their knowledge. They told me it *recently*, Mr. Tabori. You can imagine the effect that had; imagine what effect it would have had on *you*. And, well, to be honest, sir, I am trying *very* hard to find him—as any son would—and I *will*, one way or the other, with or without anyone's help. Yes, our buying a gift was a subterfuge and for that I am sorry. Truly, we apologize! This sort of thing is new to us—to me. But you have my word that we came here today in the strictest confidence and would never think of doing anything to breach your relationship or trust . . . with our grandfather, or ourselves. But even if Grandpa *were* to know we paid a visit—"

"And he *never will*," interposed the cousin.

"—he would not object. He told me a story, something he said that a general once wrote. The general cautioned his troops never to attack men who were on their way home from battle; he said men on their way home were unvanquishable. Well, I wish to bring my *father* home, sir; *I'm* on my way home, too. And nothing will stop me from getting there—from finding him! So, if you please, sir, I'd like to ask once more: is there anything else you can tell us?"

Lucy and Edward were in tears.

Mr. Tabori, not unmoved, sat down again with a sigh and smiled sagaciously. "You *are* here for a gift then—no?"

The children, puzzled at first, got his drift and vociferously agreed. Pullman yawned, shuddering his jowls.

"Then how can I help?"

"The book that was taken," said Tull. "What was it?"

"A work by William Morris—*News from Nowhere*. A utopian novel. Not my favorite of the man's, if I may."

"Do you mean the British designer William Morris?" asked Edward.

As always, Lucy was shocked by her brother's casual erudition.

"Oh, he was much more than that!" offered Mr. Tabori. "A *voluminous* intellect. Poet, weaver, socialist—*and* publisher. He founded the Kelmscott Press."

"Do you still have a copy?" asked Tull. "I mean, *another* copy? *News from—*"

"Afraid not. The Huntington has one, if you'd like to see it. Or the Clark." He leapt up, hurrying to a cabinet. "These are *all* Kelmscott. This row's vellum—calfskin. These, prenatal; those, live birth. Down here are the linens: blue-backed holland boards. That's how the *Kelmscott Chaucer* was first done: blue holland."

Blue maze, blue board, blue holland . . . what a blue mystery we weave! thought the pigtailed girl.

"So you don't have *News from No—*"

"We *do* have a Chaucer." The latter was already laid out on a table. "I hope your hands are clean," warned Mr. Tabori. "It's about ninety thousand. The cover's by Birdsall."

He showed them the prenatal pilgrims, setting out for Canterbury.

"Sir," said Tull diffidently. "Did you ever meet Marcus Weiner?" He couldn't bring himself to say "my father" again just yet.

"Oh, many times! *Interesting* character—wonderful sense of humor. Wordplay and all. Powerful voice. Great head of hair. Far-ranging mind.

Now, mind you, it wasn't uncommon for someone like him to have an 'interest'; Hollywood's always had a romance with collecting. Johnny Depp buys with us—he likes Hunter Thompson 'firsts.' Though we don't usually carry that sort of thing. Ron Bass and Tim Burton, Whoopi and 'Buffy the Vampire Slayer'—they *all* come through. But Mr. Weiner . . . well, at first I thought he was being a bit *precious*."

What's this? Was the man saying his father was a celebrity? Impossible—

"You said," Tull stammered, "that it wasn't uncommon for 'someone like him'—"

"A Hollywood person. At first I thought it precious that he was only interested in Morris . . . though after a while, I must say he proved himself *extremely* knowledgeable."

"And why would that be 'precious'—"

"Well, *you* know. Because he was an agent."

"Agent?"

"He *worked* there. Didn't you know?"

"Worked *where?*"

"Why, at William Morris! The agency—he was a hotshot. You mean that you didn't . . . but how could you *not* have—" Mr. Tabori was briefly distressed, thinking again that he'd told too much; but remembering the boy's eloquent speech, moved on. He pointed to the embossed, intertwining initials of the letterhead the children had mistaken for Marcus Weiner's. "You see? The William Morris logo."

Edward began to chortle at the sublimeness of it all.

The same helpful employee who had nearly shooed away dear Pullman now made a little show of producing *News from Nowhere* as a magician might a bouquet—freshly extracted from a *Collected Works*, which sat forgotten in the back bindery. Mr. Tabori took the volume and, with a single penetrating glance, encouraged her to leave. She did straightaway.

"I meant of course that we didn't have the volume available of *itself.* This is Longmans, Green; it must be sold in toto. It is seventy-five hundred."

"May I?" asked Edward.

Mr. Tabori handed him the volume; the cousin riffled its pages before settling on a passage from the end:

"Inexpressibly shocked, I hurried past him and
hastened along the road that led to the river and
the lower end of the village; but suddenly I saw as it
were a black cloud rolling along to meet me, like a
nightmare of my childish days; and for a while I
was conscious of nothing else than being in the
dark, and whether I was walking, or sitting, or
lying down, I could not tell. I lay in my bed in
my house at dingy Hammersmith thinking about
it all—"

As he listened, Tull seemed to hear the voice of his father, saw him
somewhere in the world agonized by myriad demons, and felt rudely
violated—as he had that afternoon with his cousins in the bedroom of
La Colonne. He seized the book, plunking it back into the hands of a startled Mr. Tabori while Lucy diplomatically intervened.

"Emerson, I'm a writer myself—of the mystery genre. But I was
wondering: do you have the Harry Potters? The original ones, from
England?—"

"That's it!" shouted Mr. Tabori, slapping his thigh. "*Dowling!*—"

"Who?"

"The 'funny name'—you made me think of it because of J. K. Row-
ling."

"Made you think of . . ."

"The *detective*—the one who reimbursed us! The detective your
grandfather hired. His name was Samson Dowling!"

CHAPTER 20

Inventories

*L*et us take a breath.

There was the introduction, pages ago, of a small detail which, in the unlikely event it has entered anyone's mind since, may have led the reader to imagine the chronicler of this tale to be underhanded. (It would not be the first time he was wrongly accused.) A train of thought, heavily freighted, was set upon a track, then without fanfare derailed.

Inspired by the unfurling of Will'm's "Strawberry Thief," the baker Gilles spontaneously shared the story of his visit to a Gallic feast with his then-fiancée—something having to do with illicit songbirds and subterranean gourmands. The divertissement had been summoned from the depths to quell the pastrymaker's nervousness around his unusual part-time employee, and he ran through it with a flourish before being heckled by the irritated giant. Just as well—Gilles had shot his anecdotal wad and would have been at a loss to continue.

Mr. Mott could not have known the strange, epic feelings he aroused in his burly listener. Right about the time he'd brought his tale around to the posh neighborhood of Marlene Dietrich and the opium eater at the door of the ancient wine cellar, Will'm found himself mentally elsewhere: twenty kilometers outside Paris to be exact, stealthily traversing a golf course during a drizzle. He saw his feet (and those of a woman, her face indistinct, gamely trailing after) step over a low barbed-wire fence, through bower and arborescent meadow. They walked awhile, then froze: in the distance stood a breathtaking apparition—a broken column made of stone. But this derelict fantasia had windows and could be lived in. While the baker droned on about crispy birds and such, Will'm remembed trodding toward the tower under billowing, storm-dirtied skies, the faceless woman tugging at his sleeve with worry. He was close enough to see the darkness within and had nearly entered when a man in short sleeves with a Gauloise stuck to his lower lip, caricature of a Frenchman, appeared on a tractor. He warned them against trespassing; so they never got to go inside.

At that very moment of recollection, an incensed Will'm resurfaced in time to cut Gilles off about his damn millet-gorged birds, barking (the perspicacious reader may recall), "That *is* the Frankish way, isn't it? Murder a thrush behind veils of civility! Truth be told, the French *are* a dishonorable and troublously shoddy race."

And so the baker's history crashed to a halt.[†]

Such embroidery is mere preamble to the aforementioned vexation: to wit, the baker's remorse over what he implied was the jilting of the "long-lost" bride-to-be (not Lani, by a long shot) who attended the fabled *fête des gourmands*. A shadow fell over him at chapter's end—did the author clumsily mean it to be Trinnie's?—as he wistfully reflected upon his double life. Amends, he said, were due! The reader of these pages knows better now, of that we are certain; still, if way back when, the very same but for a moment believed—if it is *feasible* the reader could have actually, however fleetingly, believed that the baker Gilles Mott (whose name alone too coarsely hints at things "Toulousian"), at such an early stage, was plausibly central to our tale—and, even more implausibly, if one could believe that he is still—well, then it is understandable how that reader may now turn his nose up at this red herring and feel the whole gambit to be unworthy of an author who appeared to pride himself on being sensibly meticulous; or that it was at least improvident of the latter to dredge it up here, for it may only serve to illuminate his over-reaching expository failures. If such *is* the case—if the reader is of that opinion—then there is nothing to be done. Suffice to say Gilles Mott *does* have reason to suffer, and reason to believe he has caused great

---

[†]Of his sudden, compelling memory of that ruined column (both, incomplete), Will'm could make no sense or give good context. We offer that sidebar as sheer human interest—for it is a rare, poignant, shivery thing to glimpse the metaphor of one's coming disarray, in a storybook garden to boot. That house cracked his head, then made him take up fractured residence.

suffering of another. He *will* make amends. But this is not the time or place.[†]

Let teller and listener thus reconciled, regroup—and dust themselves off to remount. That's what this chapter's about. The trail is winding, the pace leisurely; let the loping, mulish narrative carry one along.

During the Pullmanic gala's froth of fireworks, across the hill on Stradella, in surrey-fringed conversation, Edward Trotter, that wisest of boys, touched upon the extracurricular activities of his parents, pictorially pornographic and otherwise. He alluded to private prisons and Dead Baby Societies, but his blithe monologue went unheard; Tull's concerns over the mysterious monogrammed letter took precedence. We have already looked into that missive with some thoroughness so can spend this time enumerating recent powerful developments in the destiny of Joyce Trotter née Gilligan.

She sat at the dermatologist's flipping through Condé Nasts, then leaned to pull two "throwaways" from the pile. The glossy *310* had a garish photo of Katrina Trotter and Ralph Mirdling at a black-tie gala, standing beside studio titan Sherry Lansing, billionaire Gary Winnick and screenwriter Ron Bass. (All looked amiable except for the wincing Mr. M.) Joyce then opened the *Courier* to find a photo of her husband and Marcie Millard in white hardhats standing with shovels at the fence surrounding his former grade school. *That would have had to have been staged,* she thought; *not even Dodd's money made things happen that fast.*

Her eye drifted to an ad:

EXCEPTIONAL CRYPT FOR SALE

Pierce Brothers Mortuary in Westwood Village
Resting Place for a Single Casket and a Single Urn
Located in "Sanctuary of Peace"

[†]Simply because Mr. Mott's agonies are of lesser general interest than our principal players' does not rob them of meaning, for pain is pain. Consolation comes more to the earnest reader who may have been briefly hoodwinked, in a simple truism: when invariably one is misled—in book or in life—better it be for a price not too high or investment too dear. We are early enough in our history for the latter to hold true.

Crypt is at eye level, in the same enclave as
Marilyn Monroe, Truman Capote, Natalie Wood
and other legendary personalities

Price $105,000

There are no longer any other crypts available in this Sanctuary.
Don't burden your heirs with a hasty choice of your final resting place.

It gave her the biggest idea she ever had in her life.

As she drove through the cemetery gate, infused with collagen and Percodan, Joyce saw a familiar coxcombly figure at the far end of the oval drive—her father-in-law, chatting with a groundskeeper. She parked close enough to see the old man press something into the other's hand before Epitacio shut him into the Silver Seraph and spirited him away.

She of course knew of Mr. Trotter's exhaustive search for the ideal mausoleum, but had never visited the winning Westwood site. She'd never seen any of the famed funerary models either (except for the dog-houses), not having had a great interest and never, oddly, having been invited into that most legendary and exclusive of clubs: the Withdrawing Room. Amazing, she thought, to run into him at this time of day—the man truly was obsessed! Joyce watched the Rolls roll away and the homely caretaker return to raking. Then she ambled to the park office, where a receptionist quickly introduced her to Dot Campbell, the effervescent manager (she used Gilligan instead of Trotter); Ms. Campbell, in a smudged gingham, seemed ill-fitted for the part.

As they strolled the enclave past various "bench estates" and columbaria—new mausoleums were in varied stages of construction—she learned more about Ms. Campbell and her sister Ethel's pet peeves than she might have cared to. That was all right; in this instance, a kind-hearted eccentric would serve her well. SIT DOWN AND HAVE A CHAT WITH SADIE AND MORRIS was etched into a marble love seat beside two graves. Dot explained how Sadie and Morris were not yet dead but wanted the legend inscribed anyway. In funeral-world parlance, that was what they called pre-need.

Something drew her to the farthermost corner of the property, where a maintenance yard was being razed to make way for more tombs. It was lonely there, and felt colder than the rest of the grounds. When she saw a whitish pigeon wheel overhead, it reminded her of the doves at Castaic and she knew her instincts were, well, dead-on. Dot was glad the woman was interested in something family plot–size and said the work-in-progress parcel could be had for a million and a half, including a newly built adjacent shrine.

But Joyce said she wanted a simple field of grass, and besides, the unfortunately pink cenotaph held just four—not nearly enough. No: her babies needed to be in and of the earth. Well, said Dot, an unbuilt-on field *did* have its advantages—caskets could be "contumulated" or stacked vertically; if you cremated, you could fit more than a dozen. The benefactress stared at a separate grid that was going for about $500,000—at eleven by fourteen, it still seemed a bit confining . . . yet what was she expecting in the middle of Westwood? Elysium? Would she even be able to raise that sort of money to bury unknown children? She would have to incorporate her loose-knit group of "angels." They could call themselves Candlelight—the Candlelight Group. *The Candle-lighters* . . . they'd have fund-raisers and make the bigwigs give them their money. She was adamant on doing it all without Dodd's help.

Joyce felt a surge of confidence and emotion. The gesture of acquiring Westside memorial space was born not of convenience (the drive to Castaic was actually meditative) but as a way of weaving those orphans into the everyday tapestry of her—Westside—world. There was something mildly depressing about their current resting place, that arid, unincorporated outback of hinterland exurbia butt-up against the whiz and rumble of failed ride-share speed lanes, sig-alert big-rigs and CHP gunships. How magnificent it would be to bury those treasures *here*—here, not there—amid wealth of skyscraper, museum and university, far from potter's field. The poorest of forgotten children may after all help the richest of men into heaven.

When they were done, Dot let her be. She communed with Dorothy Stratten, Donna Reed and Dean Paul Martin, then with deliberation, "Mrs. Gilligan" moved closer to the groundskeeper, who now angled toward her as he raked. She struck up a casual conversation, wondering in what schemes her father-in-law had enlisted him. It was Sling Blade's peculiar fate to be linked to *all* the Trotters, without one another's knowledge.

In time Joyce returned to Pierce Brothers with Father de Kooning, whose blessings she required. The Bel-Air matron needed confirmation that her crusade didn't smack of dilettantism, that what she was considering was real and mighty and good.

The pastor mentioned meeting her sister at the Motion Picture and Television Hospital, and Joyce testily corrected him: sister-*in-law*. It seemed like she could never escape Trinnie—well, she could, but only on Trinnie's terms . . . those would be whenever she decided to leave the country or go into rehab (usually doing both at once). And when she returned, the men of this family *still* dropped everything to pend upon her every move. Now, here Joyce was with Father Tim, *her* Father Tim, whom she'd first met while doing selfless service at a godforsaken graveyard in Castaic, something Trinnie Trotter would be too stoned or bored or grandiose to *ever* do, and here he was serving her up just like that! Your *sister-in-law*, he said, was kind enough to be donating her services in designing a garden for the hospital ("kind" because even in her dereliction she was expensively renowned)—with a coy smile he called ministering at the hospital his "day job," meaning, thought Joyce, the *real* place he worked, the place that paid and sustained him, the place with a tangible, needy, dying parish, the place a thousand leagues above whatever after-school volunteer eulogizing he happened to do for dumpster babies on behalf of vainglorious society women with too much time on their hands. Her gorgeous, drug-addicted sister-in-law was donating *her* time, which was precious—precious, priceless Time and Service, making a beautiful, deathless "wandering garden"—whereas she, Joyce, the drab, laughable, very *old* in-law, the one who had to work her ass off to even look half decent, the one who cruelly brought a crippled genius into the world, was out there burying the discarded dead.

A few visits later, Joyce let it be known to Ms. Campbell that she *was* in fact a Trotter. She handed her a check for $50,000 as a deposit on a deposit—which Dot happily though confusedly accepted, noting that her father-in-law, "Mr. Louis," already *had* a plot and rather famously at that. Joyce said she was well aware, but the space she'd become interested in was for a "different" family, one she was quite close to and for which she wished to make this gift. That melted Dot's heart, triggering a lengthy, somewhat inappropriate monologue of how her sister Ethel told her of a "great *scandale*—a horrible woman bought up all the remaining cemetery space in the Hamptons—for her *own* family of course, not for *others.* A hundred and ten plots! The selfishness!" Joyce listened and clucked along before making it exceptionally clear that she did not wish her visits *or* intentions passed on to the Trotter patriarch; she would tell him in time. She assumed Ms. Campbell gossiped with employees, so took it upon herself to reiterate as much to the character we know as Sling Blade, who was surprised and impressed that she and the old man were related. For his part, he couldn't help wondering if Joyce would soon put him to work. The possibility caused him some anxiety, what with Dot being not at all shy about expressing her dissatisfaction with his growing absenteeism. The clan had him moving around so much— as occasional night watchman at various properties, for which he was on the Quincunx payroll, and sometime Mauck chauffeur, where- upon the old man tipped him lavishly—that under his breath he called them not Trotters but Gallops. He was not without his own brand of humor.

But have we gone off-trail? Then let us speed the pace.

The billionaire has been steadily adding to his ghost portfolio of empty tenements, and it bothered his wife not a little. Outlaid moneys were not the issue; such a burden Dodd Trotter could easily bear. It wasn't the cost of the forays that disturbed her but the compulsive be- havior surrounding them.

As private wealth increases, cities and states struggle for revenue. Structures once deemed historic are sold off; that is how Dodd came to own the oldest government building in Newark, the Essex County Jail (put up in 1837, it was made by the designer of the Tombs). Mr. Trotter also traveled to Poughkeepsie, Dutchess County, New York, to purchase the four-hundred-acre High Victorian Italianate Hudson River State Hospital for the Insane. He is now landlord of the crenellated asylum on the hill in Binghamton, with its trefoil-embossed stair treads and floors embedded with glass blocks; he has bought a somber, elegant bluestone palace with fifty-foot Doric columns, once the Utica State Hospital for the Mentally Ill. He acquired the Traverse City asylum (1885), too, in Michigan, another turreted affair high on the preservationist list.

Dodd Trotter leaves Detroit. From the 40,000-foot-high cocoon of his bed, he daydreams of Beverly Vista School's vast tarry playground and early-morning fog, where boys floated toward him from the mist like foretellers of doom and misfortune—wrong answers in a novelty eight ball. It strikes him as ironic that he's helping Marcie Millard and her committee refurbish the edifice, the only vacant building he has ever actually restored.

He notices a blinking light on the console. A steward peeks in and, seeing he's resting, discreetly begins to exit. The fitful sleeper inquiringly raises his head. It's your mother, says the steward, and Dodd picks up.

She is calling with today's deaths.

⁓

We've almost come full circle.

Bluey too is in bed, happy to have reached her son, imperfect as the satellite connection may be. There's a little Cessna crash in the local *Times*—a CEO and his three children—because Dodd is airborne, the item is bypassed in favor of the New York paper's listing of a one-hundred-year-old "socialite-turned-big-game-hunter and prisoner of war"; then, a famous singer Bluey never heard of, dead at forty from "total organ failure." She thinks it suspect; sounds like AIDS.

Winter sullenly pastes notices into the suede memory album. Since Pullman's birthday gala, the Icelander has been somewhat "off," so grumpy that Bluey calls her "the Winter of my discontent"—which only exacerbates her mood.

After lunch, they walk to the maze and Bluey sits on the granite bench at its entrance. (Trinnie likes that spot, too.) There, she decides to tell the helpmeet she's going to leave her something in the will. Winter scowls, but the old woman with will-o'-the-wisp hair and translucent bluish temples persists, calm and imperious enough so the younger must listen. She is going to leave her a condo, she says. It is already paid for. Winter gasps as the words sink in—and cries, because no one ever gave her anything, ever, not even the Trotters, not in the thirty-five years she has served them.

Bluey turns to stare down a wall of boxwood leading to the maze's center. She remembers reading how slaughterhouses were designed with curves so the animals couldn't see where they were heading. Panicking, she lifts her head to the sky and searches for the plane. "Dodd? Dodd? Doddie!"

Chastened, Winter walks her to the house.

⁓

Her daughter, at an AA meeting in an old wooden church on Ohio Avenue.

A homely woman stands to say she turned everything over to God and that meant "antidepressants and nicotine patches, too"—a tacit indictment of the weak hypocrites in the room who cannot do without. She says she isn't going to celebrate her AA birthday this year (Trinnie thinks: *as if anyone cares*) because her home group "forces women to put on dresses" to accept their sobriety cakes. She says she won't put on a dress for anyone.

You dyke, thought Trinnie. *You're not going to make it. You're going to die.*

She dreamed of Marcus Weiner and spent her days in the vast archives of the Withdrawing Room. Her father thought she was researching the wandering garden, but it wasn't so; she was busy unearthing blueprints and photos of the Bel-Air Colonne Détruite. Soon after her husband disappeared, Trinnie ordered that an inventory be taken of the marital house—all objects and their placement in each room painstakingly measured and documented. Everything—furnishings, clothes, books, utensils—was subsequently placed in storage.

Now, like a necromancer, she pores over the fastidious records, looking for signs of life.

CHAPTER 21

The Secret Agent

"Thanks for looking at the script," said Ralph. "But I'm on to something else now."

Tull was actually disappointed. He had found the copy of *How to Marry a Billionaire*, A Screenplay by Ralph Mirdling, Third Draft, Second Polish, A Method to His Sadness Productions, Registered at Writers Guild West—all 154 pages of it—gathering dust in the nook of his room, where the boy had abandoned it some months before.

ANGELA
(SELF-RIGHTEOUS)
YOU'RE AN UNTREATED SEXAHOLIC!

SEBASTIAN
(HEATED, WILD-EYED)
AND YOU'RE A NEW AGE PREDATOR!

It wasn't too bad a read after all. A breezy comedy involving a Beverly Hills limo driver and runaway socialite, it aspired to Lubitsch but had more the Mirdling touch.

Ralph was in the kitchen, noshing as usual. His hair shorn military-style, he looked stylishly commanding—part of a new regimen. As if taking a cue from Trinnie, he had cleaned up his act. In his shabbily chic navy-blue Costume National he looked like a survivor of Appomattox who with steady rest and diet might soon be attending the officers' ball. Today, Tull found him reassuringly unneurotic.

Pullman snored, insensate, blocking Ralph's access to the Sub-Zero. He was sleeping more than usual; his master had been meaning to take him to the vet.

"You know what they say about Danes, don't you?" asked Ralph rhetorically, gently pressing the spotted rump with the soft point of a demi-boot.

"Go ahead, Ralph. Tell me. Get it off your chest."

"Two years a young dog, two years a good dog and two years an old dog. The rest is a gift."

Pullman raised his head and derogatorily chuffed before pressing his muzzle to the humming grille of the restaurant-size freezer.

"Whatever," said Tull.

"It's plain unfair," he went on. "If you're a man, you're going to die in your seventies. *Maybe.* And if you're fucking koi, you can push the en-velope at two hundred—two fucking *centuries*, Tull, swimming about in a scummy little pond! And they love it!"

"I thought your script was really funny."

"You're a dear boy, but it's awful."

"It isn't, Rafe," he said, giving the name its rightful pronunciation. "I wouldn't shit you. I even have notes."

"Oh, by the way, it's Ralph—with an l."

"Ralph?"

"That's what I call myself now. Ralph: simple and American as they come."

"You're kidding. When did *that* happen?"

"What difference does it make?"

"But what about . . . Mirdling's Name Theorem?"

"It went the way of all flesh—don't let's dwell on it."

Tull hoisted himself onto the stainless-steel counter. "I did think the script was funny."

"It's worthless—I'll seal it in an envelope and pull it out in ten years. Have a good laugh. Actually, though, it did serve its purpose."

"What do you mean?"

"Guess I had to get something like that out of my system. Took long enough! Hey, you know who I showed it to?"

"Who?"

"Ron Bass."

"Whoa!"

"Nope. He actually read it—gave it a nice read, too. We've become pretty good friends. He's all right. I'm still not crazy about his work, but . . . you know, Ron's the one who turned me around. Gave me a whole new 'P.O.V.' Your mom and I had dinner with him, at 5 Dudley: *great* French onion soup. We met him at that sick-animal thing, you know. Very charming, *tons* of energy. And he *does* care about 'the work.' That's saying a lot."

"You showed Ron Bass your script?" he said, still disbelieving.

Ralph nodded eagerly, tucking into a king-size wedge of four-day-old mud cake. "He said I had no business writing that sort of thing, it was more like something *he* would write, but *he* would have written it *better*. I'm telling you, Tull, he's a very funny guy! 'Mirdling,' he said—that's what he calls me—'Mirdling, if you're going to do something third-rate, then for Chrissake at least do something true to yourself.' "

"I'm amazed. Next thing you know, you'll be buddying up to Robert Towne."

With that, he showed a flash of the old *Rafe*. "Oh Christ! I read yet *another* Mr. Chinatowne piece today. The Master was going on about his movie again—it's an absolute *mania*, the man can't stop! A 'classy' little essay in *Architectural Digest* . . . on and on he went about his 'nocturnal ramblings' on Western and Vermont, with the *Santa Anas* and the *water company* and all the intense bullshit–Raymond Chandler *channeling* . . . ugh! And how he took himself to a little bungalow in Catalina to hammer out that legendary first draft—oh Christ, I just want to vomit down his throat! And what about William Goldman? That vain, pontificating ass! He's worse than ol' Chinatowne! Oh *please* get cancer, Mr G., oh won't you please? With his 'nobody knows anything' . . . well, *I* know something: someone should run them both *over*—"

"So you're just going to . . . throw the script away?"

"I might do a number on it—put up some scaffolding and give it a po-mo makeover. Something closer to Charlie Kaufman. Spike and Charlie are the New Wave Wilder and Diamond. Let's hope Spike isn't as nasty as Billie, though—what a fucking monster *he* was. But *smart*. Managed to get his furry old dick pretty far up Cameron Crowe's ass, huh. I *do* think someone should teach him how to dress, though. I mean, Spike. You'd think *Sofia* would—or maybe your mother! By the way, how are you two getting along?"

"Okay."

Tull was about to do a little cathecting, but Ralph spoke first.

"I think I've entered a *very* fecund moment," he said. "I'm walking around with a *thousand* ideas. I'm telling you, man, I can't stop the flow! I'm gonna direct something on DV any minute now, I can *feel* it. How do you like this: there's a guy from Iran who's been trapped at the airport in France for ten years because of some bureaucratic snafu. True story. A *fantastic* subject, very Herzog, as in Werner—or maybe it's very Tati. Or maybe Lynch, but the *Straight Story* Lynch. Make a *fantastic* film. Then I was reading in *The Enquirer* about a travel agent *who helps people disappear*. Tells you how to fake your death, open a Swiss account—all totally legal! That could be *very* Japanese."

"How could it be legal to fake your death?"

"It is if you don't rip anyone off. Then there's this *ensemble* piece I'm thinking of, about a bunch of despots—you know, from imaginary countries—living on a wealthy street in London. They're all neighbors, kind of an outcast's *Notting Hill*. So-called kings who looted their treasuries and tortured people. Idi Amin and Papa Doc types. That could be for HBO. I'd love to create a *Sopranos,* but the dictator thing might be too harsh." Pullman hobbled out of the room in disgust. "Oh! And I want to do a comedy about a girl who's a 'G.T.A.'—know what that stands for? Genital Teaching Associate. That's a model who teaches pelvic-exam techniques to med students. I'm serious, Tull, that job actually *exists*! Ya gotta learn *some*where, baby, I am *telling* you—it's like I've been freed: my mind's *completely* opened up. When I look at those 'Rafe' scripts I wrote, it's like holding third-rate artifacts from another time. And I owe it all to Ron Bass!"

*L*et us pick up from where we left Katrina.

She is wearing a sixties Lanvin python jacket and Miguel Adrover chain-mesh halter top; setting off seriously green eyes is a multicolored pearl necklace bought at Piranesi, in Aspen, a few years back, for a quarter-million. She sets aside her Colonne excavations, nostalgically distracted by her father's collection of photographs.

The familiar images erupt, shuffled out of sync, a mess of time: Bluey, in '51, at Count Carlos (Charles) de Beistegui's costume ball at the Palais Labia on the Grand Canal, the Venetian summer before she met Louis. Cecil Beaton took the picture: her friend Daisy Fellowes came as

Marie-Antoinette, and Bluey went as lady-in-waiting, dressed like a milkmaid—they stood with the count, sweetly absurd in his sausage-curl wig. A half-dozen years later: Bluey standing with her dapper, slightly intimidated husband in the downstairs gallery of Peggy Guggenheim's astonishing palazzo among the astonishing Pollocks. Her mother first met Merce Cunningham there—and André Breton, who Trinnie later learned had been obsessed with "the Broken Column" himself, camping with the Surrealists at the Désert de Retz. A snapshot of her father in Guam, 1945; another of Louis pointing to the pig tattoo on a sailor's foot (he told her the popular mariner's notion that, like David Copperfield's caul, the mark could prevent one from drowning); again Louis, on the terrace of a Fifth Avenue penthouse showing off his Bronze Star; at the Paley wedding; then both parents, years later, with the Paleys and Cushing sisters at Round Hill. Summertime clambakes in Nantucket; messing around at Bouldereign (Carefree, Arizona); Jamaica and New Orleans; with Valentino and the Buckleys in Gstaad, and Carol Burnett at Snowmass; grinning madly at the Malaparte cliffhouse in Capri; with Jackie Gleason and Oona O'Neil at Villa Nirvana, Las Brisas . . . Palm Springs with the Nixons and Annenbergs; a hoedown at the deMenils'; Bluey in someplace like Laguna with a handsome man Trinnie had always suspected to be a lover; Louis and Bluey at their own wedding in Palm Beach. Then—standing on the pontoons of a seaplane on the lake outside their Adirondacks Great Camp, arms raised in a toast; Louis in his duds on digging machines in front of various yawning, mile-wide quarry pits; Louis during somber late-life travels to far-flung graveyards. Then came the kids: blurry black-and-whites of Dodd and Katrina behind nursery glass, haunting, smudgy little faces, swollen post-natal eyes and bundled bodies held aloft by smily-eyed, half-masked attendants for all the world to see.

Beverly Hills. The kids with new Schwinns. The kids at Point Dume. The kids in water-hose sword fights with Liz Taylor's sons in the driveway of the house on Roxbury, overlooked by a scowling, very much younger Winter. The kids in the back of the Corniche at Dolores's Drive-in, hamburgers already transferred to mahogany seat trays. Dodd, age thirteen, at the Beverly Vista graduation, standing in front of the orange-brick wall of the inner court like a prisoner about to be executed. A photo of the ten-year-old Tull riding Pullman had snuck in . . .

She stole another look at Bluey in Venice and thought, Her life has been full. Still, it distressed her to already be eulogizing.

Her eyes grew tired. She felt a hard frame beneath the remaining fan of images and pulled it out—a quote from the embattled founder of the William Morris Agency, clipped from a 1909 *Variety*. Marcus used to keep it on his desk at work.

> I will be William Morris forever. And if I must lose
> the business I have cherished, so be it. I would rather
> be William Morris and have my home and three meals
> a day and leave my name to my son—

Stuck to its underside for no rhyme or reason was the Kodak she had taken (her heart skipped a beat) of the benighted Désert de Retz on the day of their long-ago trespass. A chill came over her—she hadn't seen a photo of her Marcus in so long. He stood in the foreground of the meadowy depression, the cracked alabaster skin of the castle rising from his shoulders to crown him.

Finally, Trinnie saw the thing for what it was: the megalithic woman he'd left her for. She'd never had a chance.

She heard something and looked up—it was her son. He walked toward her through the vestibule of the great room, small steps over a floor made of 57,000 hand-carved pieces of mahogany, ebony and tulipwood, past draperies tied with leg-of-mutton passementerie, circumnavigating his grandfather's cemetery of beloved architectural models, slowing regally as he reached a grove of Chinese porcelain birds on giltwood brackets, and Fragonards resting upon a Pluvinet canapé covered in horsehair. His mother had by then tucked away the portfolio and greeted him with a smile.

He thought her ostentatiously dressed, and that concerned him; it usually presaged a leave-taking or breakdown. "What are you doing?"

"Some research."

"For the hospital garden?"

"Yes."

"How's it going?"

"Well."

"How's Bluey?"

"Not so well."

"How are you?"

"Couldn't be better."

"Can I talk?"

"Yes, you can talk!"

"It's about my father. I found out a few things."

"Such as?"

"That he was an agent. And that he worked at William Morris."

"You talked to your grandfather . . ."

"No. I just—I found out myself."

"I could have told you that. It wasn't a big secret."

"*Everything's* a secret," he reprimanded. "Anyhow, I wouldn't have asked."

"Why not?"

He lowered his eyes, wanting respect conferred upon his discretions. "But I *do* want to ask some things now."

"Ask away."

"Who was he an agent for? Actors?"

"Actors, directors, writers. He had them all."

"How did you meet him?"

"A party. At the home of a man named Ed Limato." She smiled; it had been years since she'd said that name. "Everyone went to those parties—they were great fun. I wanted to be an actress, or thought I did. For about a week."

"He was *your* agent?"

"No."

"If I mention something, will you not ask me how I found out?" She nodded. "Because I gave certain people my word." She nodded. "Do you—do you know anything about him—about Marcus—stealing a book?"

"Yes." Then: "They never brought charges."

"Because the store was reimbursed by the detective."

"You're good. You are *very* good."

She lit an American Spirit, inhaling the smoke like a native.

"I thought you stopped."

"They're organic."

"I don't *think* so."

"Whatever." She paused. "He was seeing a psychiatrist—mine, on

Bedford. Same building where Daniel Ellsberg saw *his* shrink. But you wouldn't know about Ellsberg."

"Why did he take the book?"

"He was having some . . . problems. You know, it wasn't like sticking up Van Cleef and Arpels. It was a difficult time for your father, that's all."

"Was he using drugs?"

"For what," she said, somewhat defensively.

He wavered. "Just . . . to take them."

"No."

"*You* use them."

"I'm not doing that anymore. And your father wasn't a druggie, OK? He never even smoked pot."

All the frankness made something between them relax. He saw how beautiful she was and felt his love anew. "Was I adopted?"

"Were you—*no*. Emphatically not."

"Did Father finish high school?"

"Of course he finished high school. With honors. Marcus was brilliant. He went to Oxford on a grant."

"Where's that?"

"England! Christ, Tull, you should *know* that."

"Sorry."

"That's appalling, Tull." She sucked on a Spirit, taking a deep, incredulous draft. "When he came back, he was . . . a little at sea. A friend of his worked at the agency."

"At William Morris?"

She nodded, punching out her cigarette. "Your father's friend helped get him a job in the mail room and within a few years he was a full-fledged agent. He loved the business, but I think what he really wanted was to be a writer. Marcus was a very creative man—hilarious. A great mimic. He was famous for his revue sketches at the Morris retreats." She stopped to scrutinize her son. "Why did you ask if you were adopted?"

Tull shrugged, suddenly exhausted. "I don't know."

"Because he was. Your father was."

The boy enlivened. "Who were his parents?"

"His real parents? He was never able to find out."

"Was he in an orphanage?"

"I already told you, he was adopted."

"But you have to be in an orphanage first, don't you?"

"I suppose. He never discussed it."

"Then where did he live—I mean, grow up?"

"Redlands. That's where he was raised. Lovely people."

"Have you seen them? His foster parents? I mean since."

"No."

"Was he crazy?"

She consulted the Spirit, and lit up afresh. Then: "Something happened when he was at Oxford . . . when he was a student."

"Like what?"

"He didn't talk about it much. All I knew was that he put himself in the hospital—from the pressure of exams." Pullman yawned, stretching in the doorway like a guardian-statue come alive. "And something happened in France, too, the first time we saw the tower."

She retrieved the snapshot taken at the Désert de Retz and handed it to a goggle-eyed Tull. There, short-bearded and charismatic, with open brow and fearful eyes, stood his washed-up father in front of the ruin, which itself looked beached in the bowl of a lea. He'd never seen the man before, and stifled a surge of tears that seemed to rush up from the earth like an electrical charge.

"Keep it if you like."

"*What* happened in France?"

"When we left that place, your father insisted on walking. He wouldn't get in the car. So I drove while he strolled—all the way to Versailles. It was awful. I followed alongside the way they do in those bike marathons. I had to make sure he didn't hurt himself . . . but *I* was the one who almost almost got killed. He wouldn't even *talk* to me. I checked into a little hotel—this was in Versailles—and after cajoling him like hell, he finally came in and lay down on the floor. We were in that room for days; I'm *still* shocked no one called the police. I don't think either of us slept. Anyway, Bluey knew a doctor in Paris—Bluey knew a *lot* of doctors in Paris—how we got him there I'll never remember. They finally put him under. For a whole week I kept bedside vigil at the Plaza Athénée; I just didn't want him in the hospital, which was probably a mistake. When we got Marcus to the States, we put him in a private place in Westwood on Bundy. It's not there anymore; I think it fell apart in the earthquake." She stared at her lap, wondering if she had already said too much—or if that was even possible. "They gave him shock treatment and that seemed to help. The quality of life got better anyhow.

It couldn't have been much worse! He started being his old self again. Your father and I had a lot of fun together," she said wistfully. "He and your grandpa got very close. They hardly said a word, but they loved each other—the way Louis and Pullman are when they're together. Ha! Just like Grandpa and Pullie! After a month or so, Marcus went back to work and just *flourished*. Lots of important clients: Diane Keaton, Meryl Streep. Then it started all over again, the mania, sleeplessness—the walking. Walk walk walk walk walk. Oh God, I think once he walked to Montecito. It culminated in . . ." She sighed, looking off into space. "It went on like that—relapse and recovery, relapse and recovery— and when we got married . . . you know, we didn't know anything about your grandfather's gift—it was a *very* well kept secret. We saw La Colonne for the first time on the day of our wedding, like everyone else. I can't tell you the look in your father's eyes when we emerged from the allée and saw it perched up there on the hill, waiting—for him. He shook all over, then tried to get his bearings . . . like he was having shock treatment again! Then came a look of . . . acquiescence. Tull, it was so scary to see—*the mountain had come to Mohammed.* This inescapable *thing* that in France so unhinged him had somehow taken flight across the Atlantic and set up residence, like a dream. Bizarre! Your grandfather couldn't have had any idea . . . because Marcus and I had spoken so *glowingly* of the place—it truly *was* magical, and Grandpa Lou was so taken with it, by our enthusiasm. You know how he can be. But he—your grandfather—was merely the instrument . . . I remember watching Marcus standing there smiling to himself as if—as if he finally *understood*, as if he had some *final understanding* that he was trapped, in a web—a spiderweb—I *saw* the shadow of the tower cross his face like some fairy-tale dungeon. It had come for him!"

She trembled, and Tull moved closer to take her arm. She stubbed out her cigarette, took a deep breath, and composed herself. "That must have been his thinking, anyway."

"And he left the next day?"

She nodded. "I was still sleeping."

"And that's why you took the drugs?"

She looked pale and flustered. He could see her capillaries and the fine down of her cheeks; could hear the blood beating through her veins.

"What do you mean?"

"That's why you took the drugs? Because he left you?"

She was duty-bound to answer everything now.

"I was just so . . . astonished. I thought we could—get through *any-thing.* We'd already been through so much in so short a time. But never to see him again? That he would just walk away? I hadn't considered the possibility. It wasn't an option."

A delicate hand rose to blot the tears. Tull wrapped his arms around her, imagining his mother's hot breath like a frightened calf's. Then he said all he could think to say that was true: "But he loved you."

The words hung in the air, an indisputable paradox, sad and just, with no corollary or conclusion. The Withdrawing Room fell silent save for the sound of her weeping. Pullman loped over, lowering himself at their feet—and that simple act unleashed in her a round of sobs, wails and clenches that inured Tull to manhood before he even knew what had taken place.

*N*ot all that far from the house on Saint-Cloud, on Santa Monica Boulevard's verdant north side, walked a bearded giant all in tweed. His gait slowed while he thought of his mentor John Ruskin's descent to madness—the great beacon of his generation and author of *The Stones of Venice* hallucinating in Derbyshire, foaming at the mouth in Brantwood, mute and occluded on the Kent Sands—and while he feared the same, he was willful enough to determine that would not be his fate. He must take care, if only for the girl's sake. His stride was festive and leisurely now, as one who arrives at a pleasure faire, though the ocean was really his destination. Perhaps he wasn't as vigilant as he should have been, having surmised the police would not look for him this far west.

In Beverly Hills, he paused at a "pocket park" on South Reeves to catch his breath. Other homeless were there, roosting with the requisite shopping carts and rags. He thought it made him less noticeable.

After the unfortunate summit with the baker and his wife, Will'm had returned to Angelino Heights beside himself with rage. He tore at his beard and battered his head against fragile walls like a wounded rhinoceros. He bellowed in the garden. He fell to his knees and beseeched the skies: "O darlin', darlin' girl, what have I done! What have I done!" It would not have been a good thing for a mortal to meet him during those imprecations, but there came Fitz to run his hand through Will'm's hair, with unexpectedly palliative effect.

"You've got to leave," said the pasty caseworker. Today, there seemed to be no blood in him. "The flatfoot was asking for you—look out. He *will* find you. Knew me by name he did, me, your 'running partner'— knew more about me than I know myself! So, look out, that's a *wily* man. I'd go north, Will'm—Bay Area. Big population. Cut the hair, trim the beard . . . get yourself a new set of clothes. Lay low awhile, then settle down in San Rafael or Sebastopol. I hear there's a vagrants' camp in Occidental—"

Will'm unhappily agreed, and they sat to a makeshift meal, consumed in silence.

Then he retired and plunged into sleep. A carousel of grueling, tenebrous images swam before his rhino eye, a virtual *News from Nowhere* newsreel: the Pre-Raphaelite orphan girl with nail-bitten hand resting upon a shit-stained illuminated manuscript. He heard his voice in the dream, but without English accent—the woman calling to him was not, for once, his Janey. He stood in a meadow. A man on a tractor rolled toward him, raffish cigarette stuck on lower lip. The tractor-man opened his mouth and spoke in Frankish tongue: "Monsieur," he said, "would you be so kind to consider the appointment of Chairman of the Disembodied?"

He awakened feverish. The cracks of the garage hemorrhaged cold, blinding light. Fitz was gone—nor did his faithful partner lay on the familiar bed of onerous glad rags. Will'm gathered his carpetbag and strode to the courtyard to tell his friend good-bye. No sign of him. The house was peaceful as a grave. Into the drawing room he went, calling the name of his benefactor.

The body was in the parlor, one shoe on, one shoe off, a note pinned to the grimy seersucker lapel. He stooped prayerfully to read.

Will'm—

I'm sorry we parted in such a way but you slept so soundly (I know how upset you were about the girl) I didn't have the heart to wake you for goodbyes. I didn't have the heart to tell you over dinner about Half-Dead either. I found him in the river, and know who

is the culprit; he will surely get his due but not by my hand. I have
run out of time. I buried our fighting friend at the old encampment.
There never was nor ever will be a braver, nobler soul. My "better"
Half was the best of dogs and I gave him *my* best, too—and *that,*
you will always have from me: my best. Take my advice, Will'm, and
leave this city. You are a gentle, special man and I would wish no
harm come your way . . . Half and I will welcome you, but not before your time has come. And Jesus, man! *destroy this note,* won't
you? It is incriminating.

Yours,
Geo. Fitzsimmons

A clump of excess rope lay on Fitz's shoulder like an improbable
epaulet. He tenderly pressed a knuckle to a cold cheek—the distended
eyes looked straight ahead and would not be closed. Will'm tore the note
into bits and stuffed an envelope, also addressed to him, into a pocket
without opening, then broke from the house.

He stood from the park bench and walked north on a street called
Charleville, past Beverly Drive. He *knew* this refined village—whence?
His feet, propelled by habit or instinct, marched him to a brick building
on a tree-strewn avenue called El Camino. He slowed, fixing an eye on
the sleek structure's entrance. There, he saw the symbol—XXX—and
read with astonishment the legend above the doors:

The William Morris Agency

He gathered his courage and went in.

CHAPTER 22

The Disorderly World

When Tull heard that Boulder had left her manager and was interviewing at various agencies, William Morris among them, he asked if he might tag along. He was, after all, writing a paper about the Industry; Four Winds had already bestowed curricular credits for his field trip to the teen star's downtown set. Lucy tried to glom on to the Morris outing, but Tull nixed it (three was a crowd). He put her on the investigative trail of the Redlands Weiners instead. Boulder was amused, mistakenly thinking the scion's intentions were romantic—she wasn't interested.

But maybe he *would* make a good boyfriend. Her mom said you could never sneeze at that much money. She said the Trotter family was "dynastic," so Boulder thought maybe they could just do the quirky dynastic thing—marry, then live apart. She'd keep the *hugest* loft in New York (like Claire Danes), and have Tull stay in a separate room whenever he came to town. Maybe not *so* separate; he *was* kind of cute . . . though she didn't see in him what Lucy saw—but oh my God! Claire Danes's loft! There was a photo spread in one of her mother's "shelter" rags, and it was amazing! The article said Ms. Danes stayed in the "SoHo aerie" when she wasn't busy attending Yale—that's where Jodie used to go, and Boulder was sure Jodie and Claire knew each other and that Jodie probably gave Claire *constant* shit about keeping up her grades and staying out of trouble . . . Boulder *so* wanted to live the bookish, ivied life during hiatuses from film. She had it all planned: during the week, she would sleep at the dorm, but Friday nights she'd take a train to her own private urban palace near the cool people like Christina (Ricci), Benicio and Drew. (She heard Benicio had the biggest cock, bigger even than Tobey Maguire's.) She'd live in SoHo or Chelsea, like Winona and Selma and Kirsten . . . she could probably marry Tull and get him to agree to let her even keep dating! Then she'd be a billionaire but still be able to sleep with Spanish boy-singers or anyone she pleased—and go out with famous older girlfriends to movie premieres while getting degrees in linguistics and art history and drama.

Tull's train of thought was less frivolous. As the Volvo sludged through traffic—it seemed like every street in the city was being torn up—Mrs. Langon's chitchat ran the gamut from his cousin's medical problems ("Poor boy! But to everything there is a reason") to Trinnie's Carcassone maze ("Katrina has *always* been a fascinating woman"). She even managed to rope in Dodd and Lucy. The woman loved having this boy in the car; it was like bagging Prince William.

Suddenly, they were at the redbrick citadel—for Tull, less an agency than a monument to a man long lost to the world.

He sat on the couch in a haze. Boulder was shiny and animated and called out "Hi!" to someone who whisked past. "Oh my God, that was Angelina!" The mom returned from reception and Boulder told her it was Angelina and the mom asked where and Boulder said she'd just gone out the door. A young woman appeared and invited them to "come up." Tull, now queasy and perspiring, said he'd wait. Mrs. Langon put her hand on his shoulder like a do-gooder nun with a dead man walking. "Are you OK?" she asked solicitously. He said he was fine; maybe coming down with a little something, that's all. Boulder, aloof and anxious to "go up," told her mom to just leave him alone. As they went to the elevator, Boulder asked the young woman if that in fact *was* Angelina and she said it absolutely could have been but that she would find out for certain after they "were up."

Sitting there about to vomit on the oversize Yamamoto jacket Trinnie bought him at Maxfield's, Tull felt silly and incongruous. He would wait for them outside—he needed air. He stood to get his bearings.

Idly, he took in the oil portraits by the elevators. He assumed they were agency founders, but there was no inscription. The men looked nothing like his father in the photo Trinnie had shown him.

Lost in thought, he felt his nose wrinkle. He smelled something dense, acrid and vinegary, woodsy, foul. He turned his head and saw him—a bear of a man staring straight ahead at a framed patriarch. His great jaw trembled, making the colossal beard jitter, too, and Tull thought of the nimble upside-down rabbi in Bluey's bedroom Chagall. He smiled at the boy, who for his part could not have moved a millimeter for any reason on earth. The stranger's eyes lit up with shaggy candor and kindness; a mellifluous accent pierced the decorum.

"No nameplates . . . most peculiar! Doesn't say *who* they are—now, why, son, d'you think that is?"

In short order, a guard in a blue blazer appeared behind Will'm and asked if he could be of help.

"You certainly may! Who are the gentlemen so depicted?"

"This is not a public space, sir—I have to ask you to leave."

"You don't *have* to, but you're thus compelled and so be it."

The unforgettable beast winked at the boy and was gone, with blazer shadowing after like bluish smoke.

Such encounters do indeed happen—they have before and will again. Improbable reunions occasionally find their way to newspapers or television tabloids, offering a freakish respite from "reality"; but what of the plethora of random moments, as in our own example of father and son in El Camino lobby, where interested parties are oblivious of what has transpired? Each of us has experienced the garden-variety oddity and omen—the myriad small coincidences that color our days and are usually dismissed out of hand. Yet we persist in believing such close encounters exist only in fiction—as if life itself were too orderly, too sober and practical for the improbable absurdities of mystery.[†]

By the time Topsy reached the Promenade, it was dusk. He sat by a steel prehistoric creature that spouted water into a basin. There were many of his kind there, those who lived in a roofless world, stoned and flustered, dazed by hardship and the elements, on falling-down wheelchairs and funky benches holding idiot-cards of crude implorement—

[†] Unlike their detractors, Tull and his father know nothing of fiction—they only know of the magic of this "fierce and beautiful" world. Ironically, it is the cynical reader *himself* who is threatened with fictionalization; yet such a bewitching seems unlikely, for, like characters in a threadbare novel, little has happened to these cynics, nor likely ever will. Thus may they go to their graves.

HUNGRY SICK PLEASE HELP—and there were buskers too, and drummers and dancers and pantomimists, and fat-cheeked infants, and children riding boards and silver scooters and many more who went arm in arm—whole families bejeweled and exuberant in canvas shorts and clogs, caftans and flip-flops—shameless sisters and wives, mothers half-naked in string-wear and smocks. No class was segregated and the entitled children knew no fear, nor did they disparage: perhaps *this* was earthly paradise—the alfresco community of man. The great guild's democracy touched him dearly.

He could smell the sea, but knew the beach would not be safe. Better to find the brush of a hidden highway shoulder. He was glad to be gone from downtown; it had held dominion too long. He was weak and let the crowd carry him like a river, his mind roiled by thoughts of Fitz . . . and Half Dead . . . and the lost girl . . . all paintings in a lobby now, untitled. There were new souls impinging his gallery. He could not make out any of the framed features but was determined to soon know their names.

Since her son's recent visit to the Withdrawing Room, something had begun to gnaw at her, for she too was undergoing an awakening.

She had always relied on the old man—on his practicality, good sense, fatherliness. But now his mawkish face hung before her like a vintage engraving, mocking. The slight overbite; the foppish collar; the gleam of asperity in conniving, loving eye—each conspired to say that something was quite wrong with this picture. She felt herself move downstage from gauzy darkness toward the footlights, as madwomen do in plays when their monologue has come.

She drove to the eco-industrial park in Azusa, a chain of buildings surrounding a five-hundred-acre quarry—an open pit 275 feet deep. It took more than an hour to get there; all the while his visage loomed outside her windshield like a hologram, baiting with its snarky, sharky kindnesses and muttonchopped sympathies. Mr. Trotter still came and went as she took the off-ramp and surface streets, asserting himself like a carnival barker. Trinnie thought she wouldn't be able to see the road for him.

The old man was getting his hair cut when she burst in. Having of course been told his daughter was at the gate, he eagerly commanded his minions to escort her to the office forthwith. At first, he was alarmed; he thought something might have happened—to Bluey, or the boy—then apprehension gave way to a hubris of delight at the thought of his dear Katrina wishing after all these years to pay a visit to the workplace.

He saw her twisted features, and was startled and bemused. "What is it?—"

"You found him, didn't you?"

He looked at her, dumb.

"You found Marcus!"

There was a kind of delirious gaiety to her now, as might befit a minor demon. He chuffed and sighed, glowering at the ground. Mr. Trotter palmed a hundred into the barber's hand like a card during a magic act, then removed the Art Deco ruby-studded dragonfly clasp that secured the cape around his neck; the cloth slipped off with slinky disconsolation.

"Yes," he said as everyone crept out.

Again he looked groundward, focusing almost petulantly on the thatched roofs of the huts of his own fallen hair.

"When?"

"Two years after he left you."

"Where—"

"New York."

"Where!" demanded the hell-raiser.

"Near Twig House."

She almost passed out. The old man was looking to brace her fall when a current of energy passed through her and she struck his face. He partially dodged the blow, then groaned, falling against the barber's chair. The daughter remained pitiless, retreating like a snake from its prey, waiting for the venom to take hold. He rubbed at chin and throat where he'd been hit.

"He was in jail, Katrina," he said, penitently.

The attack had at least dulled his natural impulse to ease her emotional pain. For a moment, the facts could speak for themselves, uncluttered by his heart.

"He was in jail for hurting a woman."

Trinnie silently wept. "Samson found him?"

"No—though nearly. He came very close. Was a week or so away from catching up, I'd say."

"Then how?"

"He . . . was living in the woods. He assaulted a woman—a prostitute—and they'd been hunting him. I received a call from the authorities, who were already well aware of my interest; Samson had alerted them of Marcus's flight from Los Angeles and the possibility, however remote it might be, of him showing his face. You know how much he loved the wilderness there. The sheriff knew where to look. He used to work summers at our place."

"Did you . . . see him? Did you see Marcus after he was found?"

"I went there with Samson." The old man actually poured himself a shot; one of the few times in his life he needed one. "He did not know us. What we found was—an unrecognizable man! Filthy, obese. Lice and . . . *feces* in matted hair." Each detail was like a blow to Trinnie's chest, but her father felt it vital to impart all.

"Did you ask him . . ." Her voice trailed off, unsure of its own question.

"He spoke nonsense, Katrina! In an English accent . . . and he was *violent.* He thought *we* were the police—but from another *time,* another *century.* At one point, he leapt up and tried to strangle Samson—"

"He fucking needed your help!" She collapsed on the floor, muttering, "You—you—"

"Katrina, please!"

"He was my husband!"

"He was *not*—husbands don't *do* what he did! Can't you remember what happened to you when he left? *Won't* you remember? Think about it, *please,* my darling Katrina! Remember the *agony.* The *hospitals*—the ambulances! What it *did* to your mother and me . . . what it *would* do to your son! You were just beginning to mend, Katrina! You were doing so well . . . putting it behind you. Healing yourself with your gardens—I was *not* going to be the one to drop that man down in your life again."

"That wasn't your decision!"

"It *was.* As a father, I—"

"Fuck you!"

She looked as if she might strike again, and he backed off. "He would do it again, don't you see, Katrina?"

"That was not for you to say!"

"He *would* do it! But the next time, he'd harm you. Physically."

"How do you know?" she spat, like a witch tied to a stake.

"I could *not* let that happen—"

"You don't know *anything*. He *loved* me!"

His heart nearly broke, because he saw once and for all, through that pitiable declaration, that Katrina would never—could never—be whole. "Yes, he did. Yes, he did. I believe that."

"You *believe*, in your *arrogance* . . ."

But she was too exhausted to go on. There was no energy left, not even for contempt.

"Those kind of people do *not* get better, Katrina. That is medical fact."

Trinnie stood up. He thought his daughter would leave, but instead she sat in the barber's chair, ready for the final cut.

"You said he hurt someone."

"He broke her arm. He picked her up on the road. She told the police that he said she was his wife—"

"His *wife*—" Pierced again.

"—and that he would punish her for sleeping with his best friend."

"Oh God."

"When she tried to leave the car, he struck her and she jumped out. She could have been killed, Katrina."

"What happened then?"

"He was sent to hospital. I made sure the bills were paid—it was a fine hospital, Katrina. He was there eight weeks with no improvement. I was going to move him to a more permanent place, but he escaped. We searched another year but were never able to find him."

"I'll go see his parents. Maybe the Weiners will—"

He knew where she was heading. "It's no use, Trinnie. There's been no sign. Don't you think I've been in touch with Harry and Ruth?"

"Don't I think?" she said poisonously. "Does it *matter* to the grand puppeteer what I think? Of *course* you've been in touch with the Weiners. You're all probably best of friends!"

"There was always the chance he would contact them. They understood that if he returned, I would help them—help keep him from harm's way."

"Keep him from *me*—"

"Yes! I would *not* have him coming for you! For you or my grandson . . ." He swigged another shot, then said, more calmly: "I see this fever of Toulouse's has been communicated to *you* . . . Katrina, it would be a miracle if he were alive."

"Yes it would," she said heavy-handedly. "Especially if you already killed him."

He took her comment with utter seriousness, pausing thoughtfully to demonstrate that such an act had not been entirely outside the realm of feasibility. He let the moment pass.

"Katrina," he said earnestly. "I have lost both sleep and years over this. I knew how much you loved him—how much it would have meant for you to see him again. And I love you more than life! I would not have been able to live with myself had I . . . had I done what to *you* was the 'right thing.' But I have suffered—"

"*You* have suffered!"

"Yes," he said, like a humble peasant. "And the boy should be able to find what he finds. But it's all over for me soon, don't you know, and I *will* not have regrets! I did what I thought was best for you, and would do it again."

A bony hand shakily went to the skin already purpling under his jaw.

"I would do it again!"

*J*oyce bathed her son while Dodd slept in the solarium. He was feeling the spacey effects of Neurontin, its dosage upped to 500 milligrams in the wake of a spate of recently acquired ruins—doctor's orders.

Tull told Grandpa Lou he wanted to stay at Olde CityWalk awhile. School was almost over, and it was convenient to be on Stradella cramming for finals with the cousins (nightly screenings at the Majestyk didn't hurt). Carcassone felt wrong of late; the scent of his mother's aromatherapy and perfumes filled him with dread—the scent of his mother herself. Truth be told, he was spooked. He sensed that Trinnie's latest visit was drawing to a close, and didn't want to be there when she pulled up stakes.

He went to the shrink twice a week, refusing to speak of mother *or* father. The therapist didn't seem to mind; he had all the time in the world, he said, and at $250 an hour, Tull was sure he was right. The boy did speak of Pullman, who had grown listless, and become chief repository of the analysand's worst fears. He dwelled morbidly on the topic of longevity and developed a penetrating anxiety that his noble consort, that Apollo of dogs, that "Continental Gentleman," was in fact on his last legs. (Because of the breed's short life-span, Trinnie had initially opposed the Dane's adoption, but Tull fell in love. Mother and son were at a children's party in Malibu when Greg Louganis, the famed Olympic diver, walked by with *three* at the reins. Thereafter, Epitacio chauffeured the eight-year-old boy to Mr. Louganis's hillside home almost daily; when a pup became available, he wouldn't take no for an answer.) While the therapist thought it a wonderful way to work through abandonment issues, Tull became terrified to the point of sleeplessness of losing his pet—repeated visits to the veterinarian uncovered none of the usual suspects that befell a Dane: no heartworm or Von Willebrand's or dysplasia of hips. As a preventive tool, a regimen of hedonism was prescribed—his large companion suffered Shiatsu massages three times a week. On Sundays, he took Pullman to a ranch in Carbon Canyon, where a hippie woman practiced "touch therapy"—small circular motions designed to release tension (the "form" Pullman liked most was called Clouded Leopard). The creature visited the chiropractor for adjustments; a crew in a van came to attach magnets and inject B-12 into acupuncture points along chi meridians. He was put on a diet of raw venison, bonemeal and flaxseed oil (when Lucy wasn't letting him cadge from her brother's strongbox of marzipan). Tull even brought him to a psychic, who while pronouncing him in the best of health still saw fit to prescribe Bach flower remedies and St.-John's-wort to her amenable client, and dispense Elavil samplets to "take the edge off an innate sense of sadness." Like another troubled Dane before him, the dog seemed too aware of his transitoriness on Earth—such fatal, neurotic knowledge, the psychic assured, was in the breed's collective bones. Major karmic cleansing was in order.

The two took afternoon naps beside the armillary sphere, a dog-eared copy of *When Elephants Weep: The Emotional Lives of Animals* splayed upon Tull's chest. It was thought that Pullman needed more exercise, so they hired Kali Guzman, the very same who took Diane Keaton's and Michael Ovitz's dogs on their morning runs. That was good, because Tull needed to find someone to work with the Dane in the summer while the Four Winds group was traveling. He didn't feel like going on the supersonic excursion but didn't really want to stay home, either—he wanted to get away from his mother; he wanted to get away from the ghost of his father; he wanted to get away. Still, Tull worried about leaving Pullman behind.

As he sank deeper into gloom, Lucy tried futilely to entertain by reading aloud selections from her book, but Tull was glacially indifferent to the apparent majesties of *The Mystery of the Blue Maze*. She drew solace in knowing Mr. Hookstratten had at least passed some of the pages on to a highfalutin editor in Manhattan.

After an hour of wheedling, the redhead got him to accompany her to the little hangar that had been built behind the Majestyk to house Edward's most recent diversion: a 747 simulator. You sat in front of banks of instruments while a computer initiated takeoffs and landings—the same one that pilots trained on. Lucy liked the way it projected constellations onto a "night sky"; but the best was when the computers made turbulence.

That afternoon, while fiber-optic stars bloomed outside the cockpit windshield, Lucy asked if he wanted to make out. Tull shrugged and she took that for a yes. She popped out her retainer, jumped onto his seat, and, straddling him, Frenched away. Tiny orange fuzz glowed on her upper lip as O'Hare or Heathrow or some such impossibly unnavigable complex receded into incandescent view on a virtual vector far below; he watched the vertiginous ten-thousand-light runway as they kissed. He liked the way her mouth smelled. When Tull focused on her, Lucy's lids were slammed shut in a CinemaScopic swoon. With sweaty hand she removed steamed eyeglasses—they folded up like a copper spider—without pausing in her business. Her neck, pale and faintly pulsing, looked ready for vampires. They'd been fooling around for six months now (though this was their inaugural flight) and the last few times her hand had drifted down, flopping onto his crotch with the occasional serious back-kneading of knuckles. His mind wandered during their rites and sometimes he even pretended to be with other girls, a fantasia that inevitably ended with Tull back in the Mauck kissing the homeless one called Amaryllis; in the cockpit, he would slowly open his eyes in a squint, trying to make his cousin look dark and leonine-haired. No such luck.

"Ho ho ho! Well what have we here?"

A damp-haired Edward, in chenille robe and silvery beaded hood, floated at the laddered entrance; toothy Eulogio (Epitacio's kid brother) held the boy up as if making an offer to Aztec gods. Lucy involuntarily jumped, knocking her head against the ceiling before fumbling for her spectacles.

"Oh my God, Eulogio! Look! It's incest!"

Eulogio grinned, clucking like a simpleton.

"It is *not* incest," Lucy remonstrated.

"Tell it to the court!"

Tull winced in embarrassment. "We were just . . . messing around," he said sheepishly.

"You better get *down*, Edward!" she said, sternly pulling rank; he *was* her younger brother. "Take him down, Eulogio! You'll be in *big* trouble if he falls!"

"Can't leave 'em alone for a minute!" said Edward.

There was a movie tonight at the Majestyk—*Journey to the Center of the Earth*. Eulogio carried the boy outside and set him in the buggy before going to turn on the popcorn machine. A gloating Edward waited patiently for his shamefaced cohorts, who, smoothing their skirts, soon joined him. They rode back to the cobblestone streets of Olde CityWalk.

"So," said Edward mischievously. "Ready for tomorrow?"

Tull was blank-faced.

The cousin turned to his sister. "Didn't you tell him?"

"Tell me what?"

"Do I *constantly* have to be the one to surprise you?"

"I talked to your dad's father," said Lucy.

Again, Tull was blank.

"Your *grandfather*," Edward enlightened.

"You're kidding."

"Well, you *wanted* me to find them, didn't you?" said Lucy.

"I—I guess . . ."

"You *guess*," said Edward. "Have you no concept of the amount of time and money that little maneuver of my sister's involved?"

"He's teasing, Tull. The Weiners are still in Redlands; they're listed. I got their number from 411."

"Where *is* Redlands?" asked Tull, trying to be flip.

"About an hour from here. But we don't *have* to visit," said Edward archly. "I mean, you don't really seem all that *excited*."

"No, it's cool. My father's probably been in touch with them. Then maybe we can put an end to all this."

"What*ever*," said Edward, rolling his eyes at Tull's unconvincing sangfroid. "Hey they're *your* grandparents, not mine."

"Not really. I mean, my father was adopted."

"You know, you really have an attitude problem," Edward said.

"You actually talked to them?" asked Tull of Lucy.

"Of course I talked to them. I *said* I did."

"Someone has to do the legwork," Edward said disparagingly.

"What did you tell them?" he asked Lucy.

His cousin answered instead, with campy hauteur. "That the Trotter *kinder* were descending en masse."

"Harry and Ruth Weiner!" said the braided detective, beaming. "How's *that* for Jewish?"

CHAPTER 23

To Redlands and Beyond

What's there, beyond? A thing unsearched and strange;
Not happier, but different.

— *Edward Robert Bulwer Lytton*

The arrival of the Mauck in the Riverside County suburb could not have made more of a stir than an *X-Files* alien ship. The pitch-black vehicle, abristle with various satellite dishes and antennae, was strange enough; its crew, subsequently disgorged onto the usually lonesome dead end, had a nearly traumatizing effect on neighborhood denizens, mostly children on Razors who, like tugboats, had accompanied the craft a number of blocks during its slow-speed arrival to dock.

First came the space-age spreading of the gull wings; then Epitacio exited the driver's side with impressive stoicism while his brother Eulogio, being less experienced, played to the crowd with not inconsiderable élan. The two met congenially at the MSV's rear.

The onlookers swelled to about fifteen now, including three or four adults, who, looking busily preoccupied as only adults can on a weekend, still deigned to make their way over. One of the bolder kids seemed about to make a general inquiry when he was arrested by two happenings—Harry Weiner appeared on the front porch and made a tentative albeit silent greeting to the Monasterio brothers; moments later, the hatchback rolled up with a great hydraulic whoosh to reveal the Mauck's outrageous innards.

A girl with long orange braids stood blinking at the inhabitants of this brave new world. Gambling there was oxygen in the atmosphere, Lucy decided the best thing was to step forward. From behind her came a boy of around twelve with freckly skin and hair the color of dark wine. She nervously took his arm, and he joined her in deploying the universal smile that said We Mean You No Harm. We Are Here to Learn.

Eulogio helped them down while his brother gamely supervised—first Lucy, then Tull.

And now, the real show began.

The wary mob took a great startled breath as the canopied buggy, with steady percussive bleat, began telescoping itself outward upon its iron ramp. After an étude of whirrings and pneumatic rushes of air, both ramp and cart had protruded as far as they ever would. The rubber-wheeled carriage, steered by our intrepid first cousin, lowered then suavely disconnected its own umbilicus, free of the mother ship.

It carved a cool arc over the asphalt, leaving gasps and other outbursts in its wake, for there was Edward at the wheel—or rather a small, misshapen, genderless figure in green satin mask and muumuu, its chin supported by what looked to be some sort of metal rod (like a science-fiction Jesus). The buggy drove into the street *away* from the house as if taking its leave, yet all were too astonished to follow with anything but their eyes.

By now Ruth Weiner appeared in the drive, having opened the gate that led to her backyard and covered garage. With unfailing timing, Edward, nearly a quarter of the way down the block, triumphantly returned—the cul-de-sac crowd parted for him while he waved a dashing "Hi, everyone!"—before noiselessly gliding onto the sidewalk, into the driveway and through the gate. A few younger ones nervously waved back, the way half-frightened children do at Mickey Mouse before he bounds over and sets them to tears. The neighborhood kids finally whooped it up, gleefully following his trail, yet politely stopping short of the Weiner border like Third World ragamuffins following a prince. (That would make Edward, to use a favorite expression of his aunt Trinnie's, most Fourth World indeed.) While Ruth held the gate, Epitacio, cracking a smile at last, strode through, followed by Tull, Lucy and Harry, the latter of whom was so pale that his lips were as white as his skin.

An explosion of three staccato barks caused heads to snap toward the Mauck. After a suitably dramatic moment, Pullman appeared at the rear and languidly stretched before standing, nearly tall as a man, his speckled head never more ham-size or handsomely commanding; Tull's flurry of coddling had done him well after all. Even the grown-ups scattered as he leapt from the thick Hokanson onto the street, glanced this way and that, then cantered to the driveway and through the entry, which Ruth Weiner finally fastened behind him. A jubilant crowd burst into applause, then made a beeline to the MSV, desperate to glimpse as much of the exotic orchid-filled high-tech interior as the beaming, gap-toothed Eulogio would allow.

Meanwhile, as awkward introductions were hastily made, the Trotters entered the quiet backyard and saw that a picnic table sat in readiness upon a stained-redwood deck under the shade of a tarp. The exciting details of their arrival—the built-in celebrity of Edward and his mastery, both stylish and technological, over physical misfortune—proved a beneficial distraction during what inevitably was a discomfitting moment. Tull thought Lucy wonderful in making the elderly couple feel at ease—so selfless and assured, and her efforts all for him. He felt a kind of ardor for her, shot through by pangs at how much he took her for granted; and vowed then and there he'd begin to appreciate this girl for all she was worth.

Yet watching the interplay afforded him time to step back and observe their hosts.

Summoning the ectoplasmic image of his mother's Kodak, he struggled to see his father in the bones of Mr. Weiner's physiognomy before reprimanding himself that Marcus was not of their blood. One side of the newfound grandfather's face sank down a bit as if today it had decided to sleep in. The eye was rheumy, and wept into a small yellowish crust at its corner; the same had formed like grains of dirty sand at the edges of mouth and nostril. He'd shaved as closely as he could for the event—that was touching to Tull—with some small patches on the droopy cheek bypassed or overlooked. The skin was waxen and lacked tension; the smile still bright, yet one had the sense it too would "sleep in" one day soon. Harry had dressed for the occasion in bow tie and insignia'd blazer, and this too moved young Tull. He shuffled his feet (shod in comfy old bedroom slippers) when he walked and had a faint odor to him, like brine doused in talc.

His wife, in flowery bonnet and sundress, was all loose ends. In contrast, her features were severe and controlled, more harshly "Jewish" than Harry's. Her graying hair was short as a terrier's, with nails impeccably groomed. Ruth Weiner looked like someone you wouldn't want to tangle with—a consumer-rights ombudswoman or Judge Judy type. But those looks belied; as Tull watched, she seemed more and more a woman who had unraveled.

She busied herself with small talk and place settings, barely glancing his way. He thought the call from Lucy must have been an amazing blow; under the circumstances, the lady was handling herself exceptionally well.

Epitacio lifted Edward from the buggy and sat him at table's end on a high-backed chair the old couple had thoughtfully provided—they had done their homework. Easing into it, the cousin declared the unexpected provisions to be happy ones. Hamburgers and pink lemonade were served by Ruth, who fluttered to and from the house forestalling Lucy's requests to help. Pullman was given a rather too large patty on a thick paper plate, which he dutifully ignored. When Ruth finally joined them, all fell silent, as if it were time for someone to say a few words of import or at least acknowledge this momentous event; instead, the woman stood up and began to quiver. After a stab or two at intelligibility, she hurried inside. Lucy swiveled on the bench wondering if she should follow, but Harry reassured that his wife would be fine.

So they ate awhile in silence, save the occasional honking (Eulogio allowed a few members of his appreciative audience to take liberties). Epitacio glowered in his reckless brother's direction before politely excusing himself from the table. Discussion resumed, touching on diverse topics—the especial enormity of Pullman's frame and the sage qualities of his breed; the preferred route from Bel-Air to Redlands proper and the odious state of traffic in general (a topic that naturally led to the Mauck and Edward's custom buggy)—finally settling on the cousin's costume, selected for today's occasion from a vast wardrobe handwoven by the boy himself.

When Lucy offered that he had been taught to sew by Tull's mother, Harry said, "Katrina? My goodness! How *is* she?"—reminding the children afresh of everyone's connection. But the query was somehow hollow, as was Tull's response (both came from too far a distance). Conversation trickled back to Edward and his affliction. Harry was given a cordial crash course on Apert Syndrome and related "orphans" of the craniofacial ilk. He wanted to know if the boy had had surgeries, and Edward said many, when he was younger; adenoids and tonsils removed and nasal passages enlarged to ease breathing; clubfoot, webbed toes and fingers more or less corrected; nose and cheekbones separated from skull, then reattached with metal plates, widening the space between, so new bone could fill the gap—this being accomplished by encasing the prodigy's head in a birdcage for a few months while expansion screws were slowly, torturously turned, "thus making me the person I am today. Hey—what was I expecting? The Spanish Inquisition?" Lucy and Tull laughed as always at the reference to the old Python bit, but Harry was oblivious.

Mr. Weiner asked if the kids all went to school together. Lucy chattily filled him in on Four Winds (and the upcoming summer field trip), while Tull looked anxiously toward the house. He left the table, slid open the screen door and went in. Lucy watched for a moment, then turned back to her host; she thought it a good thing that Tull and his grandmother had some time alone.

A ceiling fan turned in the cool, dark room, its Danish shelving system filled with tchotchkes. Menorahs acted as bookends to Yiddish-humor books, *New York Times* crossword-puzzle collections and the complete hardback works of Stephen King. A crocheted blanket lay across a La-Z-Boy with Harry's aluminum walker beside its pleather ottoman.

The woman who had raised his father sat upon a couch turning the pages of a photo album. Tull sat down next to her. She proffered the book as one might a Torah; delicately, he took it in hand. He stared at the picture of a boy in yarmulke and tallith.

"You look so much like him," Ruth said. She'd been crying. "Do they know you're here?"

"You mean—"

"Your mother. And grandfather."

"No. At least . . . I don't think so."

"We were so fond of her—your mother. Katrina. And Louis and Berenice." He'd never heard anyone call Bluey that before; it was all so formal and remote, the way people spoke in documentaries. "Those were happy, happy times. They met at a party, your mother and our Marcus. Did you ever hear that story? Did she ever tell you? From different walks of life but . . . que sera. God moves in mysterious ways. I thought there would be problems because of the money." She sighed and shrugged her shoulders. "Who knew? And who was I to tell them? They loved each other and that's all that mattered. I believe that to this day. It's a rare thing—if you find it, you have to hold on. When things started getting very serious between them, there were dinners. *Family* dinners. We ate! Your grandfather sent a car for us—all the way to Redlands. At first it was fun, but then we thought it too grand. With the neighbors ogling. So we drove ourselves. I'm not sure if Louis was offended, but I know that Berenice was not. I had more in common with your grandmother." She looked out toward the patio. "Harry hasn't been able to drive for over a year. I got a call from the DMV saying he'd failed his test. 'Come get your husband,' they said. That was humiliating for Harry." She sighed, then picked up the thread where she'd left it. "Your mother came from great money reserves, and your father—we owned a bakery. Two miles away. We made a nice living, but not like your grandfather! Or your uncle Dodd. That kind of money comes once in a blue moon. A lot of people who had it suddenly don't have it anymore; for a while it seemed like everyone was a billionaire! We lived modestly, but Marcus wanted for nothing. In fact, had more than most."

The screen slid open, and Mr. Weiner led Lucy in. Epitacio followed with the cousin in his arms. The old man pointed to the La-Z-Boy and Epitacio gently lowered Edward down, covering his legs with the blanket. Pullman entered and Lucy grabbed his collar to lead him out, but Ruth said it was fine for the dog to come in "as long as he didn't make a mess."

"We have wonderful photo albums," said Harry with a nod to his wife. "Wonderful memories."

Lucy's authorial heart soared—they were getting to the nitty-gritty. She resisted the urge to jot "bird notes" in the silver-edged Smythson pad (specially bought for the occasion, its covers lined in hot-pink silk); that would be tacky.

"Do you remember," said Ruth to her husband, "when we first met Edward and Lucy's parents?"

"At Trader Vic's."

"The Beverly Hilton."

"That was before Merv Griffin bought it."

"Oh goodness yes. He had a wonderful talk show—better than any of them."

"Mike Douglas had a good one."

"Merv had a marvelous singing voice."

"Mike Douglas sang, too."

"Not like Merv. Not like Merv . . . Things were *quite* serious between your mother and our Marcus by then. They had already announced their engagement."

"At the time we are speaking of," said Harry, convivially pointing at Lucy, "*you*, young lady, were a very *young* young lady!" He was starting to warm up.

"She was an *infant*—and Edward had not yet been born."

"Lucky me," came the voice from the La-Z-Boy.

"Different worlds, your father and mother," said Harry. "The Trotters were like the Cartwrights. Do you remember Ben Cartwright?" he asked of anyone who might respond. "Lorne Greene. A marvelous television show—*Bonanza*."

"Well of *course* they don't remember *Bonanza*," clucked Ruth. "They don't even show it on reruns."

Tull slowly turned the leaves of the album without really taking anything in; it was all too much.

"The wedding was so beautiful!" gushed Ruth. "And that peculiar *house* . . . we thought: why did he build them that peculiar house? When they could have had something so beautiful—anything. They could have had a ranch, a beach shack, a chalet . . . they could have had a little *bupka*. Could have had their *pick*. They saw it in France, remember, Harry? That was the story. Marcus was there all the time on business. They'd fly him out at the drop of a hat if it meant keeping one of their big clients."

"A very important agency. To this day."

"A weird, weird place. A kind of *ruin* they saw while they were over there. Well I guess Katrina showed pictures to her father—"

"Of *course* she showed him pictures," snapped Harry.

"—to your grandfather. Pictures she'd taken. And that's where he got the idea. Louis built it for them as a wedding gift. It cost a fortune!"

"Didn't he have it moved?" asked Harry. "Wasn't it moved from wherever it was?"

"No, it was *not*. Of course he didn't have it *moved*."

"I thought it had been moved, stone by stone."

"I believe it is a *French national monument*," she said, eyes beadily narrowing. "Louis Trotter has a lot of money, but not enough to buy a national monument!"

"I was sure of it."

"William Randolph Hearst he is not. You're thinking of San Simeon."

"Well that's what Hearst did, isn't it? Moved castles and churches from over there?"

Ruth hadn't the energy to continue sparring; she grabbed another album from a stack and passed it to her husband instead. He wobbily handed the tome to Lucy, who perched on the La-Z-Boy to share with her brother.

"The *time* it took to build! So painstaking. It was not the house *I* would have chosen, but . . . done with such taste, such love. Your grandfather always put your mother first, that I will say for the man. On their wedding day, he had horses and carriages and footmen—at night there was Renaissance music and torches and beautiful dancing. Was it Tony Bennett who came and sang, Harry?"

"Yes. Marvelous singer. To this day. Very active."

"It was stunning."

"A marvelous painter, too. Did you know? Tony Curtis also paints. The two painting Tonys. And Tony Quinn! He was a *marvelous* painter. Sinatra too—they all want to be painters. Isn't that funny?"

"And the *people* there—Meryl *Streep*, Goldie *Hawn*, Tom *Hanks*—"

"And this before anyone knew who he was. Tom Hanks was still struggling. But our Marcus helped him, believed in him."

"Well I don't know about that; I don't think any of those people 'struggled.' But everyone was there and everyone was *happy*—all the people your father had helped so much, all of the people who loved him. My God, I was just bowled over. To see the *impression* your father had made on these famous, famous people, who would have done *anything* for him—" She stifled a tear, putting handkerchief to mouth. "And when the . . . when the terrible thing happened—the 'disappearance'—I call it the 'disappearance'—"

"She still calls it that. To this day."

"—because what else *can* you say? Well, everyone was stunned, to put it mildly. No one even *knew* about it for the longest time. They all thought it was a long honeymoon! Louis hardly told *us*, the news was *very* late in coming. We were certain—Harry and I—that someone had hurt our boy. How else to explain? Because if he'd had second thoughts—"

"—which was not the case—"

"—but if he *had*, Marcus was certainly not the type to run away!

That wasn't his style. He had troubles in his life, but was so very *happy*—with Katrina. And in his work. In his *life*."

Tull cleared his throat. "My mother said something happened to him in England. When he was in college."

Edward and Lucy glowered at their cousin sideways; he'd been holding out on them.

"He was studying so hard," said Ruth. "So brilliant! History and literature."

"He liked to walk. A very powerful man. Powerful legs. Always liked to walk. Cleared his head."

"He didn't like to walk *that* much."

"Yes he did. Yes he did, Ruth, don't deny it. He went for a walk to Avebury."

"Harry, *please*—"

"Do you know Avebury?" he asked of the children.

"The monoliths," came the veiled voice from the La-Z-Boy.

"That's right. He walked there and *all* around. That's where the druids were—don't know how he got his fascination. Walked and walked, said it was because he couldn't sleep."

"It *was* because he couldn't sleep!" said Ruth defensively. "He was *worn-out*, that's all, from the studying. He was a scholar!"

"They put him in the hospital. Didn't tell us about it, not for a long time."

"It wasn't such a big thing, you always make it into a big thing! *Lots* of students study too hard and—"

"It *was* something, Ruth. It was *more* than 'worn-out.' There were other things, when he was younger." She winced, knowing he couldn't be stopped. "He put aluminum foil in the windows to prevent voices from coming in. That's what he said—'voices' were coming in. Sometimes they were friendly, sometimes not so friendly. Foil, all around the bedroom." He scratched his nose with trembling deliberation. "He *was* a brilliant boy. Always did wonderfully in school."

"He had an *imagination*, Harry, that's all. Why do you make such a thing?" She turned to Edward. "*You're* a brilliant boy," she implored. "You *know* how hard that can be . . ."

"Yes," said the cousin, at a loss.

"We adopted him," said Harry. "But I'm sure you already know that.

And I got damn mad—later on. Because that first time he went a little 'off' I made some . . . inquiries. Because he'd struck his mother, and that was not like him."

"Harry! He did not *strike* me—"

"Whatever he did left a bruise, and I didn't like it. Not one bit. So I talked to the adoption people, and well, you know, they sang a different song. Because it's a business, and I understand that. I'm a businessman. But these are people's lives, and it isn't right."

"They told us his mother was a student," said Ruth, resigned. "A high-strung woman having problems during the time of her college examinations. Just like our Marcus! They said they didn't know who the father was; they never do. Anyway, that's what we were told."

"Well, that was a lie," said her husband. "Because by the time I asked, see, the law had changed. They had to tell me things, they were *legally bound.* Had to turn over files. And the files told a different story. Said that his mother was a 'working girl'—"

"Harry, we don't know that's true!"

"No, but that is what is suspected, Ruth! Now, these children came a long way to hear our story and they might as well get it!" He scratched his nose and proceeded. "There's all kinds of lawsuits against that place now; Ruth and I didn't want to join the bandwagon. That's not for us. But it's a tragedy what happened in this country. Not that any of it would have made a damn difference to Ruth and me. Because we believe you do things out of *love*—you take a babe into your life not as an investment but because you have love in your heart. And you nurture that child and hope your love will carry you through. Carry the day. That is all you can hope for, any way you slice it. Now, what they said—what this gentleman finally told us—was that Marcus's mother was a 'working girl' with many troubles. Tried to do herself in a *number* of times. Gave birth to Marcus in a public toilet. Oh yes—had a few screws loose, this woman. Left him there in the trash, but the police caught up with her." Ruth began to weep, and Lucy went to her side. "Well, that's the story. Draw your own conclusions. But we loved the boy—and we'd have him again. Not sure we'd do much different, but we'd have him again. A *wonderful* boy . . . and we miss him. We've missed him so—"

It was Harry's turn to shed a tear. His sleepy side had awakened under the onslaught, and he dabbed it with a wad of Kleenex pulled from a lacquered box they'd bought in Jerusalem.

"What happened then?" asked Tull. "After he . . . disappeared? After the wedding?"

"Oh, they hired a man to find him," said Ruth. "But they never had any luck. I think that he—your grandfather—somehow blamed *us*. And it only got worse . . . because," she said with delicacy, "your mother had such misfortune. But we felt awful enough already! The embarrassment and the pain! And not knowing what happened to our boy, if he was alive or dead! Your grandfather didn't seem to take that into consideration."

"Oh I think he did, Ruth," said Harry charitably. "I think he did. It was hard for everyone."

"Well, *I* never heard it from him. Never heard it from *Berenice*. They didn't even tell us Katrina was pregnant!"

"That, I agree, was not handled well."

"It was *kept* from us. After six months it became clear that Louis wanted all ties—*anything* connected to the past—to that wedding and the heartache it brought your mother—severed. Cut right off, the way you'd cut an arm. What could we do? Such powerful people. We did our best to put the past behind us. The only time we heard about your grandfather—or your uncle Dodd—was when Harry clipped something out of the *Times*."

"Or *Forbes. The Wall Street Journal*."

"Harry subscribed to them all."

Then, said Ruth, came the terrible, wonderful thing: a friend from Chicago mailed them a page torn from *W*—standing in a garden of her own design was Katrina Trotter and her son, Toulouse. Her *son*. It cannot be! said Ruth, but the photo haunted—he looked so much like his dad—and she had it enlarged, trying to plumb its depths. Harry finally told her to call the house on Saint-Cloud, for her own peace of mind. She did, and it was like throwing sand against a stone wall. A week later they received a letter warning there would be consequences should either of them attempt to contact the boy—their grandson! So cold! They sat in their car a few blocks from the Bel-Air house as recently as a year ago, watching Tull with his dog. They dared not approach . . . how humiliating it was! She was so ashamed at the poverty of it—the inhumanity. Like ghostly sightseers, tucked away while Toulouse and Pullman romped down the hill and stole onto the wedding grounds . . . In her paranoia, Ruth imagined Marcus had long since returned and the reunited couple taken up residence in that freakish tower with the boy; that the Trotters had somehow managed to turn her own son against her, and her grandson too. Harry hated to see her do that to herself, but Ruth assured she had no more tears—until now.

Tull put his hand on hers, and the simple gesture meant all the world. "Did you ever hear from him?" he asked.

"No." Her husband stood up, excusing himself. He used the walker this time.

"But we *did* hear from Mr. Dowling—the detective who was looking for our son. In the early days he used to call at *least* once a week. Sometimes we even saw men sitting down the block in their cars. Just sitting. Waiting. I half expected to see Jack Webb! We were worried for Marcus if he *did* show up, what they'd do—Harry almost called the police on *them*. But they were decent men. I went out there and gave them pastries. Sometimes Mr. Dowling sent over tickets for a game; Mr. Weiner used to like to go to the Forum. Little gifts, too—nothing too costly. I wasn't sure if they came from your grandfather . . . I hoped they hadn't. Harry and I felt like criminals, but we didn't do anything wrong! I wouldn't have told Mr. Dowling even if I *had* heard from my son. There was not much goodwill left." Tears caught in her throat, and she apologized. "Such powerful people. Up until a few years ago, Mr. Dowling *still* called—usually right around the holidays. But no more gifts. I think he felt sorry for us."

Harry returned with a box. Handing it to Tull, he said it had come in the mail a long while back, without a note. Ruth uncomfortably poohpoohed it, asking Harry why he'd even bothered. Lucy (and Edward, much as he could) craned their necks while Tull took the lid off to reveal the copy of a book—the very same stolen from Tabori & Co. some fourteen years ago.

⌒

Tull lay down on the bed—the bed that was his father's as a boy—and stared at the ceiling much as he did in his room at Saint-Cloud, realizing Marcus would have done just that at his age: stared at *this* ceiling, *these* walls.

He heard the voices of the others, like wavelets lapping—Lucy helping Ruth in the kitchen, Edward and Mr. Weiner having a tête-à-tête. *News From Nowhere*'s ex libris proclaimed its sheaves to be PROPERTY OF MARCUS WEINER. Tull delicately fingered the book's gilt edges and felt its "prenatal calfskin" heft; he sensed the imprint of his father's hands on the blue-black vellum. He flipped through it—this place called Nowhere seemed to contain an awful lot of news. One of the photo albums piled next to him was cracked open to a portrait of the psycho-prodigal bridegroom in top hat, tails and brocaded vest, his bride in tulle and classic veil, wildly throwing rice at a Bugatti. That's what his parents had storiedly done, with playful surrealism: thrown rice at departing guests. If that were so, it meant someone would have tossed his parents a bouquet—his father would have caught it, no doubt.

His lame attempt to nap a failure, the boy sat groggily at table while the rest ate desserts: pastries made of pomegranate and almond—a specialty of the old shop, said Harry. Tull thought it the saddest, sweetest thing he'd ever tasted.

CHAPTER 24

Pixies and Tigers

Summer—El Monte at eventide. The desiccated wings of insects make for a thin layer of heavenly blisters on the high battlements of MacLaren Children's Center. The fragrance of sage, jasmine and honeysuckle fans over Mac's dusky campus grounds past a waterless pool donated by Barbra Streisand; a mural of seagull and ocean spray, insipidly anodyne; the campus boutique wherein misbegotten children trade goodness points for CDs, T-shirts and donated effluvia—locked down tight.

Eventide at Mac—dinner is done.

The volunteer grannies have all gone home.

The floors are waxed. Meds dispensed. Order all around.

The children, secure in their units.

The orphan—all orphans here!—is ensconced in Pixie cottage. That is her domain. For those her age, there are Pixies (girls) and there are Tigers (boys). Last week a Tiger huffed a hairstyling foam aerosol and died; grievous news for United Friends of the Children, who'd recently donated a batch to the brand-new beauty salon. But that's a rare thing at Mac. This is no Tunga Canyon. No Jilbos or Woolerys to be seen, at least not so far.

The orphan child—*our* orphan child—half lies on her bed, nail-bitten waif of sun-bleached hair and indomitable will, a "rainbow" child now nearly recovered from visible wounds. Syphilis has retreated from the assault of penicillin infantries; still-tender maceration of breast has drained, with only a dainty Wild Thornberrys Band-Aid as evi-

dence. Her cough is tolerable and there is no rank discharge from between fattening legs, whose calves and thighs now bear the heartening
black-and-blue memoranda of normal girlish activity. The face is filling
out nicely, ruddy cheeks made ripe by the chopping off of six licey
inches. She sleeps in a room with two others, only two, because most
Pixies insist on keeping their mattresses in the hall. They can't handle
bedrooms—any bedrooms.

Amaryllis is fully, securely, deeply in the "pop."

And sleeping without meds.

Tonight she reads in bed as in days of yore, small flashlight gripped
in smaller hand. She's uninterested in the mess of library books Dézhiree
(her staffer) brought to the Cottage from the library: *Alex, the Kid with
AIDS, My Body Is Private, The House That Crack Built.*

This is the baby with nothing to eat
Born of the girl who's killing her brain
Smoking the crack that numbs the pain
Who lives in the House That Crack Built.

She begged a volunteer grannie to find back issues of *Time* and
Newsweek. Amaryllis then made a tricked-out cradle for the scissored
magazine articles, bigger than her old cigar boxes, gluing photos to its
sides.

Tonight she's in a transport, for, scanning the articles before her,
Amaryllis knows she will soon see her babies. She always had a feeling
she would find them here, from the moment the detective announced
their destination—when she saw Mac's inviolable stone walls, she was
certain. And, besides, the baker's wife had told her it would soon come to
pass.[†]

[†] After the vagrant's disturbing visit undid and upended all her missionary work, Lani
Mott used the resources of the advocacy office at children's court to track down one Edith
Stein aka Amaryllis Kornfeld, even traveling to El Monte to visit—but to what end? What
do you want with this child? asked her CASA supervisor. Because Lani hadn't said
straight out that she wished to be the girl's advocate. That of course is what she *did* want,
more than anything, yet couldn't voice because of a lurid, niggardly fear that shamed her
no end. She had become a Court-Appointed Special Advocate in such selfless spirit of no-
blesse oblige; had cheerfully undergone the sometimes-depressing training and even put
on a little "graduates' day dessert" at the house, thoughtfully catered by Gilles. Yet

Among a plethora of fresh clippings, the Royal Kumari and even dare it be said Amaryllis's protectress Sister Benedicta, née Edith Stein, began to fade from memory. Voraciously, she carved out the text at hand: the pope had held a candlelight vigil for thousands of twentieth-century martyrs at the Colosseum in Rome. "There are so many of them!" he exclaimed. "Men and women of every land, of all ages and callings." In another scrap, she read how John Paul beatified 108 Poles who died at the hands of the Nazis, then turned around and did the same with 110 martyrs—a hundred and ten!—in a thunderstorming Warsaw mass for over a million pilgrims. How she loved this pope! On top of it, the Vatican said they were about to canonize three blacks; Vanessa Williams had already played one in a miniseries (her *TV Guide* picture graced one whole side of Amaryllis's reliquary). After all his exertions, John Paul *still* found the time to make twenty-seven new Mexican saints—before his decree, poor Mexico had had merely one.

Even popes themselves were busy being promoted. (When Amaryllis mentioned that, Dézhiree laughed and said it was like when the Academy Awards got nominated for an Emmy. Then the staffer agreed it was probably a *good* thing, and that John Paul would make a wonderful saint, because she really did like him, especially after he got shot, which, surprisingly, was news—and not good news—to Amaryllis. Seeing her long face, Dézhiree rushed to add that he'd long since recovered, and forgiven the man who attacked him.) For example, it was acknowledged that John XXIII had heroic virtues, but the Congregation wouldn't yet declare him worthy of veneration. Pius XII was on a fast track too, but there was a snag because the Jewish weren't happy—Amaryllis didn't think that boded well for her *own* cause. She didn't understand; why should the Jewish be unhappy, knowing that the Church had so proudly elevated their own Edith Stein? The Jewish were *always* unhappy, said Dézhiree. Amaryllis wondered if her father was that way.

---

more than a year later, all she had to show for her altruism was one measly case: driving a sullen teenager back and forth from a fancy residential facility to Western Dental to get a retainer. She'd made grandiose excuses to her growingly contemptuous courthouse boss—a death in the family, trouble at work—turning down case after case simply because she didn't want to travel to certain neighborhoods, where she felt she would be at physical risk. She wouldn't even go to Leimert Park! Lani Mott had said no so many times that she'd been informed that her days as an advocate were coming to an end. A fired volunteer—now, that was pretty low. But the fact remained: Lani Mott was afraid.

When she got to the lengthy piece in the *Times*—the one she'd been hoarding—there was great commotion in head and heart; all the world was hard-charging calvary and redemption and the girl's blood began to boil: the pope had declared *two children* to be Blessed, the first ever beatified by the Church who weren't martyrs! Amaryllis didn't care that the article said beatification was only bestowed on the dead—things were moving so quickly *anything* could happen. There was an actual photograph: two girls and boy, just like Amaryllis and her babies—Portuguese shepherds, from a place called Fátima, to whom the Virgin Mary had appeared in a field. She stared ravenously at the image of them clutching rosaries, sweet hands pushed together in prayer. Their eyes alone, dilated and enthralled, proved they had witnessed something awesome and eternal. It seems the three little cousins, using information the Virgin gave them, had predicted that someone would shoot John Paul long before he was even born. (She was glad Dézhiree had prepared her for the awful news.) Now, John Paul kept the bullet in a shrine. Two of the cousins died of influenza not long after the Virgin's sighting, and Amaryllis wondered why they wouldn't at least have lived a normal life span after being so touched—Dézhiree said hers was not to wonder why. But the surviving cousin was ninety-four, and that seemed to make up for it. She and John Paul smiled for the camera.

Amaryllis pasted the holy couple to the cover of her magic box. Then she said a prayer for Cindra, a Pixie attached to a respirator who slept sitting up, and a prayer for Dézhiree, and a prayer for Crystel and Shangg and Dennis the Phantom Menace, and a prayer for Jane Scull too, wherever she was, and one for Topsy—all of whom she decreed Blessed—and still another for her gone yet not forgotten mother, and of course one for her *own* little shepherds, the precious babies, with whom, God's help and John Paul's mercy allowing, she would soon be reunited . . .

She sits in front of the mural with the painted image of Martin Luther King, Jr., against a backdrop of constellated outer space. She watches a boy paint a perfectly proportioned clapboard house on the *Star Trek* cope—little house on the cosmic prairie.

Cindra in her wheelchair, facing campus. A child is only supposed to be at Mac short-term; a child must appear at children's court within fifteen days so it can be learned why he or she has not yet found a suitable placement. But Cindra's been here three years, practically a record. She's got MS, and not even one of those famous families that adopt only invalids has yet to take her on.

Amaryllis turns to look in the same direction: wild boys strut this way and that, each one trailed by a burly, unflappable staffer. "One-on-ones"—those deemed unsafe to be alone. The shadowy escorts bark corrective commands, which their charges obey in jerky protesting movements, unruly automatons staying the course.

She sits in the Learning Enhancement Center.

The Learning Enhancement Center helps kids who have neuroperceptual difficulties. All Mac kids have neuroperceptual difficulties. The teacher says such disabilities are "the hidden handicap," because most people go through life undiagnosed. The purpose of the class, she says, is to "retrain the brain"—the way it organizes information. The teacher says perceptually handicapped people are usually restless and can't control the impulse to talk or interrupt or get up and wander. They're emotionally unstable and cry over nothing or laugh uncontrollably or get too boisterous. They get easily frustrated and withdraw into themselves. The teacher says no one should feel bad about being there, because lots of famous people have neuroperceptual problems. Like Thomas Edison, Cher, Tom Cruise and Bruce Jenner. (Amaryllis hadn't heard of any of them.)

They did some tests, like making her walk on a long rail set in the ground—she pretended she was a tightrope walker at the circus. They gave her a pen and big pad of paper, and while someone read from a book, Amaryllis wrote down what they said, only she was blindfolded. They had her do a lot of bouncing on a small trampoline.

Around seventy kids are gathered because the director of the *Scream* movies is coming to talk about a movie he's planning to make about Mac.

After celebrities visited, there was always fresh "swag" at the boutique—videos and sweatshirts and key chains with movie-studio logos—and sometimes tours of Universal Studios were arranged. When celebrities came, the kids always thought there was a chance they'd be put in a major motion picture or brought on a field trip to the celebrity's house or pitied so much by the celebrity that they would be chosen from among all others for some sort of temporary home visitation sleepover that would fatefully morph into permanent placement at a Hollywood mansion.

The *Scream* man is introduced by staff. Most of the kids are shocked, because he was standing there the whole time and no one knew it. He looks like an old college professor, courtly and bespectacled and soft-spoken, with a nicely trimmed beard. Willow whispers to Amaryllis how the *Scream* man also did the movie about the monster who went into children's dreams and killed them with long finger-razors. Amaryllis missed that one. A kid asks if he really made the "Freddies" (because it was hard to believe there was a scare in him), and the *Scream* man gen-teelly acknowledges he was "the culprit." The staffer interjects that he's made *other* films, too—like the one about underprivileged inner-city kids who learn to play the violin so well that they all wind up at Carnegie Hall—and is here today to talk about the power of change and the movie he's planning on making about children like Mac children and how they can overcome adversity and realize their dreams. She tells them the woman who starred in the violin movie was nominated for an Academy Award and then introduces the dimpled lady who stands blinking and smiling beside the *Scream* man—a lady, says the staffer, who actually *did* win an Academy Award for Best Actress. The lady is old, too, and no one believes she ever won. Someone wants to know if she has the award with her, and she says normally she leaves it at home but would be sure to bring it next time. Then the boy who was painting the house on the mural shouts, "Are you the Flying Nun?" and everyone laughs and the woman with apple cheeks smiles and says yes she is, or yes she was. With great authority, someone whispers to Amaryllis that *The Flying Nun* is on TV Land. Amaryllis is embarrassed to even ask what TV Land is. Then a girl led by Dézhiree rushes up. The *Scream* man playfully scolds, "*There she is!* You're late, you're late! You'll never work in this town again!" The girl looks flustered and out of breath and makes her way to join them. There's a stir because lots of kids recognize her from television, and when Amaryllis has a good look, she gasps—it's Boulder Langon! Royal Kumari covergirl, TV superstar and friend of the boy who first called himself Toulouse . . .

The *Scream* man talks about the film he's going to make "about a place like Mac," starring Boulder and the Flying Nun, but Amaryllis doesn't hear a word: her heart pounds away as she gathers the nerve to approach her after the talk. She plays out the encounter in her head, wondering if Boulder will remember her. She was just reading about her in a magazine at the cottage—the "What's in Your Makeup Bag?" column of *Twist*, where they asked Ms. Langon that very thing. Now she stares at Boulder's Prada purse to calm herself, trying to recall the starlet's exact response, forcing herself to do a real-time inventory, neuroperceptually retraining her brain to organize data: *a Power Bar and my StarTAC,* she said, *and lots of sunscreen . . . —lots of lipsticks . . . —yes!* that's right. There were lipsticks and lotions that Boulder called "Mac" (for MacLaren?) . . .

They wanted to know when the movie would be made and if they were going to use any kids from the center. They wanted to know when he was going to make another *Scream.* They asked Boulder about *T'morrow,* her show on The WB. They asked how much money she made and where she went to school and if she had a boyfriend—everyone laughed when a cracked voice called out, "Do you want one?" Boulder said she was waiting to find a soul mate (the same thing she said in the article Amaryllis read in *All About You!*), which elicited more hoots, whistles and offers, quickly suppressed by staff. The last thing she said, with almost rehearsed gravitas, was that her "prime aspiration" was to attend a place called Yale just like her friend Claire Danes, whom she recently had the privilege of meeting at an "affiliates" luncheon at the Ritz-Carlton in Pasadena.

The *Scream* man brought some CDs and signed glossies, and the boys scrambled for them while most of the girls went over to Boulder, who signed T-shirts, forearms and scraps of paper with her name. The Flying Nun stood off to the side with the fawning staff. Amaryllis thought her best chance was to wait by the door. She stood there patiently, imagining the encounter again, but just when it looked like Boulder was about to leave, a staffer came up to Dézhiree, who then told Amaryllis she had a visitor.

"Who?"

"A *visitor,*" she slyly remonstrated.

It had to be Lani, with news of the babies.

*   *   *

When she returned to the cottage, Amaryllis was met by a Mac psychologist.

As they walked, she cheerfully engaged the girl in pleasantries, or at least tried to, before arriving at a far-corner office of the main building's second floor.

Instead of Lani, there stood a man in a brown shirt and thick brown tie. He reintroduced himself as Samson Dowling, the "public servant" who had picked her up at "the Hotel Higgins." He remarked on how pretty she looked.

"Are they taking care of you?" he bantered, with a wink to the therapist, not really expecting an answer. Amaryllis shrugged diffidently. She wanted to know if he was a policeman, and he said *kind* of— a detective. He said detectives helped find people. He asked if she really remembered him; the foundling nodded tenuously.

"That's OK," he said. "You weren't in the greatest shape. You've been through an awful lot." He said it was nice to see her looking so much healthier and what a sick little puppy she had been. Then he crinkled his eyes and asked if they could talk about her "friend."

"Lani?"

"Not Lani," he said, smiling. "The *big* fellow. Do you remember me asking about him before? Well, he's a friend of yours, at least I *think* he is, and I wanted to ask a few questions about him. Do you think that would be OK?" She nodded. "Can you tell me his name? He's a pretty unforgettable fellow from how I've heard him described! Big beard, *very* strong. Wears 'interesting-looking' suits; probably a better dresser than I am." He winked at the psychologist again. "Can you remember his name, Amaryllis?"

"Topsy . . ."

"Yes! That's right. Was Topsy a nice man?" She nodded. "You got along OK?" Another nod. "I'm going to ask you to remember a few more things, OK? Is that OK, Amaryllis? When you left your mom at the rooming house—remember how they chased after you? That must have been pretty scary, huh. When you left your mom, where did you go?"

"I don't know."

"Did you wander around awhile? You were probably frightened, and a little hungry. Did you go see Topsy?"

"He found me."

"He found you? Where?"

"The building."

"Which building? The place where we met? The empty building down the street from the St. George?" She nodded. "OK, good. Thank you for helping me answer some of these questions—that's a big help. Because I'm an older guy, and this way I don't have to run around so much. Now, after Topsy found you, what did you do? Did you talk? Did you have a little supper?—"

"We went to sleep."

Detective and psychologist exchanged glances. "You went to sleep. OK. You were tired. You were *both* probably tired. Now, I want you to be truthful with me, Amaryllis, because I'll always be truthful with *you*. OK? Fair enough. Someone saw you—you and your friend Topsy—someone saw the two of you leave that building *very* late at night. Do you remember that?" She nodded, staring at the floor. "The person who saw you and your friend said Topsy was carrying you. Was he carrying you against your will?"

Amaryllis thought he was asking *how* she was being carried; the therapist saw her confusion and intervened. "What the detective means," she said, "is did you *not want to go with him*. Did your friend *make* you—"

She shook her head vigorously, still staring groundward. A finger was now in her mouth, and she chewed it.

"Why was he carrying you, Amaryllis?" asked the detective.

"Because I was sleeping."

"Because you were sleeping. I see. OK. And where did Topsy take you?" She said nothing. "Did he take you to the bakery? Where Gilles works?" She nodded. "Did he say *why* he was taking you there?"

"He said it would be 'no good with him.' That Gilles was his friend. He said Gilles would do 'right well' by me."

"Did he mean that Gilles would take care of you?"

"He said not to say he brought me there." She looked up, her face filled with worry. "Is Topsy in trouble?"

"He *may* be," said the detective. "Would you like to help him? You would, wouldn't you. Well, he's missing and we'd like to talk to him—Gilles and Lani want to help him, too. *Everyone* wants to help him. How long did the two of you know each other?"

"Not very long."

"A month or two?" She shrugged her shoulders. "Did your mom

know him? Did he ever come see you or your mom at the motel?" She shook her head. "You said you found your mother in bed—"

Her lip began to quiver. The psychologist put a hand on the girl's shoulder. "It's all right, Amaryllis. There's nothing to be afraid of."

"Absolutely," said the detective. "I know how hard this has been. But no one's going to hurt you now, so you should just tell the truth—your friend Topsy's life may depend on it. OK? Can we go a little longer? Do you need a tissue? Let's get you a tissue." The woman handed her some Kleenex and she blew her nose.

"Amaryllis . . . did he do things for you? He did things for you, no? He was a good friend? He brought you food? Food from the bakery?" She nodded. "Did he ever bring your mother food?"

"No."

"But he—"

"He gave me food for my brother and sister."

"That was very nice of him. Very nice. Did he ever meet them?"

"No. He gave it to me and I gave it to them."

"Did he ever bring food to the motel? To the St. George?"

She shook her head. "He gave it to me."

"Where?"

"Under the bridge."

"Where he was living? Did you ever stay with him there? I mean, stay overnight? Did he ever take you anywhere?"

The psychologist chirped in: "Did he take you to the movies?"

"Lotsa great movie palaces downtown," said the detective unctuously. "Historic."

"And he never touched you, Amaryllis"—asked the psychologist—"in a way that made you feel funny? You know, that uncomfortable feeling we get in our stomachs when something isn't quite right? Sometimes when people are sick or lonely they do things like that and it makes your tummy upset—even if they don't know or mean what they're doing. Even if they're your friend. And it's not your fault, Amaryllis," she said, grinning like a moron. "It wouldn't be your fault."

"Is Topsy sick?" she asked.

"Well, we're not sure," said the detective. "That's why we want to talk to him. Now, he said not to tell anyone about leaving you at the bakery. Was there anything else he ever told you not to tell? About *any* of the things you did together? Even the good things? Did he share secrets with you, like a good friend would? Did he ever tell you he did something bad to anyone? That he hurt someone, even by mistake?"

"It's OK to tell, sweetheart. Otherwise, we won't be able to help your friend."

Amaryllis burst into tears, and the psychologist looked into Samson's eyes, signaling the meeting should end.

"Thank you, sweetheart. You've been very helpful. I didn't mean to make you cry! Amaryllis—that's a beautiful name, do you know that? Did your mother give you that name? That's a beautiful flower. A Christmas flower."

He reached into a briefcase and pulled out a stiff plastic envelope. He held it out to her; encased within was a deep-blue handkerchief speckled with gold scallop'd teardrops. "Have you ever seen this before?" he asked.

She cautiously nodded.

"Where?"

"It's Topsy's."

"Something he wore?"

"Around his neck."

"Did he give it to your mother?"

"I don't know."

Her jaw clenched and she stared at her shoes. He was losing her again.

"Know what they call it? An 'ascot.' I'd like to return it to him." He stood up, then bent to kiss her cheek. "Keep getting stronger, now—you're doin' great. Isn't she?"

"She sure is."

"Not mad at me, are you? Can I have a smile?"

Amaryllis eked one out.

"Mr. Dowling has something else to tell you," said the psychologist.

"I sure do. Saffron and Cody are coming to see you."

She looked at him, dumbfounded.

"We were able to locate them, and they're on their way."

"From what I understand," said the psychologist, "they should be here either tonight or tomorrow morning."

*   *   *

*C*ome they did, later that evening. The woman at the foster home where they'd been placed soon after their departure from the St. George could no longer take care of them. That's all that was said.

As curious as we are to observe the intimacies of the reunited, time and good taste have their limits. We shall leave them alone, for their moments together are precious and deserve exile from prying eyes. Briefly, it may be said that upon first seeing Amaryllis, the young babies, three and five years of age, were stunned and insensate, clasping each other in an odd pantomime of displaced, abject fear; then, spoken to in a persistent, cooing, complex language of animal sounds and shared remembrances, they slowly came around until the trio were overwrought to an ecstasy of desperation, Amaryllis coating them with kisses the way a mother licks her cubs clean. Even the stoic, efficient Dézhiree came undone. So let them be: allow the small, improvised party at the cottage—donated cupcakes, candles and bears all around—to proceed behind closed doors.

Such miracles happen, even at Mac.

*A*nother reunion is at hand, though not as poignant.

He had what he needed—the girl's statement about the ascot's ownership was incriminating enough for him to now seek charges of rape and murder against John Doe aka Topsy aka William. He would visit the district attorney in the morning.

When Samson returns to Rampart Detectives, he is pulled up short by the sight of a woman sitting at the end of a bolted row of hard plastic scoop-chairs. His body knows her before his mind can properly assess; one child's neuroperceptual difficulty is another man's cognitive dissonance. He takes everything in—flamboyant vintage dress and absurdly glamorous hat upon fiery, fierce-bunned hair; the business end of a stiletto tap-tap-tapping on the cigarette-burned linoleum floor.

She stands, and the air rushes out of him.

CHAPTER 25

Carved Fungi

*A*n unexpected thing happened when Trinnie and Samson sat down for supper at Ivy at the Shore: she lost focus. The manic, aggrieved woman had used her brother's office to find him—steeped in fervid self-righteousness, she had relished every step of the ambush. Yet after that first encounter, standing next to him under the fluorescent lights of Rampart, an uncanny light that made everything too real hence not real enough, after they had agreed to see each other that very night, Trinnie was all peace and love as she wended her way back to Saint-Cloud. Climbing from the bath, she felt acutely alive. She chose a simple black shift and left the house with a bounce in her step, the chill air a tonic. The top was down on the Cabriolet.

Sam Dowling was a childhood friend; well, more a friend of Dodd's. His family had been poor (they lived south of Olympic) but, like pioneers before them, were determined to give their son a Beverly Hills education. He was one of the few kids at BV—maybe the *only* one—to have gotten close to her brother, and for that Trinnie was ever grateful. He wasn't a user, either; she knew he didn't pal around with Dodd for the perks, and there were plenty. (Not that Trinnie would have cared.) Sam was a gawky, good-hearted boy, clueless in matters of money and social status, the latter of which her brother was sorely lacking. The future detective's democratic qualities and all-around innocent kindnesses were rewarded with lavish summer trips, three in a row to their Great Camp on Saranac Lake.

She knew a few things about him—that he'd married young and become a cop; that he'd been shot twice in the chest during a "routine traffic stop" and not been expected to live; that his marriage was the thing that didn't survive. When he recovered, he moved to Fiji to soul-search, with Dodd fronting him money to build a small resort for scubaholics. But law enforcement was in his blood, and Fiji was too damn peaceful. He sold the hotel, repaid his friend and returned to L.A. with an eye on a detective's shield.

He re-entered Trinnie's life when her brother called on him to mediate in the awkward business of the stolen book and then again when her husband, Marcus Weiner, the eccentric and beloved Hollywood agent, vanished into thin air.

Sam Dowling was always "interested." When he appeared on that terrible morning, standing with Louis Trotter and his children in the lobby of La Colonne—ground zero—looking so fresh and dapper, and the heiress so disheveled, anyone could see in his eyes how he was sorry-grateful the crazy man had left her at last. He tried to insinuate himself into her life, but it was not to be; soon after, she began the years of flight and exile.

"I've been reading about you," he said.

"Where?" she asked, surprised. "The AA newsletter?"

"Internet—I've asked Jeeves all about you."

"Oh shit. Google'd again."

"And that piece in *House and Garden,* about the maze. At Saint-Cloud."

"You're pretty well read for a cop."

The detective was endearingly nervous around her. Physically, his blade-like profile and droll, homespun mouth were reminiscent of Joe DiMaggio's.

"Do you ever see my brother?"

"Not recently. We talk."

"And Father?"

"Nominally." He laughed, almost to himself. "I know it's incredible, but he still keeps me on retainer. I've told him I don't want the money, but he insists."

"That's Dad."

"A good man. His health?"

"Great."

"Your mom?"

"Everyone's fine."

They spoke with bemused affection of her father's monumental funerary quest, then Trinnie broached the subject of Samson being shot (one seemed to follow the other). He said it probably hadn't been the worst thing, because it got him to slow down and reassess priorities. Trinnie thought his response a bit clichéd, then busted herself for being so cynical—*she* wasn't the one who had taken a bullet. His humor and humility won out, and held her attention. She asked if he still spoke to his wife, and Samson said no, not in years.

Since she had sat down, a familiar-looking middle-aged man had been stealing glances. Trinnie finally met his gaze; he stood and walked over. He was John Burnham, one of the heads of William Morris. A friend of Marcus Weiner's from the mail room days, Mr. Burnham politely paid his respects without referring to the debacle, adding that he would love to talk to her about designing a maze for his Hancock Park home.

When he returned to his table, Samson said, "You know, I still have feelers out for Marcus."

"I would have thought," said Trinnie, backtracking, "that you'd have stayed more in touch with my brother."

"That's not often easy—the world he moves in is a little rarefied. I mean, it's fun to joyride in his jet to some abandoned mental asylum . . . *once.*" She laughed, and it made him cocky. "But twice? A bit epic for my taste. That's your world."

"Was that a dig, Detective?"

"Sorry—that didn't come out quite right. I just meant 'to the manor born.' "

"I'm afraid my world has shrunk."

"I doubt a shrunken world could hold you, Trinnie."

He touched her hand, then withdrew it, sipping his drink. He decided to confess what she already knew. He admitted to finding her husband in the Adirondacks, rehashing everything her father had said, ending with the hospitalization and escape. The only detail she hadn't heard was how, before his capture, Marcus had taken sanctuary on cold nights at St. John's in the Wilderness, the family parish.

"I'll tell you one thing, Katrina—I think he wanted more than anything in the world not to hurt you."

"Didn't do such a good job, did he?"

Samson started to say something, but she stopped him.

They sat awhile in silence. When she asked if he'd take her to his apartment, he actually got up to flag down the waiter for the bill.

*T*rinnie had never been inside the El Royale. She always imagined the suites to be rococo in that thirties way, and maybe some were, but not Sam's. Like the detective himself, the rooms were simple, solid and unprepossessing—with the occasional flair.

They made love without niceties and she felt herself pulled through the maze. He pulled her through. The surgical scar on his chest was like a shadowy imprint of barbed wire. She sobbed and keened as they fucked, but he never stopped advancing and she was glad he didn't bother with useless questions such as what was the matter and was she OK. She felt the withheld drug of his come, hating the condom and all its second-skin safeties. This was a man she had known as a girl and now he carried her on a litter, on a bier through the bower back to the lake—hallelujah of painted summers at Twig House, Katrina and Dodd taking turns at the Chris-Craft, dizzying bounty of shimmering Saranac space, breaking the godly glass of water surrounding thirty thousand Trotter-owned acres, past great stands of maple and oak steeped in kettle ponds, bogs ringed with hemlock—past Pulpit Rock—past stone chalets and Orientalist sleeping cabins while loons and red-breasted mergansers called from their perches. Louis in black tie and Bluey in Halston sat on the boathouse porch sipping hot buttered rum from an army canteen. At nighttime, the children stormed the gates of heaven: campfires roared amid hullabaloo of square dancing, and the Dowling boy moved as if in a paradisal dream: lanterns led to the darkly dizzying mahogany-clapboard Great Camp with its diamond-fretted windows and white birch bark appliqué—marking pathways past cedar Parthenon replica—past elaborate stickwork of old icehouse to brainstorm siding of breeze-way containing the funicular; they climbed in and ascended—that's where he first kissed her, smelling girl-breath of cinnamon, spruce and beer. Their destination was the pole-worked bowling alley on the hill where Sinatra and Bobo Rockefeller played. She was twelve, and Samson, fifteen.

One summer, a servant drove them to Tear of the Clouds lake. Dodd was sick, and Sam had her all to himself. She couldn't have known what that meant; she couldn't have known anything about it. The detective never forgot the sights and sounds and smells of that day, and years later revisited those sacred waters in his mind while shrapneled body healed. When he flew back to see the jailed Marcus, he took a side trip there—to *all* the old haunts—but they were lapsed and foreign, without even the familiar desuetude of rooms after party guests have gone.

Enfolded in his arms, she felt her husband near. After all, hadn't Sam Dowling been the last to see him? Now, *she* came off the lake and was high up La Colonne, high in the boudoir of the tower before it officially sheared—holding court while their vows still held. At the El Royale, she smelled her obsession again . . . and later, at home at Saint-Cloud, as she fell asleep she too hovered over Twig House before settling into its game-stuffed den where her father kept his whimsical collection of fungi—everyone at the lake had their fungi. Mr. Trotter had commissioned a villager to inscribe one of the pieces in Latin:

> Dive, be not fearful how dark the waves flow;
> Sing through the surge, and bring pearls up to me;
> Deeper, ay, deeper; the fairest lie low.

Dodd Trotter was excited, and slightly embarrassed. Marcie Millard—and this was something one of his own attorneys subsequently confirmed—Marcie Millard said the general *feeling* was that the Board was poised to react favorably to the proposal of naming a wholly revamped Beverly Vista School in the benefactor's honor. There was *some* opposition, she said, but that was to be expected. Things were looking up, yet the question of how to live it down as far as his sister went (should the new name come to pass) whimsically asserted itself.

It was easy to see why the Board might be seduced. The new facility would include underground parking, a world-class planetarium, a theater-in-the-round (like the high school's, only larger), pool and gymnasium, a two-acre rooftop park and the kind of library where streaming-video conferencing, "smart" books, virtual homework networks and PowerPoint presentations were de rigueur. Wolfgang Puck came aboard with three menus for the cafeteria—organic, ethnic and traditional American. Yoga, fencing and Wu Shu would be offered, alongside more traditional sporting pursuits; a fund would be created to underwrite uniforms, playground equipment and musical instruments, in perpetuity. Even the backs of classroom chairs would be fitted with flat-panel screens.

The Quincunx offices weren't far from the targeted campus, and he often took his "BV walks" after lunch. Dodd apprized the Spanish duplexes, stucco dingbats and occasional multi-units on the school's periphery, then forged past the hideous dirty pink bungalows stuck on the glum, aging playground; strolled from Elm Street to Gregory Way, then to Rexford Drive—peering through the barred gate at the empty library along the way (what was sadder than an empty library?)—then on to Charleville, where sat the condemned, bell-towered auditorium. One of these early walkabouts had engendered a startling idea: what if he were to build a new P.S. template—the "Lilliputian university"? His friend the good Dr. Goodnight had shown the world it could be done with his Cary Academy in North Carolina, and Courtney Ross had made terrific inroads with *her* place in the Hamptons . . . though for a project of commensurate scale or even somewhat smaller "footprint" Dodd would need a tad more land. Just a *scoche* . . . still, he resolved to build the complex in such a way that wouldn't scare off the Board, a design that so artfully concealed its grandness that it would scarcely be noticed. In weaker moments, he thought maybe he should just have his friend Mr. Gehry wrap the whole thing in titanium, bungalows included.

He wondered: what would it take to actually purchase Beverly Vista's hundred or so surrounding residences? The duplexes couldn't go for much more than $600,000 apiece, though it wouldn't have mattered if they were $10 million. (He had the capital.) Dodd Trotter could buy up entire blocks: all the crappy five-story condos with fancy names—Rexford Plaza, Rexford House, Rexford Park—and outlying grids with private homes, too. It was a stroke of genius. He got that adrenalized, impervious feeling in blood and brain that usually presaged a buying jag, only this time it wasn't from skipping meds. He would call his consultant and let the acquisitions begin. His companies had more than sixty thousand employees now—dingbats and multi's would be purchased for secretaries to live in gratis for their first six months of employment; houses and duplexes tagged for newly relocated low-to-mid-level managers. Stealthily, he would mount his campaign—Marcie would be the only one to know. Hadn't Marlborough School in Hancock

Park done the same thing? Bought up the neighborhood for their expanding needs without anyone being the wiser? The trick was to pull it off without displacing schoolkids . . . disrupting the community was the last thing he wanted. Maybe he'd focus on buying out the *childless*, first—then snap up houses of parents with Vista students at the very *end*, just before construction commenced . . . or maybe buy the properties *now* but have everyone sign covert agreements allowing them squatters' rights until given notice to vacate; that way no one would be inconvenienced. He'd offer three times the fair market value, and if they hit a snag—if someone got stubborn and wouldn't sell—they'd sweeten the pot with Quincunx stock options. Everyone had his price.

⌒⌒⌒

"Frances-Leigh?"

"Yes, Mr. Trotter?"

"Were you able to locate him?"

"Yes sir, I was."

"Where does he live?"

"In Simi Valley."

"Isn't that, like, Cop World? What's he doing out there?"

"His son's in law enforcement."

"Son? I guess Trinnie was wrong."

"Wrong?"

"About him being a fag."

"I wouldn't know about that!"

"Did you talk to him?"

"Sure did."

"Let's call him up."

Dodd sat there in his Aeron. When she had Dr. Janklow on the line, he rocked a full minute before picking up.

"Dr. Janklow! It's Dodd Trotter."

"Well, hello!" said the voice on the other end—gone reedily eager and tentative with age. "Gee, that was quick! The woman told me you were going to call."

"How *are* you?"

"Miserable! Had cancer three times already. Cancer *loves* me."

"I'm sorry to hear it."

"I just like to bitch and moan, that's all. But I'm all right. Getting my fifth wind up here in beautiful Simi."

"Well, it's great to hear your voice."

"*You* did rather well for yourself."

"Got lucky, that's all."

"Now, I don't know if I believe *that*. Been reading about you on the Internet."

"Ugh."

"Don't worry!" he said with a laugh. "Nothing too terrible."

"Dr. Janklow, I can't tell you how often I've thought of you—what an important force you were in my life. You were always there for me."

"That's a wonderful thing. A wonderful thing to hear."

"And I wanted to call to say hello and see how you are—and if there was anything you needed."

"Well, no—unless you were thinking of dropping a few billion on me. You know, I'm set pretty well. My son's here; he and his wife and the grandchildren live close by. I'm doing all right. But now . . . what is it that *you* need, Mr. Trotter?"

That was the Dr. Janklow he remembered; the sage who gently turned the tables. "Would you—I'd love to take you to dinner."

"Well, I . . . *yes*, that would be nice! *Certainly*, yes. That's one wish I can grant! But I don't drive so well anymore . . . and I don't like imposing—"

"I'll send a car."

"It's quite a ways."

"There're a few things I'd like to talk with you about—about the school. Beverly Vista. Some thoughts and plans . . ."

"Marcie told me."

"Marcie did?"

"Oh yes—you know Marcie still keeps me up on all the doings. She's a little compulsive that way, but she *means* well. Does well by the kids, that's for sure. Always has their interests at heart. Now, Marcie said you were cooking up some *wonderful* things and I don't doubt it. But I had no idea you'd call."

"She's the one who brought me back to it."

"She'll *do* that if you're not careful! I've been knowing the Millards forever. Do you know Peter? Peter Millard?"

"I'm afraid I don't."

"Helluva surgeon."

"Well, we *are* 'cooking up' some wonderful things—and I'd like you to be a part of them."

"I'm an old man, you know. And I'm disgusted with what's going on in today's schools—all of 'em."

"We're going to change that."

"Disgusted! I don't know how I can be of help."

"Just sitting down and breaking bread with you would make a difference."

"That sounds rather biblical! Guess my age elicits that. But, Jesus, the guns changed everything. Schools have become damn shooting galleries. I retired before all that, thank God. The minute kids started bringing guns to class—well, that was just the end of the world, far as I could see."

*T*hat night, Dodd told his wife he was divesting himself of farflung ruins—his hobby had played itself out. They made love for the first time in months, and afterward Joyce nervously told him about *her* special project; how she bought land at Westwood Village Memorial Park because those babies needed a home that wasn't a potter's field. She said she hadn't yet told his father, and Dodd agreed that was probably a good thing. For the time being, anyway. He was so gentle and understanding, and it felt like they were coming to new ground. He said he needed to get back in physical shape, and she made him promise to do yoga with her at the house with Ana Forrest. They spoke of their children and general good fortune. Dodd suggested they go away on a little trip around the time the kids took off on their summer holiday. There were plenty of jets to go around.

As they fell asleep, Joyce touched his shoulder and whispered, "Thank you." She wasn't sure that he heard; she wanted it to be more than subliminal. So she said it again.

CHAPTER 26

Globe Trotters

The children were away for a whirlwind three-week tour; and while travel was Edward Aurelius Trotter's métier and he never felt more anchored than when bonds to earth were severed, the hardships he so gracefully endured amid numbered leave-takings from the softship of his father's customized cabin were notable and should be recorded for future invalids, real and imaginary.

Exactly who was part of this airborne sodality? Let us first introduce those professionally engaged. The retooled 737 came with six pilots, whose tag-team approach allowed them to enjoy more than a few sights (one might think this arrangement was on account of Dodd Trotter's largesse, when in actuality it was his wife's suggestion, being Joyce's sensible opinion that a happy, rested crew made for a safer voyage); two in-flight helpers—a hunky Greek, whom the overheated Lucy fantasized about on days when Tull was particularly distant and uncaring—and a stewardess, whose protracted, ritualized reapplication of lip gloss and outliner may as well have been a morbid surgical procedure for all the fascinated attention it received from the boys of Four Winds; a portly medical doctor by the name of Dr. Raff, who was a part-time resident of the hidden clinic at Olde CityWalk, hence well familiar with Edward's condition; two homely, overqualified nurses—whose looks still proved eminently watchable to certain of our younger captives, and who seemed on this trip to stick thermometers in more mouths than they could remember—their technical skills and general know-how being of emergency-room caliber; a physical therapist and self-proclaimed tai chi instructor (dubbed Slouching Tiger by Edward) for whom no one seemed to care and who, to his credit, cared less in return and, aside from massaging the first cousin, which he did well enough, mostly took up "carrying" duties familiar to Epitacio, Eulogio and Sling Blade, delicately hoisting the boy in his arms on request; two techies—one, an expert in upkeep, maintenance and troubleshooting of aspirators, defibrillators and assorted hose-and-pump gewgaws (an inventory that remained, thankfully, unused) and the other, a kind of practical engineer, who saw to it that Edward's portable AirBuggy, a more modest version of the bulkier trademark dry-docked at Olde CityWalk, would be up and running and not sputter out on the Via Whatever in front of Ruin XXVII; three bodyguards, charged with the security of the group and who were to be sure no kidnappings, hijackings or explosive surprises ensued; two *cuisiniers particuliers* and their assistants, all of whose glacially indifferent dispositions challenged one's romantic notions of the fiery cook-as-artist; and finally, one of Dodd Trotter's crack efficiency mavens, whose only job was to facilitate hemispheric, longitudinal and latitudinal comings and goings, VIP clearances, embassy liaisons, passports and vaccinations, baggage wranglings, concierge-strokings and hotel check-ins, general politics, skullduggeries and laundry. That would be dry-cleaning *and* fluff 'n' fold.

Let us examine the next level up. Here resides the venerable Mr. Hookstratten, whose civilian clothes and multiplicity of camera gear first severely embarrassed the children, as they weren't used to seeing him bustle about in the real world. (It felt way too intimate.) The teacher was joined by his life partner, a supposed expert in the field of celestial navigation, whose name was Reed, apropos for an attenuated, fuzzy-haired body that seemed to tilt sardonically in the wind, and who smiled at the little ones with the benevolence of a sadist who'd already poisoned their pie. There was a professor of medieval history with terrible breath, who was wont to accompany himself on guitar singing Middle English "ditties"; he was eventually exonerated, even extolled, after Edward proclaimed the man's knowledge to be authentic and of enormous range. Rounding things out came a chess-master-cum-alpinist upon whom the physical-therapist-cum-tai-chi-master instantly fixated as nemesis.

Having dispensed with the above, we now arrive at a small VIP subset: the actress Diane Keaton and her daughter, Dex—the latter already slated to be a Four Winds scholar, class of 2012. As previously noted, Tull and the actress shared a dog walker, but the ties went deeper.

Trinnie and Ms. Keaton had a reunion of sorts at the oft-referred-to Animal CAT-scan Ball, which, the reader cannot fail to recall, was attended by Ron Bass himself. Diane, a former client of Marcus Weiner, had always been captivated by Katrina (the actress being a fabled cognoscente of style, genius and tragedy) and had long followed her career in the garden journals and magazines, coincidentally even visiting some of the heiress's more acclaimed and faraway private commissions. While Mr. Bass commiserated with the now-former "Rafe" Mirdling, Trinnie poured out some of her scandalized heart to the entranced and startled Ms. Keaton, filling in the gaps of the actress's knowledge, which of necessity had been dependent on gossip and newspaper accounts read long ago, now almost forgotten. The two had lunch at Il Pastaio, and Trinnie even went so far as to accommodate her old acquaintance and newfound friend (Ms. Keaton, to her eternal regret, had been unable to attend the wedding) with a moonlit tour of the near-virginal grounds of La Colonne. In the months since the benefit, the actress had met the entire Trotter clan and become enamored of them, as anyone would. While Trinnie was the initial connection, credit must be given to Joyce (who never receives enough) for suggesting that Diane and her sweet-banged Dexter join the kids for at least part of their international campaign.

At last, then, the student body: Tull, Edward, Lucy, Boulder and eighteen of their fellows, the latter of whose individual attributes and shortcomings will remain unsung—but let us say a fair cross-section of overachievers, with archetypal brainiacs and bullies to bracket the middling. It *is* heartening to note that for the length and breadth of the voyage, there wasn't a single disciplinary problem of substance (and not a weapon, real or makeshift, brandished): the children, sensoria taxed and disoriented by constant movement through culture and time zone, shocked lungs breathing the recirculated air of an albeit opulent airship, had been transformed from jackasses into sweet, humble citizens of the world—in no time, the little dears possessed the poise and plenitude of UNICEF emissaries. They behaved with grateful worshipfulness toward their immediate hosts (Edward and his sister) while still managing to pay cousin Tull the worshiped-by-association homage or lack of it required by his given mood. Suffice to say that within mere days after the Los Angeles departure, the normally boisterous, disrespectful Four Winds mob became fine-tuned choristers, whose vocals could swing from ragtime to near liturgical at the instructive glance of any adult—or Trotter—on board. Oh, but they were good.

Let us address their itinerary. For the reader who tires of such inventories, a solution is at hand: accidental tourists may skip ahead, while the more adventurous (it is hoped, the majority) will be asked to surrender their passports forthwith. The trip will be swift—or perhaps *feel* swifter than our prefatory remarks—and cover much ground.

We are already in New Orleans; for Edward wished to visit a place where Mardi Gras masks are made.[†] The atelier outshines Olde City-Walk's by a long shot. Not that Edward is covetous—it has the opposite effect. He is utterly seduced by all manner of feather, bead and sequin. But the legendary city is oppressively humid, and this does not make anyone happy. A prearranged visit to the home of Anne Rice salves their wounds. The sequestered writer is ill and graciously sends her regrets; an extensive tour of the imposing, atmospheric grounds is offered by her handsome son, also a novelist. Lucy is at once besotted, but cannot compete with Boulder, who already whines that if she'd been old enough she was certain to have been chosen by his mother to "limn" the part Kirsten had played in *Interview with a Vampire*. *She is a snake!* thinks Lucy uncharitably of her best friend, who keeps posing and wriggling and "limning," and the young man seems fairly entranced. Disgusted, Lucy dumps Christopher Rice without him ever having known they were a couple.

England-bound. Cabin lights dimmed in readiness for sleep. The student body lay in flattened, cashmere-upholstered lounges while Tull Trotter, prompted by a certain mischievous cousin, entertains the spellbound Four Winders (and one or two anxious adults, who pretend not to listen) by reading aloud from a book of transcripts containing the black-box recordings of fatally crashed airplanes. Aside from Tull's radio-play voice, all one can hear is the drone of engines in the howling void, from

---

[†]Something must be aired, if a bit prematurely. A question may arise: Why, or how, could such an impossible array of peculiar places be visited in so short a time? An eclectica of destinations was culled from the exotic wish list that Lucy and her brother had whimsically drawn up; their father was committed to fulfilling those wishes to the letter. The logistics were a challenge, but it would get done. There is no limit to wealth and its imaginative excesses, just as there is no limit to the proscriptions of poverty—but the details of both extremes are sometimes difficult to comprehend. Just as a sixty-year-old woman might spend three days knee-deep in recycling bins so she might gather the capital to buy her grandson shoes, so may a father fly a chef from Hong Kong to Palos Verdes with ten $20,000 boxes of saliva-thread swallows' nests to make special soup for his daughter's bat mitzvah. Such is the world.

which they are separated by a metallic husk of mere inches. Edward—whose king-size head, it may be too painstakingly observed, rested upon a $2,500 oversize Legends eiderdown pillow, its feathers collected by hand from Icelandic nests so as not to harm the ducks—titters devilishly from beneath his 435-thread-count filigreed oyster-colored silk hood, while Lucy, that high-flying authoress, tries to cadge a few moments with her Smythson *Blue Maze Mystery* journal, sending a scowl or two Tull's way. Other than Edward, the only person deriving any real pleasure from this theater of cockpit cruelties is Mr. Hookstratten's consort, the very weedy Reed; Tull's tasty morsels (particularly monologues that end with pilots screaming for their mothers) elicit a steady, sardonic grin. The man is in his element.

Trinnie had insisted that while in England they visit her mentor—Randoll Coate, maze maker extraordinaire—for a tour in Gloucestershire. The extremely tall, extremely eccentric eightysomething gent was among the most amicable and learned of men (that would include Mr. Emerson Tabori) the Trotter children or for that matter the entire troupe had ever had the pleasure to meet. He spoke a great deal in phrases and whole paragraphs of other languages, and it was not a bore to wait for the enlightened translation, though sometimes the wait was very long indeed; some of the group is waiting still. At first defensive, for he was loath to have the Saint-Cloud maze upstaged, Tull gradually conceded that the Master's creations were, well, *different* and, as such, not really competitive with his mom's (or "mum's," as Lucy would have it, for while in England her pronunciation of words had subtly shifted; though to say the newly adopted accent was English would have been too generous). Some of the hedged puzzleboxes were barely three feet in height—Mr. Coate not subscribing to any hard-and-fast rules when it came to grafting his imaginative constructs onto garden or hillock.

As the Four Winders helped feed one of his egg-shaped foliated creatures bonemeal, he glanced up to ask—first in Italian, then in English—"What's the difference between a book and a labyrinth? Nothing! There *is* no difference." (He was full of koans, beans and majesty.) Lucy flushed at the revelation and instantly put pen to Smythson, certain that Merlin had just solved the Mystery of the Blue Maze. But Edward knew that Borges had said it first.

He led them deeper through a breathtaking lunar puzzle while recounting the minotaur's tale. For the children, it was like hearing it afresh; such was Randoll's art, they could almost smell the flatulence of that hairy, mythic beast. When he said "labyrinth" was thought to derive from the Minoan *labrys*, or "double-headed ax," Edward, in the tireless arms of his carrier, cursorily added (and much to their host's enchantment) that the item was most accurately defined "as a unicursal spiral to the center whereas a maze is a multicursal route: junctions and deceptions."

"Choices," added Randoll sunnily.

The old fabulist did not dawdle; like young Theseuses, they followed the thread of his erudition as best they could and in a short while found themselves within a "see-through" maze of espaliered apple and pear trees. Finally, five hundred yards farther, they traipsed amid the whimsical "Imprint of Man," an enormous boxwood footprint, the great toe of which resided on a specially created Coatesian island of an adjacent river. Ms. Keaton nearly expired with delight; it was she, with Dexter at one hand and the intoxicated Lucille Rose at the other (for, at least while on the larger Isle, that is what the braided girl demanded to be called), who spearheaded the successful search-and-rescue of a disoriented and embarrassed Mr. Hookstratten—his verdant explorations of Randoll's more complex outgrowths having been more labyrinthine than expected.

They were all put up at Leaf House, the marquess of Went's little spread in the country. It was a lovely sight to see at dusk the caravan of children and caretakers moving swiftly over roads of packed gravel on bicycles retrieved from the belly of the Boeing, vintage Schwinns and Trussardi Classics, the latter trimmed in Napa leather.[†] Edward took

---

[†]It should be noted that the Trussardis were $5,000 apiece, retail. Well, whether it should be noted or not, the author begs indulgence for his *catalogue des excès* and would argue it to be something more; that such details are relevant to this chapter and of legitimate ethnographic interest. In this vein, he will add that the eager students were cautioned to steer clear of Gothick Hall, which harbored a secretary built by Rhode Island cabinetmaker Christopher Townsend, its silver fixtures smithyed by one Samuel Casey, and recently acquired by Lord Went at Sotheby's for the not unlordly sum of £7 million. Nor were they to approach the $210,000 bottle of Château d'Yquem, personally engraved with Thomas Jefferson's initials—though grown-ups were allowed to have a look if not a taste. The good lord also happened to be a collector of *money itself*. As a hobby, he enjoyed buying uncirculated legal tender: $500, $1,000, $5,000 and $10,000 bills (he'd purchased one of the latter for around $115,000), whose value increased exponentially each year.

over the bathroom suite. Tended by a host of country elves, he soaked to heart's content in the marquess's $42,000 hand-crafted Archeo copper tub while Lucy fork-fed him grilled white peaches sprinkled with cardamom and sugar. For dinner, there were hamburgers and Black Sphinx dates; fresh sheep's-milk ricotta with warmed lemon-lime marmalade; french fries and fragile *fraises des bois* dipped in crème fraîche.

The next few days were occupied with incursions to sundry frescoed palazzi and Palladian villas along the Riviera del Brenta, between Padua and Venice. A canal side trip to the deserted fourteenth-century private chapels of Abruzzo, Ovid's birthplace, provided the occasion for a filibuster by their very own medievalist on the subject of architecture, Marcus Vitruvius Pollio and "The First House—Myth, Paradigm and the Task of Architecture," to be more exacting. Half those present nearly fainted from boredom.

But we wouldn't wish such doldrums to overtake us here; for time is precious and must be moved along, and there *are* pressing concerns in the County Los Angeles.

To summarize, these are the places the silver BBJ bullet alit, though not necessarily in the order presented: the Temple of the Tooth in Sri Lanka (resting place of the sacred molar of Buddha, snatched from the flames of his funeral pyre in 483 B.C.); the Londolozi game preserve in South Africa (where children sat on pearwood-and-leather folding chairs from Hermès under Missoni maharajah's tents, drinking Diet Pepsi from Asprey steel flasks while adults, engorged with satiny Bresse chicken, truffles *en gelée* and lavender sorbet, lazily confined themselves to Henry Beguelin chaises on faux Aubusson rugs); the Old City of Jerusalem (where Boulder, within a stone's throw of the Wailing Wall, was actually asked to sign autographs—prompting Tull to make a crack on the Via Dolorosa about the "Shroud of Tourists" which so convulsed the First Cousin that his anxious handlers began plotting routes to the nearest hospital); two sprawling villas in Marrakesh (one of which, informed Mr. Hookstratten, happened to be built by the descendants of Tolstoy; Mr. Giorgio Armani and *his* party had decamped only the night before), the base from which they sallied forth to souks, Berber villages and desert camelback excursions in the shadow of the Atlas Mountains—though Edward, hard at work weaving a "bespoke djellaba," spent most of his time sipping blood-orange juice and soaking in the *tadelakt* bath—returning late in the afternoon, where, surrounded by palm groves, yellow roses, periwinkles and plum trees, all sat on the terrace of a place called Orchard of the Shooting Star, and partook of partridge soup and swathed jellies on cloth-covered dough that had baked all night buried in sand.[†] (One evening they ate in the heart of the medina, scant tables away from King Mohamed VI.)

At each stop, they endeavored to give food and alms to the poor, and Tull always imagined to espy the face of the girl called Amaryllis, and wondered why the feeling of her had stayed with him so long.

Their last destination fittingly brought them to one of the navels of the world, where Tull underwent a great trial.

About fifteen years earlier, NASA had been kind enough to provide Easter Island with an emergency shuttle landing strip—more than commodious for the trusty 737. At descent, the children gathered excitedly by the windows to view the stone moai, which, poised upon ahu altar shelves, looked more like Polynesian-themed salt and pepper shakers than icons of mysterium. Everything smelled of sea and horses when they deplaned, and it seemed the entire town and not a few travelers had appeared to observe the peculiar invaders, of which Edward and his AirBuggy—a Sun King and his golden chariot—were the prime attraction. They took over the four-star Hanga Roa as planned.

That very day, our constituents visited the crater that provided tuff, the dense volcanic stone of the famous stoic statuary (the right tuff indeed), and it was agreed that Rano Raraku was most certainly a quarry to give the normally unflappable Grandpa Lou meditative pause. Edward was amazed and delighted to find the place littered with hundreds of discarded, unfinished moai, some without eyes, ears, mouths or arms. Lucy pronounced it all "*Très* Olde CityWalk—Workshop of the Gods!" Boulder was bored and had to be sweet-talked by Tull, which Lucy liked not a bit, into tagging along to the lapidarian caves of Orongo, anticlimactic site of the ancient Bird Man cult. (The young star's spirits sagged then rose again with Edward's allowance of a call to her theatrical agent via his Thrane & Thrane TT-3060A satphone.) Mr. Hookstratten said they used to pick clan chiefs by having warriors swim to the rock that jutted a mile offshore; the first to come back with a tern's egg strapped to his

---

[†] Against all intentions, the Keatons did not make it that far. Young Dexter's earache precluded her flying; the two graciously took their leave in Tel Aviv, and were much missed to journey's end.

forehead became Boss Man until nesting season. It was immediately proposed that a new Four Winds principal should thus be selected, and
much urging of Mr. Hookstratten to hit the drink followed. He refused.
When it looked as if Slouching Tiger and the chess-master-cum-alpinist
might dive for competing honors, the children lost interest and began
whining for supper.

It was a good thing the Boeing was well stocked, because all the island could offer were pastries, bananas, grocery-store meats and the
ubiquitous pollo con agregado. Mutiny nearly ensued when the taciturn
chefs proceeded to whip up bisque de homard and tournedos Rossini,
along with braised Swiss chard, bone marrow and cardoons and what
looked to be an obscene quantity of squid garnished with whorled,
warty celeriac. The brave Mr. Hookstratten (one could almost see egg of
tern on his brow), backed by troupes of loyal students and faculty,
protested they'd all had enough and would like hamburgers and hot
dogs instead. A heretofore timid, rubicund sommelier stepped forward
to testily note how "the goose foie gras is from Ducasse family flocks
in the Landes!"—a response which made the protesters think the
cooks had lost their minds. Even Reed was discomfitted. With the latter's
help (and this endeared him to the students, at least for the night),
Mr. Hookstratten staged an intervention involving female staff. The
women promptly got stoned. In short order, the cooks were lured to tents
deliberately pitched in the shadows of what the medievalist deemed "fertility moai" and over the course of a few otherworldly hours, six bottles
of blended L'Esprit de Courvoisier were consumed, along with Laura
Scudder's ridged chips, Southern-fried chicken and a pot-brownie
baker's dozen.

Around midnight, Tull fell into sweat-soaked sleep. A rapping at the
door of his room slowly brought him to awareness. When he answered,
the bully whom Lucy had once stood up to on Tull's behalf appeared at
the door with a half-platoon of pint-size soldiers behind him. They bade
him throw on some clothes, which he did in a fugue state before following them to the towering head that overlooked the cooks' bacchanal
with a kind of remonstrating hauteur.

They crept up a grassy slope and peered downward at this tableau:
most of the adults had disbanded, while a few still spoke softly from
within the same candlelit tent that only a week ago had been pitched

over South African soil. The detritus of plates, dishware, foodstuffs and empty bottles was all around. A body—perhaps it was Slouching Tiger's, perhaps one of the pilots', perhaps Professor Hookstratten's—lay fifty paces from the ahu, snoring vigorously. Attention was elsewhere drawn, though a wobbly Tull did not immediately join his scampering guides. What *did* comfort him was the sight of Lucy squatting nearby like a bushgirl and watching along with everyone else while a couple, half dressed, were "doing it." It scarcely mattered who they were—steward or nurse, maven or techie—it was what they did that entranced. Tull slunk to his cousin, who acknowledged him with a glance before turning back to the dark, primitive spectacle. The woman moaned and seemed, like a crab, to scuttle away. She muttered a few words in low, anguished tones, which slowly grew louder until the phrase "fuck it" was vaguely discernible; a phrase repeated in varying stages of dishabille ("it" became "me" and "me" became "you" and "you" became "me" again—and so forth). At a certain point, her demands grew so furied that those in the tent grew silent, then burst into a hail of guttural laughter before going back about their sociable business.

Perhaps it was the pork pâté or boudin noir, or maybe the blood sausage too hastily combined with six frozen mini–Milky Ways—but the world began to spin and Tull along with it. His cousin helped him return to his hotel room, a phantasmagoric journey the boy hoped never again to be forced to repeat. Luckily, the teetotaling Dr. Raff had long since turned in; Lucy summoned him; after the required palpations, acute gastroenteritis was diagnosed. Nothing was to be done. Tull emptied bowels and stomach of all they had while Lucille Rose—martyr, author, girl detective—laid on cold compresses as he lurched through the maze of his delirium. Pullman was there, and he was glad about that. They stood before the puzzle his mother had designed at Saint-Cloud and which Mr. Randoll Coate (who in his dream bore Reed's supercilious countenance) now perfunctorily dismissed. His nasty thumbnail critique amused Mr. Hookstratten and the cousins, leaving Tull hurt and betrayed. Stung by the remarks, he suddenly noticed his mother fleeing into one of the pathways. Everyone disappeared. The boy knelt to examine Pullman, who was festooned with strange open sores, and was glad they didn't seem to be causing the beast any pain. He sprinted down the dark lane toward Trinnie. Instead of reaching the heart of the labyrinth, he found himself in an open clearing—that of La Colonne Détruite.

There, his grandfather, as if orchestrating the arrangement of stones in a cemetery, directed deformed workers while they raised up more cracked columns, ragged drapes flapping like crows in the frame of each eyeless window-socket. He heard his mother call out, and ran toward one of the mysterious buildings. Inside, the furnishings were uncovered. The Dane clambered up the spiral stairs, slipping on marble as Tull overtook him. The boy reached the topmost bedroom and tentatively entered. The bathroom light was on . . .

"Dad?" Tull bolted upright. "Daddy!" he shouted, blinking sweat from his eyes.

Lucy rushed over to minister; she felt as if they were onstage in that part of a play where the invalid's fever breaks.

Seeing it was she, he became embarrassed. "I . . . I was dreaming of my father," he stammered, almost politely.

*L*ike most on board, Tull slept the entire flight back to California, with nary a ghost of present, past or future to invade unconsciousness.

Settling into the comfort of their respective homes, the youngest Trotters kept to themselves for a full week, hardly even speaking on the telephone—though, with usual aplomb, Edward sprang back in record time, the only toll paid for his resilience being a harsh and intractable case of acne.

Tull was slower to surface. He was glad to see Pullman again, but the dream had sorely spooked him; it was a while before he dared take his old friend on a constitutional in the sealed park, fearing what they might find.

CHAPTER 27

For the Child Who Is Not Present

"*I* want everyone to look for the mosasaur, OK?"

The teenage docent held a shark fin in his hand. The children reached out carefully, as if the fossil might still cause mayhem.

"And when you find the mosasaur—you'll see how really *huge* it is— when you find the mosasaur, just remember: this very *huge* creature was eaten by the much smaller *shark*."

He stroked the hooked piece of cartilage to emphasize its role as David to the mosasaur's Goliath. Then he held it in front of Amaryllis, cuing her to touch. She wouldn't, a fact not lost on Dézhiree. The fin wound up at the wheelchair, in Cindra's lap; the disabled girl squirmed and rolled her eyes in delight.

There were two MacLaren field trips that summer—the mosasaur having been encountered on a sweaty, bus-rattled fiesta to Exposition Park's stately Natural History Museum. Though nearly ruined, the coliseum abutting that place was far from Rome; a newly minted IMAX behemoth had infected adjacent buildings with its garish pastels and multiplex aesthetic. "Dancing Waters," those cheap public-space ejaculations that soak the kids during parental cigarette breaks, added to the sprucing up—all this part of the rankly meretricious, cheesily stimulating great American playground, arty and self-aggrandizing, thrilled with itself no end. The whole chain-linked grid, surrounded by a flatland of jaundiced soccer-trodden crabgrass, was supposed to be a free-spirited architectural tribute to the putative joys of Science and Learning yet was in fact an ugly hodgepodge of loading zones and dented dumpsters that no one, not even the brightest design intern, had thought to conceal from general view. But the children of MacLaren weren't critics—they were just happy to be in the "outs," roaming the cool halls of glassed-in bison and saber-tooth. The dioramas were as calming as meds.

In the three months since Amaryllis became a Pixie, she had been taken to children's court on the occasions that her stay at Mac exceeded the amount of time prescribed by law; in those same three months, two suitable placements had been found that were quickly deemed otherwise (though not at all in the league of the perilous Canyon klatch of E. Woolery).

For example, on the weekend of her arrival at the well-kept, superstuccoed home of the Barnard Tofflers of Rosemead, she was sent packing due to an allergic reaction to the family cat—severe enough to require a trip to the emergency room at the ungodly hour such trips typically demand. Rosemead was not big enough for both of them, but Mrs. Toffler would not part with her beloved. This standoff, coupled with the girl's habitual under-sheet flashlight explorations of the machinery of martyrdom, had the effect of making the whippet-size, already skittish Mrs. Toffler more skittish still. After a day or so of relative segregation from the pet, Amaryllis was remanded to Mac. To be fair, the Tofflers bought her a dress in consolation.

In the second instance, she remained with the Alfredo Quiñoneses of Diamond Bar for a relatively carefree three weeks. The rural home had a big backyard with swings, barbecue and aboveground pool. Besides Amaryllis, five children lived there, all told; two were "real" Quiñoneses, while three were adopted (a palsied one among the latter, the disabled being a sacrosanct—and lucrative—cliché of Adoption World). A few weekends in, before school began, the mellow Mr. Quiñones, aged fifty, had a coronary and died. Soon after, a wet-eyed Quiñones aunt dutifully returned Amaryllis to MacLaren, along with Palsy Girl, who barked and wept the whole ride back.

Yet the vicissitudes of an adoptee's life were nothing compared to Amaryllis's wrenching separation from the babies. Their initial reunion was short-lived; knowing the inevitable, the Mac staff was more lenient than usual in providing the star-crossed family with "together time." (Only once did Saffron ask where her mother was. "Heaven," said Amaryllis, and her sister seemed satisfied. When she inquired if it would be possible to visit that place for a picnic, Amaryllis wished her nominated to the Congregation for the Causes right then.) The age and adorableness of the babies made them "bull's-eyes": within five days of their arrival at the center, they were placed in a private home. Amaryllis dehydrated herself with tears. Lani Mott showed up to reassure that "family lawful visits" would be arranged—as the girl's official CASA (the court paperwork had just gone through), the baker's wife informed that she was "launching a third world war" to find a single placement for the three siblings so they could remain together. Everyone knew the chances of that were almost nil. But each time Amaryllis returned to Mac, she futilely asked for her Saffron and Cody, awaiting word that never came. No one would tell her where they were; she couldn't even call them on the phone.

Mac's familiar surroundings, never so wonderful, were now a lonelier haven than she could bear. Except for Cindra, the children Amaryllis had befriended earlier had long since cycled or recycled out—to hospitals, foster families or residential homes (or just plain AWOL); even counselors had moved on, never to be seen again. Favorite volunteer grannies vanished, through attrition born of old age. Against her nature, Amaryllis began to harden. She frowned and sassed through the days, and if our orphan had been a shark, she would surely have eaten a mosasaur with the same consuming indifference that Dézhiree noshed a lunchtime sandwich. Rarely anymore did she seek comfort in the Box of Saints; and went hours without speaking. She huffed air freshener with the new girl, Kristl, and grew antagonistic with staffers. For a few days she proudly sported her very own one-on-one.

At night in her bed, it didn't take much for Amaryllis to imagine the babies already in Mrs. Woolery's satanic hatchery, outfitted in his-and-her helmets, rocketing into walls or drooling on urine-soaked futons. More than once, standing before the backdrop of unfinished mural or empty Streisand pool, she came close to enlisting Kristl on a Tunga Canyon search-and-rescue. Her fearless friend was up for anything.

"Did your CASA tell you where they were?"

"She said she would."

"They're probably waiting to see if you act out. You know: they're not quite sure you're *worthy* of knowing where those babies are. *I* could find them—it's not even *legal,* keeping you separated."

"How? How could you?"

"I could find them *anytime*," said Kristl smugly, as if talking to a cretin.

Freshly fourteen, blond and sinewy, with nacreous glued-on fingernails and bleachy crosshatched suicide scars at the wrists, she was of the sorority of children of the damned (Crissie Fits of Tunga Canyon, naturally, included) fondly named after Godmother Meth: a veritable Kristall-nacht.

"I could find out when we leave."

"What do you mean?"

"We're getting *out*," she whispered.

"When?"

"Field trip on Monday. Huntington Gardens."

"Where's that?"

"Don't ask so many questions. Do you want to go or not?"

"I have court," Amaryllis said timorously.

"Court is bullshit!"

"Lani said the babies'll be there. The judge can put us together."

"That is *so much bullshit*. You are such a fucking victim! You're too *old*. They're *never* gonna put you with your brother and sister."

Amaryllis chewed on a nail. "Are you going to run away by yourself?"

"I don't know," said Kristl haughtily. "It *looks* like it, since you're such a pussy—and you *better* not say anything." Pause. She seemed to be thinking. Then: "If I find out where they are, will you go?"

"If you find out?"

"About your brother and sister! Are you retarded?"

"But how—"

"I've done *much* harder shit. Will you go?"

Amaryllis solemnly nodded her assent. "Did you hear what Dézhiree said at group? 'Yesterday is history, tomorrow is mystery, and today is a gift—that's why we call it the "present." ' Don't you *love* that?"

*A*maryllis Kornfeld, albeit in exhausted, febrile state, had first been brought to children's court for the legally mandated hearing that took place within seventy-two hours of her placement chez Woolery.

Earlymae dressed her up, restoring color to her cheeks with rouge.

Intake and Detention Control had already prepared the petition. Adjudged to be abandoned without provision for support (as the whereabouts of parent or parents was deemed unknown), the girl was thus declared under WIC300(g) to be a dependent child of the Court. Facing the bench, Mrs. Woolery threw a tanned, turquoise-jeweled arm protectively around the shoulder of her "Dillo"—the fact was that she couldn't be paid until the newbie was formally recognized by the system. So: on a scrubby hill in Monterey Park, hard by the sheriff's headquarters and impoverished fields of the defunct Sybil Brand Institute for Women, a judicial referee sat on high, surrounded by his partisans: stenographer, attorneys, social workers, dependency investigators, clerks and bailiffs. Counsel and CSW were dutifully assigned—due diligence search for parents ordered—stuffed animals proffered—tears wiped away—beleaguered child swept back to Canyon.

That was then. Now that she has returned to court, the author is compelled to freshly set the scene.

It is September, though the buildings of which we speak are anything but autumnal. They possess the artificial palette and gallingly "whimsical" tubular outcroppings popular to the aforementioned IMAX aesthetic, and proudly tout their child-friendliness. Yet no stylistic fillip, not even a swooping superimposed Bilbao, might quash the collective misery of its legion of disenfranchised guests. A plethora of female attorneys in black hose and shabby miniskirts pass through the weapons' detector, pagers vibrating in purses with the subtlety of lawn mowers. Adorning lobby walls are the homespun crayon-drawn murals and bland archival photo histories characteristic of such institutions. A vast downstairs holding pen is for charges bused in from group homes and residential-treatment facilities; nearby cells, hidden from view, are for parents in custody, most of whom attend their doomed progeny's hearings in plastic cuffs. Not infrequently, a lady lawyer will mistakenly interrupt one of her inmate clients in the middle of a bowel movement. There are no provisions for privacy.

Four floors of courtrooms, each with dockets of, say, forty cases per day. Outside, families await the bailiff's call—slovenly or nodding off, some incongruously overdressed (white chiffon and wedding lace) and overly made up; young moms' flaunty tatts peeking from shoulderless black sheaths, the latter being all-purpose "special occasion"-wear donned at funerals, graduations or dance clubs. Before they can be heard, the unfortunates must pass through an anteroom of bustling, indifferent attorneys, then sit themselves down on hard pews. Posters ring the courtroom (*102 Dalmatians, Muppets from Space, Toy Story 2*), as do fuzzy animals perched on high like in carnival booths waiting to be dispensed. Lawyers pore through the contents of murrey-colored folders bound by industrial-strength rubber bands—no one ever seems to find what they're looking for. Each towering packet (an eight-year-old in the system since birth might have a 275-page file) is eventually passed to bailiff, clerk, judge. When the music stops, the case is ruminated, then summarily ruled on; the band strikes up, packets again borne aloft and gravely scrutinized before coming to rest. Eager blackboard scrawlings and erasures chart the abbreviated pilgrim's progress of FA (father), MO (Mother), MI (Minor), PGM (Paternal Grandmother), MGM (Maternal Grandmother)—as "contests" revolve around the room in ragged circles, we note the urgent shuttlecocking of stuffed animals, yapping of translators, wider suppression of tears and the bailiff's squelching of some would-be guardian's occasional tacky, tattered outburst. Like bad bones, dates are set, reset and set again, requests brokered and broken, patience lost and sagely regained. With closed eyes we hear the murmur of de facto mothers and decertifications by the FFA; of PRCs, dispos and adjudications; of demands for interviews concerning existence or identity of fathers; of failed grades in parenting classes and noncompliance with court-ordered neurological exams; of pleadings for monitored weekend visits with discretion to liberalize; of termination of parental rights . . .

The lawyers stand when ordered to identify themselves: "Tom Friedrich for the father, who is not present!" "Lisa Gutierrez for the mother, who is not present!" "Rebekah Levy-Soweto for the child, who is not present!"—either no one is present or everyone is. And because this is America, all parties have the right to counsel: each child and each parent—real, presumed, alleged, de facto or surrogate—has that sacred right, as does even the Department itself. There can be no conflict of interest, because with conflict of interest, justice is not served: if needed, there will be *five* attorneys present—for the de factos, presumeds, allegeds and illusorys—or seven, or ten, or twenty. Sometimes the child is brought from the pen too late and misses the hearing altogether. He'd been thinking he could go home! But the Court finds by a preponderance of evidence that continued jurisdiction is necessary, because conditions exist which justify jurisdiction under WIC300, WIC364(c); Return of the Minor to the custody of the parent would create a substantial risk of detriment to the physical/emotional well-being of the minor under WIC366.2(e); Court finds reasonable efforts to reunite Minor and parents have been made and such efforts were unsuccessful; Court finds that Minor cannot be returned to the physical custody of the parents and there exists no substantial probability the Minor will be returned in six months; Court finds by clear and convincing evidence that it is not likely that the Minor can or will be adopted and orders DCFS to continue long-term foster care—

Downstairs, Amaryllis watches a scalded boy play a video game. A pudgy volunteer comes to take her up. She follows, past teens and toddlers transfixed by *The Tigger Movie* on a big-screen TV (the security guard, too, is transfixed). Lani Mott is nowhere to be seen. Amaryllis asks after her, but the volunteer only belches.

When they finally get to the court's fluorescent dugout, a lady shoves a stuffed animal into her chest. "Don't you remember me?" she asks. It's the emergency CSW who saw her at Mac when she was so sick; but today, another caseworker has been assigned. Amaryllis's lawyer comes to talk before they enter court—*not* the one who represented her during the Woolery placement back in Tunga Canyon days (and not that Amaryllis would ever recall). *This* one sweetly asks the same: "Don't you remember me?" The lawyer's perfume and long chestnut hair are familiar, but she looks like she's going to have a baby and Amaryllis doesn't remember that. Both attorney and caseworker agree the girl looks so much "prettier" than before; true enough, but what they really mean is undiseased. They fuss over her gorgeous "mane" and say she looks just like a tiger cub. That makes the attorney du jour think to get her *another* stuffed animal, but the child already is clasping a bear and anyway there aren't any close at hand. (Shocking as that might seem.) She resolves to get her one after the hearing—a kid can never have enough. Again Amaryllis asks where is Lani. Just then, the CASA enters from the wings, breathlessly apologizing for being late. Amaryllis asks about the babies, but a bailiff interrupts to invite them in. As the child is tugged into court, the pregnant attorney stuffs a business card into her pocket, insisting Amaryllis call collect if she ever needs to talk. "Here—I'll give you two," she says profligately, "so you won't lose them." She thrusts another devalued note into her tiny client's vest. In this place (like stuffed animals), such currency is always in circulation.

The judge smiles kindly while ordering the happy-faced bailiff to hand Amaryllis a tiger. He says one grandfatherly thing or another, then: *Wouldn't it be nice to be back in school?* Amaryllis nods without really listening. Now the grown-ups talk among themselves and she stares at people in the court. She doesn't hear anything said except for when the judge snaps that he cannot understand why someone so "adoptable" is still at MacLaren. It seems that it costs a lot of money to stay at MacLaren. Amaryllis struggles to listen for talk of the babies, but everything's going too fast. Lani starts in about the sibs and her efforts to launch a third world war when a man in a rumpled suit reading from a rumpled file says something about the dependent having a father who's incarcerated though not a suspect at the current time. *A father in Carcerated*—what can he mean? And who is the dependent? The father, says the rumpled man, has been "noticed" but declined to be present. But *who* noticed him? wonders Amaryllis. *Declined to be present . . .* the present is a gift—yesterday is history, tomorrow is mys— . . . the father is incarcerated in Salinas Valley . . . —talk now of requesting ongoing therapy for the girl (Medi-Cal pays two sessions a month) so a TPR can be implemented. The CSW says that Amaryllis must deal with loss and grief as evidenced by severance of contact with biological mother (deceased) and father (incarcerated), with short- and long-term goals being to engage in the process of recognizing and working through grief-related issues leading toward resolution and reinvestment in life with joy, objectives being, a) to develop a trusting relationship with a therapist as evidenced by open communication of feelings and thoughts; b) to discuss loss(es) and explore and understand how they impact current behavior; c) to identify the feelings connected to the loss(es); and d) increase ability to verbalize and experience the feeling states of loss and grief. So much loss(es) in a life so young!

Backstage again . . . dazed under full fluorescence, nails bloodily bitten. The women, including the very *latest* CSW, sagaciously realize that no one has told their client about the FA. Your FA's in jail, they say, drawing the matriarchal wagons in a circle around her, patting the mane while handing off a zebra. Zebras are a rare commodity; only the very special rate a zebra. They do *not* tell the child how anxious the police were, Detective Dowling anyway, to find the FA of MI—nor do they reiterate the business about the FA of MI not being a "suspect" *at the current time,* uneager to open the door to the business of the homicide of the MO of MI, of which the MI still thankfully seems innocent. The MI doesn't appear aware of much going on around her and rarely speaks, save to compulsively, pathetically mention her sibs (MIs #2 and #3). Nor does the caring coven enumerate how the MO of MI kept photos and letters from the jailed FA of MI in a box not dissimilar to the MI's Reliquary of Saints and Martyrs, a kind of white wooden drawer with lame little hand-painted seashells that the MO of MI got in Laguna and how the letters, written from prison and never answered, were used to trace the FA of MI, who was and still is serving a term of twenty-to-life for crimes that will remain unreported here, for they are of no relevance. It was further revealed to the MI by said coterie that the FA of MI had been "confined" since the MI was age two and was *not,* by the way, the FA of MIs #2 and #3 (aka The Babies), whose FA, MGM, MGF, PGM and PGF or any other relatives, abbreviated or not, to this day remain unknown.

As reported by the rumpled man, the barely noticeable FA of MI *was* noticed by the Court but declined to be present; and the reader may be pleased to learn he will play no further part in our tale.

CHAPTER 28

The Book of Hours

After her big day in court, Amaryllis, bereft at the thought that she would never see the babies again, planned to suckle an aerosol can till she died. If Auschwitz gas was good enough for Edith Stein, it was good enough for her—only there *wasn't* any Auschwitz gas, so Duster II would have to do. The trip to the Huntington was bumped by an expedition to the Getty, a trade-up neatly arranged through the good offices of the dimpled formerly wimpled woman they called the Flying Nun. Kristl spoke excitedly of the elevated tram one rode to get to the high-up museum and convinced her friend that death, at the very least, should be postponed.

MacLaren's census was swollen by a glut of psych-hospital refugees (Medi-Cal only paid for so much inpatient care); and while it's late in the day to introduce new players, a roll call of those visiting the Westside citadel that travertine Tuesday can be briefly sketched. There was Cindra, ensconced in her pipe-and-leather throne, respirator at full-tilt boogie; Johnathin, a gregarious, slur-speeched tween who had badly concussed himself during an "attachment disorder tantrum" (the kids called him Twappy, or Spesh, after "special needs"); Mystie (aka Lemon-AIDS), who contracted HIV after being assaulted at her mother's wedding reception; nine-year-old twins famous for being brought to court in shackles for failing to testify against their dad in an abuse case involving a sister; and Kaytwon, a ten-year-old who'd been hospitalized for raping boys and girls half his age with foreign objects. Kaytwon had been discharged to Mac after a fleece of lawyers argued it could not be proven that he possessed "the necessary intent to arouse himself or his victims."

Brave the docent and bold the plan that led these diamonds-in-the-rough through a hushed exhibit of illuminated manuscripts from the Middle Ages! Above them, robot blinds whirred open and shut, regulating the amount of sunlight to fall upon the rarities. Our children's darting attention was temporarily arrested by a few gory pages of Christ crucified, angels hovering hummingbird-like at nailed feet, precariously holding goblets to catch the spray of his blood; and sundry depictions of sinners' passage through Hell, a very gold flecked, very miniature Hell at that. Mystie's provocative query—"What did they do wrong?"—hung in the air awhile, unanswered by docent or Dézhiree. Virgins and other do-gooders elicited comments more vile than one might wish in those so youthful. Amaryllis found herself standing for quite some time before a "Sorrowful Madonna" in draped hood of indigo blue. The guide said the vines that reached above her were of columbine, which instantly provoked spirited reference to the hapless school where so many had perished. It was patiently explained that a columbine was a flower (here the docent nodded to our diminutive heroine), as was an amaryllis. Kristl was stumped by this new bit of information and glanced bashfully at her friend with a kind of flummoxed respect, as if suddenly glimpsing her true worth.

On the way out, Amaryllis stood at the final display. A woman stared demurely from the manuscript's open leaves.

"That's Hedwig," said the docent. "She was a noblewoman. She used her money to help the poor."

The matriculants, flanked by burly Mac staffers, had by now all gathered around.

"How much did she have?" asked Johnathin—twappily, dare it be said.

The docent was nonplussed.

"How much *money?*" said Kaytwon.

"Probably quite a lot, by today's standards."

"She don't look rich," sniffed the perp, sizing up the tiny painted figure as he might a "vic"; casing the page, as it were. Kristl eyed him with disdain.

"She's not wearing no fucking shoes!"

"*No language*, Kaytwon," warned Dézhiree sternly.

A displeased male staffer moved closer to the boy.

"I'm glad you pointed that out," said the docent, unfazed. "She's not wearing shoes for a reason. That's because she's an *ascetic*."

"Diabetic?" asked Johnathin, and the group—especially Cindra and the twins—broke into laughter.

"No," said the smiling docent. "That's not what *ascetic* means—"

"But that's a pretty good word, Johnathin," said Dézhiree supportively. " 'Diabetic' is a *big* word."

"Then does it means she's . . . an asshole?" remarked Kaytwon, causing the staffer to place an admonitory thick-fingered hand on his shoulder.

"An ascetic is someone who goes without common comforts, to show devotion to God."

"That would be me," whispered Dézhiree, cracking herself up.

"Why couldn't she just pray?" asked Kristl.

"She *was* praying—that was her way."

"She pray with her feet!" said Kaytwon gleefully, slapping his hands like the fins of a seal. "She put 'em together when she go to sleep!"

There were titters from the group; the staffer's grip tightened, and he shifted behind the boy, letting him feel the heft. Dézhiree was ready to move on, but the docent continued.

"They called her Blessed Hedwig. She was actually a saint."

"I ain't never heard of Saint Hedwig Day," said Mystie. "Why she ain't got no holiday?"

"Well, maybe in other parts of the world, she *does*," said Dézhiree.

Amaryllis leaned in for a closer look at the sad-eyed figure. She was clutching a rosary and what looked like a Bible, but the docent said it wasn't really a Bible at all.

"They called that a Book of Hours," he said. "Each had prayers written in it for the day—morning prayers, afternoon prayers . . . the more elaborate the book, the wealthier the owner. Families actually hired artisans—painters and craftsmen—to design them. They were very important, because they would remain in those families, sometimes for hundreds of years."

"Was she married?"

"Yes. To a man named Henry the Bearded."

Titters, in light of the docent's scraggly growth.

"Was she married to *you*?"

"Not to me, no," said their unruffled guide. "I'm not *that* old."

"Was she a nun?" asked Amaryllis.

"No, but that's a good question. She was a laywoman."

More hilarity, especially from Johnathin and the twins, while Kaytwon luridly rubbed his own tits. Dézhiree slapped his hand away and told him she'd "had it."

"Did she have any children?"

"She was married at twelve."

Kaytwon whispered to Kristl that he bet she had more pussy hair than the saint. Kristl elbowed his chest, and he stifled a cry.

"And while that's not a *good* thing, it wasn't unusual in those times."

"I like to marry *me* a twelve-year-old," said Kaytwon as their procession moved on.

"You wouldn't know what to do with one," said Kristl.

"Is that right?"

"Stick to the five-year-olds, sicko."

Amaryllis trailed after the docent in a kind of fever. "But . . . how could they call her Blessed while she was still alive? They *never* beatify the living . . . they had Devil's Advocates and a postulator and if the postulator said Hedwig had heroic virtue, the pope would make a declaration saying people could call her Venerable—then she'd beatify if she did two miracles. John Paul says now you only need *one*, unless you're a martyr. So they would canonize but *after*, only *after* she was dead—"

"Well, that's . . . now that's really exceptional! Where'd you learn so much? Have you been creeping into the research library at night?" The docent winked at Dézhiree and the orphan shrugged. "And you're exactly right—she wasn't made a saint until twenty years after her death. I said they called her Blessed, but they sure didn't while she was still with us; you are *correct*. That portrait would have been done *before* she became a saint. Now, whether she was Venerable at that point, I do not know. But that is a *very* excellent observation!"

Amaryllis cringed, feeling the sin of pride for having showboated. Kaytwon passed close and said, "Smarty-cunt."

⌒

Dézhiree sidled up to her as the tram snaked down to the parking lot. "You OK, honey?" The orphan nodded. "Got off pretty deep into that saint stuff, huh. I mean, that's *good*—you're a *real* smart girl. I just

don't think you should get too crazy with it, know what I'm sayin'?"
Amaryllis nodded, staring at her shoes. "And I know it's rough on you
being separated from your sister and brother. I know that. But you've got
a lot of people on your side pullin' for you. Tryin' to make it happen. Like
Lani—now *that's* a good lady. She don't even get paid to do what she's
doin', did you know that? But that lady *cares*, know what I'm sayin'? I
just don't want you gettin' too deep into devil's advocates and all that! I
liked that movie, by the way. Al Pacino in the subway? *Woo* that was cold!
And Keanu's my *man.* Sex-y!" She put her hand on the girl's. "But—do
you understand where I'm comin' from? Do you, Amaryllis? 'Cause
you're a smart, smart girl, know what I'm sayin'? And I want you to
start *usin'* some of that brainpower for things that are going to get you
ahead in this world. That could be computers, that could be bein' a writer,
whatever—whatever you choose. 'Cause you can do anything you want,
Amaryllis, know what I'm sayin'? Anything you want in this world, and
that's for real. You have the mind and we can get the tools. If we don't
have the tools—at Mac or *wherever*—we'll *find* 'em, OK? We'll *find* you
the tools, OK, honey? I *guarantee* that, know what I'm sayin'? Dézhiree
guarantees that. I put my money where my mouth is, OK? I just don't
want you to get caught up in lots of . . . exter-aneous saints and martyrs
and 'beetications'! I mean, that's all innneresting and has its place, but
there's a big world out there too and I'd hate you to miss it. OK, sweetheart?"

Back in the bus, the kids groused about lunch. Then Dézhiree announced the big surprise: they were all invited by the *Scream* man for
McDonald's at his production office. That was particularly good news for
Kristl, who had planned to run away during the tour but had found the
edifice escape-proof.

When they pulled in front of the nondescript Ventura Boulevard building, bushy-tailed film interns—fresh-scrubbed models of
compassion—awaited curbside to usher them in. Upstairs, a morbid display of props from his films vied with the Getty's chamber of horrors,
but the one that riveted them stood eerily alone in its Plexiglas showcase:
a burn-scarred, rubbery hand with long razors at the end of its fingers.
The *Scream* man's partner (a gracious, dimpled woman, who looked
more like Ava Gardner than she did the Flying Nun), led the children to
a conference room, where burgers, Cokes and fries sat in the middle of a
huge granite table. They dove in.

The startling thing—at least to Amaryllis—was how without much ado she suddenly found herself in the shimmery, baking sunshine of the Valley sprinting by storefronts, doglegging around Vendome and Blockbuster and Nail Time and Pick Up Stix, in this store and out the other—Pier 1, Bookstar, Strouds, Kinko's, Koo Koo Roo—zigzagging Kristl covering their trail as they forded streets wider and busier than any Amaryllis had ever known: through drugstores bright as the blinding midday sun, past delicatessens and savings & loans and marinating trash bins and ticketing policemen and old folks on their last legs, and heatstroked beggars on bus benches, until they walked miles and miles, the damp white-yellow knob of Amaryllis's wrist bone stinging from her indomitable friend's iron grip.

Finally, Kristl made a pleading call that did not look to be going well, at least not until she read the address off the pay phone to whoever was on the other end. She hung up and said her mom was coming and that was good, because the police would soon be "siccing dogs" on them. She said bloodhounds used their long ears to stir up the soil for the scent of whatever they were tracking.

The girls went to Rite Aid and busied themselves for what seemed like hours. They stole cough syrup and looked at all the makeup and perfume and laughed uncontrollably when they found an aisle that sold diapers for grown-ups. Then Kristl said they should leave, because a clerk was looking at them funny and probably thought they were going to shoplift, which of course they already had. So they went back into the deaf-and-dumb heat, walking in circles with their bad b.o.

A tattooed man roared up on a motorcycle and the girls backed off until Kristl recognized him—it was Mike. She screamed and threw her arms around him. She asked where her mom was and Mike said she had to stay in Lawndale, but he was going to take her to Topanga and Tina would come later. He handed Kristl a helmet and told her to get on. She said she wouldn't without her friend, and Mike said they would have to come back for Amaryllis in a regular car. Kristl said she wouldn't go without her friend, but Mike said she better if she didn't want him to drive her ass back to MacLaren right now. Kristl made Mike promise they'd come back in a car, and she told Amaryllis to meet them at the dumpster behind Vons and that she should hide until they came. She put on her helmet and they roared off, practically splitting the orphan's eardrums.

Feeling sorry for herself and queasy about her betrayal of Dézhiree, Amaryllis begins to cry but stops quickly enough, not wishing to draw attention. Her progress now becomes hurly-burly, scattershot, vaudevillian: in any given broiling locale, she stands weirdly stock-still, flustered; then, realizing she is making a spectacle of herself, moves on with a jerk as if given the Hook. Nowhere to go . . . so she sticks to the impossibly long alley with dumpsters all around—blue for merchants, green for residences, brown for construction debris (these, big as trucks), gray for storage, yellow for recycling—dodging them as they close in on her like the living boulders she saw on an archaic *Star Trek*. Each path of escape seems the one that will end in Carceration—in the Valley, just like her father . . .

Amaryllis wheels pell-mell through humid air, her orbit in decay, instinctively gravitating toward places where children gather, but children are the worst bloodhounds of all, and they point and whisper at the sweaty loser until she gets the Hook again, and tears across the street like a lost panicked dog, through entries of stores perceived to have rear exits; as she passes through each garishly lit refuge the air-conditioning cools her body, though is not a comfort. Plunged again into the bustle of tarry parking lots, parking lots like cities, parking lots with whole populations, rhythms, moods and laws. She slows until standing stock-still, dazed and vacant in the warpy heat, staving off tears, no longer thinking of the babies or her mother (diseased) or her father (carcerated) or Topsy or Kristl or Dézhiree or *anything*—starving, yet without a single thought of food, and shamefully peeing in the brush behind Vons, where the bluest dumpster is, at a break in the bushes that leads to a slow-moving river in a concrete bed upon whose ceasing current she would most certainly not be borne back to the past. She squats and does her business, old breast wound aching again, tears like blisters on her cheeks, thinking of Pixies as she hikes up her pants—they'd be having dinner now and talking about her (though maybe not). The lonely Box of Saints tucked in a drawer, waiting . . .

She continues her locomotion to the redundant oasis of Moorpark Park, but the grown-ups notice when she sits on the bright orange slide for a while—then off again, ashamed and horrified that she left her post and might miss her ride as nightfall comes.

*   *   *

"There she is! There! There! There!"

Headlamps light her up. Amaryllis stirs, half asleep in the bushes behind the blue dumpster, on the lip of the hillock that dips down to the river. Kristl is grabbing at her, and suddenly she finds herself in the enormous, slippery backseat of an old El Dorado. There's even a pillow back there and a chewed-up dog bone on the carpet.

"We kept *looking* for you. My mom was gonna leave!"

Tina is at the wheel. Her long, squeezed-together face reminds Amaryllis of the *Scream* masks, but more pretty than scary.

"This is *so* fucked-up, Kristl Ann! Honey, I am on *parole.*"

"But she's my *friend*—"

"You can *never* say I picked up this girl, Kristl Ann, *never.*" She turned back to Amaryllis. "You can *never* say I did this, OK? Because that's kidnapping!" To her daughter: "I'll tell you one thing, she is going back *tomorrow.*"

"Mom!—"

"And you are, too—"

"You can't!"

"Well that's just the way it's going to be!"

Kristl started to talk, but her mother said, "Shut up!" and they drove in silence along Ventura Boulevard until rattling onto the 101. Once they were on the freeway, Tina got calmer but yelled more.

"Do you even *know* what they'll do to your mother if they stop me with the two of you? Throw me in *jail,* that's what. That's right. And jail is *not* a place I want to be, *huh*-uh. *Been* there *done* that *no* way."

"I'm *sorry*—"

"We can't even go back to *Lawndale.* I can't even put you with your grandma—she's too sick. Though I may have to . . . don't you think I'm the *first* one they will call? Huh? Don't you *know* that? Well, you're fuck-ing right. Probably called *already.* I may be in violation just by not check-ing the messages! And Grandma? Would you really want to do that to your grandma? Would you, Kristl Ann? She'd call the cops on you for *sure*—you know Grandma don't put up with no shit. And why should she? That's why we're gonna be with Mike in Topanga. We can't go back home! I can't believe I'm out here in the dark with you two fugitives on my way to fucking Topanga! I had to break away from *business* to come get your friend. I'm getting my real estate license, did you know that?"

Kristl shook her mortified head.

"Do you think that's easy? Do you think *anyone* can get a real estate license? They just hand them out like candy? Here, Tina! Here's your license! You are free now to go and sell yourself a mansion! I wish. One mansion and I could buy a house. I was doing *business*, Kristl; that's why Mike had to come. You love your friend so much but not enough to say she was with you. Why didn't you say you were with your friend when you called? Huh? Huh? The *only* reason I'm here—the *only* reason, Kristl Ann—is because I know how *loyal* you are to your friend, because I *raised* you like that. And that's a nice quality. But I was doing mother-fucking *business*, do you understand?" Back to Amaryllis: "Excuse my language. I don't usually talk that way, but sometimes the situation demands it." To Kristl: "Do you *know* what kinda bills I have to pay, Kristl Ann? With your daddy in the penitentiary? He can't *help*, I'm telling you. He may *want* to, but he *can't*, OK? So it's on *me*. And, honey, you do *not* want to see your mama back in that jail either, *believe* me. I *know* she's your friend and she's real cute, but I can't be an accessory! Do you know what an accessory is? Because what you two have done is committed a crime. MacLaren Hall is an *institution,* and to leave an institution without permission as *minors* is a *crime*. They put their trust in you not to do that. They're not all bad people. Some of them care; I know they do. 'Cause they weren't *all* bad, even in jail. There's always a few rotten apples, but there's people who care, too. People that help you. Did you think I could just walk out of Central if I felt like it? It is *not* a perfect world. Do you think I could walk out of New Beginnings or *wherever* just because I didn't like the way the sheets smelled? Or the food? Or because they made me mop the damn floor? *No, I couldn't*. Because they gave me a trust and that is a *sacred* trust. And you know what? As far as the law stands, you may as well have robbed a bank and I'm the getaway."

"Mama—"

"*That's* an accessory, OK? I can't *be* that for you, do you understand, Kristl Ann? Do you ever want to come home?"

"Yeah."

"I didn't hear you."

"I said *yes*."

"That didn't sound like someone who wants to come home. That sounded like someone who doesn't *give* a shit about their mom, who's risking her *freedom* to pick up her daughter and her daughter's *friend*, who the mother doesn't even *know*—"

"Mom, I *do* want to come home—"

"Well then, act like it! And don't violate a sacred trust! *We* have a sacred trust—mother and daughter. Do you remember when you and Dakin were with me on a trial basis? And we had the dispo and they said you could stay with me? How happy you were? I worked my ass off for that! Do you think it was *fun* for me to go to school at night and hear some fucking fool who's probably molesting his kids tell me how to parent? Well it wasn't! But did I walk out? No I didn't. I maintained a stable home, Kristl Ann! I peed in a bottle for those people, OK? I did that for *you.* Would you and your friend pee in a bottle for *me?* Do you think that's fun?"

Kristl laughed and Amaryllis smiled and so did Tina, but then she got mad again.

"When someone says OK you can keep your kids, but first you have to go pee in a bottle and take these classes at night . . . when you're already tired because you have to work during the day—then they turn around and say, Hey, we're takin' your kids away anyhow! Because your daddy paid a visit and he wasn't supposed to! *I* didn't ask him over. I ain't no fucking p.o.! I ain't no police, either. What'd they expect me to do, handcuff him? Citizen's arrest? The man like to kill me. Hell, I'm afraid of that man. And he shows up and what am I supposed to do? I told the judge that, I told the lawyer that, I told the social worker, hell I stood on a street corner and shouted it. Do you think anyone gives a shit? Your father stayed on the porch, do you remember? For thirty minutes! *You* were there. It was *totally* supervised, do you remember? Thirty uninvited totally supervised minutes on the porch and that's enough to take my kids away? And the Court of Appeals *agreed* with me, did you know that? I never got any damn reunification services, I got *family maintenance.* The law says there's a *difference* between maintenance and reunification, a *big* difference! They say I already *had* my eighteen months, and that's a *crock.* But you are *not* going to blow this for me, Kristl Ann! Everything I worked for to put this family back together! I am *not* going to let it happen! I have *business,* Kristl Ann, I have business at *home* and now I can't even go back—and all because you got it in your head to shit on a mother and daughter's sacred trust. You can't just waltz in and make me an accessory! They will *not* give a real estate license to an accessory! I'm doing you and your little friend a *major* fucking favor here and I want points for that, do you understand? *Kristl you answer me—*"

"Yes yes yes, I understand! All right? OK? *Take* your fucking points, all right? Goddamnit! You can have your points! Fucking take them take them take them!"

*I*t was dark by the time they reached Topanga—another canyon. Kristl convinced her friend it wasn't anywhere near "Tunga," but only after Tina and her boyfriend concurred.

Amaryllis lay in a moldy sleeping bag on the open-air tabernacle of the deck. There were tons of insects, and the sound of animals was all around. The sky was a puddle of black ink and the discrete brilliance of galaxies confounded her. An old mangy dog, no bloodhound indeed, sniffed at them but couldn't be bothered.

Mike had his little girl with him. She was about four and slept outside with the runaways. She had a talking doll called Amazing Amy. Mike said the doll had a computer chip, so it always knew the time. At eight o'clock each morning, Amazing Amy said she wanted breakfast and if you tried to give her a little plastic pizza slice that came with the set she'd say, "Not *pizza* for *breakfast!*" Mike said there were sensors embedded in the pizza slices and in Amazing Amy's mouth, too. Sometimes she got a temperature and asked for aspirin. If you gave her pizza instead, she got mad. Mike said she cost $90.

The girls got up early and whispered awhile. Amaryllis asked if her mom was really going to call MacLaren, and Kristl said probably not, but if she did, it wouldn't be before noon. She never got it together before noon. Kristl said that maybe they should split. Then she said maybe her mom wouldn't snitch if she had "business"— if her mom was busy with business, she might not have time to deal with anything else and it would probably be easier to just let them stay in the Canyon and help with chores instead of hassling with driving them all the way back to El Monte. But Mike would have to agree, because it was his house—Kristl said Mike was on parole too, so that probably wouldn't happen, because he would get in trouble if anyone found out two underage AWOLs were staying at his house. He'd be an accessory, big-time. Amaryllis asked what parole was, and Kristl said it was when you got out of jail but still had to live by jail rules.

They went to the kitchen to look for food and, Amazing Amy aside, *did* have pizza for breakfast. They cackled and whispered and Tina shushed them from the bedroom. The little girl came in the front door with her doll and the mangy dog. The latter, casting a rheumy eye on garbage and grotty dishes, turned around and sauntered out to the deck.

For some reason, watching him go struck the girls' funny bones, and they laughed some more, then Kristl broke a glass; they winced and grew still. Her mother sprang from the bedroom. Amaryllis stared—her bush was the center of a giant spiderweb tattoo that spread across thighs and stretch-marked stomach. Tina fastened on to Kristl's arm and shoved her into the bedroom. She started screaming and Kristl screamed back and Amaryllis heard Mike tell them both to shut the fuck up. The doll said it wanted breakfast.

Amaryllis saw money and a pack of cigarettes on the floor next to a beanbag chair. She grabbed them, crept through the front door and bolted down the long gravel drive.

Shutting its sticky eyes in sleep, the old dog listened to her steps recede.

CHAPTER 29

Doggish Days

*I*t has been written that after many a summer dies the swan, but plenty happens in the seasons preceding such a lyrical demise. To wit: the heavy-bodied bird must shed its feathers before finding a mate. That is what renders it flightless.

During most of *his* season, Will'm nested. Though he never ventured to Northern California, he did take the other half of his friend Fitz's advice, trimming the wild oak tree of a beard close enough to skin so that it looked inadvertently modern (or nearly so). His accent too was shorn, the notes still melodious yet steeped in less juice; anachronisms came fewer and further between, while contemporary phrases and intonations grew like sprigs from pavement cracks. There was no explaining that. Our fugitive ruefully discarded his telltale tweeds and took to wearing a Smart & Final Iris windbreaker. He did not want for money, thanks to the deathbed bequest of the late, lamented Geo. Fitzsimmons; in the envelope that graced the blouse of the suicide lay $6,000, which Will'm did nothing to flaunt.

To what do we owe this transformation? That he was mindful of police and the continuous danger of his circumstances certainly did not explain all, for a larger part of him remained quixotic and incognizant of the threats of the world. On the streets, and with his toilet, he proved competent as always: only twice did he find himself significantly interviewed, each time by armed squadrons on horseback. Polite and sober-eyed throughout, still "in character"—but with the lambent fire of an actor more than midway through a very long run—Will'm refrained from the extemporaneous outbursts that were already so much a part of his past. In both instances, though he couldn't produce sufficient I.D., he remained apologetic and unmolested, Santa Monica on the whole being indigent-friendly; the tanned, hairy-armed cops cantered off in search of nubile beachgoers committing misdemeanors.

How, then, to explain the mellowing?

He spent hours atop a Macy's bath towel, burning his skin at the shore. The waves lapped relentlessly as is their wont; sunbathers lazed and sortied in pointillist ballet; dusk ushered in the nebulae. He imagined himself illustrated, a hero on a dead world that was tentatively beginning to flower again—saw himself standing tall under empyrean tempera of cloud-scudded sky, replete with William Morris's beloved Arthurian garb, a gleaming, high-crested morion stuffed onto thickened head, with smoky visor and ventail, fat thighs squeezed into cuisses, wearing épaulières of rubies plucked from Saturn's rings, sword and escutcheon raised against bottomless heavens filled with vessels of improbable size disgorging a-hundred-thousand-score armies of desperate, adventuresome men: celestial warriors! Will'm lay on the sand with his recumbent DNA and bore minuscule, magisterial witness to the wonder-book of yawping cosmological eye. (Science fiction pocket-book covers had forever seared the memory of a boy called Marcus Weiner, but the cryptonesic Will'm knew not whence the images came.) The pounding of surf stupefied him with reverence—any damn fool knew there had to be life elsewhere. Soon starships would hover like floating Escherian cities, ivied and fountain-filled, populated by toga'd handmaidens. "Fitz?" Will'm used to say. "We are temporal and temporary beings, nebulous childr'n on a wildly moving place!"

Like most fellow nomads, our friend enjoyed roaming the 3rd Street Promenade and varied fringes of this fair Bay City, and sitting on benches in front of the bookstores. The presence of so many volumes preening for passersby from behind the glass was heartening. One day, mused Will'm, he must use a portion of Fitz's legacy to take a cab to that downtown place where the *News from Nowhere* journal of his wandering years was stored; a taxi would be more prudent than profligate—the detective and his minions were likely to entrap him if he went on foot.

On emerging from his reverie, he found that a woman of tremendous bulk had materialized beside him. She panted and perspired, her tender dewlap trembling as she turned to address him with doleful eyes.

He could do nothing but place an arm about her shoulders—something she seemed to sorely need, for her shaking instantly ceased.

"Are you all right?" he asked.

She made a guttural sound, then sneezed. He looked at her quizzically, and she sneezed again. Coughed. Laughed. Trembled and coughed again. He laughed himself, then said: "Christ! Can you speak?"

"Ih c'n! Ih c'n! C'n spake!"

But not well enough to intelligibly give her name: Jane Scull.

"Are you—are you *hungry?*"

"Yihss! Am—am unh-gree!"

She spoke in great grunting edicts, like a cannonball angel. Dirty white hearing aids were shoved in both ears.

"Good!" he shouted. "Let's get you a Johnny Rocket's!"

Will'm stood and walked a pace, then turned to see what she was up to. She stayed rooted, staring back like a frightened child—it panged him, for her helplessness evoked his orphan-daughter Amaryllis. Seizing a clammy hand, he steered them past storefronts. Three cheeseburgers and a quantity of milk shakes were ordered (strawberry, vanilla, chocolate), for which the cashier made him pay in advance. Then all the waiters and waitresses seemed to go mad, abandoning their posts while dancing and gesticulating to the music of the little silver jukes; he'd been to this café before, but had never seen such mayhem. Of an instant, their choreographies ceased and everything returned to normal. A few patrons laughed among themselves, amused by the gaping transient couple.

That he called her Janey (a thing that made the startled girl feel as if he could read minds), was a happy coincidence to his own privately parallel world—a slew of personae now alternately burning bright and fading too within the frayed fabric of a serpentine, superbly demented history. For while Will'm had begun to molt (as established), strange plumage persisted: *wife* Jane Burden, *daughters* Jenny and Mary; *mentor* Ruskin; *boon companions* Burne-Jones and Rossetti—the latter his best friend, who, so legend had it, betrayed Mr. Morris to become Janey's paramour . . .

At dusk, they made their way to the boarded-up hotel where he'd been squatting. Jane Scull's eyes widened with delight on seeing the room, as if it were Bexleyheath itself. It *was* clean and presentable enough, with a large scrap of wax paper tacked to the wall, upon which Will'm had stenciled flowers—trademark latticework of poppy, honeysuckle and fritillaria. The work left off abruptly, its maker having lost the thread.

"Lay down awhile, girl!"

He nearly pushed her onto the futon, retrieved during a freeway-litter sally. While ecstatic to have found something like a real bed to lie down upon, *this* Jane flushed and demurred.

"I won't take advantage of you! What would you have me for? I want you to *rest*. I've some aspirin—you're feverish. Here: water. Drink!" She swallowed the pills, too, and he lit some liquor store–bought votives. "Dangerous for a woman out there, no? Brigands'll rape and leave you bleeding. Happen yet? And the *policemen*—thugs and abominations! The policemen are worse! 'Cepting the ones on horseback . . . they seem a reasonable lot. Though maybe it's the *horses* who are reasonable. But you don't have to worry now, Janey—where've you been living? Where've you had a *bath*? Or have you had one at all?"

" 'ave! 'ave uh bith!"

She would not have him think she was careless and filthy; Lord, not him!

He sat back on his heels and stared, like a director at an audition. She was all jiggling flesh and great salmon-sushi lips, thighs and buttocks tattooed with the black-and-blue fingerprints of roughhouse vagrants, and wore deep squarish patches of dirt on shoulder and hip that would take more than scouring soap to erase. She kept repeating "un-keen" (which Will'm eventually translated: "I'm clean"), her echolalia accompanied by an almost involuntary disrobing, so that suddenly she sat before him naked and quaking, breasts avalanching to either side, bruised-white mutton legs rudely splayed.

He had never seen a woman of such epic proportions, and was humbled by her offering. Gently, he covered her up and sat down at futon's edge.

"I don't need any of that, Janey—don't *want* that. It's not that I don't find you a stunner, all right? That, you most certainly are! It's just—well, you've been with *him*, haven't you? With Rossetti. And I understand it. I know I drove you to it. But you see I don't know much anymore. Don't know much about *myself*. And I don't know *you* . . . and you, well, you don't know *me*, now do you? What I'm up to. You're not as keen on my work as you once were, no? Anyhow"—he stroked his stubble, mulling a mathematical problem—"it's a while since I've been with a woman—why, I'd hardly know what to do! It's a while since I've been with *myself*! And we don't *need* do it, Janey. We don't need do it for me to look after ya, we won't have *any* of that—not for me to look after you. Is that all right? That's all right, isn't it, Janey?"

While he spoke, Ms. Scull went from puzzlement to tender acquiescence, until finally answering "ess! ess!"—a thousand times *ess*. For while she could hear little, she understood all.

From that moment on, she became exceedingly careful of her person; carried herself differently when she walked, with and without him; and modulated her outbursts, which themselves became more studiedly articulate. The corrective afflatus was not the result of "falling in love," for Jane Scull felt she had *always* loved this man, but rather a kind of self-reckoning that came upon her as would a religious vision—a sudden, inexplicable, karmic settling of accounts, a cosmic ordering and coming-to, a gyroscopic awareness that arrived with such ease and graceful surety that it would remain the rest of her days.

That night in the defunct Tropicana, they stayed up late and Will'm sang old Oxford songs. Then he lay on his back while she slept, attentive to her respirations. At half-past three, like that time at the Higgins, there were crashes and shouts and flashes of light as policemen raided the units. Will'm took her hand and ran as he'd run so often through the years—this time into the night, past the quiet pier and Camera Obscura, north along refurbished bluffs to the palisades of the California Incline.

They leapt a low wooden fence and spent the night huddled against each other on the cliffside brush of the esplanade, where, hours before, couples had lingered to watch the raked evensong of sunset skies.

*W*ill'm was fated to meet all manner of eleemosynary souls—he brought that out. A few weeks ago, he had caught the eye of a Catholic outreach worker giving away condoms and toothbrushes on the Promenade. Now, seeing the bedraggled couple the morning after their eviction, the benefactor approached.

"Do y'all need help?"

"What do you mean, sir?"

"Do y'all need a place to stay?"

Will'm shifted, stroking his cheek where once the beard had been.

Jane Scull took the man in with benign, near stately indifference—proud new wife of the Chairman of the Disembodied.

"It is possible," said Will'm, with guarded eyes.

"Y'all know SeaShelter? Over on Olympic? Salvation Army? Sure you do. Over by the buses—y'all seen the big yard with the Blue Buses?"

The voice loved to rise up, whether asking or telling.

"And what," said Will'm, "is there, sir?"

"Well, showers and beds and lockers—y'all been to St. Joseph's, haven't you?" He looked at Jane Scull and squinted. "SeaShelter'll get you a hot shower? And there's food and lockers for your personal things?"

Her eyes lit up at the mention of amenities—yet it was the idea of a locker that for Will'm was a real enticement. He would be able to retrieve his manuscript and stow it close at hand.

"I can help y'all be guests if you want to be. Y'all can stay for twenty days. They can help with medical needs, too. Would y'all be interested in being guests?"

"Possibly yes, sir." He didn't want to be a pushover, or a charity case either. But he had Janey to think of now.

"Real good then! They'll find you a job? Lotta hotels in this city now—new hotels. There's one thing you should know? They're drug- and alcohol-free? I mean, SeaShelter? That's something they don't tolerate. So they expect you to be sober?" He handed them a flyer with a map to the facility and a general list of rules and requirements. "Go stand at the gate between three and six, that's when guests are let in. Three and six in the *evening*. Best get there early? Now, one more thing is, they ask you to leave by seven-thirty each morning? Because they don't want you sleeping in? Y'all like me to go on and call ahead to say you're coming?"

The couple agreed. After the minister left, Jane threw her arms around Will'm and said, "Shower!" without impediment.

CHAPTER 30

To the Four Winds

SeaShelter is a small, clean hangar on Olympic, in the crook of the Santa Monica Freeway as it loops into PCH. Showers and lockers reside outdoors, while the structure itself contains kitchen, administrative offices and beds segregated by sex. Morning coffee and biscuits are provided, and supper too. At twenty days, guests are asked to decide whether they wish to stay on as bona-fide residents in a six-month social re-entry program. Jane and William elected to do so, becoming sterling citizens in short stead.

William was sent to a clinic for pills, the daily cluster of which had a sly way of distancing the voices of Victorian friends and family. The medications' main side effect was obesity—he now tipped the scales at three hundred pounds. Jane Scull ate less than before admission but did not lose any flesh. She was fitted with new hearing aids, and waxed indispensable with pail and mop; whereas William Marcus—for that is how he came to be known—having offered his services impromptu during a mundane culinary emergency, was drafted thereafter into the role of kitchener and off-hours pâtissier.

At the same time they thickened body and senses, swallowed prescriptions made for small miracles too: soon, the face of a wife appeared before him that was *neither* of the Janes—it was Katrina's, come not as hallucination but as odd curio, to evoke sorrow and tender sympathies. While waking or rising or even strolling with Ms. Scull, the ex-agent formed memories of himself in restaurants and exquisite cars with boisterous, passionate men. He was able to recall premieres and brises and corporate retreats, and saw the landscape of Oxford—less the

colleges of his communion with Swinburne and Ruskin, though he did
see the stones of Avebury and his own bare, bleeding feet; more, Katrina
with him at hospital . . . but perhaps at a later time than during those
English peregrinations. *Adirondacks?* He turned the queer word over in
his mouth like a taste he was trying to identify. He'd spent *lots* of time in
hospitals, it seemed. After a while, William even visualized the cul-de-
sac at Redlands, but could not remember the name of that place or the
faces of the couple who nurtured him there.

Meanwhile, Jane Scull walks the Promenade when SeaShelter
chores are done. She is alone, and that's how she wants it, for she is unwell in body, mind and spirit. There are things she cannot discuss with
anyone—not William or the shelter folk or even the street pastor, who
still visits to wish them well, the tail of each utterance lilting skyward
like a smoky question mark.

What would the Catholic have told her that she didn't already
know? He might have reiterated the sublime workings of the Lord . . .
but she *knew* His lessons and workings, though in all humility could not
understand why He would wish her to be so miserable after bestowing
her dear William—for the Lord had brought him to her, and William was
her life. It was for him that she diligently stood before the looking glass
with a self-tutored apostrophe of plosives, affricates, surds and so-
nances; it was for him she now bathed; it was for him she now breathed;
it was for him she spoke glottal poems that, because of her shyness, he
would never hear, a phonemic rhapsody of diphthongs, yaps and
rhotacisms, blubbers and brays, thunders of ictus and rictus and hail of
caesuras—electric elocutions, all for him and for hymn and for Him. For
William . . .

Weeks ago, he spoke of a spastic child—was it Jenny?—a daughter
he implied to be his own. Surely she could not have known that because
of the receding tide of his delusion, Jenny—William *Morris*'s Jenny—
had already drifted to farther shores. Yet it struck her deeply; *this* Jane
did not wish to burden him with another, a boy or girl not even his!

For it was Jilbo's: she gagged on his name.

Nearly seven months gone, but no one could tell.

Hand to belly she walked, forlorn and agitated. Distraught and devoted . . .

The dirty man approached.

"Hey, good-lookin'. Now, why you trippin'?"

She frowned at the gimp.

"Had my eye on you—big girl! *Like* that. Like a big hug. *Lot* to hug there."

She moved away, and Someone-Help-Me trailed after, or a reasonable facsimile thereof, for *he* had undergone a transformation himself, purely cosmetic, and was now called the same as the plea of his spanking-new signage: Please-Help.-Bless.

"What, too *good* for me?" he barked, taking care not to get too close. The girl could do him damage. "Watt? You sellin' it? Fuckin' *cow* with dirty titties want fuckin' *heehaw?*"

He was in her hair a block or so when Jane wheeled and almost spoke. But she didn't want to give the pest ammunition.

"Hey shit," he said, a smile metastasizing on his face. "I *like* big girls, that's all. Got a man? Man friend? Everybody need a friend. Everybody need *milk!* Yer *fine.* Cain't talk? Dat—wull, fuck *me!*" He slapped at his britches and howled through a rotten mouth. "Whoa! Got motors in your ears! Cain't *talk!* I *knew* that. Nuthin' to *say*—leas' tha's *honest!* Shit, people talk all shit any*how.*" He guffawed again. "*Like* a big girl who can't talk. But kin ya *hear?* Can ya *hear* with them motors, big-tittie girl?"

Jane lunged and grunted contemptuously, a forceful combination that took him by surprise. Adding to her unhappiness, she noticed passersby throwing sideshow stares. She strode off, and Please-Help.-Bless could not catch her.

Hobbling in her dust, he shouted, "I seen you on Pico, by Clare—hey!—you smoke?" He pulled a ratty pack of Pall Malls from a shirt pocket and, propelled by his cane, precariously offered it up. "Kin you hear me? Come on, big girl, where you stay at? Where you stay! Aw," he said, coming to a winded stop. "You cain't fuckin' hear *shit.*" He lit a cigarette. "Gonna fuck ya, big girl. Gonna fuck out yer big *cow* brains."

He laughed before darting into traffic, whereupon the shameless minstrel-show mugger courted drivers with his cardboard namesake's entreaty.

"*Is* he worse?" Tull asked.

"I don't know if he's *worse,*" said Lucy, mulling it over, "but he isn't *happy.*"

"Can't they give him antibiotics? I mean, tetracycline or whatever?"

"They *are*—they're *swabbing* stuff on him. But he's still got the intense zits. And he *picks*. It's, like, totally volcanic at this point."

Tull shook his head. "That is so fucked."

"Evidently, it's from the Apert's—I mean, the acne. I went on-line—"

"I wish I could get my hands on Mr. Fucking Apert . . . how could Edward's genes be so—shitty? It's like *nothing works*."

"Except his brain."

"Right. And that works better than anyone's."

The Four Winds term had just begun. The cousins, on a long walk from school, were strolling down Montana. Pullman loped behind, drawing the usual stares. They got a Jamba Juice and crossed the street to pick up goodies for Bluey at her favorite new confectionary haunt. Their grandmother had been furious with Gilles Mott when he dared to foist on her a pale substitute for that mouthwatering almond-and-pomegranate delight before informing her (under duress) the originals were no longer available; then one day Tull brought home some high-end morsels from Le Marmiton and, voilà, her faith in sweets and mankind was restored.

Pink pastry box in hand, the trio migrated north toward the Brentwood Country Mart.

Lucy spoke up: "My mom said Trinnie's seeing that detective. Romantically."

"Yeah."

"Is that an old thing?"

"You mean, from before?"

"Yeah."

"Maybe. I don't know."

"I mean, do you think they porked when they were younger?"

"I hate it when you use that word."

"Well, did they?"

"I told you, I don't *know*." Then: "My mother has to be with someone or she flips out."

"That's harsh," said Lucy, while agreeing to herself it was probably true. "Have you talked to him?"

"Who."

"The *detective*."

"About what."

"Your *father*."

He shook his head.

"Did she dump that guy Rafe?"

"I don't know. I guess so."

"How'd he take it?"

"I have no idea. And it's Ralph. He calls himself Ralph now."

"Don't you think it's kind of . . . weird that your mother and that detective—I mean, the guy who was searching for your—"

"Yeah I think it's weird. I fucking *hate* it. All these people reuniting after . . . *hiding* everything all these years. It makes me sick."

"It's actually kind of cool—I mean, about your mom and the cop. Very forties. You know, you shouldn't be so judgmental, Tull. Trinnie hasn't had the easiest life. You're not the *only* one stuff happened to."

"You're so *Zen*," he said nastily. "Are you a Buddha-bitch?"

"Fuck you."

She sulked, slowing her pace as they continued uphill. Pullman sniffed at the elaborately coiffed flower beds along the pricey road.

Tull turned back to make a peace offering. "He ate dinner at the house the other night—Sherlock Dowling—and I could tell Mom wanted us to talk. Wanted *me* to talk. Creepy! What am I supposed to say? 'How come you couldn't find Dad?' Or, 'Hey, can I see your gun?' "

Lucy laughed. "He's probably not such a horrible person. Anyway, *I'd* like to talk to him."

"For your book?"

"He *is* a real detective—and I *am* writing a mystery, you know."

"Oh, right! You know I am so *happy* that my personal tragedy is bringing everyone together!"

They both laughed this time.

*T*he Mauck sat in its blue-zoned berth outside Four Winds. A gull wing cantilevered over the passenger's side just enough to accommodate a chill demitasse of September air.

Edward was depressed. Today, he didn't have it in him to admire the orchids, freshly arranged; or to engage the mechanism that would eject the cushioned, canopied buggy into the scholastic world. He had or-

dered Eulogio (Epitacio was off with Grandpa Lou) to take a walk—he
didn't want to have to look at hunching, dandruffy shoulder pads while
the driver labored over his Spanish crossword. He didn't even want to
see the gang; the gang was doing well enough. All were preoccupied,
he thought somewhat sardonically; Lucy with her *bestseller,* Tull with
his *mythic search,* Boulder with her new little *film* . . . let them go with
God. Allah be praised! As for Edward, he'd had enough. He was tired
and in pain; aside from the acne, a cyst in one of his kidneys was now
saying hello. He felt sorry for himself, an indulgence he ordinarily
loathed. But today there was a moratorium on his usual rigor. Today,
Headward the First, as the witty bully had once anointed him, cried real
tears.

"You and me, Pullie, we're two of a kind," he said, kneading its neck.
The mottled dog looked up with an eye the size of a horse's.
"We're almost 'done,' aren't we? But who would I rather be . . .
would I rather be Tull, or Lucy? Eulogio? Would I rather be you? For an
hour, I would—or a day. I'd like that, Pullie, if you could arrange it. I'd
run and run like a fucker." If the Dane had any reciprocal yearnings, albeit not for running, of which he did precious little, but for living like a
sweet and damaged human king, he kept them to himself. "But you're a
healthy sovereign. You're the anomaly—you'll live forever, won't you,
Pullie?"

The dog and Grandpa Lou were his only confessors, but they were
enough. He lifted the silken hood to dab at his eyes—today would be
a gaudy blowout, a veritable Mardi Gras, a saturnalia of self-pity! He
wailed, letting loose a torrent; his body shook convulsively, chin knocking against titanium support, chronicle of a short life foretold.

Then something peculiar happened.
Shadows fell across the front seat, accompanied by a sharp intake of
astonished breath.

"Eulogio?"
For a moment, the hair of his fissured head stood on end. A tiny
thing with matted hair looked in—dirty wet chick, beneath aluminum
wing.

"Who are you!" gasped Edward, naked-faced and weeping.
He could not stop his ejaculations—water still sprang from stunned
eyes, and body still shook. She stared at the cousin with the horror of a

toddler at the fun house; yet much like before, her actions contrary to her fear, the waif found herself inside the truck.

As she walked toward him, zombie-like, Edward's tears abated while his panic grew. "You're the *girl*—the girl from before!"

Pullman tardily stood to greet her, and the sudden bigness of the beast gave her a final push off the ragged cliffs of consciousness, dropping her hard at the mouth of some faraway cove. The Dane tongued her cheek while Edward shouted for help.

Eulogio rushed in and regarded the collapsed girl with confusion. The cousin imperiously ordered him to make a getaway, and when he balked, Edward made it clear that if he did not secure the Mauck and drive off at once, he would be sacked, as would his brother, Epitacio; as would his sister, Candelaria; as would his Mexican mother and Peruvian father, wherever *they* were; as would all Monasterios who walked the earth, making sure to include Eulogio's present, past and future wives, unborn children and children's children. The reinvigorated cousin added (in Spanish, for effect) that he would then fire Christ and the Devil himself.

"*Comprendiste todo?* Then, *vamanos!*"

Neither father nor mother was home; smuggling her in wasn't a problem. A more serious hurdle would be to keep the nursing staff at bay—of late, they'd been hovering too close for comfort.

After carrying the groggy girl to his employer's apartments, poor Eulogio was upbraided further. While he did not relish his role as torturer, Edward knew how far he must go to ensure that the easygoing minor domo held his mud. Thus said, it is unnecessary to elaborate on the cousin's scoldings; they were adequate to achieve their end.

Finally, alone with the girl, an assessment was required: was she ill or simply exhausted? Amaryllis stirred fitfully on the couch, looking more frightened than anything else. He would nurse her back as one might an eaglet fallen from a nest; with medicos in residence twenty-four/seven, it would be safe enough to monitor her progress and seek immediate attention if the need arose. There was no reason to raise a flag, for now.

"My name is Edward Trotter," he said, handing her a cup of lovingly, if laboriously prepared, hot chocolate. "You, if I recall, are *Amaryllis*—like the flower. And, more vaguely, as my dear friend Tull attested, like the Texan city."

She nodded gravely at her host, as if he had exposed her last and deepest secret.

"Can you talk?" he asked. She cautiously indicated that she could. "Well then, *would* you?"

"Where am I?"

"At my home," he said, "otherwise whimsically known as the Boar's Head Inn—there's even a sign ouside: established 1843. It's where I maintain my apartments and workshop. My parents—you shan't be meeting *them*—stay in the main house; and my sister—who you *have* met—lives up the 'street,' above the Majestyk—that's the movie palace—the whole of our fair town being called Olde CityWalk and bordered by Stradella Road, which passes through the exceedingly dull principality of Bel-Air . . . itself a part of Los Angeles County, I believe. I don't think we've seceded quite yet."

The shell-shocked Amaryllis could make no sense of what he was saying. She dumbfoundedly looked to the dog, whose long, fat body now hibernated amid piles of books and dry, deformed papier-mâché.

"And *that*," he went on, "is Pullman, noblest of harlequins (remember?)—property, so to speak, of cousin Tull, né Toulouse, who I'm confident you *do* recall. At any rate, he was the first of the clan you laid eyes on. It was actually Tull who introduced us: 'us' being myself, the well-known Boulder Langon and the less-well-known Lucille Rose Trotter, sister and future novelist of note."

This time she didn't ask about his condition, which gave him leave to inquire after hers. Did she hurt anywhere? Was she feverish? Did she— yet before he could finish his examination, Amaryllis doubled over and ran to the trash, where she threw up what little she'd imbibed. With clucking self-reproach, Edward realized the poor girl was starving; cocoa may not have been the best idea. While she lay on the divan, peering at him from beneath a comforter, he rang the house kitchen for chicken broth and Popsicles.

A few days later, the cousin invited Tull and Boulder to join him and Lucy for a light supper at the Boar's Head. Edward forsook his customary face covering and, while not commenting directly, the children thought that remarkable. A molten rage of pimples had subsided, leaving a rash of burnt-out villages in its wake, their charred remains artfully covered by hypoallergenic makeup.

After heartfelt remarks on how well he looked and how buoyant seemed his spirits, the children occupied themselves with Four Winds gossip—fallout from the Easter Island faculty debauch, et alia—while young Candelaria shyly set the table. Another helper wheeled in a cart with boeuf bourguignon, yellowfoot mushrooms and Ligurian chickpea cake stowed in heated steel cabinets. A box of Le Marmiton tartes Tatins and thumbprint cookies awaited for dessert, wedged prominently between a Yupik Eskimo puppet and Julie Taymor–made goblin that Aunt Trinnie gave Edward on his last birthday. After the tossing of the mâche salad the couple was dismissed.

But a fifth place had been set.

"Who are we expecting?" asked Boulder, glancing at the empty spot.

"Wouldn't be Detective *Dowling*, would it?" added Lucy, an eyebrow archly raised. It was obvious she had in her possession an insider's "piece of intelligence"—some fresh mischief of her brother's was afoot.

"I don't *think* so," said Tull. "He's with my mom at a screening."

"Poor Rafe," said Lucy wistfully.

"It's Ralph," amended Tull.

"So easily replaced!"

"Don't worry about *him*," said Tull, blasé. Then he turned to his cousin, tired of the game. Edward smiled like a mosaic mandarin; his much-operated-upon face looked digitized. "I hope it isn't some *Jewish* thing—you know, waiting for Elijah-slash-Marcus Weiner? That would be *so* dumb. *And* boring."

"Two things I've never been accused of," he said smugly.

The invalid used a cane while meandering to an open door. He stood inside its frame and looked expectantly offstage. With not a little sense of showmanship, he faced the group again, ridiculously clearing his throat.

"Ladies and gentlemen, may I reintroduce to you . . . Amaryllis Kornfeld!"

The appearance of his father may have been the only thing to surprise Tull more than the sight of the girl, who had never really left his thoughts. The orphan haltingly entered as she had the Mauck that long-ago day, but the old terror was supplanted by a diffidence, a charming acquiescence that filled Tull's heart.

Lucy ran to shore up their guest, who in the last seventy-two hours had already regained some weight if not a good part of luster. Aside from making sure that she fed her face around the clock, Edward had steeped her in the finest of emollients, and her hair, though in need of shaping—the MacLaren "stylist" left much to be desired—seemed to grow wilder and more beautiful by the hour. Tull (he still thought of himself as Toulouse around her) now waited nervously in the reception line, directly behind Pullman, who for some intolerably annoying reason chose this very moment to spend more time with the wayward child than he ever allotted to anything, living or dead. Lucy stroked the girl's rosy gold-brown cheek while Boulder, above it all, busied herself with Edward, praising his gambit and twittering over its daring illegality.

It was Tull's turn at last. The braided detective watched as the two locked eyes; and Lucy's face became a flowery field overtaken by dark clouds. She withdrew with a forced smile, joining Boulder and her brother.

He said hello and asked if she remembered his name. When she gave it to him, he was beside himself—he would be Toulouse forevermore.

He stood and blinked, dragging upper teeth against lower lip. Finally: "How did you get here?"

"I—I came to your school."

"But how did you know—"

"Boulder visited the place I was staying." It secretly thrilled her to so casually invoke the famous name. "They asked where she went, and she said Four Winds—"

"Visited?" exclaimed Boulder, having overheard. Edward hovered blissfully, like a playwright watching from the wings. "Visited where?"

"MacLaren Children's Center."

Boulder was stymied for a second. "Oh my God! You mean that prison for kids? You were *there*?"

Amaryllis nodded. Mercilessly, Lucy smelled subplot. "But how did you escape?"

"My friend and I ran away."

Edward hobbled forth and solemnly waved, forbidding her to finish. "I am compelled to say," he began with great flair, "that by harboring this girl *sub rosa*—this innocent—we have each placed ourselves in jeopardy." He pulled a card from his embroidered tunic. "I have here the name of Amaryllis's legal counsel, which, for the record, the young fugitive offered to me unsolicited. In fact, there were *two* of the barrister's cards, were there not?" He sounded like a magician setting up a trick. "I will retain one while my lodger retains the other. Upon this card are telephone, fax and e-mail contacts. Will I attempt to get in touch? Absolutely not!"

He tore up the card as if dispensing with a ruined queen of hearts. Everyone laughed but the orphan, who smiled pathetically. Watching Amaryllis—her small joys and terrors—had for Tull quickly become a warm avocation.

They took their seats and Boulder helped lay down plates. When Tull awkwardly attempted to engage the guest of honor in conversation, Lucy ordered him to get up and serve the damn salad. Which he did.

With spirited promptings from her Mauck Daddy, Amaryllis mesmerized them with fabulist tales of woe. The numerous, thimble-size portions of cognac with which they celebrated their reunion (partly medicinal) did nothing to hinder the orphan's dizzying, colorful amplifications—alcohol or no, she had found her tongue as never before. She spoke of canyons and witches, and deaf-and-dumb supergirls (though there was much she *didn't* tell); of her father held prisoner in the forbidden Valley of Carceration and her mother now with the angels (Amaryllis said she died but wouldn't say how); and lamented over her precious babies, cruelly stolen away. There were Fátima saints and advocating devils, popes and postulators and vast stone courthouses where children were chained with leg irons to bloody stone benches; a journey to *another* canyon (not Tunga) and how she slept under the stars with a white-fanged hot-breathed coyote watching her every move then stole a motorcycle from a biker on "the parole" and crashed it on a winding canyon road then called 411 to ask for "Santa Monica's Famed Four Winds School"—that's what they called it in Boulder's *Twist* profile—she took a limousine to the address they gave but it was Saturday and no one was there and she hid for twelve days and twelve nights (actually, just the weekend) before seeing the Mauck— . . . and by the time she was done, Lucy had long abandoned her Smythson pad and with it any hope of being a teller of stories; Boulder had decided to produce and star in an

Oscar-winning film of the orphan's life; Edward was happier and hand-somer and higher than he'd been in who-knows-when; Pullman was fast asleep; and Tull—who, having come of age and into his own name, should henceforth be called Toulouse, for if Rafe Mirdling can warrant a rechristening, then so should the boy—Toulouse, a name of murky origins, which only his grandfather and Amaryllis had ever called him—well . . . our dear, suffering Toulouse was in love.

CHAPTER 31

Harvest

*T*he gang looked after her in turns—except for Boulder, who was more or less busy with shooting a film and all the important folderol that entailed—and set about her tutoring with gusto. The orphan, who turned twelve that first week of October (and was duly feted in a secret ceremony), took in the world afresh, albeit with somewhat shorter hair: as a cloak of anonymity against those who might be in pursuit, Edward had insisted a visit be paid to Frédéric Fekkai. She tearfully emerged from the salon looking like the most beautiful boy imaginable and was immediately treated to as many of Cañon Drive's 31 Flavors as she desired.[†]

Amaryllis was an eager bride. In exchange for the teaching of insipid social graces, Lucy conscripted the pint-size Scheherazade to spin yarns of a netherworld that the authoress hoped "to make her own." (The character of a wandering waif was now central to the *Blue Maze* opus.) After all, Mr. Hookstratten said the scribbler's credo was to "write what you know"; Lucy took that to mean what *others* know, too.

This was the time of Sukkoth and a great hut was constructed at school—as was a temporary dwelling on the lower Stradella campus, made from cornstalks, and hung with figs, dates, grapes, olives and pomegranates. Eager to hammily underscore the real-life exodus—Amaryllis's—unfolding before him, Toulouse edified his favorite student about the Jewish holiday in hortatory tones that promptly sickened him.

[†]Because the children adored her and truly did mean well, they could not foresee that what began as derring-do, a "homeless project" if you will, could neither be sustained nor come to good end. But they *had* rescued her and *were* so fated, thus cannot be judged.

" 'You shall dwell in booths seven days,' " he read, " 'that your generations may know that I made the *children* [italics Toulouse's] of Israel dwell in booths when I brought them out of the land of Egypt.' That's Leviticus," he said bombastically, closing the book with a flourish. He couldn't seem to help himself. Any metaphors were lost on the girl, who at the mention of Israel thought only of Edith Stein; unhappily, the open-air evergreen "booth" only served to remind her of Topsy's GE box beneath the 4th Street Bridge.

There was much recreation for Amaryllis, who, aside from swimming, skating and soccering, was not infrequently seen aboard the spotted back of Pullman, hugging his flanks while he lagged behind the fat-wheeled buggy—it wasn't the easiest thing to catch up with Edward as he careered his way over Stradella House's great expanse. The cousin would finally stop for lunch in the sukkah, where the girl held her own in conversation, showing a fine instinct and wider apprehension. She told him everything she knew about saints, an instructive amount indeed. Their encounters left him positively ebullient; even his complexion cleared.

As for Toulouse, she continued to provoke and enthrall the boy whom she had forever marked. With a sophistication that belied her years, Amaryllis experimented in both elating and angering him with as little space between as could be managed. Just when he began to shudder and his lips went bloodless and he prepared to scold, Amaryllis smiled or kissed his cheek or threw a small, sweet punch to a shoulder that made him glad he hadn't been petty—and terrified that if he ever was, she might vanish forever. It confused and upset him that he sometimes had the same anxieties about the girl that he had for Trinnie.

The gang alternated playing hooky in order to show Amaryllis the sights and buy her things—clothes and accessories that not only enhanced mood and appearance but allowed for a general blending-in with her new surroundings. It must not be forgotten that these children of privilege (as long as their schoolwork was deemed not to suffer) were afforded such leeway in their personal schedules that even at night— with cowed, overworked Eulogio at the Mauck's helm—they moved more or less with the freedom of adults. Of course Edward had always done as he pleased, especially as he got older; those who loved him wished his happiness unrestricted. On a school night, then, it was not unusual to see the foursome gorging on puu-puu platters at Trader Vic's or à table oceanside at Casa del Mar. In a two-week period, Amaryllis saw her very first concert and more movies than she had in her entire life, a slew of the latter screened at Stradella's own Majestyk, the existence of which continued to puzzle her—as did the surrealistic whole of Olde CityWalk. Some things one could never fathom. She walked on the beach for the first time too and looked through telescopes at the Observatory, forded Raging Waters, climbed Magic Mountain and went to a place called the Bowl for an evening picnic—which in fact *did* look like a bowl, but one upright and half-buried in the earth. They had their own private little outdoor room with a low fence around it, and an orchestra serenaded them under starry skies. Afterward, Toulouse suggested they drive to the motel where she had once lived, but her face darkened and he saw he had somehow trivialized her. He had not meant to make her life into another entertainment. He said he was sorry and left it at that. Why, he wondered, had he told her nothing of his own history and travails? Did he feel himself above that? He had deliberately mentioned his mother, but only to throw her off the scent of the missing dad; thankfully, she hadn't been curious enough about fathers—any fathers at all—to follow up. So at least he never lied outright about his "situation." But he was *already* ashamed, and the shame of not being candid with her shamed him further.

A few times, Amaryllis actually glimpsed the parents of her quirky hosts. One Saturday around midnight, after a hard day of designing masks in Edward's workshop and flying with Toulouse in the 747 simulator and giving Lucy her *Thousand and One Nights* fix, after a particularly arduous day of shopping and playing and eating *very* strange foods—for example, lunch consisted of raw fish and green mustard strapped by seaweed onto cubes of rice—a day made even *more* arduous by a visit to a certain bakery, whose creations so reminded her of Topsy that she burst into tears—Toulouse asked what was the matter, but she wouldn't say—around Saturday midnight, the merry twosome (Edward remained behind) abducted the girl and led her through flash-lit forest and pathway to Stradella's main house. Joyce and Dodd were having a party, and they espied them from the bushes. The first one Amaryllis noticed was a priest, whom Toulouse identified as Father de Kooning. She asked if the Flying Nun was there, laughing at her own lame joke. Mr. Hookstratten was in high spirits (the professor still tutored Dodd, currently mired in *Beowulf*), meaning he was drunk; Lucy said she could tell he was in the middle of an anecdote about their now-legendary summer vacation. There were actors and socialites and a few portly men who had managed to pull Lotus and Lamborghini from the Nasdaq heap but sported body-guards no more. Toulouse said that some of the wives were members of the Dead Baby Brigade—but his sarcasm was mostly for Edward's sake, by proxy.

Amaryllis was perplexed. When he began to explain Joyce's good works, the orphan, seeing her *own* babies before her, could bear no more and ran back through the night to the comforts of Olde CityWalk, flying straight to the duvet of her surreptitious, Black Lantern Shoppe couch.

*T*wo weeks before Halloween, Toulouse brought her to La Colonne Détruite for a day of reckoning. He gave no preamble; she was clueless about the place. He left Pullman at home—he felt a little exposed and thought things would go easier without his four-legged friend. Maybe it was Pullman's feelings he was protecting.

They ducked through the storm drain, and for a while, though not much was said, Amaryllis was sure they were breaking into a con-demned park. She was overdressed and tried hard not to soil her ensem-ble.

"My grandfather built this place for my parents."

"When?"

"Before I was born. As a wedding present."

She thought the Trotters to be truly wondrous; there seemed no end to the magical world they inhabited. All grass and sky, yet Toulouse said it had been "built"—this family worked in God-like scale! Then she saw it: on a rise at the edge of a glen stood a bewitching castle, as if dropped down from another world, another time.

"It's cracked!" she said, regarding the crown.

"It's supposed to be like that. There's another one just like it, in France."

"Another one?"

He nodded.

"But what *is* it?"

"A house."

"But why don't they live there?"

"It's a long story."

"Does *anyone* live there?"

"No—maybe one day. Maybe one day *I* will."

"You're *crazy*. Can we go inside?"

Mr. Greenjeans watched from afar as the children ran through corridors of myrtle, the fragrant shrub used during Sukkoth. On the orphan's birthday, Edward had shoved a fistful under her nose.

Amaryllis shivered as they entered the tower. She went to the staircase; Toulouse led the way. When they reached the top floor she was winded, more by unsettled feelings than exertion. As she parsed the landscape below, fear fell upon her. Then she took in the room itself—a bed was there, neatly made.

"Who stays here?"

"My mom, sometimes."

"But why?"

"I guess she misses my father."

"Is he dead?"

"No."

He wanted to tell her everything, but was blank.

She led him to the bed and took off her blouse; she thought that's why he had taken her there. Toulouse wasn't sure at first what was happening. She was full of scars and discolorations, and he thought she was going to show him something like where she got stabbed or shot with a bullet. She grabbed his hand and put it on a tit. His mouth was arid and his stomach rumbled, embarrassing him. She put her fingers down his pants. He liked the way it felt, even though everything seemed numb. She stripped off her pants and underwear.

"What are you doing?" he asked.

"Fuck me," said Amaryllis, summoning the old Airstream words like a depraved incantation. "Fuck my juicy pussy with your big fat cock."

She helped pull off his pants, and now Toulouse felt funny lying there with this girl whom he loved, starting to do sexy things he had never done, in the room of his very conception. It was too much, and he pulled away. She became more aggressive and put her mouth on him and sucked, but that felt weirdly wrong and he pushed himself back, but she wouldn't stop until he fell off the bed and shouted, "No!"

Amaryllis burst into tears and wailed, "I'm sorry! I'm sorry!" and ran down the spiral stairs without her shirt. He grabbed it, hiking his pants up as he chased after. He tackled her on the ground floor and she struggled in his arms until she couldn't anymore, and broke down again, begging his forgiveness.

⌒

Amaryllis was worried he'd tell the others; Toulouse was worried she might leave because he had pushed her away. To be truthful, he wasn't sure *how* he felt about what had happened—or what exactly had happened at all. It wasn't like the way he fooled around with Lucy; it excited him more, but was more . . . *disturbing.* She seemed to know a lot of things he didn't, and he hoped she didn't think he was some kind of fag. But he *did* feel kind of faggoty around her—the stuff she said about fucking, and the *way* she said it, put a scare in him. *Maybe it was just cultural,* he thought. As Edward might say.

As they emerged onto Carcassone, he furtively reached in his pants and touched the tip of his penis. Her mouth-wetness was still there, and some wetness, it seemed, of his own. Walking aimlessly uphill, the girl looked miserable, as if this were the end of the line. She thought of saints again to quiet herself and for the first time in weeks *really* thought of the babies, thought hard, heart-hard, almost gagging with the heartache of it, the sorrow and the guilt. Her chin twitched uncontrollably, and she soldiered forward like someone on a death march. To cheer her up—and to make sure things would be all right with them again— Toulouse suggested they visit Saint-Cloud. She'd not yet been there, and he wanted to show Amaryllis the maze: so it was, from tower to labyrinth did they go, for in childhood there is mostly myth and no middle ground.

By the time they reached the gate, they were holding hands again, sweaty and tentative, like a couple come from therapy. Toulouse had concocted a biography (she would be the daughter of a Moroccan consul whom they had met on the summer trip) should they run into anyone, which was unlikely, since Bluey rarely left her room and Grandpa Lou was in Azusa, working. His mother had gone to Palos Verdes to freshen up one of her garden creations.

As they walked through the house, Amaryllis felt herself shrinking in size. So many riches upon riches . . . and all she had to give were her shame and her nothingness. There were family pictures all around— happy, beautiful people—what did *she* have? Not even snapshots of the babies! . . . Nor a photo of her mother, dead in bed with bulging eyes, the corners of her crazy mouth stained chocolate by stomach fluids . . . Amaryllis struggled not to break and run. Watching her, feeling all her feelings, Toulouse knew right then that they should leave, but he continued on. The honeymoon was over, and he cringed; for he, Tull Trotter, né Toulouse, had been the one to end it.

Once they got outside, things improved slightly. Pullman crept from his teahouse and nuzzled her, lightening the mood. They went straight to the maze. After a month with the Trotters, the presence of a leafy backyard labyrinth was not bizarre in itself; just another ride in an amusement park that the orphan felt was soon closing, at least for her. Pullman plunged in, and the couple lazily followed.

"My mother built this—or grew it. It took about four years . . . but she wasn't here the whole time. There used to be a curtain between the maze and the house, two stories high. She didn't want anyone to see it till it was all grown. I don't know why, but none of us ever snuck in."

They walked in silence, going deeper. The tinkle from Pullman's collar could be heard through faraway intersecting hedges.

"Amaryllis, wait." She stopped without turning around. Toulouse caught up and took a long, slow breath. "Can we sit down?" He pointed to one of the stone benches lining the hedge. She sat contritely, believing the moment of excommunication had arrived. "My parents got married in that house—the place we were at. That room—that bed—is where they slept on their wedding night. And the next morning, when she woke up, he—my father—was gone. He disappeared. They hired a detective, but no one ever found him. They never told me about it. They always said he was dead, that he had a snowmobile accident in New Mexico. But it wasn't true."

"He left her?"

"They said maybe he had mental problems."

"My mom had mental problems. My dad left her, too. They never got married."

"She went kind of nuts after that. She took drugs—a *lot*. She was in and out of hospitals."

"They never found him?"

"No."

"My father's in jail. In the Valley."

"What for?"

"I don't know. They noticed him, but he declined to be present."

He kicked a stone with his foot.

"My mom was in the hospital for drugs, too," said Amaryllis.

"Where is she?"

"Someone killed her."

"Killed her?" He was incredulous. "Do they know who did it?"

"She knew lots of bad people. She sold me once to a woman, for drugs."

"God, Amaryllis!"

"Toulouse—you're not going to leave me, are you?"

"No! Why would I leave you?"

"Because of all the things that happened to me? And for what I did . . . back at the—"

"You didn't *do* anything. I even *liked* it."

"No you didn't. I only thought that—I didn't mean to—"

"It's all OK. We're going to *help* you. Edward and Lucy—"

"I don't *want* anybody's help!"

He knew it had come out wrong.

"Toulouse . . . do you love me?"

"Do I love you?"

"I want to know."

"Well—yes!" It wasn't as if he didn't; he loved her with all his heart. It was just that he'd never said that to a girl before. "I love you," he said, and it wasn't so hard. Fun, even: "I *do* love you." He put his arms around her and kissed her—rather professionally at that, thanks to the tutelage of Lucille Rose.

She started to cry. "I don't want to go back to that place. To MacLaren . . ."

"You're *not*, Amaryllis. You *won't*. You'll *never* have to go back, OK? I'll get my grandfather to—"

A scattering of pebbles through dust as Pullman kicked past, barking. A shout from the maze's entrance.

"Hey, Tull! Tull! Toulouse!" (People were actually beginning to call him that.)

"You in there?"

"Coming!" Then: "It's my mother—just stick to the story." But she'd already forgotten the story. "You don't have to talk. You're *shy*, OK? And you don't speak English that well."

Trinnie appeared at the end of the allée as a figure seen through the wrong end of an opera glass. "Ahoy!" The children walked toward her; Amaryllis smelled the familiar attar of myrtle as the lady approached. Her brown-speckled pants, white shirt, and orange hair made her look like a perfect cigarette.

"I see you have company!"

"What's your name?" whispered Toulouse, a bit frantically; a detail he'd carelessly neglected. "What's your *name?*"

Amaryllis was truly stymied; by then, the woman was upon them.

"Well, hello!"

"Mom, this is—*Amar.* We met in Marrakesh."

"I am so jealous!"

"She's the consul's daughter."

"Hello, Amar! What a lovely name. She's *gorgeous.*"

"She's only here for a few weeks."

"Well, we're happy to have you! Diane has *so* many stories—she showed me a picture of you and Dex on an elephant. Did you *know,*" she said to Toulouse, "those were the first pictures I'd seen of *le grand tour?* My *son,* Amar"—turning her full charm on the orphan—"is not very interested in photo documentation, as you may or may not know. I got him a digital camera and it just sits. I was *so* brutally envious I wasn't there—I *love* the Sahara—it was *obscene* the way I carried on, wasn't it, Tull? But I was taking care of Lauren Hutton, a dear friend of mine, who got in a terrible crash. I *adore* Marrakesh! I was there with Donna Karan and Lee Radziwill—at Dar Tamsna—that's in the Palmaraie, do you know it? Well, of course you do. Was that already eight years ago?"

The question was put to the social ether; Toulouse hated when his mother went on, dropping names like an idiot—hated that some horrible part of her was reflexively trying to impress "Amar" in order to actually insinuate herself into the exotic preteen orbit of an imaginary consul's daughter. The humility she seemed to have acquired the last few months was falling away in noisome chunks; he wondered if she was stoned.

"Did you know I was there with your grandmother? Bluey, oh yes. And Truman—how they *adored* each other! You *still* haven't read any of Truman's books, have you, Toulouse? I'll get you *A Tree of Night* . . . my God—I was about your age," she said, looking at "Amar," "when I first met that astonishing little man. So: your father's the consul! Tell me *everything.*"

"Ma, don't give her the third degree."

"I've barely said a *word* to her," she said, looking at him as if he were insane. She turned back to the girl. "We must have a dinner. Is your father here on business?"

Amaryllis stammered, but their attention was drawn to the puzzle's entrance, where Pullman caracoled, playfully ducking his head. A man in a suit walked toward them. He did not recognize the girl in the demure princess-style spaghetti-strapped silk organza dress and matching bolero, which Lucy had bought for her birthday, at Saks—and not merely because her hair was shorn and she had fattened. Seeing her in context of the Trotter's Bel-Air manse and being introduced to her, with such certainty, as the daughter of a Moroccan consul, was so wildly disparate from the circumstances of the dun-colored room in which he'd interviewed her last that Samson's mind refused to make the connection. Luckily, the girl, though recognizing the detective, was too startled to betray herself and gave away nothing but a marmoreal calm. Toulouse braced himself for the treacherous shoals of banal conversational inquiry when fortune smiled on them again—a hideous, rhythmical scream penetrated the air, panicked and desperate, soul-rending.

"It's Mother!" said Trinnie, and flew from the maze.

Samson jogged after, but when Toulouse began to follow, the orphan held him back.

CHAPTER 32

Les Miz

Bursting from the boxwood, this is what first Trinnie, then Samson, saw: Bluey, in favored negligee that unfavorably revealed her anatomy, sprinting past with spatula in hand, followed by a pink-faced Winter, the former shrieking like a parrot in maddening metronomic intervals while making a beeline for the Len Brackett–designed Pine-Lute Pavilion doghouse. Bluey clambered in double time.

"Mother! Winter, my God, what is going on?"

"I was helping with her album! She said she was hungry!"

The hyperventilating nanny looked close to collapse.

"Calm down, Winter," said Samson.

"But what *happened*—"

"I asked if she wanted breakfast in the kitchen . . . she's been locked in that bedroom for weeks . . . she said she *did*. I thought it'd be good for her!—"

"*Why* is she carrying that fucking *spatula*?"

"I was about to serve her eggs, and she *grabbed* . . . she—" (here, Winter began to lose it) "—*threw* the eggs in my face! Said I was trying to *kill* her!" The detective noticed some evidence of yellowish residue in her hair, which would support her assertions. "I was serving her *breakfast*!—"

The shrieks continued from the villa unabated, interrupted by an occasional bark.

Trinnie bent to her knees and looked in. "Pullman, you get *out* of there!"

"Why don't we call a doctor?" offered Samson.

"Mother, would you come out, please?"

"I am an old woman!" Bluey shouted. "And I will not die *today*, whether Winter likes it or not!"

The anguished Icelander looked imploringly at Samson, who gave a small nod of empathy.

"Oh my God. Mother! Do we have to call the paramedics? Is that what you want? Do you want the paramedics to go in there and grab you?"

Bluey began to shriek again and Pullman to roar, while Winter wept and Trinnie raged, and it was under this chaotic cover that the children made their getaway.

⌒⌒⌒

Approximately one hour later, in the vaulted quiet of Olde CityWalk's Majestyk Theater, an emergency summit was called. Amaryllis reverted to her watchful, closemouthed street ways, fearing, however irrationally, a reversal of fortune and speedy return to the Canyon realm of Early-mae Woolery. What she *did* share with the small circle was this: Samson Dowling was the very cop who had "arrested" her, booking her into MacLaren.

The exciting development was discussed from every possible angle. There was general discombobulation at the fact that the same man once hired by Grandpa Lou to find Marcus Weiner—the same man whose name had been first broached in the sanctum sanctorum of Tabori & Co.—the same man who had summered with Trotter *familia* before any of them were even born and now just happened to be cohabiting with their beloved aunt and mother (Toulouse averted his eyes, not wanting to "go there")—was the infernal bloodhound now after their adored Amaryllis! The diabolical enormity of it left Edward astonished and invigored, and his grateful sister ecstatic at such a plot twist; made to order and delivered by hand. Toulouse was merely angry, and mindful of Amaryllis's safety.

"It's *Les Misérables*!" cried the authorette, beside herself. "Samson is Inspector Javert! And *she*," said Lucy, turning to the orphan with what struck the latter as an accusatory air, "is Cosette! *Amaryllis is Cosette.*"

A plan was hatched. Until now, she had been shacking up in the rear parlor of the Black Lantern Book Shoppe—but that place had been deemed unsafe in the long term; Candelaria and her minions were notorious for scouring storefront innards and cobblestone without warning, especially when the children were at school. (There had already been a few close calls.) Amaryllis would now be secreted away in the attic of the cousin's apartments, an aerie accessible only by rope ladder. Seeing the look on the girl's face upon hearing his proclamation, Edward assured her there was nothing in the old belfry but discarded masks and paint-brushes, a detail that only served to frighten her more. In *this* way, reasoned Edward—the *attic* way—the likelihood of surprise attacks by Candelaria's crack troops would be severely diminished, as the invalid's quarters were strictly off-limits to the unannounced visits of parent or staff. It was agreed, then: while brother and sister breezily took to the Four Winds, Amaryllis would remain sequestered in the manner of Anne Frank (the allusion was Lucy's), at least until her freedom could be properly secured. So it was with a measure of exhilaration that the gang, excepting of course Edward and Pullman, ascended the rope like fledgling acrobats. Once she landed, Amaryllis practiced stowing the roll-up ladder, replacing the square wedge of dislocated floor that sealed her in, et cetera. Mission accomplished, shakes and hamburgers were ordered in.

What the children, precocious as they were (which was precocious indeed) yet with more a taste for melodrama than for the actual cruelties that may be visited upon us by the world—what the children could not have known was, at that very moment of mobilization, all their worst fears, fueled more by adrenaline and active imaginations than anything else, were being realized. The wheels of juvenile justice were already turning.

*A*fter much Sturm und Drang, Pullman's teahouse was restored to him. A doctor was summoned and the old woman was sedated. They bundled her up in a cashmere throw and laid her in the back of the Silver Seraph for the drive to Cedars. Louis, in sharp houndstooth coat, held her dear, limp hand, wiping periodic tears that gathered to tremble in the corner of his eyes.

When Bluey was settled in, Trinnie told the detective she was tired and not in the mood for the dinner they'd planned. He drove back to the El Royale wondering, as a younger man had earlier that very long day, if the honeymoon was over.

Samson Dowling was level-headed enough to know that Trinnie had always loomed larger for him than he for her—from even before she fell under the thumb of a ghost. He had always wanted her, and what he'd fantasized about for years had finally happened; yet they were connected through *him*, her husband, and when they made love, he had the unnerving sense of being part of a séance. Sometimes as they lay in bed afterward she would ask him, like a child, to tell her the story of how Marcus had been found at St. John's in the Wilderness or how he had looked that time when Samson first saw him or what the hospital that he and her father had taken him to was like—and how it was again that Marcus had escaped . . .

Dive, be not fearful how dark the waves flow;
Sink through the surge, and bring pearls up to me;
Deeper, ay, deeper; the fairest lie low . . .

Sitting alone with his cocktail, the detective found his mouth suddenly forming a word: "Amaryllis."

My God.

He conjured her face, then said the name aloud . . .

Amaryllis?

He dialed MacLaren. There was no one he knew on duty, so it took a while to get confirmation that, yes, Amaryllis Kornfeld had gone AWOL during a field trip last month. Jesus. How the hell could she have wound up with the Trotter kids? That meant he would have to drive over to Saint-Cloud. He would have to bother Trinnie or wake her up or do whatever—would have to tell her about the AWOL girl and bother her son about it, too. *Oh shit.* She just wouldn't be in the mood. The intrusion would seem bogus, some cockamamie bullshit he'd come up with to get next to her. If the honeymoon was over, this could be just the thing to push them into Divorce World. Still, it had to be done. We're talking about a homicide here. And a girl, a minor, a ward of the dependency court, who's *out* there. Floating.

He swigged his drink and reluctantly picked up the phone. If they stonewalled him, he'd tell the staff it was an emergency and that he needed to talk to Katrina right away.

*   *   *

*B*y ten o'clock the next morning, William had finished his baking chores in the SeaShelter kitchen. He strolled to the farmers' market on Main Street. Amid wealthy housewives, their punnets filled with feta and white mulberries, he bought his precious pomegranates. They were in season now, brick-red and unbruised and of glistening pulp. He would make a chutney for his sweet lady Jane Scull, with shallots sautéed in grapeseed oil, the red seeds folded in with molasses, kumquats and fat Jordan dates, *ras el hanout* and zest. He watched children ride the ponies—so many children!—then walked to the high-end hostelry called Shutters, where he summoned a cab. He gave the driver the Public Storage address and said he'd be making a round trip.

Eighteen months ago, he had paid in advance and had worn the key to the garage-size space about his neck ever since. The downtown structure occupied several acres beneath a swooping freeway on-ramp; guided by William's sure hand, the taxi proceeded down this lane and that, like a hearse on its way to the grave. He bade it stop, then stepped out, fitting the key with some trouble. He sweated, jigging it; the lock finally sprang. He went in.

The room was cool and empty. A rag on the floor proved on closer examination to be a rat, long extinct, bringing him briefly back to encampment days. An overturned milk crate sat in the center of the room, where he had last left it, like a prop on a stage. On top was a junky file cabinet drawer; and within, the leather-bound record of his itinerant education. He used to sit in this sanctuary and write down his thoughts, but had soon stopped all that, overcome by the Laocoönean struggle of daily life.

He reached through a spiderweb and took up the volume, opening its cover:

> ... 𝔥ereafter follows the book itself which is called 𝔑ews from 𝔑owhere, or 𝔄n 𝔈poch of 𝔕est & is written by 𝔚illiam 𝔐orris.

*J*ane visited a clinic that she thought would rid her of the child but was told it was too late. And still no one knew, no one but (horror of horrors!) Please-Help.-Bless. For they had been intimate and he had caressed her belly as Jilbo had done, and licked every place with his tongue. The baby became a third party to their intimacies; he said he could change the features of its fetal face with the tip of what he had between his legs (he never tired of dispensing this bit of folk wisdom). He went roughly in both holes, and even Jilbo had not done that. The only thing that kept her from coming completely undone was that she had not yet been with her William in a lover's way, not for lack of desire but because of his courtly, thoughtful manner. She *did* desire him (there would be time enough for that when they married), but for now did him the favor of forbearance, one William returned, for it *was* the most beautiful, refined favor, built upon Godly love. If they *had* been together as such, and she with the demon Please-Help.-Bless *after*—why, then Jane would already have thrown herself in front of a big Blue Bus! For how could she have lain with her gentleman again, after being sucked and prodded by that diseased, invidious harpy, that snide and limping carbuncle, the wheedling agent of her precious William's destruction?

The gimp had one day followed her, pinning her to a wall; though thin and rickety, there was strength in him too and what he had to say nearly crippled her.

"I know yer boy!" he rasped. She smelled the stink of his purulent gums. "I know yer boy *Topsy* from Adam! From day one! I seen you with him. He was a good boy once—helped with my sign. Then got *kinked*—like his friend with the tore-up dawg; got ridda *him,* too. Ain' *none* of 'em right in the head, jus' like you! Come down to the *beach* and shave that big *beard,* he did. Don't wear that fancy suit no more so no one'll find 'im. So what. So *shit* what. *I* find 'im. *I* know yer boy. He fuck the kiddies, that's what *he* do. Kill some lady too, thas right! They *lookin'* fer him—I'm *tight* with who's lookin', all right? Man with a gold shield. Ahm tellin' you this is *serious* shit—Gold Shield gave me the *hewhaw* to help find 'im. 'Cause I know the *streets.* Gold Shield ain' gonna *rest* 'fore he find yer boy! They look to *me,* all right? An' there I walks straight into him! An' him, with *you*—he's *yer* boy! Fuckin' you too, huh? Fuckin' an' suckin' you *an'* the kiddies, *tha's* right."

She was crying; he knew she was his.

"Throttle back, baby—s'all good. Didn't know that, did ya? Didn't know yer boy stole a li'l girl, that's what *he* did. Cleaned her pussy real good with his tong. Made it bigger too—li'l girl like uh elephant now! *Slap slap slap slap slap.* Wet wet wet wet wet. Bet *chew* tight. Bet *chew* tight like that li'l girl *used* to be. You *looks* like a cow, but ahl betchew got a

seven-year-old girlie hole! Betchew gotta hole like a calico *cat!* Best let me
at that hole or yer boy's goin' *down,* unnerstan'? They killim! Killim in
jail! Killim! Killim! Killim!" He bit her neck and dug at the crotch of her
donated skirt. "Gun let me fuck you? I *likes* big girls, ooh! Gunna haff to
take them hearing aids out to do yer ears! Make you *heer* again! And I
likes you 'cause you cain't talk, ooo! Gunna do yer mouth, ooo! An yer
ass, ooo! Gun do that li'l calico *cat* pussy, ooo! ooo! ooo!"

He had gambled and won—he owned her now. Like a hunter, he'd
watched the couple stroll the Promenade arm in arm, Jane with curls
and tendrils piled atop her head like a loopy career girl, Topsy smoking
his Rite Aid pipe. The beggar snarled at the domesticity of it, wondering
what exactly was between them. When he first had his big idea, he
wasn't sure she'd believe his accusations *or* his threats—that he was
the only thing that stood between her boyfriend and jail—he only knew
he wanted her bad enough to play it out. *Gut have that deaf-dumb cow.*
And it made perfect sense when she heard it, because Jane had always
seen that her William's eyes shone with something more than the
brushfire flames of now diminishing hallucinations; but rather, with
the awareness that someone, some*thing,* was after him—on the trail of
the man she dared call husband. She had misread whatever it was William saw gaining on him (his old life); regardless, Jane Scull would let no
harm come to her man, and it was upon that sentiment Please-Help.-
Bless preyed.

More than any of it, she felt the awful familiarity of this monster,
who was, alas, a member of her tribe, and began finally to consider that
the Lord might have made her for such men. Yet along with the shame
and agony attending such a realization came a measure of peace.

CHAPTER 33

Assisted Living

*W*hile the currents of our main story pull inexorably toward the tributaries of denouement, it is an opportune moment to look in on Mr. Dodd Trotter, whose fortunes this week have fallen, bidding him to flutter from his perch on *Forbes*'s global tree of the "world's working rich," and comfortably resettle five or six branches down. As to the wisdom of our timing, opinions as usual may vary; yet each player asserts himself in his own way, with his own urgency.

The day before his mother's eviction from chez Pullman and subsequent hospitalization, Dodd was finally on his way to meet Dr. Melvin Janklow, the genial Beverly Vista psychologist who had once talked him through the hard times of his youth. (In the few months that had elapsed since that first phone call, their dinner date had for one reason or another been postponed.) He'd flirted with the idea of Trader Vic's before discarding the Polynesian-themed restaurant as too kitschy, regardless of all the fond boyhood associations. He had Frances-Leigh make reservations at Michael's instead, at the beach.

Dodd's jet landed around six o'clock at the Van Nuys airport. He had spent the day in North Carolina, touring a private school. The Cary Academy had been built a few years before the millennium by his friend Jim Goodnight, co-founder of a data warehousing software company; Jim only had about $4 billion but, as Dodd used to joke, "that didn't make him a bad guy." The complex sat on about fifty acres—ten times that of the current BV "footprint" but only twice the size of the extended parcel that Dodd envisioned once surrounding homes and apartments were razed. The dogged CEO had built Cary from the ground up; its design technologies and dedication to learning were superb. Seeing what a determined man like Jim could do in such a short period of time absolutely impressed and inspired.

Dr. Janklow was sitting at the bar when Dodd came in. He wore a jacket with suede elbow patches, as in days of old, and rose to give his former patient a hug. The retired therapist looked on the fragile side; cancer wars had taken their toll. Dodd understood he was probably nervous, too, not being accustomed to the hoopla of a chauffeur-driven night out. They were quickly ushered to an outdoor table.

Space heaters cut the crispness in the air. Dodd politely asked the doctor (who futilely insisted on being called Mel) for a précis of his life the last thirty-odd years. The truth was, the billionaire couldn't have cared less—his indifference stemming not from callous self-absorption but from a desire to freeze Melvin Janklow in time, as he remembered him, patched-up arms warmly extended in a crinkly-eyed hello, the underground priest of a small church—Church of the School Psychologist—that had been Dodd's refuge over so many troubled semesters.

"Well, you know, I've been sick! That takes up *lots* of time. Oh Jesus—got hit with prostate, then *skin,* then *breast.* Breast cancer! That's not a typical thing, not for men. But you learn to look on the bright side: never got it in the brain, balls or palate. Saw *those* characters when I went for chemo. 'Pretty work,' as my Southern auntie used to say—ghoulish. But you don't want to hear about all *that.* Tell me about yourself, Dodd! Marcie says you're pretty high up there on the *Forbes* heap. I think that's all kind of silly myself. Do you really have that much money?"

"I have a lot, but I never see it."

Dr. Janklow was tickled. "I *like* that," he tittered. "You never *see* it! Who *wants* to see old dirty dollar bills anyhow?"

They reminisced awhile before Dodd got around to asking if he was aware of the sad state their alma mater was in, what with the seemingly permanent bungalows and school board entropy. The doctor nodded gravely and said that Marcie Millard sent him a petition bemoaning a bureaucracy that dared allow the halls of learning to remain in such prolonged post-earthquake disrepair. It was obscene. Dodd spoke of his vision for "the new BV," an academic phoenix risen from the ashes.

"Well," said the doctor, after getting an earful, "it does sound a bit grand, but why not? Why should the good folks of Beverly Hills be denied? I think it's a *hell* of an idea, David."

Dodd smilingly overlooked the misnomer.

"But what can *I* do? Now, what would you want with an old retired windbag with three cancers?"

"For me, tradition is *very* important. Dr. Janklow, if we can make this thing happen, I'd like you to have an office there—as an emeritus. You could come in whenever you like. Of course, you'd be salaried. If all this *does* come to pass—and my lawyers and friends on the school board are giving me every indication it will—I'd like *very* much if you stood alongside me during the ground-breaking." The dinner guest was flustered to speechlessness, but Dodd was just gathering steam. "I want to be able to look around and see old friends and mentors, so there's a continuum. See, I'm one of those people who *remember* things: I remember you taking the time to come to my family's house on Roxbury Drive for supper. That meant a lot to me. You didn't have to do that—no one paid you extra or wrote about it in the *Courier.* I think you just thought it might make a difference. I remember some of the other kids finding out . . . and for a few days, I felt just a little more important, a little more comfortable in my own skin."

The doctor looked sternly contemplative, as if working through a knotty math problem. "I have a confession to make." He pushed around an endive with a fork. "For *weeks* I've been racking my brain. *Who is he?*" He paused dramatically. "Who is that boy?"

Dodd's face froze in a half smile. "I'm not sure what you mean."

"Now, the only thing I can come up with is the *trauma*—I went through an awful, terrible time right about then. My wife and I were separating, a protracted thing. That's the only explanation I can give! Because even after three cancers, my mind has remained *agile* as ever. The Millards'll tell you. One thing I'm not and never have been is a forgetter."

"Forget—"

"What I am trying to say, what I feel *genuinely* terrible about, is that I *cannot remember.* Cannot remember—*you*—at all! I have *racked my brain.* I saw so *many* children, so *many* girls and boys. Had so *many* dinners—feathers in the parents' caps, but they took a toll. Oh yes they took a toll. And that was fine, I was happy to do it! Would do it *again.* If it's true that I was of some small comfort—and you said yourself it was a good, a worthwhile thing—then my, my . . . they were all good, wonderful children. Through the years. And you wouldn't have been the only one! Heavens. But where did you say you lived? Roxbury? South or north? Well, of course it would be north . . ."

"It was actually south."

"Well—but you—you say it was twice a *week* you came? How is that *possible?* Twice a week! I have racked my brain. Even looked through the yearbooks—I've got every single one—you weren't in any of the yearbooks—"

Though crestfallen, Dodd gamely rallied. "I always arranged to get sick when those picture-days came around."

The doctor laughed hollowly. "I can only say it *has* to have been because of my marital difficulties—which of course I had to shield not only from the students but from faculty as well. Took an enormous toll."

"I'm sure it will come back."

"I feel so foolish. Your *generosity*—I thought by seeing you it would jog my memory. Awful to say! It's the damnedest—what was it that we talked about? In my office . . . Did you have a specific problem?"

"I imagine it was nothing that unusual," he said cordially, "in terms of the type of thing you heard from most of the kids who came to see you. And the advice or support that you gave."

"So many of the children's troubles were alike; that's true today too, no?—hard to distinguish. Have you changed much?" Dr. Janklow squinted at him. "I mean, physically? From when you were—from those days? Because you look like the type who might have—"

"Nothing dramatic."

"It's just *extraordinary* that I can't recall! Your father wasn't in television, was he?"

*T*he next afternoon was an active one. After visiting his mother in the Louis and Bluey Trotter Family wing at Cedars, he returned home to find his old friend Samson Dowling in the living room.

Joyce sat off to one side while the detective faced the children, grouped in a semicircle on the emerald-green Roche-Bobois sectional. Edward had insisted on motoring up from the Boar's Head for the inter-

view; he would not have Olde CityWalk invaded by "the Spanish Inquisition." (Though with a secret lodger in the attic, the setting certainly
would have been more dramatic.)

Toulouse had of course already met the dapper Mr. Dowling, but
the pleasure was a first for first cousins. Needless to say, Lucille Rose
was smitten. Basking in the mannish cloud of their interlocutor's aftershave, eager for some of his authenticity to rub off on her authorial
side, she could barely contain herself; it didn't hurt that the detective,
as later described in a Smythson BIRD NOTES paean, resembled nothing
less than a "Grecian god." For his part, Edward, swathed in fine brocade,
was haughtily up for an old-fashioned game of cat-and-mouse. Only
Toulouse lagged behind, quietly, nervously, *dubiously* hoping that as
the son of the detective's ladylove he might at least be given special
dispensation—the slack would help camouflage his fear of inadvertently
giving Amaryllis away.

The gang of three stuck to their prefabricated story, of which happily enough many details were true. They had first taken pity on the
urchin, they said, after a random meeting on the set of Boulder Langon's
film some months before. When the detective asked if she had been accompanied by anyone on that day—for example a "large-built bearded
man"—the gang's denial was in easy unison. Did you invite her to the
house? *Naturally not!* came their nearly indignant response. Did she contact you? Not until way later, said Lucy—we never gave her the *where-
withal*. She showed up at school, said Edward. A servant poured coffee
for the detective and replenished a tray of Le Marmiton sweets. Edward
offered that the girl told them she had learned about Four Winds from a
magazine profile of the aforementioned Ms. Langon. ("I believe," said
the braided gumshoe-in-training, "the periodical goes by the name of
Twist.") Samson asked where the runaway had gotten her dress and
Lucy confessed she had been the culprit. A quick glance at her mother
revealed the woman looking rather charitable; even a homeless child deserved to look her best.

"You see, Detective," said Lucy, "I've been working on a project
about the disenfranchised—our whole class has. We're creating mobile
environments for 'urban nomads.' The goal is to *legitimize* the status of
the homeless in their communities. The house I designed has sleeping
quarters and a receptacle for scavenged cans and bottles. But when I saw

this girl, my project went out the window! I just wanted her to have cool clothes!"

Edward asked if they had done anything wrong—i.e., did they stand accused of aiding and abetting a crime? No, said the detective—that was a bit harsh. What you *should* have done was come to your parents and told them about the girl so that she could be properly helped. Samson turned to Toulouse, who'd been clucking and nodding his head in consternation and agreement with the others, and asked how long she had been in the group's "custody." Well, said Toulouse, not very long. The children looked from one to another, and the detective read their secrets.

Edward said to his sister through the veil: "Would you say two days or three?"

"Oh, maybe three—no more than three!"

The detective wanted to know where the girl had been staying. Edward said in the sukkah, but instantly regretted it, for that placed her at Stradella House a number of weeks back. He corrected himself by adding somewhat ridiculously that she had stayed in the *remains* of the sukkah, because, homeless as she was and accustomed to sleeping under the stars, she had declined their invitation to come indoors. Samson sipped his coffee and asked where the girl was *now*. We don't know, said Toulouse. Do you mean, said the detective, that in the last few hours she ran away?

Yes! said Lucy mindlessly.

Tull spoke up: "She didn't *say* anything—I mean to *us*—but she probably recognized you. When she saw you at the maze. My mom said that you—and she . . . [he couldn't bring himself to say "Amaryllis"]— well, that you knew each other. From some sort of detention place. So that was probably why she ran away again."

Lucy frowned while staring at her hands in remorse: "I told her I was making her a character in my new book—I'm writing a book you know, called *Mystery of the Blue Maze*. Though maybe it should be *Mysteries*. Mr. Hookstratten's already sent some chapters to a publisher in New York. He said he thought it could be big as Harry Potter!" Joyce admonished her daughter to answer the question. "Well, when I told her that I was creating a *character* loosely based on *her* . . . well I don't think she was very *happy*. Maybe *that's* why she ran away."

Edward said the orphan was already displeased at being the reluctant, somewhat humiliating subject of a school project on the indigent, to which his civic-minded sister spontaneously made a spirited defense.

In the middle of this staged ruckus, the children were startled to see Dodd smoothly if belatedly emerge from the shadows, rather like a nerdy vampire.

"You'd better tell the truth," said the billionaire, "because if you're still harboring her, then that *is* a crime. Am I correct, Sam?" The detective tilted his head ever so slightly as if to concur that, yes, by all laws of God and the land, the gentleman was correct indeed. "And if you are *not* providing the girl safe harbor," he continued, "then any vital information you withhold—information that could prove helpful to the detective in his efforts to find her—the very *act* of withholding such information may ultimately prove harmful, even *fatal*, to the child. This, a vulnerable girl whom you purport to have real feelings for! And that, I believe, *would* be a felony."

The collective pangs of guilt (each seconds long) aroused by his oration only weaved the gang's resolve into a more tightly knit revolutionary cell. They would not give her up.

Oddly, Joyce chose to accompany Edward back to Olde CityWalk, in the buggy. She knew better than to grill him further, instead remarking on how well he looked of late and how buoyant seemed his mood. She caressed the nape of his neck, and he shivered with delight.

Lucy and Toulouse sprinted to the Boar's Head like advance scouts. They rushed upstairs, to warn that they might be having "company." But this never came to pass, Joyce choosing to stroll back to the house after planting a kiss on Edward's veiled forehead.

Dodd walked the detective to his car. He suspected that Samson was dating his sister, but would never think of discussing such a thing directly; he preferred to get his gossip from his wife. They talked about the terrible business with Bluey and how Mr. Trotter was taking it—not so well—and where she might end up if home care became too "challenging." They could simply keep her at Saint-Cloud the way his father said Jennifer Jones had kept Norton Simon at the beach house during his decline; the luxurious "assisted-living" environments probably would not do. She was past all that now. The Alzheimer's facility at the Motion Picture and Television Hospital in Woodland Hills loomed hazily on the horizon, the irony being that Trinnie had almost finished the garden there.

Before Samson drove off, he expanded upon the reason for today's visit: Amaryllis Kornfeld. Her mother had been murdered, he said, and the perpetrator was probably someone who had befriended the child. The man was still at large, and that's why it was imperative that the runaway be found; if the two were in touch, she might lead him to the killer.

It occurred to Dodd that if what his old friend said was true—that the girl was "in touch" with her mother's attacker—then the children themselves might be in danger. It disturbed him that Samson hadn't played this bit of logic through. He was probably just exaggerating; it sounded like a TV thriller. Still, he would inform his staff of the situation and have them on the lookout.

He entered the house, replaying Dr. Janklow's words in his head. Was the whole world beset with memory disease? He decided not to tell his wife the details of the fiasco at Michael's. He could hardly tell himself.

They both went to bed with secrets, for that morning Joyce had gotten a call from the police about a baby found in the trash. She would name him Isaiah—the first soul the Candlelighters would lay to rest in Westwood Village.

⁓

When the cousin stepped from the elevator into his apartments, Toulouse and Lucy were literally wringing their hands in despair. The ladder dangled down from the attic; Amaryllis had fled.

After moments of furied search-party strategizing, Toulouse discovered the note scrawled on Edward's intagliated Francis-Orr stationery:

My Dearest Edward, Lucie and Tulouse,

I shuold never have come to see you and feel so terrible that you may now be in truoble now on accuont of me. You have done so much and lavvished such attention and moneys on me. I have been only greedy and have not given even much of a thouhgt to the brother and sister I left behind. I was not able to say goodbye to Pull-Man and wish you would tell him how sorry I am that I couold not show him the respekt he deserves and not thank him for the many rides he gave me on his strong and lovely back. You will always be in my memorrie. Edward, I know you will get better and be everr-thing you can be. Lucie you will be a famuos writer and I hope that when I am old you will remmeber I was some help to you along the way.

And Tulose—please forgive!

Your friend,
Amaryllis Kornfeld the Venerable

"She's going to kill herself!" cried Lucy.

"No," said her brother. "She wouldn't do that before finding 'the babies.' "

"That's what *we* should have been doing," said Toulouse, fairly frothing at the mouth, "instead of dressing her up like . . . some fucking *doll*. We should have been doing something to *reunite* them—"

"It's not too late for that," said the cousin.

"Bullshit! It *is*—it's *always* too late!"

With that, he stormed out. Lucy went after, but Edward shouted for her to let him be; and that some "fissiparousness" was to be expected.

Dusk fell as Toulouse left the main gate. Eulogio offered to drive him home, but the boy refused. The diligent servant shadowed him in a Town Car as he strode the serpentine road to Saint-Cloud.

The moon was full, and he had never felt such sorrow. The cold air stung his cheeks, but he walked so hard and fast that he soon sweatily removed his coat. She was out there somewhere alone—gone, as his father was and as his mother would be. And that was how the world ended, if you were lucky: with the jottings of your beloved's farewell. Grandma Bluey sure had it right: the world (even that of the living) was nothing but scraps of paper, an album of death notices blown hither and thither by a careless, uncaring wind. Around and around they blew, and where they landed no one knew . . .

That *was* how the world ended—in a parade of shredded paper raining down. The miserable confetti of Good-bye.

CHAPTER 34

An Early Winter

The pomegranate, or *Punica granatum*, belongs to a small tree native to Persia, where it still grows wild. Moses assured the wandering Israelites that they would one day find the fruit, along with honey, fig trees and brooks of clear water, in the Promised Land. There is, of course, the famous myth having to do with the abduction of Persephone to the underworld, whereby the winter season is born. Demeter, Hades and six pomegranate seeds play their part—but we'll leave that to various Four Winds mentors (and future professors of Dodd Trotter Middle School), for this book cannot include everything.

It is well known that the pomegranate does not easily give up its seeds and for that reason has never attained the popularity it deserves. But for William (who was not yet Marcus), such was the allure. He had always extolled the exotic fruit, staining his fingers with its scarlet juices at an early age as William Morris had stained his with inks and dyes; unlike Persephone, the suburban boy swallowed seeds in bulk.

Along this theme, another place (that had nothing to do with Mr. Morris's England) had begun to intrude on William's geographical consciousness—a place called the Red Lands. He could remember a woman making grenadine from the fruit, and syrup for cooking, and a kind fellow he thought to be his father showing him how to roll the pomegranate around the sidewalk and pierce its skin with a straw to suck the nectar. William smiled to himself, thinking he'd do the same for Jane Scull; it would make her gleeful, for like a child she was.

When he returned to the shelter in the afternoon, Janey wasn't there. He took up supper duties, then set about preparing a special dessert for her alone. William heated sugar in a saucepan until it was pale gold, then swirled the caramel; whilst adding juice from the pomegranate, the caramel steamed and hardened and he stirred until it dissolved. He made a separate bowl of arrowroot and water and ruffled that into the mix. He cooked the whole sauce until it boiled and thickened, before covering it to let it cool. At about ten that night, he blended in the carefully shucked ruby-colored seeds of the ancient fruit, and when someone said Janey'd come back, he spooned the caramel sauce over three scoops of vanilla Häagen-Dazs.

Bowl in hand, he was suddenly disquieted—he had been so preoccupied with pith and pip and memories of the Red Lands that he hadn't given proper weight to her uncustomary absence. Earlier, he had taken one of the counselor's casual asides (that Janey was at a sobriety meeting at Clare) at face value, knowing full well she refused to attend those peculiar, mandatory gatherings with anyone but him. William found her sitting on a bench inside the shelter's chain-link enclosure and saw immediately that she was in no mood for treats. She was pale and drawn, and drawn in on herself too.

"Janey, what is it? Are you unwell?" Her body shook, and she could not get a word out. "Shall I call a doctor?"

Her dress had a smear of crimson, as if one of his fruits had been crushed down there, and William, in his naïveté, thought her embarrassed by some menstrual clumsiness. But in fact she had come from her chores with Please-Help.-Bless, who was particularly indifferent to her frailties that night and had made her suffer greatly.

She glanced at the dessert offering, then stood up, kissed William's cheek and took to her bed until morning.

*B*luey came home. A conspiracy of sophisticated scans revealed the disease to be at an alarmingly advanced stage, the brain under siege by a riot of dementia; memories and faces had begun their anarchic stampede from tear-gas clouds of vanishing or misbegotten cells, while moods and emotions cowered, blackjacked in the rainy, atrophied back alleys of the cavum septum pellucidum (which was not so pellucid, or even lucid, anymore). Toulouse wasn't sure what all the fuss was about—Grandma was still Grandma, more or less. At least, to him.

He strolled with the old woman along the perimeter of the maze (a metaphor too tidy by half, yet unavoidable when inviting a faddish archetype into one's backyard). Those with the disease of forgetting enjoyed their wanderings, as monks had done in meditation labyrinths of old—though enlightenment was not the thing awaiting Bluey Trotter at puzzle's end.

"The strange thing is, I remember *everything*—from half a century ago. Though sometimes I can't remember my *name*," she said, and smiled. "But I *do* recall the oddest details. San Francisco, 1947. A piece of jade I bought at Gump's—clear as a bell. The amazing thing is, I haven't thought about that jade *or* Gump's in a hundred years. Vic Bergeron—that was 'Trader Vic'—and George Mardikian . . . the *restaurants,* Toulouse. I'm so glad you've started calling yourself that! Baghdad by the Bay—oh, Tull, it was just . . . *creamy,* like those pastries I love. Or a late de Kooning—do you know who that is? The painter, not the pastor. He had a rough time of it mentally, too. Do you know what San Francisco was like back then? There seemed to be no *people* there—just women in long white gloves. Swans . . . like the movie *Vertigo.* Oh, but Kim Novak was a beauty. But you've never *seen Vertigo,* have you, Tull? Of course you haven't. Your mother *loved* that city; that wasn't until so much later. But *then! 1947!* Oh good Lord, it was *heaven*—it was *all* heaven. And Capri!" she gasped. "How can I describe for you Capri? I remember the little chalk scribblings the boys made on the cliffside rocks, boys just your age. See them clear as day. You've heard of Capri? Well of *course* you have! My world traveler! Good Lord, you've been to more places than *I* have."

She stopped near a leafy inlet and drew her fingers through her grandson's hair. Pullman came over, and Toulouse watched a tiny shock wave of fear enlarge her eyes until the dog passed. She hadn't recognized the animal.

They walked some more in silence, until reaching the side of the maze farthest from the house. "My parents never wanted me to marry him, you know. To them he was a trashman, a digger of holes. A mole. Worse: a *clotheshorse* mole! Now, *your* father, well, the situation was . . . those people—those *Redlands* people had no money, but what difference did it make? We didn't care about that. One thing your grandmother is *not* is a snob. And your father . . . Marcus seemed a bit 'lost,' no? He had his Oxford side, St. John's and all, and then he had his Hollywood side. Very Jewish that way. Well, we didn't give a yap about *any* of it, your grandfather and I. We only wanted Trinnie to be happy." She traced a line with her foot in the pebbly ground. "Your father . . . well—what was meant to be was meant to be. He was not *mentally correct.* Do you love him?" The question took him aback. Again, with a rakish smile: "Do you love him?"

"Grandma, I've never even met him!"

"I'm sure you will," she said, with a pixie's amusement.

"Sometimes I wish Lucy never told me he was . . . alive."

"Oh, but *someone* would have. And you'd have been angry, no? Lucy is a great friend, no? You love Lucy, don't you?"

"Yes."

They passed a second entrance to the box hedge, and Bluey gave an inquiring side glance.

"Don't think I'll go in—not today."

She gathered herself on a stone bench. He sat down beside her.

"Do you know what is *truly* distressing?" She had the hollow, watery eyes of an excommunicant. "The thing I'm terrified of?—"

"Grandma, what is it?"

He thought she would burst into tears.

"You promise you won't say anything to anyone?"

"I promise."

"Are you certain, Toulouse? Because I don't want this to get back to your mother! And I sure as hell don't want Louis bothered by it."

"I won't," he said, genuinely wanting to ease her agony. "I wouldn't tell *anyone.*"

She leaned in his ear and whispered: "We are running out of money."

Toulouse was nonplussed; under contagion of the old woman's derangement, he struggled to understand. He'd never given money much thought—its running-outs *or* running-ins.

"But . . . did someone *say* it?"

"No! No! Of *course* not! Of course no one *said* it. No one ever *says* it. No one ever says *anything.* It's something I *know* and it does *not* need ratification *or* ratiocination. But I *cannot* discuss this with your grandfather, do you understand? Because that *will* 'hasten' me—in their eyes. They'll send me away! Did you know Louis bought a set of buttons at auction for twenty-three thousand dollars? A set of buttons, Toulouse! From the Court of Louis the Fourteenth. He collects anything with 'Louis' attached, such is his *vanitas*—'vanity of vanities,' sayeth the Preacher. And to what end? How are we to maintain the house, Toulouse? Do you *know* what that man hoards in his den? (You *should* know; you're in there enough.) More than Croesus, that's what! And your *mother* is cut from the same cloth. I told them to sell that house—that crazy cracked tower. I told them *years* ago. What good does it do just sitting there? Do you know what that land is *worth*? Families could live there fourteen times over! But your mother and grandfather would rather keep a haunted house. Well now *I've* come to haunt *them—I'll* make them pinch a penny!"

"Grandma, let's go back."

"You cannot breathe a *word*—"

"I wouldn't."

She began to weep.

"Your uncle Dodd . . . I had such hopes for your uncle Dodd—that *he* would be the one to restore us. But he spends so much! Lord, he flies around in a plane that costs millions and millions—you need an entire crew and every one of those crew-people have their own lifestyles that must be maintained. And you have to *pay!* You're supporting a whole *city* of people you don't even know! Joyce says she makes him take pills so he won't spend the money—his wife is an *angel.* But I *do* think they may be worse off than we are! The market is *constantly crashing.* But you wouldn't know it from talking to Uncle Dodd! No you wouldn't. He's got his head in the sand, Tullie . . . Do you think they'll ask for anything? Do you think they'll ask Grandpa for money? That would be a terrible calamity. Because we simply do not have it!"

"*M*r. Trotter?" She stood outside the Withdrawing Room like a child. "Mr. Trotter, may I come in?"

The old man was surprised, and pleased to see her. "Yes, Winter, of course."

"I won't take too much of your time."

"Not at all, come in! Come in." He was having his drink, and strolling amid the little tombs. "How's our girl doing?"

"Not so bad today. Keeps to her scrapbooks." She smiled rather painfully. "Says we lost one of the notices—that I misplaced it. Sometimes she even says I steal them."

"Never was a shy one!" he said. "Always spoke her mind."

"Spends most her time looking, looking, looking—then forgets what she's looking *for*."

He chuffed and clucked and shook his head. "Invidious disease."

He sipped at his sherry and offered her some, surprised when she acceded.

Winter looked around at the room's wonders, and he handed her a glass. He knew she had more to say. She'd been under a great strain and perhaps wanted a sabbatical; the timing could not be more inopportune.

"And how are *you* bearing up, Winter?"

"Me, sir? I'm all right. I've been through it before—with an aunt. In Reykjavík. But it's not an easy thing . . ."

"No. Not an easy thing."

"Mr. Trotter . . . there's something been on my mind. And I—I wanted to talk it over."

"Yes! Anything, Winter! Please!"

"Well, some months ago Mrs. Trotter said she bought me something. And I was *very* glad and *very* grateful of it at the time but now . . . now that her troubles seem to have gotten so much worse—"

"What did she buy you, Winter?" he asked, genuinely curious.

"Well, sir, she said—she said it was a condo."

"A condo?"

"Yessir. A condominium."

He chuffed and looked thoughtfully into the air. "Where?"

"I don't know, Mr. Trotter. I never asked."

"I see. And . . . well, she never mentioned—never mentioned any details?"

"No, sir. Not a word." She looked at the ground, as if at a loss; he thought he would help her along.

"And you want to know if the papers are in order . . ." Winter looked up, confused. "You're concerned that with the onset of Bluey's 'difficulties,' the paperwork or records of ownership might be, shall we say, *in flux*."

"No sir, I—"

He chuffed, trying to lighten the mood, which had become a trifle morbid. "Perhaps *that's* the thing she thinks you've misplaced—perhaps that's what she's been searching for. I'll look into it, Winter, you have my word. And I'm glad you came to me. It's an absolutely valid concern."

"But, Mr. Trotter, you misunderstand!"

"Oh?"

"I don't care about any condo—I never have! I never asked for any-thing and never expected anything in all my years with the family! But, sir—if she *did* do this thing—if she *did* buy this place for me—which was quite unusual in that she'd never done anything like it before in the thirty-five—if she *did* do this thing on account of—her 'difficulties,' as you said—if she bought this thing for me and doesn't remember or never meant to in the *first* place . . . or *wouldn't* have if not for her 'difficulties'—"

The old man stopped her short. He chuffed a bit, and fiddled with a cuff link before meeting her eye.

"Winter, I am truly sorry if I jumped to conclusions. I *do* understand you now and it's so good of you. Forgive me. Because there *are* people who prey on—not you, certainly not!—but in the time since all these 'difficulties' came to a head, so to speak, I have learned that my wife—that Bluey has written checks in the last six months to various charita-ble organizations, some of which have proved dubious. Some of these came from phone solicitations. There are whole armies of people, it seems, who prey on people such as my wife. We are actively going over all her transactions of the past year. We are doing it at this very moment. So I appreciate you coming to me, Winter. And I assure you everything will be looked into."

"You won't say anything to her, will you, Mr. Trotter? About my concerns?"

"Of course not," he said, putting an arm around her.

"Thank you! Thank you so much."

"Thank *you*, Winter. Now, get some rest. You look tired."

"I will, sir. The night nurses have just arrived."

"I'm going to move them in, Winter—we need three shifts. Two isn't enough. Because it's far too much for you, now isn't it?" He felt an on-rush of emotion for this selfless woman, who had served so long and so well. "We need three shifts, and we need the people already here so we're not at the mercy of waiting—so *you* don't have to wait. Extra pairs of eyes to watch over her . . . so you're free to go to your room and look at television. Or to the Village to take in a movie. And not be burdened by waiting for someone to show up. That's already in the works."

"Thank you, sir."

He gave her a hug and ushered her out before she had a chance to start bawling.

*J*ane Scull heard a commotion. Some lights came on, and she was confused. Was it morning? She climbed down from her bunk, rubbing her eyes. Then looked up: horror! She ran to William, now surrounded by policemen, hands fastened behind his back.

"It's all right, Janey! It's all right."

A staffperson restrained her while a lady cop stood between Jane and her beau.

"*Uttt? Cant ake youuuh!*" Now all the hours spent enunciating before the mirror were for naught. She trundled after, and William asked an officer if he might please say a word to his frightened friend. Seeing that he was peaceable, they allowed a supervised moment before locking him away.

"Janey darling, it's a mistake—I'll be back, don't worry! Don't *cry*, there's no *reason* for it. I left ice cream in the freezer with a special topping. You'll have some, won't you?"

She nodded and composed herself to speak as best she could. He leaned to her mouth and had trouble understanding, but at the last moment, just before they made him go, his eyes flashed righteously—she was asking if he'd hurt a girl, a little girl! That's why she thought they had come for him . . .

"Janey, Janey, who told you such a thing? That child was my life! I did everything I could to help her!" He was flabbergasted, and numbly took in those gathered around as if they were picadors and he had been one hundred times lanced. "Who would tell you such a thing?" They pulled him away, and William had no time to explain. "Now, don't you worry your pretty head," he shouted. "D'you hear? I have done *nothing*, Janey! [His refutation being general, for he knew not why they had come for him, either.] Have your ice cream in the morning and by the time you finish, I'll be home!"

As the handcuffed giant awkwardly insinuated himself into the backseat, an officer held a palm over his head in the baptismal gesture that ushered the doomed into custody.

"See to my personal things, Janey! My book—see that it's safe!"

She nodded vigorously, while the staffers held her back, and cried when the black-and-white peeled away, joyful with what she'd known in her heart all along: her William was bighearted and tender and good. Her William was the Lord's child, and innocent too! She would visit Please-Help.-Bless once more, *then* have dessert—and by the time she finished the very last spoonful, her man would be forever home.

CHAPTER 35

Probable Cause

*T*he very next morning, Samson Dowling drove downtown to in-terview the prisoner, who was being held on charges of murder and rape. Arraignment wasn't until Tuesday, and a public defender would not be appointed before then; the client would be shackled and al-ready in court on the occasion of that first meet.

After the MacLaren interview, his gut told him it was unlikely that the suspect (who since the arrest had reluctantly identified himself as Wil-liam Marcus) had participated in any nefarious acts, sexual or otherwise, involving the girl. He would no doubt be cleared of such accusations—but that was the least of the prisoner's worries.

Regarding the murder, Samson had a few threadbare theories. He believed the defendant was in a relationship with the deceased and that there had been a squabble over money or drugs—perhaps even a classic sex-gone-bad scenario escalating to homicide. Things got a little murkier after that. One of his thoughts was that after the killing, a remorseful "Mr. Marcus" aided the girl as a kind of penance. Yet what troubled the detective most were the vicious circumstances surrounding the mother's death.

The coroner's report concluded that the woman had been raped postmortem. Amaryllis had told intake workers that her brother and sis-ter were crawling on the bed when she came home to find the body, meaning they had been either in the kitchenette or the room itself while the crimes were being committed. Whether they were sound asleep or not meant little; their sheer presence betrayed a coldness on the part of the killer that was unsettling.

Other details nagged. Investigators were unable to lift prints from the scene; it was the detective's experience that in a case like this, such fastidiousness (given the low-life players) was unusual to say the least. In other words, there was a degree of professionalism involved. Then there was the actual method of strangulation, accomplished by ligatures of uncommon complexity. What was the meaning of it?

But the most damning piece of evidence was the navy-blue ascot. Amaryllis had corroborated that it belonged to William Marcus aka Topsy; and while the silken item—stuffed deep in the victim's throat—had not been the instrument of her death, it revealed yet another layer of brutality.

Samson found himself high in the Twin Towers, sitting opposite a weather-beaten mountain of Caucasian male, roughly forty-five years of age, with long, slender fingers on delicate hands and cool, gray eyes. His informant (whom the detective paid off and hoped never to have dealings with again) had accurately conveyed that since relocating to the beach, the formerly hirsute "Mr. Marcus" was now in fact close-shaven; Samson wished he'd at least gotten a glimpse of that near-legendary beard, for it had helped him better form a picture these last few months. William Marcus was assumed to be an alias but would have to be lived with until the computers told them otherwise.[†]

He began rather delicately, for his instincts told him there was no other way to approach the creature before him; but soon he was asking anything he wanted, for something in the man made him want to rush to the heart of things. Where had he been living before the beach? Had he bivouac'd downtown, under a bridge? Had he ever worked for a man named Gilles Mott in a Temple Street bakery for pocket money? Did he bring a young girl there? And where did he meet that selfsame girl? Was it the girl's mother who introduced them?

The mind is a mysterious, plastic thing and never ceases to invent

---

[†] It was more than a decade since our detainee had been fingerprinted at a far smaller jail in upstate New York; those records, if they even still existed, may never have been entered into the national identity bank. *That* Marcus was lighter by nearly a hundred and twenty pounds and resembled a hunter from the Pleistocene epoch; *this* one was in his own manner as much a missing link. Neither resembled the man to whom Samson had been first introduced by Katrina Trotter.

itself; it can plod faithfully along with a yeoman's awareness or sparkle with exquisite brilliance before losing its way. It learns and relearns with startling agility but, like any Thoroughbred, likes to be put through its paces. As implausible as it may seem, had Detective Dowling not lately gone through the mental gymnastics of connecting the dots between the short-haired "consul's daughter" recently met at the Saint-Cloud maze and the pallid little beast he had once driven from Hotel Higgins to MacLaren—if his brain had not been suchwise jarred, then his sudden and precipitous recognition of the lost soul before him might never have occurred at all—this being a roundabout way of explaining why midway into the thirty-minute interview his eyes glazed and his pulse quickened. What tipped him over? The odd, vaguely anglicized turn of phrase—remnants of an accent heard long-ago in Adirondacks interrogations? Intuition of familiar bones beneath fleshy mask before him? Or the ineffable thing of Trinnie's voodoo upon Samson's séanced heart . . . it was—it was—it was—

"Marcus?"

"Yes?"

"You're Marcus Weiner."

"Man, who?"

"You *are* him."

Whether he knew or knew not, and if so by and what degree, William wasn't ready to abandon his post.

"Marcus! It's *Samson*," he said, pointing rather absurdly to his own chest. "Samson *Dowling—Dodd's* friend. Dodd *Trotter*—"

He glowered and said, "Sir, do not challenge me!"

The detective took a long breath, and retrenched. "Look: I want to help you."

"Man, I am not desirous of your help!"

"Do you not know that your name is Marcus Weiner? That you have a family? And that you've been missing thirteen years? Do you not know this?"

SeaShelter, the morning after. An agitated SeaStaff bristles: can it possibly be that William, *their* William, eccentric lord of the kitchen and shining rehab poster boy, was actually a fugitive wanted in connection with the heinous murder of a downtown woman some months back? And that wasn't all! Rumor had it that on top of it, he was being charged with the kidnapping and molestation of—suddenly paranoid, one of the day managers thought it prudent to pay a visit to Le Marmiton and gather up any items extant that were William-made. Only days before, the Montana Avenue bakery had bought a half-dozen jars of pomegranate preserves, along with his trademark thumbprint cookies ladled with the fruit's special sauce; such was their popularity that all had sold out. The woman behind the counter was glad to see the representative so she could order some more. The SeaStaffer anxiously scanned the shelves for potentially poisoned goods and, as he left, made an empty promise that a delivery would soon be on its way.

Jane Scull was devastated. SeaShelter "guests," whom she thought of as friends, now declared with aplomb that William—whose pastries and foodstuffs they'd so greedily inhaled, and who had patiently adjudicated their squabbles and poignantly attended their subliterate tales of woe, and who had transcribed in careful calligraphic hand all their wretched poetries—their William, *her* William, was a strangler and a child-fucker who was going to fry!

She had an important question for Please-Help.-Bless.

Upon her request, a counselor opened William's locker so Jane could retrieve *News from Nowhere,* wrapped in oilcloth and tightly bound with twine; her plan was to bring it to him in the afternoon. The same staffer had been good enough to draw a map showing how to get to the jail, albeit the wrong jail, but it's the thought that counts. She put the book in her backpack, then launched for Pico Boulevard and environs.

She walked for hours, but there was no sight of him. Maybe he was done with her and had moved on to the next case—he was, after all, or so he said, a professional informant. "Me and Gold Shield, we's a team!" She would not mention the woman they said her William had killed, for she wished to hear no lies about that, nor would she bother to tell him it was not true about William touching the girl; she already felt ashamed for not having gone to her man right away to tell him of the blackmailer. She had let herself be raped instead. She felt so agonized and traitorous and diseased on so many fronts—no, she would not press the outrageous innocence of her William's case, not with that devil, nor with anyone else. She knew that in jail a murderer might be well regarded but the "other" kind, the child-bothering kind was . . . the thing Jane wanted to know, *needed* to know, was: *would her William be killed in jail?* For that's what he had said . . .

Killim! Killim! Killim—

It was more than her heart could bear! Why *did* the devil say such a thing? And how would he *know?* She could not rely on her William being released, for the wheels of justice move slowly and the maulers of children are guilty until proven innocent. She knew nothing of the girl—could it be his daughter?—knew nothing of anything but her William. Was it possible the devil had made up a story just so they would kill him? That her William's life was in *his* hands? But how, how! And there, in Tujunga, was Jilbo—Jilbo, who'd fathered her child, *his* hands on all the little ones . . . and her William in jail, this devil in her holes and Jilbo free as a dirty bird! She would talk to Gold Shield—*My William is going to be killed!* she would say. *And that should not happen to a man when he is in jail, especially an innocent who is awaiting his trial. It is* not *right, it is not* supposed *to happen* . . . She would find Gold Shield when she visited the prison. Jane bit her lip in recrimination; she should have asked for him on the night of the arrest. Selfishness! The police were all around and she could have talked to Gold Shield *then,* could have talked to any one of them . . . but she was busy blubbering instead; busy getting assurances from her true love that he was not a molester of children—assurances that he was not a devil—when she took *this* devil's assurances whenever he liked—collecting her husband's startled consolations: that's how she'd spent their last moments together. As if anything her William might have done (no matter how immoral) could ever make a difference, or injure her love for him.

There he was ahead, crossing the street called Speedway, a buzzard with a brown-bagged bottle of wine. He grinned and licked his chops. He was drunk, and some German tourists watched him paw her tits.

"Ahm *hun-nuh-gree,* you slappy cow bitch," he said, mimicking her impediment. "An' *horrr-neee.* Wanna puts muh *whole haid* in there! Thinks you kin fits a whole haid? How 'bout a whole *fist?* How 'bout *two* fists? Two-fisted love!" The crapulent fiend pulled from the bottle and cackled.

She took his hand and said, "Want. Too. Fuck."

She nearly dragged him down the sidewalk, and he got such a kick out of her ardor that now and then he broke free, girlishly collapsing in laughter, hacking and wheezing and pointing. "The bitch in love! The bitch *love* me! Now howda ya like that!" Like an underworld Music Man, he almost burst into song.

She led him through the cyclone fence surrounding the depredated rooms of the Tropicana. The structure had been gutted and prep'd for re-building, but there were no guards or workers. Jane took Please-Help.-Bless upstairs—still bent over gleefully, he pulled from his wine—to the very same room she had shared with her William on their first night to-gether. The mattress was gone and the space looked altogether different than it had before, and of that she was grateful.

This was the first time in a room for Jane and Please-Help.-Bless too. When he fucked her, it was usually behind the scratchy freeway brush near Lincoln and Olympic, a block or so from SeaShelter. He liked it when the people in cars could see them going at it.

"You looks thin—did I ball that kid outta you? Shit! How 'bout that! I fuck him right outta you, huh? You *likes* that. Don' need no abortion *now*. Here it is, slappy-cow: the lean, mean 'bortion machine!" He un-buckled his pants and she lay down while hiking up her skirt. "You *love* me, don' chew? You love me *now*, now ain't that a bitch? She love me! She wanta *fuck* me! She *love* to fuck her daddy!"

She would tell her William everything now, every terrible thing she'd done, and risk him leaving her. She would risk it all, because that was the only way they could begin anew. She would tell William every-thing, and if he said it was too terrible and that they could never see each other again, she would just walk away and kill herself without him ever knowing. (She would never want him to think he had anything to do with such an act.) And if he told her to go to the police and confess what she had done, she would. They would arrest her for her crimes and she would be able to sleep again. She would at least be able to see her William—there were probably jails that held men and women under the same roof, like at SeaShelter. Maybe they could serve their time then leave jail together and come back to Santa Monica to start over. They could stay on the beach-bluffs awhile before checking in to the shelter, like that night they left the hotel after the raid.

She wet herself down there with spit, and Please-Help.-Bless spat wine on her too and opened her up with dirty fingers. "You look *good*," he said, turning her over and forcing his way in. "Ooh but you stank! Shit, you stank. Somethin' like to crawl up there and *die*. Maybe the baby did! Heh heh. Naw—I think you dropped that baby. It *good* you dropped that baby 'cause you thin now. You a thin cow. What'd that little peesuhshit have, cock or pussy? 'Cause if it had a pussy, you shoulda *saved* it for me."

He grew quiet while he worked, and let go of the bottle.

"Pweeze," said Jane, trying her best to enunciate. "Why yoo seh they killum."

"Shut up, bitch. Shut up whileye fuck."

"Yooo seh dey killum in pwih-sun. They *killum*—"

"Oh yeah!" He picked up the bottle and swigged while jimmying himself in. "Thas *right* they gun killum! That turn you on? They prolly killim right now while I fucks you! Man a menace! Das why I pull him off thuh streets! *I* do that. *I* have the pow-uh! Gold Shield lissen to *me*. Them boys in the joint, they find out he fuck kiddies, they killum good and slow! They gun *rape rape rape* jus' like I rape *yoh* ass. He gun bleed like *you* bleed 'cept he ain' gonna drop no *baby*."

"Buh you canh *stop* them—"

"Now, why *would* I, *bitch*? Now shut tha fuck up. Ain' gonna stop *nuthin'*. They killum! Killum! Killum!"—the word capping each painful thrust. *"Killum! Killum! Killum! Killum! Killum! Kil—"*

In the midst of his transport, Please-Help.-Bless stopped dead— or nearly so, for Jane Scull had plunged a knife deep into his bowels. The smell of perforated belly erupted in her sensitive nostrils, pelting like a weapon itself. She used the knife William had bought her for protection; the same that had cut the umbilicus in the bathroom at McDonald's.

Please-Help.-Bless stared into her eyes, lips clamped, shaking like a zealot. It was then, with him seizing beneath her, that she uttered the fruit of weeks of diligent elocutionary practice: *"You—are—dy—ing."* His body retracted, crab-like. The bottle was still in his hand and shattered against the wall. He slashed at her throat, which opened like a well of water everlasting. She was gone before him, though not by long.

Her weight acted as a full-body tourniquet, so that when he wriggled out from beneath, impaled on her dagger, a bucket of blood and insides poured forth. He slipped and slid as he stood on the killing floor. It is said we revert to infancy at the time of our death; the vagrant reverted only to the name by which he first was known.

"Someone help me!" he cried from the door frame.

And that was the end of him.

*A*maryllis's farewell lay on the floor in the middle of the cousin's apartments, and they paced around it—even Edward hobbled about—like lost hikers awakened to a final campfire extinguished by careless neglect. Toulouse accused Edward of being cavalier *and* Machiavellian; Edward accused Toulouse of being lovesick, needy and vain; Lucy accused both of being hypocrites and was in turn lambasted for having the gall to be secretly relieved that the girl was gone, to which the outraged mystery writer responded by sobbing hysterically while hurling various items against the walls of Boar's Head Inn proper. To make matters worse, an oblivious Boulder showed up on a film break and spoke blithely of her crush on Joaquin Phoenix and how she had gone to Diane Keaton's house for dinner and held the *Annie Hall* Oscar in her hand.

Toulouse left in a huff and walked up the hill to Saint-Cloud. The Dane's gait seemed wobbly, and he thought: *That's all I need. For Pullman to up and die on me* . . . He had failed her; he had failed everyone. He remembered the girl's misery on meandering up this very slope—that was the day he pushed her away, the day he wasn't man enough to do the thing his mother and father had done in that very room. A day that would live in infamy.

Then came the revelation, as they passed the gate at La Colonne: *she had taken refuge there*—there, in the master suite, she awaited!

Boy and dog raced through the hole in the hedge, charging at tower's entrance. "Amaryllis!" he cried, past boxwood and yew. "Amaryllis!" He sprinted up the spiral stairs. "Amaryllis! Amaryllis! Amaryllis!" But where would he spirit her? It would be too strange and impractical to keep her *here*; they couldn't hide from Mr. Greenjeans. And Stradella and Saint-Cloud were bridges already burned . . . he would need to come up with something brand-new—maybe this time he'd leave Edward and Lucy out of it. No: he'd *never* be able to pull that off. Maybe he would just tell his mom . . .

Things were as they had left them. Toulouse went to the window and looked out. He imagined seeing Amaryllis far below, coquettishly staring back at him; he thought of Trinnie and how desolate she must have felt that morning, searching the meadow with newlywed eyes. He called her name a few more times, then feebly ducked his head into the rooms on each floor. His instincts had been so wrong; what a surprise.

Again, he climbed the hill to his grandfather's house. He resolved that he *would* tell Trinnie, not so much because it was in her power to find the girl (he was convinced Samson Dowling would prove up to the task), but rather to selfishly enlist her aid in restoring Amaryllis to his world once she was back in captivity. Toulouse knew his mother would be unable to resist, especially if he confessed his love for the foundling; a quintessential romantic, she'd always been one to nurse a broken-winged sparrow. He would play on her ample reservoirs of parental guilt—anything to make the woman throw her bountiful energies into pulling Amaryllis from the county quicksand. The timing wasn't great. The Trotters were consumed by the Bluey crisis, and no one had been thrilled with the adopt-a-homeless-child episode; it was generally agreed that Toulouse and his cousins had abused their privilege and the family's trust. Even Edward was in the doghouse, though perversely enjoying his "grounded" status.

He arrived in time for dinner and was startled to find an old couple at table with Trinnie and Grandpa Lou. It took a moment to place them—Harry and Ruth, the Weiners of Redlands! Introductions were made before Trinnie knowingly turned to her son and uttered the kind of arch drawing-room cliché that set the new, improved Ralph Mirdling's teeth on edge: "I see that you've already met."

CHAPTER 36

Reunions

"*A*ren't you curious about our guests? I mean, what they're doing here?"

Trinnie was making sport, but her son wasn't receptive.

"It's a *wonderful* thing that we're here," said Ruth. "Wonderful!"

"I can't believe it myself," offered Harry. The spiffed-up face still drooped on one side but was so closely shaven (Ruth had done the job) that his cheeks looked like marzipan. "This marvelous house—hasn't changed! Nothing has changed."

"Nothing, and everything! Well, aren't you *wondering*, Toulouse?" his mother asked mischievously.

"Now, don't bother the boy!" said Grandpa Lou.

"The Weiners graciously consented to come to dinner tonight so that I could make amends." She looked at her son with near-religious gravitas. "It's important to make amends. Do you know what 'amends' are, Toulouse?"

"Of course he knows!" exclaimed Ruth, beaming.

"But does he *really*—"

"Why talk to the boy like that, Katrina?" chuffed Louis, stabbing a forkful of quail salad.

"He's *extremely* intelligent," Ruth went on. "Like his cousin Edward." She was thrilled to be sitting there dropping names and having discourse with . . . family! "Why, I couldn't even *follow* some of the things that child discussed!"

"Marvelous boys," said Harry, soaking an endive in Persian mulberry sauce. "Marvelous *minds*."

"Now, don't bother him, Katrina!"

"Father, he'll be fine!" She gently mussed Toulouse's hair with her fingertips, then took a breath, centering herself. "There's an old saying—Ralph told it to me—back when he was still Rafe! But it's a beautiful saying: 'When someone plants a tree under which they will never sit, that's how you know civilization has arrived.' "

"That's lovely," said Ruth, putting her hand on her husband's.

"And quite pertinent," said Harry, "for a designer of gardens."

"It's Greek—he probably read it during his *Poetics* period. Remember, Tull?" Then, to the Weiners: "Rafe is an old paramour. And so is Ralph!"

"A very *young* old paramour," said Toulouse.

"Oh!" said Ruth. She liked a little spice.

Trinnie eyed her son with mock reproach. Then: "He wrote for the movies, or was trying to, anyway. I think he was convinced that Aristotle could teach him something about screenwriting."

"Now he prefers the ancient philosopher Ron Bass."

Trinnie gave him another look.

"I wonder what Detective Dowling reads," he cattily mused. Toulouse was on a roll.

She ignored the remark and turned to her affable in-laws, who, for their part, were somewhat confused by the banter. "The Greeks knew how to keep it real," she said. (His mother's hip-hopisms made the boy squirm.) "I share this, to illustrate something about amends—that they always come too late." She lifted her glass of cranberry juice to the Weiners in *salud;* Grandpa Lou looked up, hastily raising his own. "Tonight, I have planted a tree. It was meant to be planted long ago, but never took root." She winced, blinking back maudlin tears as she addressed their visitors. "I hope that . . . now that you know the tree is *here,* you'll feel free to sit under it when you like, and avail yourself of the shade."

Toulouse thought he was going to be sick. "You're not even making sense!"

"It is *never* too late," said Ruth ingratiatingly. "And it's very *nice* what you've done, Katrina—to call after all this time and have us here for this *lovely* dinner."

"To send a *car,*" added Harry, adjusting a crepitant knee to throw his comment Louis's way.

"It could not have been easy," said Ruth. "It *has* not been easy—for any of us!"

"It has not been easy, no. And least of all for Marcus!" Only Harry could have pulled off such a remark. He reached for the gold raspberry vinaigrette; a server jumped into the fray, handing over a Chinese porcelain sauceboat.

"My son—*your grandson*—has taught me so much," said Trinnie. "He taught me not to run and hide; I've been doing that long enough. Though he probably doesn't know it—I hope he does—though he probably doesn't know it, his mother loves him more than anything." She fussed with his hair again, and he blushed in spite of himself. "*Toulouse* is why the two of you are here tonight. And I just want to be as brave as he has been—and to make my amends. To ask his forgiveness again—and *yours*, for shutting you out. For taking this light—this lamp, my son, and hiding him away! For closing the door on his beautiful grandparents because of my own self-indulgent . . . I am *praying* the fences can be mended. I am praying you will sit beneath this tree that I have—"

"That's enough!" said Louis, not to chastise, but to protect her from further shaming herself in the depths of such sorrows—he knew how low she could go. "But very well spoken. Very well spoken."

"Oh, Katrina!" cried Ruth, unable to hold back. "Please don't! We already *love* you—aren't we family? Aren't we still family? Haven't we always *been?*"

"Yes! But say you forgive me, Ruth! Harry . . . just *say* it—"

"Katrina!" barked her father.

"Well of course we forgive, dear! Now, we need to put this all *behind* us—"

"Listen to the lady, Trinnie!" chuffed Louis. "That's a wise lady—listen to her."

"She *is* wise," said Harry, who never stopped munching his quail. "Always has been."

Trinnie recovered herself. "Did you know that Toulouse never even mentioned that he'd been to see you?"

"Isn't that something?" gushed Harry. "That's how *I'd* have played it—close to the vest!"

After a few choice queries, he realized that his mother's dinner invitation had been coincidental to the Redlands excursion and not because of it. (He'd been thinking the cousins had tattled.) He was impressed—and less pleased with himself all around.

"Well, well!" said Louis, spontaneously pushing back his chair to stand in greeting—for Bluey had come from the kitchen in chenille robe and silky hairpiece. Shadowed by Winter, she bore a silver tray of butter-laden sweets.

"How marvelous!" said Ruth, and really meant it. The appearance of the old woman moved her; she'd always had a fondness for Berenice in her heart and had been genuinely unhappy to learn of the recent downturn. Harry echoed his wife's enthusiasms with bird-like perorations.

"Mother," said Louis. "Do you remember the Weiners? Harry and Ruth?" He wished he could take it back, for his tone was too much the one used with a child.

"Yes of course!" she said contemptuously. "Marcus's folks!"

"You look so lovely!" said Ruth.

"Beautiful, beautiful!" said Harry. For some reason, everyone was shouting.

"Mother," said Trinnie. "Some of us are trying to diet. What evils have you brought to tempt us with?"

"No one says you have to have any," said Bluey.

A server went to relieve her of the heavy tray, but Louis did that instead, setting it on the table with Harry's valiant, if tottering, help.

The old woman approached the couple, who received her as subjects would a dogaressa. Leaning over, she whispered: "My daughter—in case you haven't already noticed—tends to think she's the center of the known universe."

*W*hy is it that, in lull or interlude, we so often turn to Dodd Trotter? Well, why not? As someone once said, attention must be paid. Besides—no one close to our story is going anywhere, at least not for the moment.

William Marcus is in jail for the weekend, at minimum; and Trinnie has made amends, so all's well with *her* world. The detective is in turmoil for a number of reasons, but so be it—his discomfort won't last. Toulouse and Pullman are at rest, the former reading a book, head propped on the pinkish mottled bellows of the belly of that loyal beast. Bluey is well fed, well loved and unafraid, the briny waters of dementia having mysteriously receded; Mr. Trotter is in her good favor again and sits upon the Duxiana duvet cross-legged, helping with the mordant scrapbook after having packed Winter off to the movies. At Stradella House, Joyce has just received a curious call: the dumpster baby she'd been forewarned of and whose burial she had already begun to plan— the first for the Candlelighters' Westwood site—the soul she had named Isaiah—wasn't dead at all. Rumors of the castaway's demise were deemed exaggerated enough to make page three of the California section of the *Times* (the article said a police dispatcher had jumped the gun). Joyce thought it a wonderful omen. She celebrated with a rubdown at Aida Thibiant, followed by a smattering of Restylane to smooth the facial furrows.

So: no one is going anywhere, and all is relatively well. Even Amaryllis is being looked after, or at least looked *into*. Then why not follow Dodd into a hastily organized luncheon? It is one of the last events on his calendar before pressing business swallows him up.

A casual reunion of sorts; he walks the few short blocks down Cañon to Spago. Marcie Millard held the last—the official—coming-together, Beverly Vista's twenty-fifth, at her home in Benedict Canyon. Grade-school reunions are uncommon, but attendance was surprisingly high. They barbecued and the Vistonians sang Christmas carols once belted forth in the lobby of the Beverly Wilshire Hotel; a few graying alumni who won the fertility lotto brought their newborns. Marcie made hilarious I.D. tags from yearbook photos and everyone had a high old time. (Just recently she sent Frances-Leigh a newsletter with photos and funny captions of the event; the note that accompanied said, "Call me stupid, but I literally did not know how to get in touch!")

There had been a flurry of excitement surrounding the Vista re-build, and Dodd Trotter's felicitous participation only added to the buzz. Marcie said a decision would be made by the Board any day now; meanwhile, his agents had already made a number of quiet bids on property surrounding the school. They were batting a thousand, with over twenty separate units bought and fifteen more in escrow.

Marcie thought it timely for the Vista Vets to meet and greet the new crop of movers and shakers, whose children were current enrollees— and it couldn't hurt to informally invite some of the Board and their spouses. Dodd shook a lot of hands, and was gratified to meet the well-shod, multiethnic parents of kids who were flowering in the greenhouse of a new millennium. Only one of them commented on the school being named after him and Dodd brushed it off, not wishing to call attention. He'd been pillow-talking with Joyce lately and had decided (Marcie's cheerleading aside) that if renaming BV was going to be a deal breaker, then he'd simply accede to the Board's wishes and forge ahead as planned. They could call the thing George W. Bush Elementary for all he cared—this wasn't about ego; this was about the children. This was about tradition, values, education. Joyce said, you know you're sounding more like a politician each day. But she reveled in her husband's newfound serenity, not knowing whether to thank God or the psychopharmacologist.

"Are you Dodd Trotter?" asked a bald, portly man. This time, Marcie hadn't made I.D. badges.

"Yes, I am."

"My God. I'm Val DeWitt!"

As the billionaire pumped his hand, a memory flooded back. Val DeWitt was the once-hardbodied boy who got him in a playground headlock that lasted almost twenty minutes. Other students artfully encircled so the P.E. instructor couldn't see; Dodd had almost blacked out. He'd often dredged that image up through the years as a symbol of what he had managed to overcome—he saw the two of them in stone, timeless victim and oppressor, a frieze of everything unjust and unexpected that the world had to offer.

"I just wanted to congratulate you on your amazing success," said Val. "I'm kind of a geek freak—I guess I was into it more before the bubble burst. I've read about you the last few years and saw the article in *Forbes*—I think *everybody* saw that article. It was seminal! You guys became a hobby of mine. But this is actually the first time I've ever met a billionaire! Well, now wait a minute—that's not true: I just saw Marvin Davis inside, sitting on his special chair. But he doesn't count. And I didn't actually go *up* to him. I don't even think he's in the top *hundred* anymore—you're still way up there, no? Quincunx is holding its own. I guess you and Gates and Ellison and all those guys'll do OK no matter how low the Nasdaq goes. But I'm being a bore! I hope you don't mind! Thanks for letting me say hello."

He started to edge away, and Dodd grabbed his arm. "No, not at all— and what are you doing these days, Val?"

"I own a restaurant—two, really—in Northern California. I'm afraid I operate on a slightly smaller scale than you."

"Restaurants: that's a *very* difficult undertaking. Super–high risk. What are they called?"

"DeWitt's—not very imaginative. We're actually pretty well known in the Bay Area. I'm only in L.A. today to sample the goods; they have some *amazing* wines here. Spago's has a master sommelier. Not too many people know that—there's only around forty in the whole country. Do you know Mike? He's the sommelier. By the way, you should try the La Tâche. It's only about a grand per bottle—you can afford it!"

"Have you kept in touch with Marcie?" he asked perfunctorily.

"Who?"

"Marcie. Marcie Millard."

"Now, *that's* a name from the past . . ."

"She organized the luncheon."

"What luncheon?"

"You mean, you didn't know this was a Vista event?"

"Vista?"

"Beverly Vista—we're having a bit of a precelebration."

"For what?"

"I'm rebuilding the old school. All the people here"—he nodded at the patio—"they're all BV alumni."

"Now wait a minute. Hold on. *You* went to Beverly Vista?"

"Oh come on, Val."

"No way."

"Don't tell me you don't remember the headlock."

"Headlock?"

"Yeah, the damn headlock. The mythic fucking headlock. Bruised my damn windpipe."

"There is no way I went to school with Dodd Trotter!"

"You *absolutely* did," said Dodd, almost jovially. What did any of it matter now? "And I've the psychic scars to prove it."

Just then, Marcie came over. Dodd began to introduce them, but there was no need—Marcie effusively declared she'd had a crush on fatboy since second grade. He left them to their flirtation and eased his way to the rest room.

He sat in a stall and scrolled through his BlackBerry. Frances-Leigh said his mother had called; she seemed to be reaching out to him less often, even when there was a "big" death in the news. Dodd felt a pang of guilt, and promised himself he would spend more time at Saint-Cloud. It was anyone's guess how much longer she'd be living there.

The men at the urinals spoke some kind of Arabic. He heard his name—*Doahd Trotter*—stranded like an oasis amid melodiously guttural consonants. One of them laughed, shifting to English, the accent clipped and British.

"No one can remember him? But how is it possible?"

"I'm telling you," said his friend. "I spoke to the crazy woman— Marzie. And she said *no one* can recall. He is the Invisible Man!"

"As long as he puts his money where his mouth is, what difference can it make? He is going to build a hell of a thing."

"I don't know if you want your money where that mouth is," he said nonsensically. "You don't know where that mouth has been!"

"He is *not* the Invisible Man—he is the *Indivisible Man*. Because he will never divide that pile of money up."

"Oh!" laughed the other. "Ho! The Indivisible Man! The Indivisible Man! Oh! Ho!"

There was more unintelligible Semitic discourse; urinals flushed and faucets turned at sink. As they toweled their hands, Dodd heard his name mentioned once more amid the babble, and then *Forbes* and then "*number twenty-three.*"

"I am predicting I too will be on the list—in the privacy of my home, I will soon make number two!"

They laughed all the way out.

On Sunday afternoon, the detective drove to Broad Beach and limped around an empty lot. He felt it would be irresponsible to share what he suspected—what he *knew*—before the computers gave confirmation. That could take a week, maybe more.

What if he was wrong? What if he was just lovelorn and in the wake of the perceived "breakup" with Trinnie had superimposed all this foolishness onto the wrong man? *That's insane*—it *was* Marcus, he was certain . . . but what if he was withholding information from the family because deep down he was angry that the ghostly rival of his affections had returned to the scene? His predicament was even worse than when he had gotten shot; at least then, his role was clear-cut. There were pills to take and wounds to swab—the healing was visible. It behooved him to convey the weird development to his client, Louis Trotter (after all, he was still on the payroll); that was the right and happy solution. He fantasized breaking the news to Trinnie, but that wasn't his place, as martyred or heroic as it would make him feel.

Samson headed back down PCH. He called Saint-Cloud and asked to speak to Mr. Trotter. The old man wasn't home, but a servant patched him through to the Silver Seraph. That part of the highway was dicey when it came to cell phones; they could barely hear each other.

"Samson?"

"Yes! I need to talk to you."

"Where————you?"

"Around————bu."

"Where?"

"Malibu——Malibu!"

"Do you————where the————Dining Car is?"

"The what?"

"The Pacific Dining Car!"

"Yes! On W————?"

"The Pacific Dining Car!"

"On Wilshire!"

"Yes!"

The detective said he would see him there, but the phone was already dead.

By the time he arrived, his employer was seated in a bar banquette. He looked like someone who'd just been in a hit-and-run. As Samson slid into the booth, the barkeep brought another martini and it was just in time, because Mr. Trotter had downed the one at hand.

"I have something to tell you," said the old man. To fortify himself, he swallowed the contents of the glass. "I—I—well, Samson, what I mean to say is—is—is . . . that I found our Marcus!"

CHAPTER 37

Twin Towers

*H*ere is the tale Louis Trotter disgorged.

He explained how, at their reconciliatory dinner with the Weiners, they had been graced with Bluey's presence and how they partook of "sweetmeats arranged upon a tray given her six decades ago by the redoubtable Peggy Guggenheim herself." The offerings were delicious, but what had truly captivated, to the extent of rendering Ruth Weiner strangely mute, were certain thumbprint cookies smeared with pomegranate jam. At first they had thought she was choking, but when Mrs. Weiner recovered she took another bite and then another, rolling crumbs and syrup on her palate until she literally slapped the table.

"It's Marcus!" she cried. When asked what on earth she meant, Ruth averred that those cookies were aptly named, for whoever made them could be identified with the same precision a fingerprint afforded—there being now no question in her mind that her son, Marcus Weiner, had cooked this jam *and* the buttery indentations wherein each dollop rested; after a somber retasting, her husband, Harry, with as much resolve but less volubility, concurred.

At the moment of epiphany, it so happened that Trinnie was in the powder room and Toulouse was checking on Pullman, who was mistakenly thought to have cried out in pain (it was only Winter's television). It is to Louis Trotter's credit that the Redlands woman was so quickly heeded—with alacrity, he told them the secret must be kept from Trinnie and the boy (and anyone else); in the morning he would take immediate steps to find the delicacy's maker. The impromptu pact helped soften the bedeviling shock of Ruth's discovery, so that when Trinnie returned from the loo, she couldn't put enough of a finger *or* thumb on what was amiss to dare wonder out loud, instead ascribing any residual awkwardness to the Weiners' valiant efforts to be gracious after so many years of snubbing and callous disregard—in other words, true to Bluey's admonition, Trinnie put it all on *herself*. Louis feared his wife might blurt something out, but she was an absolute dream, ingenuously engaging the in-laws in conversation that allowed them to forget, or at least cover over, the bizarre revelation. Perhaps she never fully absorbed the implications of Ruth's outburst; and even if Bluey *had* said something, it would have sounded "off" enough to be easily quashed and ignored.

The old man had not been sleeping well since Bluey's travails and, keeping to form, fared poorly that night. He was completely dressed by six o'clock Sunday morning and took his coffee on the terrace. The top button of his shirt—part of a $35,000 set of Lagerfeld-designed diamond-encrusted camellias—remained irksomely undone. He would have a word or two with the ladies at Brown's, the dry cleaners, because he was having trouble closing his top buttons, especially on the last batch of shirts sent over.

When patience no longer held, Epitacio drove him to Le Marmiton, where they sat in the Silver Seraph for a full hour awaiting the doors of the bakery to open. When they did, Mr. Trotter examined the cases, but there were no thumbprints to be seen. He smiled gnomishly—a grin that frightened children but merely put adults off, at least until they know who they were dealing with—telling the girl behind the counter that he'd recently sampled a marvelous cookie which he was positive had been bought from this very establishment, smeared with the unforgettable jelly of an ancient fruit, et cetera, et cetera. She was only a part-time worker, she said. She disappeared, and voices were heard from a back room. The girl returned with a shrug, and just when the old man was about to imperiously reclaim his just desserts or go down trying, a youngish Mediterranean, with deep black tendrils and the annoyed look of someone awakened several hours before he had a right to be, entered—no, *filled*—the small main room.

"We cannot get any more," he said, sounding very French.

"Really!" The old man's blood was up; he was on the scent. "And tell me why is that?"

"The person now doesn't make. We have *tried*—but we cannot."

"Then do you know where I might find him?"

"I have many things to do this morning—" He smiled in such a way to indicate that the old man had already seen the best of him by far.

With a thuggish toss of his head, our would-be customer beckoned the Frenchman to come out of earshot of the girl.

"If you tell me where I can find this man, I will give you a thousand dollars in cash. Now."

To prove his point, he reached into his pocket and pulled out just that—nothing more, nothing less.

"I am not a whore," said the waiter with a smile, "but today, you make me one!" To emphasize that he meant business, Mr. Trotter palmed the notes into the Frenchman's hand. "He is a very gifted man, who lives at a shelter—a place for the homeless people. It sounds I know to be quite bizarre. But he is a very great pâtissier."

"But *where*—"

"They call the habitation SeaShelter—it is one word. Olympic Boulevard, near where are the big Blue Buses."

"Do you know his name?"

"It is William. I do not know more."

"Thank you, sir!"

"Anytime! *Au revoir!*"

Things didn't go as easily at "the habitation" as at the bakery. Mr. Trotter *did* cut strange enough a figure to warrant immediate attention; the weird visitor had to be reckoned with. The presence of the Rolls and its liveried driver elicited stares from staff and resident alike, and cluckings that weren't all that far afield from the old man's chuffs.

He stood in SeaShelter by the seashore's shiny aluminum shell, prepared to shellac a SeaStaffer. A frowning African American informed him that the gentleman to whom he referred was no longer in residence and that his whereabouts were unknown and confidential (which struck the old man as contradictory). The interviewees were naturally cynical and suspicious, and this morning even more so, not being a happy group after having been told that the body of Jane Scull had been found in a squat with its throat slashed. They didn't know what to make of this old freak, and their patience grew thin as the layers of one of William's mille-feuilles; Mr. Trotter *was* making inquiries about cookies and jam and whatnot, the entire subject of which they were still mildly paranoid. The digger's instincts told him that an offer of moneys would not go down well, and he retreated to the leather wings of the Seraph to plot his next move.

Slowly, the car wheeled away from the tiny receiving area. A quarter of a block later, his driver remarked that a gesticulating bum was flagging them down. They turned the corner and Mr. Trotter opened his window; Epitacio cautioned him to be wary.

"You tryin' to find William?" He looked sixty years old but was probably closer to forty, with washed-out Dust Bowl features. His pants were cinched by rope, like a dancer in an Agnes de Mille ballet.

"William? Why—yes!"

"They arrested him. Took him away. Police took him away." Before the last few words were out of his mouth, the indigent had accepted a one-hundred-dollar bill, pre-folded with the artistry of origami and slipped so silkily into the weathered hand that the old man knew enough to apply some pressure (unnecessary for, say, a doorman) so its recipient would at least know that a bill had been passed.

Not half an hour later, he was inside the Santa Monica police station—

At this point, he interrupted himself and apologized to Samson for not having called him straightaway. He waved at the barkeep for another drink. It was the *speed* at which things were happening that took him by surprise, he said, and filled him with a treasure hunter's euphoria. The detective, who had been struggling to suppress his *own* shockingly pertinent "intelligences," fleetingly wondered how Mr. Trotter would have gained access to the prisoner, who was no longer even in SMPD custody. Clarification was swift in coming. It seemed that a captain of the latter precinct knew the famed philanthropist from his profligate donations to various policemen's balls, leagues and benefits (his grandchildren did after all attend school in that beachside city); some years back, Mr. Trotter had offered to build a gymnasium for the officers—a kingly gesture declined for legal reasons but the generosity of which was never forgotten by the thin blue line. After a family friend (then Patrolman Dowling) was shot in the line of duty, the paterfamilias let it be known that anonymous funds would be available through the Trotter Family Foundation in cases of pediatric emergency or catastrophic family illness, in perpetuity. More than a few of the fraternity had availed themselves. When the reason for his presence at the precinct was told, one can imagine the eagerness with which its soldiers volunteered their aid. The aforementioned captain made some inquiries and quickly ascertained an "aka William"—arrested at the SeaShelter hangar in the early-morning hours—had already been transferred to Twin Towers on the charge of murder. When Mr. Trotter relayed his "extreme interest" in the fate of the suspect, the captain took it upon himself to escort the dapper figure downtown, as his shift was anyways ending. There, in the desolate landscape behind Union Station, on the seventh floor of an off-pink edifice, Louis caught a glimpse—for that is all he said he wanted—of the man who had once been (and was still) his son-in-law. He knew immediately it was him; that was the digger's gift. He had a sixth sense for bodies and the same for the ground in which those bodies would one day lie.

As the detective began *his* side of the serpentine tale—how he was the officer who happened to have been assigned months ago to the very case in which the arrestee now prominently figured, and how the arrestee was a suspect in the murder of a woman who happened to be the mother of the same girl who'd been harbored by his own grandchildren—well, as Samson began to unwrap and exhibit these astonishments, the old man listened with a preternatural interest that turned preternaturally painful; clutching his throat, he collapsed. He rallied in time to greet the paramedics, declining their offer to ferry him to St. John's. (The world was filled with St. John'ses.) Epitacio, he said, would take him to Cedars. Within minutes, the chauffeur had alerted the emergency room to their imminent arrival; Mr. Trotter's internist was on his way; VIP liaisons were dispatched and a deluxe room prepared. Samson wished to accompany him in the Rolls, but the old man insisted that he follow, which of course he did, though not before quietly advising Epitacio to take the quickest route to UCLA if so much as the shade of a need grew apparent.

Mr. Trotter, never one for hospitals, even those with wings graced by his name, refused to be admitted. He had no fever. His throat was sore, and gave him some trouble swallowing; he was routinely cultured for strep. Bedford Drive's pre-eminent ENT man was enlisted to examine the tycoon, and palpated the mass (the thing that had been giving his topmost buttons their workout), declaring it to be something more than a swollen gland, though how much more he couldn't say. It was not "pulsatile," yet it didn't *feel* like a tumor, and that was odd; they would have to rule one out. The medics weren't happy with the headstrong patient taking his leave, but wangled a promise that he would return later in the week for an outpatient biopsy.

*O*n Monday, the digger burrowed into "the case." Powerhouse attorneys were hired to represent the captive, who naturally proclaimed innocence in all matters relating to the grotesque assault and death—and subsequent rape—of a prostitute and drug addict called Millicent "Geri" Kornfeld. Per Detective Dowling's instructions, the Adirondack Park sheriffs of Essex County, New York, had already been contacted, and while those lawmen were able to dredge up a record of his detention, the defendant's fingerprints proved more elusive; they had some more rummaging to do. As far as anyone knew, Marcus Weiner had never been enlisted in the military, so the detective's fears might indeed be realized—there was the chance that an official identification would never be made. He remembered seeing a French movie about a man who returned to a village claiming to be someone he wasn't; by the end no one, not even family and old lovers, knew truth from fiction.

Now that aka William had "lawyered up," Samson Dowling received a call from said legal counsel, telling him to have no further contact with the defendant. Even though it was a "friendly" notice—they knew of his special connection to the case—Samson got depressed. But he gladly told them all he knew: of his informant, whose whereabouts were unknown, and how the victim's daughter, AWOL from MacLaren at this time, had some months ago identified the telltale ascot as having belonged to the suspect.

A meeting with his son-in-law could easily have been arranged, but the benefactor felt his place for now was behind the scenes. At his prompting, a medical team examined the prisoner; the psychopharmacologist who looked after Dodd was enlisted to provide one or two cutting-edge prescriptions cropped from the latest harvest of smart-bomb antipsychotics. The old man didn't wish the story leaked to press, so made sure that the more celebrated attorneys on the team avoided the arraignment. (He himself chose not to come.) Eulogio embarked for Redlands to pick up Harry and Ruth, who Mr. Trotter felt should be present.

Tuesday morning, the defense met with judge in chambers. They informed him the suspect had been I.D.'d by his father-in-law, who had in fact engaged their services on the defendant's behalf; no further details relating to their unusual employer were discussed. (The judge listened with a glacial reserve broken only at the mention of the famous surname, when an eyebrow rose involuntarily with near comic effect.) Mr. Weiner, they added, had been diagnosed as schizophrenic, but a full psychiatric evaluation was not yet complete. One of the lawyers then remarked that the parents of aka William Marcus aka Marcus Weiner would be in attendance this morning and would provide definitive witness to his identity, though it had been roughly fourteen years since they'd seen their son last.

Once in court, the ascot was presented as damning evidence and a trial date was set. DNA had been collected from the victim shortly after her death; a sample from the defendant was ordered for comparison. In spite of eloquent pleas and the unusual circumstances surrounding the detainee, owing to the nature of the crime and aka William Marcus aka Marcus Weiner's alleged flight from the facility in upstate New York, bail was firmly denied.

After the prisoner was led away, the judge asked if Ruth and Harry Weiner—their names had been written down for him at the preliminary meeting—were in court. They eagerly stood, or it should be said that Ruth eagerly stood, followed by her less spry mate. The judge asked if they knew the accused.

"He is my son," said Ruth, voice quavering. An expensive attorney on each side held her steady. She cleared her throat and said again, "Your Honor, he is my son!"

That afternoon, Epitacio drove them to Twin Towers. Visitors waited to see loved ones, but it had been so arranged that the elderly couple would be spared the queue. Harry peered through the tinted glass of the Silver Seraph at the men with tattooed foreheads loitering across the street from jail, and remarked how they looked like prisoners themselves. He puzzled over them while Ruth remained silent. The skin of her chest was stretched so taut she feared it might split open at any moment, like papyrus—with each inhalation, her caged lungs shook as if invaded by moths.

Neither remembered much of the half hour or so that passed from the time they stepped from car to visitors' room.

There was a metal grille between them, and he was shackled.

He sat down and they all blinked at each other.

Harry was the first to speak. "Son?"

Sitting opposite the enormous stranger, the retired baker had a momentary doubt; but then the roots of his boy, so to speak, grew toward him as in time-lapse photography—tiny green buds rapidly bloomed, stems thickened and curled themselves about the elder's ankles, tugging him closer.

"Marcus . . ." said Ruth, hand rushing to mouth, unable to conceal her emotions. She was certain as only a mother could be. "Do you know who we are?"

He nodded solemnly.

Ruth suppressed another outburst.

Most of the men on the seventh floor were sedated and Marcus was no exception. But thanks to his remarkable constitution and the intervention of private shrinks, he'd managed to elude the zombified look worn by most of his cell mates.

"You," he said, rather diffidently, "are the people from the Red Lands."

"Redlands?" said Harry, with great enthusiasm. "Redlands, yes! Still the same house! Though the bakery's gone—we sold it."

"Harry!" chastised Ruth, not wishing her son to be overrun by extraneous detail—particularly that of loss, in any way, shape or form. "We ate some of your jam . . . you made the jam, didn't you? The pomegranates—"

He looked them in the eye and smiled—the seed-stained smile of their precocious boy, who at Toulouse's age could play the cello with thick, agile fingers; who took the bus to the Vagabond near MacArthur Park to see the entire oeuvre of Buñuel; who dragged them to the Huntington's Japanese moon bridge—and exhibitions of branchy intricacies perpetrated by William Morris & Company.

"Yes!" he said, and laughed, not the laugh of a madman but of a man come home. "Yes, I made the jam. Didja like it?"

"Oh yes!" they said in chorus. It was marvelous! Better than they'd ever had! Much better than your mother's! Always *had* been—

They laughed some more, and then his tremendous body undulated as he sobbed.

Not being able to reach out to him was for Ruth a fine torment. "We're here now, Marcus!" she said. "We're here!"

"She's right—listen to her. You're home now, son!"

Marcus dried his eyes, having calmed a bit after a look from one of the guards. "I don't know you—or, suffer me, *barely* do—or much of what has happened for such a long time . . . I know that you are from the Red Lands—"

"Redlands," corrected Harry enthusiastically, until Ruth kicked his foot.

"—that you are from the *Redlands*, and have been kind enough to see me . . . I *do* remember you—but there are so *many* memories that I don't know what's real and what's conjured. I *was* at Oxford, no?" he asked, with faint English affectation. "But at another time than Rossetti and my friends?"

"Yes! Yes! You were at Oxford!" cried Ruth.

"You see? Things are coming back!" exulted Harry.

"The medicine will help you."

"The medicine!" said Harry.

The keeper indicated that their time together had ended.

"We'll see you through," said his father.

Ruth was without words, squinting at him as he stood because she could not bear to see her boy in chains.

He smiled as they led him away, turning at the last moment to shout, *"Bon appétit!"*

We chose to ignore a certain gentleman who attended the arraignment (a few rows behind the Weiners) because, well, parents take precedence.

That "silhouette"was none other than Gilles Mott, whom the reader already knows to be the current owner of an establishment once held in highest esteem by that grandest of dames, Bluey Twisselmann Trotter, an establishment now prominent on her shit list. For when the erstwhile Topsy abandoned ship so did the old woman, eventually finding succor at Montana Avenue's Le Marmiton. Fortunately for Gilles, the two establishments were not in any direct competition.

The baker and his wife were contacted by Detective Dowling on the Sunday following Marcus's arrest, the latter occurring scant days after the remarkable sighting of Amaryllis at Saint-Cloud. Without much embroidery, he informed them of the charges being brought; but the real purpose of the call was to apprise the couple of the girl's dire straits. Lani told him she was already aware of the AWOL, having learned about it the hard way when arriving at MacLaren for a scheduled visit. And, no, Amaryllis hadn't been in touch.

The detective and the Motts weren't exactly strangers. After the MacLaren psychologist told her of his interview with Amaryllis, the feisty CASA had taken the liberty of dropping by Rampart unannounced to introduce herself (she had of course accompanied the child there once before; as far as Lani was concerned, she and the detective were practically colleagues). She told him all about her husband's long-term relationship with the suspect, and naturally Samson wanted to hear more, for until then his only real character witness had been the execrable signboard beggar. So he took them to lunch at the Pantry. There, both husband and wife reiterated the peculiar history, including their last, rather strained encounter—how incensed the man had been that they'd "turned the girl over." Lani was a little surprised that none of this information had been conveyed, because the Motts had dutifully spoken to a policeman after William's tirade regarding the child. (Though her instincts told her he wasn't a predator, her role as CASA still demanded that she let such developments be known through official channels; she was sworn to the court, and so legally bound.) The detective merely said that sometimes "things fall through the cracks."

Now, starved for information, Lani and Gilles swamped him with questions about the imprisonment. Between the two of them, they felt oddly responsible for the woes that had befallen that unforgettable Victorian gent.

It may be recalled that after William had made a fuss about their handling of the girl, Lani had been overcome by remorse. She had, in her own mind, self-righteously passed the "social" buck—she, Lani Mott, who was capable of ruining a Sunday brunch with a strident serenade against the *L.A. Times* or the corruption of the MTA or the soul-killing hypocrisy of the child welfare system or what have you. Yet what did she have to show for her coffeehouse activism? She'd become a volunteer at children's court (her friends never heard the end of it) but had spent a year saying no: *no* to advocating for this child and *no* to advocating for that . . . and then, as fate would have it, came her big chance—an orphan dropped at their very door, a discarded little *being*—and what had she done? Obediantly called the hotline, strictly by the CASA book . . .

the useless right thing. She may as well have phoned the SPCA and had the child picked up in a perforated metal box. Lani Mott had barely gotten her hands dirty. And everything she had done for the girl since (none of which seemed enough) was to atone for that moment at Frenchie's when William—crazy, stinky, delusional William—had delivered a moral coup d'état.

Husband Gilles had his own cross to bear, for *he* had been the one to have strong suspicions that William was a molester or child aggravator or whatever; and too, that day at the Pantry, had blindly accepted the detective's assertion of the vagrant's involvement in the murder of Ms. Kornfeld. When Samson called that Sunday after the arrest and Gilles broached the touchy subject of an "inappropriate relationship with the girl," the detective tersely said that as a result of his interview with the child herself, "nothing like that was on the table." ("I told you so," interjected his wife.) He wouldn't elaborate, but Gilles got the sense it wasn't the type of situation—not that Gilles had claims of knowing anything about the machinations of the law *or* its enforcers—where the charges of rape and homicide eclipsed or took precedence over a middling one of, say, child-bothering, thus rendering the issue moot; instead, the baker inferred from Samson's tone that such an accusation was bogus and insupportable and had no basis in fact. Suddenly, Gilles felt like a snitch—as if he had perversely betrayed his original instincts, and done a good man a great wrong.

That night, after each took long, reflective soaking baths, the baker and his wife split an Ambien and fell into troubled sleep.

*L*est our chronicle lean too heavily upon the travails of a certain child of nail-bitten hand, a child who has already had her goodly share of sorrow, a quick and painless exegesis of that hapless girl's travels will here be provided, though more painless for some than for others.

Needless to say, upon her fleeing the Boar's Head attic, things didn't go any better. Amaryllis, venerable and nearly Blessed, fell in with a coven of runaway skeevs who favored Promenade benches by day and the debris-strewn husk of a condemned mental-health center by night. Their style in clothing ran to Goth, but a strain neither Morris nor Ruskin would recognize. She spent two fun-filled nights in Skeevy Hollow before being chased down by policemen, one of whose legs was bitten so hard that she had to be concussed into releasing her jaws—and got a hairline fracture for her trouble. Convalescence occurred in the lockdown unit of a psychiatric hospital in Alhambra. Once she emerged from the torpor of head trauma, the fiercely combative girl was given enough meds to become a bona-fide member of Mrs. Woolery's tribe; she peed and bled (for menses had come) with the best of them.

Inside of a week, news of her reappearance had in its own excruciatingly random, slipshod way devolved to the stalwart Lani Mott, she of the special-advocates' office berthed just inside the lobby of children's court. Mrs. Mott convened with her supervisor, and a stratagem was devised. It was agreed that a visit to the Alhambra hospital must be paid and the child's physical and mental state assessed, in view to finding a suitable placement—if not a private home (which seemed an impossible goal), then, say, a ranch-like environment for wayward children— perhaps even one out of state. Lani put her boss to work, then got her briefcase in order.

She packed a blue wallet of special business cards with the CASA "heart" logo and made sure to carry a copy of the signed notice from the Superior Court of the State of California for the County of Los Angeles Juvenile Court identifying her as the child's Guardian Ad Litem of record.

When she saw Amaryllis, she was sickened. The girl drooled and could barely keep her head up. There were deep scratches on the insides of her arms. "Did you make these?" asked Lani over and over. She couldn't figure out whether the poor thing was nodding or shaking her head. "Amaryllis, do you know who I am?" Finally, Lani abandoned the interview and told a nurse that she wished to speak with the doctor.

After waiting more than forty minutes, she asked again and was confronted by a different attendant.

"What is it you want?"

"I've already told the woman."

"What woman."

"A nurse. I didn't get her name."

"Well I'm the one in charge. So you better talk to *me*."

She took a breath, and girded herself for battle. "I would like to speak with the prescribing physician."

"That isn't possible."

"Oh? And why is that?"

"He isn't *here*. Who *are* you again?"

"I am an officer of the court."

"An officer of—"

"*Of the court.* I would like to speak to Amaryllis Kornfeld's psychiatrist and I would like to speak to him *now.* If he is in this building and you're not telling me that, then you are potentially in a world of trouble."

"Don't you threaten me. May I see some I.D.?"

Lani handed her the court order and her driver's license.

"Do you work with that detective?"

"What detective is that?" Lani asked.

"The one who came to see her. Well, obviously you don't," she said disdainfully, "because otherwise you would know what I'm talking about. Just wait here please."

The nurse walked off with the documents, but Lani stopped her and said the driver's license would have to stay.

Lani assumed the bitch had been talking about Detective Dowling, and tried not to get angry at him for having left her in the dark. Though someone might have at least phoned the CASA office; he was probably just overwhelmed, like everybody else. But these were matters of life or death, and it would have been nice to have gotten a call.

Some moments later, the nurse returned Lani's papers and told her the doctor would see her, but only for a moment, as he was "about to lead group."

The psychiatrist then appeared. He was around fifty and looked as if he'd been napping. He wore tennis shoes, Dockers and a faded madras sport shirt.

"I'm Dr. Fishman. What can I do for you?"

"Dr. Fishman, I'm Lani Mott. I just met with one of your patients, Amaryllis Kornfeld—"

"Are you a relative?"

"No, I am not. And she looked like *hell*. What have you been giving her?"

The psychiatrist actually laughed in her face. She felt a mote of his spittle cool on her cheek but made no move to acknowledge it.

"That's confidential information. If you're not a relative, I can't even talk to you."

"Is that right?"

"That's right. That's a state law."

"Are you going to tell me about the law?"

"Listen, I don't know who you are, but—"

"The nurse didn't tell you?"

"If you're not a relative, you're wasting your time. Even if you *were* a relative, there is certain information I can't even legally share with a parent."

"Let me tell you something about the law, all right, Doctor? Are you listening? I am a Court Appointed Special Advocate! Do you think I'm playing a game here? *You* may be playing a game, but I'm too old for that. You've never run into someone like me, have you? Now, I'm not accusing you of anything, Doctor, but that girl could barely speak! She was drooling, OK? Now, I want to know what she's on and the reason she's on it, OK?"

"When she was admitted," he said, like a child about to tear the wing off a bug, "she was dysphoric and circumlocutory. Do you know what that means, Miss—"

"It's *Mrs.* And I'm not here for a DSM symposium. I need you to tell me some things, Doctor. You can tell me *now* or you can tell me in the morning, when a marshal comes down to make an official demand. The judge will want to know why you were uncooperative—do you really want to be under that kind of scrutiny? Maybe you'd like to read this." She thrust the order at him while reciting from memory. " 'WIC section 106: Upon presentation of this order, the CASA shall be permitted to inspect and copy any records of any agency, hospital, school, organization, division or department of the state, physician and surgeon, nurse, other health care provider, psychologist, *psychiatrist* [italics hers], police department or mental health clinic relating to the child in the above matter without the consent of the child or the child's parent.' Do you think they could have made it any clearer, Dr. Fishbein?"

"Fishman," he said with a dyspeptic grin, while giving the papers a cursory glance. "I'll have to go find the records."

"I'll need a copy."

"If I can find them, I'll make you one."

"We'll do this however you'd like."

"Is this *60 Minutes*?" He smirked again, but less convincingly.

"Joke all you like, Doctor. But if I don't leave with a copy of those records, it won't *be* a joke, I assure you. I hope for *your* sake they reflect a full physical examination of that child before she was given whatever drugs you so 'confidentially' prescribed. I hope for *your* sake you didn't phone those drugs in from a steakhouse. And I hope when I come back tomorrow, she's in better shape than she's in now."

"I'll need half an hour."

"Good. Because half an hour's all I've got."

Twenty minutes later, back in the Volvo with records in hand, Lani's body shook uncontrollably. She called Gilles on her purple Nokia and gave a mighty war whoop when he answered—then chattered like a fool all the way home. She told him she felt like Erin Brockovich.

They went to a neighborhood cucina to celebrate her empowerment. After a few drinks, she solemnly confessed her shame at having once abdicated her responsibilities to the girl, and how the jailed man, whom she considered the child's *real* caretaker, had been correct in upbraiding her and that she had grown to admire and respect him immeasurably for that. There are consequences to our actions, she kept saying. There are *repercussions* . . . Emboldened by alcohol, she passionately suggested that William, for whatever reason, was being *railroaded*—and her husband was glad to see her back in good form and good rant, diatribing against injustices wrought upon innocents, spinning Chomskyesque conspiracies of politics and the media. He loved her more than ever.

Quiet and introspective until now, Gilles spoke up. Slowly swirling the wine in his glass, he said he had failed to give his friend the benefit of the doubt regarding any "untoward activities" with the girl—and for that, he felt bad. But something else was troubling him that he was compelled to share. Gilles said that after their Sunday call he had spoken with the detective again, who had told him that an ascot belonging to William—identified as such by Amaryllis herself—had been found stuffed in the victim's throat. How to explain?

Lani swallowed her drink and closed her eyes like a mystic in mourning for the folly of the whole race of man. Smiling, she set the glass down and seamlessly uttered the words that finally vanquished all his remaining doubts:

"We are going to save that little girl."

CHAPTER 38

Awakening

*A*t the arraignment, the letter was passed to aka William's lawyers, who forwarded it to Twin Towers. Various official eyes had been already upon it by the time it reached the prisoner's:

Dear William,

They would not let me visit, so I am writing this to you. Lani and I feel so awful that you are in that place, and would like to help in any way we can. Lani is trying to aid Amarillys, just as you wanted us to from the very beginning. But she is in "the System" now and believe me it doesn't make things any easier. We know there is trouble regarding a woman who passed away, but we do not know anything about it and hope you were not involved, and if you were, that perhaps the reason was that you were not in your "right mind" or maybe even that you were protecting the girl. Because we have heard terrible things about that woman. (Who I believe to be—*was*—Amarillys's mother.) We will visit you as soon as is allowed. I was at the arraignment and once I learned that only a relation would be able to visit, I gave this to Detective S. Dowling (who I believe you know) to pass on. We even tried sending croissants and pastries, not so good as yours I'm afraid, but they said it was forbidden. You have all our best wishes.

Gilles and Lani,
Your "amis" at Frenchie's

He read the missive twice more, and, after a baffled interlude, began to assemble the pieces.

Amarillys . . . the girl! They were speaking of the *girl*, his *angel* . . . —Lani and Gilles—those kind, gentle people—the Frankish baker who had given him work, honest work, and paid him an honest wage. His wife—*Lani*, he read again—who'd merely done what she felt was right by the child and for which aka Topsy aka William Morris *Marcus* (here, he pounded his fist on the wall of the cell, for he knew not even his own name) had wantonly berated her. And what had this clot of aliases done in the first place but drop the pitiful orphan off in the early-morning hours beside a trash bin and shove her toward his benefactor—what nobility!

He kicked and slapped at his cell, then sat on the bed and hung his head. He picked up the page again.

is in "the System" now . . .

"The System" . . . did he mean the girl was—*the little girl is in jail.* The horror of it! His friend Fitz had told him so! He remembered now: the girl had been captured in a dragnet—

He stood and read the letter some more while he paced. *Amarillys*, in *jail* . . . —he imagined her as a fish, flopping and expiring on the ground, and wished to tear his hair out. But the worst part, the *very* worst, was to read the words

(Who I believe to be—*was*—Amarillys's mother.)

But *how*—how could it be? Phantasmagoric! The detective (and Fitz too) had been trying to tell him, but it never made any sense. *Now* it came together, and he felt like an amnesiac struck by a rain of blows to the head that restored an old order, an order transformed to new. All of Dowling's queries . . . and those of the lawyers—were about the woman who lay dead in the St. George by *his* hand—the dear child's mother! By *Topsy's* hand. Suddenly, it stood to reason. He'd been seen carrying the orphan off, a block from where the murder was committed . . . could it be? Could it really? That he was in this place—these Towers—that he was in *"the System"*—for killing the mother of his adored Amaryllis?

Hellish abomination! Then that would mean the woman's death had led to the *girl's* being in "the System" too . . .

"Guard!" he cried. "Guard! Guard! Guard! Guard! Guard!"

The detective—or the baker Gilles and his wife—or the parents from the Red Lands—*someone* must arrange for him to visit the child so he could tell her he hadn't touched a *hair* on that woman's head, and let her see he was whole and humble and still in the world for her! She would bury her head in his arms and cry as she used to; and then if he was very brave, he would tell her that her dear Topsy was nevermore. He would tell her who he was—or was becoming.

A man named Marcus Weiner.

*A*s much as the author, out of sheer affection, would like to drop in on those Bel-Air denizens who, being out of earshot of Grannie Ruth's revelation, remained unaware of the dramatic return of Marcus Weiner—namely Katrina and Toulouse—the propulsion of narrative demands that such a visit be postponed. We will concentrate instead on a triad of developments that occurred in the ten days that followed the arraignment and which significantly altered the course of *California* v. *aka William Marcus.*

The DNA extracted from the suspect failed to match that found in the vagina and anus of the deceased. This alone was not definitive proof that Mr. Marcus wasn't the murderer: an accomplice still could have committed the rape. But the defense rightfully considered the results more than a good thing. The troublesome ascot still nettled.

Shortly after the laboratory returned its findings, Amaryllis was discharged from the Alhambra infirmary and returned to MacLaren, where she lashed out bitterly against the entire staff, not even sparing true-blue Dézhiree, who no longer recognized the girl and mourned a relative innocence lost. When a visitor from the district attorney's office told her that she would have to appear in court to identify the ascot belonging to her friend, Amaryllis told him to eat shit and die, a command which, to his credit, was omitted from his report.

Lani was the only one she allowed near. The earnest CASA came each day and eventually told Amaryllis of an idea she and her husband had—they wanted her to come live with them. Amaryllis was startled and suspicious, but it would have been impossible to misinterpret Mrs. Mott's resolve. The child pretended not to heed and let three days pass before inquiring when such a move might occur. The CASA said it depended on her behavior, for that was the gauge used by the court in such actions. She told Amaryllis that the court's decision would be handled with particular care, as in this case living in their home would be the first step in a formal adoption. She and Gilles had already begun classes with the goal of accreditation.

"You would adopt me?" she asked.

"Absolutely. No hesitation."

"What happens if you don't want to do it anymore?"

"We don't change our minds like that."

"What if I do something bad or you move away?"

"You'd move *with* us. Once we make a decision, that's it, OK? We don't turn our backs on it—we don't turn our backs on *you*. If you do something 'bad,' we'll just deal."

"What if you die?"

"I'm not expecting to."

"Neither was my mother."

"I know that, honey." She put her hand on Amaryllis's, and the girl let it stay. "What happened to your mother is very sad, and very . . . unusual. Things *do* happen in this world—people get sick, people go nuts, people die. People get killed. But I think I have a relatively long life ahead of me. At least I *like* to think that," she laughed. "I'd like *you* to think that. This would be an adoption, OK? That's permanent. That's how the courts look at it, and that's how *we* look at it. It's forever. I want *you* to look at it like that, too—for better or for worse, in sickness and in health."

"What about the babies?"

"If you're with us, in a stable home, the chances are good—*definitely* better than where we're at now—that we could establish regular visits."

"Would you adopt them?"

"I don't even know if that's in the realm of the possible; I'm not sure what their status is. Your brother and sister may be happy where they are."

"They're not!"

"You don't know that."

"They're *not* happy!"

"One thing at a time, OK, Amaryllis? Let's worry about *you* right now—then we'll see about them." The girl relaxed, seeming to go with the logic of it. "For me, for *us,* we'd like to have you in our home because we love you. And we would hope you love us, or learn to. So I want you to think about it."

"How can you love me?"

"What do you mean?"

"You don't know me."

"Of course I know you."

"Only for a *little.* You didn't *raise* me. You can't suddenly love me."

"I can—and I do. You see, Amaryllis, I believe a person can *decide* . . . can make the *decision* to love. And then love follows."

Over time—a short time, for children and the human heart always astonish by the speed with which they heal—Amaryllis lowered her guard. She asked Lani where she lived and where she would be going to school. She asked if she could have a bicycle and a computer. She asked if she would be able to have friends sleep over and even mentioned, albeit briefly, a certain group of children who had taken care of her during her travels (and travails) . . . but discreetly said no more.

When she felt the girl was ready, Lani eased "Topsy" into their conversation (she knew that was how he was known to her). She questioned her about the same things William's lawyers did when they visited the child at Mac—but from a different place.

Amaryllis repeated that Topsy had never, in her knowledge, come to the motel where she lived with her mom and the babies. How then, asked Lani, did his ascot make its appearance there? (The silken tie was the one thing left that, forgiving the phrase, stuck in the CASA's craw; naturally, she withheld referring to the place from which it made its grisly "coming-out.")

She related how one day under the bridge, after Topsy had provided food for herself and the babies, the wind had brought a chill; the sun was setting and he worried she had no sweater. He gave her the ascot to wrap about her neck. Amaryllis loved its shininess and golden teardrops and kept it to wrap around her Box of Saints. She never gave it back. In a separate matter, she said there *had* been visitors to the St. George suite—but ones she had never mentioned and was unsure she ever would. They were unspeakable.

Lani conveyed all this to the detective, who put her in touch with the defense—it was the CASA's feeling that she could get the girl to testify to as much in court. The attorneys were concerned it still wasn't enough to clear him; the testimony of a combative child, diagnosed as "labile and hypervigilant" and "with flight of ideas," currently being weaned from Effexor, Neurontin, Ativan and Cogentin, was not the most convincing.

At this juncture, as it is wont to, a deus ex machina explained all.

Samson Dowling was awakened by an early-morning call from Jerry Whittle, a coroner's assistant whom he had known for years. Whittle was a funny, meticulous eccentric who, at the age of forty-nine, still lived with his mother in San Marino. He visited the detective regularly after he got shot, and made Samson laugh and forget his pain awhile. When he was discharged, the odd couple went to ball games and barbershops together, and had the occasional steak and martini at Musso & Frank's. Whittle aspired to writing but could never settle on a niche: he liked the idea of creating a mystery series based on a coroner's assistant, a kind of bush-league Kay Scarpetta, but also had a mind to tackle a book of ruminative essays in the *Death to Dust* or *How We Die* mode, or maybe even a precious memoir along the lines of the one by that well-known fellow who called himself a "mortician poet."

Whittle had been the first from the coroner's office to arrive at the scene of the Kornfeld homicide. He took tissue samples and scrapings—it was he who had discovered the ascot in the throat, drawing an excited parallel to the pupae similarly found in *The Silence of the Lambs*—and snapped photos of the deceased, which he added to his collection (he'd flirted with publishing a volume of Weegee-type photographs, getting someone like DeLillo or Ellroy to write the text).

"I'm telling you, Sam, I'm looking at both sets of photographs. Now. As we speak."

"What are you saying?"

"The *knots*, Sam, the knots are the same."

"The knots in the ascot?" He was still foggy.

"No, Sam! There *were* no knots in the ascot—Jesus, what kind of detective *are* you? The knots in the sheet the woman was strangled with. They're *manropes*—"

"Manropes?"

"Manropes. They're one and the same."

"The same as *what*?" asked Samson testily. He'd been dreaming so pleasantly only minutes before.

"The same as the knots in the tie of the guy who killed himself."

"*Which* guy, Jerry? Who are you talking about?"

"The *suicide*, on Carroll Avenue—George Fitzsimmons!"

*I*n fact, Mr. Whittle was correct; the knots *were* unique.[†] A macabre death-scene photo of the former DCFS worker, on the floor of his Victorian parlor, was shown to the frog-like Korean manager of the St. George, who quickly affirmed the deceased had indeed visited Geri Kornfeld more than once and during said visits tied a maimed dog to the sidewalk's rusted-out newspaper rack. The attorneys of Marcus Weiner (for that is how the defendant was now addressed) obtained an order from the court to draw DNA samples from the body of Fitzsimmons, which had not yet been (and never would be) claimed.

A few expository things happened "offstage" that will never be known by the players in our drama but should be passed on for the sake of thoroughness—it is hoped that for even the less curious reader the by-product may give a parenthetical frisson. The man who had once thought of himself entirely as William Morris (and still did, to a much smaller degree) was a naïf incapable of imagining the horrors that might befall a child, while the once honorable Geo. Fitzsimmons, late, great and faded pride of the Department of Children and Family Services, was capable indeed. His eyes had seen too much. When he first met Amaryllis at the 4th Street Bridge encampment, he saw things in *hers* that had mercifully eluded the gentleman who hailed from Merton Abbey on the River Wandle. He saw she was on her way to being half dead, and that he might rescue her as he had his own four-legged beauty. So he befriended her mother and gave Geri money to sleep with him; and did not begrudge himself enjoyment of that act. Now, because he suspected but had no proof, and because Geo. Fitzsimmons (ever professional) must be certain, he eventually solicited the woman to let him have the daughter to himself for an hour to do what he liked. He named an amount, and after token protestation, she took the money—a

---

[†] It would not be the first time that a criminal, living or dead, was "tripped up" in like fashion, and will likely not be the last; though one can be sure that *this* history's done with the knotty device. While admitting such an artifice to be a hardy staple of the mystery genre in days gone by, the author would hope that while there is plenty of mystery in our tale, there is less genre too.

princessly sum of ten one-dollar bills. He asked if she'd ever made such arrangements before, and she was reluctant to say, but was forthcoming after Fitz withheld the pipe. There *was* a lady, she said with playacted hesitation, to convey that while she wasn't at all happy about what she had been forced to do to survive (to put food and crack on the table), that while she wasn't happy, at least it was a *woman*—no offense to Mr. Fitzsimmons, because she could tell he would not hurt her girl. He was not a pervert, she said—then asked, Was he? She would be in the room with them anyway, she said, now flaunting her motherly instincts. That, she said, was "non-negotiable." But the thing she was telling him before (her daughter with the woman) was the only time. And her daughter was stoned, she said she made sure of that, so as not to know what was happening or even remember if she did. *What a humanitarian.* He withheld the pipe some more—and when she told of the others who had had the girl, some for what Fitz determined was less than a lungful, he choked the life from her with a bedsheet of cinches he'd learned from his father, so that in *this* instance it can never be said that any sins were passed on. Then he surprised himself by sodomizing the body—and that was the moment he married Death. For he suddenly knew in the same way that Jane Scull had when she lay with Please-Help.-Bless that his life was done and that he was three-quarters gone; the demise of his dog made it whole.

*L*ouis Trotter found her strolling the far side of the Saint-Cloud property near the cutting shed. When she saw him, Trinnie smiled warmly—she was losing a mother, but he was losing a friend and lover of half a century. She kissed him, and his face, an odd mask of worry and resignation, looked mildly electrified. She thought he had come to speak of Bluey, soon to be transferred to the Motion Picture and Television Hospital; shrieking by night and by day, she had entered the phase caregivers euphemistically call "fecal play." It was nearly too much for the hired hands, and simply too much for Winter and the household to bear.

"She'll be much better once she's settled, Father, you'll see. And I'll be there all the time, looking after the garden. It's my garden," she said, smiling some more. "Remember?"

"That I do! That I do. Katrina—I don't know how to say this." She saw how troubled he was, and her concerns about Bluey were quickly supplanted by the irrational terror that something had happened to her son. As she opened her mouth in a gasp of inquiry, he said, "We found Marcus. He was arrested . . ."

"Arrested—" she could not catch her breath "—for—"

"For a crime he did not commit. He's been cleared."

"Where—*where*—"

"I don't think you should see him just now—"

"Where!"

He grabbed her shoulders with a force that took even him by surprise. "Katrina—I am telling you this because I do not wish to repeat my mistake of so many years ago."

She went pure white, and her hair was already dank with sweat; he had a vision of her as one of Edward's Kabuki puppets.

"Oh, Father . . ."

She shivered in his arms like a stranded person airlifted from a great height.

He stroked her and softly spoke. "He will not leave this time. He is not . . . wild. He is—he is not *Marcus*—but—well, I'm not sure who he is. And I'm not sure *he* knows, either. Harry and Ruth have seen him; it was because of Ruth we were able to track him down."

"Did he . . . did he mention me?" It was all she could think to ask.

"Katrina—I'm not sure how . . . *intact* he is."

"Have you seen him?"

He shook his head adamantly. "Only Samson. Marcus didn't remember him. Or didn't let on."

"Is he still in jail?"

"He's been released. I've put him somewhere under guard, for his own sake. The doctors are tending him now; he has lived his life on the streets and bears the scars. Though he seems quite pleased and grateful to be free."

She licked the sweet salt of tears from her lips and grew strangely calm. "Father," she uttered. "I wish it were all a dream . . . I'm like Tull now! Suddenly, I don't know anymore. I know how I was when I came to see you that day at work—so *crazed*. But *now*—now I'm not sure I even want him to *be* here—"

He took her shoulders again, but this time it was his gaze alone that held her. "You mustn't say it, Katrina—mustn't even think it. You will face this man, I'll help you. Listen to me! Long ago I told you my grand-son would come into a piece of intelligence and that it would be your duty to be candid. That, you were: with a dignity that absolutely floored me—took me marvelously by surprise. You will face this man with the courage you've shown since you faced Toulouse. You will face your hus-band, Katrina! And settle the books once and for all."

At that moment—and if here we *do* lapse into genre, it is hoped we can be forgiven—she fainted dead away.

CHAPTER 39

Thanksgivings

Dear is the memory of our wedded lives,
And dear the last embraces of our wives
And their warm tears: but all hath suffered change:
For surely now our household hearths are cold:
Our sons inherit us: our looks are strange:
And we should come like ghosts to trouble joy.

—*Alfred, Lord Tennyson*

*I*n comparison to Marcus's previous lodging, the Hotel Bel-Air—though more an antacid pink than Red House—was most congenial (at least it was no Big House). He occupied a large series of rooms and was never left alone.

He even cooked for the men who guarded him, wearing a dainty, ill-size apron about his waist for the task. He made a mean pomegranate sabayon—the color of which resembled the aforementioned bismuthal lodgings—that when poured over mille-feuille pillows melted in the mouth like stardust.

The entourage of healers was vast: psychotherapists and physicians, nutritionists and body-workers, barbers and manicurists and of course the hulking men in well-tailored suits who stood at the door with tiny earpieces, as if covertly auditing the drone of a bureaucratic god. He did not find the circumstances at all oppressive, and actually marveled at the suite's wallpaper and chintz, which though not topflight had the effect of reminding him of patterns designed by that distinctive genius with whom he once shared such affinity and ardor, and from whom he felt himself sadly receding each fallish Californian day, days marked less by chill and chimney smoke than by the sight of the hostelry's storybook swans.

For after a week had passed, Louis Trotter, at the urging of his son-in-law's mental-health supernumeraries, declared it a fine idea for him to stroll the grounds with the men in suits as chaperons. Tourists and other passersby must have thought him to be a King Nerd who had bottomed out à la Brian Wilson when, in fact, Marcus's world had gone from "lockdown" sandbox to oysters indeed.

The education—or re-education—of Mr. Weiner proceeded with uncommon speed. He had always been an apt pupil, but now that it was his own life he was studying, he did his homework with especial rigor, unclouded by hallucination.[†]

With the case happily resolved, the detective was allowed to come and go as he pleased, and the expansion upon their already cordial bond was mutually healing. They made small talk and took their meals by the patio or pool. Out of the blue, Marcus spoke of wishing to visit the new cathedral downtown before it was filled with "tiresome" parishioners; he had a fondness for empty churches. Along that vein, he unleashed an impassioned filibuster on "the preservation of ancient buildings," radiantly evoking St. John's in the Wilderness—his sanctuary in the early fugitive days of his Adirondack unraveling. Just as Samson was wondering if he should delve into that episode, Marcus himself brought up the arrest, even referring to the detective's "official" visits those many years ago.

"No Twin Towers that," he said, with gentle irony. "The woman—the one who said I struck her? Crazy as a loon! I never raised a hand to a woman in my life! Beaten by a 'john,' she was. But I was in *terrible* shape—oh, terrible. Wasn't I, Sam? Oh good Lord."

"How did you wind up there, anyway? I thought you'd hardly visited Twig House before the wedding."

"How? Don't know. Some things—a *lot* of things—are just lost. We *did* go there once or twice; the lakes always had a strong and lovely pull. Tear o' the Clouds . . . been up there, Sam?"

"Not in a long while."

"Perhaps because it was Essex County—I have ties there, you know. Across the Atlantic." He brought himself up. "Or *had* ties, should I say. I'm *losing* some of those old ties," he said, with a wink of apprehension.

So they sat or sunned or strolled among the swans, talking of this and that: a bit about Mr. Trotter and the twenty-four-cylinder, $3 million, quarter-million-ton, two-stories-high earthmover he'd bought, with tires that dwarfed a man—and a bit about Dodd—and a bit about the movie world and popular culture—but never a word of their

---

[†]Thanks to the efficient plasma-protein bindings of Olanzapine.

shared true love. Sometimes they watched television, an activity interrupted by the hilarious regularity of Marcus's "Oh, good God!" outbursts. Once, a film featuring his old client Tom Hanks and a bulldog
came on through the satellite dish and Marcus was riveted. "That's
Tom," he said. "By God, that's Tom, isn't it?" He said it over and over.
"But the story—it's mad, isn't it? But charming! But absolutely mad."
(He was still determining what and who was crazy, and when and if it
was all right to say or be so.) At night, while the men in suits sat before
the droning tube, he lay on his bed staring at the letter from Gilles,
exhausted—there was so much to do, and yet it seemed he'd forgotten
how to do *anything*. A torrent of thoughts and schemes and projects
rushed to his head, just as they had in the William Morris mind-set of
old. But he was sorely paralyzed; and could not go marathon-walking,
even if he had a mind to.

Harry and Ruth delivered a trove of picture albums, and Marcus
soon ran "Red" and "Lands" together like a native, no longer infusing his
boyhood community with comic biblical import. Though images of himself as a toddler left him scratching his head, he began to scrutinize the
souvenirs with a growing titillation—bar mitzvah photos were of exorbitant interest, like clandestine documents detailing the arcane rites of
Guinean tribes. Delicately, with Polaroid and Kodachrome time line, the
Weiners drew him toward adulthood. He loved the snapshots taken at
the Huntington—here they huddled at the foot of the Japanese bridge;
there, crouched at the lily pond. Young Marcus stood in the library of
that great institution beside a tapestry, and his older self brought it
closer and cooed, as if recognizing something he had woven with his
own hands.

His parents were grateful to be asked the random personal
question—for example, What happened to his father's face? "I had a
stroke, son," Harry said. "But it hasn't slowed me a whit."

Marcus nodded and cooed, like an acolyte handed a koan.

Ruth brought pomegranate preserves made especially for him; he
slathered them on a cracker, wincing as they hit the palate—the three
had a good laugh about that, because even thirty years ago he had not
liked her results. The men in suits admired the jelly well enough and
were given some to take home. The men in suits seemed to eat pretty
much anything.

Ruth Weiner left the wedding album home, for a mother's instincts told her it was too soon. But Harry, rascal that he was, managed to smuggle something past—not that his wife knew, even in hindsight, that she would have objected. One day at the Bel-Air, he presented his son with a package wrapped in rice paper. Marcus tore it open and stared blinkingly at *News from Nowhere*, the very book that Toulouse, whose existence was still unknown to him, had held in his hands not long ago.

The former agent hung his head and remembered. (But could not remember why or when he had mailed it to Redlands.) This was the thing he'd been accused of stealing, and *had* stolen, but had lied about when confronted; not even his parents knew of that episode—nor was their son aware that Mr. Trotter, using Detective Dowling as a go-between, had compensated the aggrieved booksellers shortly after his final flight. The longer he held it, the heavier it became, its history soaking his cells the way certain medicines act on the muscles of a horse when sponged upon its coat; for this book of William Morris's marked a kind of beginning of the end. He had taken its name for his own diary . . .

He pressed the book to his chest and sunk into the divan, disconsolate. Ruth and Harry rallied futilely around him. His mother suggested it was time to go home, but when she tried to take the book, thinking it had already vexed him enough, he resisted, so Harry told her to let it be.

That night, instead of Gilles's letter, he turned the utopian novel over in his large hands. He examined the frontispiece.

Ex Libris
This Book Belongs to Marcus Weiner

XXX

He was beset by nausea, disgusted by the pretentious ass, the wag who thought a juxtaposition of names—William Morris the showman and William Morris the designer—so incredibly amusing; it was himself he hated. His mind regurgitated an agency mosaic: a speedy mail-room apprenticeship; staff retreats in Santa Barbara; romantic weekends at San Ysidro Ranch (though he wasn't at all certain it *was* a ranch, and couldn't remember who used to go there with him); openings of restaurants and openings of films and openings of little retail palaces filled with ruinously expensive clothes; first-class flights to visit clients the world over—Fiji, Ireland, Paris—lavish vacation jaunts to Venice and Sri Lanka, pyramids and power spots and the thousand wonders of lava beach, fjord and dune; cay, cwm, atoll. All those breakfasts and lunches and screenings with desperately self-assured faces, famous and egregiously unknown. A name wafted back: John Burnham, the colleague to whom he had told his premonitory dream of becoming Chairman of the Disembodied . . . —but the whole of these meandering mental aerobics, though invaluable to his rehabilitation, would not lead him to Katrina, for too much scar tissue had formed.

Other matters weighed heavily upon him, specifically one that took precedence even over the fate of the orphan girl, and had been stirred by his parents' restoration of the forbidden fruit of his kleptistic act—the *other* "News from Nowhere," *his* news, needed to be retrieved, for it was a vital piece to the great puzzle of where and what he had been. He had already layed his hands on it, with his little cab ride; and the timing of the trip to Public Storage—coming just before his arrest—seemed a powerful omen. He only hoped the journal (Weiner's, not Morris's) would be intelligible. Like the proverbial man who in the middle of sleep jots down the secret of the universe only to find jibberish in the morning, Marcus feared that the diary, ten years in the making, might be useless. Sometimes long-buried things decay when exposed to light and air.

Now each time he saw the hidden earpieces of the men in suits, he thought of her.

He *would* retrieve his manuscript, and Jane Scull in the bargain.

*M*arcus had not yet visited with the old man, though on his release from the Towers, they had spoken by phone.

He knew Louis Trotter to be his "father-in-law," but the scarring earlier noted made him subject to a selective dysphasia that robbed things of context and meaning. Still, such were Mr. Trotter's patriarchal powers (and so genuine his concern for this creature) that Marcus relied on him for all manner of "pieces of intelligence." So it was not unusual that he asked his mentor to grant a furlough to visit his dear friend Jane so that he could get back the journal she had in safekeeping; it had been his last request of her. He also told Mr. Trotter it would not be a bad thing for him to help this woman, as she was disabled and might benefit even more than *he* from the quality of care so kindly made available; and as she—his Janey—was the most decent, hard-luck being he'd ever known and he would do anything for her if ever he had the means. (This, he offered with characteristic charm and humility, not wishing to tax Mr. Trotter's energies or goodwill.) When the old man consulted Marcus's therapist on whether a small road trip would be kosher, the lady raised a flag, astutely hypothesizing—for she was no slouch, and even knew her Victoriana—that this new "Jane" (if she existed at all) might in fact be a delusionary stand-in for the *other:* the Jane Burden of William Morris, the famously adulterous wife of which therapist and client had had numerous discussions early on, in fresh-from-Twin-Towers pre-Zyprexa days. He had been doing so well; she wanted to be sure he wasn't mixing himself up with Morris again or confusing Jane Burden with Katrina Trotter—or some such combination. If this *were* the case, the analyst coolly cautioned that Mr. Weiner's lauded progress would need to be reassessed. They went to his son-in-law's rooms to talk over the matter. Mr. Trotter was glad to see Marcus good-naturedly assure both himself and therapist alike that Jane, unburdened—*this* Jane—was indeed the very special, very dear Jane Scull, boon companion and erstwhile shelter mate. The digger stopped short of deeper inquiry, wisely deciding it was none of his damn business.

It would have been easy to enlist one of the men in suits for this particular bit of business, but Mr. Trotter's unfailing instincts told him otherwise. Because the Monasterio brothers were busy enough with dynastic chores, he called up Sling Blade and for a not inconsequential "palming" had him escort Marcus to SeaShelter. (The moonlighting caretaker had been forced to call in sick; and while Dot Campbell was displeased, she strenuously offered to bring chicken soup to his Culver City apartment—an offer as strenuously rebuffed.) Some of the more conservative advisers warned that an outside visit was premature and that he should be accompanied by two guards at least. The old man waved them off. He had his concerns but was learning to let go; if Marcus ran away again, perhaps then it had been in the stars all along. Louis Trotter would do his best and could do no more.

When they arrived at the Olympic Boulevard sanctuary, things were as they had always seemed. The hangar was mostly empty, as residents were not allowed indoors during the day. The skeleton staff greeted Marcus with vacant looks. They didn't recognize him, for he had lost a great deal of weight (less as a consequence of imprisonment than of the nefarious conspiracies of nutritionist and trainer). He still wore donated clothes, but of a different ilk than prior castoffs; Mr. Trotter's tailor, Ray Montalvo, had made stylishly incremental adjustments to a number of long dark coats and crisp white shirts sent over from Barneys and Maxfield's.

The quondam boarder finally introduced himself, but that was no good either, because he used "Marcus Weiner." A few of the staffers squinted hard before moving closer. "It's William!" he shouted at last—they recoiled, startled and uncomprehending, yet captivated nonetheless. Sling Blade handily jumped in to clarify, and had never strung more words together in his life: Mr. Weiner—*William*—had subsequently been cleared of all charges, he said officiously, and was now a free man. On recovering from their initial shock (having long since envisioned their once-favorite "guest" to be comfortably ensconced on death row), the staffers extended a warm and courteous welcome, and soon a half-dozen gathered around. Curiously, they asked no details of crime or exoneration but *did* somewhat skittishly presume that he had returned to pick up where he left off. The counselor who not long ago had scanned Le Marmiton's shelves for tainted treats spoke up, half joking that an official notice of his "acquittal" would have to be presented before William—*Mr. Weiner*—might actually be reassigned bed and locker. Before Marcus could respond, Sling Blade, with great aplomb, said the gentleman would most definitely *not* be returning, for his benefactor had arranged that he be *well* taken care of pending the results of a "massive action against the state involving matters of false arrest, false imprisonment and police brutality, not to mention libel, slander and defamation of character." The staff took this bulletin with appropriate solemnity.

Now off the hook, they let Marcus know their outrage at the Gestapo-like actions of the SMPD and their cynicism upon hearing the charges proffered. They were free to share with him their hysteria after he'd been hauled away—they were only human!—and how anxious they had been for a while about the, ahem, *quality* of his desserts, for they wondered if, aside from being an (alleged) strangler and a rapist, he wasn't a (potential) poisoner to boot—it all sounded so silly now, so screwball!—and how they'd been unsuccessful in their attempts to retrieve the cookies and pastries, because there weren't any left. That's how popular the damn things were! (There was money lying around somewhere for William, they assured, royalties on goods sold.) And how they checked the newspaper each day for reports of victims . . . the lawsuits they imagined! Did you ever see the Keystone Kops? asked one of the staffers, rhetorically. Well, that was us—for a while, anyway.

Even Marcus joined in the laughter.

As Sling Blade had remained stoic, one of the counselors on a more serious note reminded that they had become purveyors of his confections because they wished him to get a leg up, and their intentions had been pure from the beginning—and that he had been the most successful guest to have ever passed through shelter doors. Seeing how at least *William* was still convivial, they pulled up chairs as he extemporized on his prison ordeal.

"They call the place Twin Towers, and a more evil set of twins you're unlikely to meet! It wasn't easy receiving visitors, and frankly, I'm glad for it—I wouldn't have wanted Janey to see me that way, all shackled up. It would have upset her no end."

They looked at him, and looked away too.

"What is it, then?"

The one who had first discovered his talents with a saucepan took Marcus by the arm and walked him away. "There is bad news."

"Let me have it, man!"

"Jane . . . is dead. She was murdered. It happened the day after your arrest."

"My arrest?" He repeated it, as if it related to someone else. "How—"

"In the old Tropicana . . . that's where they found her. A man killed her—"

"The Tropicana? A man . . . —*what* man?"

"I don't know. She killed him, too—stabbed him dead."

"Stabbed him—" He said the phrase over and again, like someone frantically trying to recall a crucial code by saying key words aloud. "Stabbed *who*?—"

"The man who attacked her."

Sling Blade, that Ph.D. of misery, had been eavesdropping, and moved closer to put a hand on Marcus's biceps for support.

"We're sorry, William. She was doing so great. Of course, she wasn't happy about you being arrested . . . When I went to identify her—one of the officers who found the body recognized Jane from having seen her on the night they took *you*—I claimed her property. She had a knapsack, and that was all. We've got her hearing aids, if you want them. She had something of yours—she was on her way to the jail to give it to you."

An associate had already fetched the item, stowed in a slick gray garbage bag with a built-in bright yellow cinch, and passed it to the one doing all the talking. It was handed to Marcus, who gingerly looked inside.

"That's it, no?" asked the counselor. "What we gave her from your locker?"

Marcus reached into the bag and pulled out his diary, still wrapped in grocery paper and hemp. There was a brown smear of blood on it.

"Isn't that what you asked Jane to bring you? She was probably on her way when she got mixed up with the man who attacked her."

Slipped beneath the frayed string was an envelope addressed "To my Darling Will."

*C*oulouse fled to Stradella House for Thanksgiving supper as the mood at Saint-Cloud was forbidding. His mother had taken to bed, and the self-righteous boy guessed drugs were at fault. Bluey was dragged kicking and screaming all the way to Alzheimer's World; Grandpa Lou took her absence hard.

We lied when saying Toulouse "fled"—the old man ordered him to go, knowing the domestic air to be clouded even more than usual. The truth was he didn't want Trinnie blabbing to the boy about the reappearance of his dad, which in her current state she was resoundingly capable of.

The cousins took this forced reunion as a welcome rapprochement. In short order, with much thanks to Pullman (a natural icebreaker), the three were together again as if never parted. They caught up on various enterprises, and gossiped, too—about a few "pieces of intelligence" regarding Trinnie's beaux. The first, from Toulouse, seemed anticlimactic on the telling: the detective and his mother had definitively broken it off. Lucy was particularly thrilled, never having completely gotten over her crush; now and then during class, her pulse quickened while daydreaming that she had Mr. Dowling in the 747 ready for takeoff. The second bit of news was more delicious. As it turned out, the Screenwriter Formerly Known as Rafe had struck paydirt and was now actually dating Diane

Keaton. Edward said the great actress had even asked him to punch up the movie she was directing (featuring Boulder Langon as the juvenile lead). But there was no discussion of the runaway girl; the subject was too radioactive. Toulouse slept in the main house, and took great care in avoiding Olde CityWalk altogether—the mere thought of the Boar's Head garret and the perfect picture of that sad-eyed gamine staring down through its trapdoor were enough to cause a catch in his throat.

In the late afternoon, they gathered at table. Joyce shabbily asked where his mother was on this Thanksgiving Day, and Toulouse, not half because Amaryllis was still on his mind, spontaneously said, "A dinner for orphans." Lucy nearly choked on her marshmallow'd yams; Edward grinned—*touché*—for his cousin had killed two birds with one stone: not only had he boldly referenced their illicit boarder, but he had also stood on Joyce's nerve by implying that Trinnie would be more inclined to help the abandoned living than the abandoned dead.

But his comment had a deeper meaning—at meal's end, he promptly announced that he wished to go home.

He thanked his hosts and said heartfelt good-byes to Lucy and Edward. That was the wondrous thing of being their age; they hadn't yet the sophistication to shut a final door—whereas in adulthood bruised feelings born of shared adversity become the stuff of feud, and mysteriously acquire permanence. The spite of children is truly child's play; grown-ups hate for all eternity.

*T*he light in his mother's room was on, and he decorously rapped at the door. She softly asked if it was Winter (who'd been told she could stay on indefinitely even though Bluey would not return) and was surprised when Toulouse answered.

He slipped in with her assent.

Trinnie lay in bed in the dark, in a crumb-stained Ghesquière caftan. She asked him to hand her a glass of water. She looked druggy.

"Are you sick?"

"No—why? And why are you looking at me like that?"

"Are you . . . taking drugs?"

"No, I'm *not* taking drugs. Are *you*? You're not being very respectful. I'm tired. And I don't feel well."

"That's what you say when you're taking drugs."

"I thought you were with Lucy and Edward."

"I wanted to come home. I need to talk to you."

"You mean you need to *torture* me—I told you: I'm not taking anything, OK?"

"I wanted to talk to you about the girl."

"What girl?"

"Amaryllis. The one Samson was looking for."

"What about her? You didn't get her pregnant, did you?"

"No," he said, bringing all his youthful contempt and puritanism to bear. "I want you to talk to Samson. I need to know if they found her."

"You really like that wild child, don't you? 'The diplomat's daughter.' "

He shyly nodded, averting his eyes.

"C'mere."

He crawled into bed and snuggled up. "I'm worried about her—I just feel like it was all my fault. We could have worked it out, couldn't we? Grandpa could have made it so Amaryllis could have stayed . . ."

"You can't save the world, Toulouse. And you can't save everyone in it."

"I don't *want* to save everyone—I just want to save *her.*"

"People have their own lives, their own destinies. Their own karma."

He didn't want to hear any of her negative mysticism. "I—I just worry that I'll never *see* her again. Like—you and Dad . . . only I didn't get a chance to really know her. At least you and Dad—at least you got *married*—"

He didn't want to hurt her; he thought to himself how he was always ruining everything.

She blew her nose and looked at him with a face disfigured by irresolution. "Oh, Toulouse! You should know this, you should know this . . . —but I promised your grandfather I wouldn't say!"

His heart stuck in his throat. "They found her . . . something *happened*—"

"I can't, I can't!" she said, scurrying to light a cigarette. She was wild-eyed now. "I said I wouldn't, but I can't keep it from you! I promised him—but I can't!"

"She's dead, she's dead!" he cried. He stood and shouted—*demanded* to know: "Who killed her!"

"Tull, it's your father—your father came back, Tull! He came back, he came back, he came back!"

He reeled away, and only the wall held him up. His mother nattered on, sobbing and mumbling and blowing her nose as she rushed to the bathroom, then out again, inadvertently exposing one tit, then another. In his shock, he heard only a few isolated phrases: "jail for murder," "Grandpa got him sprung," "four hundred pounds!"

That night he stayed in the Dane's great villa, curled into the dog like a pup. As Half Dead before him, Toulouse licked his wounds in preparation for war.

CHAPTER 40

Phantoms and Convocations

*L*ouis Trotter ignored the calls from his physicians. He'd been feeling much better since the emergency-room visit; his collar buttons were even fastening again. While such indifference to "follow-up" was perhaps unwise, it should not of necessity be considered a harbinger of doom—the old man had survived all manner of assault to his various systems, in degrees both large and small. It would take a lot to bring him down.

He busied himself with Bluey, who was still settling in—if that's the appropriate phrase when all the settling is done for you, and nearly against your will. He held her hand and occasionally ducked or broke away when the going got rough; then clucked and chuffed and asked of her his pet question over the years: "And how, little girl Blue, do you like your new digs?" (The thin humor of this being that she had always called him the digger.) "I don't like them at all," she said cogently and it pierced him through and through.

She asked why he had put her there, and while Louis remorsefully pondered a reply, Bluey shouted he was trying to kill her and that she'd fix his wagon good. She reached in her diaper, pulled out a hand smeared with feces and gave chase. The dapper old man dodged and parried as nurses in arm-length latex gloves scrambled—Marx Brothers by way of Dante.

The staff was careful around him, because they knew he was a donor and had billions and that his daughter had even designed the wandering garden; but Louis still worried about what they'd do to his wife when he wasn't there. He would have to hire special people to stand around, like NATO observers; more men in suits. No . . . best not to meddle. He was horrified to find himself comforted by the fact that Bluey bruised easily—a handy indicator of skulduggeries. Maybe he would install a webcam in her room so that he could watch her from Saint-Cloud. (He thought of a friend whose wife had lost her mind. The suspicious man set up a secret camera to document the abuse—as it had turned out, the one being abused was the nurse.)

He rushed out, unable to bear any more. Passing through the doors, he found Winter on her way in; they could hear Bluey's chilling chorus of "I'm afraid!"s.

"Can't they give her something, Winter? Why don't they give her something to knock her out?"

"I'll go see about it, Mr. Trotter. Don't you worry."

He sat by himself on a bench. He had yet to share with the old nanny any details relating to the purchase of the "condominium." He wasn't sure how to bring it up; there was time enough for that. There would be time . . . But it was real. The condo was very real.

He surveyed his daughter's handiwork. A profusion of honey locust trees with underplantings of fern and Siberian iris abounded, in the intimate style of a sixteenth-century garden; lining the Yorkstone path were bluebells, cosmos and mini-narcissus. Senescent creatures walked this eternal return of heavenly road—more surreal by far than anything made of yellow brick—waxen-skinned foragers on a looped and loopy veldt.

*C*he boy waited impatiently in the foyer—Mr. Trotter could not help noticing him from the living room, where he entertained his fiftyish, rumpled guest. About half an hour later, he ushered the visitor to the door, where they exchanged earnest good-byes.

Upon entering the Withdrawing Room, he saw his grandson among the grove of tombstone maquettes. One look told him all he needed. "I see you've spoken to your mother."

Toulouse nodded glumly. His face was puffy from worry and sleeplessness; a rough night in the doghouse all around.

His grandfather pursed his lips, a habit carried over from business—

a "hardball" rictus unpleasantly familiar to those who had sparred with him on the corporate level. "What would you like me to do?"

"I want to see him."

"He's not ready for that, Toulouse."

"Is he sick?"

"That's a complicated question, isn't it?"

"It doesn't *sound* complicated."

"Let's say he's getting better."

"What's wrong with him? Is it the schizophrenia?"

His grandfather laughed, then chuffed. "You might put it that way! But he has the best care now and the doctors are seeing to his every need."

"Was he in jail?"

"He was."

"For murder?"

"For a crime he did not commit. That is why he was released."

"What crime?"

"That is irrelevant."

"Has Mother been to visit him?"

"No. Refuses to—and I'm glad. I don't think he's ready to see *any-one*." He added, "I don't think *she's* ready."

"Is it true he weighs four hundred pounds?"

"He's not that heavy." He laughed, knowing whence the exaggeration came. "A nutritionist has his diet completely under control."

"Then why can't I see him?" The boy dug in; he had his grandfather's genes after all.

"Because it is not the time," said the old man insistently.

"If it wasn't for me," said Toulouse, scowling, "you would never even have *found* him!"

"How's that?"

"*I'm* the one who called Harry and Ruth—"

"I know it. And you shouldn't have imposed on them that way."

"They were *glad* we went to see them. And *I'm* the one who bought the jellies that reminded her of him! *I'm* the one who wanted to find my father in the *first* place! No one else did—"

"You know that isn't true, Toulouse."

"But it *is* true! No one wanted to find him *enough*. And *you* didn't want Mother to marry him in the first place! And *she* didn't care—it was better for her with him gone. That way, she could be happy taking her precious drugs! If he did come back, what would her excuse be *then?*"

Though his words stung, the old man stifled a swell of pride at the boy's sagacity. "That's enough now! You're far too young to sit in judgment of me, let alone your mother. You will see your father *in time*—and that will be soon enough. Do a few months really matter? Do you want to ambush the man before he's ready? Are you that selfish, Toulouse? I don't think so. He *is* your father, regardless of how he behaved in the past. He has been pursued by *Furies,* and now we are trying to chase those demons away. Or as many as we can. He needs *all* his energy for that struggle, do you understand? I don't want him derailed by certain— well, let's just say I want him stronger before he has any more shocks. For you *will* be a shock to him. Now, do we have a deal? You agree that you will see your father when *he's* ready?" He held out his hand, and the boy grudgingly shook it. Toulouse had been persuaded; his grandfather's logic was sound.

"Deal."

"Good. And not a word of this to anyone—not Lucy or Edward—not *anyone.* And leave your mother alone about it! What you said about her is true; before she sees him, she has to shed lots of dead skin. And it's not an easy thing. But she's holding up. Doing *damn* well, she is."

He put an arm upon the boy's shoulder while walking him out.

When they reached the door, Toulouse looked into his eyes. "I'm so sorry about Grandma," he said sweetly. "I'd like to visit her soon."

"She'd love that." He was moved by the youngster's politesse, for that was another visit of large proportion that needed the old man's sanction. "Epitacio will take you whenever you like." He leaned to kiss his head. "You're a wonderful boy, Toulouse. You've a strange lot in life, but you're unforgettable. I am proud you're my grandson, and will do anything I can for you in the years I have left."

*W*hile Toulouse acceded to his grandfather's wishes, his pact did not prevent him from listening in on a visit paid his mother by the lovelorn detective. Though Trinnie remained beguilingly, if morosely, in bed for the occasion, her son's efforts were made easier by an open door. He assumed Samson had left it that way on purpose, to let his mother know he didn't have any big ideas.

After the usual awkward chitchat of the recently estranged, Trinnie inquired after her husband (she knew Samson had been spending time with him). He affably responded, happy to have alit on familiar ground. It was all very conversational; one would never have suspected the extraordinarily baroque details involved. The detective told her that Marcus had a "pretty good setup over there." Toulouse hoped "there" would be named, and was not disappointed.

The Hotel Bel-Air wasn't far—the boy felt the flush of the downhill walk, and the flush of illicitness too, not dissimilar from the feeling that had overtaken him when he had first climbed through the broken hedge of La Colonne. He had promised Grandpa Lou not to interfere and would keep that promise; yet, as in the trespass of the forbidding park on Carcassone Way, he seemed powerless to stop his legs from propelling him forward.

He waved to Kevin, who knew him well from two years of Pullmanesque peregrinations. The valet let him park the dog by a sleeping Ferrari while he went in to investigate.

Toulouse struck out over the bridge, glancing down to the postcard pond with its swan fantasia. His plan was to dash through the small lobby and walk to the pool, then back past the bar and restaurant in hopes of "seeing something." Before he had the chance, he noticed a figure crouching at the edge of the water. It was Sling Blade, who vied for the attentions of the long-neck'd, floating beauties while grinning at some remark a man nearby had tossed off. The man laughed, the laughter itself as full-bodied as the throat from which it poured out—

Toulouse froze. Was it?—it must be—it *was . . .* it was!—*him.* Him.

He was looking at his father.

Then came a shock from another direction: "Toulouse?"

Boulder fairly tackled him.

"What are *you* doing here?" she asked, her face frozen in a country-club smile that said: Celebrities Only.

He couldn't answer; he couldn't speak.

"Are you *rolling?* Oh my God, you look like you're rolling!"

"What?" he managed.

"Like you took E."

"E?"

"Ecstasy, stupid. Anyway, I'm just *kidding . . .*"

"Boulder, I have to—I have to go . . ."

"*Diane's* here, with Dex. Don't you want to say hello? You *have* to. We're having a brunch—we have the same agent now, isn't it cool? I signed with William Morris!"

*H*s recent events were too much to assimilate alone, Toulouse was forced to throw himself on the mercy of the court of Olde City-Walk, his rationale being that Lucy and Edward had been in on the search for his father from the very beginning and that, to this date anyway, the suppression of family secrets had done the Trotter clan no apparent good. Like in the early days, the musketeers convened in Edward's apartments—and that, beginning with Trinnie's boudoir confession, is where he brought them up to speed.

"Oh my God!" cried Lucy. "Why didn't you tell us!"

Toulouse instantly regretted having opened his mouth. "I'm telling you *now*. I just found out! Grandpa would kill—"

"I cannot believe you *saw* him and didn't say anything! Weren't you dying to go up to him?"

"And say what? Hey, how ya doin'? It's me, your son! You know—the one Mom had after you flipped out."

"But how could you at least not—"

"Lucille Rose," said her brother. "Please chill."

The wise guy had spoken. The eyes of Oracle Ed blinked languidly above the veil. "None of this comes as a great surprise," he continued with studied nonchalance. "I believe I came into that 'piece of intelligence'—as Grandpa Lou would say—some days ago."

"Don't tell me you knew all along," said Toulouse, prepared to be at once astonished and betrayed.

"Edward!" she rebuked. "You knew and didn't tell us?"

"I had all the ingredients but didn't have a recipe—until now. See, for the last week or so, Dad's been acting *very* strange. At first I thought it was fallout from the Alzheimer's. That he was getting 'emotional.' But then I happened to learn from Eulogio (you know how close we've become) that he's been shepherding dear old Pops to—guess where? The Hotel Bel-Air."

"But Grandpa said no one knew—"

"I assumed he was having a dalliance. I thought, *Good for him*—because he sure doesn't get enough at home!"

"Edward," said his sister. "That is *so mean.*"

"When I implied as much out loud, Eulogio said he didn't think a woman was involved. So then I thought: it's a man!"

"Ed -ward!"

He squealed with delight. "Now *why*, pray tell, asked I of Eulogio, why would you think a woman was not involved? Getting information from that fellow is like pulling dumpster-baby teeth. (Well, maybe harder.) Because each time he drove him there, Eulogio responded, each time he drove *Señor Dodd*, he would later see him strolling about the pond with a heavyset man whose features were much as you described."

"Fuck!" spat Toulouse. "The whole *world* knows!"

"The immediate family—and I'm certain Grandpa Lou has taken pains to *keep* it immediate—is hardly the whole world, Toulouse. So chill."

"We *have* to go there," said Lucy, fiendishly agog at the plotty new developments. Tonight her Smythson would get a workout.

"I *glossed* it," said the cousin, kicking himself. "I thought it was just one of Dodd's pasty Seattle friends holed up in Tinseltown incognito to do a little bullshit consulting on the middle-school project—you know, Billionaire-Boys'-Club stuff. But then it came back to me . . . one night at dinner last week—remember, Lucy?—Father received a phone call. He stepped away from the table, which was rare; had to be Grandpa Lou. He listened for a second, then shot two words back to the phone." Edward paused dramatically. " 'John Burnham.' "

"Yes!" said Lucy knowingly, though just then she wasn't sure *what* she knew.

"John Burnham?" Toulouse was lost.

"Then Grandpa said something else, because Father's forehead wrinkled up and he asked: 'When?' "

" 'When?' " echoed Toulouse.

"Yes!" cried Lucy. "He said, 'When?'!"

"—and at *this* point, Joyce was listening *very* carefully. Her ear was moving toward the receiver like it was going to fucking *dock* with it. Then Father says, 'Did they speak?' "

"Into the phone?"

"Into the phone."

" 'Did they speak?' "

"Yes!" corroborated Lucy, with great excitement. "And then Dad said, [she lowered her voice in imitation] *'I'll take care of it.'* "

" 'I'll take care of it'?" said Toulouse, sounding—and feeling—like a simpleton.

"Exactly. *'I'll take care of it.'* "

"What is this, *The Sopranos?*"

"Who *is* John Burnham?" begged Lucy of her brother.

Edward shoved a cappuccino truffle under the veil and crunched. "I didn't put it together until Boulder called to gossip about Tull snubbing her at the Bel-Air. After she got it out of her system, she went on and on about how she and Diane Keaton had the same agent—John Burnham! That night, I innocently mentioned Mr. Burnham to Mother during a bath. There was a long pause—I mean *long.* Then she said, 'He was best man at their wedding.' Just like that."

Toulouse sagely nodded.

"What does it mean?" said Lucy, beside herself. "What does it *mean?*"

Toulouse filled in the blanks. "Mr. Burnham must have run into my father at the hotel—must have recognized him. They probably spoke, and that's what the phone call was about. Sling Blade—or some other 'handler'—probably saw it and reported back."

"Bingo," said Edward.

"I guess the cat really *is* out of the bag," said Toulouse.

"Not if Grandpa Lou can help it," said the cousin. "And, believe me—he can help it."

*T*he gentleman Louis Trotter had received in his living room *was* the inimitable Mr. Burnham, a higher-up at the William Morris Agency at that time, invited to Saint-Cloud to give express assurance that he would not give away the unexpected return of a fragile old friend—and that if he had already discussed it with, say, a colleague, then would he be so kind to cover his tracks by declaring himself to have been mistaken. Marcus Weiner was by no means the center of Mr. Burnham's world; thus far, he had only mentioned the brief encounter to Ms.

Keaton, his client and confidante. (The actress had of course already told him about her summer holiday with the kids—and of her affection for the profligately talented Katrina; Mr. Burnham had said hello to the latter not so long ago at Ivy at the Shore and found her alluring. Recently divorced, he was on the lookout, but his halfhearted entreaties to Ms. Keaton to play matchmaker had been ignored.) He felt the Trotters were a shade on the paranoid side, but appreciated their sensitivities. A thing like this could attract unwanted press.

This is what led to their summit: after being informed by his father of the swan-side run-in, uneventful of itself yet fraught with potentially hazardous repercussions if not quickly contained, Dodd cold-called the agent, who was also by chance an alumnus of Beverly Vista, albeit some years ahead of him. Mr. Burnham was tickled; having the eccentric billionaire on one's phone sheet was somewhat of a coup. Dodd quickly gave him the lowdown—while the jailing and other convolutions were withheld, the saga of an ongoing recovery from debilitating mental illness was not. Mr. Burnham was more than happy to comply with the request to, as they say, put a sock in it. He *was* somewhat taken aback when Dodd, in a transparent and superfluous effort to solidify the agent's trust, brought up the sketchy idea of a future creative alliance between Quincunx and the Morris agency—something in the digital realm or perhaps an interactive project that might tie in with his plans to rejuvenate old BV. (Until now, Mr. Burnham had been unaware that they had that place in common.) Dodd ended by saying his father was eager to meet him face-to-face. An interview at Saint-Cloud was arranged. As reported earlier, that conference was amicable, leaving Trotter the Elder much at ease. Again Mr. Burnham felt it odd, for he had already given his word; but he had always wanted to meet the legendary digger nonetheless, and seized the opportunity, which did not disappoint.

There was no longer any sense, not that there had been in the first place, in keeping Marcus at the Bel-Air. Mr. Trotter hadn't properly thought it through—the hotel was still a watering hole of the industry his son-in-law had once taken for his own. Though Marcus's appearance had radically transformed since his show business days, the digger of course had recognized him at once, at his most ragged and obese; it only stood to reason that others, all the Burnham types, would follow suit as he shrank closer to his former dimensions.

A house in Montecito was secured. Marcus decamped with ear-piece'd retinue, and the Bel-Air lodgings were no more.

The old man now obediently turned his attention to a flurry of medical procedures thus far avoided. He was strapped to a chair while a needle poked about the small mass in his neck (for it had lazily returned) in an unpleasant and futile attempt to extract cells. After forty-five min-utes, Mr. Trotter thought he might faint and said as much; the doctor stepped away with a flourish while of a sudden the chair went upside down with a great metallic whir so the blood could rush to his head. (He hadn't been quite ready for that little trick.) All told, the frustrated man spent more than an hour trying to get what he needed—and what he needled—but, failing miserably, could do nothing but schedule an MRI. Mr. Trotter smiled on his way out in such a way that the medic felt he had undergone a nasty procedure himself.

*M*idweek and mid-December now, and all is weirdly well at the house on Saint-Cloud. For Trinnie, the swelling, so to speak, has gone down. She busies herself with the wandering garden, which has become a kind of obsession. The old woman has not yet taken to its winding path, but her daughter prepares for her arrival through daily diligence and micromanagement of fountain and flora, belying the fact that she herself has utterly lost her way. (It is the Trotters' special gift to grow or build the family metaphors.) As for Bluey, she has calmed somewhat, Winter's presence being no small reason. But the Icelander is adrift, shell-shocked by the change of venue. Mr. Trotter finally con-firmed that the mystery condo was real; when he began to elaborate, she stopped him, as it would have been vulgar to evince curiosity. Still, his wife's generous bequeathment made the days lighter and filled her with gratitude.

*D*rawing on "intelligences" gleaned from his kind patron, Marcus Weiner embarks on a sacred mission.

Around nine o'clock one chilly Wednesday morning, he leaves the 1930s Lutah Maria Riggs–designed Montecito aerie and sets out by chauffeured car for Boyle Heights, a rough, historic neighborhood not far east of the bridge that had once sheltered him. He does not look like the same man who left the Hotel Bel-Air as mysteriously as he arrived; he carries forty pounds less, and there's a spring to both step and mind that is decidedly un-Victorian. A kind of contemporary reason has returned, along with memories of life before Gypsydom. The therapist has kept a watchful eye out for relapse. Ready to triage, she is lying in wait to cushion his fall when the classic epiphany comes: when the patient realizes the scope of all that has been robbed him and can never be recovered—time, tide and loved ones—but with Marcus, such frissons seem to come and go like trains at a station, leaving him sadder but wiser, morose but not marooned. (Mr. Trotter is unsurprised at his son-in-law's stamina and resolve.) So today—this dreary, exalted Wednesday morning—our bighearted pilgrim is on a numinous journey, preapproved by all those concerned. His shrink would like him to corral that elusive nineties' warhorse called closure; but *he* wishes simply to say good-bye.

And the boy? He has decided that if he cannot see his father, he will at least see Amaryllis. He called the detective to ask where she was; Toulouse had become seriously "proactive." Samson stonewalled—any information about the girl or her whereabouts, he said, was confidential. Besides, he added, you kids caused enough trouble. He went on to say how cruel it was to expose a girl like that to so many luxuries; how it was *his* opinion the children had been selfish and condescending "from day one"; how the boy's demands to see her—"your very *tone* in this conversation"—showed him to be selfish, impetuous and "entitled" still. In other words, the detective gave Toulouse a piece of his mind. Our hero did not feel at all well after their conversation and to make himself better, wrote the diatribe off as Samson's spleen at being spurned.

The very same children the detective maligned now gather at Olde CityWalk for yet another in a series of pre-holiday feasts. As Christmas approaches, Stradella House is busy with charity lunches and dinners and the attendant tours, so it is not unusual for the cousins to look out the gingerbread window above the Boar's Head Inn and see groups of strangers nosing about or passing by in special trams. (The Majestyk has screened *It's a Wonderful Life* more than once to benefit Joyce's Candlelighters.) Lucy is the only one who appears to relish the intrusions of the outside world, though Pullman never seems to mind the endless gaggle of awed spectators, who fuss over him as if he were a unicorn. On wintry nights, cobblestone backstreets fill with carolers and caterers' torches and carriages pulled by draft horses; the scene is set for Lucille Rose to imagine it really *is* the London of H. G. Wells and his time machine, a London soon to be expanded upon by an irresistible series of mystery books to be known the world over simply as *Blue Maze.*

At Toulouse's request, his braided cousin, who had tirelessly transcribed the orphan's outpourings for future novelistic use, took to the Smythsonian archives and in no time at all located Amaryllis's AWOL reference—the marble-hearted institution from which she had escaped. The infamous Mac (Lucy's footnote: "short for MacLaren Children's Center. In common usage") was in a distant town called El Monte.

Toulouse suggested they call the place forthwith. Edward, shrouded in white linen and suffering nobly through a holiday pestilence of acne, barked that it was useless to ring the place up—they should board the MSV instead and hope for a sighting. They could lie in wait just as Amaryllis had outside Four Winds; with gull wings extended, the rescue party should be easy enough for the prisoner to spot (Edward as yet being unaware of the height of MacLaren's walls). Better yet, they'd come bearing Yuletide gifts and offertories for the fucked-up little foundlings—a veritable Trojan Mauck.

"You know," said Edward to his cousin, "we haven't talked about this . . ." He waited until he had their full attention. "It's actually pretty intense."

Toulouse was thinking he was finally going to announce the date of his facial surgery.

"I haven't told you either, Lucy."

"Then tell us!" said the girl, with customary exasperation. *"Just tell us, Edward."*

"Well . . . think back. To the day of our wonderful interrogation by the good detective Dowling. Now, *if* you recall, the detective was *wondering* . . . if the girl—Amaryllis—had ever been seen in the company of a certain *bearded* gentleman—" He swiveled his head toward his sister. "You're supposed to be the *author.* You're supposed to *listen.* Have Inspector Javert's comments been forgotten?"

"Bearded?" said Toulouse. "I don't remember him saying anything about a bearded—"

Lucy frantically flipped through her BIRD NOTES. "He's right, he's right! The detective asked if she was *with* someone—that first time we met . . . remember, Toulouse? He wanted to know if she was with someone when she came to Boulder's movie set—here!" She reached a pertinent passage in the Smythsonian transcript: " 'A *large-built bearded man . . .' "*

"Very good!" shouted Edward.

"What are you saying?" asked Toulouse.

"What I am saying is . . . that your *father*—and this is going to come as a bit of a shock—your father befriended Amaryllis on skid row. He took *care* of her: you know, brought her food, looked after her and so forth."

"That is bullshit!"

"But here's the shocker. Maybe you'd better sit down . . ."

"Tell me!" said the apoplectic boy. "You better fucking tell me *now*!"

"Edward, *tell* us—"

"And you *better* not be bullshitting!"

"Well . . . you see, it was Amaryllis's *mother* who Marcus was accused of murdering. *That's* why he was in jail."

Lucy gasped and was so overcome that she lay on the floor to steady herself. Toulouse fought the impulse to knock down his cousin, and was glad he didn't, for the consequences would have been dire.

"But who—who told you this?" snapped Toulouse, like a lawyer on the losing side. He'd gone white as Edward's veil.

"I wish I could say I deduced it myself, but I can't. It was Mother who spilled the beans, during a bath—that's when her guard's down. She tells me everything during a bath."

Toulouse began to gibber. "I can't—I can't believe—murdering her *mother* . . . my father!—fed her? looked after? you mean to say she was actually *friends* with—" He went on like that, much as a sensitive piece of equipment that had been dropped on its head.

"It's karma," said Edward, sounding like his aunt. (The whole world sounded more like Trinnie every day.) "What goes around comes around."

What came around just then was Sling Blade, preceded by a rap at the door. Due to complicated dynastic interweavings, the caretaker had a knack for popping up when family members least expected; yet precisely because of such ubiquity, his presence was never puzzled over. Sling Blade informed that he had come to borrow the MSV as per their grandfather's hasty request. Edward was outraged, or pretended as much—before a sixth sense that "intrigue" was afoot won out.

"And *why*," said the cousin, having a bit of sport, "would Grandpa Lou be suddenly inclined to joyride in the Mauck?"

"It's not for your grandpa," he answered, one-upping.

"Really!" said Edward, like a Roman toying with a slave boy. "Then who *is* it for? Is it for *you*, Blade?" They'd somehow stopped calling him by the full appellation, for the groundless fear he might take offense.

"That fellow in Santa Barbara."

Eureka! Edward winked at Toulouse, who had not by a long shot recovered from the blow delivered only minutes before.

"Which fellow?" asked the boy.

"You know who he's talking about," said the cousin snidely.

The caretaker became circumspect. "I'm going to stay out of everybody's business."

"Well then, why does he need the Mauck?" asked Toulouse.

"Town Car broke down on the freeway somewhere."

"He's driving *himself*?" asked the astonished Lucy.

"I didn't say that. Car broke down over in the Valley. Gonna go pick him up."

Sling Blade was unaware of the blood ties between Toulouse and the agreeable "fellow" he occasionally ferried from one place to another. (He never thought to ask his employer about the big man; that was his way.) Mr. Trotter didn't wish Marcus to know about the boy—not yet—so had kept the cognoscenti to a minimum. That way, there'd be less chance of a slipup. He had already issued a rather stern warning to the Weiners, but was concerned that Harry and Ruth would inadvertently *kvell* about their grandson to Marcus before he was psychologically prepared to "deal."

Sling Blade asked if he might use the rest room, and was pointed the way.

When he disappeared, an agitated Edward lifted his gauzy mask. "Toulouse, this is *it*. This is fate! You've *got* to get in the Mauck!" Lucy and Toulouse gaped at him. "I'm *telling* you—go! Hide in the Mauck! You want to see your father, don't you?"

"But—" stammered Toulouse, "hide *where*?"

"In the media cabinet! It's totally empty—they're swapping out the components. Take my *sister* if you're so scared. There's room for both of you!"

"Oh my God . . ." hissed Lucy, like air rushing from a tire.

"I can't—" said Toulouse.

"Then you'll *never* see him! And you'll always remember this day! You're the one who found him, OK? And they're doing what they *always* do—conducting business on *their* time and at *their* convenience. It's your *right*, don't you get it? What if he runs away again? You don't think that could happen? What will you say then?"

"Come on, Toulouse, let's hide in the closet!"

"But what if he—"

Edward shook his head dismissively. "Aw, he's *chickenshit*."

"Why don't you just go *fuck* yourself, Edward?"

He had never spoken like that to his cousin, and the goad quickly replaced the veil, not out of effrontery but rather to conceal a classic if malformed Cheshire grin.

In mere sweaty minutes, Lucy and Toulouse stood still as hostages upon the plush carpet and chopped wiring-conduit remains of the Mauck media center bowels. The plucky scamp took the opportunity to stick her tongue down his throat; he was about to push her away when suddenly she started.

"Oh my God, I left my pad! Be right back!"

She bolted from the truck just as Sling Blade entered the garage, lifting the gull wing to clamber in. In a blur of moments, he had switched on the engine, secured the passenger door and backed out into the circular drive.

Toulouse would tell him it was only a prank—after they passed through the gate, he'd reveal himself, then have Sling Blade drive him home. (He only hoped the caretaker wouldn't be so startled by his presence that he'd swerve into something.) But how would he live it down to his cousin? He would have to say Sling Blade heard him cough and *that's* how he was discovered. Or maybe that he'd gotten an electric shock from one of the exposed wires and had cried out . . .

Sling Blade turned on the radio and began to sing the way people do when they're alone. Being a stowaway was more fun than he'd thought; he was *glad* Lucy had left. He could smell her on his upper lip, and wiped a residue of saliva away with his cuff. His driver bantered with the guards as the Stradella delivery gate was raised, and then they were on the open road, winding toward the West Gate.

Toulouse thought of the immigrant boy he had once read about, hiding in the wheel well of a jet to escape his country, and for some reason that made him think of the trip to Easter Island—he could see Edward in the AirBuggy, stalwartly motoring among great stone moai. The impossible revelation of a "street" bond between his father and Amaryllis brought to mind the dinner they had all shared at Trader Vic's . . . His thoughts continued willy-nilly: on their way to Cedars, Lucy was in the midst of telling him his father was still alive—then he tasted pomegranate jelly, and blood in his mouth too, unleashed by the fist of the Four Winds bully. He winced at the sight of his mother weeping in bed, fearful to meet the man whose absence had governed her aborted life.

By the time he emerged from his reveries, Sling Blade had already steered the Mauck onto the 405, past the hulking hillside clinic of the Getty (where Amaryllis had communed with gilt-edged saints, and devils too), and joined the artery of the eastbound Ventura. He would go the distance now; there was nothing to fear. He would *not* be a cowering Trinnie . . . hadn't he been watered by his grandfather's blood? They had all seen his dad, every single one: Burnham and Uncle Dodd and Sling Blade, even the Monasterios—was he, Toulouse Trotter, the very *son*, less than them? He stewed in the cabinet, raging at Grandpa Lou for so elegantly bamboozling him. *Your father's not ready,* he said . . . as if anyone ever was. As if anyone in this whole fucked-up scenario *could* be. When the old man accused him of being selfish—just as the detective had! they were a coven, conspiring together!—it had caught the boy off guard. Wily, clever old man! Now he'd had enough. Edward was right; fate dictated the moment. It was his time and his right, and he would lay claim.

Sling Blade muttered, "There they are, there they are," and the Mauck slowed, edging to the shoulder. "Stay in there, stay in there, you dumb fuck."

Toulouse wondered who he was talking about; maybe his father was stepping from the disabled car. Maybe his father would be struck down by a drunk or a Caltrans truck and that would be the end of it.

He opened the door of the cabinet and listened a moment to the voices beneath the drone of speeding traffic. Hunching over, he crept out to peer through the tinted window. A tow was attaching itself to the Town Car while Sling Blade and a suited man spoke; the boy assumed he was his father's chauffeur. That was when he saw Marcus Weiner heading for the Mauck.

He panicked and ran back to the closet. Fate now dictated that his bravado was no more; he whispered imprecations and prayed he wouldn't sob or soil his pants. He could hear Sling Blade helping with the door, and the carriage was rocked by the weight of entry. What if out of sheer curiosity his father opened the closet and found him hiding there? Toulouse knew little about the man's disease: maybe schizophrenics didn't *like* jack-in-the-box surprises and reacted violently, even bloodily. Hadn't the man recently been fingered for homicide? He never heard details . . . maybe he'd been released on a technicality and was guilty after all—that would be a fitting end to the saga of Toulouse Trotter's poignant search: torn to shreds à la Hannibal by his mentally deranged dad! Lucy would have to run a fresh proposal by Mr. Hookstratten. Might not be appropriate for the kiddies.

Marcus lowered himself in the captain's chair with a grunt. It seemed the man in the suit would be staying behind with Triple-A. "We'll be fine," he heard Sling Blade call out, to which the man responded, "Oh, they know I'm not going ahead with y'all—no one has a problem with that." The Mauck shook again as the caretaker entered through the passenger side and pulled the door down after him. He opened the fridge and got an Evian for Marcus, who thanked him.

Toulouse sat cross-legged in the darkness. If he never saw his father face-to-face, at least he'd had *this* proximity, at once horrifying and intimate. He could hear the rider's breath, and even a few low farts. Occasionally, Sling Blade made small talk or inquired if his passenger wished to hear music. Toulouse wondered where they were going. His plan was to escape as soon as they reached their destination, but that might be difficult if it was a secure area—say, an airport runway. They'd probably get gas or stretch their legs soon enough . . . but why *would* they? Onboard facilities were more than adequate, and Sling Blade had most likely received instructions discouraging pit stops.

The big man began to hum, and Toulouse was swamped by embarrassment and self-loathing. His grandfather was right; he *was* selfish. How could he have let Edward manipulate him into this absurd, potentially cruel enterprise? Hiding in the closet like an a-hole! Incredibly, he had just been told of the mind-blowing ties between the girl—his beloved—and the father he had staked everything to find . . . Amaryllis, whom this mysterious being had nurtured (according to Edward), would never have stooped so low; Dad raised her with more dignity than that. But here *he* was, the putative son, quailing in the media cabinet. For shame! He would have to have a "sit-down" with Grandpa Lou. He would tell him he had decided it was unnecessary to meet the gentleman who had sired him—and that all he wished was for Mr. Weiner to stabilize and move on to some measure of happiness; that initiating the search had been a terrible experiment in egotism which had caused irreparable harm to his mother in the process. He would hereafter devote his life to good works. During their study of religion at Four Winds, the students learned of a monastery in the heart of Hollywood filled with cloistered Benedictine nuns. Perhaps there was an equivalent place for boys. He would live a life of seclusion as penance for his tomfoolery, and in time, after demonstrating proper maturity, might oversee a vast trust established by the Trotter Family Foundation to help those afflicted by mental illness—and homeless children, too. He could administer the moneys without ever leaving the confines of his austere spiritual haven.

Having achieved a near-beatific state during his musings, Toulouse managed to remain calm upon realizing that the MSV had glided off the freeway and was downshifting toward what felt like an end point. Not five minutes later, his feelings were borne out.

The Mauck came to rest. He waited a few minutes after the men had left before emerging from the closet. He moved slowly through the cabin and could smell the not unpleasant, musky imprint of his father; he shivered again with shame.

He crept outside and looked around. They were in some kind of urban park, on a gently sloping grassy hill. At the crest of that hill was a building with a tall smokestack. He saw the figures of Sling Blade and his father sitting on a bench, waiting. Toulouse left the parking area and walked down to the street. There was a graffiti'd sign at the entry— CREMATORIUM—and now he could see that a cemetery abutted the place he'd just been. It stretched for blocks. The surrounding neighborhood looked bleak and dangerous. He had left his StarTAC at Stradella; he would need to find a pay phone to call the cousins, to make Eulogio pick him up. Instead, he retraced his footsteps until he was again beside the MSV.

"Jesus, what are you doing?"

Sling Blade, who had just emerged from the Mauck with two bottles of Evian, barreled toward him.

"It was just a joke! I didn't mean to . . ."

"But how did you—"

"I hid in the closet!" he said nervously. "We were just messing around, Blade—it was just a joke! I was going to come out, but you pulled away . . ."

"A joke! Just a joke that's gonna get me fired!"

"It's *OK*. I'll take a *cab*—"

"The *hell* you will," said the caretaker, forcefully grabbing his arm. "You come with me!"

"No!—"

"That's all I need! You getting a *drive-by*. Now, come on!"

"But what do we say? What do we tell *him*—"

Sling Blade scratched his head; the boy's overweening concern about an alibi for the sake of "the heavyset fellow" never even registered. "We'll just say that—that you're my *nephew*." He cringed at the inadequacy of it all. "Oh *shit*. God*damnit*, Toulouse! Why'd you do this stupid thing? We'll just say you're my nephew, OK? No!—*Dot's* nephew! You're Dot's nephew—Dot's my boss. We'll say she lives around here, OK? You knew where I was gonna be and came around to say hello. Or no! You *saw* me—like a coincidence. He won't ask any questions; he's a little disturbed. When we're finished here, I'll take the 10 and drop you near the Getty. And if you tell your grandfather—"

There was little chance that he would.

Toulouse followed him into the chimney-building like one condemned. "What is this place?"

"It's where they burn up bodies."

When they reached Mr. Weiner, he was talking to a man who held a shoe box filled with human remains under his arm. The shoe-box man took in Toulouse with vague disapproval, but the boy wouldn't meet his eye—or anyone else's. Marcus never gave his son a glance.

Because of this obliviousness, and because Sling Blade's scowls gradually subsided, Toulouse had the opportunity to scrutinize the burly character now standing at a lectern skimming a ledger of the dead and holding what looked to be a prayerbook in his hand. How handsome his father was, he thought—already much thinner than the day he saw him at the Bel-Air, and with a powerful magnetism about him, though his eyes were red and his face swollen and ruddy from weeping. His suit was finely cut yet capacious as a tent. He looked wise and kind and fierce, too; he was no one to tangle with, yet that's all the boy wanted to do.

"Her name is Scull, not Scall," said Marcus matter-of-factly after examining the log. Their host said nothing and made no move to correct the entry. "Well, I'll see her now." He daubed at his nose with a handkerchief and walked outside.

Toulouse watched him thread his way down the hill; keeping a discreet distance, the boy struck out on his own. There were no tombstones, but he noticed markers embedded in the grass, with years instead of names, memorialized: 1978, 1983, 1991. His father squatted down to touch one. Then Sling Blade strenuously motioned for Toulouse to return to the Mauck.

On the way back, he saw beer bottles washed up at the bottom of a chain-link fence, the sediment of small-time paganism.

They left the parking area without discussion and pulled into the street. Toulouse felt at once numb and giddily relieved—for better or for worse, the mysterious man who happened to be his father now seemed more novelty than threat. He was cocky enough to think it might be time for Sling Blade to make an introduction. He was about to nudge the caretaker when Marcus Weiner began an oratory of tears that jolted both boy and driver from their seats.

"Janey! Janey, my Janey! What did they do to you?" He tore at his hair; a worried Sling Blade looked in his rearview and was at least assured that the man had wits enough to have used his seat belt. "Why'd they do it to you, Janey? Why? My darling, my darling!" He wailed and snorted and thrashed about. The book he'd been carrying fell to the floor, and with it the envelope that was tucked inside:

To my Darling Will . . .

The caretaker, though inured to the trappings of grief, to its keens and waterworks, and bodies lowered into the earth, could not help but grimace at the force of his rider's pain. There was beauty in it, too—just as in the gnarled olive trees of Westwood Memorial Park. Toulouse was all gooseflesh, like a riptide had sucked off his clothes.

Sling Blade glanced sidewise at the boy, pleased at the demonstration of humility. He saw that Toulouse was sorely moved by this stranger, and such maturity in one so young unexpectedly moved him too. Came the caterwauling and lamentations: now melodious, now atonal, now piano, now forte, monolithic arpeggios of sorrow lit by plaintive trills—grace notes singing the leitmotif: *Janey, why!*

He took the Sunset off-ramp and left the boy just south of Sunset. When Toulouse began the walk to Saint-Cloud, he thought, *Surely this life of ours is a dream—and those who said otherwise could not even aspire to be phantoms of a phantom world.*

CHAPTER 41

Worries and Wrinkles

*A*s the Candlelighters became better-known (just the previous month they had settled into the top floor of a charming little building the Trotter family owned on Brentwood's tony San Vicente), the group received calls from friendly police departments alerting them to bitsy bodies recovered from all manner of tide and trash. This time, as earlier reported, a well-meaning soul jumped the gun; the overeager dispatcher had received half-baked information from a hospital worker but passed it on to the ladies anyway. Happy, red-faced retractions abounded.

Joyce was determined to meet the infant she had named Isaiah but was now calling Lazarus—the Candlelighters' own "lucky angel." She got in touch with the newborn's foster parents, Rachel Hirschberg and Cammy Donato, a gregarious lesbian couple living in the Palisades, late-thirtysomethings who'd been planning to go the in-vitro route until reading the *Times* item about the McDonald's Miracle Baby Doe. They had been touched, just as Joyce was by her first Baby Doe almost two years before.

Rachel and Cammy were eager to soak up the stories-behind-the-story of their baby's almost novelistic arrival into the world and eagerly invited Mrs. Trotter to tea.† Joyce came in Chanel armor, bearing duffels of baby Pratesi, sweet little frog boots and English-made tattersall shirts

---

†Mercifully, they would never know of a woman named Jane Scull and the sorrows she endured.

DHL'd from the Magic Wardrobe in Virginia. The Candlelighters' CEO was not disappointed by the mascot's sweet disposition or his astonished, resurrected eyes. She was absolutely taken with every single Rembrandt-drawn hair of his fuzzy, sweet-smelling head.

When Rachel surprised by saying he was yet to be christened, Joyce underwent a welter of emotions she hadn't experienced since the perilous birth of her own son; he too went unnamed for a while. The baby, jaundiced and malformed, barely left the ICU with his life (aside from ten thousand other afflictions, he had swallowed amniotic fluid and was vomiting blood)—it seemed there were two teams working full-time: one to keep him afloat and the other (Bluey and Dodd and various shrinks) to keep Joyce from going under.

Staring at Lazarus, tickling his perfect pinkness while he wrapped a Lilliputian hand around her finger, an old sickening riff sang in her head: this was how she had expected Edward to look. This was what she had dreamed. But the miracle was theirs—a spectacularly healthy fast-food discard, born of who knew what godless monster, snatched up by ebullient, shorthaired queers.

Her son had stayed in the hospital for three months, while she remained bedridden at Stradella. It was Winter who visited him, and Winter whom all the nurses knew, and Winter who sat for hours by the incubator after intubations and bloody cut-downs, and Winter who gave Joyce progress reports that she listened to from bed as a grinch would a poorly written fairy tale.

Then one day without warning he was home. He stayed with the Jamaican RN and Oahuan doula in the faraway "servant and sick wing."

Joyce didn't touch him for a year. It wasn't until he was four that she even tried to bathe him, as a dutiful if reluctant penance. He was so damaged that she barely had the stomach. How had anyone expected her to give him a name?

*I*n the noisy steel cask of the MRI, Louis Trotter had much to mull over. A long time coming, Bluey's grim predicament had nonetheless taken him by surprise; he could not buy her comfort, or even assess her agonies. If she had a cancer, he might help her rally to blast the thing away—or end it all, if that's what she'd wanted. But this! A once fearless woman now possessed by terrors, trembling with each breath in horror that her mouth had become a broken window to let robbers in . . . With a violent twitch, he pushed the picture of her away.

He drifted in the diagnostic tube. What was this thing if not a coffin? The digger was, thankfully, not a claustrophobe; no Valium, please. For this particular procedure he was in his element.

He had other concerns—to wit, the grandchildren. Not the girl—he had no worries about the girl to speak of. Lucille Rose possessed an enormous heart and a head for figures, too; a buoyant, practical child certain to have buoyant, practical passions. A dreamer and a nester at once, she was not prodigal, and relished in absorbing the best parts of those around her. She would live to be 102. But the boys . . . the boys.

Shortly after the existence of Toulouse's father had been revealed, Edward asked that they convene. When the old man suggested the Withdrawing Room, he demurred, nominating the site of his grandfather's future memorial instead. Onlookers whispered while the curious pair strolled past the neatly mowed graves of Natalie Wood and Donna Reed.

The boy said he was tired and quite often in pain and had, like his confessor, been preparing a long while for his death. He could share these things, he said, because he knew the rigor and care with which his grandfather had pursued *his* final home. Edward said he too wished *"la última casa"*—the last house—to be aesthetically pleasing, and that he'd spent quite a lot of time studying Saint-Cloud's funerary-commission maquettes. He asked Grandpa Lou into the Mauck (Epitacio had parked adjacent to Irving "Swifty" Lazar) to show him clippings of tombs, stelae and catafalques collected over the last eighteen months, and expressed his desire to be buried in this very park so that his sister and beloved cousin Toulouse might be near him.

Louis Trotter, for all his end-point obsessions, was for *life*. He was always on the loamy side of life; he had dug the earth for its living riches and would keep on digging to provide for his grandchildren and their children, too—yet in this instance the boy's wizardry had transformed the old man into a ghoulish handmaiden. This was a sudden, unwelcome fillip given his heretofore charming role as "afterlife hobbyist," and he felt some guilt because of it. Had he really imagined that his years-long pursuit of a resting place (the mention of which family members assiduously avoided) would go unnoticed by this most brilliant and fragile boy? They were closer than kin that way; Edward, in his superior fashion, had simply made his grandfather do the legwork.

On the day already discussed, the boy left his collection of "memorabilia" with Grandpa Lou, and while he hadn't looked at them since, he often revisited the events of that afternoon. They had been distracted by the infernally meddlesome Dot Campbell, who'd prattled on about talk shows and orphan diseases; Mr. Trotter pretended to be irritated but was secretly relieved, for the gracious child had been unbearably poignant and he needed to step away. He let out a string of chuffs and walked over to Sling Blade to arrange for the caretaker to accompany the kids on their one and only group field trip to La Colonne.

He had never followed up on their discussion, and it nagged him that his grandson might be planning a "dramatic" exit. But he didn't know *how* to follow up on such complicity; he loved that boy and respected him and knew he was doomed, just as he himself was doomed. (As were we all.) Edward had sung his graveside song with such profound elegance and economy that—well, it wasn't the old man's style to hand him a pep talk or send him to therapy, as his mother would have done. Who could ever really know how that child suffered? So he let it go. Whenever he saw Edward, at school events or family dinners, there was a wantonness between them, the shorthand charisma of a very married couple who had made their vows on the Day of the Dead.

He ruminated on it as Epitacio drove him from Cedars to the Westwood Village Memorial Park. On the car phone, the doctor said the MRI results were inconclusive. They would need to shoot dye through an artery and see what they could see. Mr. Trotter was surprised that with all the fancy equipment, there was still no clear resolution—so to speak.

Sling Blade, who was raking leaves near the Candlelighters' parcel, ran over when he saw him stepping from the Rolls.

"What happened?" asked Mr. Trotter as he approached with more than a little speed.

Sling Blade went blank.

"You never told me what happened!"

"You mean—"

"I mean with Mr. Weiner!" he said with great annoyance. "What do you think I mean?"

"Oh! Yessir!" he said bashfully. Then he leaned on his rake and remembered. "Well, we went there, sir."

"To Boyle Heights," he prompted.

"Yessir."

"And there's a large cemetery there . . ."

"Yessir."

"Was it the old Jewish one?"[†]

"I don't know, sir. We didn't go *there*, anyway. We went to the other one, next door."

"I see." He stroked his chin, already intrigued.

"We went inside—there was a book there. And her name was written in it."

"A book?"

"Yessir. More like a ledger."

"A *ledger*," he said, fascinated. "With 'Jane Scull' written down . . ."

"*Scall*. It was a misprint. Your friend—Mr. Weiner mentioned it, but I don't think they'll do anything about it."

"And then?"

"He went and paid his respects."

"Went over to the *grave*?" The old man chuffed and strained at the caretaker's appalling dearth of detail.

"Yessir. Kneeled down. Had his book with him."

"What book?"

"You know—that book he got when I took him to the shelter. The *Nowhere* book."

"And the grave?"

"The grave, sir?"

"Man, tell me! What was the grave like? Describe the headstone!"

"Headstone? Oh no, sir—there was nothing like that."

"No headstone?"

"No sir. They don't do it like that there."

"Then how *do* they do it?" he asked imperiously.

[†]His son-in-law's East Los Angeles outing had provided the old man an opportunity to indulge his natural curiosity of local burial grounds while at the same time catching up on Marcus's doings.

"With little markers on the ground. Little markers with the year written on them."

"The year? Just the year?"

"Yessir."

"Just the year? And no names?"

"It's all grass, just like this." He pointed to the cemetery flats. "No names or headstones—just little markers with the year."

Mr. Trotter seemed shocked at the simplicity of the concept, and again set to stroking his chin. He then reached into his vest pocket and pulled out a gold money clip whose teeth clamped onto a sheaf of hundreds like a feral dog's. He loosened a few bills and palmed them toward Sling Blade.

"No, sir, not today," said the caretaker, retreating.

"And why?"

"It's all right, sir."

"Don't be a fool!"

"I can't, sir, not today."

"Is it your pride?"

"No, sir—"

"But I didn't *pay* you for the day you drove him there! I don't like people doing things for free. Now take it!"

"Sir, something happened," he said, still stepping back, head hung low. "It was my fault, and I didn't tell you about it. And I don't want to take your money."

"Happened? *What* happened?"

"The boy, sir—Toulouse. He went along."

"He went what?—"

Epitacio started in their direction; the old man's posture had turned apoplectic enough to hint at a return trip to the diagnostic center whence they had come.

"It was a mistake, sir—a game, he said. He was hiding in the Mauck."

"Hiding?"

"Climbed in, evidently, when I picked up the truck at Stradella. Hid in the cabinet the whole way, sir! Didn't even know he was *there* till we got where we were going. Then he asked me to send him home in a taxi, but I wouldn't let him, sir, no sir, so he stayed on. Sat in the front seat."

"My God. Did they speak?"

"Who, sir?" (The old man had forgotten the caretaker was in the dark.) "You mean, Mr. Weiner and the boy? Why no, sir, they didn't. But he was terribly upset."

"The boy?"

"Why no, sir—Mr. Weiner was. Over his loss. Cried all the way to Santa Barbara. Never stopped! I don't think he even *noticed* the boy."

"Now, isn't that something!—"

The old man scratched his chin, which was, to Sling Blade's observation, auspicious.

"But the boy was very respectful, sir, I'll say that. You would have been proud." He nodded his head, saying more than he knew. "*Honored* the man, very much so. Honored him."

"That little son of a bitch." Mr. Trotter grew contemplative before shrugging his shoulders. "Well—I suppose there's no stopping him . . . a *stowaway!*"

"My fault, sir. Should've checked. But, you see, I'd left the kids only two minutes before. I was *sure* they were all still in that room when I—"

Both caretaker and chauffeur were surprised to see his scowl replaced by a leprechaun's grin, ear to ear. A laugh issued forth that neither had heard before; like a bee to nectar drawn, Dot Campbell dive-bombed from a hundred yards. Epitacio hustled to shut the door after the old man, who had jauntily climbed in front. As Dot came in for a landing, he uncharacteristically ordered his driver to brake.

"Hello, Mrs. Campbell!" he said, convulsed.

"Hello, Mr. Trotter! Happy mood today?"

"Happy, happy, yes! Happy indeed! And why wouldn't I be? My little son of a bitch grandson is a *stowaway!*"

---

*W*e will soon return to star-crossed father and son, remaining at their side for the duration (more or less) of our tale. But first the author must digress. Let us turn our attentions to an old—not *so* very old—standby, whose fortunes had fallen significantly enough in the last forty days to displace him to the rankling of *Forbes*'s number thirty-seven. It can be sworn that he will never fall much farther than that.

Dodd Trotter descended upon Stradella House, having just returned from India, St. Petersburg and Seoul. He was on the phone with his mother, who was resting comfortably at her Woodland Hills cottage complex, Winter and the gilded book of obituaries faithfully at hand.

"Did you see the picture, Doddie?" asked the old woman.

"What picture, Mother?"

"In the paper today."

"I've just come home—didn't get a chance to look. Is it in the *Times?*"

"So handsome."

"Who, Mother?"

"There's a beautiful loafer with a tassel lying there."

"The *Times?* New York or L.A.?"

"Do you remember the loafers we used to get you from Church's, Doddie?"

"I do."

"This loafer—it's just lying there on the platform. Right where people wait for the subway. A couple got married. Young, handsome couple. I think he worked in public relations. They have *money.* They took the train to get married. Impetuous. One of those spontaneous things. *Fun.* And, suddenly, he doesn't feel so well and he goes outside—the space between cars? For fresh air, Doddie. And they think he just—well, they're not sure! Electrocuted. So handsome! You should see the picture."

"That's awful."

"And, Doddie, another race-car driver died. Not a very well known one—they all die the same way now. You see, they're very good at restraining their *bodies,* but they don't have anything that holds the *head* or the *neck,* so when they crash, they just go wild in there. Those cars are like little cages, Doddie! They gush blood from their mouths and noses like a fire hydrant. Terrible. The people who get to them first—a *horrible* thing. Because you see, Doddie, they keep that image in their heads for years. Just like water from a hydrant; that's how they all say it looks. In ten seconds you're completely emptied out." Before he could speak, she began to sing, a soft thread that tightened into steel wire. " 'Woodenhead Jones was uh-fat and uh-funny, dumber than sticks and stones . . . an' that's just why the kids all called him Woodenhead Puddin'-head Jones!' "

"—Mother?—"

" 'Teacher told his *mother* she would take him by the *hand—teach* him a thing or *two . . .* like his older *brother* he began to under-*stand,* he learned ev'ry-*thing* she ever *knew!'*—"

"Mother? Are you all right?"

The old nanny wrestled the phone away and assured him she just needed to be fed. Bluey shrieked like a zoo monkey, berating and mimicking Winter as she hung up.

<hr/>

Dodd asked the driver to take him to his office in Beverly Hills before going home.

When he passed through the lobby, the guard said his secretary was in. That wasn't unusual, even on a Sunday (though Dodd discouraged it). Frances-Leigh, a widow, didn't exactly need the extra income; even with the bears having raided the picnic, she still held some $7 million in Quincunx stock.

Her face fell when she saw him.

"What's wrong?" he asked.

"Marcie Millard just called. I'm not quite sure why she called *here,* on the weekend . . ."

"That's obvious—she didn't want to talk to anyone. What did she say?"

Frances-Leigh took a breath. "She said the Board said they weren't going to go ahead with the proposal. She said they made a decision to restore and rebuild and draw from city funds."

"When did they make that decision?"

"Well, they hadn't made it officially, but she said she'd spoken to three members over the weekend and they said that naming the school after you would be impossible—politically *and* legally—and that they were going to deal with everything on Wednesday. She sounded *very* upset."

"That's just so asinine—I mean, if that's the focus. It's just crazy. Because my name on that school has never been an issue."

"I told her that."

"I couldn't have made that clearer to Marcie *or* the Board."

"She said the Board was very flattered by your—your vision of—

your commitment—this is what she said—and they were going to call—
they wanted to talk to you about a sculpture garden—Marcie said *something* about a sculpture garden, her kids were screaming in the back and
I could hardly hear—a sculpture garden or maybe a fountain they were
thinking about having in front of the school, you know, as you go into
the main entrance . . ."

"We'll get the attorneys into it in the morning."

Frances-Leigh closed her lips in solidarity. She knew how much the
project meant to him; it had become his grand passion. And so *noble*—it
didn't seem fair. She rested her hand on the museum-board base of the
maquette.

A Frank Gehry–designed gallery space crowned the rooftop park like
an ecstatic, silvery wimple. Dodd's plan was to revolve paintings
through from his collection—Ruscha and Matisse in spring, van Gogh
and Fischl in summer, Rothko and Chardin in fall, Pollock and Rembrandt in winter—so that students could *live* amidst art instead of having to do the museum dance.

"Well, maybe it's not over—they'd be *crazy* not to build it, especially
with the economy in the shape it's in. They can't afford *not* to." She
wasn't even sure he was listening. "We still have a ton of options. We
could quietly bring it to the media . . . let public opinion decide."

"No," he said vigorously. "I'd get ripped a new asshole, pardon my
French. *Why isn't he doing this for the impoverished? Why is he lavishing
money on the already rich?*"

"Your record speaks for itself. The Quincunx educational fund has
already given away seventy million dollars in scholarships—"

"Oh, they don't care about that. Here's the better copy: BILLIONAIRE
BULLISH ON VANITY SHRINE FOR SPOILED BRATS. You know—the Xanadu angle.
Maybe I should just call it a Holocaust museum–*cum*–teaching institute—
that way *nobody'd* bitch! They'd greenlight it right away." He laughed,
then became mindful of his secretary; he didn't want to appear too bitter. "I appreciate your feelings, Frances-Leigh, but this was supposed to
be a very personal project. You know that's how I wanted it—from the
beginning. Check your egos at the door. That's why we needed to go
under the radar." He sighed, lightly tracing the arc of the nun's habit
with his finger. "Sometimes we live in a little world, filled with little people. And little people don't like big dreams."

She nodded, still feeling the affront. "It's just so disappointing. I mean, *people*. People are disappointing."

"A sculpture garden, huh. What a shame," he said with a droll little smile. And then he left, without taking a final look at the perfect mock-up of what the design team had discreetly labeled

DODD TROTTER MIDDLE SCHOOL

CHAPTER 42

An Epistolary Homecoming

Trinnie decided to stay in Rancho Mirage through New Year's, getting massaged six ways from Christmas Sunday. She asked Toulouse to come, but he declined. He wanted to be with the cousins.

What with Bluey's crucifixion and Marcus's resurrection, the holiday felt more like Easter anyway; family spirits were rather low. They stayed in town (everyone but Trinnie—who wasn't, in actual Trinnie terms, really *out* of town), which was highly unusual at year's end. The trauma of recent events put the dynasty on a kind of tornado watch. They hunkered down, ready to take to the cellars.

On yuletide morning, presents were exchanged at Olde CityWalk, with the most gold stars going to Lucy for her gift to her brother. During their summer hegira, the budding author picked up an exquisite weave of Mor Pakh cotton, rayon and peacock feather in Morocco and had prevailed upon Isaac Mizrahi (an old friend of her aunt's) to design a light-hearted caftan—which Edward adored on sight.

Among the *cadeaux* Lucille Rose was happy to receive in turn were a bouquet of pens (among them a spiderwebbed Montblanc Octavian and a saffron-colored Omas, which paid tribute to both Buddha and the Dalai Lama) and a Louis Vuitton writing-desk trunk bestowed by Edward, in the style of the original commissioned by Leopold Stokowski. Such tools may do a young writer no harm.

Toulouse was showered with his favorites—bunches of nineteenth-century ivory bananas carved in half-peel and eerie, delicate watercolor eye portraits set in stickpins (the preceding from Edward). Lucy offered bounty for his mother—part of such largesse being that her cousin was permitted to claim that he had selected them himself—that included a truffle shaver and a bamboo-handled sterling-silver fruit-and-flower cutter. But the most precious gift, at least as far as Lucy was concerned, she saved for last, and dramatically ushered him into the Black Lantern Book Shoppe to impart: standing under hastily rigged mistletoe, she gave him everything she had.

At around two o'clock, just as Pullman was opening his own spectacular goodies (including an old-fashioned milk bucket full of his favorite white truffles), Candelaria Monasterio clopped across the cobblestones to greet the merry gang. She told Toulouse that his grandfather had asked for him; Eulogio was waiting to drive him home.

Lucy wanted to know if he had something for Grandpa Lou. Toulouse shamefacedly admitted he hadn't. At her wise suggestion, and with her brother's wholehearted assent, he made the sacrifice and selected a stickpin with the painted eye of Napoleon's brother. It would do well for a dandified old man. The cunning Edward threw in a bottle of Sassicaia.

When he arrived at Saint-Cloud, the front door was open. Toulouse went in, calling for his grandfather—he knew Trinnie wouldn't be back for at least a week. He set down the gifts, and Pullman galloped into the yard.

The defining moments of our lives are usually so called in retrospect; they rarely arrive with the unmistakability of an Olympian entering a vast arena, torch held high, to the applause of thousands. The worn epigram of the power of journey over destination still holds—and held still at the first official meeting of father and son.

Marcus and Toulouse found themselves not six feet apart, in the grassy neutral zone between the descending marble steps of Saint-Cloud and a *tonnelle* of pear trees that led to the formal parterres. They shifted on their feet like shy dancers at a cotillion while Mr. Trotter, a damp towel placed to his neck like a compress, made the introductions.

Mr. Weiner had been told about the existence of the boy at a special afternoon briefing in Montecito; a full complement of therapists had been employed to shore up their client if need be, while a battery of men in suits waited in the wings. Even Harry and Ruth were there to lend support. The old man himself refreshed Marcus's memory of the wedding (over past weeks, his son-in-law had recalled much on his own that he hadn't yet shared); his rash leave-taking; how his wife had gone on to make the best life for herself and her son that she could. Mr. Trotter said Katrina was aware of his return but was not yet prepared to see him. When Marcus asked if she had ever filed for divorce, the same therapists who had presented a united front were at odds as to whether this was a healthy question, but the old man thought it absolutely on point.

What impressed the experts most (aside from his equanimity in the face of these formidable bulletins) was that the client's main concern appeared to be for his son's well-being. He wanted to know how much Toulouse had been told and was keenly interested in the boy's current emotional state and general response to his arrival on the scene. His patron said "it hadn't been easy for him"; at that Marcus gravely nodded his head, emitting the closest thing to a Trotterian chuff that those gathered had ever heard. During this session—a session in which even professionals dropped their defenses and became teary-eyed as the client, flanked by his parents, spoke elegantly of time lost and time never to be regained—Marcus pronounced the words *my Katy* for the first time in more than a decade (for that is what he had always called Katrina). Remarkably, he even commented on "that dreadful tower." But then he looked to the old man and said apologetically, "It was the most beautiful thing a father could ever have done for a daughter—I wish *I'd* been as beautiful for her."

Marcus asked after her health and was satisfied by what he was told. He wished to be given the boy's name, and smiled delicately upon hearing it. "Might I see him?" His patron said that was the purpose of this meeting; the time was nigh, and they were seeking his thoughts about a rendezvous. "Yes," he said, with a great sigh. "I'd very *much* like to see the boy." The old man wished to tell him he had already in effect met Toulouse during the trip to Boyle Heights, but the shrinks had thought better of it, cautiously theorizing that the client might misinterpret the child's adventure as backhanded or spurious. If, they said, when he met his son he recognized him from that trip (which seemed doubtful), well, that would be something else.

And so it was he'd come to Saint-Cloud seventy pounds lighter than in SeaShelter days. As said, the epigram still held, at least for Toulouse, who felt oddly let down and now understood his mother's reluctance toward reunion. After all, he was in *her* camp—he too had been abandoned.

A quick handshake—followed by an awkward span, which felt at least as long as the years his father had been away.

After an elision of chuffs, Mr. Trotter spoke up. "Well! I felt it best to just bring the two of you together."

The boy rocked uncomfortably on his feet.

"Do you go to school, son?" asked the stranger. He had rehearsed the opener for an hour or so.

"Yes."

"And where would that be?"

"Four Winds."

"Sorry?"

"It's called Four Winds," he said impatiently. "In Santa Monica."

"I see. That's where I stayed awhile—over by the freeway. And what do you study there?"

"All kinds of things."

Marcus solemnly nodded.

"Pull! Pullman!" Toulouse upbraided the dog, who was absurdly frolicking through the bushes; it irked his master no end that the Dane should be exhibiting such freakish sprightliness. A fresh torment.

"Large dog, he," said Marcus.

"Pullman!"

The disobedient leviathan finally cantered to his side and, with a single fart, laid himself down.

"Ho!" said Marcus, smiling at the dog as if awaiting another outburst.

"I really should go—I'm supposed to be with the cousins."

"Toulouse!" said Grandpa Lou sternly. "Talk with your father a little—"

"What should I say?" shot back the boy.

"It's all right," said Marcus. "Another time."

"You didn't even *see* me!" said Toulouse contemptuously. "I was in the Mauck, and you didn't even *see* me!"

"The Mauck?"

"The truck that took you to that grave," said Mr. Trotter.

Without missing a beat, Marcus said, "Of course I saw you."

"Bullshit!"

The old man restrained himself. He expected the waters to be a little choppy.

"I didn't mention it," Marcus went on coolly, "because I feared it was something you weren't glad about. Did you hide away? I did that once at your age—at the Huntington, in San Marino. Holed up in the library, clear through to the next morning. Scared all hell out of my parents."

"I'm gonna go," said Toulouse, flustered.

"All right, son."

He ran to the house, Pullman leaping ahead.

He heard his father shout after him, not without emotion, "I'm sorry, boy! I'm so sorry about everything!"

When Toulouse ran off, a somber mood washed over this stranger in a strange land—a wave of what philosophers have called ontological sadness. (A phrase that of itself can make one wistful.) He floated on that tide like a creepy jellyfish whose tentacles wished to caress but had only managed to sting the flesh of a small bodysurfing boy: *Toulouse* . . .

Toulouse!

That would be from the tattoo he got in Paris (he was hypo-manic at the time) after they first saw La Colonne Détruite—

It was still stretched across his shoulder, bleached by sun and hard times, a silly thing Katrina ill-advisedly took to heart after he fled the *other* tower, the Frankish one's better half, on Carcassone Way . . .

Toulouse: he would not have wished that for his son—a name born from a loser's pun—but so be it. Pay the piper. His mind caromed between wife and boy, and the old man let him be.

When his son-in-law vanished into the maze, Mr. Trotter had a nagging fear he would end his life somewhere within. Holding the towel-wrapped ice pack to his neck, he slowly climbed the steps that led to the house. Suddenly, Marcus burst from the boxwood asking for pen and paper, and watercolors, too, if they were to be had. Mr. Trotter enthusi-astically conducted him to the Withdrawing Room, where the visitor spent scant moments marveling at treasures before settling down to business.

During the next few hours, each time he was looked in upon, the man was hard at work. Candelaria brought food, which he barely touched. Around eight in the evening, he blotted what he'd made and requested a large envelope. He said he was tired and wished to be driven home.

"I want you to know how much I appreciate all you've done," Mar-cus said, standing at the Town Car. "Plucking me from prison and ar-ranging it so I could visit my dear Janey. You've looked after me, and I shan't forget it."

The old man couldn't help but wonder if he was saying good-bye.

"And bringing me together with the boy! That was sure a noble, risky thing and cannot have been easy. Bold! Can't say I would have done it myself."

Louis chuffed, stroking his chin. "He'll come around," he said. "The boy'll come around."

"I'd like that—I'd like it fine! But I'm not so sure. The unbreakable *does* break; I know it too well."

"I don't want you to be discouraged. I wouldn't want—"

"I left him once," said Marcus, as if reading his mind. "I shall not leave him again."

"Time," abbreviated the old man. "Time."

"You'll give the boy my package, then?" he said, proffering the enve-lope.

"Of course."

"Does—does she know I came today?"

"No."

"And will you tell her?"

He nodded. "I am going to tell her that I brought you here to meet your son."

Marcus sighed. "*When* you talk to her—to Katy—ask if I might write to her."

"I'm sure that would be fine."

"I would not like to presume. I imposed my absence on her; and don't wish to impose my comeback. But would you please, sir, mind just telling her that I wanted to put down some thoughts? And that I'd like to share them with her, if she's willing? And that it is not incumbent on her to respond?"

"Yes. I'll tell her."

"It is not incumbent on her . . ."

Words failed him and so they embraced—and any trepidations the old man had of having done the wrong thing by bringing him to Saint-Cloud dissolved as smoke into air.

*C*ull opened his eyes just before midnight. The air was stagnant and fetid; the wind of the dozing Dane was rank.

Life was strange. For most of the year, since learning that his father was alive, he'd been like someone convalescing after a blow to the head. And now that they had finally met, he felt no different from before he knew the man existed. He rummaged his brain for the few times he'd seen him: from a distance at the Hotel Bel-Air . . . crouching over a grave . . . wailing in the back of the Mauck . . . then pressing his flesh in the backyard of Saint-Cloud (the backyard!), and all of it seemed like a dream or—dare he say it—a *hallucination.* The very word struck fear in the heart of him. How many times in as many months had he awakened from troubled sleep to rev search engines for chat rooms and bulletin boards on the p-(key)word: "psychosis."

Edward, that paragon of cynical morbidity, had giddily helped fuel the theory that somewhere an errant gene-spore was already shooting tendrils into the plant box of Toulouse's brain. It was a concern he never mentioned, not to his shrink (whom he'd stopped seeing anyway), not to his mother (she was already crazy), not even to Pullman, to whom he dared tell everything. He had read somewhere that, like Apert, schizophrenia usually skipped generations . . . or maybe he just imagined having read that. Maybe he'd hallucinated it. A kind of pre-psychotic disposition—"prodromal," one of the websites called it—would even explain his blasé, somewhat irritated reaction to the man he shook hands with at the maze.

Toulouse wondered if he should begin taking medication. The therapist had had him on antidepressants, but he'd balked, because the pills made him dry-mouthed and nauseous. A kind of virtual shame engulfed him as he slipped through the Internet's cracks—the same morti-

fication he knew he would feel on becoming homeless. That seemed a
fait accompli . . . anyway, was there any real difference between what
had happened to Bluey and what had happened to his father?
Alzheimer's *and* schizophrenia were busy coursing through his veins! At
least his dad could be treated—or managed . . . *maybe.* He imagined himself in ten years living downtown in rags like those men he saw in boxes
when they visited Boulder. Lice in his hair, toothless, falling-down pants
smeared with shit, ready for a little recreational fecal-play. Sores on his
head from AIDS . . . scarred and scabbed from cop beatings, and a hundred broken-bottle scuffles. There would come Edward and Lucy in the
Mauck, all grown-up, searching. He'd be rescued just as Grandpa Lou had
rescued Marcus, and they would let him stay in Edward's long-vacant
rooms above the Boar's Head Inn—he would live out his days watching
movies at the Majestyk, tended by male nurses who'd suck his dick after
doping him up. But maybe the cousins *wouldn't* be so kind. Maybe they'd
by then have become Scientologists or militant throwbacks to the pre-
millennial concept of "tough love" and Toulouse would be farmed out to
an asylum. One of Uncle Dodd's empty asylums! Or maybe the Trotters
would build another wing where Bluey was and he could just hang with
his demented grandmother, both of them heavily sedated, walking arm
in arm on the infinity road that wended through the garden his by-then-
probably-even-more-famous mother had once designed—

The overheated boy decided to take a purgative dip in the pool when
he noticed the envelope that had been slid under the door some hours
before. He picked it up and read the elaborate scrawl: *For My Son.*

He was seriously spooked.

Was his father still there, on the grounds, in the house? Worse: was
he actually staying over? *No!* . . . the same panic he had felt while hiding
in the Mauck overtook him—as in a horror film, Marcus Weiner would
burst in and shake him to death like a newborn in the hands of a wigged-
out au pair. Shamed again, he ascribed his thoughts to the hysterical,
nay, *prodromal,* throes of incipient psychosis, until he was fully beside
himself once more—

He opened the door.

And stood in the hall, letting the quietude of the upper floors restore
his pulse to a reasonable rate. While there *was* a certain flamboyance in
bringing the man to Saint-Cloud, Toulouse was convinced it would have

been uncharacteristically reckless of his grandfather to have organized a sleepover—especially after his churlish response to the visitor's clumsy overtures. The gambit had been an unmitigated failure.

He closed the door and bolted it. He raced to bed, still nervously clutching the heavy leaf of stationery with the Trotter family crest. Upon it was an elegant, forthright cursive, beautifully engraved and colored in. He drew it to his nose and sniffed the damp paint, instantly becalmed.

Dearest son,

    I robbed myself of having known you—and this, along with having done harm to your mother's heart, has broken mine. But you must be assured that even should you choose not to know ME or speak with me again, and while I would be utterly respectful of your feelings, I shall never leave you and shall always honour you as my progeny; for you are a brave and wondrous boy—this I know without having been told. You have nothing to fear from me, for I have only the deepest and most abiding awe for a boy called Toulouse. Awe, and a father's kindest love!

                        Marcus

    PS: I have had it with the JINNAS; they will not take me away again. (Ask your grandfather about the latter; it is not a raving but rather a metaphor.) SALUD!

He had plenty to ponder on the ride back to Montecito.

A part of him wished to vanish again. In his mind, with only Jane Scull for companionship, he walked dark, faceless streets searching for cardboard to build a home. He saw them warmed by the blistering sidewalk fires of skid row as they made their way back to the bridge encampment, where they peacefully supped on all manner of discarded delicacies. Yet he knew he could never go back to such a life now, and would die before trying.

The boy! He believed—yes, he did—that it was the very *same* boy he had seen in the agency lobby some months back. They were, the both of them, staring at . . . William Morris! Marcus had turned to the child and remarked—no, inquired—why it was that there were no nameplates to identify the painted men. Why indeed! *That's* what this thicket of a wicked, ineffable life sorely needed: captions and nameplates.

As they rushed along the coast through the night air, moon roof open, he read the letter again, for the last time:

> My Darling Will—Her is the Booke you wantd me to Look after. And I have kild the man who did tern you in and also akuse you of Terible things that shold not be saed of anie personn. He saed you wold be Kild in jael and I had to reek Vengenke. He is the saem man who has taken me to Bed by Forse. I did this with him becos he Threaded you with Vengenke—he sae he kno you from downtow. But wen you were takken by the Poliec, it did not matter Any mor. Also, I am carieing a Chylde. I am sory to say it is not yurs. It is a Man what rapid me. But not the Man who I kild. I am telling Evry-thgn you now tho it Hurtts me so, Will! Becos yuou must kno! I am NTO a Hore. I am a good womon who have Terible Luch. I am lovin you So Muc now, Will! I have ridden this with out help from the Bu-tifull Gremar Book you gav me and wich I will hav ben Stuedyingy soon. I thot you mite lik to know that, Signned, Your Own Jane Scull.

> Ps. I hav bin told ttha in TWIN TOWWER JAIL, one of the TOWWERS JAILS is for Woman. So if you feele I shold Tern Mysel in for the Kiling, we cold vissit, If that is alowd.

> Pss. I hav left this note instedt of Seeing you and wantd too so muche. but I cuold not say these Things to yor face? and thot you wolde not Love me anymor. I hop I am wrong. Plaese rite bak soon.

> From Yor deerest friend, who loves You as a Wif. Jane

He told Eulogio to pull into a beachside lot. The driver hesitated; Marcus said he had to urinate. He stepped into the Santa Ana night, loud with ocean, and walked to the sand.

Suddenly fearing for his rider's safety, Eulogio chased after. "Where you going? Mr. Marcus! Where you going, please!"

He strode into the waves. As they rushed his calves, he tore the letter to pieces, scattering it to sea. He wanted to scatter himself with it, but no: he would not leave again. There were too many people he owed, living and dead.

At Montecito, another letter in the chain awaited. It lay on a bedside table and was from his wife.

CHAPTER 43

Words Alone

But O, sick children of the world,
Of all the many changing things
In dreary dancing past us whirled
To the cracked tune that Chronos sings
Words alone are certain good.

—W. B. Yeats

A FIRST LETTER

[Indian Wells]

Marcus—I hardly know where to begin. ~~I'm writing this for myself~~—I fled the holidays to a favorite desert spa but now I'm housesitting for a client who's in a balmier place. It's been done up rather Balinese, Rangooney(?) too, with Tabriz rugs, Tang-this and Ming-that. In the middle of it all—or should I say the front—the long low fascia trimmed in copper. Not very "me" but then that's probably a good thing.

Funny, but I have begun writing you, in my head anyhow, at least a hundred times in the last month but now the stars, literally, seem right. There's a mystic hair-raising wind peculiar to this corridor that shivers the soul—always a spur to confessionals. I'm seated at a white linen outdoor table beside a great black maw of golf course. A handsome young man in a rather frayed monkey suit just brought me a steak and (nonalcohol) martini—O God, suddenly I'm writing short stories again, trying to please the professors with an undergrad lyrical turn of phrase—

I can't care, or I'll never write a word. I don't even know who you are—but Father tells me you're making terrific progress and I'm happy for you because I can't imagine the horrors you've endured in your odyssey. I've had my share of agony and if I sometimes did not know or bother where I was, I always had the luxury (curse?) of money and a roof over my head. Maybe those things aren't so important after all; tho I don't wish to be presumptuous and romanticize what happened to you. That's always been my impulse, isn't it? I fight it still—finding the "Zen" bit in what for you was surely catastrophic. It was catastrophic for me too. Anyway, Father assured he's given over scant details to you of my life after we married; since I seem to know a bit about <u>yours</u>, it's only fair I attempt to enlighten.

I traveled quite a bit at first

(two hours later now) the morning you vanished, a part of me vanished too (oh, hideous cliché!). For a while, I naturally feared for your life, because the disappearance made no sense. How could it? Initially, we thought you'd been kidnapped—did Father tell you how certain he was he would be contacted for ransom? As for shell-shocked me, I retreated to the topmost room of that dreadful tower, all the while hating that we'd ever discovered the Colonne. Bluey finally pried me out. Doctors gave me pills for depression and pills for sleep; I didn't learn I was pregnant till ten weeks later (my period had stopped but I chalked that up to the general trauma—is this Too Much Information?) and all those enforced Rx's gave me a fright I'd done damage to our son . . .

Is this painful to read? Or do you feel nothing? Do you even remember who I am or what we had together? I ask not to wound you, but—truly, Marcus, I don't wish to make you suffer but I <u>must</u> talk aloud in the tribal sense and free myself from that castle aerie. What could be more painful than what has already happened? I'd like to try to impart the history of the years since you left, without malice—I have no "malicious intent." If my words are crude, forgive me. You were always the writer in the family.

My life became a "psychological" melodrama—I drew comfort telling myself you'd had a prescient glimpse of something awful, and you feared you might hurt me and <u>that</u> is why you went away . . . some dream you had that night of our wedding, that perhaps you saw yourself tossing me from the bloody tower; I was very Gothic!—~~had to tell myself you loved me that much.~~ I know now there was no real explanation and never will be; I've always detested people who search for motive. Your illness is a cunning one but as your progress attests, the miracles of modern medicine may finally be rooting it out

nothing to do all those years but kneel at the altar of your un-fathomable illness. I understood for the first time why my brother collects abandoned buildings—there's a purity and a longing for something frozen between what-once-was and what-will-never-be-again. That's what the tower became for me. I took to visiting it at night and still sometimes do (but haven't for months)—now I <u>do</u> tell too much! Always my flaw. <u>Your</u> flaw was that you resembled those in my tribe—the tribe that tells too much—when in fact you told too <u>little</u> or said nothing at all with your torrent of words.

It wasn't your fault . . .

I left L.A., <u>had</u> to, but where could I go? On top of everything, I was so embarrassed! The ego dies hard. I couldn't deal with talking to my society "friends" (all of whom flew in for the wedding)—because of my silence, some very <u>strange</u> rumors began to circulate about what had happened . . . drugs and satanic murders and what-have-you—I didn't want to know! It was quite the Hollywood scandale. I flew around the world, morning (and mourning) sick-ness in every time zone. <u>Absolutely crazed</u>—even retracing the footsteps of our Paris trip—at least I had the good sense not to re-visit the Colonne, for that would have finished me off—and wound up at the Plaza Athénée, literally back in our old suite, immobilized. Do you remember when I kept vigil there after your long walk to Versailles? Our son was born at La Croix Saint-Simon . . . I named him Toulouse—after your little joke. By then, the joke of my life seemed utterly cosmic . . . and there was something spritely about "Toulouse," something playful and musical and unburdening.

~~I knew I had to get him home because I was secretly planning to become Debra Winger from The Sheltering Sky and go wandering in the desert (somewhere a bit more exotic than where I am now) and get boffed by gorgeous nomads until I lost my mind. So I dropped off our Toulouse at Saint-Cloud and began my peregrina-tions . . .~~

I've scanned the above and see I'm babbling like an ass so I'll do the noble, foolish thing and give this to the driver to take to Montecito—tho I'd rather give it to one of those pigeons who specialize in airmail delivery. Feels like a message in a bottle. There I go mixing metaphors again. I do not wish you to answer this—it was not written to begin a correspondence. I don't mean that to sound passive-aggressive; you've probably had enough of "jargon"!

I will not read anything you write so please do not bother—I wrote this for <u>myself</u>. The worst part is, I know that if I was still seeing a therapist myself, he'd applaud me!

Wishing You the Best,
Katrina Trotter

A SECOND LETTER

Marcus,

<u>Please</u> discount what I wrote. Clearly, there is too much—and too little—to put in a letter. I feel now I was overwrought; there has been so much pent up in my mind. I shouldn't have sent it but it was too late to get back. The shrinks say that one is supposed to write those things then burn them, or put them in the mailbox with no address . . . how ~~typical of me to fuck it up.~~ There is really nothing that can be said. I <u>do</u> wish you well, and hope I did not stir anything up that will make things difficult for you; or any more difficult than they already are. I reiterate that was not my intention. I do, sincerely, wish you the best.

Katrina Trotter

A THIRD LETTER

M.—I feel my last entry did not say all I wished. I'm writing this final "installment" to say I am attached to you, not only through our son, but because I've spent so many years feeling your absence. I told Toulouse a lie—that you were dead—and in truth it was a half-lie, because you were all but dead to me, and to him. But in time he found out otherwise, as I suppose I knew he would, and set out to find you. He is an amazing boy. Marcus, if you feel you'd like to see him that is up to Toulouse and, of course, my father, to arrange. I would not stand in the way of that. So when I said I do not wish to see or hear from you, I didn't want you to draw the impression I was ruling over you or would hold back my son from visiting. That is not who I am or what I'm about.

I wanted to clarify this because I would not like to wake up one morning and be told you have gone again without seeing our son, if in fact a visit is something <u>he too</u> would like to have. If Toulouse wished to see you but did not because of an impression you got from one of my letters, I would never forgive myself.

I just wanted to make that clear, as I felt it wasn't from the previous correspondence. I hope you are continuing to make progress and remain well, and that nothing I have written is puzzling or upsetting to you.

It has been a great help to be able to write these things down and send them. Perhaps I have made a mistake. If indeed I have, then forgive me. I do not wish a response; I wish things were different, or that I felt differently, but I have long since moved on in my head and in my heart.

Sincerely,
Katrina

A FIRST LETTER

Dearest Katrina,

How kind your letters were, how kind and thoughtful, and how difficult it has been for me not to answer them; I have been mindful of your emotions, and of course, of the boy's, and feel a great pang of selfishness in now breaking my silence—but I must, just as you, put some things down! If this returns unopened, so be it; I will make the next entry to my journal instead, a notebook which I have kept for many years and entitled "News from Nowhere." Aptly named it is too, for that is the very strange place I resided all this live-long time. Until now.

I remember everything about you. While I appreciate your delicacy in referring to the powerful forces that conspired to have me living homelessly and somewhat deranged these past years, reading your words (which I have, over and over, in the wee hours of the night)—"Or do you feel nothing? Do you even remember who I am or what we had?"—has caused much sorrow. And I do not wish you had not written them. I encourage you—implore you—to set down, if you've a mind, every little miserable thing, to the end. It is a help rather than a hindrance. I stand on the prow of a ship now, in the head wind; each memory that slaps my face and stings my eye also revivifies, and makes me more human. I never felt that I lost my humanity in that other incarnation; but I did lose the one who was closest to me. I do not think it unwise you told the boy I was a goner; I might have done the same. What else could you have said? Please do not badger yourself over decisions and choices made in the wake of that upheaval.

In my travels, I met a wondrous dog named "Half Dead"—and so it was, as you wrote, that I had become. But Half Dead was a scrapper, and a good soul; I think I'm made of the same stuff.

Your father has been a godsend. He greets me without judgment, and I am moved by him—as I was moved by your courageous outpourings. I will understand if you do not choose to respond to my unsolicited phrases; be assured then, I will not bother you any more.

Your words about our son were sorely needed when they arrived. I thank you for them. You can be assured too that I will not impose myself on the boy, or badger him. I feel that I am here by the lights of some strange god, and will do nothing to fall from his graces. I hope I have not forever fallen from yours—and remain,

Marcus

A SECOND LETTER

Dear Katrina,

I hope I did not say anything to put you off; I mean, anything untoward or presumptuous. I've raked over the letter in my head and wish like hell I hadn't written "dearest" at the onset; it was improper to imply an intimacy I long ago forsook. There are other things I wish I hadn't said but I don't desire to make this a catalogue. I'm not even certain that my letter was read; perhaps it would be better for both of us that it wasn't. I do not mean to sound neurotic because that is not how I feel; I am merely mindful of not making false steps—I imagine that would be impossible! I waited a week or so before sending this out—I thought perhaps my first letter might be returned, and if not, that perhaps your father would have passed on a hint that any such correspondence from me was unwelcome. Which, of course, I would honor. But as I heard nothing, and received nothing back, I will humbly set down just a few short thoughts.

The medication I have been taking (thanks again to Louis) has worked wonders. Luckily, I am a fine candidate, neurologically, for such treatment. I have lost quite a bit of weight and am feeling rather fit. I don't mean to boast. My life has settled in here; I go to the sea with my "men," and often cook us lunch on the beach, which they invariably declare most saporific. (Do you remember the tall chef's hat you once gave me?) My mother and father have been to see me. They look old, and poor Harry had a stroke. But he is soldiering on—

This IS diabolically difficult. You were so right when you said there was "too much and too little" to put in a letter. My God. Do you know that you never left my thoughts, ~~Katy~~? Katrina? It is just that, in my disordered world, you had become someone else, someone called "Janey"—Jane Morris, the wife of William, that genius of English design. I cannot elaborate for now, for it is painful to set this down, because it is shaming; my illness is shaming and shameful. But the one thing I wished to say is that I never felt I would have harmed you. I do not have that in me. I am not wounded by your mentioning it; it seems a reasonable explanation for what you called an unfathomable thing. I have tried myself to piece together that night and that morning and the months that followed, but it is as if something ruptured. I only see colors and a drizzle before my eyes—and the Tower itself. I remember the Tower receding as I ran, like a giant struck dumb and immobilized. It was the TOWER, it seems, and not you, from which I was running. The Tower had become a conspirator—against us, and our happiness. The Tower had to be placated. It was such a beauteous thing; we are often trapped within wondrous designs, without explanation (the intricate patterns of Mr. Morris's tapestries being a felicitous example of this most unfelicitous condition). Even then, as I struggled in panic to escape, it loomed over me, gorgeous and well-made. I feel nothing for it now; should I be walked to that place this very hour, I am certain it would have no court or sway. It never was an icon of superstition for me, nor did it have a demonic voice—it simply became something that must be jettisoned, or it would have crushed the world. It is, as you said, unfathomable, and unfathomable to me now.

But I always thought of you, Katrina, and NEVER wished you harm nor thought I could be harm's instrument. I ask for your forbearance and forgiveness and will not write if that is what you so desire. And I would not leave again without the boy's "consent"; would not even dream of it. But it was wise and motherly for you to say what you did. I remain

Yours,
Marcus Weiner

A FOURTH LETTER

Saint-Cloud

Dear Marcus,

I thank you for your letters; and yes, of course, I read them. And yes, of course, I hesitated in responding, for a number of reasons—the primary being that I don't want to lead you on. Any exchange might somehow charge off, by itself and without warning, in a wrong direction. You are mending now and I would not wish to contribute to anything that deters from that. You must spend your time in exercise and meditation, not in composing letters to me—letters that, if I can be blunt—cannot lead to anything. Our thoughts, I think (and I am not sure I have many left!) would probably best be confined to personal diaries. No?

As said, I did not initially respond, because I didn't want you to get the wrong impression—that any kind of romance could be rekindled. If this sounds vain, then let it—I may as well be "up-front" and put all the cards on the table (forgive the cliché). For I am past all that, Marcus. Another reason for my hesitance was I'd hope that if it <u>did</u> come to pass that you saw Toulouse—that you were serious when you said "I would not leave without the boy's consent"—then I became suddenly fearful you might misinterpret my "interest" (i.e. any sort of correspondence) and <u>that</u> would become the driving influence on your decision to remain, at least for the time being, here in Los Angeles . . . or in our lives or however one wants to put it. "Waiting for the next letter," so to say. I know this might sound monstrously egocentric but I must speak my mind. I know you have affection for the boy but as you have not yet met him, he is still an abstract. He might better remain that. I am hoping that by making it VERY clear that I do not wish to pursue anything romantic—or anything really at all—that you will—if that is the main thing that was holding you here—that you will leave this city before seeing our son. In other words, I can't know your motivations, and while I <u>do</u> believe you're a good soul, and <u>always</u> believed that (and always will), I would not condemn or judge if you felt you should move on—cut your losses so to speak. Your seeing Toulouse cannot be contigent on something between us which is not (& I suppose was never) meant to be. I'm sorry to speak so crudely but I am protective of my son. If after reading this you <u>do</u> have a mind to leave then I implore you do so <u>before</u> seeing him. For what good would it do, other than to perversely appease a curiosity?

(It is a day-and-a-half later.) I let this sit awhile, because I felt a bit self-righteous upon finishing. I'll add this to it, rather than attempting to revise; I don't think I have it in me to revise anything anymore.

Perhaps I "spoke" too soon. If you <u>are</u> planning on going away ~~again~~ it might actually be a "far better thing" for you to actually meet with Toulouse, so you can (both) "get it out of your system." I don't want to be the Gestapo.

I suppose there aren't any rules, are there? So for me at this point to try and make them seems a little arrogant. I do not mean to sound all over the map, and am sorry for that. But I am

Sincerely,
Trinnie Trotter

A THIRD LETTER

Dear~~est~~ K,

First off, may I say how gladdened I am you took the time to read my letters, and also took time to so thoughtfully respond.

Secondly, your point on the "romantic" front is well-taken. Katrina, I think the world of you, but promise I do not harbor such ~~il-lusions~~ notions. You are to me—aside from being the mother of my son, which is itself a new and astonishing complication—like a friend with whom I once shared many things, turbulent and joyous, and with whom I have recently had the pleasure and good fortune to make reacquaintance.

As for the boy—I can't say they are forever dead but whatever demons drove me—well, they are so quiet or at least now so distant that I can't make them out against the general landscape. Perhaps they lie in wait, as on that long-ago morning; perhaps they've met their match in therapist's pharmacopia. But your point was, as usual, well-made, and well-taken.

I see the above was a bit unclear. What I meant to say was that the sirens do not call. Not anymore. And that I have not commingled your presence—the existence of you—with the boy's. And that my head is on straight about it.

[three hours later] Katy, I must now divulge something which it now seems clear you've not been told—I have met the boy. ~~I know that~~

[one hour later] If I have violated a confidence, so be it—it does me no good to part with information which my sponsor, my father-in-law if I may, might rather I had kept to myself. He never said as much, mind you, so I don't feel the complete opprobrium of betrayal; still, he has been so kind and I am uncomfortably shy in exposing him. But I fear if you WERE told—you may be in possession of such knowledge at this reading for all I know—if you WERE told and I did not mention this development, you might feel again wronged by me and have fuel for myriad resentments and suspicions. I do not wish such emotions to come between us. It has been difficult enough.

Katy, I do not know what goes on at this time between you and Louis; but I do believe that your father, for reasons which I shall put forth in a moment, must have had the very same thoughts as you regarding the urgency of a summit between Toulouse and myself, and so arranged a meeting on Christmas Day. (He had his own "intelligences" for believing the boy was in fact ready to see me, or ready as he might be.) An opportunity to meet him on home ground dovetailed with your absence; why he decided on Saint-Cloud I am uncertain. He had brought me there to show the maze, and we were then, I had been told, to move on to the Hotel Bel-Air for a rendezvous with our son. But then your father felt poorly and rubbed a bit at his neck as if something pained him so we stayed instead and cold tea was brought for him to drink and a wet towel to lay on like a poultice.

The most peculiar thing was that I had already "met" the boy without having known it (this is the "intelligence" of which I spoke). You see, I had a grievous chore to attend to and the vehicle called the Mawk was borrowed when our own broke down. When Toulouse found out I was to be onboard, he stowed away. It was such a sad errand for me, Katy, that I saw him but did not really notice, and thought he belonged to the the driver, Mr. Blade. In any case, I was certainly not introduced. When Louis learned of it, he said to himself what I imagine to be the very same thing you put to letter: well, that the two (or at least Toulouse) should "get it out of their systems."

Anyway, I won't go on much more just now—I'm only hoping THIS piece of intelligence, as dear Louis might say, finds you in a charitable, forgiving moment of your day. Lay the blame on me if you wish, for I can bear it, especially from you, but your father was not at fault. He is the best of men, with the best intentions. Katrina, forgive me! My words sound rife with patronization, but I'd rather be back on the streets, mindless and unhinged, if they were to be taken as such, which is the furthest from how they are meant!

Earnestly, and with
~~Devotion~~ Respect

MW

P.S. I recall that Louis was emphatic in voicing his desire that you should know that meeting took place; perhaps he has not yet found the right time to convey what transpired. I hope the time I found—and took—was not the wrong one.

A FOURTH LETTER

Katrina,

I understand your silence. In my fear you would sever contact, I selfishly failed to even mention how the meeting with ~~our son~~ Toulouse went. It did not go all that bad. I made inquiries of his schooling and while the boy was reticent to engage in much discussion, he was clearly not afraid, or intimidated. This, I know, does not sound valedictory or sanguine—but is relevant in that he might have heard many unfounded but terrifying rumors about his father.

I have not seen him since, though I long to. I am leaving it to Louis—and to you—and to the boy himself of course—to decide otherwise. I know that you desired to limit your correspondence with me and I don't wish it to seem I am enlisting you into some sort of contract where I await your delegations; this is so damn difficult, Katy.

I will leave you in peace and am sorry to have disturbed you but felt compelled to send this corollary.

May you have a Good Day,
Marcus

A FIFTH LETTER

January 24th
The Post Ranch Inn

Dear Marcus,

It is all right about you meeting Toulouse; how could it be otherwise? Didn't I suggest it in my letter? I <u>was</u> taken aback that it happened at Saint-Cloud, and accept your explanation (with some concern as to Father's health. I have since called his physicians). But I'm not sure why he had you there at all. I <u>do</u> respect your relationship with Louis and have not mentioned the "incident" for precisely that reason, though it is not my job to protect anyone. (It was one of the housekeepers who told me you were there.) Nor could your telling me have any repercussions; Dad might have half-understood you would pass it along to me anyway. He does know we ~~are~~ have corresponded. He isn't so petty—nor am I. It's just that I am not feeling very close to him at this moment. I would ask you though, for my sake, to decline any further invitations to Saint-Cloud; if you are to see Toulouse, I feel it should be on neutral ground. ~~Our son~~ He needs to feel safe in the house where he lives; by "safe," I mean, Toulouse needs to be secure there won't be any big surprises thrown at him there. Surely, you understand?

I am traveling and shall not be returning letters. It is probably best we break this off.

Wishing you the Best,
Trinnie

A FIFTH LETTER

February 10

Katy,

Thank you for your response, and of course, I will not revisit the house—as you wish. Thus far, a request for an encore has not been received! Not to worry.

And yes, sadly, I accede to your desire to end our exchange. I hope this will not prevent you from thinking well of me, and at least on occasion, too. I have a long road ahead to be sure. I am getting to know my parents again and will soon make the trip to Redlands. I am catching up on the historical goings-on of this country and the world since I went in abeyance—am finding the computers absolutely extraordinary. I've been shown how to play some astonishing games on the keyboard by the boys—around here we call them "the men in suits"—and am already whupping them, to their great chagrin. Have been to a few films in the Westwood Village (how that place has changed!). I've seen the most elaborate cartoons, where the characters look almost as real as people. They are also apparently made by the computers.

All told, I've lost nearly 80 pounds in the last 4 months—no mean feat, considering the side effects of the medication I am currently prescribed tend to seriously enhance one's avoirdupois . . . Soon I'll be wearing Louis's fancy hand-me-downs!

That was in jest—

I've taken to reading Variety and am staggered at the amount of money films now take in. And the venues! Three thousand theaters, all at once

I know I shan't "speak" to you, so am trying to cram much in . . . forgive my foolish mouth (and pen) while it tries, and fails, so valiantly to keep up with my heart. Please have a splendid journey, Katy, WHEREVER you may go! And may you be secure in the knowledge there are those who value your great, tremendous spirit and demand nothing of you—and so—and so

You have my everlasting admiration, support, and dare I say, Love. Please, know that I will always be

~~Your Hu~~
Your great good Friend,
Marcus Weiner

CHAPTER 44

Close to Home

You have been mine before,—
How long ago I may not know:
But just when at that swallow's soar
Your neck turned so,
Some veil did fall,—I knew it all of yore.

—*Dante Gabriel Rossetti*

*M*arcus put away his wife's letters but couldn't help think of her, especially while leafing through the garden of his Montecito home. Though Louis said his daughter had never set foot on the property, the husband felt her hand there nonetheless: in the purplish echinacea, magenta cosmos and—most powerfully—in the white bridal veil of *Dendrobium superbum.* He spent an inordinate time watching caterpillars fatten on parsley before attaining their samadhi posture, necks arc'd to twig, perfect yellow-green sarcophagi suspended by strands of silk. In time, the single wing of a black swallowtail previewed through a diaphanous cocoon; then out it came, lucky enough to have dodged the wasp.

He went around picking up snails as when he was a boy, gently provoking them to retract their gelatinous antennae. One of the suited men had shown him a magazine article about a certain parasite that began its life cycle beneath the shell of one of those curious creatures. When the host was eaten by a fish, the parasite sent a pulse through the fish's brain, commanding it to surface, thus increasing the odds of being plucked from the water by a gull. There was beauty, he thought, in being snatched heavenward from the deep blue sea. For so many years he'd marched to schizophrenia's viral drum—what was each living thing, he thought, if not a parasite of God? Now he was free; he'd been commanded to surface. A great bird was bearing him aloft.

One morning, Marcus had a dream that made him rush to the ocean for cleansing. He had conjured the tower—and Katrina on their wedding bed. He came in her and was still ejaculating when he woke up.

He went out far enough to make his chaperons briefly consider stripping for a rescue before he turned around and bodysurfed to shore like a doughy crate. As he strode from the heavy water, the Great Dane he had met at Saint-Cloud nearly knocked him over before taking a desultory romp in the foam. A small figure trudged tentatively forward, dappling the sand with its footprints. A suited man handed Marcus a towel as the boy approached.

"Hello!"

"Hello!"

"We went to the house. They said I could find you here."

"And they were right!"

The boy was staring at the tattooed heart that encircled his name. Marcus dipped down to give him a better look.

"Want to come in? The water's fine."

Toulouse hesitated.

"Not too cold today—are you a swimmer?"

"Mostly in pools. But I like to Boogie-board."

"Do you? We've got one right there!" He pointed to the fiberglass plank, stuck in the sand like a shark's fin.

Toulouse cracked a smile.

"Well come on, then!"

"But I don't have a suit—"

"You've got skivvies, don't you? *That*'ll do—there isn't a soul around! And these gentlemen," he ribbed, with a wink to his keepers, "well, they don't count!"

—————

"Oh my God, Edward, are they taking off their clothes?" She strained her eyes mightily. Lucy and her brother had stayed behind in the parking lot, where they sat in the buggy like tourists in a safari park.

"Incredible."

"*Edward*, let me *see*," she cried, grabbing at his binoculars.

She tugged again, but he was busy getting his magnified jollies; the fabric of the Mizrahi Christmas shroud bunched atop the lenses like a soft, thick cord. He relented his hold.

While Lucy adjusted focus, Sling Blade rolled up his trouser legs and blissfully ambled in the sand.

"Oh my God," said Lucy. "They're going in?"

"Yes," he said. "It's . . . beautiful."

Edward watched with naked eyes, transfixed, the veil held up by a gloved, sequined finger. He lowered the cloth, and on its way to his chin, the Moroccan weave blotted tears from his eyes.

The scene was primeval: the father, a large, pale mammal, with the jittery seed of his progeny floating near, ducked under the greenest crepuscular swell, the very air aglimmer from a drunk philanthropist sun who carelessly cast a trillion coins down. (You could see the milky wave's arterial underside.) Edward thought of his own father, Dodd, a man who'd been here all along—on Stradella Road—*not* a swimmer, and with whom he would never float in seas real or imagined. He envisioned the body of his grandfather on a bier, cast onto wavelets, lapping toward oblivion, then drifted back to the iroko tub where his mother bathed him—he could summon all the years spent soaking there—and closed his eyes, wondering how it might feel to be in the ocean with *her:* a baptizing and a going-away, bobbing in the deep with Toulouse and Marcus and Trinnie and Lucy—Pullie and Bluey and Grandpa Lou. Winter and the Monasterios . . .

"They're coming out!" cried Lucy.

Like bizarre cabana boys, a row of suited men held bath towels in readiness.

"Let's go to the Mauck," said Edward, who was himself just surfacing.

"But *why?* Don't you want to meet him?"

"Do you want them to see us gaping?" he snapped. "Jesus, Lucy, they've hardly met—allow them some dignity!"

Apprehending him stirred by forces larger than the ones at hand, she sheepishly trailed after while Edward steered the buggy to the ramp. It docked and was pneumatically lifted.

Holding a tidy package of dry clothing above his head as they descended the low dune that overlooked the lot, a shivering, towelwrapped Toulouse proposed a jaunt to Bel-Air. (The plan all along was to introduce Mr. Weiner to the peerless pleasures of Olde CityWalk. The cousins had wisely chosen a day when the in-laws were out of town.) Marcus enthusiastically agreed, begging the chance to first run home so he might make himself more presentable. It was exciting as hell to be courted by his son.

While Pullman leapt ahead, entering the MSV through the passenger side, Toulouse confessed to having brought his cousins and hoped Marcus didn't mind. The man proclaimed it a delight. Seconds later, the dear, inquisitive face of Lucille Rose hung like a small pink lantern beneath the Mauck's open wing, the long neck attached to a body still hidden in that amazing vehicle's recesses. Mr. Weiner caught a glimpse but was diverted by the arrival of Sling Blade, who threw his old acquaintance a cocky salute. Lucy had by then retreated—and Edward was nowhere to be seen.

The small convoy left the lot, with Marcus in the Town Car ahead. Edward busied himself in the lavatory while Toulouse gingerly removed the sand between his toes and quietly mused; he still tingled from the sea and from other things, too, and the corners of his eyes stung from salt.

Lucy could contain herself no more. "Well, what did you talk about?"

"Not too much. We mostly swam."

"Not in the water—on the way *back*."

"Not too much. He said he was glad to see me."

"Did he mention her?"

"Who."

"Trinnie!" she exclaimed, marveling, but not in a charmed way, at his laconic mien. "Your *mother*—"

"No."

He started in on the other foot, and she wanted to slap him. "Did you tell him about us?"

"What do you mean?"

"Does he know we're *here*? That we came with you?"

"He saw you, didn't he?" he said grumpily.

"I wasn't sure."

"I *told* him. He already knows all about you *anyway*. Your dad's fucking told him everything, I'm sure."

"Knowing about us is different from us just having invited ourselves along, OK? That could be construed as rude."

Edward clumsily exited the bathroom.

"What *I* want to find out," his sister continued, "is why he went to that cemetery in East L.A." She was convinced that a chapter—if not her whole book—hinged upon that particular puzzle's solution.

"Lucy," Edward interjected. "Would you please just stop?"

"Edward, why are you so angry with me? It's for my *book.*"

"Are you a writer or a journalist?"

"A writer," she said, with a mixture of pride and caution.

"Well, I'm not sure if you're either—but if you *think* you're a writer, then *act* like one. Some things are better left as mystery."

She sulked. "It's interesting, that's all. I mean, him going there. The possible reasons. Whatever."

They arrived in Montecito and waited while Marcus readied himself. One of the men in suits poked a head in to invite them for refreshments at the house; another bade them stretch their legs on the manicured grounds. Only Pullman took them up on their offers.

After an interlude, that very animal shot back to the Mauck from the outside world. At the same time, there were boomy voices and, without warning, Mr. Weiner clambered aboard, causing immediate discomfort and general paralysis. He was still an enormous man in many ways, but a superbly dressed one, and his face, slapped with fine aftershave, shone with health, wit and good tidings. He had the stubble of a beard on him and had come from the shower—his hair glowed too and the tousled locks tangled and stormed so that for the life of him he resembled Neptune on holiday—and he filled up the Mauck in such a way that it felt close to bursting.

Toulouse made introductions and his father shook hands all around, taking care not to pulverize any mitts. Edward was disarmed by the air of diffidence and politesse that accompanied this fellow freak of nature; and the trace of an English accent, threadbare yet aristocratic, along with the old-fashioned cadence of speech further lifted his sour mood. Lucy developed a crush on the spot, even larger than her erstwhile devotions to the detective—it would be fair to say that *all* the children had their crush, if one can call it that; for they felt like lost, weary travelers emerging from a jungle clearing to encounter a smiling tribal chief of legendary wisdom and largesse. However we may define it, Marcus reciprocated, and was happily crushed himself.

They gave him the captain's chair; he already knew its contours. He nestled in with an exhalation of comfort, and Sling Blade motored off.

The first cousin offered their celebrated guest sparkling water, and when he assented, Lucy scurried to the fridge. Toulouse took a crystal glass from a cabinet. After inordinate fussing with an ice bucket, two bottles of Perrier (deemed "flat" by Lucy's eagle eye) were discarded; when a third green vessel reached his prodigious palm, it looked like a dollhouse prop. He sipped and nodded approvingly—relief all around.

"Who's in the closet?" he finally asked. The children were confounded. "Do you mean to say no one's hiding in the closet? Scandalous!" He smiled—and the children smiled, then laughed—and felt completely at ease. It was like a merry tree-house club in there.

Marcus was grateful that his son had reached out, and was eager to be "sane" and accessible—which of course, for all intents and purposes, he now was. He was moved by Edward's fractured physique and the outlandish ways that he compensated for his lot in the world; the vestigial Victorian was particularly captivated by the ornamental intricacies of pattern-design and dye he'd availed himself of to be swathed from prying eyes. For his part, the cousin found Mr. Weiner to be unpretentiously imposing. In his presence, Edward felt like one of those bent trees that, managing to survive an eruption, is now forever in the good graces of the volcano gods.

When he democratically turned his attention toward Lucy and spoke of her book, she blushed, frowning at Toulouse for having said so much (when it was her own proud father who'd betrayed her). But the bearish magus distracted her by apotheosizing the Blue Maze—what an evocative title it was, how he'd already visited the one at Saint-Cloud and been duly impressed, what a fine centerpiece for a mystery it'd make, and so forth. He made her feel as if she were already on a bestseller's tour. His interest was piqued when Edward brought up the venerable Mr. Coate, a master "labyrinther" met on their globe-trotting sojourn.

Half an hour from Bel-Air, Marcus gave a tender précis of the lost years leading to his imprisonment and subsequent liberation at the hands of their grandfather, the estimable Louis Aherne Trotter. He was compelled to add that after the storm there came a glorious rainbow of trainers, dietitians and pill-pushers (for whom he had a more dignified name), the latter dispensing compounds which altered, in a subtle and marvelous way, the very chemistry of his brain—allowing him to take stock of his life and start anew. No mention was made of his estranged wife, and that was fine for all concerned. The children were relieved that Marcus Weiner knew enough not to throw open every door.

"Are you aware," asked Edward, "that we know Amaryllis? Amaryllis Kornfeld?"

Toulouse didn't seem thrilled to hear her name; he wasn't sure what might annoy his father (he would soon enough learn that little did) and was wary of upsetting the apple cart, such as it was—a very large cart indeed.

"Oh yes! I had been apprised of that by Mr. Dowling."

The detective had in fact been the first to enlighten Marcus to that curiously entwined history, even going so far as to suggest that it not be dwelled on in the case of an encounter with the children. Marcus grinned, adding nothing further—which again seemed a fine thing all around.

Candelaria had lunch waiting (a salad with pomegranate dressing, served in his honor), set upon a table smack in the cobblestone middle of the main thoroughfare of Olde CityWalk, and Marcus had a wonderful time with nephew, niece and son. But he could not relax, for his brow impulsively furrowed at the thought of sleeping in a box on a street less luxurious than this. With that spasmodic image came others, like falling dominoes: the orphan girl, and the guard who had come upon them in their hideout, and Janey too—and Fitz and Half Dead, and the kind baker Gilles—then last of all Katy, *his* Katy hovering for a millisecond before him: *I am traveling and shall not be returning letters. It is probably best we break this off.* He shook away the faces and felt some comfort that the children were not the wiser.

They popped corn and watched a movie at the Majestyk (Boulder's latest, yet to be released) but still Marcus couldn't enjoy himself, having now succumbed to the chaotic melancholy that had visited him earlier. The portraits—and feelings—returned with such force that he thought he might sob and frighten his hosts, ruining everything. So he was relieved when Candelaria half whispered to the boy that his mother had returned from New York and ordered him back to Saint-Cloud, pronto.

Marcus seized the opportunity to stroll into the light, where he took some restorative breaths and crouched beneath the theater's overhanging marquee.

Toulouse came out moments later. "It's OK—I don't have to go home."

"But your mother asked for you."

"That doesn't mean I have to go."

"You mightn't be so cavalier, Toulouse—if I may say it respectfully. She's your mother and has done the best she could. Always *has* done that very thing: her best. Loves you deeply, boy. Has done much more than I." The last said without a trace of self-pity.

He was not unaffected by his father's words, and appeared resigned. Just then Eulogio materialized, jangling his keys at Toulouse and grinning like an ass. Meanwhile, Sling Blade revved up the Mauck for the drive back to Montecito.

"Son—would you say adieu to your cousins for me? They're fine, fine children. That Edward is a heartbreaker! And Lucille—she'll make an exceptional authoress, she will: *big* brain on her. You value them, don't you, boy? They love you! They love you with everything they have, and that's rare. But you give it back to them, don't you? I know you do. You've a great gift that way. You've your mother's gift." He gathered his son to him, and Toulouse tucked his head into the brocaded vest. "I hope to see you again, son. I'm here now—I shan't leave you."

"Have you talked to Mother?"

"We've corresponded. But we have not seen each other."

"Is she—was she mad—was she *angry* with you . . ."

"She was civil. She was—kind." He bent on his knee to face the boy. "Thank you, Toulouse. Thank you for your courage, for coming to see me today. I am a very lucky man."

He kissed him on the cheek, and the child wiped a tear as Marcus climbed into the Mauck. Lucy saw this last bit of business but with uncharacteristic restraint did not rush to her cousin, who watched his father pull away, preferring to step discreetly backward into the fastness of the movie palace instead.

*R*ather than return to Santa Barbara straightaway, Marcus had a request. He knew (because the old man had told him) of the famed Louis Trotter funerary commission; just as he knew of the parcel in Westwood where his benefactor would eventually make his "digs." He was also aware that his driver was its general caretaker, and was curious about the place. But there was something more. Since the burial of Jane Scull, he had had a powerful, pointedly unmorbid desire to visit a graveyard, to loiter in a place twice removed from her tragedy, abstract enough to absorb his grief over all those lost to him.

At the moment Sling Blade was revealed by the ascending gull wing, Dot Campbell, in an outfit that worked much too hard to be called a leisure suit, charged at the errant employee, who had not even bothered this time to leave a scrap of paper behind explaining his absence. He took his scolding, then muttered the provenance of their guest; she was miraculously assuaged. The caretaker was then free to give Mr. Weiner a tour of the sanctuary, while his overlord graciously hung back.

Marcus spent a while pacing the grassy roof, so to speak, of the patriarch's "last house." When both roof and pacer had enough, Sling Blade vainly suggested that they examine the stones of various celebs; yet even Dorothy Stratten held insufficient allure. As a kind of consolation, his guide walked them to the furthermost real estate Joyce had purchased under Candlelighters' aegis; then swore his guest to secrecy before divulging Mrs. Trotter's mission. He held Mr. Weiner in thrall while weaving the peculiar tale of dumpster babies, identities unknown.

Marcus winced at the irony—if he would not come to potter's field, potter's field would come to him.

"Did you see your father?"

"Yeah."

"Is he well?"

"He's all right."

"Did he say anything . . . weird?"

"No," he said, displeased by her comment.

"Don't get defensive," she said, a little ruffled. "I guess it *is* pretty romantic—having a father return from the urban wild. The mental outback. I can't compete with that."

"I didn't realize there was a competition," he said frigidly. Silence, then: "Have *you* talked to him?"

He'd heard his father's side and now wanted to hear hers.

"He wrote some letters—strange but sweet. I thought it best not to continue. It didn't seem healthy."

"He's trying really hard. The pills seem to be working."

"Good. Good for him." She lit a cigarette and took the deepest inhalation he'd ever seen.

"You're smoking again."

"Toulouse, I just want you to be careful. You're a big boy and he *is* your father . . . But we're not talking about someone who has something that's necessarily *curable.* I don't want to see you hurt. Any more than you've been already."

"I'm OK."

"You're OK *now.* The disease that your father has—is not something you can *predict.* There are relapses. And whatevers. And I just don't want you to have false hopes. But you do what you like . . . And I'm *not* saying seeing him is wrong—I don't want to give you a double message, which I guess is what I'm doing. It's just that . . . we don't know if he'll be here when we wake up."

"Will *you?*" Her jaw tightened. "You've been traveling a lot lately. And you're smoking again."

"You're *not* my jailer. Look," she said contritely. "I didn't even want to talk to you about any of this." She took another long, fidgety drag. "And that girl is staying with a social worker."

"Girl?—"

"The *girl,*" she said, rolling her eyes. "Amaryllis. The woman gave me her e-mail, if you want to write."

CHAPTER 45

Termination of Parental Rights

ull added lanimottCASA@hotmail.com to his computer's address book but went no further. He didn't even tell the cousins.
His birthday was at the end of the month, and he toyed with the idea of
inviting her, as a surprise. The appearance of his father in his life had
only heightened his desire to "do right" by Amaryllis; it seemed capricious and immoral to leave her behind like so much memory roadkill. He
was glad he had set her rediscovery into motion. But words and courage
would not come, and he let a week pass before sending the following:

> From: "Toulouse Trotter" <harlequinboy@home.com>
> To: "Amaryllis" <lanimottCASA@hotmail.com>
> Subject: No Subject
>
> to whom it may concern,
>
> is this the home of amaryllis kornfeld? i was given this e-address
> by my mother, katrina trotter. i believe she spoke personally to
> whoever is on the other end. my name is toulouse trotter and
> amaryllis is a friend.
>
> is she currently living there? thank you

Lani was charmed but a little nervous about passing the message on.

Not long ago, Detective Dowling, in his steadfast role of liaison, had called to give the most amazing account of her foster daughter's high-end layover in the Westside world. Lani, needless to say, was thunderstruck by Amaryllis's society connections. But the new mother, still very much finding her way with her fragile, complicated ward, was initially hesitant to help the children connect the dots.[†]

But how, one may wonder, did the orphan effect her transition to the Motts' comfy Franklin Hills home? Here, for once, the author will make a long story short.

It has already been noted that the idea of adoption formed early in the head of the baker's wife, as a consequence of her dressing-down by the man who once went by the name of William; she had begun the three-month foster-care-licensing process forthwith. As a CASA, Lani already had an inside track, and her supervisor helped her through the rough patches. Soon after accreditation, a "walk-on hearing" was arranged whereby notice was given to the Department regarding the request for immediate placement of the child, Amaryllis Kornfeld, with foster parents, namely Gilles and Lani Karoubian-Mott, who were, as interested parties both formally and informally attested, loving and caring professionals, not to mention college grads. The court agreed to release the child to the Mott household pending the longer process of adoption,

---

[†]Once Trinnie had decided to aid her son, Detective Dowling contacted the Motts (who had not let up in asking after Marcus anyway) and laid the whole astonishing thing out: how, *independent* of aka William, the street-savvy waif had insinuated herself into the bosom of the Trotter clan. That was a mind-blower. Lani subsequently had a lively conversation with Katrina Berenice Trotter, who was funny, easygoing and acerbic. (By the time they spoke, the CASA extraordinaire had supplemented her working knowledge of the famous family with numerous Internet forays.) When Lani discreetly referred to the almost supernatural far-fetchedness of Marcus and Amaryllis's skid-row alliance—without mentioning anything relating to his incarceration—Trinnie said indeed it *was* a weird thing, but her voice was flat and distracted and she made a dry cliché about life sometimes being stranger than fiction. Yet before they got off the phone, Trinnie had warmed to the topic. She said she'd debated about putting the kids in touch at all, then decided it would be unfair to be censorious. They were *good* kids, she said, and without having met her "Tull," Lani wholeheartedly agreed. Toulouse—his "full" name, the mom explained—had intermittently spoken of Amaryllis for months, but Trinnie said that until rather recently, the adults were of a mind that there had been enough excitement surrounding the girl already. So at first, she wasn't eager to reward the delinquent clique's behavior by tying their special friend to Marcus Weiner in nearly cosmic fashion. Things were different now, she said. They had stabilized; months had passed, and the phantasmagoric aspect of it had diminished. Everyone seemed to be getting on with their lives.

which would likely remain uncontested and be expedited by public counsel.

With a doctor's close supervision, Lani weaned Amaryllis off the residual drugs prescribed during her final stint at MacLaren and reestablished regular visits with the girl's brother and sister, who lived in a modest home overshadowed by tall electrical towers (the kind favored in fifties alien-invasion flicks) in the city of Lawndale. Amaryllis was enrolled in a progressive district school and in short time won kudos for her special project on saints, with its gold-flecked illuminated text, laminated articles on Sister Benedicta née Edith Stein and an ingeniously imagined diorama of the inner sanctum of the Vatican's Congregation for the Causes of Saints. She made new friends and, aside from the occasional tantrum and teacher-bidden time-out, her recovery was remarkably swift. After school, Amaryllis liked to sit on a stone pillar of the Shakespeare Bridge, overlooking a gully filled with quaint houses. (A generously proportioned lady hanging clothes on the line invariably reminded her of Jane Scull.)

As it happened, Lani and Gilles had tried for several months to stage a reunion between themselves and Marcus Weiner but were stonewalled by his attorneys. Said counsel, protective of their client's recovery, to say the least, could not have cared less about personal relationships formed during that particular era of Mr. Weiner's troubled life. Phone calls to Detective Dowling went unreturned in kind, though in all fairness Samson was swamped by cases old and new, and found nothing pressing about the resolute couple's nostalgic urges. At Montecito, Marcus had asked after the baker (and Amaryllis too), but the detective was chary about starting an egg hunt; there was enough omelette on his old friend's plate as it was. He *did* go so far as to discuss the matter with Mr. Trotter, who thoughtfully turned things over to the crack psychotherapeutic team. It was their continued and vaunted opinion that the patient should remain focused on reconstructing his life via insights attained through examination of childhood events—the memories of which were now surfacing nicely—and that it would be premature and counterproductive to revisit street bonds formed while in full delusion.

After a series of long talks with her husband, Lani finally caved. When she handed over Toulouse's e-mail address, Amaryllis nearly fainted. The child instantly set to composing a trial response in longhand but found the composition as difficult as her suitor had, and as torturous too, for both possessed an elastic sense of time and keenly believed that every minute that passed without them somehow communicating exponentially decreased the chance they would ever see each other again. (So it goes with the very young.) Fortunately, girls are bolder; Amaryllis wrote everything out by suppertime, and her foster mother agreed to let her sit before the keyboard in privacy—though not before a forthright discussion about Master Trotter and his cousins, whose rescue efforts, she reminded, certainly helped in the short term but had had more dubious results as her respite stretched on. For Lani, the bottom line was that Bel-Air was a seductive place, but "you've got to keep it real." She borrowed that phrase from Trinnie, who had dropped it during their chat.

We will not divulge the content of that first e-mail offering or summarize Toulouse's reply, nor hers after that, nor his that followed—what soon became a deliriously ungrammatical outpouring of gossip, jokes and sweet nothings. But all those nothings added up, and Lani soon curfewed her use of the iMac.

*T*he sudden death of Edward Trotter obliterated upcoming birthday festivities and cast an apocalyptic pall over both Bel-Air houses.

The body was found by a gardener on a far-side Stradella path, leaning on the seat of the buggy that, without fanfare, had lumbered into a stand of hawthorn. Doctor and nurse reached him within minutes but were of no use. Dodd was 45,000 feet in the air when informed; Joyce had to be hospitalized for two days, for she could not catch her breath. Trinnie was at her best during such adversity and would not allow herself to feel the loss, because there were myriad details to which no one else possessed the sobriety to attend. Assured by her steeliness, the old man retreated to the Withdrawing Room in private grief. Bluey, of course, would not be told.

When Toulouse first saw Lucy after the event, she embraced him, then broke away and screamed. She ran off, and he took after her—they fell to the ground and locked on to each other, breath fetid, as if the caverns of their mouths held Edward's beating heart. Pullman yelped and groaned and for two days was seen near the Boar's Head Inn retching like a drunk.

The two cousins would not leave each other's side, and grew giddy with the endless looping catharsis of horror and tears: they kissed hotly and deeply, laughing and sobbing in between, plumbing each other's depths for their beloved boy. Adults came and went. Lucy and Toulouse hid awhile in the coolness of the Majestyk—they could not yet bear to enter the workshop, with its masks and cowls and bolts of fabric, let alone Edward's apartments, which they felt should be decreed sacred ground and fenced in like La Colonne. Who would ever have the courage to go up there? Trinnie would, of course (and found a sheaf of papers in the bedroom whose striking contents will shortly be disclosed).

When she stepped from the Inn, the children huddled expectantly, as if she might tell them it was all a mistake; that Edward was resting comfortably in a toile caftan. Instead, she glided forward and held out her arms, which they took to like lost babes and promptly began another round of tremors and tears, the crowns of their heads now smacked by the salty droplets of Trinnie's own. All she said was, "I know, I know," and she really did—she knew, and they were glad—*everyone* was glad—that she knew and that she was there.

The cousins spent the next few days watching grown-ups emerge from the house to embrace or smoke or chat among themselves in low tones, or merely to meditate. First would come Dodd, with Trinnie, who held him; then Epitacio and kin, respectfully scurrying on this or that errand; and Grandpa Lou, with private sector–types, whom they did not recognize. Still others—old money and vanished new new money (and just plain money too); fashion mavens and designers who had loved Edward so; a cadre of their grandfather's funerary architects (Mr. Koolhaas included); sundry politicians; imperishable icons (Bluey's dear friend Rosamond Bernier), socialites and blue bloods—famous of themselves who went mostly unrecognized too.

One time they even saw Joyce. She was hugging Trinnie, and while they thought it unnatural, they were glad nonetheless, for she didn't look at all well. She was led back to the house by poor Winter, who, since the death, had been shuttling between Saint-Cloud and Alzheimer's World, and whom the children had never seen demonstrate such quintessentially Icelandic reserve. Ushered into the darkness of the tomb-like master bedroom, Lucy visited with her mother ten minutes at a time. Few words were spoken and a uniformed nurse was always present, tucked into a shadowy niche like some kind of low-caste devil.

There was some trouble over the funeral. The papers Trinnie found in Edward's apartments were copies of those in the packet he'd given his grandfather months before: etchings and photo montages of memorials, ancient and modern. But there was something else—a letter addressed to his aunt. For a change of heart had taken place in the time since he first made his desires known to the old man.

During long baths, mother and son spoke of many things. Joyce told him how she had bought land in Westwood for the abandoned babies, an incursive notion that suddenly appealed to Edward immensely, but for reasons other than charitableness. He thought there was something gorgeously heretical about it; he had found his new "gang." His grandfather, he reasoned (and all this he carefully set down in the letter TO MY AUNTIE), would be injured by his decision, yet still he'd forever be just a stone's throw away, so to speak, from that kindly old digger . . . It was the perfect *anonymity* of it that had enraptured him and bloomed during his ablutions; he, who had always been stared at and singled out, in wealth and infirmity—he, who had been surrounded by untold riches, would now make his home in the unglamorous swales of the park's Siberia, surrounded by unnamed discards—the very ones he used to mock!

The unfortunate task of disclosing his wishes to the old man fell naturally to Trinnie. He shot the messenger, then reloaded, initially appalled that his daughter-in-law had sneakily purchased mass graves in the very spot it had taken him years to select. It was hostile and underhanded—but worse than that, it *contaminated* . . . she had connivingly hauled her cut-rate bleeding heart onto *his* domain and now would ask him to soak himself in its tainted fluids as they leached down into the very earth intended to encoffin him, and he would not have it! And that her *son*—his *grandson,* a *Trotter,* and the noblest of the lot—would be buried alongside the murdered children of addicts and criminals, born of rotten wombs! Hadn't the boy come to him with a plan not long ago? He had said that he wished to be interred somewhere beauteous, beside his grandpa—those were *his* words, *his* instincts. TO MY AUNTIE be damned! It was obvious he'd been unduly influenced . . . but why? Why would she want that for him? Some born-again conversion? Was it possibly true she could *be* such a crazy cunt? Who was she but a spinster—a non-executive secretary at Trotter Waste Systems—and a shitty one at that—a tired, dried-out fuck who had preyed upon his son and made a lucky last-ditch marriage. He would see her in court! At any rate, the boy was still a minor and such an "instrument" could be superseded. He paced the Withdrawing Room like a wounded bull. He had loved that child . . . he had made a promise to him, and would keep it!

In their agony, neither party would relent. Joyce descended on her husband, who diplomatically remained neutral. *Does your father think that we're making this up?* They'd shown him the letter—tantamount to a last will and testament, it could not be ignored. Did he really imagine that because of his own narcissistic obsession with the "aesthetics" of death she would fly in the face of her son's final wishes? Did he think she was one of his toadies? That she would capitulate? Was he so arrogant to assume that she had had no discourse with her son, *her* son, no quiet intimacies wherein he confessed his desires? He had even dared throw at her the circumstances of the difficult birth and her "selfish sequestration"—how cruel of him, how merciless! It only strengthened her resolve. Weeks ago, when Edward shared his plan, she had brought Dodd in on it; now he had told his father as much, but the old asshole only spat and raged. You are simply siding with your wife! he said. During a fiasco of a "mediation," Father de Kooning predictably made no headway; and Mr. Trotter warned the by now co-dependent chorus of Montecito therapists not to come near him. (On a drive to Woodland Hills, Dodd hatched a bizarre peacekeeping compromise: the boy would be cremated and kept in a fourth-century Scythian vase in the lobby of the Majestyk. It was good he kept the brainstorm to himself.)

Word of the passing found Marcus much aggrieved. He phoned his son to say how sorry he was, and Toulouse cried, softly thanking him. He asked if he was coming to the service. Marcus said he'd very much like to, but feared it would make his mother uncomfortable; this wasn't the time for additional drama. The boy understood, appreciating his sensitivities in the matter. Marcus said, *"Bon courage,"* and hung up.

The funeral, held on what was perhaps the dreariest Sunday in the history of the basin if not the world, was a horrific affair. Such was their fervor that the mourners threatened at any given moment to break out in mass insanity, as in storied incidents of villages poisoned by ergot-laced water. The park was ringed by bodyguards, for there was a large contingent of press (he had been, after all, a royal son) and principals wore swatches of fabric, torn from Edward's shrouds, pinned to their clothes in the manner of Orthodox Jews. Even Pullman wore a papier-mâché mask contrived by Lucy and Toulouse to sit on his shoulders so that it devoutly faced the sky. Dot Campbell's skirt, blouse and coat were poignantly mismatched; Sling Blade wore a suit, his first ever, purchased for the occasion. It was also a first for Dot to see a zoned-out look in the haggard caretaker's eye, as if he had finally had enough of death. He drove the Mauck to the cemetery as per Dodd's instructions, and lowered the buggy from its berth; once grounded, it sat like an otherworldly catafalque. The sight of it sent a fresh wave of despair through those gathered.

Joyce, in lenses dark as obsidian, was supported on one side by Dodd and on the other by Trinnie (appropriately Edwardian, in a high-collared Branquinho waistcoat), with Father de Kooning and the vigilant Candelaria in tow. She sporadically stopped sobbing to aver, as if in the middle of a daymare, "I never named him! I named the babies—but never him!"—spectacularly moving and bathetic at once. She wore Prada, except for the distinctive veil that fell on her face: a favorite of Edward's, it was inelegantly poised and made for a grotesquely comic effect. A row of votive Candlelighters stood close to the parcel where Edward would be laid, while the lesbians from the Palisades hovered nearby, perturbed and guilt-stricken, as if all this might have been avoided if the Lord had taken their boy instead. (Fortunately, the son of Jane Scull was on his best behavior throughout the ceremonies, although, upon her catching sight of the bundle she had dubbed Lazarus, the same could not be said of Mrs. Trotter.) Then Winter's heel broke and she fell with a thud; Frances-Leigh, and two from the deceased's Olde CityWalk health-care team rushed to her aid, but Epitacio and his brother adroitly won out. She rubbed her ankle and smiled as they helped her stand, and spent the remainder of the event partly unshod, anchored by the somber, handsome brothers.

Louis Trotter, incensed and betrayed, did not attend; he was the digger after all, and had that in him. He would visit his grandson another time, away from the circus, and let a moment pass before contemplating legal action to move the boy to more hallowed ground. He visited Bluey instead, who was in fine form, and sat with her on a bench along the path of the wandering garden.

The Weiners stood a respectful distance off until Trinnie waved them closer. Ruth helped Harry navigate the gravestones and he kept reaching for his yarmulke, which, ill-clipped, threatened to tumble from his head. Detective Dowling passed Lucy and Toulouse—he smiled at the girl, and her face lit up through her sorrow—and Trinnie greeted him warmly. When she embraced Ralph Mirdling, who had come to pay respects with his friend Ron Bass, Samson stepped back and stared contemplatively at the ground. He was going to say hello to Dodd but would have to wait, for the billionaire was consumed with ministering to his wife.

There were photo flashes as Diane Keaton walked through the gate on the arm of John Burnham (she and Ralph were still seeing each other but had decided to arrive separately), and it was only a coincidence that Boulder Langon and her mother arrived just after. The starlet gave the wannest of smiles to the paparazzi before hurrying along to join the group from Four Winds—Mr. Hookstratten, his lanky friend Reed and the teachers and nurses and flight crew from the world tour. All the globe-trotting kids were there, too, shocked and shivering, deflowered by death.

Trinnie stoically held the hands of son and niece, and, as the casket was lowered, at last began to fall apart. When she saw them watching her, she smiled like a valiant dying superhero: "He loved you," she said. "He so loved you!"

While his mother gently released the warm water of a sea sponge over his spindly chest, Edward used to speak of the potter's field his cousin visited that famed stowaway afternoon. Toulouse had told him the plaques were inscribed with years instead of names—that's what Edward said *he* wanted. But she couldn't bear to listen—and could not bear it *now*, could not bear to have him in the earth without his name as a marker. She had violated her son's request and begged his forgiveness. Joyce felt a bottomless pang of loneliness for him, but soon there would be others crowding around—the "gang." She knew how sardonic yet welcoming he would be. He would disperse their fears like doves into the air, and call them by their new names.

The first clump of earth was shoveled in.

*　　*　　*

*A*fter the funeral, a large reception was held on Stradella. Cavernous tents were pitched over heroic amounts of food, and visitors—some, there for the first time, marveling at the cobblestoned village—filed through the Boar's Head to admire the masks Edward had created and the tidy rows of those he'd been crafting at the time of his death. (Candelaria and her elves had made the place spotless.) Ordinarily, such trespass would be anathema, but Lucy and Toulouse felt expansive as the crowds ogled deferentially; they stood to the side like proud curators, their burden for the moment lightened as it was shared.

Trinnie accepted a number of hugs, then pleaded exhaustion and told her son she was going home. Now her grief arrived, borne aloft by the pallbearers of her relatively young life's every regretful moment. Our stay on earth was suddenly exposed as tenuous at best, and of exceeding short term—what if it had been Toulouse they were busy burying? She shuddered at the ease with which the image came. She was perverse; she had no regard for the sanctity of this world or any other; she was a wastrel who ruined everything she touched. Marcus had an excuse! He had myth and pathology on his side—and yet, there he was doing the brave thing, battling his demons, bloody and unbowed. For her, it was business as usual: still playing in the garden and flirting with disaster. Edward was stone-dead and now, on top of everything, Toulouse must factor *that* in, his fragile worldview further rocked. At least he had the role model of his father, a father at war, kind and courtly, fervid, mysterious, brimming with remorse and amends—real amends—back from a hell ten thousand times worse than any of the self-pitying, insipidly pornographic soap operas this brassy golden girl's rehabs had ever provided. There *she* was, a twat ingenue who could only be counted on to pick up her toys and vanish, and who dared feel justified because that's what *he*, Marcus, husband and eternal old flame, had done . . . done to *her.*

The men in suits waved Trinnie through. She saw him right away, stepping from the Town Car; he must have arrived only moments before. Dressed in dark navy, with a great shock of hair and a week's growth of beard, he wore a recherché vulnerability that drew her in.

"Excuse me," she said. "I'm looking for Marcus Weiner."

Startled by this roan-headed woman (handsome and exotic to him as well) and unable to put the pieces together, he said, with a smile both broad and nervous, "I am Marcus Weiner."

"It's Trinnie."

He still looked perplexed, so she held out her hand.

"Katrina Trotter. We were once married."

CHAPTER 46

Forgotten Prayers

"This is so strange!"

"Yes."

"Your letters were nice."

"It was difficult—to know what to say."

"It's difficult *now.*"

"Yes!"

They sat under a pergola near—appropriately enough—the "Tête-à-Tête" Narcissi.

"So: you were William Morris."

"Yes."

"It's funny—not funny but odd."

"It *is* funny."

"It *is.* And kind of fascinating."

"He *was* an interesting man. He and his circle."

"You already knew a lot about him."

"Yes."

"From when you were at Oxford."

"Yes indeed."

"He went to Oxford, too, no?"

"Yes. And I learned a good deal more—I mean, through the years. Firsthand! So to speak."

"You were always making jokes about 'the two Williams.' When you were an agent."

"The joke was on me, I'm afraid."

He smiled disarmingly while she laughed. "You've got a bit of an accent there."

"They tell me it's fading."

"I like it. I mean, it's not too bad on you." She took cigarettes from her purse. "Mind if I smoke?"

"Not at all!"

"Do you know who has a lot of Morris pieces? Andrew Lloyd Webber, the composer. He did *Evita* and *Cats.*"

"Oh yes."

"He's a tremendous collector of the Pre-Raphaelites."

"Is he?"

Marcus seemed quite thrilled, which he actually was, but more because this woman was finally in front of his eyes. Though he did not yet know what that meant.

"Oh yes. I did one of his gardens, in London."

"*Really.* Whereabouts?"

"Belgravia. He's got Burne-Jones tapestries—"

"My, my!"

"And portraits of Jane, Morris's wife—"

"Jane Burden."

"Well, of course you know who Jane is," she said, chastising herself. "He's got a portrait of her by Rossetti."

"Now, *there* was a character. A wicked, wonderful character, Rossetti. Loved the low life, that one. Took tremendous walks—like Dickens that way."

A pause wherein it was tacitly acknowledged that Marcus was a well-known—or at least inveterate—walker himself.

"How do you find Santa Barbara?"

"Very tranquil. The beach is lovely—a tonic. Though part of me misses the city, vile as it's become."

"The bustle."

The bustle, he concurred. They fell silent again.

"Are you hungry?" he asked. "I can cook something."

"No thank you. I'm not sure how long I—how long I should stay. The children—"

"Of course."

"And Joyce isn't well."

Pause.

"What a horrible, terrible thing. Someone so gifted and so young."

"Toulouse said you met him—Edward."

"He came up with his sister when the boy and I had a swim in the ocean. We all rode back together to the house on Stradella. He was a bit introverted, Edward—I drew him out. And now it feels like he may have had a . . . foreshadowing. He seemed to be very special that way."

"He was an *extraordinary* boy."

Her voice was beginning to lilt and dip like a bird on wing; it was contagious.

"And how is our—how is Toulouse bearing up?"

"All right, I think. Thank God he and Lucy have each other."

"A marvelous girl, that. So perspicacious."

"Neither has experienced a death before. With you . . . it was different. I told Toulouse from an early age—" She stopped herself, not wishing to repeat what she'd already written in a letter. Besides, it was gauche.

"I'm so sorry about all of it, Trinnie." He amended himself by saying, "Katrina." Then: "I'm sorry about it all the time."

"No, please. I didn't mean to sound callous."

"Not at all, not at all."

"With what happened to their grandmother . . . well, it's been a difficult year. And it's not half over."

A pause.

"You look well! You look fit."

"They work me out all right up here. Still a ways to go though, still a ways to go. There's a marvelous gymnasium on the other side of the property, overlooking the pool. I've had my share of time in *that* body of water. Do you swim?"

"Oh yes."

"It's marvelous. I'm dropping stones on a daily basis." Pause. "I meant to say pounds. How is your father bearing up? I've been worried—haven't seen or spoken to him. He was quite close to the boy, no?"

"It's a bit of a mess."

"In what way?"

"He didn't come."

"Come?"

"To the funeral."

"I can't imagine!—"

"I suppose you haven't heard."

"He's ill?"

"No. There was a bit of controversy—over the placement of the *grave*, of all things."

"How strange!"

"It's one of those awful, ridiculous *family* things. I'm sure it will make its way to the A&E biography."

The reference was lost on him, but he let it rest.

There was a long pause.

"Are you certain you wouldn't like me to cook you something?"

"I really shouldn't stay."

"It'd be no trouble."

"That's all right."

"Not even a salad? You're sure, now?"

"No thanks."

"Yesterday I made a pot of turkey chowder; don't know exactly *why*, but I was very much in the mood. The *réchauffé*'s always better, no? Wouldn't take but a minute—"

"I should probably get back."

"Well—it was good of you to come."

"Goodness had nothing to do with it. As they say."

"I'm glad you did anyway."

"I'm not sure what we do now—where we go from here."

"As my half-dozen psychiatrists would urge me to say: 'I think that's OK.' "

They had a laugh. They stood and he awkwardly shook her hand. Not much voltage there—none of the anarchic, voluptuous ardor that a death sometimes confers in its wake. Still, Trinnie felt herself cleave toward family, the sacramental, primal pull of blood.

They walked in silence along the side of the house until reaching her car.

"Did you ever hear that saying about answered prayers?"

"No," he said, curious.

"I think it was Saint Theresa—according to Truman Capote, any-way." She groped for the quote. " 'More tears are shed over answered prayers than unanswered ones.' Or something like that."

"Is that what I am, Katrina?" he asked, callow and open-faced. "An answered prayer?"

She smiled, with kindness and sorrow. "More a forgotten one, Marcus. I wonder if anyone ever said anything about tears shed over prayers that were forgotten."

*C*here may be those who feel the transformation of Marcus Weiner improbably contrived (though it is hoped the cynical reader would have long since abandoned our tale). For the skeptic who has held on, stubborn as he is dubious, the author merely suggests—for nothing is being sold here—that there is ample precedent to Mr. Weiner's awakening and that the precedent has a name: Mystery.† We will leave it at that.

The day of the funeral, Marcus kept an appointment he thought would not be fitting to cancel. Besides, he could be of no solace to his son moping around the Santa Barbara estate. The men in suits knew how to reach him and had an explicit directive to do so should Toulouse need his counsel or company.

When Trinnie saw him stepping from the Town Car, he had just returned from an emotional reunion with none other than Amaryllis Kornfeld.

It has been noted that on Samson's Montecito visits, Marcus used to inquire after the girl—and was delighted when the detective eventually called to say she was living in the home of his old friend the baker. He felt guilty about not having replied to Gilles Mott's kind note while in jail—and over his shabby treatment of Mrs. Mott, too. After all, the man had been faultlessly generous in providing sustenance in food and moneys, which in turn allowed Marcus to feed that poor soul and her brood. Now

---

†It would not be fair to pause in our narrative in order to give a lecture on the miraculous and recuperative powers of the human spirit or the unknowable chemical capabilities of the brain. Suffice to say that while Bluey began to shed memory as a feverish person would her clothes, the son-in-law eagerly, and with a growing sense of adventure, gathered up whichever of his own discarded garments could be found.

fate had decreed that Amaryllis be properly with them—just as "Topsy" had wished all along. He owed the couple a debt and was, naturally, anxious to visit his onetime ward. He owed *her*, too, for she had been as an angelic tutor, rousing and nurturing in him all the feelings he now had for his discovered son.

Much as the children had been, Marcus was of course astounded to learn the connection between Amaryllis and the Trotter kids; yet because so much of his life had seemed, and still seemed, a dream, it struck him as being perfectly right. He thanked the detective for enlightening him, and was glad he'd been told before Edward had brought it up.

At the risk of further complication (from which the author has never shied), it is important to note that Amaryllis had herself not yet been apprised of "Topsy's" tortuous connection to the Trotter *familia;* as a stipulation of his being allowed e-mail privileges, Trinnie had forbidden her son to share the revelation. She said things were already messy enough. When a date for a rendezvous had been set, Lani called Marcus to reiterate that he was not to bring any of it up, just yet—they would tell their foster daughter in time.

Marcus had other concerns; he wondered if the child even remembered him. Lani assured that since being told of the impending visit, "Topsy" had been very much in the girl's thoughts. Yet with youngsters, she added, one never really knew.

That afternoon Marcus sported the same staid, bespoke ensemble worn for court appearances. When he stepped from the car, he was concerned that his formality might be misinterpreted as high-handed. Gilles rushed out to greet him, dispelling all worries with a deep-dish hug. He explained that Lani and Amaryllis had taken Felix to the vet after the cat had "got into" some flea-control gel. He was in the middle of cooking, or at least midwifing, a meal Lani had begun—and quickly enlisted a neighbor to watch the stove while they dashed to the bakery. Gilles said he'd forgotten something.

"Fancy!" he said, getting a load of the Lincoln and its driver.

"Don't have a license yet—Mr. Trotter's been kind enough to allow me use of the car. Shall we avail ourselves?"

"Hell, yes! Let's avail away! Always *knew* you'd make it to the top, William!" He hesitated. "Shouldn't call you that, huh?"

"William's fine."

"No—you're *Marcus*. But Amaryllis still calls you Topsy."

"Does she?" He smiled, pleased that she called him anything at all.

"Well, let's hurry—they should be home before too long. Don't want to keep 'em waiting!"

They climbed in the Town Car and wound toward Beverly Boulevard, Gilles hamming it up like they were a float in the Rose Bowl parade. The chauffeur pulled into the alley behind Frenchie's, right around where he'd left off the orphan girl nearly a year ago. Marcus loitered halfway between car and dumpster while the baker went in. For a moment, he had that hunted feeling and needed to remind himself he was no longer a wanted man. He almost went inside for old times' sake but thought better of it; Gilles emerged holding a soiled pink box tied with thin white string.

The Volvo was there when they got back. Amaryllis bounded out to tell Gilles that Felix would be all right but needed to stay over for observation.

"Good, good, good—now, say hello to an old friend."

"Hello," she said, staring at Marcus.

"Hello!"

He smiled and hung back, not wishing to crowd her. She looked beautiful—so much *longer* than when he had carried her on his back from the Higgins—with shorter hair, and some fat on her, too.

"Well, don't you know who it is?" the baker said.

"It's Topsy," said the girl nonchalantly, as if idly identifying a photograph. Lani called from the kitchen, and Amaryllis sprinted off, disappearing through the front door.

Marcus asked the baker if he felt the visit was a good idea. Gilles reassured that she was shy and had actually been awaiting him with great anticipation. That made him feel somewhat better, but he wasn't sure if it was puffery. He followed his friend into the house.

Lani served lunch in the backyard (roasted guinea hen stuffed with nutmeg and parsley) on a glass-topped wrought-iron table set with wildflowers. Marcus even drank a glass of wine, which he usually eschewed owing to various meds. Table talk skirted anything related to hard times, and while now and then he caught the girl staring at him with a kind of formidable acuity, it was readily apparent that they would share no intimacies—at least not here. His focus drifted. Toward the end of the meal, Amaryllis brought up the place called MacLaren and told her mother how much she wanted to go for a visit, especially to see Dézhiree. Plates were bused while Gilles went inside to arrange the surprise.

For a moment, the two were alone. He told her how pretty she looked, and she deadpanned that he looked "different." She asked where his beard had gone and remarked that he was a good deal thinner than she remembered. He laughed, but she only smiled, and by then Gilles had returned with a tray of desserts: mille-feuille of custard, almonds and honey. By the taste of it, he could tell the flour had been rolled "hot"—Marcus always made sure, as his father had taught him, to run his hands under cool water while evening out the layers. Still, it was a lovely, magnanimous gesture, true to the baker's form. Lani returned with little cups of espresso and partook herself of the lemony Moscato d'Asti.

Soaking in the sun (he'd hung his coat on the back of the chair), his broad face dappled by leaf shadow and the skittish attentions of a silver fritillary—soaking up all the space and time the four of them had traveled since being apart—well, Marcus thought it more than a small miracle.

Suddenly, it was over. The men smoked cigars while Amaryllis helped at the sink, though Lani shooed her away (she wanted her outside, with their guest). Gilles asked about his arrest and imprisonment, then talked all kinds of harmless nonsense about his fascinating recovery and how if he should write the whole incredible story up in screenplay form it would win fourteen Oscars, and so on. Marcus heard raised voices; then Lani's alone. She was talking to the girl, not harshly but firmly.

When mother and daughter re-emerged from the wings, Lani announced it would be a wonderful idea for Amaryllis to show her old friend the Shakespeare Bridge.

"No, no," said Marcus, mindful of the girl's feelings. "Another time, another time!"

"Go with her. It's nice to walk," said Lani.

"Go!" said the expansive Gilles. "You should see it!"

"Oh, the bridge won't go away! I'm sure Amaryllis has other things to do," he said guilelessly.

"I'd *like* to show you," she volunteered.

He was surprised, because she sounded quite sincere. Only human, Marcus had mistaken a child's nervousness on seeing a mythical figure from her own Dark Ages as a sign of indifference. He grabbed his coat, and they set off, first passing through the coolness of the house.

Lani stopped him just inside the front door.

"*Tell* her," she whispered, "about who you *are*—if you want to. I mean, she should *know*. I mean, the hell with it—when she came to stay with us, I said, 'No secrets!' But you do what you like."

~

They walked through the neighborhood in relative silence, but this time the girl led the way, unlike long-ago peregrinations. Watching her chug along on her own steam as an independent (if still tiny) person, he couldn't suppress a smile.

After a time, she spoke. "You don't talk with an accent anymore."

"Did I have a thick one? I didn't think it was too bad."

"It *was*," Amaryllis said, and he saw her roll her eyes. "Were you just pretending?"

"I wouldn't say I was pretending—I really did feel I was someone else."

"Were you crazy?"

"Did I seem crazy?"

"No."

"I don't think so, no. I think that—that I had *concerns*—preoccupations, if you will . . . that others—well, *most* people—don't have."

"You were in jail," she said, not looking back at him.

"I was. A terrible place."

"The detective thought you killed my mother."

"Yes."

"The lawyers came and talked to me."

"I was grateful for what you told them about the scarf."

"But you *didn't* kill her." She looked him tentatively in the eye, wanting him to tell her what she already knew.

"No, Amaryllis, I didn't. To be accused of something like that was the hardest thing. And that it was your mother—"

"But they found the person who did it."

"Yes."

"The man who owned Half Dead?"

"Yes."

"He was your friend?"

"He was."

"Did you know that he killed her?"

"I did not—and was shocked when they told me. I had no idea he was capable of such a thing. Did you ever meet Mr. Fitzsimmons at the encampment?"

She nodded. Then: "He used to come around with that dog. He tied him up outside when he came to see her. She always made me go leave, but I never played with that dog."

"I wanted to call you the moment I found out what they were accusing me of. I couldn't believe it! But they wouldn't allow me. And then so many things happened . . . I moved to a hotel—and then to a house on the coast, where I now live. I finally got my wits about me and the energy to come see you. I ask your forgiveness for the delay."

They had reached the bridge, and sat down on its bulwark.

"Not as big as the one on Fourth Street, is it?" he said.

"I like it better."

She stared into the canyon. The spirit of the child he knew was hidden by armature grown these past rough seasons. Cars rumbled by, and they watched birds and planes and insects. The world was filled with flying things.

"Do you like living with Gilles and Lani?"

She nodded.

"Marvelous people. Good souls. Have you seen your brother and sister?"

"Uh-huh. They live in Lawndale."

"Lawndale. Now, where is Lawndale?"

"I don't know. It takes an hour to get there—no, maybe a half hour. We're going to California Adventure next month."

"Very good, very good."

"Where do *you* live?"

"Santa Barbara—a place called Montecito, actually."

"Where's that?"

"Up north, about ninety minutes."

"Is it near Tunga?"

"Well, I'm not really sure!"

"Does the man drive you everywhere?"

"Until I get a license."

"Are you rich?"

"No. But the people taking care of me are."

"I met some friends when I went AWOL from Mac—MacLaren. They were *really* rich. I met Boulder Langon, the actress."

"I see. And how is school for you?"

"Fine."

"Have you made many friends?"

She nodded.

"Do you have a boyfriend?"

She shrugged.

"Is that a yes?"

"Sort of."

"Does he go to your school?"

"He goes in Santa Monica."

"You like him."

She nodded. "He stopped e-mailing me."

"He did?"

"A week ago—but I think his mom probably made him. He's one of the friends I had when I went AWOL. She probably thinks I'm bad. They are *so* rich."

Marcus heard Lani's words in his head, then felt the crushing onslaught of unseen forces. "Amaryllis, there's something I want to tell you."

She turned to him, unnerved; she thought he might confess to the murder of her mother after all. "About what."

"There was a boy called Edward . . . you knew him, no? He was a friend of Toulouse, the one you speak of."

"Did my—did *Lani* tell you?" she asked, readying herself to be angry with the woman for having betrayed details of her private life.

"Edward wore a brace and colorful scarves . . ."

"Edward and Lucy: the cousins!" she said excitedly. "And Lucy's writing a book—"

"Yes. Well, you see, Amaryllis—it's just that Edward died last week. And that's why Toulouse hasn't written you."

"Died? But how?"

"He'd been sick most his life, as you know. You remember what a hard time he had just getting—"

"Oh! Oh!"

Amaryllis fidgeted, scanning the horizon as if for an exit so that she could go AWOL from the world. He steadied her, softly placing a paw on her forearm.

He poured everything out, hoping she might grasp it. She made him repeat a few things, and when it seemed she finally understood—or had at least absorbed the fact of his blood connection to Toulouse—well, it was simply too much.

"Oh, Topsy," she murmured, clinging to him as she used to—he had worried things would never be the same between them. She stroked the stubble of his cheeks as if trying to summon back the beard. "Topsy . . ."

He reached into his pocket and pulled out a Baggie with a treat baked especially for her. Like in old encampment days, the child's nail-bitten fingers dug greedily into the foggy, nectar'd sack; and after a while her crying ceased and her breathing became measured as she spooned all manna of crumbs to her mouth.

CHAPTER 47

The Wheel

[Note: for the sake of fluency, the author has taken the liberty to correct certain
errors of typography and usage, of which there were a goodly amount; and
begs the reader's indulgence. If the girl at times seems precocious in expression,
it can be reminded that she was a seasoned reader of newspapers and magazines, and also possessed a natural abundance of expressive gifts.]

From: "Amaryllis" <lanimottCASA@hotmail.com
To: "Toulouse Trotter" <harlequinboy@home.com
Subject: No Subject

dearest toulouse, it has taken many hours to put these thoughts
to paper—i have only recently heard of your most terrible tragedy.
i have learned everything (please forgive my "abominable" typing—
I am sorry but i don't yet know how to use the spell-check). what a
wonderful boy he was! if you do not wish to write back it will be ok.
i know you must be suffering so. i'm sorry i didn't write you during
the week but was playing a stupid game, waiting for you to write
ME first. i DO know everything now—even that my oldest and dearest friend topsy is your father (!). he is such a good man and saved
my live! and the babies too, i think. you are blessed even if it
seems that god has done something so unfair by taking dearest
edward away. he is with the angels now, and should be a saint if
john paul has anything to say about it. PLEASE write soon and
again, i am sorry for being "petulant." love, amaryllis

ps my love to pull-man

From: "Toulouse Trotter" <harlequinboy@home.com
To: "Amaryllis" <lanimottCASA@hotmail.com
Subject: No Subject

amaryllis, thank you for your note and i'm sorry it has been so long to get back. i didn't even check my email for the longest time. since you already know, i will tell you now that i DID know my father was the man who had helped you—i knew but made a vow not to say it and i hope you will forgive me. but it is something i did not know for the longest time either. it took edward, as usual, to put the pieces together. actually, and i don't think he would mind me telling you this, edward put the pieces together with the help of his MOTHER, who actually TOLD him (!) (did your foster mother tell you?) edward said that you and my father already knowing each another was "karma." have you ever heard of karma? it seems to be a buddhist concept. lucy and i are still trying to adjust to him not being here—as if that will ever be possible. most of the time it feels like he is away at the hospital (where he used to go periodically). sometimes lucy and i drive around in the buggy—we tied one of his scarves at the end of the antenna so that it flaps like a flag—or just lie around his house. (we have not yet gone thru the ceiling trapdoor into your old room) that way, we feel his presence near. we avoid the workshop too because it is still a bit eerie to see all of his masks. we always keep a seat for him at the majestyk when we screen movies. it is the empty one between us. there are no longer doctors and nurses everywhere and that's a good thing but joyce (edward's mother) is having a hard time so there's usually one nurse here at night who stays in the main residence. lucy has had sleepovers at saint-cloud a lot. (the place you were nearly "arrested" at, remember??!!) sincerely, toulouse

ps. she has been depressed and her parents want her to take a drug for it. that is so insane! (she has assured me she most certainly will not take a single pill because it would make her gain weight.) also, she has not been writing her book.

pps pullman sends his love

From: "Amaryllis" <lanimottCASA@hotmail.com
To: "Toulouse Trotter" <harlequinboy@home.com
Subject: No Subject

dearest toulouse. thank you for writing back so promptly. i apologize for spelling your name incorrectly in my previous note. you are SUCH a good speller! lani has shown me how to use the spell-check but i'm worried their are words it does not include. no, my foster mom did not tell me but we have since talked about it and she thinks it is AMAZING. how is everything? i hope you are feeling better. yes, things will never be the same without him but you must cherish the time you had with edward while he was here—which i know you and lucy already do. (I don't mean I am condescendant.) i looked up karma on the internet. it said that the universe is a wheel and that all its creatures turned upon the wheel and that you couldn't leave the wheel until you realized you were part of brahma? but what IS brahma. i have done my share of studying of the religions especially the field of those who are in line for sainthood. i have studied the royal kumari, but the lives they lead are so different than this experience of the wheel—they return to their villages after they are done. i guess that is getting off the wheel but in a different way?

i'm sorry but the spel-check does not work today
love, amaryllis

From: "Amaryllis" <lanimottCASA@hotmail.com
To: "Toulouse Trotter" <harlequinboy@home.com
Subject: No Subject

dear DEAREST toulouse, they have also beatified TWO popes. one of them has met resistance because it was reported that he called the jewish "dogs." we should all be such wonderful "dogs" as pull-man, so that is a complement?

From: "Amaryllis" <lanimottCASA@hotmail.com
To: "Toulouse Trotter" <harlequinboy@home.com
Subject: No Subject

ps—i'm sorry i pressed *send* before i wanted to ask why are you called harliquinboy?

From: "Toulouse Trotter" <harlequinboy@home.com
To: "Amaryllis" <lanimottCASA@hotmail.com
Subject: a swami sandwich on rye

pullman is of the harlequin breed of great danes. edward always thought harlequinboy was dumb but i like it because it reminds me of pullie. besides, so many email names are already taken it gets boring trying to be clever.

do you think you will ever get your own account? and do you think that your foster mom ever "E-avesdrops"?

i was very interested in what you wrote. it made me thing of pullman too though it bothered me to read on one of the *karma* websites that people of "evil" were in danger of being reborn as dogs or pigs, both of whom i feel to be often more advanced than animals of the "human" variety. if that is their true belief then I would think twice about becoming a buddhist. one thing i did read i thought pretty interesting. it was called the *law of the last thought* and said the thoughts or ideas that come to a person at the time of his death are responsible for his next life. what if a person who is in the middle of realizing how to make the perfect potato chip suddenly dies?!!? or what if a person forces himself to think "i will live forever" during his last moment. it made me wonder what EDWARD'S last thought was and i can't help but think it was something really mean & witty. at least i hope it was. your friend, toulouse

p.s. i was also wondering if pullman could have a thought, and what that thought might be. aside from food!

pps i can just see edward as a swami, with a turban of his own design. it's funny but when i think of him now, i never picture him with his face covered and i never see the brace. i just see him normal, and able to move around. corny, huh.

From: "Toulouse Trotter" <harlequinboy@home.com
To: "Amaryllis" <lanimottCASA@hotmail.com
Subject: internet superhighway fatalities

i forgot to tell you this weird thing that happened while i was searching "*karma*" i suddenly get this bizarre message on my computer: **unexpected trappable error. a fatal error occurred in an external object.** it was like the computer was trying to explain karma! or at least PART of karma, i guess. it was very nearly the computer's "last thought"!!! i wonder what my computer was before it was a computer. maybe a dishwasher?!! kinda rad, huh. i wonder what they mean by *trappable* tho.

my mom owes me a birthday party. maybe we can see each other?

have you spoken to my father? i see him a lot now but don't like to ask him about you. (not that i don't want to) he DID say he saw you, and the motts. he said you told him you were actually looking for him that day you met me and my cousins on boulder's movie. how weird is THAT? it made me sad to think of you back then so all alone. but you had him and he had you and that's the main thing, no? and then you met US.

From: "Toulouse Trotter" <harlequinboy@home.com
To: "Amaryllis" <lanimottCASA@hotmail.com
Subject: i-mail

we should do instant mail?

From: "Amaryllis" <lanimottCASA@hotmail.com
To: "Toulouse Trotter" <harlequinboy@home.com
Subject: SORRY SORRY SORRY!!!!!!!!!!!!

my dearest DEAREST darling toulouse, i am SO SO SORRY i did
not write yesterday but i was with my brother and sister at california adventure. there is a limousine ride where they make you feel
like a star arriving at a premiere and i so thought of boulder! on
another ride we got wet wet wet!!! the babies were SO HAPPY.

when when WHEN was your BIRTHDAY??????????? what sign are
you? are you 14 yet?

i did talk to topsy last week but only on the phone. /i still call him
that because that is what he used to call himself./ i told him about
the day i met you and boulder and everyone. how is she? i want to
see the movie she made. is she making others? did you know that
she visited mac (the place i was staying and went a.w.o.l. from?
but i never got a chance to talk to her.) but i think i may have told
you that already. topsy told me he sees you a lot and that makes
me glad. but do you think WE could see each other soon? i want
to give you a birthday KISS. i have not talked to my foster parents
about it yet. (and NO, lani would NEVER read what you wrote me.
she knows i would KILL her. just kidding.) but i don't think they
would say no. would your mother? we could go to trader joe's, the
place we all went to dinner that was polynesian. the food was SO
GOOD!!!! i have to go—lani says i MUST do homewwork. she has
threatened to RESTRICT my email if I don't go RIGHT NOW! your
friend and love, amaryllis

p.s. that was SO INTERESTING about what happened when you
looked for karma. i guess it was your karma?!! and i KNOW what
pull-man's last thought would be: how to EAT the perfect potato
chip!!!!!!!!!!!!!!!!

From: "Amaryllis" <lanimottCASA@hotmail.com
To: "Toulouse Trotter" <harlequinboy@home.com
Subject: re: i-mail

lani is so freaked about computers that she only has HOTMAIL and cannot do INSTANT. I think INSTANT is available on HOT-MAIL but lani doesn't know how to do it and i think the other person has to have HOTMAIL too.

love, amaryllis

From: "Toulouse Trotter" <harlequinboy@home.com
To: "Amaryllis" <lanimottCASA@hotmail.com
Subject: summer RULES

hi, am. that's short for amaryllis. my mother always shortens names—she used to call me "tull" but not so much anymore. now everyone calls me mostly toulouse. my father kind of named me that. but there was a famous french painter too called toulouse lautrec. he was short in stature but amazing. he has a tattoo about it (my father, not the short painter) which is actually a very bad french pun. if i call you am, you can say "i think therefore i am." that's a bad pun too. guess it runs in the family.

i was fourteen in march. i am an aries—the ram. (i think therefore, i ram. sorry!!!!!) are you thirteen yet?

my father and i are spending more time together and he and my mom have seen each other too. but all of us haven't really been to-gether at the same time because i think my mom is being some-what protective of me, but mostly of herself. (occasionally she sees him when he's picking me up or dropping me off and i can tell by the way they look at each other that they still love that maybe they are still in love.) my grandfather seems happier too because my grandma bluey is doing better. she has alzheimer's. did i tell you that he was actually going to sue my aunt joyce (ed-ward's mother; grandpa's daughter-in-law) so that he could dig up eddie's grave and bury him over on "his side"? how fucked up is THAT? i think he's getting a little crazy in his old age. it runs in the family, you know. meanwhile my aunt is busy burying babies that are donated to her after police find them in dumpsters. (she is burying the babies on "edward's side," which further freaks my grandfather out.) what a family!!!!! the trotters are INSANE

i am really glad you are spending time with your brother and sis. they must be SO HAPPY. in a way, i think it is good they were so young when all those bad things happened to them. sometimes i think that is a blessing but maybe i am wrong.

i think my father may be moving back from santa barbara soon. my uncle dodd owns a lot of houses near his old grammar school and i think my dad father is going to move into one. i don't think he enjoys living his life with such opulence and that house in santa barbara is a real mansion. i think he gets lonely up there too. also, his main psychotherapist is in beverly hills. living in one of my uncle's houses, he can pretty much walk everywhere he needs to go. also, he is getting rid of those men who were always around him for whatever reason—making sure he didn't go apeshit!!! or whatever. i think maybe he will keep just ONE of them but mostly in case he needs to drive somewhere. the man can take him. (my dad still doesn't have a license. that makes two of us.)

i would VERY much like to see you and mentioned it to mom. i think she may have spoken to lani already? maybe not so don't mention it to YOUR mom. it will be summer soon and trinnie was talking about taking us (me and lucy) to the adirondacks. my grandfather has owned a house (it is called *twig house*) there for i think forty years. wouldn't it be cool if you could go! but maybe you have plans for the summer and are going to school or something. your foster parents might object.

the name of that place we all went to was trader vic's and it is the COOLEST. the sundaes are called SNOWBALLS, remember? it's so hard thinking of a summer without edward. i've never had one before.

ps. does "foster parents" sound lame?
love, Toulouse

From: "Amaryllis" <lanimottCASA@hotmail.com
To: "Toulouse Trotter" <harlequinboy@home.com
Subject: oh my god, said am

oh my god toulouse summer at that place with you and lucy would be so cool & crazy!!! i didn't mention anything to lani yet.

i am a libra. i will be thirteen in five months. i will cook dinner for you.

what is a "french pun"?

i am very sorry about the alzheimer's and have looked it up on the internet.

i went with my brother and sister went to the OLD disneyland. my brother is soooo cute!!! (my sister is too) they were on the roger rabbit. did you know a bunch of kids died on it? my friends at school say people die on it all the time, like once a week, but everyone is paid by the lawyers not to talk about it. toulouse— there is something i wanted to speak about to you but if you don't want to then it is ok. that time when we went to that weird tower and i acted in a certain way and you told me to stop. i have felt so bad about it and want you to know that is not the way i am. i really care about you and it hurts me to think that YOU might think i am someone else than i really am. i don't know what was wrong with me that day. i would like you to one day be my boyfriend and would not want you to think i was a *ho* even though i acted in a slutty way. i am so absolutely NOT!

and oh oh oh! my mother just came in the room and said she talked to YOUR mom and that we could see each other

SOON!!!!!!!!!!!!! (she said it will be *supervised*) that is, if you still want to after i brought up that old thing that happened in the tower. but anyway, if you still want to see me, i can't wait!!!!!!! xxxxxxxxxxxxxooooooooooooo your ***MORE*** than friend, AM ("am" i in love?)

p.s. it is ok to say *foster parents* but you can just say parents too.

From: "Amaryllis" <lanimottCASA@hotmail.com
To: "Toulouse Trotter" <harlequinboy@home.com
Subject: sorry

dearest Toulouse, please forgive me if i discussed things that you would rather me not to bring up ever again. when i said that i wanted you to one day be my boyfriend, that can be in the very distant future if at all. i will wait until you feel it is the right time, if ever. until then, i will never talk about you being my boyfriend again. your FRIEND, i am and will always be . . . amaryllis

p.s. xxxxxxxxxooooooooo
p.s.s. xxoo

From: "Toulouse Trotter" <harlequinboy@home.com
To: "Amaryllis" <lanimottCASA@hotmail.com
Subject: No Subject

dear amar, (wasn't that your "moroccan" name?!) i am sorry i haven't written a full email in awhile but things got "hairy" because lucy read your last letter! she came over to see pullman and i wasn't home so she SNOOPED. she wouldn't even tell me what was wrong for about TWO HOURS later and then she totally freaked out. she always acted like she was my girlfriend but i don't feel that way toward her. (i don't love her the way that i like you.) i was mad at her for snooping but then i felt bad because she has been through so much and the fact that we have been emailing (you and i) and i haven't even told her about it not that it is any of her business. and that you said certain things that made her very JEALOUS . . .

i told trinnie about it and she and lucy had a "heart-to-heart"—she went with her to iceland! there was a party for that singer bjork who my mom is big friends with (bjork even met edward once). now I'M the one who is jealous! but they called from granppa's jet and mom says lucy is ok. trinnie can be great for lifting people's spirits like that—but when MOM goes down, there's no one who can do the same for her. she IS feeling better in general about her life, i think, because things are going well with my dad. he is making great progress and mom has been helping him decorate his house. (did i tell you he moved?) one night he even had my mom and diane keaton over for dinner. (she was in both of the "godfathers" and used to be my father's client.) have to go now but i think our moms have spoken about us going to magic mountain or disneyland?

From: "Amaryllis" <lanimottCASA@hotmail.com
To: "Toulouse Trotter" <harlequinboy@home.com
Subject: LOVE

to my dearest boyfriend toulouse, i LOVE LOVE LOVED disneyland! and when you kissed me behind the roger rabbit!!!!!!!!!!!!!!!!!!!!!!!!!!!!!!!!!
!!
!!
!!
!!
!!
!!
!!
!!XXXXXXXXXXXXX
XXXXXXXXXXXXXXXXXXXXXXXXXXXXXXXXXXXXXXXXXXX
XXXXXXXXXXXXXXXXXXXXXXXXXXXXXXXXXXXXXXXXXXXXXX
XXX
XXXXXXXXXXXXXXXXXXXXXXXXXXXXXXXXXXXXXXXXXXXXXX
XXX
XXXXXXXXXXXXXXXXXXXXXXXXXXXXXXXXXXXXXXXXXXXXXXX
XXX

XXXXXXXXXXXXXXXXXXXXXXXXXXXXXXXXXXXXXXXXXXXXXXXX
XXX
XXXXXXXXXXXXXXXXXXXXXXXXXXXXXXXXXXXXXXXXXXXXXXXX
XXX
OOOOOOOOOOOOOOOOOOOOOOOOOOOOOOOOOOOOOOOOOOOOO
OOO
OOOOOOOOOOOOOOOOOOOOOOOOOOOOOOOOOOOOOOOOOOOOO
OOO
OOOOOOOOOOOOOOOOOOOOOOOOOOOOOOOOOOOOOOOOOOOOO
OOO
OOOOOOOOOOOOOOOOOOOOOOOOOOOOOOOOOOOOOOOOOOOOO
OOO
OOOOOOOOOOOOOOOOOOOOOOOOOOOOOOOOOOOOOOOOOOOOO
OOO
OOOOOOOOOOOOOOOOOOOOOOOOOOOOOOOOOOOOOOOOOOOOO
OOO
OOOOOOOOOOOOOOOOOOOOOOOOOOOOOOOOOOOOOOOOOOOOO
OOO
OOOOOOOOOOOOOOOOOOOOOOOOOOOOOOOOOOOOOOOOOOOOO
OOO
OOOOOOOOOOOOOOOOOOOOOOOOOOOOOOOOOOOOOOOOOOOOO
OOO

L O V E

  L O V E

L O V E

amaryllis (am) (your little tiger)

From: "Amaryllis" <lanimottCASA@hotmail.com
To: "Toulouse Trotter" <harlequinboy@home.com
Subject: LITTLE TIGER LOVE

i miss pullie! he is sooooooooo cute! i like him to slobber on me!!!!!
did you know there was a famous dog from paris who was made a
saint by the people? but there is someone else i miss MUCH,
MUCH more. and he is a boy. and that boy is YOU. i LOVE YOU

From: "Toulouse Trotter" <harlequinboy@home.com
To: "Amaryllis" <lanimottCASA@hotmail.com
Subject: No Subject

dear l.t., I had lots of fun too. my mom likes lani and gilles very
much and said that the next time we see each other, my dad
would like to even come. LOVE, tull (toulouse)

```
         *         *

     *  *  *    *  *  *

  *  *  *  *  *  *  *  **

    *  *  *  *  *  *  *

      *  *  *  *  *

        *  *  *  *

          *  *  *

             *
```

From: "Amaryllis" <lanimottCASA@hotmail.com
To: "Toulouse Trotter" <harlequinboy@home.com
Subject: LOVE

```
        !!!!                    !!!!
     !!!!!!!!!!!!!            !!!!!!!!!!!!!!
  !!!!!!!!!!!!!!!!!!!!!    !!!!!!!!!!!!!!!!!!!!!
!!!!!!!!!!!!!!!!!!!!!!!!!!!!!!!!!!!!!!!!!!!!!!!!!!!!!
!!!!!!!!!!!!!!!!!!!!!!!!!!!!!!!!!!!!!!!!!!!!!!!!!!!!!!
!!!!!!!!!!!!!!!!!!!!!!!!!!!!!!!!!!!!!!!!!!!!!!!!!!!!!!!
!!!!!!!!!!!!!!!!!!!!!!!!!!!!!!!!!!!!!!!!!!!!!!!!!!!!!!!
 !!!!!!!!!!!!!!!!!!!!!!!!!!!!!!!!!!!!!!!!!!!!!!!!!!!!
  !!!!!!!!!!!!!!!!!!!!!!!!!!!!!!!!!!!!!!!!!!!!!!!!!!
   !!!!!!!!!!!!!!!!!!!!!!!!!!!!!!!!!!!!!!!!!!!!!!!!
    !!!!!!!!!!!!!!!!!!!!!!!!!!!!!!!!!!!!!!!!!!!!!
     !!!!!!!!!!!!!!!!!!!!!!!!!!!!!!!!!!!!!!!!!!
      !!!!!!!!!!!!!!!!!!!!!!!!!!!!!!!!!!!!!!!
       !!!!!!!!!!!!!!!!!!!!!!!!!!!!!!!!!!!!
        !!!!!!!!!!!!!!!!!!!!!!!!!!!!!!!!!!
         !!!!!!!!!!!!!!!!!!!!!!!!!!!!!!!
          !!!!!!!!!!!!!!!!!!!!!!!!!!!!
           !!!!!!!!!!!!!!!!!!!!!!!!!
            !!!!!!!!!!!!!!!!!!!!!!!
             !!!!!!!!!!!!!!!!!!!
              !!!!!!!!!!!!!!!
               !!!!!!!!!!!!
                !!!!!!!!!
                 !!!!!!
                  !!!!
                   !
```

!!!!   !!!!

!!!!!!!!!!!!!   !!!!!!!!!!!!!

!!!!!!!!!!!!!!!!!!!   !!!!!!!!!!!!!!!!!!!

!!

!!!

!!!

!!

!!!

!!!

!!!!!!!!!!!!!!!!!!!!!!!!!!!!!!!!!!!!!!!

!!!!!!!!!!!!!!!!!!!!!!!!!!!!!!!!!!!!!

!!!!!!!!!!!!!!!!!!!!!!!!!!!!!!!!!!!

!!!!!!!!!!!!!!!!!!!!!!!!!!!!!!!!!

!!!!!!!!!!!!!!!!!!!!!!!!!!!!!!!

!!!!!!!!!!!!!!!!!!!!!!!!!!!!!

!!!!!!!!!!!!!!!!!!!!!!!!!!!

!!!!!!!!!!!!!!!!!!!!!!!!!

!!!!!!!!!!!!!!!!!!!!!!!

!!!!!!!!!!!!!!!!!!!

!!!!!!!!!!!!!!!!

!!!!!!!!!!!!!

!!!!!!!!!!

!!!!!!!

!!!!!

!

!!!!   !!!!

!!!!!!!!!!!!!   !!!!!!!!!!!!!!

!!!!!!!!!!!!!!!!!!!!!   !!!!!!!!!!!!!!!!!!!!

!!!

!!!!!!!!!!!!!!!!!!!!!!!!!!!!!!! !!!!!!!!!!!!!!!!!!!!!

!!

!!!!!!!!!!!!!!!!!!!!!!!!!!!!!!!!!!!!! !!!!!!!!!!!!!!!!!!!!!!!

!!!

!!!

!!

!!

!!

!!!!!!!!!!!!!!!!!!!!!!!!!!!!!!!!!!!!!!

!!!!!!!!!!!!!!!!!!!!!!!!!!!!!!!!!!!!

!!!!!!!!!!!!!!!!!!!!!!!!!!!!!!!!!

!!!!!!!!!!!!!!!!!!!!!!!!!!!!!!

!!!!!!!!!!!!!!!!!!!!!!!!!!!!

!!!!!!!!!!!!!!!!!!!!!!!!!

!!!!!!!!!!!!!!!!!!!!!!

!!!!!!!!!!!!!!!!!!!

!!!!!!!!!!!!!!!

!!!!!!!!!!!

!!!!!!!

!!!!!

!

CHAPTER 48

Aftershocks

"I didn't want to tell you," said Lucy, one windswept August afternoon.

She had invited Toulouse to join her in the latest addition to what she called Stradella Fields, a charming Russian-style gazebo crammed with more pinecones and willow-work than Twig House itself, and not far from where Edward had been found in the wayward buggy. Afternoon tea was something new for her, as were many things English. For most of the summer, she'd affected an accent that could only be called a poignant variation on the real thing. Lucille Rose, as she insisted on being called, put a cool face on her passionate interest in the Royals (especially Lady Sarah Chatto), and was surprisingly fluent in the languages of, say, Damien Hirst or Hussein Chalayan. She devoured back issues of *Hello!* and once, when Epitacio drove them home from a visit with Toulouse's father, they detoured around the Beverly Hills Farmers' Market on Cañon Drive—seeing fruit sellers in their stalls, she turned up her nose and hissed, "Look at those yobbish costermongers!"

Settling back on the silk mohair club chair beside the *vert de mer* fireplace, Lucy took a sip from her cup, then scrunched her brow. "I didn't want to tell you, but it looks as though I'm going to be living in Europe."

Toulouse nearly choked on his crumpet. "What do you mean?"

"England, mostly—that's where I'll be going to school."

"But how? *Why—*"

"When Trinnie and I were in Iceland, we met the Hectares. As in

Lord Hectare. They are bloody rich. I got on quite well with Amanda—she's their daughter. And they asked if I wanted to come stay with them."

"Staying with them is one thing. Living is another."

"Then bugger it all, Toulouse, they asked if I wanted to *live* with them, OK? It's not like they don't have room—they just bought Sutton Place for forty million pounds. It's a bleeding castle."

"Bleeding or bloody?"

"They're so rich it's *both*, you arse. We'll be going to Monte Carlo first; they have a cliff house Aunt Trinnie says is *très* Belle Époque. They're quite friendly with the Grimaldis, you know. We're going to see Charlotte, Princess Caroline's daughter—we're almost the same age. She's got a bulldog called Romeo, isn't that sweet? I so love a little bulldog! And one of Lord Hectare's best friends is the man whose family makes ink for all the world currencies. Isn't that brilliant?"

$\mathcal{W}$e shall return to the cousins in a moment, for the above scene is not yet done; but first a little context should be provided, as months have gone by that were relatively unaccounted for.

The departed invalid-genius became both muse and, daresay, mascot for Toulouse and his parents, offering his imprimatur to the baby steps that the reborn family took each day. They invoked him often; the boy became a sacred spot in their secret garden, a wistful, contemplative presence that eased not only the sorrow of his being gone but that of their own sad history. Practicing a gentle psychomancy, Toulouse felt closer to him than ever.

Yet as one family knitted together (two, if we include the Motts), another unraveled in the wake of his passage. Joyce emerged from paralysis to throw herself into work with manic compulsion. The Candlelighters bought up more ground (all that was left, in fact) at the Westwood park, but awakened more phantoms than were put to rest. For it was no longer the cracked tower that haunted her neighborhood but rather the empty monuments of Olde CityWalk—not to mention the east wing of the main house, where sat the tub in which she had poured water over her son's bird-like, terminal frame. In the hour of the wolf, it was not unusual for Winter to awaken Dodd on the intercom with news that Candelaria had espied the mistress barefoot and febrile, moondancing about the Mauck with its ghostly incubus of buggy within. When, to break the terrible cycle, the doleful billionaire sold off both vehicles without warning, Joyce took to her bed for weeks.

Each day, she visited his grave, which by late summer was surrounded by others, who kept their respectful distance; she could not bear anything encroaching on Edward just yet. As in Castaic, the dumpster tribeschildren were given biblical names, and the Candlelighters (which now included the Palisades lesbians, who had since made Joyce godmother of their son) stuck colorful pinwheels in the fresh plots, with tiny name-banners attached. Whirligigs spun in the wind, and Dot thought them a welcome addition, even though she knew they brought much grief to the eldest Trotter, whose visits to his own humble memorial had for the most part quit. Her sister Ethel said it was a family affair and to stay out of it, which she did.

Among Edward's papers was an epigram the boy had lifted from the pages of his Roman middle-namesake (a name bestowed by his grandfather); he had pasted it on a photo-montage of stones like an epitaph. Joyce thought the text to be morbid, but dutifully had a plaque engraved and set in the ground—a guilty compromise for having betrayed his dream of anonymity:

EDWARD AURELIUS TROTTER 1990–2001

"Soon you will have forgotten the world,
and soon the world will have forgotten you."

After a few months, the old man returned to the park and for the first time attended his grandson's grave. He was disgusted by its meagerness. The tacky windmills whirred in the periphery of his vision, but he refused to acknowledge them. Still, he was moved by the inscription—at least she got *something* right.

Louis Trotter had actually taken the initial steps of filing a suit to disinter the boy and bring him "home"—but the lawyers (if one can imagine), not to mention Katrina, were strongly opposed. Trinnie even brought their old friend Dr. Kindman to bear and warned her father flat-out that she would never speak to him again if he dared follow through with such an action. Besides, she asked, where would Edward be traveling but to another empty field? She had a point. After all these years, the great patriarch couldn't decide on a memorial for himself, let alone for his grandson. What it came down to, then, was pride and entitlement. In life and in death, it seemed always to come to that.

He began bringing the boy flowers. One afternoon, he even trod the Candlelighters' turf for a closer look at the "charity cases." Mr. Trotter clasped his hands at his lower back, clucking and chuffing in *largo. How freakish and asinine!* he thought. *Selfish devil-woman.* . . . He kicked himself for having hired her in the first place—none of this might have happened! But then Edward mightn't have happened, either. His lip began to tremble with the sadness of it.

With the skillfully combined efforts of Dot and Sling Blade, warring parties were given hints as to when one or the other would most likely be paying respects; in short order, a schedule was mentally drawn and strictly adhered to. Thus, the old man and his daughter-in-law were never to see each other at that cemetery—or anywhere else, for that matter—again.

༄

The reader has not yet been treated to any private moments between the departed wunderkind and his dad, and for good reason. They did not have many. (Though somewhat awkward in each other's presence, they adored one another no end.) What they *did* have was an arrangement; the charter and by-laws of their corporation, so to speak, had been drawn up at Edward's birth and become a living, immanent article of faith. The father, neurotic in a way diametrically opposed to his wife's dysfunction, had sworn to his Maker he would always be there for his son, a declaration never voided.

But let us dig a little deeper for those who may wonder what effect Edward's loss had upon a man whose emotions, even under normal conditions, seemed inscrutable at best. Dodd's worst fear was to have taken his son for granted. Perhaps more than anyone, he had been cognizant of Edward's mortality, but hadn't the courage to face it head-on, preferring instead to shower him with the outrageous comforts that only material things can provide. In other words, he was afraid he hadn't shown the boy enough affection. A psychiatrist briefly consulted some weeks after Edward's passing helped the billionaire (who, because of recent fluctuations, had fallen on the *Forbes* list to number forty-one but would give his detractors much comeuppance in coming quarters) to recognize that he had demonstrated his love in the best and deepest way he could—and that Edward had surely felt it. Wiping an eye, Dodd was certain this was true, and left the man's office satisfied.

At around this time, the motive behind his collection of empty buildings came home to roost. When he learned that his son had been researching his own demise all along, he thought: *how strange are these Trotter men.* Each obsessed with death or the trappings thereof—for what was an empty building but a monument to the once-alive? Those were *his* monuments, *Dodd's* cenotaphs and sepulchres, spread across the land. At escrow, he felt the same tidy relief one did upon inoculation against disease (the disease of death). In the past five years he had acquired nearly eighty companies, spinning off or turning over those that couldn't be absorbed by the healthy corporate body. He despised himself when on weak or dismal days—and by a kind of accountant's synaptic legerdemain—he took comfort in regarding Edward as a gloriously failed acquisition.

*L*ucille Rose generally suffered in silence, evincing the characteristics her grandfather had attributed to her some pages back. But the overarching one—his observation that she gleaned from the best of those whom she knew and loved—held fast and true, for in mourning she showed an uncommon valor: such a trait was Edward's gift, and what he would have wished of her. It can be recalled that Mr. Trotter made note of his granddaughter's big-heartedness and this too held true, even though that heart was like a river that had changed course so it would not flood her brother's land—for there was a moment upon his death when she could not control the waters, which threatened to engulf both her and his memory. The trip to Iceland was the right cure for that, and to her aunt she would always be grateful. In time, the river would run near Edward again, as sure and strong as the Thames, and would never leave him.

So: in the Russian gazebo she told her cousin she would soon be living the expatriate's life. A fleet of planes at the heiress's disposal guaranteed that no one in the Trotter clan—or outside, for that matter, i.e., such indispensables as Boulder Langon—would ever be more than a half day away. Yet Lucille Rose (who would in a matter of weeks pluck out the thorny Lucille and become a mere Rose) still somehow managed to make Toulouse feel that prohibition and embargo were in the air and that he might not see her for years—or at least not until she was an older woman of eighteen or twenty.

"Would you come with me, Toulouse?" she asked demurely.

He thought she meant England.

Tea had cooled, and by the time Candelaria arrived with hot water, they were already heading toward Olde CityWalk. Lucille Rose clutched her new snakeskin Smythson—Amanda Hectare said python was the "rage"—while Pullman gambol'd about, and she slapped and kissed and fussed over the creature all the way to the Boar's Head. "Oh oh oh!" she cried (very Liz Taylor in *National Velvet*). "*You're* the one I'm *really* going to miss! Oh, Pullie, *you're* the one! *You're* the one!"

"What's going to happen to your book?" asked Toulouse.

"I don't know," she said cavalierly. "I sort of lost interest . . . now I just mostly use it to jot down places I want to go and people I'd like to meet." She shook the python pad like a tambourine. "I'm not sure I really want to be an actual *writer* anymore—unless it's for a magazine, like *British Vogue*. Oh, *bugger* it all! I mean, I'm *good* and everything, but . . . I talked to Mr. Hookstratten, and he was *very* upset. He had *brilliant* plans for *Blue Maze*. But as Grandma Bluey has sung before: *Que sera, sera!* Besides, if I *still* want to, England will only make my writing better. I mean, *all* the brilliant writers are from England. The Brontës, the Austens, Emily Dickinson . . . and bloody Shakespeare!"

"Emily Dickinson is not from England."

"Well, *Dick*-ens is, so bugger off!"

When she led them past the Boar's Head *and* the Majestyk, Toulouse wondered what she was up to.

"Anyway," she said, "I never did really 'crack the case.' "

"Case? What do you mean?"

"The mystery. What *was* the 'mystery' of the Blue Maze?"

"Well *maybe*," he said, shrugging his shoulders, "maybe the mystery was that there *is* no mystery."

She stopped in her tracks, as if giving his suggestion the gravest consideration—for a moment, Toulouse thought he'd saved the day and handed her a reason to live again. Jumping for joy, she could at last go back to being plain old Bel-Air Lucy. They would ride together to school as they always had, and everything—well, *most* everything—would be just like it used to be.

"Too cliché," she said.

He followed her to the hangar.

The 747 simulator was being picked up Monday and given to a charitable group. Lucille Rose climbed the stairs, turning midway to see if he had followed.

"Where shall we go?" asked the randy aviatrix, once they had settled in. It was dark; only the instruments were illuminated. "Oh my God—Heathrow, of course!"

She punched something in, and the cockpit began its subtle gyrations.

She reached over and kissed him. He unbuttoned her blouse and, for the first time ever, saw her breasts. She dropped his hand to her thigh, then moved it up. Her face was hot and tears sprang from her eyes. He watched her as they kissed like he always had, certain she was distressed by the same recollection: Edward surprising and embarrassing them as they groped in the plane. But that was far from her mind. She loved him so, yet he loved another—the orphan girl—and there wasn't a thing in the world she could do. (Her brother was dead, and there was nothing she could do about that, either.) She was truly excited about leaving. England lit up before her, tactile and redolent: she had already dreamed herself there and could smell its trees, soot and chilled air. She was inordinately excited for her life . . . but she bloody *loved* Toulouse Trotter and always would, with every fiber and filament of her body, with every red hair she had and with the red blood that beat through her bloody, bleeding over–river-run heart—nothing to do about it, nothing to do . . .

Oh bugger! Oh bollocks! Oh brilliant! *Oh, Toulouse*—

But that wasn't why she threw herself at him now . . . he would not want her for her little tits or for the pulse that shook her neck like explosives deep within a building being demolished; he would not want her for the thing she guided his fingers toward, and would not want her for her smile or kindnesses or funny girl-detective ways. He would not want her for any of that. No: he loved another, and she could not change what wasn't meant to be. Just now she wanted what *she* wanted—merely to touch him, to breathe in his smell and his hair and feel his clumsy hands stumble-bum over her. Not, as her aunt might have put it, such a terrible way to say good-bye.

CHAPTER 49

Pied-à-Terre

oulouse began his last year at Four Winds feeling very much older, and more philosophical, too. During one of Mr. Hookstratten's lectures, he stared out a window and mused on the capriciousness of this life. The mature student played a mental parlor game, imagining he was eleven years old again, sitting cross-legged on a hill. Peering into a crystal ball, he saw himself just as he was now, in Mr. Hookstratten's class during a lecture, musing through a window. The ball then showed him walking the campus alone. "But where," he asked of a wizened old warlock, "are my cousins?" "Edward is dead," said the Merlin. "And Lucille Rose has moved to England." The images in the crystal swirled and changed: there was Toulouse romping with Pullman at a house in the flats, just south of Wilshire. His mother turned into the drive in a Mercedes G-wagen, while a handsome bear of a man in corduroy slacks, tweed vest and smudged cook's apron barreled out the front door to greet her. "And who," asked the mesmerized child, "is *that?*" "Why, your father, of course!" said the mage. "But," stammered the boy, "my father is dead—" A final figure materialized in the ether: Amaryllis. But by then class was over. Toulouse gathered up his books, passing Mr. Hookstratten on the way out.

"How is your cousin Lucy?" asked the teacher with a smile.

"Fine."

"She's in London? Or was it Monaco."

"London, sir," he said, giving his enunciation an *Oliver* twist. "Living the bloody high life!"

"Well, give her my love—she's much missed. And tell her Mr. Hookstratten said, 'Keep writing!' " He shuffled his papers, then posed a daring afterthought: "And your father? Is he well?"

"Bloody well, sir. Bloody well."

As Toulouse emerged from the Hall, a shiver of autumnal breezes brought the scent of chimney smoke and the haunting frisson that only the end of a year can deliver; an unsettled, gnawing feeling that when the music of Time stops (and starts up again, soon enough), one just might be left without a chair. Yet as Lucille Rose "smelled" England, so did Toulouse intuit a whole cosmos awaiting him, grown-up and filled with adventure. Students ran or walked past on the way to their *own* thrilling destinies; some nodded in recognition, fellow ships nearly launched. The knowledge that his father had returned was by now common and somewhat secondhand. The occasional mockeries had stopped. He wondered if the general restraint had been tied to Edward's death—maybe not. Everyone was busy enough with sails and rigging, readying their vessels for the full-masted world.

*W*hen his brother-in-law left Montecito, Dodd was happy enough to provide him with new lodgings. The redbrick colonial was on South Cañon, between Gregory and Charleville, and within a few weeks had been graced by Trinnie's sure touch—funky Moorish tapestries hung on wood-paneled walls that overlooked a sly, swank mishmash of furnishings from the sixties of the last two centuries. The backyard garden was deliciously, deliriously remade, with a charming little brook that meandered through creeper and feverfew.

Though Mr. Trotter provided his son-in-law with a generous allowance so that he could begin to manage his own affairs, Marcus retained the frugality he'd exercised on the streets (and still had a not insignificant amount left over from the once Right Honorable Geo. Fitzsimmons's original bequest); so he was well fixed to treat his boy to marathon movie binges and snackathons. Within the dreaded claustrophobic cineplexes—Marcus beguilingly called them "charnel houses"—our fearless duo leapfrogged from theater to theater, dodging an incessant barrage of special effects and silver-screen profanities. (He was sad his beloved Wilshire Boulevard mecca—the Vagabond, that old Buñuelian bastion of youth—was no more, yet gladdened the lake at MacArthur Park appeared in great good health). They went bargain bookstore–hunting for inexpensive treasures to fill the groaning shelves that lined most rooms of what his father had sardonically christened Cañon Manor. They even journeyed to Tabori & Co. There, after Toulouse made "improper introductions" (Marcus's witticism), Emerson was startled to be the recipient of profuse apologies in regards to the infamously stolen volume, which the scholar accepted (the apologies) on behalf of his belated brother. The wide-eyed visitor, still Victorian in taste and sensibility, marveled at the establishment's Gothic arches and spent a full hour lingering over the pages of the *Kelmscott Chaucer*—Mr. William Morris's pride and joy.

Toulouse accompanied him to Redlands, where the boy had the surreal experience of rediscovering the childhood bedroom of his father (the same one he had napped in on a prior visit) through the very eyes of the man responsible by half for bringing him into the world. Marcus made his folks a succulent osso bucco with risotto alla Milanese before embarking on a bicycle tour of old haunts. (Redlands, oddly enough, was famed for its Victorian homes.) They camped in Joshua Tree. He showed his son the Dog Star, Sirius, and spoke intimately of Magellanic clouds buffeted by stellar wind, nostalgically perusing the sky as he once did from the lonesome beaches of Santa Monica, as if it was *there* whence he'd hailed—not Redlands or England or Misery House—now so far away from home. On the way back to L.A. they went to Huntington Gardens—there was a Morris exhibit that his father assiduously avoided but whose presence seemed to galvanize him nonetheless, for suddenly he got the urge to visit the 4th Street Bridge. Off they trooped, and made a walkabout to that encampment and other spots of local lore and legend: the motel where Amaryllis had lived with her mother, and the Higgins, too (now property of Quincunx Holdings), where he and the girl once rendezvous'd—on to the magnificent cathedral (in those days barely a shadow of its current self) that had replaced dear old St. Vib. He told him how he piggybacked their friend alongside its fence in the wee small hours of night, saving the whole of the story for another time.

At dusk, the Town Car stealthily skirted the Twin Towers, then rolled by thousands of homeless in cardboard shacks. Watching the street bonfires scared Toulouse, and he leaned into his dad. Before long, Marcus had guided them to the alley behind Frenchie's, where the boy took over. Recovering his courage, he directed the driver to double-back to the SRO where the children and Amaryllis had first met—but in the darkness, the former movie set could not be found.

" *H*re you certain?" she asked, with not a little superstition. They were stepping from Katrina's G-wagen; Pullman had already leapt out. "You're *sure* this is a good idea?"

"Well—actually, no! But we've got the boy here. The boy will keep us from harm, won't you?" He winked, but Toulouse didn't wink back; seeing his father was having sport, he merely smiled. "And if the boy won't, then Pullie will!"

Mr. Greenjeans had left for the day and the heavy, corroded gates of La Colonne Détruite were flung open in readiness.

Toulouse lugged a picnic basket filled with delicacies. Pomegranates were in season again, and Marcus had poached Shinseiki pears with caramel sauce made from the ruby-studded fruit. They'd packed bread from Poilâne, a small round of Époisses (his father said it was Napoleon's favorite) and a Solengo, one of Tuscany's finest.[†]

"Pullman and I have been coming here for years," said Toulouse, by way of small talk to calm his mother's nerves. "I mean, before I even knew anything."

"Beautiful," said Marcus, breathlessly taking it in. "Untouched! Exactly as I remembered."

As they walked in deeper, past skedges and box globes, hornbeams and hedges of hawthorn, viburnum, rhamnus and sweet briar, silence overtook them; the little family got soaked in the lush, peculiar meadow kingdom as a cotton pad in chloroform. Beyond the allée, the great cracked tower hove into view above the swales. The smile plastered on his father's face struck Toulouse as garishly bogus, and his mother had the same stilted, artificial look—like goo-gooing pedestrians who lean over a pram only to find themselves nose-to-nose with Rosemary's baby.

"That was quite a wedding we had here!" he awkwardly exclaimed (and somewhat ridiculously, too, thought Toulouse), not so much halfhearted as half winded by the sight of the castle before him. He

---

[†]Of late, Katrina allowed herself the occasional social drink; and while it may seem politically incorrect to note, her decision was—and remained—a most sober one.

had slain the dragons of psychotic delusion—and still there was this: like something out of Piranesi run riot, it should have had the sense to confine itself to Mr. Trotter's Withdrawing Room wall.

"Yes," said Katrina, privately undergoing her own swampish dishabille. "Amazing!" she averred. (Her reading was hollow and stagey.)

His father turned to him. "Horses and carriages—the works!"

"We have pictures!" said Katrina, taking up the slack. "I've never shown you pictures, Toulouse?"

"I saw some at Grandma Weiner's."

"Well!" said Marcus, rubbing his hands together. "Shall we have a walk around it?"

"Yes! Let's."

It was like watching a car wreck. Toulouse set the basket down, and his father handed him the colorful blanket he'd been carrying. The boy thought it better to let them wander alone. He took out food and drink, linen and silverware, arranging things as best he could; he even tore a sprig of flowers from a bush and laid it fetchingly upon the spread. He watched his parents glance at the tower like fitful tourists as they strolled. They held hands intermittently. When they reached the entrance, they stood in suspended wonderment—then laughed, declining the open invitation of its mouth. Their laughter broke the mood, and Toulouse rushed over. At least, he thought, they had the good sense to know it wasn't yet time to explore; in his worst imaginings, he saw them swallowed up, never to return.

*W*ithin a week, the couple returned sans Toulouse. In earlier days, Lucille Rose would surely have found them perfect subjects for a book cover, though she would no doubt have bestowed them flashlights, the more dramatically to ascend the spiral staircase at midnight hour. As it was, husband and wife performed their excavations in the reassuring light of day.

They ventured forth in much the same way that Toulouse first had—with titillated innocence, fearless and inspired. They giggled a lot and delinquently skidded around corners. Only upon entering the master suite, did they allow their mood to become something more layered. The sheets on the mattress Katrina had put down months ago were mussed, as if a body had lain there only hours before, calling to mind all manner of curious comings and goings; when she confessed, as she had in her letter, that she had drawn comfort from staying here—*here*, on this very bed—Marcus rushed to the loo to compose himself. Trinnie was at the window reclaiming the empty, verdant vista (unchanged from so many years past) when she suddenly realized how quiet it was and panicked that her husband would evaporate, or already had. She shivered and moaned aloud, and then he came toward her. He held her awhile before they descended.

*E*mboldened, she asked him to Mexico. They stayed in separate rooms, sharing a canary-yellow villa choked with elephant's ear and guayabi trees whose lanky branches sprang from saffron-colored brush. They took long walks on the beach and siesta'd in a strangler-vined palapa overlooking Careyes Bay. Under its thatched roof, she told him how La Colonne was shuttered after he'd gone, and how everything inside had been finically accounted for and fastidiously stored away.

"Do you mean, it all still exists? As it was?"

She nodded. "I think that I—well, I *hoped* you'd be back. I thought you might have suffered a memory loss . . . I don't know *what* I was thinking. I was crazy. When you came—*if* you came back—I was going to return everything to how it was. To jog your . . . it's silly, I know . . . so that it would be as if you never—I still have the maps the curators made of each room, showing where everything was—because I didn't want photos taken. Like little art pieces, really. They're in Father's study."

"There's something ineffable in that," he said softly. "It pierces my heart."

She held him, kissing the tears. Then his body awakened, and he trembled with desire. He lifted her blouse and kissed her there.

"But"—she felt so lurid to be bringing it up!—"have you . . . have you been tested?"

He didn't know what she meant. "What I mean is, well—you've been—you were on the streets for so many years . . . have you been tested? At one of the clinics?"

"Do you mean, for a disease?"

"Well—yes. For AIDS, mostly . . . for *anything.* I don't have any condoms." She cringed, but soldiered on. "Have—have you—did the doctors—did the doctors give you a test? I mean, at the jail. Or Father must have had them—"

"I have not been with any woman since you, Katy."

She had not expected that response in a million years.

"But how?"

"That part of me closed down."

"But that woman . . . the one you visited at the cemetery—"

"Jane Scull? I wasn't with her that way. I loved her dearly, but was not with her like that at all."

"Oh!"

"What is it?" he asked tenderly.

"But I *have*, Marcus."

"Have?"

"Other men! I *have*—"

She sobbed in his arms, feeling very Mary Magdalene—then grew ravenous.

"*M*arcus, there's something I want to talk to you about."

"Anything, sir!"

The former colleagues had been rehashing the good old days at Morris. It wasn't John Burnham's first time chez Weiner; just last week, Marcus and his wife had invited the agent for dinner with Diane Keaton and Gus Van Sant (another Burnham client). The group had salivated over their host's seared Kobe rib eye, DHL'd the day before from Japan.

"This might sound a little *unusual*, but—what you've been through—your *life*—is really kind of . . . amazing. Have you thought of doing anything with it?"

"Doing anything?"

"Writing it down."

"The baker said I should try that very thing!"

"The baker?"

"Gilles Mott. Said I'd win an Oscar—some such claptrap. One of my therapists encouraged me to keep a journal. Used to do just that. Afraid I haven't been very religious about it lately."

"You wrote?"

"Oh yes, kept a book for years."

"While you were out there?"

"Yes."

"A journal . . ."

"Called *News from Nowhere.*"

"I *love* that. Would I be able to see it? 'For my eyes only.' Or, if it's too personal—"

"Not at all. I have it somewhere, hidden in the house. Give me a day to find it! Become somewhat of a rabbit warren here, I'm afraid."

"You know, Gus really loved meeting you. He mentioned something to me that might be kind of an amazing opportunity. I think he's interested in doing a film about you."

"A film?"

"Did you have a chance to see *Good Will Hunting?*"

"Not since you spoke of it. Been a bit derelict. Toulouse and I were going to rent it."

"You really should look at it."

"Katy said it's quite marvelous."

"It's a wonderful film—*aside* from the fact that it's Gus. *Good Will* took a lot of people by surprise, because it was mainstream without really *being* mainstream. And this from the man who made *Drugstore Cowboy* and *My Own Private Idaho.* Not exactly Middle America! Gus can do it all."

He screwed up his eyes and said, "Now, what do you mean, John, when you say he wants to make a film about me?"

"Gus was incredibly moved by your story—your journey. He's looking for something to do next. He wants to do something 'smaller,' and I think this could be it—though this might be a little 'bigger' than what he's looking for . . . but I think it could *totally* work. There's a book called *A Beautiful Mind*, have you heard of it? At one point, Gus was interested in developing it—it's a pretty amazing story. Ron Howard did it. Russell Crowe. It's about a professor at Princeton—a true story—who kind of dropped out for twenty years because of his schizophrenia. They let him roam the campus, that sort of thing. He wasn't *violent* or anything—is it weird for me to be talking about this?"

"Not at all, John! Talk away!"

"Then he had this incredible recovery and they wound up giving him the Nobel Prize in economics."

"I don't think there's a likely chance of such a thing happening in my case," said Marcus sardonically. "Though if they gave a prize for walking, I might get one."

"I mention it because I think that while Gus is *drawn* to that kind of screenplay or book—stories with certain 'elements'—the fact that this one, your story, is so personable . . . and I don't think he wants to do the whole campus thing again, which he's done and which *A Beautiful Mind* kind of heavily gets into. He wants to go more the Charlie Kaufman route. But what I needed to know, what I wanted to ask was, would you be interested in him pursuing that? Because Gus was very specific about not wanting to offend or intrude. And *I*, certainly, as your friend—and possible agent!—wouldn't want you to become involved in anything that's going to make you uncomfortable. I wouldn't even bring something like this to the table if it was anyone but Gus. He expressed the interest; I didn't pitch him. Gus is a genius. He gets it. He's an artist. And *Good Will* made about $250 million! I asked if you'd written anything for two reasons. One, because that's something I would be interested in reading personally and possibly passing to someone in New York if we felt there was a book there, or if you felt a book could be something that might help you or be valuable in your recovery or journey or process. Or even if you just wanted to do a book to see what it felt like to be an author who suddenly has a book on the shelves. Because—bam!—you're a best-selling author. The agency could do that. And, two, because Gus would be totally open to you writing the screenplay."

"Me? John, you're kidding!"

"There's a tremendous 'independent' focus, and we are *very* strong in that area. Gus bridges both worlds. Do I think that with his help you could write a great script? Absolutely. The old rules don't apply. And, Marcus: if you write the same way you talk, the potential is amazing."

"Well, I'm flattered, John—I think." He chuckled. "And if you'd like me to meet with Gus, I'd be more than happy to. A very interesting man, very humble. I like that."

Marcus walked Burnham to his scintillating Facel-Vega. They chatted about their kids, and the agent asked after his father-in-law.

"Marcus," said Burnham. "Would you *please* come by?"

"Come by?"

"The agency—whenever it feels right. I think it'd be great, or *interesting* anyway, for you to see the changes that have happened since you were away."

"You're not going to offer me a job, are you, John?"

"It crossed my mind." They had a laugh. "Seriously, though, lots of people you knew are still doin' their thing. Doing very well, too. Let me throw you a little coming-out."

"Ah. The medicated debutante."

Burnham smiled as he switched on the engine. "Gus called me four times the day after our dinner. He was really moved—that story you told about the dream you had . . . about the 'disembodied'—"

"The Chairman of the Disembodied."

"The Chairman of the Disembodied! *Great* title, don't you think? You could call the book or the movie that—*The Chairman of the Disembodied.* I *love* that. Anyway, it really blew Gus's mind."

"Well, it surely blew mine," he said. Burnham waved good-bye, then mischievously peeled some rubber.

Marcus repeated the words sotto voce: "it surely blew mine."

CHAPTER 50

Misery House

Carry me out
Into the wind and the sunshine,
Into the beautiful world.

—W. E. Henley

Toulouse and Amaryllis returned to the maze to complete the tour interrupted months ago. They strolled within its tall borders, and had no fear of becoming lost. Pullman lay at the entrance, supremely bored.

He confessed his indiscretion with Lucille Rose on the eve of her crossing "the Pond" (as his cousin liked to put it), and Amaryllis didn't seem to mind; she had won the war, so it was easy to concede a battle or two. She kissed him deeply, in front of the inset Rodin, to show her willingness to forgive and forget.

"I've been thinking about something," she said. "And I don't want you to make fun of me."

"I wouldn't."

"Promise?"

"I promise."

"I've been thinking about John Paul."

"John Paul George and Ringo?"

"I *told* you not to make fun of me."

"Sorry."

"I was talking about the pope. I used to do a lot of thinking about John Paul, and I had this idea . . . you promise you won't make fun?"

"I won't. I swear."

"Well for a long time—a *long* time—I wanted to be a saint. I wanted him to *make* me a saint. But I thought only Catholic people could be made into saints and they had to have lived a long time ago. Like centuries. Then I found out it wasn't true and John Paul wanted to make as

many saints as he could, so he changed all the rules. Now you only need
one miracle for beatification, and one for canonization—that's when he
makes you a saint."

"You don't have to be dead?"

"I *thought* you did, but John Paul says no. John Paul is rad! He even
made eighty-seven *Chinese* people saints. And he canonized a society
lady from Philadelphia—someone just like Joyce."

"So what are you saying?"

"I bet your grandfather would be able to meet John Paul. He could
fly to the Vatican on his plane. If the pope was too busy or sick or
whatever—then your grandfather could give the Vatican money or build
an orphanage. Something to get his attention. Then John Paul would
have to meet with him."

"Meet with him? For what?"

"For Edward."

Toulouse just looked at her.

"Edward was a martyr to the Apert—martyrs don't even *need* miracles to get beatified. Then John Paul could put him on a fast track."

"Amaryllis, are you kidding?"

"I told you not to laugh!"

"I'm not. But a saint . . ."

"Edward *was* a saint."

"But you said you needed a miracle to be 'canon—' "

"There *is* a miracle—it came to me when I was with my brother and
sister at California Adventure. I think Edward was put here for a reason,
and no one knew it but him. He was put here for Joyce so she would take
care of those babies! The ones people throw in the trash. Otherwise, why
would she have done that, Toulouse? Why would she have even *started* to
do it? It was because of *him,* because of *Edward,* and I think he must have
known all along. Remember how you said at the funeral she was crying
because she never named him? That's the proof! He had no name because he was pure. It's like he was 'of God'—how do you give God a
name? And don't make fun of me! And *now* Joyce names those poor little
babies, Toulouse, that's her life's work! She made a potter's field in a rich
man's graveyard. For a woman like that—and I don't even know her
that well, but I *do* know what you and Lucy and Edward always said
about her—for a rich lady who doesn't care about anyone and who just
gets face-lifts, for a rich lady like that to bury those dumpster babies and

give them names, to make *that* her life's work, well, that *is* a miracle, isn't it, Toulouse? Isn't it? Isn't that a miracle?"

*M*arcus met with Van Sant, and with a writer from *Vanity Fair.* But one had nothing to do with the other.

The meetings took place at the William Morris Agency on El Camino Drive. This time, he stared at the oil paintings of the founders to his heart's content.

He was greeted warmly, if as a kind of charismatic curio, by the many to whom he was introduced. He was frankly startled that he ever had a passion for anything that went on in this cold brick building; though appreciative of Burnham's intentions, he would soon put an end to the misguided efforts of his gemütlich old friend. Marcus found it amusing that the agent actually harbored the fantasy that he might wish to return, in whatever capacity, to the world of "talent"—as what? Mental-Health liaison? The Van Sant business he didn't particularly mind; Gus was the real article, and he'd let that play itself out, to be sociable. He *would* say no to *Vanity Fair*; when he told Burnham—"*Say no to* Vanity Fair"—the unintentioned hilarity of the command made them split a gut. But a line had been drawn in the sand and Burnham understood. Trinnie couldn't have been happier; his behavior in the matter was the ultimate proof of sanity.

*O*n Christmas morning, he arranged to meet Trinnie, Toulouse and his father-in-law at Saint-Cloud. It was a joyous surprise when he rolled up in a pristine aqua-blue Chevy convertible (a Bel-Air, fittingly), having passed his driver's exam a mere three days before. Mr. Trotter declined, so he took his wife and son for a spin to the beach. They drove all the way to Palos Verdes, then around the peacock-infested peninsula to Portuguese Bend. They ate hamburgers and watched surfers.

Trinnie had her own surprise. At dusk, after dropping off the boy, they switched seats and she drove downhill to Carcassone Way. The cold wind snapped at their burnished cheeks, and they were happy. When they reached the driveway of La Colonne, she pushed the remote on her key chain and the gate swung open; the padlock days were no more.

"I had to do this," she said as they walked the short distance to the tower. "I know I'm insane—but I had to."

Entering the house, still lit by a stubbornly dying sun, Marcus slowly apperceived. It was filled with housewarming furniture and just-opened gifts, ribbons and wrappers torn off in a careless bacchanal. The kitchen was redolent of "leftovers," painstakingly re-created only this morning by Saint-Cloud chefs from archival recipes, their exact placement on stove, pot and dishes culled from "crime-scene" sketches commissioned by La Colonne curators—the same white-truffle risotto cooked in the late hours of their wedding night after a first round of lovemaking. The sheer recovered memory of it all, the audaciously micromanaged *authenticity* . . . the touching, nearly macabre care his wife had poured into presentation and conceit—part spectacle, part performance-theater—sent Marcus's heart to stifle his throat.

He went up to view her handiwork, with Trinnie nervously trailing after. Whenever he smiled or shook his head in wonderment, she did the same; and when the light that shone from his face darkened at some fleeting, unvoiced thought, she inadvertently mimicked his mood like the most sorrowful of mimes. Occasionally, he bent to the floor to retrieve an article of clothing or slip of paper—say, a receipt from '87 with his signature—and muttered his astonishment, to which Trinnie would say with an anxious smile, "I know, I know—I'm *insane*, I *told* you . . ." Then he would calm her with a caress or a look of such kindness that she thought: *now we can truly face anything.*

More investigations: darting in and out of cupboard and closet, drawer, nook and cranny (most of the middle floors were empty, as Louis had only provisionally furnished "lobby" and topmost floor), and for a moment it seemed like the very air of that time was transported intact from some fabulous interdimensional holding zone, flying mites, motes and all. It took his breath away and reminded him of the daring, the scope and wild apprehension, of the girl he'd left behind: remarkable creature! Naturally, he'd have been drawn to her, and she to him with his cracked mind—that was her passion and folly—and now here they were strolling through the crackedness of both, room by room, floor by floor, until they reached the master suite. *This* time there sat the four-poster in the Moroccan style, the one they had made Toulouse in. He swore he could smell their young bodies there.

By now it was dark. He sat on the bed, and Trinnie lit candles as she had years ago. They took off their clothes, eager and ritualized. When he came in her, she was sure she had conceived again.

"Shall we stay over?" he said.

"It's like that horror film, isn't it?" she laughed. "*The House on Haunted Hill?* You know—if you can *remain* without being scared shitless you win the inheritance."

They listened to the wind and soon he drifted to sleep. She stared at his rugged, beautiful face, and it was not hard to imagine that he had never gone away. Fourteen years . . . what was fourteen years in the scheme of things?

The jealous moon glared, all full of itself. "If he's gone in the morning," it seemed to say, "then you'll belong to me forever." Trinnie told the moon it had a deal.

$\mathcal{M}$orning, with its inescapable light—and majestic indifference. Morning, unbecoming—neither birth nor death nor even Time itself can woo it. Morning: that outruns the lightest of heart, and makes undone the rest.

She heard Marcus brushing his teeth. She was glad she hadn't re-connected the phones; she shivered with the memory of her father's calls—then Dodd's—then her father's—then Samson's—and her father's and Dodd's again and Bluey's and Samson's and her father's again and again and again until she could pick up no more. Bluey and Winter had finally come and spirited her to Saint-Cloud.

He appeared in the rococo door frame and smiled, toothbrush in hand. She ran and wrapped her legs around him like a child, so her feet touched soles at the small of his back; he carried her down that way—for all four flights they were conjoined—then walked her to the vast lawn, where they spun around and around, their dervish movements banishing anything that remained of old specters—that tragic and be-fuddled young woman who had searched futilely for her Gothic groom.

"Hey! Hey!"

Epitacio smiled frantically, waving from the Silver Seraph as it raced up the drive. The first thing that went through Trinnie's mind was that her disapproving father had gotten wind of what she'd been up to (from one of the archivists) and was perhaps in the throes of a sympathetic panic that Marcus had disappeared again. But she didn't see the old man on the passenger side.

As he got closer, Epitacio looked to be in a state—his smile wasn't a smile at all. "It's your father—"

"What . . ."

"He's at Cedars!"

"Oh my God."

Marcus opened the door and pushed his wife in. "Take us there!" he commanded.

They were barefoot and barely dressed.

*W*hen they arrived, Dodd and Winter were in the waiting room of the ICU. Epitacio was dispatched to bring the Weiners clothes from both Saint-Cloud and Cañon Manor; in the meantime, his-and-her VIP-suite bathrobes were proffered.

"What happened?" asked Trinnie.

"Winter found him—Dad was in the Withdrawing Room. He collapsed. He was on the floor."

"For how long?"

"We don't know!" said Winter.

Dodd put an arm around the woman to shore her up. His secretary, Frances-Leigh, came in, then hung back.

"The paramedics worked on him for a while. They had trouble getting him—Dad's heart wouldn't . . ."

Trinnie closed her eyes and groaned.

Four doctors came to the lounge, including the retired Dr. Kindman, who counted himself as Louis Trotter's oldest friend. He had treated her as a little girl, and now she went to him for comfort. He clasped her hand while the head man spoke in low, thoughtful tones. "He's unconscious at this time."

"But—what exactly happened!" said Trinnie.

"Your father," he continued, "has suffered a hemorrhage."

"Is he going to die?" Dodd asked.

"I don't know. He's fighting. The next forty-eight hours are critical."

"Can we see him?"

"Yes, of course."

Dodd left the room and squeezed the secretary's hand as he walked by. Trinnie followed, then grabbed her husband's arm, saying, "I want you to come." Winter and Frances-Leigh stayed behind, huddling together like refugees.

Mr. Trotter lay in a tangled, blood-flecked, intubated nest. After covering the old man's catheterized penis with a sheet, Marcus stood sentry at the foot of the bed. Dodd, who was not good at this, shifted uncomfortably on the sidelines. Trinnie pulled up a chair and sat beside her dad, holding his hand in hers, smiling and cooing and murmuring that everything would be all right. Her cheeks glistened with tears and she wiped his face. She was certain that his eyes had welled up since their arrival.

"It's OK, Papa, it's OK! We're here. Dodd and me—and Marcus too. We love you so much! Are you in pain, Papa? If you're in pain, squeeze once for yes and twice for no. Are you in pain? You're not in pain? You're not in pain? That's good then—he's not in pain. That's good . . . is there anything else you need? Do you need water, Papa? Would you like some water?"

One of the nurses said he was being "hydrated" but that Trinnie could daub his mouth with a damp towelette, which she did.

"Is that better, Papa? Because we don't want you thirsty. Maybe we could get them to put some scotch in that IV bag, huh. Would you like that, Papa? Can you arrange that, Dodd? Because I think it'd be very cool." She smiled at her brother, then at her husband; she was heartbreaking. "We stayed in the tower last night, Papa. The house you built for our wedding. Can you believe it? We stayed all night and it was so beautiful . . . I put everything back the way it was—all the things you gave us, all the antiques . . . we slept like babies! Didn't we, Marcus?" She drew the towelette across his forehead. "Oh, Papa, I love you so much! You can't—what will I *do* without you? What will *any* of us do?"

He opened his eyes and smiled.

"Hello, Papa! Hello, baby! It's your girl! He's awake!" she shouted to one of the nurses. "Dodd, he smiled at me! Did you see? Did you see him smile?"

When she turned back to him, he was smiling no more. "See? You'll be fine now, Papa. We won't let you leave just yet, will we, Dodd?"

"No, no we won't. There is just no way."

"And besides—you haven't picked your memorial yet!" she said, laughing through her tears. "Has he, Dodd?"

"He sure hasn't."

"So you *can't* leave, Papa, you just *can't*. What would the woman at the cemetery say? What was her name, Dodd?"

"Dot."

"Dot—that's right. What a sweet, funny lady. Well, Dot would have a conniption. Wouldn't she, Papa?"

Dr. Kindman interrupted to say that the men needed to perform a procedure and the family could come back in twenty minutes.

Trinnie caressed her father's brow. Only one eye was open now; he looked like a gnome whose forest had burned. She bent to kiss his cheek.

During her ministrations, Dodd's attention was drawn to his father's shriveled hand. As the four fingers twitched in unison, he had a shock of recognition, for what he saw he believed to be no purposeless tremor but rather the unmistakable trademark gesture belonging to Louis Aherne Trotter and Louis Aherne Trotter alone—a four-fingered last hurrah that for decades had slipped untold C-notes into the welcoming palms of bellboys, valets, barbers, doormen, gardeners, footmen, chefs, cabbies, housemaids and shine boys.

Forty-five minutes later, that very hand—having passed off its final currency to God, say, as a grateful token for His services—grew still. And the digger dug no more.

*C*he funeral was a small, intimate affair, in keeping with the wishes of the deceased. There was no wake, and no ceremony for employees or shareholders.

When Mr. Trotter crumpled, he was in the Withdrawing Room beside the welter of miniatures. The latest model—Ryue Nishizawa's corrugated-steel tomb interlaced with slats of ipé, ash, piranha pine and ebonized afromosia (which the architect had titled "Open Plan")—had broken his fall and was broken in turn. The family chose not to make that a portent; the old man's choice of memorial remained more cryptic than ever.

Trinnie's idea, which no one challenged, was to bury him in the plain green field of his plot; in six months, the family would select from the commissions and build a structure there as he had wished. The irony of this arrangement—"the temporary contemporary," as Trinnie called it in lighter moments—was that for now, the patriarch's resting place was even more austere, more anonymous, if you will, than his grandson's once-controversial domain.

Joyce elected to pay her respects, and everyone was fine with that. Rose, as she now called herself, flew in from London, looking older if not wiser. She was now in meager though spirited possession of an English accent, and peppered her conversation (outside the cemetery, anyway) with a superabundance of "shite"s and "bollocks." She wasted no time in letting Toulouse know that there was a plenitude of "Etonians" in her life—"and some of them, Royals." Naturally, Marcus and his parents were in attendance; Rose greeted them warmly, as a princess moving through an infirmary.

Trinnie had asked the Motts to please come, and the family stood alongside the man they had once known as William Morris. Amaryllis insisted on wearing the birthday dress Lucy had bought her while she was on the lam, and that proved prescient; though its style was inappropriate for the occasion, the haughty expat was moved by the homage and was more easily able to renew her affections for "the other woman."

Samson cut short a snorkeling trip in Fiji. He brought a "date," an aging-starlet type, and Trinnie thought that rude but figured he was making some kind of I'm-over-you statement. The thwarted detective was partly redeemed when the gal was later introduced as his ex-wife.

Aside from immediate family members (and Winter, who was not having a good year at all), those hit hardest stood in a group, shivering and bereft: Epitacio, Sling Blade and Dot. The disconsolate chauffeur wept openly, and not since his father had cried over Jane Scull had Toulouse seen such a cruel and alarming thing. His sobs came like great perverted sneezes followed by a train of *Ohs!* that conspired to sound like a protracted guffaw—one simply could not look away. Sling Blade's grief took a different tack. His face contorted in a frozen Mardi Gras smile reminiscent of one of the cousin's workshop masks while he rocked back and forth on his heels and hung on to his elbows for all his life. Now and then a hand leapt to the opposite biceps and scoured it, as if he were a freezing person trying to warm himself.

Perhaps the most poignant of all was Ms. Campbell. So distraught was the parkland guardian that her sister Ethel had been summoned from the East. Though she knew Mr. Trotter to be repulsed by her fashion sense, Dot was too unmoored and dispirited to dress in his honor, and wound up in the most grotesque costume misery could select, on or off the rack. (Ethel did not fare much better.) As many people were touched as they were chagrined by the clownish sight of her.

When the body had been lowered, inevitably calling to mind the whirligig boy across the way—when they had taken turns shoveling dirt over the box—after all had stepped back in respectful contemplation—that is when the final mourner arrived.

Pullman loped to the grave and no one interfered. He circled, tentatively poking his head in the airspace above. Seeing the great hole, he used a paw to push in a clod; if that weren't enough, roundly and ceremonially chuffed. Some of the mourners swore they heard the old man chuff in return.

CHAPTER 51

Restless

*A*n autopsy revealed that Louis Trotter had exsanguinated into his thoracic cavity. Trinnie attended a meeting at the law firm that had represented her father for thirty-five years. It was suggested that Cedars-Sinai be sued for employing what the attorneys characterized as a "fatally non-aggressive" treatment plan, the assertion being that their client had died of medical inaction.

An aneurysm such as his was rare, and the doctors hadn't caught it; they had attempted to rule out cancer or thyroiditis instead. They admitted being frustrated in their efforts to extract cells during the initial outpatient procedure, and the pathologists now had an understanding of why they had failed. It was speculated that some months ago, a microscopic tear in the decedent's arterial wall had caused a leakage of blood—the root of Mr. Trotter's difficulty in closing his collars. The hole had spontaneously repaired and the blood resorbed. Such a "rip" may have had its origin years ago, and been caused by trauma; a car accident or what have you. (There *had* been a collision with a taxi in Mallorca, but that was in '85.) The innominate artery had been weakened and filled with "turbulent" blood flow, then burst from its capsule underneath the collarbone that day as the old man leafed through the pages of a recently acquired twelfth-century bestiary.

Trinnie knew that her father never had any use for hospitals; he was a lousy, irascible patient and saw doctors on his terms, not theirs. He had lived a long and wonderful life and would not have wished a drawn-out lawsuit to be part of his legacy. So while Trinnie was amused that a quantity of physicians were shitting their pants, she forbade the lawyers to proceed.

*O*n ten o'clock Wednesday morning, they left Burbank by private jet. When they returned, approximately three and a half hours later, they were married—again. The oldlyweds agreed to tell no one, not even Toulouse.

Why had Trinnie proposed (for Marcus would not have dared)? The reasons were manifold. She was thrilled at the effect he was having on her son. It was as if some magnificent chunk of the boy had been restored—perhaps his heart. He seemed more *alive* with his daddy in the world, more at ease, more boyish, more manly, more everything. It may have been her pride that colored what she saw, but Trinnie knew he respected Marcus's native intelligence and eagerly sought him out for all manner of arcana, and was usually more than satisfied with the response. Seeing them together like that—student and mentor—was a *coup de foudre.*

Yet it wasn't just the child they shared. She was forced to admit to her therapist that her husband's psychosis had always made him more perversely attractive; now it pulled her in deeper still, potentiated by the feeling she had in her bones that he would never leave her—them— again. In the time since his return, Trinnie had become convinced the wrenching dislocation that had transpired between them was actually a *good* thing; they were now in possession of their own "personal myth," portable and custom-made, to which they'd been fated, and fated to recover from, too. The past would hold no dominion, and they would be infinitely richer for it.

In other words, she had fallen in love for a second time.

The therapist had some concerns. (They always do.)

The most compelling reason for repeating those vows was the death of her father. The digger had always felt guilty for not having protected her from the beginning; he had built La Colonne out of hubris, and it became their tomb. It didn't matter that his feelings were irrational—to marry Marcus again would close the circle, and give the old man absolution. Hadn't she told him on his deathbed that they'd spent the night there? Hadn't the corner of his mouth turned up in a smile?

She had lost a man to the tower just as before—sacrificed so the other might stay.

"*G*randma!" shouted Lucy, running to Bluey's arms.

Though her name was now officially Rose, she had graciously agreed to fall back on the birth moniker so as not to further confuse our dear cottage resident. The old woman looked stricken; Lucy had forgotten (and Toulouse had failed to remind her) that Bluey didn't take well to noise or abrupt movement. Even the girl's clothes were loud—a Lacroix jigsaw-print mini with red tights and lime-green ankle boots. Her grandmother smiled and softened, yet didn't say a word. Lucy had enough for both of them.

"Oh, Grandma, I have so much to tell you!" Her accent was still cheap, but she wore it like the crown jewels. "England is so bloody wonderful! Aunt Trinnie said"—"aunt" being pronounced as in the first syllable of "entourage"—"Aunt Trinnie said you used to go there all the time. That you were a 'regular'—crossing the Pond on the *Queen Mary*, I mean. Very posh: *Port Outward Starboard Home*. Did you know that's what 'posh' stood for, Toulouse? At least you weren't on the *Titanic*! Aunt Trinnie said you were like a heroine out of Henry James—I'm halfway through *Portrait of a Lady*, and it's *so you*."

They set out for the wandering garden. Bluey, having twisted her ankle, now used a wheeled walker to get around; its front legs were thrust through tennis balls, to let it glide. She had lost a good deal of weight and constantly drew her tongue—dried-out from incontinence meds—over chapped lips in a futile attempt to moisten them. She cleared her throat incessantly, as if to dislodge foodstuff caught within, because the Haldol prescribed to squelch her delusions affected the ability to swallow. But she still looked elegant, due to Winter's heroic ministrations. She wore her favorite Bill Blass and as usual was scrupulously done up for the children's visit.

The girl with straightened hair didn't seem to register any of the sadder nuances that Bluey presented. The cousins had been to visit a number of times since their grandfather's funeral, and Toulouse was, frankly, sickened by the caricature his relation had become. He hoped it to be a passing phase—he'd heard enough about Miss Hectare and her lord- and ladyships to last a lifetime. Lucy had flaunted the aquamarine ring "Amanda let me borrow" and couldn't help but inform that it had cost five thousand quid and was designed by none other than the estimable Jade Jagger. He'd seen the charm bracelet she wore around her neck as well—*s*p*o*i*l*m*e*—and heard her prattle on about ludicrous chocolate boxes ringed in Chloé fringed denim that "Stella McCartney created at just four hundred apiece. They say *Eat Me* on the lid, and they're giving all the proceeds to breast cancer! Isn't that brilliant?" She'd exchanged her python Smythson for a fire-engine-red one with the snooty gold cover engravature:

LONDON

PARIS

MILAN

NEW YORK

She spoke wantonly of fashion, like a pathetic imitation of his mom—how her "completely knackered" clique all wore Chanel and Ghost and Uth and how she and Amanda went to a Moroccan-style wedding and a Hilton girl took her bloody blouse off and then they went to Paris (the city, not the girl) and sat behind Angelina Jolie and Jennifer Lopez watching models in nun's habits and $70,000 dresses, throats fakely slashed, sashay through fifteenth-century churches on bloodred catwalks—oh, but the "shows" were great fun! Her highest aspiration was to spin records at parties. She said she was meeting lots of boys who thought she was older. They all wanted to "bonk" and she'd actually "snogged" with a twenty-seven-year-old broker at Billie Piper's nineteenth birthday at the Papagaio.

"They're all wankers, for the most part—poseurs. They come up to you straightaway and make their proposition. And you just stand there, gob-smacked. Amanda's older, so she gets hit on more. They're bleeding idiots! Poofs and poseurs! Tossers! Off their heads! They look you straight in the 'porkpies'—that means 'eyes.' It's Cockney-rhyming slang, haven't you heard of that, Toulouse? It's *great* fun. They look you in the porkpies, even the ones with rotten 'boat races'—'boat race' means 'face.' And I thought English boys would be so . . . unaggressive! I was *wrong*, they are seemingly *so* un-English. Bounders! Oh, and Grandma!" She turned to Bluey, as if they were all on a talk show. "We went to the most *amazing* party at Badminton. Have you been? It's where the duke of Beaufort lives. Lady Hectare's *brilliant* friends with Bunter and Tracy—Bunter's the duke's son. And Bobby is *so cute.* He's only twelve, but he's an earl, the earl of Glamorgan or something. There were *huge* amounts of marquesses and marchionesses, viscounts and countesses and even a bishop—the bishop of Kensington, I think. The *houses* there. They are *castles,* they are *manors,* Stradella is shite! Stradella is naff! Oh, Toulouse! I forgot—there was a Spanish infanta there too! But we never met her. Oh, bollocks. We were too busy painting our faces and being wicked! The duke's wife is a landscape artist, just like Aunt Trinnie. They have a nanny from New Zealand who *so* reminded me of Winter . . . and the marquess of Bath was there—Alex, I think he's called—he's friends with your mom. Oh! And do you *know* who showed up? The marquess of Went! Remember when we were at Leaf House with Edward and that old man showed us the maze? Well, that was *his* property—I mean, the marquess of Went. But the marquess of *Bath* is so *cute,* looks like a bloody wizard. And he's witty! And he wears the most *brilliant* vests and ties—and lives at Longleat with the marchioness— they're 'trouble and strife'—that's husband and wife. But Amanda said Lord Bath has *lots* of wives—'wifelets,' I think he calls them. He's like a Mormon. Do they call that 'polygamous'? Oh, Toulouse, he's the *most* brilliant hippie! Longleat's open to the public. It would be like having crowds troop through Olde CityWalk, but that's the way they do it, because the upkeep is so expensive. They even have a *zoo* there, and bollocks if there isn't a gorilla living on an island *gob-smack* in the middle of the lake . . . oh it's posh and posh-totty. There are lions and tigers and rhinos and giraffes—and even a railway! Capability Brown did the landscaping, Trinnie told me all about her. Didn't Trinnie tell you about Capability Brown? Capability did Sutton Place too, that's the Hectares'. It's in Surrey—Surrey with a bloody fringe on top! *Capability Brown* and *Gertrude Jekyll* . . . aren't they the queerest, most brilliant names? Oh don't make a face, Toulouse, you look like an arse. Anyway, the duke had this very fab party and ordered everyone to wear purple leather and suede. Well, maybe it wasn't the duke's party, maybe it was his son's. And there was an entirely *different* brilliant gathering where the men wore tuxedos and went *shooting.* Foxes? Or maybe birds—I'm not sure. These people are *super* multitaskers! They're brilliant! And there are *ghosts* in that house, Grandma—I say 'house' but it's more like a small *country*—it's like fifty thousand acres! Lauren Bush was there, and

Madonna, and the prince of Bourbon too. (Amanda calls him the Prince of Scotch and Soda, but not to his face.) Everyone got bloody well off their heads and played polo and it started to rain cats and dogs and the duke had a helicopter hover over the wicket so it wouldn't pour on the pitch. Oh, Toulouse, you *have* to meet the Dent-Brocklehursts! Then Henry did a little dance and it stopped pouring! It was brilliant. Jemma introduced me to George Harrison, of the Beatles? I had no idea who he was! Amanda said he was stabbed or something, and he looks a hundred years old. Got cancer, too. A gray, gray man. Amanda and I were in the kitchen and she said, 'You've just met one of the Beatles,' and *I* said, 'Bob's your uncle!' When I go back next week, we're going to a party at Gatcombe Park. And guess who's having it: Zara Phillips! She's Princess Anne's daughter but doesn't 'wear' a title, isn't that so fab? Got a pierced tongue, Zara does—Amanda and I are thinking of getting *ours* pierced. But don't you *dare* say anything to your mum, Toulouse, or I'll be fit to—"

She couldn't help but notice that her grandmother was now leaning on the walker with her elbows and reaching out with both arms—rather plaintively at that. Lucy regarded her with a slightly confused smile; thinking that she wished to be held, the young socialite put a stiff upper lip on it while she and Toulouse maneuvered the old woman from her encumbrance. Now free, they embraced—and Bluey began to scream. No ordinary outburst, but a high-pitched bone-rattling ululation that startled the girl and filled her with horror. (Winter later reported that it usually happened at night and was the cause of some wonderment, because once begun, the siren could last up to fourteen hours without relenting or even varying much in pitch. Even those who had seen their share of screamers were astonished at the suprahuman outpouring.)

Lucy tried to break away, but found the old woman's grip to be formidable. Toulouse did what he could to pry them apart but was fearful of injuring his grandmother, who now fell atop the girl, pinning her to the hard ground, while other residents made their way over like querulous zombies.

"Tull!" she cried. "Tull, help me! Help me!" To add insult to injury, Bluey began to sing—" '*All of the kids—to teacher carried—candy and ice cream cones—but who do you think the teacher married? Wood'nhead Pudd'nhead Jones!*' "—all happening in a blink yet feeling like an eternity to the child trapped beneath. Winter, who'd been taking a much-earned respite in the commissary, was on her way back when she saw the commotion through a garden fence. By the time she'd passed through the gate and emerged to the wandering path, the staff was already lifting Bluey from her traumatized guest, whose stylish retro print was soaked in the former's pungent urine.

Winter and Toulouse helped her up as the old woman was led away. The smelly rubberneckers muttered oaths and inanities as they dispersed to rejoin traffic on the sumptuously topiaried loop.

"Are you all right?" asked Winter.

Lucy stood there, stunned.

"She didn't mean it. She doesn't know what she's doing . . . she didn't know who you were—"

Lucille Rose, who had by now wandered a short way down the path, turned and looked at her—at both of them—then tightly closed her eyes as if to teleport herself to another place.

Winter came closer.

Lucy screamed her *own* little scream, but it didn't last—then ran like the devil to the car.

*C*he Trotter women were having a time of it.

Trinnie hadn't been the same since returning from *another* wedding—an old rehab chum's, in Manhattan. She took to her room without explanation and wouldn't speak to anyone, not even Marcus, who had shown himself to be an easy confidant. She shed twenty pounds in half as many days and was sleeping barely two hours a night. Out of suicidal desperation, she finally called Samson and said it was urgent that she see him.

When the detective arrived at Saint-Cloud, the feeling was of a city deserted. Trinnie had ordered the staff away; she could no longer tolerate their accusatory eyes.

"What's wrong? My God, what's happened?"

She stood at the door, emaciated and trembling. He'd never seen her so haunted.

"Oh, Sam!" she said, glomming on to his jacket. "Something terrible—something so *horrible* . . ."

"Is it Marcus? Did he leave?"

"No—no! Marcus is *fine* . . . better than *ever.*"

"Then Toulouse—"

"No," she said, frantically shaking her head. "They're all fine. It's *me* this time, Sam, it's me . . ."

She led him outside to the flagstone terrace, where she had laid a possum on a delicate porcelain plate. Its breath was labored; it was clearly dying.

"I think he fell from the roof. Look how sweet he is! Poor thing can't breathe . . . do you think he's going to die? He's just a baby. Where's his mother, Sam? Maybe he's just playing possum, no? I put out some peanut butter—they're supposed to like peanut butter. That's not such a bad thing to smell if you have to die, is it, Sam? That's not such a bad thing to be smelling before he . . ."

She began to sob. He helped her to the wrought-iron divan.

"Trinnie—tell me what's wrong. What's happened?"

"I was in New York last week . . . and I saw something from the hotel, on the street. Oh, Sam, I *saw* something!—"

"Tell me."

"—and things have been going so *well*, Sam! That's what's so— that's what's so *crazy* . . . but it's always like that, isn't it? Just when you think everything's great!"

"Trinnie, you have to calm down. Try to—"

"A man and woman . . . arguing. It must have been two in the morning. Two or three. You know New York—these *dramas* playing themselves out . . . junkies and whatever. Like some awful play—you hear everything. The streets are like canyons, everything echoes. Especially if you're high up—and they . . . the man, he kept walking away. He didn't want to listen anymore. And she kept coming after him, like a harridan—and . . . it *was* like a play—some stupid Sam Shepard— because each time they moved in front of a town house, the lights would come on—you know, those automatic lights in front of houses that get triggered when you . . . —so as they walked, each house lit them up in pools of—oh, Sam! You don't *know*, you don't *know*, you don't *know!*"

"Tell me, Trinnie," he said, his tone nearly harsh.

"At a certain point, the man walked away and the woman came after—he turned—and she . . . hit his neck. And he fell backward . . ."

"She used a knife?—"

"No, no, nothing like that! With her *hand*—a fist, *something*. I don't know. I couldn't *see*."

"The police came?"

"No! No! You don't understand! *No one can understand.* Oh I am fucked I am fucked I am fucked! Sam . . . when I went to see my father last year—maybe it was the year before—when I went to see him at the quarry—I went to see him because I found out that he—it was after you told me the two of you found Marcus—I was so *angry*—and he was getting his hair cut when I came in, Sam, so *helpless* and so *small* and I struck him with my *hand* on his *little neck*! I was so angry and my hand just lashed out and I hit him *hard,* Sam, hard enough for him to fall back and I *know* that I hurt him! And he couldn't button his shirts after that— do you remember? He couldn't button his shirts! And then Marcus told me . . . Marcus said that when he met Toulouse for the first time—I was in the desert—Marcus wrote in a letter that when he met Toulouse at Saint-Cloud, Papa was holding a towel to his neck like a poultice . . . he was holding a towel there! And I never pursued it! I said I would but I didn't! And the doctors—Sam, the doctors said the tear in his vein came from a blow! They asked if he'd been in a car crash—they said sometimes this sort of thing can happen as a result of an accident or a fight. But I didn't think of it—I didn't *remember,* Sam, until I saw that dreadful couple on the street! And I sat in the lawyers' office feeling so smug, so *benevolent* because I didn't want the hospital to be sued. The hospital— when it was *me*! Oh, Sam, I killed him, I really did! And what I want to know—what I *need* to know—from *you*—the reason why I asked you here, what I need to know—because that would be catastrophic—what I need to know is if they can put me in prison. Because I couldn't survive that, Sam—I couldn't survive! After everything we've been through, Sam, with Marcus and Toulouse, for it to end this way! But I *did* kill him, Sam, I killed my father! Toulouse's grandpa! Toulouse and Lucy and poor Edward's—Bluey's *husband* . . . oh, Sam Sam Sam, the way he *looked* at me in the ICU—his eyes suddenly opened and he *smiled* at me and I think he was smiling because he realized I didn't know what I'd done and he would have wanted to spare me from that knowledge because he would *have* to have known that me *knowing* something like that—well I simply could not *live*—and so he was glad that I—but now I *do* know, Sam, I *do* know—everything!—and oh, Sam Sam, what am I going to do, what am I going to do, what am I going to do?"

*   *   *

*M*arcus wasn't overly concerned by his wife's prolonged absence. Always careful not to make demands, he had resolved to calmly subjugate himself to her moods. He thought it best to maintain an attitude that at least on its surface was High Victorian laissez-faire.

He took to visiting the Westwood cemetery on a daily basis. It was a decent walk from his Cañon Drive home, and he enjoyed the sloping stretch of Wilshire Boulevard that bisected the country club. Sometimes you could see deer behind the fence butting heads.

He befriended Dot Campbell, who found him winning, and a great comfort.[†] His sartorial style reminded her of Mr. Trotter's in that it was a tad antiquated—a "bespoke" lapel, golden fob or the unusual cut of a pocket amicably connoting another era (she wasn't always sure which).

[†] [*All but the most persnickety of voyagers are here advised to skip this lengthy, if final, footnote; or at least come back another day, for it has no pertinence to our main story, nor does it desire to disturb the secret rhythms of denouement*—"Ed."] Before disclosing this almost whimsical piece of intelligence, the author wishes to note that the perfect reader does not exist; and while some whose hands turn these pages may come close, certain ideals should as such remain hypothetical. All right then. A long while back (long enough that it may translate to weeks in the life of one who has attended this volume) it was learned that Gilles Mott had a fiancée with whom he mistakenly ventured to a certain (or uncertain) Parisian cellar in which a sophisticated group partook of roasted songbird—but of this incident we've already heard enough. What matters here is that he implied, songbird or no, that said fiancée was subsequently jilted. The author did not think much of this indiscretion then nor does he now; it is the baker himself who belabored it. As a remorseful pastime, he had long dreamed of making amends to that aggrieved and vanished girl, and to his amazement, opportunity finally knocked. That "girl," alas, was Dorothea "Dot" Campbell—or so a careful study of her features and dress (for even then, at the time of their affiance, she was well on her way to fashion infamy and remained undeterred by the raiments of the City of Light) during Louis Trotter's services bade him believe. Knowing that the time and place were inappropriate, he remained undaunted, for he knew full well he would never have the gumption to return. Immediately following the burial, Gilles Mott confirmed she was indeed the womanly version of the one he had ditched not two weeks after their illicit dinner in an arrondissement whose numeric designation remained forgotten even then. Dot watched blank-faced (gob-smacked, as Lucille Rose might have put it) as the baker stood on her turf and launched into one of the more stupendous mea culpas of our time—after which he went rigid, expecting to nobly bear the brunt of a physical blow. Instead, her clear and simple response freed him. Ms. Campbell said she *did* remember and always felt he'd done her a great service, for it was within the same month of the "lucky breakup" that she met the love of her life, the courtly, handsome (and short-lived) Byron Campbell, inventor and engineer, whose romantic attributes were such that the memory of past dalliance or promised betrothal (there were many, she assured with a wink) were completely and utterly obliterated. Upon hearing this, Gilles Mott was so relieved that he ventured a flirtatious remark, but was cut off when she excused herself with the finality of a debutante detaching herself from a cipher. A final footnote deserves a final epigram: it was Marcus Aurelius who wrote: "How ludicrous and unrealistic is he who is astonished at anything that happens in life!"

Sometimes he came with Toulouse, but more often he was alone, and strolled the grounds scrutinizing stones and taking the air. He occasionally knelt to read an inscription but was not one of those tedious hobbyists who with paper and charcoal make imprints of headstone faces.

Marcus often walked alongside the caretaker while the latter performed his duties, and sometimes (though Dot frowned on it) the burly companion assisted with a rake. He was happy to talk with Sling Blade about the old man, and it seemed to relieve them both of pent-up sorrows. Marcus was especially intrigued by the Candlelighters' parcel, with its whirling grave markers—he counted more than twenty now. He never failed to brush Edward's plaque with the tips of his fingers and say, "Sleep well, son. Sleep well."

Invariably, he ended his visit with a walk to where the digger lay. There was no memorial as yet, but that wasn't what disturbed him (for even the portraits of the founders of William Morris bore no names). The man had spent so many years imagining a monument, and Trinnie would soon make her decision—but how? By what lights? And who had the right? Perhaps they should just leave things as they were, he thought. Perhaps in the end it was best that Mr. Trotter take a note from the Candlelighters and join his grandson in oblivion.

Whenever he left that place, always in dusky hour, when a chill stole through the gate, Marcus felt no peace—and was certain that it did not bode well for the migrant, entrepreneurial spirit of his dear, departed benefactor.

"Doddie?"

"Mother! Hello—"

"Doddie, I'm so glad I reached you!"

"Are you OK? Is everything OK?"

"Yes, yes, wonderful! Where—where are you?"

"I'm on my way to India, Mother."

"India!"

"Can you believe it?"

"How wonderful!"

"I'll only be gone a few days."

"A few days! But why on earth *India*?"

"We have factories there. Quincunx has factories there."

"Well now, *that's* really something."

"How are you feeling?"

"I'm clear today!"

"That's so great. You sound wonderful."

"I'm not *afraid* today! And Winter's here—she's been so marvelous."

"Winter's a terrific lady."

"I haven't been the hostess with the mostess. In fact, I've been a royal pain in the you-know-what!"

"She understands, Mother. She understands . . . God, it's so great to *talk* to you like this. To hear you sounding so—"

"I *can* talk, you know. People seem to have written me off."

"No one's written you off. That would be an impossibility."

"Doddie . . ."

"What is it, Mother?"

"Doddie, I know that Louis isn't here. That my dear Louis is gone."

"Did one of the nurses tell you that?"

"No, no. There are certain things a person doesn't have to be told. And I say: what's so great about this little blue planet anyway, that's what *I* say! Doddie, did I tell you that marvelous little aphorism of Winter's? God is wringing his hands. He's sitting on a bench in the clouds, wringing his hands. 'I'm in love with an atheist,' he says, tears *streaming* down his cheeks onto that long white beard. 'I'm in love with an atheist who lives in New York—but she doesn't even know I exist!' Isn't that marvelous, Doddie?"

"It's a *wonderful* joke."

"It's not a joke, it's an aphorism."

"I laugh every time you tell it."

"Oh, don't be so stupid."

"I'll come see you, soon as I get back. Thursday, all right? I'll bring you something, would you like that? I'll bring you a sari."

"I'm so sorry."

"Mother? I didn't hear you. What did you—"

"I'm so sorry, said she, but we're not accepting saris today."

He laughed. "It's *great* to hear you like this. To hear your sense of humor again."

"Doddie, how are we fixed for cash?"

"We're fine, Mother."

"I don't want you spending all your money on that plane."

"Can't happen."

"Why don't you get rid of that plane and fly American Airlines?"

"I actually *save* money with the jet, Mother."

"Oh."

"So I don't want you to worry."

"Doddie—there's something I read in the paper—while I have you on the phone . . . did you hear about Lillian Hammersmith? A *glorious* dancer. Friend of Alice's—Astor. Had a house in Rhinebeck, one of those fancy places high on a hill. I always wanted your father to buy in Rhinebeck, but he was obsessed with the Adirondack 'style,' had to have his Great Camp. But, my *God,* Hudson Valley was grand. So green, so stately! Alice had fireplaces in the bathrooms, and *that,* I think, is the greatest luxury known to man. If you stood in the backyard, you could see the Roosevelts on one side and the Stuyvesants on the other."

"Mother? I'm sorry, I didn't . . . what was the last thing you said?"

"Ninety-*two* she was, poor Lillian. That's marvelous genes, isn't it? A *great,* great friend of Bill's—and Tennessee's—and Cecil and Evelyn too. They were *all* at Rhinebeck. Well as you can imagine I was *deeply* impressed. I was barely twenty-five!"

"Little hard to hear you, Mother. Connection isn't good."

"The *Times* didn't say how she passed away—at that age, they never do! It's considered poor form. But it seems she held on to her money, and I'm glad for that. Doddie . . ."

"Yes, Mother? I can hear you now."

"There's someone else who passed on."

He was certain now that she knew about Edward too, and girded himself to respond.

"Do you remember Bluey Trotter? Née Twisselmann, of the Pittsburgh Twisselmanns? She married Louis Trotter, the Bel-Air waste-removal king."

"Mother?"

"Doddie, can you hear me?"

"Yes—"

"Because I know how busy you are . . ."

"I'm not busy at all. I just couldn't understand what you—"

"*Bluey Trotter née Twisselmann.* Have you already heard?"

"Heard what, Mother?"

"She passed, Doddie! And so young. Well, relatively—do you

remember her? We all seem to have lost touch. I wanted you to know before you read about it or heard it from a stranger."

"I don't know what you're saying."

"Don't be stupid, Doddie! You're always so stupid!"

"Is Winter there?"

"I'm telling you that she *passed*. But I know how busy you are."

"Mom, can you please put Winter on?"

"I'll let you go, dear. You take care now, Puddin'-head."

"Can you just let me talk to Winter a second?"

"I just wanted you to know so you wouldn't read about it in the paper. So don't be sorry. Say hello to the Indians, said she, and don't be 'sari'!"

CHAPTER 52

At the End of the Day

What in the midst lay but the Tower itself?
The round squat turret, blind as the fool's heart,
Built of brown stone, without a counterpart
In the whole world . . .

—Robert Browning

*I*t was Marcus who made the suggestion that proved pivotal to his wife's recovery.

When Samson Dowling confided the putative reason behind her breakdown, Marcus quickly formed a stratagem in keeping with the nimble warriorship of his storied agenting days. A summit with Dr. Kindman was held at his magnificently restored Pasadenan Greene & Greene. Digger and Duffer had first met in the Pacific Theater, before an agreement was struck stateside; Mr. Trotter would make his friend filthy rich if the latter would deign to improve his golf game. (Each held up his end fairly well.) More than anyone, Dr. Kindman had been privy to the panoramic events comprising *toutes les affaires Trotter.* He was present at the births of Katrina and Dodd, who in turn came to know him as a frequent dinner guest (and Twig House crony, too—he canoed with the best of them). Suffice to say he was close at hand while a third generation was brought into the world, some with more trouble than others, and was a great comfort to the parents of Edward, seeing them through the difficult times and always making sure they had access to the best care available.

The good Dr. Kindman had in fact intervened on Trinnie's behalf when it seemed that her fiancé might benefit from a little professional counseling after the incident of the stolen book, and was the very same Mr. Trotter thought to call to La Colonne on that faraway, inconsolable morning to administer tranquilizers to his wounded girl. And while the old man had demurred in asking his advice on the matter of the collars that would not button, Dr. Kindman *had* been furnished with a blow-by-blow of Marcus Weiner's extraordinary Twin Towers adventure. Upon his release, the physician spent several afternoons at the Hotel Bel-Air and subsequently Montecito, feasting on the ex-convict's truffled grits and mango'd foie gras. (Though it has already been shown that his "family" credentials could not be more impeccable, it should be noted that Dr. Kindman still made the once-a-week trip to Woodland Hills and wandered there with Bluey, who never screamed in his presence. He was at bedside the exact moment Louis chuffed off this mortal coil.)

As Marcus laid the whole thing out over coffee, the doctor knew early on where he was heading, for he understood the headstrong woman's sensitivities and always felt the needless torture she had inflicted upon herself throughout the years to be a crying shame—this latest being "the topper." While it was arguable that the physical blow she had inflicted upon her father was the contributing factor, or even the cause, of his death, Dr. Kindman (and of course Marcus) realized that in order to secure her peace of mind, such a thing would need be indelibly disproven, which it, naturally, could not. An alternative course of action was proposed. By the end of the day the very pathologist who had given Trinnie the news of the fateful arterial "rip" stood in great officialdom before her hospital bed with a raft of MRI, CAT scan and "autopsy" results (the latter had not actually been performed) while Marcus, Dr. Kindman, two psychiatrists and three others from Mr. Trotter's health team hung fire.

Trinnie sat with knees drawn to chest, like a despondent bookend.

It is unnecessary to go into any great particulars regarding the tender machinations that led to the assembly's cogently convincing refutation of an earlier-stated now wholly "speculative" cause of death, or the passionate assertion of the "absolute impossibility" of such a blow having played any part in said demise. The true culprit, they averred, lay in a pre-existing condition of which Dr. Kindman and the deceased himself had been long aware, a condition for which our carefully prepared team had gathered enough corollating data to sway the grandest of grand juries. It *is* enough to say that these were men whose predilection and training was to do no harm, or, at least, to ease human suffering, and that the situation at hand—a distraught, borderline-delusional woman who needed to hear certain things in order to get on with her life—brought out their very best.

The present company, some of whom were already well disposed toward Trinnie for not having sued them, was beholden to her father for his selfless disbursement of grants and private research fundings, large amounts of which had yet to be released. In other words, they depended on the largesse of the executor of the estate, a role that happened to be filled by none other than Dr. Kindman, a detail offered here without irony or cynicism and not meant to dilute the wonderful thing they did that drizzly, gray afternoon. Which was: they lied. They lied to Katrina Trotter. They lied to save her—she tenuously came to life before their eyes—and in so doing, were born again to the qualities of healing and mercy which most had forgotten (or left by the wayside), the very things that first inspired them to take the Hippocratic Oath. They lied, and slept like babes that night, awakening to a day that was new. They were full of grace and heroic virtue, and whether that venerable mood lasted an hour, a week or forever is of no concern here. This is all that mattered: in the course of twenty-odd minutes, a diabolical, potentially fatal burden was lifted from Trinnie's frail shoulders by her husband and his cohorts—an ingenious act of merciful aplomb that could not have been orchestrated any better by Louis Trotter himself.

We *are* that malleable, usually punishing ourselves for no good reason, and are happy-go-lucky and indifferent while leaving sorrow and havoc in our wake.

*C*rinnie divided her time between the presidential suite of the Peninsula Hotel and Cañon Manor (where Toulouse was installed), for the solitariness of Saint-Cloud was too much to bear. Over the next few months, the seeds the doctors had planted finally took root so that, looking back, she could recall the time she thought herself a patricide as one recalled the paranoid Technicolor of a fever dream. Slowly, her father's memory was able to take its rightful, benevolent, quietly riotous place in her garden.

The social cachet of the Weiners, steadfastly building after fits and starts, achieved a kind of flash point with the publication of "The Man Who Would Be William Morris" in *Vanity Fair.* John Burnham felt terrible for having initially provided access, but there was nothing he or anyone in his circle could do to quash the piece. The profile, one of those lush, quasi-literary tabloidal numbers that tipped their hat to Oliver

Sacks, contained a treasury of La Colonne wedding photos and even Weiner juvenilia (to wit, a grainy shot of the boy staring directly to camera, Portrait of the Itinerant Schizophrenic as a Very Young Man). What disturbed Marcus most was that the writer had duped poor Harry into handing one of the old albums over. He thought that unforgivable, but graciously shook it off, for he was glad just to be whole again, and reunited with his family. Besides, a certain amount of notoriety accompanying their "coming-out" (as Burnham put it) was inevitable; the agent in him was savvy enough to know the publicity apparatus would soon enough move on to fresher prey. The article was optioned as a feature film, but certain forces—which did not exclude the artful designs of Dodd Trotter or, for that matter, those of Mr. Burnham himself—had conspired to guarantee that nothing would ever come of it.

*M*arcus, who still took his constitutionals to and from the cemetery, one day found Joyce crouching over her son's grave, agitated beyond the norm.

"Are you all right, girl? What is it?"

"I'm just heartsick—some heavy equipment came through here, and look what happened."

The plaque had cracked in two, with only the bottom-most half remaining. It now read:

90–2001

rgotten the world,
nd soon the world will have forgotten you."

"It's going to take three weeks to repair."

"What a shame! What a shame . . ." They knelt there staring at it awhile before he spoke up. "Joyce—have you been to potter's field?"

She looked at him blankly, thinking he spoke in metaphor.

"The potter's field in Boyle Heights."

"No."

"A dear friend of mine was buried there. Do you know how they do it, at potter's field?"

"Yes. Edward told me . . ."

"No names—not even an apothegm! Only dates. They keep markers, markers with the year etched upon it."

"I don't think I could do that to him."

He had only been trying to make things better, but had made them worse instead. "Oh, I wasn't suggesting it, Joyce. Oh, not at all!"

"I know you weren't, Marcus. It's just that . . . I feel it's so important—*apart* from honoring him—you know, that he was *here*—that he was *with* us . . . It's a way of saying: 'The world will not forget you.' "

"Oh, I doubt Edward would ever feel he could be forgotten, ma'am." He saw that he'd wounded her again. "But surely you're right, surely you're right. Names *are* very important—I should know. I've had more than one!"

She smiled, and felt his warmth. She had sold this man short—had called him crazy and unwashed and a bad father in the bargain, the major kink in her sordid sister-in-law's dissolute life. But he was the sanest of the lot. She so appreciated him visiting her son each day. He was unmorbidly comfortable with death, and that made Joyce more comfortable too. He never judged her.

Only days before, something strange had happened. After receiving a frantic call, she had invited Rachel, one of the lesbian moms, to Stradella House for lunch. The frazzled woman showed up with the baby, saying Cammy left her for a man and that she had no idea as to her "wife" 's current whereabouts. She asked point-blank if Joyce—being the infant's godmother—would "look after him" for a few weeks while she went east. Her mother was dying, and Rachel said she didn't feel up to the task of caring for the boy in the midst of deathbed duties. While she spoke, she glanced nervously about the house, like a slave girl soon to be banished. *Take him!* her flitting eyes seemed to cry. *You could take* ten thousand—*this place could fit them all.*

She called him Ketchum; the name the Palisades ladies had given him simply wouldn't do.

Winter moved to Stradella to help out. She and Joyce almost had heart attacks—it was scary and messy and hysterical fantastic fun; it was *life*, tiny and needy, pissy and shitty and squalling—and she found herself actually looking forward to coming home from Pilates or Aida

Thibiant or Candlelighters, and that was a big change, because since Dodd had moved to the Hotel Bel-Air after telling her he was in love with his assistant, Frances-Leigh, she had found the house and haunted Olde CityWalk grounds to be a far less amenable place than where her son lay anonymously (for now) buried. The absurd thing was, she was living the life of some kind of sitcom: the rich lady of a certain age whose husband leaves her for the secretary and who inherits a toss-away baby—throw in a nanny, she joked to Winter, and you've got an old-fashioned prime-time hit! She felt like Bea-fucking-Arthur. It made her laugh, and anything that could do that had to be good.

Ketchum's presence healed them both, for Winter had been at wit's end; Bluey's condition had deteriorated exponentially and was a horror to behold (she thanked God Mr. Trotter could no longer bear witness). When Trinnie finally decamped, Saint-Cloud became a very creepy place to lay one's head; though Winter kept the television on all night long and slept on the living room couch, she still felt as if Jack Nicholson were going to come axing his way through the front door. At least there was life on Stradella, and new life at that. Joyce let her stay in any room she liked, and it almost felt like a holiday. Still, when she made herself dinner, she fell to musing about the condo Bluey had promised, wondering if it would vanish, as Mr. Trotter had, into thin air.

*O*f course, now that Toulouse's hormones were racing, Amaryllis was no longer interested—well, she was, but not in the kind of explorations that had taken place some months ago in the penthouse of La Colonne. Then, Toulouse had been a gentleman, wise and respectful beyond his years; *now*, thinking back on that precocious moment, he merely wished to shoot himself. He'd become obsessed with her, and the evil thing was that she knew it. She fussed over him just enough (her attentions falling sadly short of the cockpit grapplings with his English cousin, which now seemed stupendously pornographic) to keep him from going bananas.

They saw each other at least twice a week. Toulouse lived for Friday afternoons, when he found himself being driven over the Shakespeare Bridge to the home of his true love, now legally known as Amaryllis Kornfeld-Mott (the hyphen had been her idea). He stood at her door, warmly greeted by Lani or Gilles, feeling spiffy in his sporty Costume National Homme. The object of his devotion invariably summoned him to her room to present a clipping or two—this week, her particular favorites being the piece in the *Journal* about a woman whose actual job was to sniff the leather of new Mercedeses, and an item in the *Times* detailing the amount his uncle had lost in a recent week of trading ($237,198,940, to be precise—Toulouse gulped, but did his best to remain cool). They would then stampede to the Silver Seraph and be delivered to Cañon Manor, where their sagacious host had spent all day preparing the most heavenly food known to man. When Trinnie was there, it was fun, but a different kind of fun, because Marcus was always sweetly mindful of her and charmingly distracted; in other words, she came first. Toulouse thought that was how it should be, and it gave him pleasure to see them laughing and joking and holding hands. Though in fine general spirits, his mother still walked beneath a cloud, as if not yet fully recovered from the years. The boy was certain—the *children* were certain—she'd come around.

On other nights, Trinnie's absence was sorely felt but soon blotted out by food and revelry and the spellbinding tales of a shadowy world—a street world, one that Amaryllis of all people had shared. Toulouse was envious; when his father spoke of carrying her on his back through the night, he may as well have been describing a magic carpet ride. Sometimes the details were so vivid Toulouse felt he might somehow insert himself so that Marcus would remember a time when the *three* of them had had some such adventure. Just when the boy's desperation nearly drove him to recount some pathetic anecdote from his own life (shoplifting from 7-Eleven came to mind), Marcus sagely saw fit to weave another web, only this time one whose weave Amaryllis had not been part of. She would listen enrapt, her eyes wide as her suitor's, even reaching for Toulouse's hand during the telling—then all would be right with the world again.

The ride back to Franklin Hills would be quiet, with a kiss stolen here and there in the rare moments Epitacio avoided peering into the rearview.

Weekends were devoted to the babies. There was usually a large group—Gilles and Lani, Candelaria and her niños, Cody and Saffron and their foster parents, along with their other three wards—and off they'd go in a minivan to Downtown Disneyland or the San Diego Zoo. Sometimes they made a day of it at Stradella, and Trinnie hired a circus with acrobats and elephants and sword-swallowers too. After barbecue they would trip to the Majestyk for a noisy matinée. Of course Winter brought Ketchum, and everyone was glad to see Joyce looking so well again.

It was good for Toulouse to wander Olde CityWalk. Since Lucy left, there hadn't been much reason to visit; he'd even built up something of an aversion to the place, as in the time Amaryllis vanished from her hideaway. But now it was like walking inside one of the dreams he still had about Edward—dreams that left him feeling warm and reassured when he awakened, and without melancholy. He would grab Amaryllis and break away from the crowd, stealing into the Boar's Head to survey the workshop, where masks still hung as if awaiting selection by their master for the new school day . . . then they would creep upstairs to the "apartments" where so many schemes had been hatched and secrets revealed.

Toulouse poked open the trapdoor, and they climbed to her old safe house.

She looked around with a shiver of nostalgia. He kissed her and she let him.

"Amaryllis," he said.

There was a catch in his throat, and she noticed how he'd gone a little pale.

"I wanted to ask you—I wanted to know if you would think about the idea—or the *possibility* . . . and it doesn't have to be, well, it *couldn't* be something that would happen now or even very soon but—something that would happen maybe in the *future* . . . well, I wanted to know if you would think about thinking about the idea of us—of us eventually getting married. I mean, years from now. When we are older or after college or whenever you—whenever you thought that might be something you wanted to think about or maybe say yes to in the future but not necessarily now."

She took his hands and looked him in the eye.

"I *do* love you, Toulouse," she said. "I always have. And I always will."

She kissed him and ran to the ladder to rejoin the group, now in general tumult over a tightrope walker's derring-do.

That night he lay in bed more tortured than ever. No amount of careful analysis could yield a definitive result: had she said yes or no?

Was it an undying—or a sisterly—proclamation? Luckily, sleep laid siege to the conundrum and put it to rest until the fresh misery of morning.

*I*t was true that Dodd Trotter had fallen in love with his secretary, but one could not hold it against him. He had been loyal to Joyce for as long as humanly possible, and remained so in his fashion; unlike his wife, he had no dumpster babies with which to sublimate his grief. Frances-Leigh was a good woman. She was devoted to his happiness.

Trinnie asked her brother for help. She had decided to sell La Colonne Détruite, or rather sell the property where the broken tower resided, for no buyer could be expected to preserve such a monument. Nor would she wish it preserved—to that end, she had even considered tearing it down before putting the park up for auction. Strangely, Trinnie found she could no longer set foot in the place. Bluey was right; they should have sold and subdivided years ago. All the furniture and items so mathematically arranged were carted off to storage, to be sold on another day. Next on the list was Saint-Cloud—everything must go. She wanted no more shrines or mazes in her life.

Dodd had an agenda of his own. He decided to move the corporate headquarters out of Beverly Hills. His son and father were dead and his daughter was living in England; his mother did not know anymore who he was; and the last of his worries—his rolling-stone sister—was safely anchored by Marcus and Toulouse. It was all right now for him to begin afresh, away from the nexus of his old life. To her credit, Frances-Leigh argued against the move. Conservative by nature, she felt it more symbolic than practical.

The dream of revamping Beverly Vista was dead too. There would be no rooftop gallery, no Puckish cafeteria, no starstruck planetarium or fiber-optic learning center powered by truck-size servers buried underground—no Sage Hill, no Ross Institute, no Cary Academy—no footprint or imprint, only misprint. There would be no thinking outside the box, only thinking *inside* the box. Probably what his dad was doing right about now, he darkly joked (Frances-Leigh didn't think it so funny). That's all the imperial Beverly Hills school district knew how to do anyway, he said: think inside the box.

The Quincunx Holding Company undauntedly continued to acquire rectangles of real estate in the Beverly Vista matrix and was now in possession of nearly one hundred houses and apartment units. Like an embittered dramaturge (but more like a broker calling in margins), the billionaire ordered the division to take possession of the deeded homes that surrounded the school. It would be a three-month process, for that was the amount of time the tenants—former owners who had continued to "squat" on the properties—agreed they would need in order to move, upon notice to vacate. (Many of the homes whose original owners had already taken the money and run were currently inhabited by Quincunx employees.) Within six weeks, Dodd Trotter's hydra-headed enterprise had transplanted itself to Northern California, and the eighty or so employee-participants of the Middle School Adjunct Residency Program had followed, leaving empty residences behind.

A series of increasingly frantic calls to the Quincunx CEO from honorary PTA president Marcie Millard went unreturned. As one by one the dwellings around the school went dark—and the student body dwindled accordingly—Dodd Trotter's disappearing act became fuel for the media. Stories of the unfolding suburban debacle invariably contained two sides: that the celebrated nerd had avenged himself *Carrie*-like on an ungrateful school district for failing to allow him to remake the alma mater in his own image (and name), and the counterspin being that any reports to this effect were patently absurd, the vacancies an unfortunate by-product of a recessionary downsizing. For a few months the Trotters, Dodd in particular, endured more scrutiny than may have been desired. They would endure.

Neither the *New York Times Magazine* cover ("An Unsentimental Education") nor the intercession of various moguls, senators and billionaire busybodies—most of them friends and colleagues or at least high-level acquaintances of Dodd's and his father's—did anything to sway him. His lawyers said the courts would eventually force Quincunx to sell off the marooned properties, but such a decision might take two years, at least. By then the paint would have faded and the lawns died, and Dodd Trotter's interest along with them. He never held on to the empty buildings in his portfolio for longer than that anyhow.

When approached by outraged do-gooders, Trinnie chose not to get involved. Was she supposed to have an opinion? Did they think she was going to get big feelings over her kooky brother's little stunt? She actually *liked* it when Dodd took some kind of action; the more bizarre, the merrier. Anyhow, who gave a shit. Beverly Hills could go fuck itself. He had always been there for her, and had suffered his own terrible losses; she would stand by him. She didn't think it was any of her business to meddle—hers or anyone else's.

*O*ne weekend, after paying a purely social visit to Marcus at Cañon Manor, Dodd took a dusk-time walk to old BV. For a half-mile around ground zero, there was the eerie absence of customary sights, sounds and smells—the lived-in-ness of a neighborhood. A few cars idled here and there while tourists snapped pictures of loved ones posing in the driveways of vacant houses as if they were their own. City-leased klieg lights lined the sidewalks to ward off vandalism. He saw a few media vans rumble past, and private patrol cars. Some of the news teams were from other countries.

When he was sure no one saw him, Dodd entered the apartment building on the corner of Rexford and Charleville. He passed the dry lobby fountain and rode an elevator to the fourth floor. Using a master key to gain entry to one of the empty units, he walked out to the patio that overlooked the darkening playground where the ugly bungalows still held dominion.

He watched the night fall.

Coda

Now sleep, the land of houses,
And dead night holds the street,
And there thou liest, my baby,
And sleepest soft and sweet;
My man is away for a while . . .

—William Morris

With some reluctance, the author concedes that he has reached the end of his story. The garden will be frozen in time and yet, paradoxically, grow wild outside these pages. Some last trimmings are in order.

At the age of eighteen, Lucille Rose Trotter gave her hand to the son of Lord Tryeferne, thereby becoming the fairest component of that entity known in English society sheets as the Hon Travis and Lucille Rose Tryeferne. Through an unfortunate act of terrorism, she somewhat prematurely became Lady Tryeferne and Lady Tryeferne she would remain, through miscarriage and divorce and romantic entanglements thick and thin. Our dear cousin, who wore braids when we first met, would not settle down until her mid-twenties, when, after the usual diversions—stints at fashion and auction houses, jewelry designing, handbag making, hospice working and even finally a passing stab at children's-book authoring—she regained her senses and went to work for her dad. Taking to Quincunx like koi to water, she quickly proved herself to be more than a nepotistic adornment, and those who doubted her talents certainly suffered, though not for long; Mrs. Tryeferne (she detached the aristocratic handle in the workplace) had a way of wielding a blade so that its business was done before there was time to notice a spot of blood.

She had always gotten on well with Frances-Leigh, who was endeared by the girl's bossiness, especially after a star turn as the former secretary's maid-of-honor at the most spectacular Scottish castle anyone in the world had ever seen. (Her father had bought it especially for the wedding ceremony and the three-day gala that followed.) Lady Tryeferne—or Our Lady of the Tryeferne, as Trinnie liked to call her—was also keen on South Sea pearls, and looked more and more like her auntie each day: lanky, freckle-flecked, willowy and red, red, red, with a keen look in her eye that made one fear she knew, or at least had known, too much. Now, whether the lady would one day have children—she had no hankering to marry again, nor did she pine for the patter of little feet upon marble—is not for us to guess; though she did take the loss of the child she had conceived with Travis as an omen, and was sorely reminded of the bittersweet genes that had ushered her brother into the world. (It mattered little that she'd been told she was no likelier to have a child with Apert than anyone else.) While Lucille Rose could not imagine another Edward in spirit, she *could* conjure one in body; that would have been a terrible thing to inflict upon anyone. So she put off thoughts of childbearing for a while and told herself she was doing the responsible thing. But time is on her side. Her life, we can say with certainty, shall be a long one, with never a use for a wandering garden.

She found her mother's adoption of the McDonald's baby galling. In *her* mind, he hadn't so much been adopted as co-opted—a fledgling, deputized into Edward's memory posse. It was just so blatant and, as she put it to friends, "unattractive"; happily, such judgments coincided with the arrival of that age when a young girl cultivates her innate desire to cannibalize or at least crucify the woman who bore and raised her (the very woman who, in therapists' undying jargon, "had done the best she could"). Well, Lucille Rose did *her* best to loathe her put-upon mom. Yet each time she saw Ketchum, he was a little bit bigger and a little bit older, and a bit more affectionate, too, until Lucy (that's what she let him call her) began to see him as a person in his own right rather than a substitute for the loveliest, most poetic soul she'd ever known. Watching Joyce with the boy, watching her chide and correct, hold and fuss, watching her *love* in a way the woman had never been able to with Edward (not to mention Lucy herself), she grew to respect and forgive, and to imagine her mother anew. It brought her close to godliness, for she finally untied what up till then had been the banal knot of Christian charity: that to save a life—such as Ketchum's had been saved—to love for love's sake alone created a chain reaction that truly changed the world. During yoga, or in moments of repose, Lady Tryeferne felt herself on the receiving end of her mother's selfless act and was invigorated to start her own "chain"—when and where and whatever that might be. Her heart overflowed with hope and abundance.

It was true that Joyce had never been happier. When Dodd came to town, they caught up over drinks at swank Brentwood hideaways, a routine Frances-Leigh lobbied for and was immensely satisfied to see take hold. The amazing thing was, they even flirted. Yet on the romantic front, Joyce had no time or desire. Her life was filled by Ketchum and the others—her Westwood children. Men fluttered around like butterflies, but she was no collector; she took her leave from fancy fund-raisers on the arm of Father de Kooning, her walker and biggest fan, and that was just fine.

*S*hortly after his move to Cañon Manor, Marcus Weiner spent many a Saturday at Frenchie's, refining and embellishing his prodigious gifts. The first thing he did was re-create the Persephone, the original pastry that had drawn Bluey in years ago, making sure it was delivered to her cottage at the Motion Picture and Television Hospital in Woodland Hills. According to Winter, whenever the old woman partook of that favored treat, she broke lustily into song and a certain woodenheaded Mr. Jones was invariably invoked.

One person who particularly benefited from Marcus's drop-ins was none other than the proprietor's daughter. Amaryllis Kornfeld-Mott proved herself a studious yet inventive helper, with the knack of being one step ahead of her tutor, even when at his most unpredictably daring. Sometimes he challenged her—threw down the gauntlet and stood back, hands clasped behind him like a Russian maestro commanding a scherzo to be played at speeds beyond human capability—in this case, the prodigy pulled it off and then some. They simply took over, relegating Gilles to the front register, and the only thing left for him was to get coffee and cupcakes for the old folks who shuffled in. During lulls, the poor baker tried to small-talk, but so involved was the pair that they wouldn't even notice; if they did, he was shooed away forthwith. Back at his post, he heard Marcus roar at his pupil or clap with delight upon tasting her morsels, and the coffee-sipping pensioners wondered what the hell was going on. The pâtissier got carried away enough that he often forgot to remove his old-style tweed coat, which became dusted with confectionary powders as a field by snow. Even when Amaryllis was enrolled in Pitzer College, she came home on weekends to see Cody and Saffron, and to attend master classes with the man she loved as a father—the man who had once fed her and the babies and who carried her on his back, where she would forever in both their eyes remain.

Toulouse was still in love. It was unnecessary to remind her of the pledge he had made—she knew full well his feelings. She *did* love him, but could not jump, as Lucy had with Travis Tryeferne; perhaps, thought Amaryllis gloomily, that was her flaw. The truth was, too much had happened in her young life for her to ever have a passionate, clear-cut feeling. Eroticism and emotions had been commingled, and mangled too, and ghosts conspired to put a governor on her ability to sort it all out. Things had been done to her of which she never told a soul. Eventually, she would, thus opening a door to the world; it can be assumed that Toulouse Trotter would be standing there, first in line, in forthright, timorous fashion, holding a slender stalk of honeysuckle and passionflowers. She would let him in. But that time was not now, nor would it be for some years. There would be other loves and other heartaches for both, the lesser ones which they'd share as best friends do. By *that* time (the time they found each other), Amaryllis would have consecrated a Westside Frenchie's, hard by Le Marmiton, and its wafery creations would make her name—and bake it too.

What *was* Toulouse Trotter doing while the door to her heart remained closed (or at least secured against entry of all but an occasional breeze of sweet nothings)? Well, he was doing the things that young people do while casting about for "meaning." Taking a leaf from Lucy's earliest Smythson, he attempted to write what he thought to be a touching absurdist play about his cousin, called *Prince Headward* (after careful consideration, the somewhat sacrilegious title was revised to *Edward the First*). Sadly, the title was its high point. He traveled the world, notching this and that power spot on his belt, taking care to avoid places visited during the famous Four Winds holiday—not an altogether easy task. He became enamored of Cambodia and New Guinea, Java and Madagascar, Abu Dhabi and the Maldives, Zanzibar and Nepal, and kept the river on his right during the requisite near-death, near-homosexual experiences of an inveterate adventurer; he had dalliances with nymphomaniacal girls who spoke pidgin English; he sometimes stayed with families who thought him a poor vagabond—in short, got up to all the normal mischief that could be expected of any self-respecting scion.

He never stayed away too long (whenever home, he bunked at Cañon Manor), and sent his parents a raft of letters, which Trinnie thought so wonderful she threatened to have published under the title *Off the Road.* Particularly savored was the antic account of Toulouse's re-enactment of his father's legendary walk from Oxford to the great earthwork of Silbury Hill, a path William Morris himself had once trod as an undergrad. He called his dispatches "News from Anywhere," a nod to the log Marcus kept all those years and had long ago given him for safekeeping—a gesture so intimate that his son had immediately handed it over to Harry and Ruth.

The young man at last fell upon the career of medical doctor, with a specialty in maxillofacial reconstruction; he had no stomach for blood, so it didn't pan out. His studies *did* get him writing again, penning thoughts on morbidity and mortality (which had become a clichéd literary genre in itself)—but the trenchant, tender quality of Dr. Trotter's observations proved anomalous, and anomalously marketable at that. Now wisely engaged in dermatological pursuits, he wrote as elegantly of lupus as he did of childhood acne, though readers generally conceded his finest essay to date concerned a dog—his own.

Toulouse had meant to meditate on his cousin's infirmity but wound up memorializing Pullman instead. In "A Harlequin Romance," he wrote how as a boy his mother had tried to put him off Great Danes, owing to the breed's short life-span, and recounted that tragicomic year of vicarious hypochondria wherein Pullman was needled, massaged and therapized. But the dog turned eight, then ten, then twelve, then fourteen . . . an age thought impossible for the breed.

Then he disappeared.

At first, Toulouse thought that in a misguided act of charity, his mother and the Monasterios had taken it upon themselves to incinerate the finally dead creature and concoct a story of his mysterious departure. But they withered under his interrogations—he had after all inherited the digger's formidable "nose"—and the young man concluded that if they *had* been responsible, they'd have surely come clean under his assault.

He had gory theories galore: someone had struck the dog with a car then buried him in a literal cover-up—or that Pullman had collapsed and fallen into a street-maintenance dugout, where the body was inadvertently mutilated by pipe cutters or whatnot, then simply buried by workers out of sheer expediency. Awakening in the middle of the night from a dream, he was certain the dog was in the maze, but would then remember it had been uprooted and that the house on Saint-Cloud was no more.

*A*bout a year after Marcus moved to Cañon Manor, Trinnie began taking lovers again, as she had all those years he was absent. If Marcus knew, he kept his feelings close; she was a good mother and a good friend and he had no right to tell her anything. Their own lovemaking had come and gone like a freakish meteorological event that would never recur. (She had been wrong when she thought she conceived in the tower on their return; the doctors said she was now barren.) Katrina Berenice Trotter Weiner made excuses, telling herself they just needed time. He was having relapses—an accent had crept back to his voice, and the tailor Montalvo called to say that Marcus had ordered a dozen suits in "the bespoke Victorian cut." The bill was to be sent to a certain W. Morris of Kelmscott Manor. But the details of his infirmity no longer seduced—once the stained glass was broken, the rebuilt church could not allure. When she left for Slovakia (Ralph Mirdling and Ms. Keaton had since broken up and he was directing a film there) and stayed six weeks, husband and wife spoke twice a day, and that gave Marcus great joy. Sometimes when she returned from her travels, she was so exhausted that he nursed her. Once she almost needed to be hospitalized again, and he brought her to Cañon Manor because she couldn't sleep. She paced like a wraith at all hours, muttering in a fugue state, "I killed him! I killed him—it was *my* blow that killed him!" He shushed and kissed and rocked her in his arms; it was so beautiful and so awful that the boy could hardly watch.

*L*a Colonne Détruite outlived all the Trotter residences. Ironically, it was Marcus who exhorted for its preservation, as had William Morris for the preservation of cathedrals "and other ancient buildings." (He had in fact been acting as a kind of informal curator for the structures in his brother-in-law's shrinking portfolio of skeletal landmarks.) He argued that the broken tower was simply too grand a curiosity to demolish. But there was another, far more compelling, reason not to tear it down.

Marcus Weiner continued to frequent the Westwood cemetery—why beat about the bush? It may now be said that with the dotty Ms. Campbell's blessing, Mr. Weiner eventually took over the duties of Sling Blade, who, as the result of a small inheritance left him by Louis Trotter, renounced his career as park caretaker. (Mr. Blade was unsure of his future and needed time to lay fallow; he was, as he put it, "on sabbatical." More certain of their path were the indomitable Monasterios: Epitacio, Eulogio and Candelaria. With money bequeathed them by Edward—who, aside from having feelings of great affection, had harbored a residuum of guilt for having forced them to betray their employers in the matter of the AWOL orphan—the hardworking family bought a fleet of Town Cars and founded a livery company, which they christened, in eccentric yet poignant homage, E. A. Trotter & Sons.) He raked and watered and polished, pointing tourists toward celebrity stones—but never got over a gnawing sense of incompletion during his "unquiet" peregrinations of the digger's monumentless greens.

On a day in which the Santa Ana winds lived up to all the morose and mystical things ever written about them, Marcus called a meeting between himself, Dodd and his "Katy" in which he made a proposition so startling and bizarre it could not be ignored. After much thought, much *agonizing* thought, he said, he'd come to conclude that the body of Louis Trotter should be exhumed and reburied on the grounds of La Colonne—or better still, burned there and thrown to the winds.

Brother and sister thought he'd gone mad yet again. But as the minutes ticked on, then the hours and the days, they realized it was the most sound and gorgeous of proposals. Louis Trotter would finally have a memorial that was fitting, or, to put a finer point on it, fit for the digger's grandiose, quixotic imaginings.

And so it was achieved—the hows and whens and legalities thereof have no import here. A small service was performed on what was now most assuredly Carcassone Way. In years thereafter, only one family member would ever set foot upon those strange and hallowed grounds again.

*   *   *

*W*hen he turned twenty-eight, Dr. Trotter made the trip to Redlands. Ruth had died the year before, and Harry was looked after
by around-the-clock nurses, their salaries paid by the estate of Louis
Trotter. He was frail but comfortable.

Suddenly, the journal was back in his hands. He went to the swing-
ing couch on the porch and opened it. The pages were empty of handwritten text but filled with aged clippings and photos: *Variety* blurbs,
rare-book-auction announcements, Oxfordiana, SRO rooming-house
vouchers, Frenchie's receipts for payment of services rendered (signed
by "G. Mott")—that sort of sad miscellany. For years, the son had had his
own ideas of what was between the covers of *News from Nowhere*, fueled
in part by Marcus's occasional references to "the work," something of
high literary merit, a tour de force with bravura passages offering insights of a life hard lived, hard fought and hard-won. Like an archaeolo-
gist in virgin tombs, he expected to uncover whole sections of cramped
cursive—the *cacoëthes scribendi* that is the hallmark of any schizophrenic worth his salt—and had already envisioned himself in New
York while his father took the stage amid thunderous applause to collect
his National Book Award from Philip Roth. As a parting gift, Harry gave
him a manila envelope of photographs, some of which he'd looked at
more than fifteen years ago while sitting on the couch beside Grandma
Ruth—and again, in his father's boyhood bedroom.

With the ragtag anthology on the seat beside him, the doctor drove
directly to La Colonne. He ducked through the privet as he once did with
Pullman (he had ordered the illicit entry never to be repaired). Approaching the tower, he pretended to see the great speckled jowl of that
"continental gentleman" jut neatly from the ocular penthouse window.
He could hear chuffing in the air; the ashes of his grandfather—and
Bluey too—had long since been scattered through the meadow, and
God-knew-what innumerable castle niches that sweet-soul'd couple had
found, white-gray smudges on the cracked stones of eternity. He imagined them all inside: Edward coquettishly swathed in tulle, Trinnie and
Marcus on their wedding, and Amaryllis and his boyhood self, awkwardly groping. The property was eventually to be given to the city as a
public park maintained in perpetuity by the family trust, and he did not

think he would visit until then, when its history would be softened by time and the impersonal mass of the world.

He reached into the envelope and pulled out a photo of his parents standing before the tower throwing rice on departing guests. As he left La Colonne, he brushed the tiny blossoms from his coat, thinking how much they looked like the celebratory grains of farewell.

*Y*es, his accent had returned full-blown, as had most of his bulk and prodigious physical energy—he did the work of ten men around the graveyard, and it had never looked better. He supervised new plantings (some at the suggestion of his wife) and carved beautiful flowers into the wooden benches, painting them so subtly that their effect was visible only at close inspection. In other words, he was mindful of the visitors, whether tourists or mourners, and would do nothing to intrude upon or upset the spirit of place. The caretaker would not disturb or senselessly upgrade that which was already aesthetically pleasing; he would, as he put it, "have no part of grimthorpery."

He still hung his hat at Cañon Manor—though its quietus would never be the same. The Beverly Vista neighborhood had begun to thrive again, as the courts had forced Quincunx to divest its residential holdings. And though Dot discouraged it, sometimes Will'm (or Topsy, if you like; either will do) stayed in a small shed on the edge of the Candle-lighters' plot, one he'd done up in trompe l'oeil so that it looked like a modest Gothic church. (Mr. John Ruskin might have approved.) The gregarious and immensely knowledgeable "Big Will'm" was sought out by those who came to visit the park's more famous dead, and was given a generous write-up in the *Times* that did not allude to his provenance. He was especially beloved by children, who found him a rowdy, eccentric delight. In that role alone, Dot found him a terrific asset.

One day he saw a familiar face by the columbaria. It was Winter. He hadn't seen her in a while and asked how she'd been. Well, said the nanny, she'd done "a bang-up job with my Ketchum," who now happened to be off raising hell at some Swiss boarding school or other—then she smiled wistfully and said he really had turned out to be a brilliant, considerate, wonderful boy. She said she was going home. She looked older but was still elegant, and the crystal blue of her eyes made one think that most of her had already departed for northern climes. He spoke animatedly of her imminent return to Iceland and of the great sagas born there—how he, William Morris, longed to go back and translate more of its epics. (The first publication, he said, had met with great success.) Aside from those assertions, for which she'd been prepared by Toulouse, she found him eminently sane, if eminently Victorian too.

He wondered what she was doing over by the tall drawers of the dead. The caretaker assumed she was here to see the boy, since her employers had been scattered to the Bel-Air winds. Yet Edward lay some forty yards off from the place that held her attention. Perhaps, he thought, she was meditating and wandering a bit as she did, girding herself for the approach to his grave.

"I'm thinking of selling mine," she said, out of nowhere.

"Selling? What do you mean, woman?"

"When she died, Mrs. Trotter left me a crypt. I knew about it for years—sort of. She always called it a 'condominium.' " Marcus laughed, without meanness. " 'I've got a wonderful condo for you!' she said. And Mr. Trotter—dear man—confirmed it. I thought it was some three-bedroom high-rise in Century City, but it turned out to be something else entirely, didn't it? Well . . . that's what you get when you start thinking grand." She looked at one of the upper slots. "Dot said someone might give me a hundred and fifty thousand for it."

"I think it's a damn fine idea, ma'am—sell it! Otherwise it's here, waiting on you. *Sell* it. And when it's *your* time, have 'em hurl you into a crevasse in the motherland! That's what *I'd* do."

"Maybe so, Marcus. Maybe so."

"It's Will'm," he said kindly. "If you please."

They strolled over to the Candlelighters' land.

"My, look how full it is."

"Over two hundred babes now," he said.

She looked down at Edward's plaque, void of his name. "How did *that* happen?"

"Something fell on it, years ago. Broke it in two. I told Joyce to leave it be—t'was an omen. I think she felt funny at first, but now she *has* left it. As she should! A very busy woman, Joyce—a *good* woman. But I don't think Edward would have wished to stand out, no? He'd want to be just like the rest. 'No favored treatment for me!' he'd say."

There was indeed a whirligig stuck in the dirt, with *Edward* brushed upon it in delicate script, along with the names of legions of others.

They walked toward the gate where her car was parked, and stared at Louis Trotter's former plot. It was wide and green.

"Is it going to stay empty?"

"I've been talking to Katrina," said Will'm. "Had a marvelous thought. What if the Westwood land is simply donated to those Candle-lighters? For, God knows, there will never be enough space for the poor kiddies." A gleam came into his eye. "And then I set to cogitating: wouldn't it be wondrous to have *another* little parkland for these babes? If it were up to *me*, I'd stash the whole lot of 'em up at La Colonne—how many thousands of small souls might we there set at rest! I think it sits pretty well with Mr. Trotter now; I mean, having them here in the Westwood. Wouldn't spring them on him up *there* just yet—no, ma'am! Might have 'imself a sore fit . . . but I *do* think he wouldn't begrudge 'em that, not here, anyway. I think all's forgiven—or is on its way to being—all round!"

She smiled and shook his hand, but he embraced her instead. He smelled like some great musky elf, and Winter's heart leapt in her chest for the mysteries of the world. She watched him a long time in her mirror, waving as she pulled away. Then some children tugged at him, Lilliputians at Gulliver, and he went along.

Winter laughed as she sped toward the 405. It *was* an extraordinary idea, but she wasn't as confident as Marcus that Mr. Trotter would approve—oh but to hell with it! Maybe she'd sign her condo over to the Candlelighters. They could probably fit a dozen in there.

She laughed again with wet eyes, imagining the entire cemetery, and broken tower too, overrun with tiny bodies—invaded by those holy homeless souls, thrown out before they were ever named.

About the Author

BRUCE WAGNER is a novelist and film director. He lives in Los Angeles.